The Chinatown Death Cloud Peril

Paul Malmont

Simon & Schuster
New York London Toronto Sydney

SIMON & SCHUSTER
Rockefeller Center
1230 Avenue of the Americas
New York, NY 10020

This book is a work of fiction. Names, characters, places, and incidents either are products of the author's imagination or are used fictitiously. Any resemblance to actual events or locales or persons, living or dead, is entirely coincidental.

For information about special discounts for bulk purchases,
please contact Simon & Schuster Special Sales at
1-800-456-6798 or business@simonandschuster.com

DESIGNED BY LAUREN SIMONETTI

Manufactured in the United States of America

1 3 5 7 9 10 8 6 4 2

Library of Congress Cataloging-in-Publication Data

Malmont, Paul.
The Chinatown death cloud peril / Paul Malmont.
p. cm.
1. Gibson, Walter Brown, 1897-—Fiction. 2. Dent, Lester, 1904–1959—Fiction.
3. Authors, American—20th century—Fiction. I. Title.
PS3613.A457C47 2006
813'.6—dc22 2006042205

ISBN-13: 978-0-7432-8785-2
ISBN-10: 0-7432-8785-1

To my son, Nathaniel,
for getting me up early all those mornings so I could write this
and bearing with me while I did

To my wife, Audrey,
for my sons, and for so many other wonderful ways you have shared
your life with me

To Forrest Barrett
and
William Putch,
old teachers gone but never forgotten

The Chinatown Death Cloud Peril

My little son is crying out for nourishment—
O Alice, Alice, what shall I do?

—Edgar Rice Burroughs

We know how Gods are made.

—Jack London

Introduction

It is called the Pulp Era.

An era is like a book in that it has a title, its own unique exposition, characters, a beginning, a middle, an ending, a theme, and maybe a moral. And just as heroes and villains in a book do not realize they are in a story, so you cannot know the title or themes of the time in which you live. You may think you know. You may even hope to contribute to the story line, or be a witness to the ending. But even if you did, you would not know. Only after those days have passed can one discern the form, voices, and meaning of those days. Then the era can be given a title because titles are how we refer to times passed and stories told. The Pulp Era.

In other times and places—Imperial China, for example—an emperor could declare his own era while he was living in it. When Li Shimin, Emperor of the Temple and Library, decided that China was in a period of divine richness, then from that day on everyone was living in the Divine Richness Era. At least until the next emperor decreed the dawning of a new era.

In China this prerogative was considered a literary expression on the part of the emperor. The known world, after all, was his, and he could tell his story about it as he saw fit. As this known world is mine to tell about as I see fit. I am the Emperor of the Light and Darkness, and this is the Pulp Era.

You may recognize some of the heroes and villains of this era, but recognizing a vaguely familiar face is not the same as rediscovering a long-lost friend. I will introduce you to some old friends of mine, and make their days come alive again. I will let their voices speak and let their hearts fill with life one more time. An era, like a book, can be forgotten. Days, like pages, crumble into dust. Stories, like memories, fade away.

In this account I will offer you these lives, their stories, their shared events, that time with as much truth as they deserve. But saying that I will tell the truth about them is not the same as saying that I will tell you truth. In order to exercise my imperial prerogative I have to let shadows fall between fact and fiction. These friends, several of whom were writers, would have been among the first to remind me to never let the facts get in the way of a good story, and so I will not. The reader will determine what is truth and what is fiction.

In the end it's just a story.

But if you ask me, it's all true.

Issue 1:
Curse of the Golden Vulture

Episode One

"YOU THINK life can't be like the pulps?" Walter Gibson asked the other man. "Let me tell you a story. You tell me where real ends and pulp begins." The cigarette in his left hand suddenly disappeared.

The young man, whose most distinguishing characteristic, in spite of his stocky build and shock of red hair, was his powerfully forward-thrusted jaw, blinked in mild surprise at the magic trick, then nodded agreeably. "All right," Ron Hubbard said.

The cigarette, a filterless Chesterfield, reappeared in Gibson's right hand. He took a long sip from his whiskey and washed it down with a sip of beer and an involuntary shudder. He was getting drunk and it was too early. He knew it. He didn't even want to be here tonight. Well, he did want to be in the White Horse Tavern drinking. But he didn't want to be here drinking with the youthful and ambitious president of the American Fiction Guild, who had been hectoring him relentlessly to speak about his writing at the weekly gathering of pulp mag writers in the Grand Salon of the old Hotel Knickerbocker. John Nanovic, his ed at Street & Smith, had begged, pleaded, and in the end agreed to pay for a few of this evening's drinks if he would agree to do it. Nanovic had told Gibson that it was important for him, as the number one bestselling mag writer in America, to take an interest in the new writers, the young writers. To help groom them. Gibson felt that what Nanovic really wanted him to do was to find his successor in case he stumbled in front of a trolley car some drunken evening. Ultimately he had to admit that it was a fair concern for an editor to have about him.

So, here he was having drinks with Lafayette Ron Hubbard, a writer of moderately popular but pedestrian (in Gibson's opinion) westerns, and at twenty-five, fifteen years younger than he. One of the new writers. One of the young ones. They were seated at a small table next to the bar and treating themselves to waiter service. Hubbard was one of those writers who acted like they really cared about writing and had launched into a theory that the sort of adventure pulp Gibson wrote was somehow less valid than the westerns and two-fisted tales he wrote because at least his stories were based on history or reality.

Gibson knew the kid was impressed by him. Hubbard had practically been begging him for a sit-down for weeks. Every now and then Gibson would see Hubbard looking around the saloon as if he could recognize somebody he knew who might come over and interrupt the conversation. If that had happened, he might then have the opportunity to say to them, "Excuse me, but can't you see I'm having drinks with Walter Gibson? That's right, the guy who writes *The Shadow Magazine.* Well, I know *The Shadow* byline is Maxwell Grant, but that's a company name, a Street & Smith name. Trust me. Walter Gibson is Maxwell Grant. Walter Gibson writes *The Shadow Magazine.* We're just talking about writing." But he recognized no one and no one recognized him.

Gibson had seen several writers that he knew come through already; the Street & Smith building was just up the road at Fifteenth and Seventh, and the tavern was popular with writers who had just been roughed up by eds and by the eds who had applied the beating. George Bruce, the air-ace writer, had been and gone; Elmer Smith, the rocket jock, and Norvell Page, the fright guy, were still drinking in a corner. But he hadn't invited either to join them. As a rule Gibson didn't like other mag writers; he found them too self-denigrating yet self-important at the same time. He much preferred the company of the magicians whose books and articles he often ghosted.

He kind of liked Hubbard, though. The kid was eager and acted like he thought his shit smelled like roses, a confidence most other writers lacked. In a one-draft world a man had to believe that every word he wrote was right. Gibson knew he had quickly muscled out old Arthur Brooks, a man Gibson had no use for whatsoever, who as head of the Guild had run the organization as a lazy gentlemen's social club. Hubbard had plans for the Guild, but Gibson didn't really care to know what they were. He knew that Hubbard had lived in New York for several years a while back with a wife and a daughter, and that they had all moved back to Washington State for a while, and that he had left them behind in Washington and come back to New York alone just a few months ago. Gibson could only venture a guess why; the Depression had made it so that sometimes a man couldn't afford to bring his family with him when he went looking for work. But the last thing Gibson wanted to do was ask another man why he had left his wife and child.

"What's real? What's pulp? Right, Ron?" He unbuttoned his collar and loosened his tie knot. "Okay. Here's a story. For the sake of argument, let's call it the Tale of the Sweet Flower War. This is a story filled with blood and cruelty and fear and mystery and love and passion and vengeance and villains," he said. "It began with the arrival of a strange mist which rolled in from the harbor and seemed to fill the streets of Chinatown. Those who were superstitious felt it was the cloak of death. Those who weren't superstitious, and their numbers were few, only felt it was another reason to hate living here." Walter spoke rapidly; the hard emphasis of his consonants tended to resemble a staccato drumbeat, and his fingers twitched mildly as he spoke, involuntarily typing his words onto the table or against his leg or into the air as fast as he spoke them. Gibson's energy always seemed to keep him in motion. His friend Harry Houdini had once told him he seemed to vibrate, even when he was standing still.

"Here Chinatown? Or San Francisco's?" Hubbard asked with a vaguely worldly air that implied he had traveled some in his time and knew both intimately: a warning to Gibson that he'd better have his facts straight.

"New York. Here." The tone of Gibson's voice let Hubbard know not to interrupt the storytelling again unless it was something important. "The deadly fog rolled over the tiny enclave thirty years ago during the great tong wars, when the red flag of war flew over the tallest building in Chinatown."

"Tong?" Hubbard made the same mistake again and winced a little, knowing that Gibson's next breath would have explained it.

"Ancient organizations with mysterious roots going way back in Chinese history. Brutal, cruel, and sadistic. Mostly they imported opium, slave girls, and indentured workers from China.

"In 1909, the year of the menacing mist, the biggest tong in America was the On Leong group. They controlled everything in the matter of things Chinese from Frisco to New York. There were other tongs around at the time, but the only serious rivals were the Hip Sing. Their boss was a fella about your age, everyone knew him as Mock Duck, and he had a habit, when he got into a brawl, of whipping out two pistols, closing his eyes, and firing blindly until everyone was dead or running for their lives. You can laugh if you want, but legend had it that this was a very effective street-fighting technique.

"Well, those that said that something sinister would emerge from the shadow which had fallen over Chinatown were right. One day Sweet Flower came to town. Now she was, by all accounts, a beautiful and delicate virgin. She had remarkable long, slender fingers and could play a variety of Chinese instruments with skill and grace. A slave, of course, smuggled in by a slaver and probably destined for a life of prostitution. But one of the On Leong leaders saw her, fell in love with her, and he had his men steal her from the slaver. Or rescue her, if you prefer. And, he married her. She was sixteen, and on her wedding night he possessed her in every way that a man can possess a woman. And she was happy with her station in life.

"At first, all the slaver wanted was proper restitution for his loss. But the On Leong man refused to pay for what he considered to be true love. He told the slaver to go to hell. The slaver went to another tong, the Hip Sing. A truce was declared and the two parties sat down for formal negotiations. Now this was at a time when the tong fighters, the hatchet men, the *boo how doy,* were killing each other at the rate of two or three a week. So for these two tongs to actually sit down together in the same room and hold a peaceful discussion . . ." He made a futile gesture. "Chinatown did not hold its collective breath."

"The negotiations did not go well for the Hip Sing. Once again, they were told in no uncertain terms where they and their demands could go. All things considered, it's pretty remarkable that any man walked out of the tearoom alive that day. That night, however, was a different story. While her husband slept, someone broke into their house and cut off each and every one of Sweet Flower's slender and delicate little fingers."

"Mock Duck?"

The White Horse Tavern served its own blend of scotch, and each bottle was topped by a cork with a white tin horse rearing up. There was a cork on their table now; it was usually given to the customer who had put the polish on a bottle, and he had, several drinks ago. Gibson picked it up now, idly playing with it.

"Maybe. It was probably the vile slaver. And, in fact, Mock Duck delivered him over to the On Leong for whatever justice they chose to administer. But it wasn't enough and over the next couple of months, over fifty men from both sides were killed, and hundreds more were crippled or maimed in the fighting. Now what's really incredible about this is that we're talking about a neighborhood that takes up maybe a square mile and is made up of only a dozen or so streets. So relatively, it's a truly gruesome amount of men carving each other up."

"Hundreds! C'mon! That's pulp."

Gibson cleared his throat. "In those days the center of Chinese social life was the old Chinese Theater. It's still there; you can go down and see it for yourself. It's all boarded up now.

"At the time of the Sweet Flower War there was a famous comedian named Ah Hoon. Famous among the Chinese. An ugly clown of a man. Loyal to the On Leong. His grand finale was, and this supposedly laid them in the aisles, an impersonation of Mock Duck firing his guns blindly until he would roll over, ass over teakettle. Guess you had to be there, right? That's what the Hip Sing thought too. They were losing this war badly and now they were being made fun of in public by a clown. Word went out that Ah Hoon was a dead man and he would never see the sun rise after his next performance.

"Even though City Hall never went out of its way to keep one Chinaman from killing another, the rising tide of blood was starting to offend the sensibilities of the rest of the city. This bald-faced death threat was just the opportunity the cops had been looking for to show that they could handle a few uppity Chinese. That night they turned up at the theater in force. There were probably more Irish in Chinatown altogether that night than there were in all the bars in Brooklyn. The chief of police himself escorted Ah Hoon from his apartment to the theater. I imagine a load of innocent Chinese men took a whopping nightstick to the head for looking this way or that to some cop's dislike, but there was going to be law and order on Doyers Street.

"Poor Ah Hoon didn't even want to do his act that night! When he heard he was a marked man, he wanted to take the next train out of town, but the cops and the On Leong made him take the stage that night. They had something to prove. He didn't. But he waited in the wings and sweated through the acrobats leaping over each other. He agonized through the singer's songs, trying to peer into the darkness to see where the bullet or knife or hatchet was going to come from. He probably came close to having a heart attack every time the gas lamps sputtered and popped downstage. But all the time the cops and the On Leong men reassured him that all would be well. He was protected. He would live.

"Can you imagine anyone having a better reason to have stage fright than poor Ah Hoon? He walked out onstage that night and the first person he saw front and center was Mock Duck, grinning up at him.

But there were the American police to the left and right of his mortal enemy. Ah Hoon took a deep breath, wished he were in a faraway place, and dove into his act. He didn't change a word and by all accounts he was very, very funny that night. Even Mock Duck laughed at the impersonation. When it was time for the curtain call, the police swept him offstage before his first bow and an encore was out of the question. The point had been made: Ah Hoon had survived the performance.

"Well, the On Leong men went wild that night. Fireworks exploded in the sky over Chinatown, their brightness dimmed somewhat by the eerie fog. Hip Sing men were burned in effigy and humiliated in songs and jeers. To the On Leong men, the survival of Ah Hoon had proven that the Hip Sing were no longer the threat they had once posed and that the war was won. Meanwhile the cops hustled Ah Hoon to a cheap room in a cheap hotel next to the theater. They had rented it just to ensure that nothing would happen to tarnish their reputation as protectors of the weak and innocent and funny.

"The apartment had just one room. Everyone on the floor used the same washroom at the far end of the hall. The other apartments along the hall had been cleared of occupants for the night. Didn't matter if they had paid in advance, lived there for years, or had no place else to go. They were rousted. There were no closets in the room, but several small cupboards. There was a bed. There was one window, but it had been jammed into a stuck position for years. A two-inch gap let a little air into the stuffy room, but the window could be neither forced open wider nor lowered more. Three stories down was a dead-end alleyway barely the width of a broad-shouldered man. Three cops were positioned at its mouth, preventing any entrance. Opposite the window, about three feet away, was the solid brick wall of a building. That particular side was unmarred by a single door or window, featureless and rising another four stories beyond Ah Hoon's floor. Cops on foot and horseback blocked the front and back entrance to the hotel. Ten officers stood in the hallway outside Ah Hoon's room. A big Swede cop of impeccable moral fiber, at least of no discernible vice, was placed before Ah Hoon's door.

"An hour after sunrise, the chief of police led a phalanx of reporters, photographers, reformers, and politicians past the few remaining On Leong revelers, into the hotel, up to the third floor, down the line of ten cops standing at attention, and up to the big Swede. The chief of police himself proudly opened the door to introduce Ah Hoon to the rest of his life and announce to the world that the resolve of the Hip Sing tong had been broken and that peace would reign forever and for all time in Chinatown.

"The bullet hole had made a perfect dot in the center of Ah Hoon's forehead, giving the appearance of a third eye. He sat cross-legged on his bed, stiff and cold in a pool of his own drying blood. Legend has it that it wasn't even a bullet hole, it was the touch of a demon.

"Flies were already buzzing curiously about his head, which faced the single window. Still opposite a solid brick wall. Still jammed at less than two inches open. And as the chief of police roared his outrage and the flashbulbs popped, and as the word spread through Chinatown like a flash fire that the Sweet Flower War was over and the Hip Sing, not the On Leong, had won, and as an entirely new celebration began, the wide-eyed expression on Ah Hoon's face seemed to say one simple thing:

"Now that's funny!"

Gibson closed his fist around the tin stallion and reopened it. It had vanished. "The winds changed that morning, and after months of coldly clinging to every nail and stone and board, the Chinatown death cloud rolled back out to sea and vanished as completely as the life from Ah Hoon's body." He closed his fingers into a fist again and then opened them suddenly. A fresh cigarette, tip glowing, now lay crooked between his first two fingers. A simple French drop with a flourish for dramatic punctuation. His tale was told. He inhaled the smoke deeply and waited for the reaction. He could tell a lot about a fella by the way he reacted to a story or a magic trick. They either bought it, didn't, or tried to find some little flaw that could let them feel like they hadn't been conned into enjoying it when they really had. He figured Hubbard for the last type.

"The cops were in on it."

Gibson was right. "They weren't. And you forgot what I asked in the first place," he reminded Hubbard, the booze making him sound more arrogant than he wanted to be. "I asked you to tell me what's real and what's pulp."

"Well." Hubbard thought a moment. "The way Mock Duck fired his guns sounded kind of pulp."

Gibson shook his head. "True story."

"When all her fingers got cut off?"

Again Gibson shook his head.

"What happened to Sweet Flower?" Hubbard asked.

Gibson shrugged. "No one knows. Some say she may have killed herself. Others suppose her husband kept her sequestered in his house until he died. But no one really knows."

It looked like Hubbard was about to speak again when he was suddenly interrupted by a strong cough from the bar behind him. When they looked to see who had coughed, the man began to speak.

"Actually, it's not fairly common knowledge, so I'm not surprised you passed over this, Mr. Gibson, but Sweet Flower, considered defiled, was driven from the house of her husband and ended up living at the mercy of others."

Gibson looked at the tall man leaning against the bar placidly smoking his pipe and found himself gritting his teeth. What the hell brought *him* out tonight?

"It's a trick question," said a man from behind them. "Because the whole story is true. If it were pulp it would have a better ending."

Dent.

"It's real if it's a lie. If it's a pack of lies," Lester Dent said with definitive superiority, "it's a pulp."

Gibson tried not to let his expression change. Dent. Here. Tonight. What were the odds? Everyone said he was a teetotaler anyway. But here he was in the White Horse hoisting a mug of beer and looking as smug as an ape on a pile of bananas. Of course there was a good chance that Dent had dropped off his latest *Doc Savage* manuscript at Street & Smith earlier and decided to celebrate with a beer. For a moment Gibson wondered just how many books Dent was up to, then decided he didn't care. At that moment.

"Not to say that there can't be true stories in pulps, but most true stories don't have good endings. Pulps need great endings. Mr. Gibson's tale doesn't have a good ending. In fact, it has no ending. The problem with the Tale of the Sweet Flower War is that Mr. Gibson ends it just when it's about to turn into pulp."

Gibson felt his blood rising. "I can't believe you're going to lecture me on what makes great pulp. I am pulp."

"You're not pulp. The Shadow is pulp. Doc Savage is pulp. In fact, I will tell you what makes pulp. Of course there's blood, cruelty, fear, mystery, vengeance, heroes, and villains. That's just a good foundation. To make true pulp, really great stomach-churning, white-knuckle, turn-your-hair-white pulp, you have to fill it with a pack of outright lies. Secret identities and disguises." Dent began ticking off the items on his fingers to emphasize the point he was making. "The Yellow Peril. Superweapons. Global schemes. Hideous deaths. Cliff-hanging escapes. These are the packs of lies you won't find in any slick or glossy or literary hardcover bestseller. Horrors from the grave. Lost lands. Overwhelming odds. Impossible heroics. Unflagging courage. Oh, and I almost forgot! Guntotin', lingo-slingin' cowboys." He looked at Ron with a mischievous smile, knowing that Hubbard was guilty of perpetrating more than his share of outlandish cowboy tales. "Can't be a true pulp without a genuine gun-slingin', tabaccy-spattin' cowboy, right, Ron?"

As if charged by the sudden burst of electrical tension in the air, Hubbard's gregariousness had increased substantially. He was practically bursting with joy at the fact that Lester Dent knew his name. "That's right, Mr. Dent!" he said loudly and eagerly, nodding like Nipper responding to his master's voice over the Victrola.

Mr. Dent? What was it about the guy that made the kids like Hubbard call him Mr. Dent while he, Walter, was always Walt or Gib or, God forbid, occasionally Wally? Sure, Dent had a good ten years on

Hubbard, but Gibson was still a few years older than Dent. It had to be the height.

Gibson, who barely cracked five eight, had never grown accustomed to being the short man. Gibson had heard from eds and other writers that Lester was the athletic type who liked sailing and mountain climbing. Gibson didn't know if it was true or not but Dent certainly was broad-shouldered as well as tall. Sitting in a chair now as Dent loomed nearby only encouraged his sense of resentment that Dent had shown up here to ruin his night. Dent hadn't even bothered to take his overcoat off. And Christ, he was smoking his damn pipe like some longhair! Couldn't he smoke cigarettes like a normal man? Only eds and socialists smoked pipes.

"Walter." Dent nodded after a long pause in which he seemed to scrutinize Gibson through his thick glasses. His broad mustache twitched in the vaguest manner. Dent, thought Gibson, was tweaking him. Gibson felt the alcohol pulsing through his veins. It was a sensation that began at the back of his neck. He shouldn't have started on the shots so early.

Dent's eyes then flicked back to Hubbard and his hard expression seemed to soften. "It's all about the formula. Just throw enough of the right lies into the mix and add a great ending, and that's the formula for a pulp."

Dent spoke with a flattened midwestern intonation. Gibson tried to remember if he knew whether or not Dent was from Illinois. Dent's inflections were more rough-hewn, he decided, even less sophisticated than Illinois. Arkansas, possibly. Then he remembered. Missouri. Nanovic had told him that once. Definitely Missouri. "To make the Tale of the Sweet Flower War pulp you would have to find out that Ah Hoon's enemies had released a venomous snake into the room through an old mouse hole; what everyone thought was a bullet hole was actually a bite, and the cops never even looked for the serpent, which remained coiled behind a radiator."

"Excuse me. So the Sweet Flower War. It's true? Both of you know about it?" Hubbard asked, looking concerned.

Both men nodded simultaneously.

"What I want to know is how come I never heard of it?" He looked from Gibson to Dent. "And do you know what really happened to Ah Hoon?"

"I don't have a clue. Then again I've never tried to pass the Sweet Flower War off as a pulp. But if I wanted to know for sure, I'd start by going down to Chinatown and doing some research. Right, Walter? You used to be a newspaperman. Weren't you the cub reporter who exclusively interviewed Al Capone behind bars? You know how to research a story. And you used to know how to get that ending." He looked directly at Hubbard. "That's the kind of work you have to do if you want to be a good enough writer to get yourself out of the pulp biz and into the glossies, slicks, and hardcovers. Where the real writing matters."

Gibson took a long drag on his cigarette and blew the cloud in Dent's direction. He knew Dent's beef with him, but he was not going to rise to the bait. He just wasn't going to do it.

"Well, that Sweet Flower yarn. It's a helluva story," Hubbard said to them. "You fellas, uh, mind if I take a crack at writing it? I believe I'd like to."

"Well, I'll tell you, Ron," Gibson said, "the reason the Sweet Flower War was on my mind tonight was that it just inspired a big part of the Shadow story I just dropped off today. *The Art of Murder.* There's a locked-room murder in it which was inspired by the Sweet Flower War. And Lester, you'll be happy to know that I propose a solution. A pulp solution."

In his latest book, his 217th, The Shadow, the hero who knows what evil lurks in the hearts of men, had set out to solve a series of murders which had taken place in the Metropolitan Museum of Art. Priceless antiquities arriving from distant lands had been stolen from a locked vault deep within the museum, while guards inside the vault had been found dead come the morning. Slinking from dark corner to dark corner without making a sound, ink-black in his greatcoat and slouch hat, becoming nearly invisible by merely acting invisible, The

Shadow had penetrated the museum, eluded the well-meaning guards, and entered the vault, where he had, earlier that day as Lamont Cranston, his millionaire playboy alter ego, made a big show of donating a lost Rembrandt. The door had slammed shut behind him: The Shadow had been betrayed by one of his very own agents, the dedicated and devoted who owed him their lives, men and women whose vigilance constantly provided him with information from every corner of the city, and who carried out his orders without question. Except for this one, who had turned rogue.

Sometime before the dawn the vault door had opened and the sinister crime lord behind the plot had entered and, to his delight, laid eyes upon the murdered corpse of The Shadow, enemy to the criminal demimonde. As his hands had fallen upon his new prize, The Shadow's eerie laugh—a haunting, piercing, maddening sound which rattled in the black minds of the guilty—had filled the air around him. But the corpse remained still. The crime lord shut himself in the room, knowing it would be safe. At that moment, The Shadow revealed the key to the mystery. A secret panel under the floor flipped up and The Shadow leapt out, nickel-plated .45s drawn. The corpse in The Shadow's coat had been none other than the traitorous agent, who had been lying in wait under the floor. When he had attacked, The Shadow's justice had been swift and merciless, as it would now be with this evildoer. The struggle to the death began.

In the morning, when the museum guards opened the locked room, three dead bodies were found inside beside a note from the mysterious Shadow explaining all, identifying the villains, and giving directions to the location of the rest of the stolen art. In the resulting confusion and general throng of visitors to the scene of the crime to examine the secret hiding spot, no one had noticed as one of the corpses suddenly arose and vanished into the crowd. Later, no one would be able to say for sure whether there had actually been a third body.

"Trapdoor? Not bad. It's pulp." Dent puffed on his pipe. "Of course, I went completely pulp when I proposed a solution in the very first issue of *Doc Savage.* I had a Mayan with a rifle scale the girders of the unfinished top floors of the Chrysler Building and take a shot at Doc Savage, who was ten blocks away. Of course, he missed because his target was a decoy statue. I'm sure you read it, Mr. Gibson. It was just six years ago. Right after the Golden Vulture disappeared."

And there it was. The Golden Vulture. He'd brought it up. All of a sudden Gibson could sense Dent's particular dislike of him. It was there in his penetrating gaze, and Gibson felt a sudden rising pang of guilt, which he tried to force back down with angry self-righteousness.

"The Golden Vulture," Hubbard interrupted. "What's that?"

"Like the Sweet Flower War, it's a story that's become a legend. And like the murder of Ah Hoon, it's something only two people know the truth about. The one who held the gun and the one who got shot."

Gibson leapt to his feet. He was quivering with anger. "Why don't you call a spade a spade and tell me what you want to say, Dent?"

Dent took a step forward from the bar and drew himself up and over Gibson, looking down at him. "I just did. Anyway, it's all just spilled ink, Mr. Gibson," Dent said. He put his beer stein down in front of Hubbard, who, having been oblivious to the tension, was now registering an expression of complete surprise at their open hostility. "I believe I'm done," Dent said. "I'll see you around."

"Not around, Dent." Gibson put the palm of his hand on Dent's chest. For a moment Gibson thought that the brick wall he could feel under Dent's jacket and shirt was muscle, but then he realized what his palm was on. If Dent had placed his hand on Gibson's chest, he would have felt the same thing. A Street & Smith–issued notebook was always next to a pulp writer's heart. "Behind. You'll always be behind me. The number two. They're not making Hollywood movies of Doc Savage. Doc's not on the radio. The Shadow is. My Shadow." People were starting to look over at them. Gibson saw men he knew recognize him, whisper about him. He didn't care. It was time to put Lester Dent in his place. "And you can forget about cracking the glossies. You ain't gonna see your name on the cover of the *Saturday Evening Post* or the *New Yorker.* 'Cause you're just a nickel-a-word pulp monkey like me, selling daydreams at wholesale prices to soda jerkers in Boise and schoolboys in Kansas City while your house name, Kenneth Robeson, gets all the glory! So take that, and your Doc Savage oath, and blow it out your pipe."

Gibson knew Dent would take the first swing. When he swiped at him, Gibson was going to try to punch his lights out with one hit. He even had the spot on his chin that he was going to go after. Then the big man would probably pummel him into a pulp. He had only been in a few scraps in his life, two of those in the army and one in the Bowery, but those had been years ago. On the plus side he had come out of those dustups better than the other guys. Instead of making an aggressive move, Dent looked passively down at the floor for a moment. For some reason this made Gibson even angrier. Why wouldn't the guy just put his mitts up?

"I may not be Jack London, or Ernest Hemingway, but I will make it out of the pulps and into the glossies," he said. He put on his hat, his eyes almost disappearing beneath the brim. Then he nodded toward Ron. "Ron, it was nice seeing you."

Ron cast about for something to say. "How about coming by the Knickerbocker on Friday?"

"Your pulp writers mixer? I just might." Dent puffed on his pipe to make sure it was burning. Without looking at Gibson he said, "That soda jerker and that schoolboy? They're good people. Until I get out of the pulps they'll get my best month after month. I know you're happy to just do pulp—that's the big difference between us—but are you still giving your readers your best?" He walked slowly around the table, deliberately in no hurry as he headed toward the door.

"Holy . . . ," muttered Hubbard as Gibson dropped into his chair and swallowed another drink.

"Yep." Gibson sighed. The anger was evaporating. The gaze of the spectators was moving on. "A regular Algonquin roundtable here at the White Horse Tavern. Without the sex. Or the witty banter. But mostly without the sex."

"What the hell was that about?"

"*The Golden Vulture.* It's his beef with me."

"So what's the Golden Vulture? A legend? A statue like the Maltese Falcon?"

"It's a story. Just a goddamned book." He wanted to say that it was something that he felt bad about but he couldn't bring himself to admit it. "When you get the number one and number two bestselling writers in America together, there's bound to be some rivalries. Some misunderstandings. Some shit."

"Why don't you try and straighten things out with him?"

Gibson shrugged. "Because I'm still number one and Doc Savage is still number two."

"You mean Lester Dent?"

"Of course."

He waited for Hubbard's contemptuous response. Something deserved that would just wither his spirit. He still felt like he needed the pounding from the fight with Dent that he hadn't received. Combat might have vindicated him, at least restored his honor. Instead he had received nothing from his rival but a lecture. His own notebook felt heavy in his breast pocket against his chest. He carried it out of habit, but had he made any entries in it lately? Weren't all the notes and observations in it kind of stale? Maybe Dent was right. Maybe he hadn't been delivering his best lately.

Instead the young man asked, "Do you guys really make a nickel a word? 'Cause I'm only making two and a half cents. What do you think I can do to make more?"

Gibson decided at that moment, as Hubbard spoke, that not only was Nanovic going to pay for all the drinks tonight, but the ed was about to drop a substantial down payment on his future bar tab.

"I got a boat back in Washington. Sure do miss her," Hubbard rattled on. "You know, I went to China once. It was okay. You get better Chinese food here, though."

Gibson smiled to himself. Like any pulp writer worth his salt, Hubbard told his tales well and half-believed his own bullshit. Believing was essential.

"Tell me all about China," Gibson said. And as the other writer launched into what was sure to be a wildly entertaining story full of plausible lies, gratuitous distortions, and outrageous half-truths, he ordered another round.

Episode Two

HOWARD LOVECRAFT knew he was going to die. It was a horrible thing to know.

He had always been obsessed with his death. Even as a child he had imagined, in evocatively vivid detail, what his funeral would be like. The eight-year-old Howard had envisioned an open-casket viewing in the small Providence chapel his family attended. There would be lots of candles, an imported pipe organ (the chapel only had a tinny piano), and a tiny mahogany coffin lined with red silk. He would be serenely beautiful in a very adult black suit with long pants, and nestled on a soft, white satin pillow. There would be no wailing or cries of despair, only gentle weeping and perhaps a whispered apology from Howard's father for the way his choices in life had led directly to his son's present state.

In his teens, perhaps to compensate for his growing shyness and awkwardness in all situations not directly involving any family member, Howard had imagined his funerals as grand expressions: New Orleans jazz parades with a solemn procession accompanied by a somber *thomp-thomp* cadence on the way to Swan Point Cemetery, the citizens of Providence lining the streets, and then a boisterous explosion of music and celebration upon its return. There had been a somber midnight burial accompanied by a distant bagpipe player shrouded in graveyard mist. He had even conceived of an elaborate and very satisfying Viking funeral to be launched in fiery fury from the shores of the Cape; its light would be a beacon to the cod fleet through a long, dark night. In later years, after he had forgotten most of his fantasy scenarios, he still would occasionally recall this one fondly and with approval. He had in the end, however, made other arrangements.

Lightning was followed, after a count to ten, by thunder. The heart of the storm was five miles away. Wisps of Bing Crosby's voice reached him like puffs of a gentle breeze from a distant land. Someone had tuned the RCA a floor below to a Broadway song review show and Bing was singing a Cole Porter tune that had been big last year, "You're the Top." Howard couldn't remember what show it was from. It might have been a movie, as well. Howard didn't go to the theater or the pictures.

Howard desperately wanted a cigarette. The last bout of wracking spasms had ended and the pain had receded somewhat. He knew the agony would return, worse each time, forcing him to curl up into a moaning ball, but before it happened, he needed a smoke to steady and prepare himself. He forced himself to climb out of the uncomfortable bed. His cigarettes sat on a table on the other side of the hospital room. The green and white tiles were refreshingly cool against his feet. His legs were a little wobbly, but he crossed the room with the stability and dignity requisite of a scion of the Phillips line. His mother would have been proud of how her little boy was holding up under the strain. He had been very proper. A good Phillips. She would have liked to have known that he had risen to the occasion.

He lit his cigarette and willed himself to the open window, where he exhaled his first lungful out into the night. The cold rain fell in great sluicing torrents, spattering heavily across the parking lot. If he put his hand out into the night air, even if only for an instant, he would draw it back as wet as if he had plunged it into the pitcher of water near his bedside. The next bursting crack of lightning was followed by an ominous flickering in the lights in his room. Dependable as ever—a mere rumor of heavy weather could cause the Providence power system to collapse. He watched, fascinated, as the lightbulbs struggled to regain their brightness for a moment, only to dim again. Electricity delivery in Providence was not an exact science; it was more of a game of chance. The lightbulbs seemed to settle into drawing less electricity than before, and though they flickered erratically, the light they provided seemed somewhat steady. He let the cool, damp air caress the long, gaunt face that children had always taunted him about, calling him "horse" or "Man o' War."

The cigarette tasted good. Great, in fact.

He wanted his mother.

For a moment he thought he heard her voice, but then he realized with disappointment that it was her sister, his Aunt Annie, in the hallway. She was pleading with the doctor for more information about her nephew's condition. She wasn't convinced about the stomach cancer diagnosis. Howard smiled grimly. Of course she was right; no one gets stomach cancer in three days. He had had to lie and tell her that for months now he'd been feeling pains in his gut which he'd been ignoring. She still didn't understand how he could become so ill so fast. That's what she was pestering the doctor about in the hallway. Aunt Annie was sweet and good but not the smartest of her sisters, and now she had grown old as well and the afflictions of her age were often upon her mind. She and Howard had lived together in Providence in the devastating years since his mother had died raving beyond the bounds of human sanity in the asylum.

Howard had given Aunt Annie complicated instructions to be executed upon his death. He was worried that she was nearing a point of hysteria which would incapacitate her when he needed her the most. For the first time in his life, now that he was dying, he had real plans.

Outside, standing at the edge of a pool of light from a streetlamp, a man was looking up at the hospital. At Howard's room. His hat was pulled down to conceal his face and his open coat blew around him in the wind. A haunter, Howard thought. A haunter in the dark. From far off he thought he could hear a man laughing wildly; someone must have switched the RCA to *The Shadow.* It was Sunday night, after all. The man staring at his room was swallowed by sudden darkness the next instant when the lights of Providence dimmed again. The strangest thought emerged in Howard's mind—that perhaps it had actually been The Shadow. His old friend Walter Gibson's Shadow, come to pay his last respects. A flash of lightning illuminated the area where the man had been standing, and Howard was startled to see that he had vanished completely from sight. He cursed his imagination, the instrument which he had called upon so many times in the past to deliver him to literary greatness but which had only offered up a dark mythology that the world had ignored resoundingly. So many times, as he sat down at the typewriter, he had begged for the story that issued forth to be about something that was, well, if not normal, then at least something that normal people wanted to read. But in the end, he wrote what he was miserably and helplessly compelled to. And now, as he waited to die, with no more words to write, his own mind did not have even the dignity to offer up hallucinations of his own creation, only The Shadow. Although this was mortifying, he had to admit that in the end, that vision was ultimately preferable to his own creation, the great dark god Cthulhu, with his dripping tentacled mouth and dreams which caused madness.

Madness.

His father had died insane as well. For five years when Howard was still a young boy, his father had been locked away in a hospital in Chicago. For five years Howard had been told that his father had been paralyzed in an accident and lay in a dark slumbering coma. For five years while Howard had prayed every night that his father would awaken and return home refreshed, his father had staggered around a gray hospital room, naked and shorn and screaming at phantoms. Aunt Annie had finally told him the truth about his father and the cause of his terrible dementia, syphilis, only in the past year. She could bear the shame alone no longer.

Howard closed his mind against the sound of Aunt Annie's voice in the hallway. Stomach cancer. He had assumed he would die in the grip of madness as his parents did, but as another great crashing wave of pain broke over him, he realized he had rarely experienced such mental clarity. He had to protect his aunt the way she and her two sisters, including his mother, youngest of the three, had protected him about his father. He had been able to grow up under the romantic delusion that his noble father was only trapped in a dark spell like an old king in a legend and that any day might bring his return. His aunts and his mother had given him hope at an age when he had needed hope. When he could still believe. Now he could protect Aunt Annie. By dying.

The six-minute smoke. That's how they advertised his Lucky Strike cigarettes, and he was three minutes into it. There was another flash, the bolt of lightning clearly visible across the skyline. The thunder followed quickly—five seconds. Two and a half miles away. The hospital wing was quiet now. Aunt Annie had followed his doctor out of earshot, still pleading with him to help Howard.

Death would be cold.

He looked at his reflection in the mirror: his long face, always somewhat equine, was now a skull barely covered by a thin layer of barely living tissue. His eyes were wild circular orbs, gleaming and alive against the dying flesh. He felt the emotion roll up from deep inside him; it rocked his body as much as the pain had a moment before. Tears began to fall onto his cheeks. Sadness. He felt sadness and regret for the moments off his life. He missed ever knowing how it felt to be loved by a father—his father. He wished he had made a success out of his marriage, had been a better husband, had found a way to love Sonia and be loved by her. Why a divorce? There had been love there. Where was she now? Chicago? Cleveland? Back in New York? And how would she find out about him? And what would she think? Would she shed more tears than he was shedding now? She had wanted a different path for them than the one he had chosen and clung to. A writer. As if that career could restore his family name to the station his mother had dreamt of. Perhaps had he risen to the stature of Mark Twain. But what a mess he had made of that. Not even good enough to be considered a second-rate Poe. He had written the worst tales for the lowest of the low—the pulps—and even they had shunned him. If only he had had the sense to stop early on. Become a professor of English or a journalist or anything but a failure to his family. He had always thought there was more time. There should have been. If only his path hadn't forced him to translate research papers from science to English at the Providence Medical Lab. He never would have discovered that damned island. Never would have made that nightmare trip. Never would have entered the abyss. Never would have had to find himself facing the cold. If only—

If only his mother were still alive.

"Howard." He heard his name spoken aloud and it startled him. He twisted around, the motion painful. The voice hadn't belonged to his doctor.

His eyes fell upon the figure of the person who had called his name, his murderer. The man suspended himself in the doorway on shaking arms. Rainwater dripped from his soaked coat. He clutched a dripping felt fedora in one clawlike fist. His head was bare and water drops slid easily over his bald, fleshy scalp. Howard could see that their skin shared the same nearly translucent yellow coloring, arteries clearly visible beneath. The man's deadening eyes were shining and desperate, like cold, hard anthracite. Jeffords. Howard realized instantly that it had been Jeffords he had seen outside in the flash of lightning, and not any Shadow, and he knew why the glimpse had caused him to shudder. In another instant the thought crossed his mind that the two of them might be mistaken for a pair of syphilitics and he was afraid that people might think he had died like his father after all.

"You sneak son of a bitch," Jeffords hissed at him. To Howard, Jeffords didn't look nearly as afflicted as his own reflection had. Of course, Jeffords had been farther away when all hell broke loose and was a more robustly healthy man to begin with than Howard had ever been. "Where is it?" Why, he might live on for days yet. In agony, Howard pleasantly assured himself. But he would still be able to perpetrate great harm to Aunt Annie in that time. That's what Howard could protect her from. Jeffords. And Towers.

Howard sighed. He thought it would be an extremely defiant gesture to light up another cigarette now and have a puff before answering; to show Jeffords that he was no longer afraid of him. But the cigarettes were still on the table and he was still by the window. And he was still afraid of Jeffords. Terrified. He held his hands open to indicate that he had nothing for Jeffords. "Gone," he said simply.

"You misguided bastard!" Jeffords took a couple of steps into the room and looked around as if he expected to see what he was looking for just lying around. "Don't bullshit me."

"I'm not," Howard explained. "It wouldn't have done us any good anyhow. Don't you understand that? Look at us. We never had enough time. None of us did."

A look of understanding, horrified understanding, dawned across Jeffords's face. His shoulders sagged as if all hope were being crushed out of him. He looked at Howard as if trying to make sense of this strange, dying little man. He clapped a hand to his forehead. Jeffords always prided himself on being a problem solver, Howard remembered. He was now a problem for the man to solve.

Howard felt he had to make another attempt to explain himself. "Short of going back to the isle, destroying *this* was the only thing I could think of."

"The only thing! The only thing! Christ, Lovecraft! I might have thought of something." He took a couple of steps closer.

"Your thoughts on the matter were perfectly clear." Howard could see that Jeffords's despair was beginning to turn into something more menacing. He wished he would hear Aunt Annie's voice and the doctor's in the hall again. He swallowed hard; even that was painful. "I was saving it from you."

"You've killed us both," he said. "You're a goddamned murderer."

Howard stared at him. Then he shrugged. "I didn't take us to the isle."

Jeffords leapt at him. Howard was so surprised he could only blink. Jeffords's hands wrapped around his throat. Howard was still so uncomprehending of the actual events unfolding upon him that he had time to think that Jeffords's hands were soft and smelled like Ivory soap and Burma-Shave. This was in the time that it took for their bodies to fall, ungainly, to the floor. Howard's elbow cracked upon impact, bearing the full weight of his own sickened body, and Jeffords's. The shock and knowledge of the imminent awesome pain made him open his mouth to gasp in air. That's when he understood he was being choked to death. He found his body's urge to struggle. The pain in his chest grew. He could feel his body panicking; his legs began kicking. His arms began pawing at Jeffords. Something exploded in his chest. Still his mind resisted.

"I'm going to hunt you down in hell, Lovecraft." Jeffords's face was turning red from the exertion. It made his sickly skin glow orange, like that of a deranged jack-o'-lantern.

Howard's gaping mouth began to turn up at the edges. He was trying to grin. Saliva drooled from the corners of his mouth. His chest began to convulse. Jeffords pulled his hands back, unsure of himself. Howard sucked in a gale of air, which instantly escaped from him in a whooping laugh.

It was the best he had ever felt. Jeffords was looking at him queerly. Howard owed him an explanation for his good humor.

"I've got other plans," he whispered, his voice a croak. There were red spots floating in his vision. He could barely see. He couldn't breathe well at all. It wasn't even his windpipe; some mechanism in his chest was not drawing air. He could feel his grin, though. He had a lot to look forward to.

He heard a scream which sounded as if it came from the bottom of the deepest ocean. Aunt Annie. She was so far away. He could feel Jeffords lift himself from his body. His body instinctively tried to draw itself into a fetal position, trying to find some kind of protection from the pain without and within. Some of the redness cleared from his vision. He saw Jeffords's feet running away from him. He saw Aunt Annie and the doctor, their faces aghast, in the doorway. Saw Jeffords push past them. The doctor in pursuit. Aunt Annie's hand in his. She looked like his mother. His mother should have been here when he died. He should have been with her when she died.

"Our Father, who art in heaven," she began softly. Tears were beginning to fall from her eyes. He could feel his writer's mind, ever present, struggling to preserve all the little details of the moment. There were shouts down the corridor. Aunt Annie smelled of lavender. The floor needed grout in between the tiles. Agony was beautiful. "Hallowed be thy name."

He shook his head at her. She stopped praying. His mouth moved, trying to form words. She leaned in. She was weeping now; it would be hard for her to understand him. He knew she felt as if she had failed her sister and failed their entire family line. He clutched her hand harder, trying to reassure her, staring into her eyes. From far away he heard music. She understood that he needed to communicate and stifled her sobbing.

"Is it cold?" he asked her, desperately. "Is it?" Everything depended upon that.

She nodded. "It's very cold."

A moment before he died, he wished the moment of death would bring some clarity or enlightenment or revelation. But there would be nothing.

That was his last thought.

It was cold.

EPISODE THREE

WORD ON the street was John Campbell had work for writers. And that was the word The Flash needed to hear.

The Flash paused by the newsstand at the corner of Seventh Avenue at the edge of the Street & Smith building to look for Campbell's mag. This particular newsstand, run by a set of old Italian twins, had all the mags put out that month—not just by Street & Smith, the biggest publisher in the world, but Popular, Frank A. Munsey, Clayton, Thrilling, Culture, and Pro-Distributors Publishing. There were over two hundred mags decorating their stalls this month. Two hundred titles. The newsstand looked like an ink truck had crashed into it. A sharpster could tell instantly how well any given mag was selling by where it stood on the racks of this newsstand. If that same sharpster knew whether or not a certain mag was hot, said sharpster might have an angle on squeezing more than a penny a word out of that mag's ed. The Flash considered himself a sharpster.

Astounding Stories, Campbell's mag, wasn't hanging on a clip from a clothesline out in front like the very best-selling titles, the hero books like *Doc Savage* or *The Shadow* or *G-8 and His Battle Aces,* but it was clearly visible, full cover on display, on the first rack above the slicks like *Collier's* and *Vanity Fair* and the *New Yorker,* and the chewing gums and chocolate bars. On the same row as *Astounding* were some of the other bestsellers that month, titles that were flying out of newsstands, soda shops, and drugstores all across America: *The Spider, Thrilling Detective, Adventure, Thrilling Adventures, Amazing Stories, Blue Book, Weird Tales, Dime Mystery, Phantom Detective,* and the granddaddy of them all, still going strong after more than forty years, *Argosy.*

The cover of each and every mag on the newsstand was a brilliant four-color explosion of breathtaking action captured forever in a frozen moment of suspense: the instant before a righteous fist impacted against a gnarled and snarling face; a plane spiraling disastrously toward earth as its hero struggled to untangle his parachute from its tail; Art Deco skyscrapers crumbling under a devastating alien onslaught. The Flash loved the mags' cover art, though he knew how much it was derided within the industry and without. He knew it was what sold the mags to begin with and then kept folks coming back to find out what was in them. Ten *million* of them a month. Each buying an average of three mags. That meant that thirty million pulps, give or take, were being read by America each and every month! It was the cheapest and most popular form of entertainment in the country, and as long as the covers beckoned from the newsstands, it would continue to be so.

Behind the first row were the mags that still sold consistently well but just were not gangbusters. Their bold legends were clearly visible but most of the artwork was covered by other mags. The Flash was disheartened to see that many of these titles were westerns and two-fisted tales—his bread and butter. *Thrilling Western,* for example, had done well by him and he by it, but it would never pay more than two and a half cents a word. Same for *All-American Stories* and *Thrilling Wonder Stories.* None of them had broken out while he had been writing for them. Probably none of them ever would.

The third row of mags were all pulled up from behind the second row so men could see the mags that boys couldn't bring home. In addition to the mushy *Love, True Love, Romance,* and *True Romance* titles were *Spicy Adventure Stories, Spicy Mystery Stories, Spicy Detective Stories,* even

Spicy Western Stories published by a man named Donenfeld. Their cover artists were inventive in coming up with endlessly daring ways to put glamorous and scantily clad women in harm's way. They knew how to deliver the goods. These were the mags that had imperiled the entire industry recently, as Mayor La Guardia was so offended by their lurid scenes that he was threatening to have the garbagemen rip them from the newsstands as they executed their rounds. Some of them were making good on the mayor's threats. Some newsstand owners had recently taken to ripping the covers from the pulps before placing them on the racks, as if that would help. The Flash had certainly never written for any of the mags on this row, but their covers had given him plenty of stimulating moments. Every writer he knew had a stash of the men's mags in one of his desk drawers.

He had also never written, nor would ever condescend to write, for the final row. This was the row whose titles were mostly blocked by the arousing arrangement of the men's mags before them. Here were the shudder and menace mags like *Terror Tales, Horror Stories, Strange Detective Mysteries* (Who was strange? The detectives or the mysteries?), *Eerie Stories,* and others. Dreck. The bottom of the bottom of the literary barrel. This was the ghetto where that Lovecraft fellow had tried to eke out a name for himself. An assortment of dark perversions and decadences, never permeated by the light of a well-written phrase or inspiring insight. Many of these mags were the literary equivalent of the filthy eight-page Tijuana bibles the old Italians hid under their newspapers and would sell you if you asked for the "funnies." He supposed that somebody must be reading them. Publishers ran their mags on a slim profit margin that didn't allow for much misjudgment of the public's desires. If a mag slipped only one month, it could be gone from the stands the next, its publisher bankrupt, its eds pounding the pavement and looking for work.

He knew in his bones he was destined for the top tier. After all, he was The Flash. Sometimes (when an ed demanded) he was also Kurt von Rachen, L. Ron Hubbard, and Frederick Engelhardt. But he liked The Flash best of all. Of course it wasn't a name he published under, like the others. It was a nickname given to him by his agent, Ed Bodin, because he could write so damn fast. He liked The Flash a hell of a sight better than Red, which was what he had most often been nicknamed until he embarked on his writing career, on account of his shock of thick red hair. But these days, Red was gone and no one in New York or Hollywood need ever know that he had existed. There was only The Flash.

Fact is, he earned the name outright. He was blazingly fast at turning out stories. Like a machine. He wrote faster than anyone he knew, except maybe Gibson. And Dent. It was just like when he had been a boy in Montana and could read earlier and faster than anyone else. He took great pride in his ability to write fast, and to hell with writer's block. Sometimes he felt like he was a river of words, that they flowed out of him with unimaginable force to soak the pages churning through his Remington. It was as if his imagination was fed by a deep spring. He had every confidence that the wellspring would never run dry. Why should it? It hadn't yet. He knew his mind and never doubted it.

Gibson's story about the Sweet Flower War had been pretty damn good, all right, he thought. He could use a killer story like that to bust things wide open. But if both Gibson and Dent had drawn on it, they'd know where it came from if he wrote it again, even if he used a pen name. Still, it was tough to let that one go. Really good stories were hard to come by.

These days, every two weeks, he had a new story to sell to the mags. It wasn't easy. It was righteously hard work, tougher than laying tracks or stowing cargo had ever been. But he did it because he loved writing. He loved using his mind and his fingertips to move mountains, shape the universe, wreak havoc. Rewriting? If a fella knew what he was doing the first time, he wouldn't have to rewrite. Muses? Hell, fear of starvation was the name of his muse. He didn't hold with the theories about motivation, which he overheard other writers talking about at his Knickerbocker gatherings; his characters *knew* what to do. They knew from right and wrong, good and evil. That's all you needed to know about someone to know what they would do. Besides, there wasn't time for motivation. Not when the eds were trying to chisel a guy. The only way to make money in this industry was to write as best a sharpster could, as fast as he could.

His writing had attracted attention too. He actually had a small but loyal group of readers. The eds heard from them occasionally when they would write in and demand more Hubbard. Even if a few of those letters were actually written by The Flash himself, that didn't devalue the bona fide original and unsolicited letters that the eds would receive. His dim glow of fame, within the limited sphere of the mags, had at least made it a little easier to sell stories. When eds received a Hubbard story, they didn't have to read it too carefully anymore. His name on the cover page was a mark of recognized quality. They could publish it easily and it would help sell. Which was the name of the game. So that was one thing he had over both Gibson and Dent: although they were top sellers, nobody in America knew who they were; they were hidden behind house names, Maxwell Grant and Kenneth Robeson. He, on the other hand, was becoming known by his own name.

The top tier, that was his destiny. He knew he'd get there. He loved the pulp business like no one else he knew. Most of the writers he knew were cynical about it, embarrassed by where their fortunes and talents had abandoned them and damned by their ambitions. They longed to be published in hardcover. Read in libraries. Discussed in cafés. They longed to be lionized like the legendary Street & Smith writers: Horatio Alger, Upton Sinclair, Theodore Dreiser, and, most of all, Jack London. The Flash didn't crave the stature of those alumni, or even of Dent and Gibson. Particularly those two men, he felt, were his peers, who owed their elevated positions to the benefits of age and timing more than talent. When he looked desirously at another's career, and chose to emulate its course, the writer could only be Edgar Rice Burroughs.

Tarzana. The thought of it practically made him sigh with longing. Burroughs's ape-man had practically ushered in the pulp age, as publishers sprang up all over the place to try and produce a successful imitation. Through careful control Burroughs had parlayed the character in the funny papers, movies, toys, and games, not to mention a seemingly endless string of new novels and their lucrative international translations. With the money he had made doing this, he had turned around and bought himself a kingdom. A whole valley in California! Just outside of Los Angeles. He built and sold houses on the land to the suckers who wanted to get out of the city. He ran the town council. He was king of the pulp jungle.

Just before the decision to move back to New York had been made, The Flash had been in Hollywood writing a serial movie adventure, *The Secret of Treasure Island.* He had made the pilgrimage to the promised land of Tarzana and seen for himself what it had to offer. It was peaceful and bucolic in the California way. Fragrant orange trees basked in the warm sun, shading the little backyards behind the small houses Burroughs had built and sold.

He could do better, he had decided as he strolled down the elm-lined sidewalks of Tarzana. He had tried to meet Burroughs but the people at his gatehouse said he was otherwise engaged. Imagine being too busy to meet The Flash! He suspected that Burroughs, now an elderly man, might be jealous of The Flash's youth and vitality. Burroughs was richer than Croesus. He had created an empire. By simply writing! Now why wouldn't The Flash himself aspire to do the same?

Tarzana.

To get there he knew he first had to jump from the second row to the clothesline. *Astounding Stories* looked like it might finally be the way. Campbell had already moved it from the second row to the first. It just needed a push to get to the top tier. Then maybe The Flash could land a hero mag for himself.

He turned from the newsstand. It was much colder in New York than it had been a few months ago in Hollywood. A fell winter wind blew off the dank Hudson River, which he could see just west of him. The wind stung the ears and eyes, and he turned up his collar, wishing he had had time to pack a heavier coat. Upon his return from Hollywood, he hadn't even made it up the stone path from the front gate to the white door of his house in Bremerton, Washington, before his wife, Polly, had turned him away. He had had an affair with a starlet, and a jealous former lover of hers had written his wife a letter, ratting him out. He loved his wife and loved being married, and he didn't feel he deserved to be banished from their household just because he had done something stupid out of loneliness. The suitcase he had brought with him to his hotel in New York was the same one he had been carrying when she had appeared in tears upon their front porch. In it then, and now carefully arrayed on his cabinet in the hotel, was an untouched brand-new teddy bear for his son, Ron Jr.; and a china doll for his daughter, Catherine.

Damn, it was cold. He looked at the faces of the men hovering outside the Street & Smith building—anxious men, expectant men, hopeful men. Men who hoped to be able to slip a story to a passing ed in exchange for a few bucks or a break. He realized that no matter how many times the radio played "Happy Days Are Here Again!" or Roosevelt spoke about the next New Deal, the Depression was not over. Especially not for these men. These were the penny-a-word men. Most of them had other jobs and were here on their lunch hour. Some of them spent an entire day out here, trying to scribble stories in notebooks as they waited. The Flash felt a moment of dread. This was the fate that awaited him if he fell to the third row, or farther. Even a guy with talent could end up like Lovecraft. In truth he knew that his moments of weakness, as with that actress, could put him out here on the street faster than failure to anticipate the public taste ever could.

He walked past the line of men, aware that they were staring at him. A tall, gawky teen tried to foist some pages on him but stepped back at the last moment. The teen looked at his face eagerly and then his face fell as he realized that The Flash wasn't an ed. Just a writer.

Francis Scott Street and Francis Shubael Smith had founded the company which took their names in 1855. The firm had made its home in this seven-story, block-long building fifteen years before The Flash was born. Even outside it was possible to feel the deep and persistent thrumming vibrations of the enormous printers, rolling and pounding below the street in the basement; and the binders, which folded the cheap pulp paper into four sections to make a book. Farther up the street he could see the trucks at the loading docks, and the teamsters tossing the bales of freshly printed pulps into them. Some of them were down to their undershirts, even in the chill air, and their coarse language and rough joking reinforced for The Flash that the pulp business was hard work. From the discipline and determination it took to write pulps to the aggressive tactics it took to get them published and onto the newsstands, it was a man's job. He knew of no women pulp writers—even the romances were written by men—and he couldn't name a female artist or ed to save his life. Not that there weren't women in pulps. There were assistants and secretaries.

God, that actress! What had he been thinking?

He put his hand on the door and opened it up. The security guard inside waved him on in. His tenure as president of the Guild had granted him certain privileges; easy access to the Street & Smith building was one of them. The reception lobby was faded and dark. The walls were brown from years of cigarette and cigar smoke (The Flash detested smoking). The carpet was worn from years of shuffling feet. The wood desk was scuffed, and the club chairs were leaking stuffing. In spite of the scent of smoke, he loved it all. He headed for the elevator.

She had had long, loose blond hair and staggering blue eyes and she smelled like an orange grove on the Malibu shores at sunset. She was California incarnate. When he had first been introduced to her on the set, she had been dressed in the wardrobe of an explorer, with tight beige jodhpurs and a crisp white blouse that accented the dark tan of her cleavage. Later he would find that skin to be smooth and warm, covering muscles toned by years spent splashing through the surf. She was utterly without restraint, introducing him to situations and sensations he had never even dreamt of. Her red lips and sharp tongue had peppered his body with kisses; she had devoured him in every way. He had tried to match her enthusiasm; after all, he was a young man in his prime. Not even his own wife had made him feel so powerful in bed as this fierce Hollywood creature.

With a practiced twist of the wrist, the uniformed operator stopped the elevator at the second floor. The cacophony that hit The Flash when the door slid open made him wince. A man wearing a vest and ink-stained apron stepped onto the elevator, carrying a heavy tray of spent lead slugs and space bands. The Flash saw dozens of men just like him sitting in front of machines with giant rollers—the linotype machines. The men were endlessly keying in letter combinations to create the lines of text which would be used to make the molds for the pages the presses waited to print. Hubbard watched with fascination as the man at the station nearest to him slammed a lever back to force his finished page mold, all the letters backwards, into the next level, where molten metal would flow over it and create a mirror cast. This was the room where the type became hot, where the words became real.

The linotype man took the ride to the third floor, the sorting room, where his tray of slugs would be cleaned and sorted by men standing at wooden bins and prepared for the next round. The man gave him a dead-eye look. He didn't care that The Flash was a writer. He didn't care about the pulps. His father when he worked here probably hadn't cared about the mags that they had then, called "dime novels," and even earlier than that, the "penny dreadfuls." If Street & Smith decided tomorrow to print Bibles, he'd show up and carry letters for the Bibles. Just a job. The man exited at the next floor with a bored look at The Flash. Then the operator drew the door shut and the elevator rose again, ascending to the publishing floor, where The Flash stepped off. Campbell's office was at the far end of the long, dark wood-paneled corridor. To his left was the archive, which held the fifty years of manuscripts published by the house. On his right were offices for writers, artists, and eds. The floor above him, the top floor, held the management offices, where guys like Henry Ralston worked. The money men. The men who owned The Shadow and Doc Savage.

He shook the tangle of thoughts of Polly and Hollywood from his head. It was time to be The Flash and The Flash was here to sell. He strode with confidence down the hall.

He passed a life-size poster sign of Walter Gibson holding a typewriter. The advertisement boasted that Street & Smith writer Gibson had been recognized as holding the record for writing the most words ever, over a million, about a single character—The Shadow. The man's output was staggering. And so was his impact. Before The Shadow's appearance, all the top tier mags were detective stories. Within a year of The Shadow's first issue all the bestseller mags were heroic avengers who did more than solve a crime; they combated it. It was as if the nation as a whole had decided in one collective moment that they were tired of justice being served after the fact; they wanted it dished out in advance. They didn't want someone to just look out for them, in the middle of this Depression; they wanted someone to protect them. And the pulps were more than willing to accommodate them. According to the poster, Walter Gibson had achieved greatness on his Smith Corona. The Flash sniffed at the numbers. He was easily turning out a hundred thousand words a month, in his estimation. Okay, they weren't about a single character, but he was certainly on track to set some sort of record. If only he had a hero mag, then he would earn the record and the endorsement money.

He sure wished he had a killer idea like that Sweet Flower mystery. He had to admit that he wasn't very good at tracking down stories like that and using them the way Gibson and Dent seemed to. That was one of the reasons the Street & Smith style suited him so well; here most of the ideas, sometimes even the outlines, for stories of the sort he wrote were provided by the eds. It was just the writer's work to put the words to them. He relied much more on his imagination than his life to just make up the goods. So far the words kept bubbling up.

"John Campbell?" He knocked on the door. On its window were stenciled the words ASTOUNDING AND AMAZING. He knocked again. The Flash's palms were sweating. He needed to win Campbell over. He needed something big. Something bold. Something with great heroes, horrifying villains, and beautiful dames. Something astounding and amazing. He heard a rustle from behind the door, a smooth whisper of pages turning.

"Yeah?" The door flew open and the young ed appeared. He was big man, nearly as tall as Lester Dent, and barrel-chested. The Flash caught a glimpse of paper everywhere, both the yellowish browns of cheap pulp and the richer whites of typewriter stock, as if both the newsstand and the men peddling their stories on the sidewalk below had exploded in a blizzard of scattered pages and spilled ink across every available surface in Campbell's office including the floor.

"Ron Hubbard." He stuck out his hand. Campbell took hold of it and gave it a powerful shake. To Hubbard he appeared to be one of those types that advertisers liked to call a man-on-the-go.

"Hubbard," he said. He was either Hubbard's age or younger. "I hear you're a writer."

"As a matter of fact," said The Flash, matching Campbell's grip with vigor and confidence, "I am."

Episode Four

"AND NOW," the tall thin man with the thatch of white hair announced, his voice ringing out fiercely, "I will attempt to save this sinful woman from the eternal inferno of hell itself!"

The woman held on to a velvet rope for dear life. Below her was a pool of roiling fire. A tendril of sputtering flame climbed busily up the rope, leaving charred strands behind. The woman recoiled in fear and tried to pull herself up but it was clear that her grip was slipping.

"Of course, as every righteous soul knows, the path to salvation lies through the fire." He threw his arms wildly toward the woman, and fireballs leapt from his fingertips. The rope snapped and the woman dropped into the roiling conflagration far faster than anyone could possibly have anticipated. Books and movies have convinced people that a rescuing hand can reach a falling person in the nick of time, but the truth is that the speed is breathtaking and that the moment of rescue is nearly impossible. Voices cried out in terror from onlookers male and female. The fire vanished in a cloud of smoke and heavenly birds flapping into the darkness, and great gasps were heard. The woman floated in the air in the very spot where the flames had been an instant before. She was dressed in a gown of shimmering light, which surrounded her in angelic radiance. The man gestured and slowly the woman descended, as if controlled by a mysterious energy emanating from his hands.

As her feet touched the floor, the audience at the Majestic Theater erupted in rapturous applause. Elderly women fanned themselves excitedly with their programs. Couples turned to each other to express their astounded disbelief. Gibson applauded along. He had seen Blackstone perform the Salvation of Miss Molly illusion dozens of times, and it never failed to impress him with its artful deception and its ability to captivate and impress an audience.

The fireballs from the fingertips were a dazzling new wrinkle, however, and an inspired flourish. He made a mental note to try to figure out how it was done as soon as possible. A flash powder effect was common enough, but he had never heard of one being detonated from what he assumed was some kind of handheld or wrist-attached apparatus. Flash powder was extremely volatile stuff. Anytime the size of a load of powder was doubled, its explosive force multiplied eightfold. Just four ounces, handled recklessly, could do more than remove a limb or an extremity; it could dismember a person. To keep quantities of the explosive somehow attached to reservoirs on his person in close proximity to an igniter was an invitation to disaster for a lesser magician than Blackstone and a reminder to Gibson why his old friend's name was on the marquee.

The bewitching showgirl, one of the bevy of show beauties, bowed and slipped quickly off the stage, no doubt to make another costume change. Blackstone theatrically dabbed some droplets of sweat from his brow with a silk and drank in the applause as he transformed the innocent piece of cloth into the dancing handkerchief, one of his signature pieces. The premiere so far had been brilliant and Gibson could see how much his old friend was enjoying himself.

Gibson had been introduced to Blackstone soon after ghosting biographies for Houdini and Thurston about a decade before. The two had become friends and had collaborated on seven books and dozens of magazine articles about magic over the years.

As Blackstone held the stage, alone in a single spotlight, Gibson could imagine the hullabaloo backstage. Blackstone's team of technicians and performers numbered around fifty; the intense stillness of the man onstage belied the havoc that Gibson imagined was happening mere feet from his back. Blackstone adjusted his bow tie, drew a finger across his thin mustache, then held up his hands in a call for silence, his long fingers spread wide. "Ladies and gentleman," he said in a strong stage voice. "We have a great treat for you tonight. The name of the Great Raymond is known to many of you, as it is throughout the world, as one of the legendary magicians of our time." There was a smattering of applause as some audience members placed the name, although Gibson recognized that Blackstone was being gracious to a brother magician.

Maurice Raymond had been an eclectic yet middling professional magician at his career's apogee, which was more than a few years past now. Just one of that great number of mediocre but serviceable magicians who had sprung up out of nowhere in the previous decade during magic's explosive boom in popularity, performers with no discernible original style—and more importantly, no signature tricks—of their own. Their survival seemed to depend upon presenting budget-conscious versions of the fantastic illusions created by the masters—Thurston, Houdini, Blackstone—to a populace who would never be able to afford to see them otherwise.

"As you may know," Blackstone continued, "this master showman has recently retired from the stage in order to pursue certain occult studies of the deepest and most profound nature."

Once again Harry Blackstone was being charitable. Raymond's shows had declined in quality because of his unwillingness to develop new tricks, and he had quit touring because producers would no longer bankroll his moth-eaten productions. Even though magic shows were not as popular as they had been ten years ago, the public still expected to see new and fabulous extravaganzas, but the Great Raymond had emptied every trick he could from his dusty old bag. Blackstone had surmised to Gibson that with fewer magicians around to crib acts from, Raymond had been unable to sustain his show. Furthermore,

Gibson knew, as Blackstone did and the audience surely did not, that the Great Raymond was ailing.

Blackstone continued in the spotlight, his Michigan accent flattening some of the rounder sounds, "We are thrilled that he has been gracious enough to loan us a special pleasure for the duration of our American tour. She was trained in her mystic art by the greatest of all mentalists, El Cheiro, far from civilization, high in the Peruvian mountains. She has read the minds of kings and queens, emperors and shahs, viceroys and chancellors, presidents and prime ministers. And tonight, ladies and gentlemen, she just might read yours. For seven years she has been one of the star attractions of the Great Raymond's show, as well as his partner in wedlock, and we are proud that she has deigned to join the Blackstone Spectacular for a limited engagement."

Gibson knew she was now part of the show because with Raymond's show in mothballs, Blackstone had been able to sign her at a farm foreclosure price. And she was worth so much more.

"Please give one of your legendary New York welcomes for the woman whose mentalist abilities are sure to convince you of the existence of higher planes of reality, of the existence of worlds unseen and unknown, of the existence of spirits who see all and know all."

A low, mysterious melody began wafting from the orchestra pit, summoning imagined memories of far-flung tropical islands floating on the black Pacific Ocean in the deep of night. "I bring you the astounding, the shocking, the mystifying, the enlightening, the terrifying, the Dragon Lady from the Tibetan Orient, Pearlitzka!"

The spotlight winked out on Blackstone, and another light, hung above the stage, blinked on. It shone into the eyes of the audience. A woman was silhouetted in its beam. Her arms were held high, her back was arched, and her legs were poised in a dancer's position. Light fabric extended from her wrists to the sides of her body, giving her appearance some slight resemblance to a Chinese fan. Gibson could see the rise and fall of her breasts neatly outlined in the light.

"Spirits from the nether regions speak to me of things seen and unseen, of the knowable and unknowable." The girl's husky voice seemed to float out of the air around her. Her arms drew to her side and she turned downstage, a sylph in the light, and bowed. As she stood upright, the house spotlight caught her in its clutches and revealed her to all. Gibson's heart skipped a beat as the light drew out her features.

The woman looked like an Asian of uncommon beauty. Her exquisite baby-doll face was painted white with greasepaint, great swooping teardrops of red Oriental makeup accenting her almond-shaped eyes. Her black hair was piled on her head and held in place with a number of long, thin metal spikes. Her long curved nails were lacquered red. The silk Chinese dress with open sleeves was slit up its side, occasionally revealing the breathtaking legs of a dancer. The silk clung to her skin in a smooth, coolly sensual way.

A stagehand wheeled a rectangular object onto the stage. It was one of the ticket stub boxes from the lobby.

"The spirits will select some of you this evening and tell of things past and present and future." Her voice was light, strong, and clear. "For some of you the things they have to say may be enlightening; for others, terrifying. Only the spirits can know what they know and why they know it. It is for us, the living, to determine what we shall do with the knowledge they choose to share." She unlocked the stub box and extended her arm into it. The audience tittered expectantly; few things enlivened an audience like allowing them to participate in a magic show. Whether being hypnotized, choosing cards, or inspecting chains, the civilians loved to be part of the act.

If they thought about it for two seconds, Gibson thought, they could figure it all out. The box was obviously just a ruse. All the stubs would have the same seat number on them. She could call any number she wanted to, when it came down to it; whoever she called up would obviously be a plant. But the audience was here to be entertained, and surrendering the human desire (or was it an American desire?) to know how everything worked was key to the theater.

"The spirits have spoken!" Pearlitzka called from the stage. Gibson watched everyone look around. "Will the person sitting in seat E2 be kind enough to join me onstage?"

A hand tapped him on the shoulder. "Hey, buddy," a voice whispered in his ear, "that's you! You're in E2!"

"It's only a letter and a number, E2. It shouldn't be hard to find yourself. Of course I could just let the spirits come bring you to me." Her voice had a ring that tickled the base of his spine. He stood up suddenly and waved.

"There he is. There's the one whom the spirits have chosen!" Gibson's palms were sweating, and he swallowed, nervously. He looked back to the exit, which got a laugh. Then he shrugged and gamely marched up the aisle toward the orchestra pit, where an assistant was waiting to direct him up the stage steps.

The beautiful young woman had his hand in an instant and gave it a surprisingly reassuring, and strong, squeeze. Her hand was small and soft. She smelled of sandalwood and jasmine. She looked younger onstage than she had from the auditorium. Her makeup was perfect. Completely in control of the stage, she turned both of them so their bodies faced the audience.

"Do we know each other?" she asked.

He shook his head. There were twitters and whispers from the audience before him. It was hard to see past the footlights and make out faces.

"Do you have a name?" she asked.

He nodded. This time there were guffaws.

"Well, don't keep it to yourself. How about sharing?"

"Walter Gibson," he said sheepishly, and the audience rewarded him with some light applause. He wondered whether if he had said the name Maxwell Grant, it would have garnered more applause than his own name did. Here he stood, the number one bestselling writer in America, creator of the most popular show on radio, and no one even knew who he was.

"You don't mind if I call you Walter, do you, Walter? All right, Walter. Let's see why the spirits have chosen you this evening." She took several steps back from him. He glanced down into the orchestra pit. Some of the musicians were sneaking looks up the slit of her dress. "You work with your hands, they tell me."

"Yeah," he said, not in the least surprised.

"You're not a laborer. You're some kind of skilled craftsman, a sculptor or carpenter. Something that combines the mind and the hands, right?

"I suppose."

"Wait, it's coming to me. It's not about making something physical; you're more in the nature of an artist or a writer."

He nodded. "I'm a writer."

The audience applauded. She peered at him closely, scrutinizing him. He knew what she was doing. Shotgunning. The technique, adapted by magicians from an old spiritualist routine popular at the end of the last century, required throwing a large amount of random information at the mark and letting them pick out what seemed personally relevant. In their astonishment they would tend to forget about all the other questions and choices that were presented to them and focus on the ones that seemed to concern them. For example, stating that a dead relative was trying to contact a mark was usually a safe place to start because everyone always has a dead relative. Then it was a matter of calling out relatives until a match was found. If one rattled off enough relatives, sooner or later the right one would be hit upon. Shotgunning was occasionally referred to as the Barnum Effect, because it played off people's vanity and desire to believe that someone would actually want to have meaningful contact with them from beyond the grave. People tended to believe a lie told to them about themselves if it was a flattering lie. And to tell a person that someone they had loved was trying to break the boundaries between heaven and earth just to tell them where the fried chicken recipe was hidden was quite flattering indeed.

Her green eyes were lively but critical. Her approach, which had started off in typical fashion, had become fairly specific. She was an expert shotgunner. Maybe the best he had ever seen. "The spirits tell me you carry one picture in your wallet at all times. Do they tell me truly?"

"Yes." How had she known that? He was beginning to feel vaguely uneasy.

"And that picture is . . . I see . . . There is someone far away. Someone who loves you. The spirits are showing me a little boy. He wears shorts and is holding a baseball."

Reluctantly Gibson slipped his fingers into his wallet and pulled out a photo. The audience broke into applause.

"A little boy, ladies and gentleman. Walter, the spirits want you to know that he . . . Robert . . . thinks of you often and sends his love."

The audience applauded with great enthusiasm. He tucked the picture back into his wallet without saying a word or even glancing at it. Pearlitzka tried to take his hand. He wriggled his fingers free. She seized it and led him in a bow. He turned to leave but she held on to his hand. She looked at him and a puzzled expression crossed her face. She held up her free hand. "It appears the spirits have more for Walter from the world beyond," she said.

"That's okay," he said. "They've said quite enough."

She was silent for a moment. A long moment. Long enough for the audience to begin to grow uneasy. The orchestra vamped. She studied him closely. "Someone you know is dying," she said at last. Her voice had dropped into a much lower register. "He's dying." She closed her eyes; the spectral voice made his flesh shiver. "He's dying right now and he's so afraid. It's so cold."

The audience began to murmur. Someone coughed, nervously.

"No," he said with a shrug. "I don't think anyone I know is dying."

"The spirits are afraid," she said, and her voice was hollow and cold. "The spirits want you to know that . . . he refuses to cross over. His soul is trapped between our plane and theirs. They are trying to help him but he won't go. He won't admit he's dead. He says he was murdered! You have to help him! There are lives to save. You have to help."

He could feel the audience slip away from her. He looked at her face and realized she had lost the thread of her patter; she seemed distracted. "Help who?" he said, loudly. "The only one dying here is me!" The drummer rapped out a rim shot for him; the sound of it plucked at her stage instincts.

She recovered in an instant and looked at the audience. "Obviously a comedy writer!" she told her audience with a wink, and they applauded. But her hand had turned cold and damp with sweat. She released him and he retreated to the safety of his seat as quickly as he could, while she summoned the next willing mark to the stage.

His heart was pounding. He felt a tap on his shoulder. It was the man sitting behind again who had alerted him to his fate a little while ago. "Hey, pal," the man said, "too bad she's married, huh?"

"Yeah," he replied, angry at the man and angrier at Pearlitzka. "Tough."

Episode Five

"How did you know about my son?" he demanded.

"What?"

"Robert! How did you know I had that picture in my wallet?" he said to her later, back in his apartment. She was naked and glistening in sweat which had soaked even into her loosened hair, giving her a wild leonine look. He was naked too and lying on the floor, where he had landed after falling off the couch.

"The spirits," she said, still trying to catch her breath. Litzka was beautiful. He thought so now as he looked at her in his apartment. How could he have helped himself? Of course she wasn't an Oriental. She was from Mount Carmel, Pennsylvania. The makeup was a disguise, again created by her husband to play upon certain feelings he knew American men had toward Asian women, which ultimately served to further misdirect them. Without the stage makeup her Kewpie-doll face had an innocent, open, vulnerable appearance. Except for her eyes. Her eyes were wise and experienced.

"I don't buy it."

"I am a little bit psychic, after all," she said, with a mildly offended tone. "Just last month the spirits warned me not to get on a train and it got trapped in the Rockies for three days because of an avalanche. And they were trying to tell me something about a friend of yours."

"Litzka," he said, sitting up. That was what most people called her instead of the mouthier Pearlitzka. Actually, her real name was Pearl Beatrice Gonser Raymond, but she hadn't gone by that in years—not since the Great Raymond had anointed her Pearlitzka. "I don't buy your psychic bit. I never have. I'm serious. Now how did you find out about my son?"

She sighed, finally—hating, as all magicians did, to divulge even the tiniest secret. "That's easy. I went through your wallet when we were in Silver Springs."

Silver Springs. Florida.

He had never meant to start an affair with a married woman. He had never wanted to make time with the wife of someone he knew. But he had. In Silver Springs.

Blackstone's company was preparing a series of shows in Miami for the snowbirds, the rich New Englanders who traveled to the southland to winter. This yearly destination was always a lucrative engagement for the tour, so Blackstone's customary demands for flawless execution were always greatly amplified. Among his many concerns: his backers spent the season in Miami and, despite their participation, this was the only time during the year when they took an active interest in the show that always reaped them a profit. Facing such myriad distractions, he was unable to spend as much time with Gibson as he had anticipated when he first suggested that Gibson come to Miami and cowrite a new book with him. So Gibson had spent much time watching rehearsals in the showroom of the Eden Roc Hotel and much more time at the hotel bar. He had spent so much time there, in fact, that the hotel had invited him to leave his typewriter on the bar so he could walk right in and begin his work.

He had met her once before at a Society of American Magicians meeting, when she had first appeared on the arm of Raymond, and he had agreed with the assembled brotherhood that the old magician was lucky to have found himself such a dish. But he hadn't realized how that pale, pert face disguised her mischievously bright and clever spirit until they had spent time in Florida. She was new to Blackstone's company and was having trouble breaking into the tight-knit group. Gibson was an outsider as well. And that was the first thing they had in common.

He had tried avoiding her for several days. But the attraction was too apparent to both of them, and so to make sure that he would not add any more pressure to his friend's hectic production, he slipped out of town.

He had driven his Ford Tudor north, away from the coastal cities, toward the sparsely populated wet wilderness which lay inland beyond the swamps and Seminole Indian jungles until, late in the evening, when he could drive no farther, he discovered Silver Springs. A simple hotel sign had compelled him to turn off the road. He had never been to this oasis before, had never even known of its existence, but as he stood watching a heron rise over the waters bubbling up from deep beneath his feet to form the Crystal River, he felt as if this wild place were his very own.

Upon checking in he had discovered that a Hollywood movie crew was staying at the small hotel, which clung to the bank of the deep springs. Evidently the waters of Silver Springs were so clear that they were perfect for underwater photography, better than anywhere else in America. He spent the next day watching the crew film swimming scenes, and that night he spied on Johnny Weissmuller and Maureen O'Sullivan as they dined at the Angebilt Hotel's restaurant. They were sleek, sophisticated, glowing from their tans. Gibson knew many famous magicians, and theater and radio actors, but there had been something about being in the presence of bona fide *movie stars* that captivated his attention. He had watched their every move all evening long, fascinated to see them in color, and to hear Weissmuller speaking in complete, articulate sentences. O'Sullivan smiled at Walter more than once. She had a slight Irish accent. The chimp who played Cheetah had pissed on the dance floor and chased the singer from the stage.

That night there was a knock at his hotel room door. Litzka stood in his doorway, hair damp and wild from the tropical rainstorms that swept through Florida on a daily basis. Her eyes were filled with desperation and longing. Her lips trembled. The thought had crossed his mind to just close the door on her. She wouldn't have spoken a word if he had; she would have just left.

"You chose the only woman in the world you can't run away from," she had said.

He had let her in.

"What would you have done if I had taken the picture out?" he said to her, casting off the memories of Florida.

She shook her head. "That picture has been in your wallet for years. I knew you wouldn't." She flung herself on him and he kissed her roughly. "Weren't you surprised, though?"

"It's not what we rehearsed!"

"That's what you're mad about? That I improvised? Really, Walter?"

"You were really improvising up a storm tonight," he said. "Between that and your message from the grave, I just felt like I was out there flapping like a screen door in a twister."

She looked down and seemed to be studying her red-lacquered fingernails. He heard a scratching from the other side of his living room. "China Boy is messing up my pulps."

With a sharp cry meant to startle the bird, she leaped up and ran across his apartment to where China Boy was scratching the cover off a recent issue of *The Shadow.* He watched her strong, naked body with fascination. "Bad China Boy!" She picked him up and tucked his head under his wing. "Go to sleep." She gently rocked the chicken back and forth and it stopped moving.

"That bird's a pain in the ass!"

"He's showing an interest in your work. I think you should encourage that."

Gibson shrugged and pulled himself onto the couch, wrapping the blanket around himself. "I'm pretty hungry. If he does any more damage around here I might just fricassee him."

She gasped with mock horror and put the sleeping bird in the basket she used to transport him from place to place. Everyplace to everyplace, Gibson corrected himself; she went nowhere without her lucky bird. The scraggly bantam had been part of her act until, at the height of their career, Raymond had decided that the psychic chicken act just didn't suit the dignity of their status and had sidelined him.

"Sorry," she said to Walter as she straightened up the damaged mags. "Why are they called pulps?"

"Well," he said. "It all began with a wasp."

"A wasp?"

"The kind that stings you, right?" He was still angry with her. But maybe she was right about him and he could share a little more of himself with her. "You see, paper used to be very expensive, much more like a cloth than what we have now. In fact, paper was made from the cotton fibers in rags and worn-out clothing. It was expensive and slow to make. Then one day a Frenchman, René de Réaumur, noticed wasps building a nest in the eaves of his house. He studied the wasps as they chewed up wood. They were mixing it with chemicals in their saliva, which created a moist mass of fibers that, when it dried, resembled the paper made from cloth. He experimented with sawdust and chemical glues until he came up with a fairly good facsimile of what the wasp was spitting up. When he pressed it through a roller, it made a nice sheet of paper.

"Now a lot of people since have put their two cents' worth in and come up with some pretty fancy ways of making paper nicer, and more expensive—adding bleaches, for example. But for our mags to be cost-effective they need to be cheap, and that means hiring the cheapest writers, using the cheapest ink, and buying the cheapest paper. The paper we use is pretty much like the original wood pulp process inspired by the wasp. Hence, the pulps."

"Oh." She brushed a loose feather from her arm. She came back to Gibson and stretched out along his side. "Pulps have a bad reputation. Like actresses."

"That's because they're both fast and cheap but they look good doing it."

"Hey!"

"I don't aim to educate or enlighten, so by that measure I guess pulps don't pass as literature. But if it's entertainment you want, a little bit of showbiz, I got that over literature any day of the week. And as long as I can write and be read, and get paid for it, I'm a happy man."

She snuggled her head into the crook of his arm and for some time they simply dozed. Hovering just above the place where dreams begin, he let the memories of Silver Springs swirl around him.

"What's he like?" he heard her asking him now, and his consciousness raced up to meet her. Dawn light was burning away the night and made her gleaming eyes seem even more penetrating, as if she really could read his mind. And for all he knew, when it came down to it, maybe she could.

"Who?" He was groggy.

"Your son. Robert?"

"I don't know. I haven't seen him in years."

"Why not?"

He tried to talk but couldn't. His throat had closed up on him. He was only able to give her a mute shrug.

"Why not?" she said again, insisting.

"I can't talk about it," he managed to croak.

"No, Walter," she said, "you *won't* talk about it."

And suddenly she was getting dressed, pulling on the garters and affixing the clasps to the stockings, the gold silk Chinese gown she had worn to the premiere party gliding smoothly over her body. "You won't talk about it."

"What do you want me to say? What do you need to know about me? Do you need to know that I'm a bad man? That I turned out not to be the man I thought I once could be? I'm just the man that I am. The kind of man who walks out on his wife and son and never sees them again? The kind of man who steals another man's wife?"

"You didn't steal me!"

"What more do you need to know about me? My desk is over there. There are some personal papers in the drawers. I'll go back to sleep and you can sneak over and have a look! They'll tell you all about my divorce. Look for the words 'alienation of affection.' What that means is that my wife stopped loving me because I wasn't happy being a newspaper reporter and I made her life miserable because I was miserable."

She stared at him in silence for a long moment. He thought she would say something, but she didn't. He could see in her eyes that he was changing from someone she knew to someone she didn't recognize and didn't want to be in the room with.

"I'm sorry," he said. "Litzka! Honey! Wait!"

She was already at the door. The basket with the slumbering rooster swung from her hand. He went to the door to stop her.

"Hang on a second," he said. "I didn't mean it like that, and just wait!"

But she stepped into the hallway. She turned to look back at him and for a moment he remembered again how she had looked in that doorway at Silver Springs months ago and how she had whispered, "I love you," as she slid past him when he hadn't closed the door on her.

"Do you believe I'm a little bit psychic?" she asked him suddenly.

"No."

"Then I must be a complete liar," she said and turned away. He slipped on his trousers and then ran down to the hall where she waited for the elevator. Then he stood there mute, dumb, as the cage rattled wearily down toward them. He kept searching for something to say, knowing that there were words in his head that could make things right. Where had his words gone?

She entered the elevator and refused to look at him even as the doors closed. He stood there and listened as it descended the shaft; he heard the echo of its doors as it opened onto the lobby of the Hotel Des Artistes, where he rented the biggest apartment.

He waited for a long moment hoping that the elevator would spring to life again and rise and the doors would open to reveal Litzka and she would listen to him. Because he knew what he would say to her.

He had the words now.

Episode Six

Norma Dent held a martini in her hand as she hunted for Dutch Schultz's lost treasure.

"Who shot you?"

"I don't know."

"How many shots were fired?"

"I don't know."

"How many?"

"Two thousand."

Last year he had been gunned down at the Palace Chophouse in Newark. Sometime prior to that, his accomplices were now admitting in testimony, he had buried a steel chest full of, according to those same accomplices, stacks of thousand-dollar bills, jewels, gold, and stock certificates estimated to be worth millions of dollars. Stolen from the honest, decent citizens of New York, as well as some of its dishonest and corrupt ones.

"Please crack down on the Chinaman's friends and Hitler's commander. I am sore and I am going up and I am going to give you honey if I can. Mother is the best bet and don't let Satan draw you too fast."

"What did the big fellow shoot you for?"

"Over a million—five million dollars."

Five million dollars in treasure.

He had been shot in the stomach. It took him four agonizing days in his hospital bed to die. Newark cops had been with him the entire time, writing down his ramblings and confessions as he slipped in and out of feverish delirium. The transcript had finally been published in the *New York Herald,* despite the best efforts of the police to keep it from the press. While they may have hoped his words would provide insight into the underworld, Norma knew they contained the key to his treasure.

"Control yourself."

"But I am dying.

"No, you are not."

"Then pull me out. I am half crazy. They won't let me get up. They dyed my shoes. Open those shoes. Give me something. I am so sick. Give me some water, the only thing I want. Open this up and break it so I can touch you. Danny, please get me in the car. Please mother, you pick me up now. Please, you know me. No. Don't you scare me. Please let me up. If you do this, you can go on and jump right here in the lake."

The lake. Was that a clue? Norma wondered. His accomplice, Lulu Rosenkrantz, had claimed that he and Schultz had buried the treasure near a grove of pine trees near the town of Phoenicia in the Catskills. The atlas open on Norma's lap indicated that an Esopus Creek ran between Phoenicia and Kingston, the only body of water directly in the vicinity that Lulu Rosenkrantz claimed to have visited. Schultz alluded to water more than once in his ramblings. Water was the key, she decided. The treasure was buried near the creek, which in the mind and on the lips of a dying man could become a lake.

"Police, mamma, Helen, mother, please take me out. I will settle the indictment. Come on, open the soap duckets. The chimney sweeps. Talk to the sword. Shut up! You got a big mouth! Please help me up, Henry! Max, come over here! French-Canadian bean soup. I want to pay. Let them leave me alone."

She felt her face flush with the thrill of discovery. She took another sip of her martini. The gin was crisp with the scent of juniper. The doctor had told her it was okay now for her to drink occasionally, so she made sure to follow doctor's orders.

Norma Dent loved treasure hunts and this promised to be a big one. It didn't matter to her that she had never found any treasure; the thrill was in finding clues, tying loose ends together, trying to get into the mind of someone who could stash their secrets away. Together the Dents had embarked on a number of quests. They had explored the ingeniously booby-trap-rigged shaft on Nova Scotia's Oak Island, presumably the resting place of Captain Kidd's wealth; hiked the fields of Georgia's Chennault Plantation in search of the lost gold of the Confederacy; and sailed the *Albatross* across the sapphire-blue waters of Cuba seeking the Spanish golden tablet. Each time she felt as if she had come closer than ever before to realizing her dream. Now here was a treasure practically in her own backyard. The winter had been long and heavy, so the creek might be frozen over, the ground hard. But it could be right there waiting for them. But then again, it was so much effort.

She sighed and laid the newspaper clipping across the atlas, then closed the old book. She swept an errant lock of her long blond hair out of her face and tucked it behind her ear, feeling the surging treasure passion recede. Maybe in the spring she'd be ready. Or by summer.

A sharp metallic snap echoed through the apartment, interrupting the steady rat-a-tat-tat beat of Lester at his typewriter which was the daily background noise of her life. Suddenly she could hear the traffic from West Seventy-sixth Street below her, the distant hoot of steamships on the Hudson, and the ratcheting clank of the elevators in the hall. The apartment, which seemed so warm and alive while he was writing, instantly chilled. She waited expectantly, knowing what had happened. Lester had been typing so hard and so fast that one of the strikers had snapped off and whizzed across the room. Whenever this happened she always half expected, as she did now with a wince, that the flying sliver of metal would impale Lester. At least he wore glasses, so his eyes were protected. She waited, knowing for certain what was happening in his tiny office. Lester, still writing his story in his head, would remove the page he had been working on and place the broken typewriter on the floor to the right side of his desk. Then he would turn to the left side of his desk, where he kept several cases of new typewriters. He would open up a new box; place it on his desk; roll in the page of paper, which made very reassuring clicks; then begin to type again, trying to get his fingers to catch up with his mind, which was already racing pages ahead into its story. Or if he were out of typewriters and Elizabeth, his secretary, was around, he would simply dictate as she wrote in shorthand. But she was off today, and Lester would fend for himself. Norma listened for the sound of a new box opening. Instead, she was startled when Lester cleared his throat in the doorway behind her.

"How are you feeling?" he asked in his low, deep voice. She still felt his soft rumble in her toes—the same way she had when she had responded to an ad for a Western Union clerk back in Carrolton, Missouri, and Lester had answered the phone. God, she thought, that was thirteen years ago. Lester almost never raised his voice over that whispery rumble, yet she never had trouble hearing him, even in a crowded restaurant or on the noisy elevated train.

"I'm okay," she shrugged, sipping at the martini. She saw him furrow his brow in concern. She knew it had been difficult for him to understand how so much more of her mind and heart had suffered than her body. The blood, the physical pain—he could understand that, she knew. He could act on that, and he had. During the emergency of the miscarriage and the traumatic recovery afterward, he had responded swiftly, with decisive, caring purpose. It was only later, during the long fall and the cold of early winter, that she could sense his occasional frustration and impatience with her. Because he didn't understand. It had happened to him too, it was true. And she knew she had to acknowledge that he had lost too. But what had he really lost? A figment of a future? Not a life that he could feel within him the way she had.

She had wanted four children. She had ended up with four miscarriages. Her doctor had told her that her uterus wouldn't support life, that it was a hostile environment. What a horrible thing to say to a woman.

On the coffee table she could still see the edge of the cover of the one present she had allowed herself to purchase when she first realized she was pregnant this last time. It was a children's book which had been published just around Christmastime: *And to Think That I Saw It on Mulberry Street.* It had been purchased in hope. Now it was buried under a mound of *Doc Savage* magazines which she had meant to read but hadn't.

She had lost another life in blood, and this time nearly lost hers as well. And in the months since the miscarriage, while her body mended, while she spent her days in dark places removing that child from her dreams of the future, she had grown angry at Lester for being there too much and not being there enough. It wasn't that he was angry with her, but maybe she wanted him to be. Maybe she wanted him to scream at her, tell her it was her fault, that she had made a mess of everything because of who she was. Recently, while making a pot roast (because cooking seemed to be the only thing she did lately), she realized that she had been waiting for the past six months for him to blame her. She wanted him to be angry with her, yell at her to stop wallowing. She wanted him to deck the doctors with a patented Doc Savage double-fisted haymaker to the jaw and set everything right. But that wasn't Lester. Although strong and dependable and loving with her, he had never been a forceful person. And in the end it wouldn't have fixed her.

So she had dug herself out of her hole. Somewhat. She had begun by focusing on things other than her loss. For example, making sure that Lester had proper meals at the right time was an important step. It was a small goal she could achieve on a daily basis, and a more realistic goal than finding a lost treasure.

"I'm going to go out tonight," he said, "to a Fiction Guild meeting at the Knickerbocker."

"Okay." She nodded. "I have ham steak for dinner."

After a hesitation in which he only blinked three or four times, he said, "I thought we might go down to Chinatown this weekend and visit Mr. Yee's." And by that she knew that he couldn't care less about ham steaks or pot roasts.

Mr. Yee's was one of their touchstone places in the city. On their first night in New York four years ago they had taken the wrong train and ended up in Chinatown in a blizzard. It was as far from La Plata, Missouri, as either of them had ever been; it might as well have been China, as lost and lonely as they were then. Mr. Yee had been one of the few brave souls to keep his restaurant open and had welcomed them graciously. Treating them as his special guests, he had brought forth to their table a large tank holding live fish and asked them to make a selection. She could still remember how grateful she felt that someone could be nice to her in a city that everyone had warned them about. He had been as thrilled to have customers that night as they had been to find a warm and friendly place: his restaurant had only been open a week. They talked to him for hours, and listened, as he told them all about how to get around their new adopted city. Mr. Yee had been their particular friend ever since, and Lester consulted with him often on the Chinese details that gave the Doc Savage books a special level of authenticity.

He chewed on his pipe stem and waited for her to answer. He wasn't used to her taking her time to make a decision.

"Let's move to New York so I can be a pulp mag writer for Street & Smith. They've already hired me to write a Shadow story for them and I did it. It's called The Golden Vulture. *Walter Gibson, the fella that usually writes The Shadow, just has to sign off on it and they're gonna run it. John Nanovic says there could be a whole lot of work for me up there."*

"That sounds nice. Let's go."

He would go to Mr. Yee's without her if she didn't want to go; she knew that. Lately he had been going out more and more on his own. He had recently come home in a foul mood from an evening at a bar where some of his fellow pulp writers went. He was disinclined to discuss his night, but he had spent the next day looking through his old story file instead of writing. At the end of the day he had mailed off several stories to the *Saturday Evening Post.* She wished he could be satisfied writing *Doc Savage.* He was more successful than almost any other writer in America. But she knew how much he wanted public recognition of his talents under his own name, how much he despised being forced to publish under the name Kenneth Robeson. He craved, with a depth she could only imagine, the vindication of being published in one of the so-called classier magazines. She understood that about as well as he understood her pain, she supposed. After so many years of marriage it was good that they still had things they needed to learn about each other.

"Is this about something you're writing?" She always liked to help him research his stories, help open the doors which lead to adventure. Well, she used to. She hadn't even been able to bring herself around enough to be able to read the last three issues of *Doc Savage.*

"Sort of."

There was something else, she was sure of it. But his face was nearly impassive. She looked at the yellow corner of the children's book on the coffee table. A pang of sadness and fear stabbed at her, but she said, "You know, I've missed his dumplings. That sounds nice."

She hoped it would be. She hadn't left the apartment in six months.

Episode Seven

"Did you know Howard Lovecraft?" Dr. Elmer Smith asked him.

The Flash shook his head, as did the other men at his table. Bob Hogan, who wrote the *G-8 and His Battle Aces* hero series, shrugged; his angular, bony shoulders bounced up and down beneath his suit. "Who was he?"

"He wrote a few things for the shudders."

"I never even heard of him," Hogan said.

"Yeah, he never broke through," Smith said. "And he didn't live here in New York. He lived in Providence." He was a heavyset man; his girth was an occupational hazard. Doc Smith was a pulp writer, but he was also a real scientist, a chemist, who created tasty mixes for the Dawn Doughnut Company. He could always be counted upon to bring fresh samples of his newest creations to the Knickerbocker get-togethers. Tonight the big boxes of blueberry dunkers were being received with great enthusiasm. Not so much for the coffee-strawberry.

Smith wasn't the only one afflicted with an expansive waistline. The Flash looked around the room. Fat and hemorrhoids were the plagues of his field. Even the skinny men in the room shared another common misery with the fat ones: their shoulders were all stooped and the head of each and every one hung from his neck so it looked as if the room were full of strange, gray vultures. This was the ultimate reward for hunching over a typewriter for long, hard hours. The Flash shifted his weight, straightening his posture, feeling the tendons crack in his neck as he did so. When he was rich he would have a masseuse and a chef on staff. And he would dictate his stories from a comfortable position, perhaps on a sofa, to a secretary.

Smith continued, "His stories were all about ancient horrible monsters from outer space who have been on earth in a state of suspended animation for eons waiting for the day when their leader would arrive and help them to take over the world. Meanwhile, while they sleep, their dreams have enough power to drive men insane. Very strange stuff. Full of reanimated corpses and shuffling dread fish creatures and mysterious, fog-bound islands that don't appear on any chart."

"Sounds surefire. Surprising that stuff didn't sell," The Flash said with a tone of enlightened disdain. He reached for a blueberry doughnut, his third, but he hoped that the other men hadn't seen him take the first one and would think it was only his second. He looked around the room. The turnout tonight was quite good; he nodded to himself. Four tables full of writers, drinking coffee and talking about writing. Some of them were very successful, like Hogan and Smith; some were just starting out, like his friend Al van Vogt, who had recently moved to New York from Canada to rustle up more work. Then there were the grizzled old veterans like the Brit, Talbot Mundy, who claimed to have tramped around the whole of the Empire, hunted tigers in Afghanistan, fought in the Boer War, and published his first adventure story in *The Scrap Book* in 1911. The Flash had been reading Mundy's stories since he was a little boy and was always thrilled whenever he could spend time in the man's company.

A low rumble made the chandeliers shake and tinkle. It had been a while since they had been cleaned well; the Knickerbocker was no longer in its prime, and dust trickled down in a slow flurry. He covered his coffee cup. Knowing that the vibration was caused by the subway which ran under the hotel didn't exactly reassure him. The shudder felt too much like the earthquakes he had known so well back in Washington. He didn't trust the subway and only took cabs or the el. Tonight he had taken the trolley to the hotel on the corner of Forty-second and Broadway. Once upon a more elegant time the Knickerbocker had been part of the social pulse of the highest levels of the Manhattan elite. Now it was just another stop for the merchant class.

"He and Robert Howard were good friends," Smith continued his impromptu eulogy.

"Aw jeez! Was he a suicide too?" asked Norman Daniels, a man who was often hired by publishers looking to imitate the success of *Doc Savage* or *The Shadow.* Howard, a *Weird Tales* writer who over the last ten years had authored a series of bold adventures about a mythical land traveled by a fearsome, amoral barbarian named Conan, had put a bullet into his brain with a .38 Colt revolver last year outside his home in Texas. Rumor had it that he had been upset by the irreversible coma his mother had slid into. He had been only thirty years old.

Smith shook his head. "Some kind of cancer, I heard. But here's the weird thing they both had in common." He lowered his voice and the men at the table leaned in to hear him. "They both lived at home with their mothers."

They all looked uncomfortably at each other, aware why Smith had lowered his voice. One by one they all snuck glances at Cornell Woolrich, the skinny, nervously fey detective writer who had begun his writing career in *Black Mask,* the pulp started by H. L. Mencken that had launched the career of the West Coast gumshoe pulp writer Dash Hammett into the stratosphere. Hollywood made movies of Hammett's stories and real publishers put his books in libraries and bookstores. Woolrich's star was rising as well; he now sold almost exclusively to the slicks, and there was gossip of a nice novel deal in the works (a novel, The Flash thought, how great would it be to have the stories he wrote considered fine enough to be novels instead of just pulps), but he still stayed tight with his pulp friends. The great Fitzgerald himself had taken an interest in Woolrich's writing and had tried to persuade him to make a move to Hollywood. Woolrich refused to leave the Harlem hotel he lived in with his mother, who sat by his side now, possessively brushing imagined lint from his ill-fitted suit. The Flash had to admit that some very strange people were attracted to writing as a profession. They couldn't all be as normal as he.

He wondered why some of these other fellas wrote. Smith, for example, had a great job and with his skills as a chemist could find all kinds of interesting work even if the American public suddenly rejected tasty doughnuts, so why was he here? There had to be better hobbies. And the same question applied to the perennial second-story man Emile Tepperman, over there under the chandelier with all the crystal missing. His meager monthly returns, cashwise, couldn't compensate him for the effort he put into his silly Purple Invasion stories. He even seemed content with his place providing filler for other magazines. Maybe one Friday night he, The Flash, might introduce the topic of muses and see what these men had to say about that subject. He was sure it would be interesting. But tonight he had prepared a different topic for their discussion. It was time to introduce it.

The Flash excused himself from the table and moved to the lectern at the head of the room and raised his arms. "Gentlemen, gentlemen! Can I have your attention, please?" Smith clanked his spoon against his coffee cup and others picked up the call to attention. The Flash waited for the room to settle down and all eyes to be upon him. "Thanks all for coming and thanks for all getting your dues in to me on time. Let's thank Dr. Smith for the doughnuts!" Everyone applauded. Smith heaved himself up and took a bow.

The Flash continued, "There's no real news on the Guild front this time out. We're always looking for new members, of course, so if you've got any buddies, bring 'em along." A latecomer was entering the room. He removed his fedora and The Flash grinned. Lester Dent had come after all.

The big man looked a little lost. The Flash gave him a little wave, inviting him to join their table. Dent nodded and made his way to the table. The Flash could see the other writers sneaking furtive, envious looks at him. Of the men in the room, probably only Hogan and Woolrich had achieved a somewhat comparable level of financial success. Many of the men in here were second-story men, the guys who wrote the filler tales that ensured each book was the proper length each month.

Then he started to worry that his beckoning gesture to Dent had been too eager and enthusiastic. Had he looked foolish? It was important that he represent the Guild with dignity. Until he had campaigned for and won the presidency, the Guild hadn't functioned as anything more than a glorified social club for men who, by the very nature of their work, spent their days in isolation. In the few months of his tenure he had been able to institute a few changes, including the circulation of a newsletter and the quiet distribution of a few Guild dues bucks to some established writers who had hit a streak of bad luck. He wasn't trying to turn the Guild into some kind of commie labor union and he had no intention of going up against the powers that be at Street & Smith in any kind of negotiation. When it came to wages, it was every man for himself. He just thought that it was a good way for guys who had crossed a certain professional threshold to look out for one another.

The Flash continued as Dent took a seat at his table, next to Smith. "So let's get down to why we're really here tonight. Taking over the world!"

It got a great laugh and he grinned. If he had acted like a giddy fanatic when he had seen Dent, then it had been forgotten.

"A lot of us write about how to do it. Death rays. Vast armies. Rocket-powered missiles. Plagues. Lots of our characters have designs on the world. Our masters of menace: The Octopus, Doc Death, Doctor Satan, Dr. Yen Sen, Shiwan Khan, Fu Manchu, Wu Fang. What I want to discuss this evening is, what does someone do with the world once they've achieved their goal of world domination? Why do I think this is a relevant topic? Even to those of us who write cowboy stories?

"Hitler."

There was a snort of derision from somewhere in the room. The Flash shrugged. "I know it seems ludicrous. But since he shredded the

Treaty of Versailles and moved troops into the Rhineland and has started building his forces, it made me start thinking that if someone could make a run at it, he could. If not the whole world, then three continents at least—Europe, Asia, and Africa. So, in trying to figure out if it is really possible for someone like Hitler to do it, I decided to backtrack and ask the question of all of you, would it be worth it? Could you, in fact, rule the world?

"Of course, I mean in the pulp sense. Say you managed to take over the world. What happens the next day? What kind of organization would you need to manage it? Would you have to be accountable in any way to anybody? How would you suppress an uprising of opposition which occurs on the other side of the world? Could you enjoy it? In short, to come back around to its relevance to Hitler, is ruling the world actually worth the effort? Go to it!"

He sat down as the room began to buzz with conversation again. He didn't know if they were discussing his topic, but he certainly hoped so. He shook Dent's hand. "Lester Dent! Glad you could make it. You know everybody here?" The Flash was thrilled that Lester had come. Adding him to the Guild would only burnish its reputation, which would help improve the image and status of its members, and by extension, its president.

Lester nodded. "Sure." He tore a chunk of fried dough from a dunker and before any of the surprised men at the table, Smith included, could stop him, he had popped it into his mouth. Conversation at the table stopped. He chewed unsuspectingly for a moment and then his jaws stopped moving. "Is that mint?"

Smith nodded. Dent shrugged and swallowed. Then he took a second bite. "You fellas talk about writing here. I've got a question for you. Anyone know the origin of the expression 'and the horse you rode in on'? As in, 'to hell with you and the horse you rode in on'? I was writing that today and I got to wondering where it had actually come from."

"Nick Carter?" The Flash said, reminding them of the first Street & Smith hero, who had fathered their profession. "From the days of the real Old West."

"I first heard it during a poker game in Texas," Smith said. "So that could be it."

"Like everything else," Hogan interjected, "it's from Shakespeare. 'Some hilding fellow, that had stolen the horse he rode in on.' Not sure which play, though."

"Thanks, Bob. Maybe I'll try and work that tidbit in. Somehow." He pulled out his pipe and a leather tobacco pouch. Unlike his hat and suit and watch, which looked new and expensive, The Flash noted, both the pipe and pouch were old and worn. Dent packed and lit the pipe. Its stem was well chewed. He pointed it at The Flash. A thin tendril of smoke leaked out of its small opening. "You know, Mrs. Dent and I made an accidental detour into the Reich last summer on our trip to Europe."

"Sounds like fun," The Flash offered. He wished he had been so adventurous as to visit Germany. Dent must have come up with some great story ideas there. He decided he should travel more.

"Nazi soldiers shot up our car and chased us back across Bavaria."

"Oh."

"Let me ask you something, Lester." Hogan was scratched at his balding head. "I always wondered how you came up with Doc Savage."

"Well. Nanovic wanted a new Shadow series. Only better. So I took some of that and then I came across some articles by an old Street & Smith writer named Richard Henry Savage, who fought in Loring's Egyptian army in 1861. He turned in some fine stories of his time over there, and when he came back he became an engineer, a lawyer, and a playwright. So he was kind of interesting too. I don't know, maybe that's it. Soon after reading about Savage, I woke up with an image of Hercules riding on the running board of a car down Broadway toward some great adventure. Sure, laugh at that. It's kind of funny. But it's important for kids to know about Hercules and I don't know if they even teach mythology like that in schools anymore like they did when we were young.

"Like I said, when I woke up there he stood, bigger than life, as big as myth, standing in front of my eyes with a brown wool coat over his shoulders instead of a lion's hide, a ripped shirt revealing skin tanned during exploits in equatorial jungles and deserts. And my fingers began to get that itch." Every man at the table nodded knowingly. "Then I had to use my imagination."

"Is there much of you personally in there?" Hogan asked him.

Dent shot the man a look of scoffing derision. "You mean like that Miller fella in *Tropic of Cancer*!" That got almost as big a laugh from the table as The Flash's crack had. Almost. "Hell no! I make stuff up. That's what they pay me for."

"I meant," continued Hogan, unperturbed, "for example, that Doc's own father created a physical and mental regimen designed to turn him into a superhuman. He turned his own son into a science experiment. Do you think he has any problems with that?"

"Why would he? His father made him a hero."

"But do you draw on your own life to make stuff like that up?"

"I see what you're saying. No. My own father couldn't read a book and didn't care if I learned to. So no." He smiled, gazing into the bowl of his pipe as if reading tea leaves. "Not in the least."

No one seemed to want to pick up the dropped thread of conversation. "How do you think Ah Hoon died?" The Flash heard himself asking Dent.

"What's that about?" Smith asked, curious.

The Flash quickly explained the story of the Sweet Flower mystery up to its unresolved ending. For a moment he felt as if his telling the story had revealed an ending, but when he got there, the story trailed off just as it had when Gibson told it. The ending The Flash thought he was going to come up with just wasn't good enough. He shrugged and bailed out with a cryptic-seeming "We may never know."

"Hooey," Dent snorted. "There's an ending to this story, maybe even a great one. I don't yet know how Ah Hoon was killed but I've been turning it over in my head a great deal. And I tell you what. I'm going to find out. That's what Walter Gibson should have done before he even started telling that story. I'm gonna find out and I'm gonna bring it back here and get up in front of all of you and tell you what happened."

The Flash now wished he had kept his mouth shut. Why hadn't he just thought of solving the Sweet Flower mystery himself instead of asking Lester Dent's opinion?

"And then"—Dent grinned and puffed on his pipe contentedly—"I'm gonna write up the greatest pulp ever."

Episode Eight

"SO, WALTER Gibson did not create The Shadow, eh? But one could say that The Shadow created Walter Gibson," said George Rozen, with his tone of Viennese presumption. He was painting a cover for an upcoming issue of *The Shadow,* and blood seemed to flow from his fine brush as if it had pierced an artery in the hand that was holding it. "Without Walter Gibson would there still be a Shadow? Without The Shadow, would there be a Walter Gibson?"

"I don't know about that," Walter replied, "but without The Shadow there would certainly be no Maxwell Grant." Walter had cleared some old canvases from his desk and was lying on it while Rozen painted. He didn't have much to offer the talented painter by way of inspiration or motivation, but the two men enjoyed each other's company. He had been in a foul mood since Litzka had deserted him and he didn't particularly want to be alone with himself. He could have gone to the Fiction Guild meeting at the Knickerbocker, but he didn't particularly want to be around anyone else either. Sequestering himself in his office while Rozen painted was the perfect compromise. Rozen's work could be a focus for both of them, offering conversation-free seclusion and the security of companionship at the same time. Except that for some reason Rozen was feeling expansively garrulous today.

Gibson watched as a little bit more of The Shadow disappeared under paint. Strict with its resources, Street & Smith made all its artists get as much use out of stretched muslin as possible. This meant that the gloriously violent covers like the ones Walter had moved out of his way and the dozens more lying around the studio had all been painted over at least twice, and all were destined to be painted over at least once more. Then they would be thrown out.

Rozen was the only artist ensconced on this floor, on editors' row, but great sunlight poured through the large south-facing windows all day long, and Gibson had pressed Nanovic until he had given up and allowed Rozen to paint up here instead of in the large bullpen on the third floor with all the other artists. The argument was easy to make. Rozen was the best artist Street & Smith had, he painted the covers for the biggest mag the house had, and he deserved the light.

The Shadow glared righteously at Gibson from the paintings, silver-black eyes flashing vengeance and retribution. There were dozens of canvases around his office, so the malevolent pupils blazed at him from every corner of the room; he shifted his head slightly to get a different perspective. The steely eyes above the character's hawklike nose followed him. Walter shuddered and closed his eyes for a moment. The image of The Shadow's glare hovered before his closed lids—alive, penetrating, and judging. He gasped and opened his eyes, suddenly shaking. There had been a few times since the creation of The Shadow that he had felt as if the character were real—this brief flicker had been one of those—and it always made his blood run cold. It meant The Shadow wanted something.

He dragged his gaze from the old paintings and turned to watch the silver-haired old man concentrate on his art. The artist had originally based his conception of The Shadow on the profile of one of Street & Smith's art directors, but over the last few years the character had taken on a life of its own.

"Where do you get that?" Walter asked him. "The inspiration?"

The old Austrian shrugged. "From The Shadow. Same as you, right?"

The only artist in town who gave George Jerome Rozen a run for his money was his own brother, Jerome George Rozen, the second-best cover painter at Street & Smith. All Walter or his ed, Nanovic, needed to give Rozen was a thirty-second story rundown and then he was off to the races, creating the luminous and disturbing covers that did as much to sell the mag as the stories themselves did. More, in some months.

"Well, if he's lurking around, I haven't heard from him lately."

Gibson knew that his efforts of late hadn't been his best. He'd even hired a ghost for the first time, a guy named Tinsley, to pick up one of the two books he had to deliver each and every month. That's why Dent's needling had really worked its way under his skin. He had been having problems with endings in particular.

"Not since Kent Allard, yes?"

"That's right. That whole Allard thing."

"What brought that on?"

"I still don't even know."

"I think The Shadow spoke to you, is what I think."

"I'm sure that's it." The painter either missed or ignored Gibson's sarcasm.

That Allard thing. An incident of creative impulsiveness he was still doing penance for. One morning it had come to him in a burst which Rozen might call inspiration and the result was *The Shadow Unmasks.* For seven years, readers had been told that The Shadow was actually secretly Lamont Cranston, playboy about town. In *The Shadow Unmasks,* Gibson had taken his readers' expectations and thrown them out the window. What they discovered behind Rozen's cover was that it had all been a lie. Cranston, it was revealed, was merely a disguise. The Shadow's true identity was Kent Allard. Possibly. The implication was that Allard was only a disguise as well. Maybe seven years of success had made his eds complacent: Nanovic claimed to have read the tale, but Gibson suspected he hadn't. When it ran, the vocal reaction from the fans was loud. Very loud. They didn't like it. They considered it an outrageous betrayal akin to Arthur Conan Doyle's pitching Sherlock Holmes over Reichenbach Falls. By the time the scope and extent of the outrage were clearly expressed by the incoming mail, several more issues had run with the Allard subplot and it was too late to turn back. There would be no stopping of the presses.

Street & Smith's management had been furious. Nanovic had taken a lot of heat and had passed most of it along to Gibson. He continued to, in fact. The scrutiny he was under was intense. The only reason Gibson kept his job was that the mags sold better *after* the Allard revelation than before! Gibson was glad of the success; it felt somewhat vindicating. The only problem was that when someone asked him why he had done it, why he had messed with a successful formula, he had no answer for them. He had no idea what had compelled him. The whole Allard thing was just there for the telling and he had told it.

Since that incident he had felt a vague unease while he was writing, as if he doubted his own process. It hadn't been as easy to let the powerful torrent of words conduct his fingers. If he were to be honest with himself, the torrent had slowed considerably. Maybe he could crank out 100,000 words a month right now—more than most writers and just enough for him to keep up with work, but compared to his usual output, a mere trickle. It wasn't just the distraction of the affair with Litzka, with all its inherent emotional turmoil; he had been feeling this way for some time now. In fact, the compulsion, the need, to inflict some sensation on himself, to stab at himself or pummel himself in order to feel anything, emerged at the same time as Kent Allard. He had begun the affair with Litzka hot on the heels of Allard's first appearance. Nineteen thirty-six had been one for the books. Nineteen thirty-seven was shaping up to be one hell of a sequel.

The Shadow's eyes were following him again. The words, the images, the stories—they weren't his to control anymore; they were just coming from someplace within and he didn't know where or how. At the same time he also knew not to question the process too deeply or it might just vanish altogether on him. Then where would he be? Out on his ass while Nanovic, his ed, tossed the mag, *his mag,* to some two-and-a-half-cent hack like Hubbard.

The thought of Hubbard getting his mitts on *The Shadow* made Walter grimace. He could almost feel the kid's triumphant gloat. Hubbard was an okay writer, and blazing fast, but his ambition was greater than his talent and he had none of the skills needed to wrestle The Shadow to the page. Walter shook his head to clear it. Between Litzka and his writing problems he had enough to worry about. He didn't really have time to worry about Hubbard or whether or not The Shadow's eyes were watching him. "Scotch?" he asked, knowing the answer.

"Of course." Rozen was from the Old World and had developed no puritan sense of impropriety about drinking before the sun set. Or even before the clock struck noon. Gibson heaved himself off the desk and pulled a bottle of White Horse scotch whiskey from the drawer where he had stashed it. He splashed the brown liquid into two vaguely clean glasses and handed one to Rozen. Then the two of them stood back to look at the cover for *The Shadow of Death.*

"Christ almighty," Gibson breathed. "That is one son of a bitch of a painting."

It was one of Rozen's favorite themes, The Shadow face-to-face with Death. In his paintings the characters mirrored each other's nature. Many times they had met before; Death had lurked in tarot cards, behind Broadway curtains, in warehouse rafters, whispering in the ears of cruel-mouthed thugs. If The Shadow lacked an arch-nemesis within the pages of the mag, he never lacked for one on the cover. Against a background of flames and smoke, the two rivals challenged each other once again. One eye glittered, rolling loosely in the ivory skull. A skeletal hand held the book of Life and Death and with a bony finger he touched the word *Shadow,* written in flame on the page of Death. The Shadow seemed like a dark Lucifer about to take the throne of fate with a .45 and a sneer while Death appeared on the verge of taking his retribution upon the hero for usurping his role on Earth and sending more souls to hell than he. Only a slight turn of The Shadow's head gave any indication of his recognition of his mortality. He might prevail this time, as he had before, but he was only human; sooner or later his enemy would have him.

"Brother," Gibson said, impressed. "I wish I could write what you paint."

"At least no codes this time," Rozen replied, stirring up some red paint. Gibson loved codes and often included them in his stories. When he did, he liked Rozen to place messages on the cover for his readers to solve. Rozen hated painting the intricate symbols or numbers and letter sequences that Gibson required at those times.

"Don't tempt me."

"So, Walter. How about we finish up and go to Rosoff's for some steak and beers?"

"I can't," he said. "I have to go to a funeral."

"Whose? Anyone I know?"

"Howard Lovecraft. Ring a bell?"

Rozen shook his head. "A writer?"

"He tried."

"I never heard of him."

"Not many did. I have to go up to Providence for the funeral. I wasn't even going to go because I didn't really know him all that well, although he could write letters like nobody's business. But his aunt sent me a telegram asking me to attend. His will asked for me specifically. So . . . At least I can get some writing done on the train."

"A new Shadow book?"

"Probably. I'm far enough behind that I ought to get crackin' on one, that's for sure. I don't know, George. Maybe I'm just tired of writing about The Shadow. Maybe I just need a break. I've been doing it steady for seven years now."

"Ha!" Rozen grinned. "The Shadow won't let you."

The comment made Gibson give a little jerk. "What do you mean?"

"Without you? *Pfft!* No Shadow. Maybe he won't like that."

"I kind of miss investigating and reporting. I used to be quite the reporter back in my Philadelphia days. You know when Al Capone was being held at the federal prison there before his sentencing I was the only reporter he allowed to come interview him? It's true. He was a big Houdini fan and had read the autobiography I wrote for him, *Houdini's Escapes,* and he wanted me to do the same for him. Got him to tell me the really great stuff. His whole life story from Brooklyn to Chicago was right there on the paper. I was like his priest and he was the sinner making a confession."

"I have never heard of this book. What happened to it?"

"Well, unfortunately, old, sick, fat Al confessed a little too much. After the first few articles were published in the paper, his lawyers were able to seize my notes and do God knows what with them. Probably burned them. To be fair, the things he told me about would have had his ass in the electric chair before the ink dried on the book. Ah, the stories I could tell you, brother, if only I weren't afraid a lawyer would jump out of that spittoon there and serve me. But you know what? Every Christmas I get a card from old Al over in Alcatraz, so don't believe he's as brain-addled and feeble as he lets on to the papers. He's a canny son of a bitch."

"If that kind of writing excites you, then you should find a way to do it. If your muse lets you. Of course, I would miss our collaborations. No one else here will take a drink in the afternoon."

Taking the hint, or taking it as a hint, Gibson refilled their glasses. "It ain't easy finding a subject as interesting as Houdini, or Blackstone, or Capone to write about. They broke the mold when they made those guys. To be honest, I'm more interesting than most of the famous people I meet now and I wouldn't want to read *my* autobiography. So until I meet someone who really captures my attention I'll keep making up characters to write about."

"So how does a reporter from Philadelphia arrive at all this?" Rozen made an exaggerated gesture of showing off the entire office. It looked as if a bomb had recently been detonated in its center.

"Houdini again. Okay, so about seven years ago Street & Smith decided to start advertising on the radio. They sponsored a program called the *Detective Story Hour* and every week they would take a story from one of the mags and turn it into a radio play and put it on the air.

And the host of the show, some actor, decided it would be clever if he called himself The Shadow. He'd put out these messages to his agents. Say things like, "Agent 57, be on alert. Report to me immediately any skulduggery in the Bowery," and things like that. And you know how people are about the radio. They started wondering if The Shadow was real and whether or not, at least, he had a mag of his own. So Ralston and Nanovic cooked up a little story for their new hero series, and they had liked my Houdini book, and they knew because of my magic articles that I could write really fast. They sent me a telegram making me an offer. I caught the train up and here I am. At the mercy, as you say, of my muse!

"Now I'm stuck. Pays too well for me to be doing anything else, but not well enough that I don't have to do it."

Rozen nodded in commiseration and picked up his paintbrush to add a few sparks here and there. Gibson poured himself another drink and sat on the edge of his desk. To this day he attempted to maintain the illusion that The Shadow was real. Each month's story was printed "as told to" instead of "written by" Maxwell Grant. He looked out the window toward lower Manhattan. The winter had been so brutally cold that sheets of ice had formed on the Hudson River all the way to the Battery. Folks said it was the same on the Brooklyn side with the East River. He had never seen a winter in New York cold enough for that to happen.

He wanted to call Litzka before he left and try to explain himself to her. But he knew she would then want to see him this evening, and he had to go to Providence. She would think he was pushing her off again and get even more mad at him. It might be better to wait until he came back to talk to her. He thought about sending her some flowers at the theater, but the things he needed to say to her couldn't be said with a card and flowers. For a second or two he envied Lester Dent; now there was a man who seemed to have made a good, strong marriage and wasn't plagued by the absurd impulses of women.

Rozen cleared his throat, indicating that he was finished. "So," he asked, stepping aside, "how would you know if this person or that person is worth writing about should you meet him? How do you know if someone is a Houdini or a Capone? Do you know, as your Shadow knows, what lurks in their hearts?"

Who knows what evil lurks in the hearts of men? The Shadow knows. It was the catchphrase of the day. It was on the lips of every American. Thanks to the radio shows, they now knew to follow the statement with The Shadow's signature maniacal laugh. Walter thought for a moment about the inspiration of the phrase. There had been a German magician of the previous century, Alexander Herrmann, who billed himself as "the man who knows." What exactly he knew was up to the audience to divine, but that simple sentence had outlived the man and Gibson had always wanted to write about a character who lived up to that title. When he finally had been able, in his first description of The Shadow, to begin the sentence, "Who knows," he had been surprised to see his fingers type, "what evil lurks in the hearts of men?" It sounded sinister and right.

Gibson stared at the painting. The Shadow's eyes were going to give more than one kid a memory that would last a lifetime. Years from now those kids, grown to manhood with The Shadow long forgotten, would wake up from nightmares and wonder where those piercing eyes that haunted them came from. He knew.

"Yes," he finally answered.

Issue 2:
I Am Providence

Episode Nine

THE LEGEND of Zhang Mei, the Dragon of Terror and Peril, begins in this way:

The man who would be his father was a Manchu and he rode from the west, from the Nulu'erhu Mountains, across the windswept, snowy plains of Lianoning Province behind Zhang Zuolin, the warlord. With him were three hundred militia men, temple-trained in Northern Shaolin mountain fighting techniques. *Chua'an fa* had turned their muscles into wood and their skin into iron. No sword could cut them and no bullet could pierce them.

They swept into the village of the woman who would be his mother just past dawn and put to the sword all the men who had accepted the god of the ocean men. The man who would be his father took the woman who would be his mother to be his second wife. His first had produced no sons.

When the moon was new and black, the warriors, including the man who was his father, rode out from the village. Zhang Zuolin turned his men south toward Beijing. Toward the war. Toward the foreign invaders.

It was the year 4597, the Year of the Rat. And the men of the Fists of Righteousness and Harmony rode to glory.

Episode Ten

"YOU KNOW why the streets of Chinatown are curved?" Lester was asking, or rather telling, Norma. Trying to listen, she neatly sidestepped a slop-smelling gap in the cobblestones. She was wearing her smart brown leather button-up boots today and was not about to get rotting cabbage leaf on them—even if that meant she occasionally had to put all her attention on where she was stepping and ignore Lester's ongoing travelogue. She was wearing the gray wool dress she had bought last winter at Gimbel's; it made her feel very attractive. And nothing in Chinatown, no stain from sauce or slime or oil, no drop of cabbage-filled puddle water, was going to stop her from feeling that way about herself today, finally.

"To confuse the hell out of all the demons," he continued, oblivious to her street gymnastics, although he always seemed to have a helpful arm out for her, instinctively. He was wearing a brown tweed suit which she had bought him, and which she thought made him look very dashing. She felt they must seem quite the pair.

The shadows of the low buildings hung heavily over the sidewalks in the late afternoon. Her long legs kept pace with his swinging stride as they left the Quong Yuen Shing and Company store and headed south on Mott Street. Lester loved doing research in the little market and it was always their first stop upon entering the exotic enclave below Canal Street. While Norma fingered the delicate silks and carved ivory and jade figurines, he would prowl beneath the store's ornate bower, carved from oak and stained with years of tobacco smoke, discovering exotic herbs and medicine and testing the bemused patience of the owner with questions about their Chinese names and powers. Astragalus (*huang qi*) for the heart; ginseng (*ren shen*) for fertility and diabetes; skullcap for hay fever; angelica (*dong quai*) for anemia; and licorice (*mi gan cao*) for infections, hepatitis, and colic. Bia Yia Pian pills and Ping Chua pills for strong lungs; Bu Zhong Yi Qi Tang for the health of "delicate" areas. The stranger the better, as far as Lester was concerned. It was all ammo for the gun. Clark "Doc" Savage Jr. was, among many other things, the greatest chemist in the world, and it behooved his creator to know as much about as many interesting substances as possible.

Lester towered over most of the men on the street around him, and he forged easily through the crowd. "That's the headquarters of the On Leong tong." He pointed out a nondescript building across the street. "They protect the laundrymen."

"I thought the tongs were gone."

"Not gone. Just rehabilitated."

There was never any room to move in Chinatown. The streets were narrow and clogged with Chinese, mostly men, who seemed to have a total disregard for anyone's personal space. Every now and then a sullen-faced Chinaman would careen off Lester like a small marble hitting a big one.

A new blue Packard squeezed past a double-parked horse-drawn cart; the horse didn't even twitch an ear at its horn blasts. Two men were unloading eviscerated whitish-pink pig carcasses from the back of the cart and tossing them into bins. Other men were rolling the full bins of porcine husks to different destinations within their enclave, the cobblestones causing the hind legs to rattle against the sides of the bins like thick drumsticks.

Across the street a bloated Irish cop, his uniform too tight, his face as red as the crimson on the many prosperity banners which hung in shop windows, was angrily berating a fishmonger. Norma could not tell what he was so angry about, but she thought that his tipping over a bushel of crabs was uncalled for. An elderly woman rushed from the fishmonger's stall pleading loudly and carrying some fish wrapped in paper. The cop patted her patronizingly on the head, took the fish, and swaggered up the street.

Norma turned to Lester. "You should get his badge number and report him."

She saw the tiniest crinkle of a wince at the corner of his eyes. He didn't want to do it; it would interrupt his plans. He didn't want to, but he would.

"Never mind," she said. She didn't want to turn their excursion into an incident. "Let's not get involved."

His quickening resolve turned into relief, and as they headed away from confrontation, he picked up his discourse on Chinatown. She could tell that Lester was excited to have her out. He spoke rapidly as if he were trying to distract her, keep her mind from turning inward. She didn't mind; she appreciated his efforts on her behalf. And it was good to be out, stretching her muscles.

He turned them left onto Pell Street, passing around a steam cart selling huge white puffy rolls full of sweet pork. Pell was even darker and narrower than the cramped thoroughfare of Mott Street. The stores were smaller, more Chinese, more mysterious; red banners hung from doors and windows, adorned with gold symbols of blessing or curse. Chinese gods sat in windows holding sticks of richly smoking incense.

Lester pointed out another building, taller and newer than its surroundings. "Another tong building," he said. "We're in Hip Sing territory now. This is their street."

"It doesn't feel any different."

He looked at her for a moment before realizing that she was making a joke. His face relaxed and his mustache crinkled as he grinned. "Hard to believe what a man will decide to fight for, isn't it? But a few years back these streets were red with tong warrior blood and visitors sometimes had to step over the bodies to go about their business."

It never ceased to amaze her how much Lester knew about so many things. He never stopped investigating or reading and his curiosity was limitless. Once he discovered an interest in a subject, he would obsessively devour all he could about it until he was an expert. The knowledge he acquired flowed from his mind into his stories. Not only was Doc Savage a chemist and a scientist and a global explorer; the men who kept his company were also remarkably accomplished in the fields of electricity, architecture, engineering, and law. Lester always tried to sneak information he thought boys needed into his mags. Millions of American boys knew about the malaria-resistant and ultraviolet properties of quinine, the writ of habeas corpus, the benefit of calisthenics, the virtues of Eastern meditation, the cultures of South America and the Caribbean, the steel cage construction of the skyscrapers, the history of the lost Maya, the physics of positive and negative electrons, and the use of the word *superamalgamated* as an expression of amazement through Doc and his band of merry adventurers: Monk and Ham and Renny and Long Tom and Johnny. But most of all they knew about friendship, courage, and loyalty.

These were the qualities she was most proud of Lester for working into *Doc Savage,* and exactly the qualities which were missing from his other stories, although he could never see that. She knew he put down the Doc Savage series as mere formula, but she thought there was an integrity to the work that made it better than he thought it was. Lester Dent wasn't happy being Kenneth Robeson; he wasn't even all that satisfied being Lester Dent. He wanted to be John Steinbeck.

They walked on past the utterly unthreatening building. She was disappointed that no one even glowered at them. At the intersection of Pell and Doyers, Lester paused.

"Where are we going?" she asked. "Mr. Yee's is down farther."

She saw the look in his eye again, the one he had had in the living room a few days ago. Something was eating him. He was obsessing about something he wanted to know about. She looked at his fingers and they were twitching, already typing out words on an imaginary typewriter.

"I ran into Walter Gibson the other night," he said, his eyes wandering down the street looking for something.

"I hope you gave him a piece of your mind."

"Maybe a little piece."

"Good! I would have punched him."

"Maybe it's time to let bygones be bygones."

"Bygones. He nearly ruined us. He tried to keep you from having a chance at writing."

"First of all, by getting Nanovic not to publish *The Golden Vulture,* which I got paid four hundred fifty dollars for, by the way, he may have done me a favor. I didn't have to be his substitute writer."

"Some favor."

"If I had been writing Shadow stories, I never would have come up with Doc. And think how different our lives would be."

"He still had your very first story squashed, which was wrong of him to do because it was your big break. Thank God you were talented enough to land another break. But I don't see how you can forgive him."

"Oh, I'm not trying to forgive," Lester assured her. "I want to get one up on him."

"How?"

He stared down the block for a long moment. "I just want to take a look at something, real quick," he said at last. She nodded, but he didn't even notice. He was writing. He set off down Doyers and she hurried to keep up. He headed toward an aged building standing by itself by an alleyway. She followed, still fuming about Walter Gibson, whom she had never met and knew only as the man who had denied her husband his first steady writing job.

The old building was boarded up with rotting black planks which smelled of oily pitch. The remnants of a faded marquee still clung stubbornly to the bricks over the row of double doors. Any glass in the windows had long since been pried away and covered over with tar paper; any trace of elegance in its façade was erased. It stood as an aching spot to be avoided, like a sore tooth. As an indication of its diseased state, the sidewalk before it was empty, as if the locals allowed the awareness of its existence to intrude upon their single-minded missions and purposes and avoided it instinctively by crossing the street or finding alternate routes. Even in the middle of one of the busiest neighborhoods in the busiest city in the world, it exuded vapors of quiet desertion. They were almost entirely alone as they approached it.

"What is it?" she asked. Her pulse was quickening; her thoughts of Walter Gibson were fading away. Lester's interest in the building was infectious. She felt a surge of treasure-hunting excitement, a feeling she could never get by sitting on her chesterfield doing research. She felt the weight of the last six months melting away.

"The Chinese Theater," he replied.

"It's beautiful!" she exclaimed.

"I guess it kind of is." He showed only a passing interest in the building, preferring to investigate its surroundings. "It ran Chinese plays and operas for almost thirty years. The Salvation Army then tried to run a soup kitchen out of it, but nobody came. In the end it was a burlesque house, until La Guardia closed all of those down about five years ago. And now it's just abandoned.

"You know there are secret tunnels leading to and from this spot? They run all under Chinatown. A tong man could sneak in, whisper a garrote around a rival's neck while he watched the show, and *shneek!*" He made a deathly horrific face. "Meet your ancestors. Then it's back into the tunnels. The Irish cops think they've got a lid on it up here, but it's down below, where they'll never go, where you can find the real Chinatown. The gambling, the brothels, the opium dens, the slavers. It's happening in rivers and torrents below us."

"Sounds like a brilliant story."

"Story! It would need to be a novel! An exposé ripping the cobblestones off Chinatown and getting the first real look into the demimonde."

"That's your plan for getting back at Mr. Gibson? A novel?"

"No," he said. "I'm just trying to find the ending to a story." He looked the building up and down. "The boardinghouse was over here," he muttered.

"What boardinghouse?" she responded. But he didn't answer. Now that he was engaged, no matter what the outward Lester said or did, the inward Lester would be preoccupied with writing the next book. The words would have to be in place when he sat down at the typewriter so they could stream out in an uninterrupted flow onto the page. He walked off to the left side of the building, still muttering to himself. There was a gap about two feet wide, big enough for garbage cans and not much else, separating the windowless wall of the Chinese Theater from the tenement building on the other side. Lester stood in contemplation.

Norma lost interest quickly in his woolgathering. He could have the boardinghouse, whatever it was, all to himself. She was falling in love with this old, faded beauty. She walked along the front of the theater, running a hand along what was left of the ornamentation which had once adorned its pillars; once powerful long, thin dragons had wound their way around them but they had been chipped at and worn away to the point that they had become nothing more than mere worms.

Long, heavy beams had been posted with spikes over the front doors to the theater years ago. The beams were rough yet soft, slowly rotting away under the constant assault of the city's elements. Gaps appeared between the planking, and wondering if she could see anything beyond, she stepped up to the hole, mindful not to actually touch the smelly wood, and tried to peer into the darkness. She assumed that the closed doors of the theater would be behind the boards, but the blackness between the cracks indicated that at least one of the doors had swung open or fallen off its hinges at some point. She could make out vague shapes in the gloom but nothing that she could recognize properly.

Deep in the darkness something golden winked at her.

Something glittered, like a lone firefly just seen out of the corner of the eye—a momentary flash that had probably never really happened at all. Startled, she pulled her face back and looked around as if she had done something wrong. She leaned her head back to the position it had been before. She saw the flash again.

Excited, she reluctantly pulled herself away and ran to the side of the building where she had left her husband. Lester was trying and failing to scale the gap between the buildings by placing his hands and feet against the opposing walls and forcing himself upward. He was grunting with exertion and red-faced with frustration. The sight almost made her forget her own discovery. She watched in befuddled amusement as he strained and skidded obsessively against the bricks.

She was going to tell him not to rip his suit but she felt it would only be adding insult to his somewhat embarrassing struggle. She knew she'd read about this someday and it would all probably make sense. Watching Lester in this small space jogged her memory. There was a bigger alley on the other side of the theater. Set into the wall of the theater on that side was a stage door. She backed away from Lester, hoping no one they knew was in Chinatown that day; then she trotted quickly past the front of the theater to the other side.

The alley was dark. Distant sounds of pots being rattled came down from somewhere in the windows high above her. The shrill, high-pitched yammer of a faraway, very angry Chinese woman echoed through the air. The stage door was just to her left, but the alley continued on until it ended at the door of another building. A red lightbulb above the doorway was lit, as if the people behind that door were ignorant of the daylight.

She tested the doorknob on the stage door. To her surprise it responded with an affirmative twist and click. She gave the other door at the end of the alley another look and decided that no one was going to come out that portal anytime soon. She gave the door a little push and it opened with a rusty squeal onto the darkness of the Chinese Theater. As she stared into the gaping darkness spreading before her, she took a step back. Why had she come out? She should never have left the safety of her home. It wasn't too late. She could turn now and get Lester and return. To what? The chicken thawing in her sink? The pace of her heart was quickening. She didn't want to cook. She wanted to see.

The thick, sweet smell of ages-old incense greeted her as she waited for her eyes to adjust to the contrast of the auditorium's darkness against the light pouring in through the door. It seemed as if much, if not most, of the light was absorbed by a decade's worth of dust leaping into the air as she introduced oxygen into its vacuum. She stepped farther into the theater. Above her was a balcony floor. At its edge the room opened up to a cavernous yawn. Most of the seats were gone, but individual rows still remained like teeth in a jawbone. Torch lanterns that had been twisted in an attempt to wrest them away once upon a time were still affixed to the walls. The stage raked up from the brick proscenium arch. Thick rope hung like hemp cobwebs from the rafters. Tattered canvas backdrops and rotten set pieces lay scattered about the auditorium, some of them quite large—relics of performances decades old. But towering over all in its exotic glory was the object sitting center stage, her glittering attractor. She walked compulsively toward it, passing through pagodas painted on aged wood, across a muslin scrap depiction of the Great Wall, and emerging from a bamboo grove to see it clearly. So this is what it feels like to discover treasure, she thought.

The statue was gold, of that she was certain. She hadn't worked at the jewelry counter of the Rike's department store when she was sixteen and not come to know gold when she saw it. The figure of the man seated on a drapery-covered throne was nearly a dozen feet tall, she guessed. In appearance and presence it was horrible. Its angry face was dominated by a gaping mouth which forced its chin down to its chest. The body was draped in robes. In one hand the statue held a vase and in the other an upright sword which spired over its head. Both also appeared to have been forged of gold.

She stood before it at the lip of the stage gazing up as it seemed to look over her at an invisible congregation. How long had it sat here waiting for an audience? Well, it had her now.

"Hey!"

She spun around, choking back a gasp. Lester stood in the doorway. "That is the ugliest Buddha I've ever seen!"

"It's not a Buddha," she said. "It's treasure. A real treasure."

"It's just an old piece of set dressing."

She climbed up onto the stage. "Look how old it is. It's practically ancient."

"I don't think you ought to mess around with it," he cautioned her.

She knew that if it had been his discovery, he would already have been prying samples off to bring to a jeweler. She felt a small, fierce stab of pride; this was hers! She rubbed a hand slowly down the statue's arm. "There's not a speck of dust on it. Everything else is covered in dust, but this is spotless." She held up her fingers for him to inspect.

"Someone's been cleaning it," he said, looking toward her feet. From where she now stood she could see that recent footprints had been left in the thick dust. They came from and led back to the stage left wing, but they seemed to stop short of the statue. A wide expanse of dust surrounding the pedestal of leaping lions was undisturbed. She was about to tell Lester this when something insectlike hummed past her ear. As if the entire world had suddenly grown thick and slow, she saw Lester's expression change from concern to shock as his gaze moved from her to somewhere past her left shoulder.

The man emerging from the shadows of the wings was Chinese, but he had about him an attitude that was markedly different from the humbled westernized men on the streets just outside. He was dressed in a black variation of the standard gray pajamas that many Chinese men wore; around his waist the shirt was cinched with a tight yellow sash.

His contempt for them was palpable. He swung a length of chain in a long arc by his right side. It hummed in a hypnotically threatening way. In the same instant she took all this in, she realized that he must have already launched this at her once, that what had flicked past her ear had not been an insect but had, in fact, been the tip of the swinging chain.

"Nee how ma," she heard Lester greet the man. Everything was happening so slowly and too fast at the same time. She wondered why Lester would be asking a man who had just tried to whip her with a

chain how he was, and then she realized that the chain had moved so fast that Lester probably hadn't seen it. She heard the chord of the chain deepen and knew it was a moment away from lashing out again. She felt the speed of the world return to normal as her head snapped around to Lester.

"Don't just stand there!" she said simply. And then she flung herself toward the edge of the stage. In motion, she could feel the last of the chain as it whisked past her hair. There was a hollow metallic clang as the chain struck the statue.

They were frequent dancers at the Rainbow Room and Roseland. Lester was accustomed to the weight of her body in motion; his hands caught her waist and he used her momentum to swing her to her feet. She could see that the Chinese man had a grip on the long chain which stretched out from his hand in a straight line. Its other, more lethal end, a spike about seven inches long, was embedded in the soft gold of the statue. His expression hadn't changed at all.

Lester spun her around, in control now. They sprinted for the door. They heard the chain hit the stage but there was no time to look back. They burst into the gloom of dusk. She could hear the man angrily slam the door open again, for their impact had caused it to swing back closed. The sidewalk was still ominously empty. They raced toward Pell Street, to people and to the welcoming neon sign of Mr. Yee's. She looked back. The man was gaining on them.

They plowed into the human traffic at the intersection. Lester kept a viselike grip on her hand. Her calves were beginning to ache from running in heels and she began to have trouble catching her breath. Lester pulled her into the street. Cars squealed to a halt as they darted across. The uneven cobblestones didn't help her balance, and Lester nearly threw her up to the sidewalk. She couldn't run another step. She knew Lester knew too. She wanted him to keep running but she couldn't speak.

Lester did the last thing she, and probably the man chasing them, expected. He stopped. The man was so close behind them he didn't have time to react. Lester drew his arm back, his large hand clenched in anger, and he threw the first punch Norma had ever seen him throw. She could hear the threads in the shoulder of his jacket tear apart as his arm snapped out and his fist made contact with the man's jaw.

The man's face stopped instantly, but his feet continued the skid he had begun to try to stop himself. The impact threw his head back as his legs propelled his body forward, until, for a moment, his body seemed parallel to the pavement, suspended at the end of Lester's arm. Then he collapsed to the ground. There were murmurs of surprise from the bystanders. At least, Norma thought as Lester grabbed her again, he had knocked that nasty look off the man's face.

Lester was staring at the end of his fist, still suspended steadily in space several feet away from his nose. He gave a low whistle of amazement. In the stillness of the moment the eerie, floating, melodyless tune seemed to be the only sound in New York.

"Let's go." She snatched a handful of his jacket.

"Did you see that?" he said as he stumbled after her through the crowd toward a familiar destination.

"So lovely," she had time to reply.

"Mr. and Mrs. Dent!" Mr. Yee greeted them outside his shop enthusiastically, waving off the small crowd of spectators. Norma looked back and saw that the man had managed to crawl off into the shadows somewhere. Life had returned to normal so quickly that except for her throbbing legs and Lester's ripped jacket, there was no outward indication of any trouble. *"How boo how?"*

"No," Lester said, massaging his swelling knuckles, *"boo how doy!"*

Mr. Yee's ever-pleasant demeanor never changed. "The *boo how doy* are long gone, Mr. Dent."

"I'm telling you, Mr. Yee," Lester replied. "Mrs. Dent and I just met living history in all his glory. An honest-to-God hatchet man. In fact, I knocked him ass over teakettle!"

He began to tell the story of the chase but Norma interrupted. "Mr. Yee? Where are your dumplings?" She caught her breath and drew *And to Think That I Saw It on Mulberry Street* from her handbag. She had wrapped it in colored crepe paper. "I have something for them."

"Of course, Mrs. Dent, please come in off the street." He ushered her into the building, where hugs and squeals of delight from little Monk and Ham, Mr. Yee's dumplings, greeted her.

Episode Eleven

The boy, who was known only as Gousheng, dog food, left his village behind him and set off on the harvesters' path through the rice paddies. The evenly spaced sprouts were growing in water that smelled dank and old. It was the smell of his grandmother, who worked these paddies. He hated his grandmother, who, in addition to smelling like cow dung, was shrill and quick to anger and favored his cousins before him because he was a bastard and his mother was dead.

The summer day was brilliant and clear. The sun was high in a sky with few clouds. If his cousins or friends were with him, the day's fun would be to try to knock one another into the knee-deep, muck-filled water. This contest could last for hours.

A water buffalo gazed sagely at him, a huge wooden yoke upon its back. The ticks on its flank were swollen nuggets, the size of his thumb. The boy knew what the weight of the yoke around the beast's neck felt like. It felt like his grandmother's burning hatred.

He came across the ridge to a copse on the far bank of the paddy. He stepped easily up the hill and looked around. From here he could see no one from his village. The buzzing of bees and the distant cry of cranes were the only sounds he could hear. The old women of the village (there were no old men, or any men, only boys) said that the thicket was haunted by demons and that no one should ever go there. So he escaped there whenever he could, for he knew no one would follow. He crept deeper into the grove of trees, pushing into the darkness for the clearing he knew lay ahead.

The temple was ancient, older than any old thing he had ever seen in his village, which meant that it was older than anything he had ever seen. There were stones embedded deep in the earth, grass growing up nearly over them. The clay tiles of the roof were gone in places. He knew there were no demons here.

Inside the temple were old stone statues of gods that he had never heard of and that no one worshipped anymore. Most had toppled from their bases ages ago and lay crumbling on a hard wooden floor. Their hands embraced holes carved through the centers of their chests in some ancient symbol of heavenly illumination. The large statue, still upright against the back wall, fascinated him in particular. This god's face was not serene and meditative, like the faces of the others. It was wrathful. He liked to pretend that he was this god's priest, and the caretaker of his temple, and here the people of his village could come to him for the interpretation of the whims of the gods, and he would instruct them that the gods would favor them if they were to drive his grandmother from the village or harness her to a yoke.

The sound of the horse snorting interrupted his daydream. He ran from the temple. A strong hand grabbed his shoulder and threw him to the ground. The sun was behind the demon and made it hard to see him when the boy looked up from the ground. His head hurt. He kicked out at the demon, his foot connecting with wooden shin armor. He couldn't fight this. He thought about the beautiful day, the secret grove, his temple with its gods, his one god in particular, and he thought of his grandmother and the yoke on the water buffalo and realized he had nothing much more to live for and that this was a nice place to die. He smiled and closed his eyes, for he knew his life was over.

"Your father, who was my cousin, has died," spoke the demon into his darkness. His voice was hard and commanding, but gentle. "I have come for you. You will sit behind me in my saddle and we shall ride from here together."

"I shall never return here?"

"No," said the demon. "You will find a new home."

"Would my grandmother be able to find me?"

The demon laughed. It was fearsome and warm at the same time. "You will never see your grandmother again."

The boy opened his eyes. "I will come with you," he said, and the demon held out his hand to help him up.

And so the boy, who had been known in the village only as Gousheng, dog food, was adopted into the clan of the warlord Zuolin and took his surname, Zhang. But he was also given a name that honored his father's spirit as a warrior who fights against the foreign invaders. His new name was now Zhang Mei. But he would not be known as the Dragon of Terror and Peril for many years yet.

Episode Twelve

"JESUS CHRIST!"

Walter could tell that Hubbard was a little impressed by his personal Pullman car.

"Holy jeez!"

He knew it was impressive.

"Son of a bitch!"

He had bought it to impress. "Like it?"

"Hell!"

"I couldn't tell." He threw his hat on the banquette. "Well. Come on in and make yourself at home. It's not the distance to Providence that wears you out. It's all the stops at nowhere in between."

It had taken a couple of days to get the car hitched up to the New York and New England Railroad, over from its usual place on the Seaboard Air Line Railroad, where Gibson used it to make frequent runs down to Miami. Often on those occasions when he wasn't heading south, the railroad would rent the car out for him. This arrangement had already paid for the car. Yesterday, Friday, the car had been floated on a tug from the Oak Point rail yard in the Bronx to the New York Central rail yard at Seventy-second Street on the Hudson, where they were now boarding it to get to Providence and Lovecraft's funeral tomorrow.

A Negro porter opened the door separating the living quarters, which they were in, from the sleeping quarters, and said, "Welcome aboard, Mr. Gibson," with his smile of familiar affection.

"Hi, Chester," Gibson greeted him back. "How're the ladies?"

"Same as usual, Mr. Gibson. They all want me richer or deader. Or both." Chester traveled with the car; tending to it often meant living in it. In the year since Gibson had hired him, Chester had kept the car as neat and trim as any ship.

Through Orson Welles, Gibson had met a number of people involved in the Federal Theatre Project and the Works Progress Administration. One of them had mentioned a talented young writer who had the misfortune to be both a Negro and a prison parolee but was on the straight and narrow and would work honestly and hard. Gibson had hired him with the words, "There's typewriters in the car and lots of paper and lots more spare time. A man could put all that to some kind of use." Gibson didn't know whether or not the man had put it to good use because the car was always immaculately prepared for him whenever he arrived.

Chester hopped off the train to get their luggage from the nearby cab. He moved with an old, slow limp. The story was that he had fallen down an elevator shaft at some point in his life, before prison, and busted his leg up.

Gibson hung his coat on a hanger and put it in the small closet. He hadn't traveled recently and the scents of varnish and polish made him smile. It was one of those particular combinations of favorite smells that he always remembered that he had forgotten once he remembered it.

"God damn!" There was a heavy thump behind him as Hubbard stumbled around the car. Being in a coach was kind of like being on a boat. There was never quite enough room and it took some getting used to.

The walls of the lounge room were paneled with dark cherrywood, and the Persian rugs on the floor were deep red, so even though the glow of the oil lamps seemed to be swallowed up, the room remained comfortable and warm. A leather banquette, a pair of leather club chairs, a sideboard with liquor decanters, and a small bookcase stocked with books on magic made up most of the furnishings. There was a small workbench supplied with tools of the trade where Gibson could tinker with magic tricks. If he had any time on this trip, he intended to continue his efforts to re-create Blackstone's astonishing exploding fireball effect, which had stymied him for months.

Unless he could bring himself to write.

At the end of the room, beside the corridor to the main cabins, galley, and head, was another small desk set. A typewriter sat on it with a fresh sheet of paper in the roller. Thanks, Chester, he thought. Thanks for reminding me. Next to the typewriter lay a neat stack of the latest mags in case he would rather read than write.

Gibson went straight to the desk and opened one of the drawers. Good. He was pretty sure he had left a half-finished manuscript here after a trip to Chicago many months ago, and seeing the papers confirmed that he had. One of the reasons he was taking the overnight train was that it took a roundabout route and made many stops, so it wouldn't pull into Providence until late morning, giving him plenty of time to work on this book. Or start a new one. He flipped to the back page and read the last sentence to see if it would remind him what he'd been writing: "Lamont Cranston had a premonition of Death." For a moment he stared at the words, which appeared halfway down the page. He turned the phrase over in his mind, whittling it down until just one word remained: *premonition.* Had Litzka really had a premonition of Howard's death?

He put the thought out of his head and instead focused on the work that had to be done. He'd be able to finish the book on this trip. And maybe he'd start something new. Something different.

If only Hubbard gave him a break.

"How much did you spend on this? Are you still making payments? Can I borrow it sometime?"

There was something else rolling around in the drawer. At first

Gibson thought it was a cigarette, but it wasn't one he had rolled. He picked it up and sniffed it. Reefer. Interesting. Without putting it down he looked at the mag on the top of the stack. It was the recent issue of *Bronzeman,* one of the only Negro pulps. This particular mag was actually published in Harlem. Underneath the striking image of a handsome Negro—face turned to the sun, sleeves rolled up, indicating readiness to work or to join the revolution—was the list of names of this issue's story writers. He saw Chester's name and smiled, guessing that Chester had been planning to throw himself a little debut party. Looking at the reefer stick and the mag, he knew that Chester would probably be moving on soon. Gibson would read the story and congratulate Chester, but the two of them would never speak of the marijuana that went missing on the run to Providence.

He'd smoked the stuff once or twice before and hadn't seen any demons. Anyway, maybe this would help him relax. After all, he hadn't slept for nights, ever since the theater, and Litzka and her disturbing premonition. And the booze just wasn't cutting it.

Sleep? Hadn't he been thinking about writing all night moments ago? To sleep or write, the writer's eternal boxing match. If sleep weren't such a damn good fighter, there would be a lot more books to read.

"Do they make these to order or can you buy them from a showroom?"

He wasn't quite certain how Hubbard had managed to invite himself. He certainly was a persuasive and ingratiating little son of a bitch. If writing didn't work out for him, Gibson suspected politics would. One minute Gibson was in his office making travel arrangements and the next Hubbard was offering to tag along. As the president of the American Fiction Guild, Hubbard felt it was important that a representative pay his respects to one of their fallen own.

"You ever read Howard?" Gibson asked, surprised that he didn't already know whether Hubbard had any knowledge of Lovecraft.

"Sure. Nothing that comes to mind right now. But folks say he was good. Doc Smith says he was great."

"Yeah." Gibson felt like telling him that he didn't have to lie.

Howard's stories were hard to find and even harder to like. Gibson moved to the sideboard and held up a decanter of scotch. Hubbard nodded and Gibson poured.

"Yeah," Gibson continued. "He was good. Could have been the next Edgar Allan Poe. He was that good." Lovecraft—just another writer passing from obscurity to oblivion.

"What happened?"

"Well, I guess most Americans think we already have one Poe too many."

"Oh." Hubbard settled easily into one of the club chairs. "How'd you meet him?"

Gibson looked out at the sun setting over the Hudson River. The ice was thick and silvery in the pinkish light; boats wound their way through channels hacked through it. "Our wives," he said. "Our wives introduced us."

"You're married?" Hubbard was surprised.

"I was."

"I know what that's like."

"You're divorced?"

Hubbard shook his head. "My wife threw me out. She heard I had an affair with an actress out in Hollywood."

"How'd she hear that?"

"Well, it was true, for one thing. What a mistake! Walt, I'm telling you . . ." He stopped, carried away with his memories. "My lawyer calls it a trial separation. She'll take me back when she cools off. I hope so anyways. I miss my damn kids."

"Didn't want to go back to your actress?"

"Well, the picture didn't really do what everyone hoped. So . . ." He trailed off for a moment. "I s'pose she's screwing the next writer by now. So's Hollywood, for that matter."

Gibson smiled and loosened his tie. Hubbard could be an agreeable person when he wasn't trying to shine a fella on.

Hubbard sighed. Then he gave a dismissive flip of his hand. "So how'd your wives introduce you?"

"When I was married, I used to get lots of fan letters." He paused, then decided to back up a little bit. "Lovecraft was a huge letter writer. He spent as much time writing letters during the day as you or I do writing our stories. Anything or anyone that struck his fancy would get a letter. So he started writing me because he liked my codes which I stuck in some of the books. I was working on one of those at the time, so I sent him a special code key for it. I gave him his own layer so everyone who had the code key that I published in the story would read it one way, but only he could read it another. I've done that occasionally for other people who are interested in the codes. It's a good brain teaser for me to write one code that has two keys. Y'know, I'd just stick in something personal like, 'Hi, Howard. Ain't scotch swell? Drink more scotch.'"

With a whistle and a shudder, the train began to move. Gibson continued, "Howard was a really smart guy. Self-taught about biology and math, in particular. He had always wanted to be a scientist, but he'd had to drop out of college and I guess he was embarrassed about that so he tried to make up for it by learning and doing these little experiments.

"He loved the codes and he would keep writing me. I got a letter a week, mostly about writing and how frustrating he found it. He never asked me to read his stories, which he could hardly ever get published. But he talked about them and he spoke about writing as if he were a bestseller.

"After a while I was getting so busy with my books that my wife started reading and answering my mail. She came across a letter from Howard telling me that he and his wife were moving to New York and she was going to open a hat store. Well, among other things, my wife loved hats. I think for about three months she single-handedly kept that store open. So, she and Sonia, Howard's wife, were getting together and eventually we went out to visit them in Red Hook and I met Howard.

"It was obvious that this was a nervous guy. I guess his family was blue-blooded. So Red Hook was a real comedown for him and I think he really resented it; all the immigrant Italians distressed him in particular. I don't think he had ever been really exposed to anything even vaguely foreign or exotic. I think he was humiliated by the poverty of their apartment and their neighborhood and their life. He was kind of a momma's boy and Sonia really tried to mother him. She didn't exactly cut his steak for him, but fairly close. We had drinks a couple of times after that. He was just miserable in New York. I think he hated that his wife had to work. Even though he was where the mags were, he couldn't get his stories published on any kind of regular basis. I mean, even *Weird Tales* has a limit to how far they'll actually push 'weird.' And his stuff was weird. Y'know. Poe weird." He trailed off.

"I tried to get him a gig before things got too bad. *Weird Tales* had a license from Harry Houdini to print some of his true adventure stories. And by true, I mean completely made up. Harry asked me if I could do it, but I was too busy with The Shadow. So I recommended Howard. So he met with Harry and wrote a crackerjack little story called "Imprisoned with the Pharaohs." Well, we all thought this was going to be the big one. He waited for it to be published so the eds could really discover him.

"Of course, first *Tales* decided it was a good spring issue fit, and it was winter. Then in the spring they decided maybe it was a better summer story. So they sat on it. Howard didn't get that things like this happen all the time."

Hubbard nodded; he had stories all over town that were waiting for publication for one reason or another.

"I told him to get busy and write another story. And another. And another. Take the fact that he got paid well for this one as a sign of encouragement. He really wanted to see that story in print, more than anything. Really thought it was going to break his career in a really big way. But it just took too long. And when it finally did get published, it didn't even get the cover.

"The bigger problem was that Harry hadn't read the story before it was published, and he didn't like it. In the story his character keeps fainting from sheer terror. He found that rather unmanly. Houdini never faints! And he never asked Lovecraft to write for him again.

"I don't think Howard could take it here anymore. He left Sonia and moved back to Providence. I'd get a letter from him every now and then. He took a job writing science papers at some research lab. Once or twice a year he'd publish a story in the shudders and he'd let me know. I'd write him back in our code, y'know, just a short, secret note of congratulations."

"What happened to his wife?"

"I don't know. My marriage . . ." He let it hang, unwilling to talk to Hubbard about it. "Lose the wife, lose her friends, y'know?"

Hubbard nodded empathetically.

Gibson rose, swaying gently with the rhythm of the train. He could hear Chester in the main cabin unpacking his bags.

"I'm going to try and get some work done," he said, moving to the desk set.

"Sure thing," said Hubbard. "Pretend I'm not here."

Gibson took a seat and lit a cigarette.

"What's your story called?" Hubbard was stretching out on the sofa with one of the books from the cabinet: *The Great Raymond Presents 200 Tricks You Can Do!*

Gibson took a long drag on his cigarette and stared at the cover of the book in Hubbard's hands. Seeing the cover of the book he had ghosted with the elderly magician five years ago gave him a pang of guilt.

"*Murder Rides the Rails,*" he said, trying to remember more about the unfinished book.

Hubbard stuck out his lower lip in thought, as if he had heard better. He thumbed through the book. "I saw Lester Dent at the Knickerbocker. Said he was thinking about trying to solve the Ah Hoon mystery."

"Mystery. History. I wish him luck."

Gibson looked at that last line again.

. . . premonition of Death.

He took a long swallow from his glass. Why was Lamont Cranston having a premonition of Death? Where had Gibson been intending to take that thought? His glass was empty, so he rose and went for a refill, turning the words around in his head. Should he have called Litzka? Maybe he'd compose a telegram to her and have Chester pass it along to the conductor to be sent at the next stop.

"What do you think happened?"

"To what?"

"To Ah Hoon. What do you think happened?"

"I think for the purposes of the story I was telling it doesn't really matter and if old Lester Dent wants to try and dig up something, then that's his story to tell. I'm ready to start the next one."

"What's your secret?" Hubbard asked a while later from behind the book. Gibson gritted his teeth. Just because a man's not typing and is staring out the window watching the Hudson Valley open up to him doesn't mean he's not writing, he wanted to blurt out.

"How do you keep cranking out the words? You gotta have a secret is what I figure. I mean, I can write a lot. But you. Everyone says you're like a machine."

Gibson shrugged. "Sure, a machine," he said. "I don't know about secrets but there's some tricks I keep in mind that keep problems from getting in my way and stopping my flow.

"Don't worry about getting it right, just get it on paper. Never, ever try to describe New York in its entirety, only by blocks, neighborhoods, or atmosphere. I never use the word *occasionally* because I can never spell it right.

"When you write about a dame always start with what her legs look like. 'Dashing' is the quickest way to describe a hero. 'Hirsute' is the quickest way to describe a villain. Never take a job from an ed who says he'll pay you better next time around after you earn your stripes; he'll never respect you and he'll just toss you scraps from there on in. And he'll never pay you better. Never.

"Don't try and write a whole book at once. Throw everything you know on the page. Only write a story that you really know, because only you can come up with the right ending. Don't steal a story; you'll be found out. Keep writing. Don't stop. Ever. Because there's always the chance that you won't start again."

. . . a premonition . . .

He had it! The book had been started before the Allard thing. But Gibson must have already been toying with the idea in the back of his mind and let it spill out onto the page. Lamont's premonition had been about his death as a character. That would never do. His fingers began to move against the keys. He struck out the line and started a new sentence.

"Although The Shadow wore many disguises, he would always be Lamont Cranston, and when he laughed, weak men would experience a premonition of their death."

"That's better," he muttered to himself.

Hubbard arched an eyebrow and then returned to his book.

Gibson wrote like the train itself—relentlessly, driving forward into the night. Long after Hubbard had turned in, he slammed away at the typewriter keys. The pages began to pile up. The skin on his fingertips cracked, then bled. When he finally lit the reefer cigarette early in the morning, he watched with interest as the thin paper turned red from blood which hissed and bubbled away into tiny wisps of steam as it burned.

Episode Thirteen

THE PIGS had screamed all night.

Mei had been unable to sleep. Even if he hadn't been so excited, the sounds of the tormented pigs would have kept him up anyway. So he was alert to the sound of someone creeping down the hall to his sleeping chamber.

"He's coming," Xueling whispered from the door.

Mei threw his cover off and leapt up. He was already dressed.

Of his eight adopted brothers, Xueling was the closest in age to him. He was also his closest friend. The two studied many things together, from history to sword fighting to riding to languages such as French (it was important to know the language of diplomacy) and English (it was more important to know the language of the foreign invaders).

They padded silently together through the halls of Shenyang Palace. Mei was bigger and faster than Xueling and most other boys his age, and Xueling had to quicken his pace to keep up. Dawn had yet to arrive and everyone but the guards was asleep.

There was a man awake, however, standing near the entrance awaiting the sun: Mi-Ying, the diplomat from Beijing, who counseled their father on the intricacies of dealing with the Russians and Japanese who flocked to his court like goldfish to crumbs.

"Your father is triumphant. The foreign invaders have been driven from the land. It is only a shame that you are not old enough to be at your father's side at his victory," he said to them.

"There are many battles yet to fight," Xueling said back to him coldly. "Though China is divided by civil wars, an emperor will sit in Beijing yet again."

"Indeed." The diplomat nodded and took a step aside so the boys could pass him. His eyes were dark and mercenary, and malice and contempt lurked behind his thin, unctuous smile. Mei could feel the man's hard eyes driving into his back as he retreated into the dark of the hall.

They entered the courtyard with its eight pavilions. The sky was lightening and the stars were winking out. The cool dew on the flagstones made his feet tingle. They ran up the stairs of the Phoenix Tower. At the top of the turret they could see the vast palace below them, across the city, even to the land beyond.

Slaughtered pigs on raised platforms lined the wide, tree-lined road which led toward the palace gate. The heralds had arrived yesterday at noon the previous day with word of the victory. Each house had been commanded to produce an animal for the feast. The pigs were decorated with painted symbols of victory, flower blossoms filled their eyes and mouths, and colorful flags were staked into their flanks. Many were draped with firecrackers.

"Look," said Mei. His eyes were sharper than Xueling's. He pointed into the distance. A cloud rose on the horizon. "Dust," he added. "Our father comes. He will be at the gates by midday, at the head of an army of triumph."

"Someday," his brother said, "we will ride with him into Beijing, and China will be saved."

Mei nodded. He knew Xueling was wise for his age. Xueling could grasp the vastness of China's history and dilemmas at times when he could not. But then he also knew that there were things he saw that Xueling did not. He knew for example that devious Mi-Ying profited from the dealings he recommended to Zuolin. Mei also knew that Mi-Ying hated them all. He knew this because he recognized his grandmother's cruelty in Mi-Ying's eyes. Xueling would not know hatred like this. Xueling was as oblivious to this side of human nature as the dead pigs had been to their fate.

The two boys turned to watch the sun break through the great cloud rising in the east. The Emperor of the Northern Lands was returning home to his sons.

Episode Fourteen

"Opium? So that's what that smell I smelled was?" Lester asked.

"Yes," Mr. Lee nodded. "*Fook yuen.* Opium. There is a notorious opium den underneath the theater for many years. Men descend through the door at the back of the alley." He sat back and contemplated Mr. and Mrs. Dent. "You should not have gone into the theater. It is a very bad place. You are very lucky you were not hurt."

Mr. Yee's restaurant wasn't the fanciest restaurant in Chinatown but it wasn't one of Chinatown's many cheap noodle houses either. There were always fresh red cotton cloths for every table and the savory green tea was served in painted porcelain pots, not tin. The aromas of fresh garlic, scallions, and vinegar filled the air. Every now and then a rich smoky blast of sizzling peppers would issue forth from the kitchen, causing guests to clear their throats. Dozens of framed pictures of China's landscapes and history, and of Chinese immigrants in America from the railroad age on, hung on the walls. Candles burned at the foot of a small Buddha statue in a shuttered box at the back of the restaurant.

An old man sat at a table near the front window, having dinner with a much younger man. Neither of them spoke to, or even seemed to acknowledge the existence of, his companion. Next to them, on a table near the door, sat a fresh metal pail. A flyer was pasted to the pail. Every now and then a person would open the door, drop some change or a bill into the bucket, and then leave. On the other side of the window, Chinatown had neatly made the transition from late afternoon to night. The women had taken their shopping home and the men were out running the errands that men do after dinner.

Monk stared Norma down over the last few pot stickers on the plate. The boys' mother had died in labor giving birth to the second child. Norma had nicknamed the children Ham and Monk after two of Lester's most popular characters, Doc's comic relief companions. The names seemed to suit them. In the books Brigadier General Theodore Marley Brooks, or Ham, was a fussy and supercilious lawyer who carried a sword sheathed in a dandy's cane. Gorilla-shaped Lieutenant Colonel Andrew Blodgett "Monk" Mayfair was his opposite in every way except his brilliance; his field was chemistry. The elder boy, Ham, who was eight, was fastidious and somber and unusually erudite for a child. Monk, who was four, was strong and messy and thought nothing was funnier than tweaking the sensibilities of his older brother, to his father's amusement. In return, they had dubbed Lester and Norma Mr. and Mrs. Doc.

Although Monk had probably eaten three times his weight in pot stickers during his short life, he wanted nothing more than one of the savory, steamed wrapper-around-pork-rolls which lay on a bed of cabbage between him and Norma. He made moon eyes at it and then her, and back and forth, trying to get some indication from her that it would be safe to attack the pot sticker. What complicated matters was that he had already managed to cadge one from her, but it had slipped from his hands and landed with a slightly greasy plop on the tiled floor. The look he gave her now was intended to make her aware that he understood the responsibility of being entrusted with the next pot sticker, and that its fate would be entirely different.

Meanwhile Ham, also sitting at the table, studying the *Doc Savage* magazines Norma had brought him, would periodically look up with disdain at his brother's scheming. Norma took great delight in stretching out the suspense for both boys.

"The *boo how doy.* The highbinders. The hatchet men. They don't really exist in Chinatown anymore," Mr. Yee explained to Lester. "There has been a truce between the Hip Sing and the On Leong for almost ten years, and the smaller tongs such as the Sam Yip and others have really died away.

"Look over there." He indicated the two men at the front of the restaurant. "My uncle is a Hip Sing man. Does he look like a fearsome gangster to you? I am a Hip Sing man. Am I not your brother? Why, right this moment my uncle and his friend, a diplomat from the consul general's office here in New York, are discussing the upcoming Unity Parade in which we Chinese here in this land will show our solidarity with our families fighting the Japanese back in China. The consul general himself, a great man, will be the grand marshal," he added proudly, "and he will take the money we have raised back with him to our people who are in desperate need. It was not until mere months ago that the remaining warlords and the Communists set aside their difference with the old Imperialists and began to fight the Japanese invasion. And that only happened because Chiang Kai-shek was kidnapped by the last warlords and forced into an alliance at the threat of his life. Meanwhile, Japan advances every day and the Chinese people go hungry."

Norma looked toward the two men, who were still stoically eating. Any discussion appeared to be taking place on a purely metaphysical plane.

"Unlike in China, the old feuds have died out here. The face of Chinatown today is one of unity. Being peaceful and prosperous together in the Chinatowns across the Golden Mountain is the only way we have to convince your government to lift the Exclusion Act and bring our refugee families here."

"What's a Confucian hat?" Monk asked.

"Exclusion Act," his brother snorted. "It means no Chinese in America. Unless you're born here. It's the law."

"Father wasn't born here," Monk said defiantly.

"Through the graces of my uncle who already lived here, I entered," their father told them. He gazed toward the front of the restaurant for a moment, recalling his journey. "I sailed across the Pacific Ocean and then I had to make my way all across Canada, which is almost as big as the whole America, and much colder. And I was just a little older than your brother when I did it. By myself."

"They can't make us go back to China, can they?" Monk asked, plainly worried.

"Of course not!" said Norma. "I would never let them take you. Because you're my dumplings and I love you. And your father makes the best pot stickers in the world and I love them too!"

"Which do you love better? Pot stickers or dumplings?" Monk was laughing. Ham looked up from his magazine, invested in the answer as well. Norma laughed at Monk and the great pot sticker–dumpling debate was joined.

While Norma and the dumplings teased each other, Lester turned to Yee. "You ever hear of a fella by the name of Ah Hoon?"

"Ah Hoon?" Mr. Yee began to laugh in a most good-natured manner. "Ah Hoon!"

The old man at the table by the front caught Yee's eye with a gesture so subtle that Norma nearly missed it. "Excuse me," he said, rising, wiping away a tear. He went toward the table.

"Who's Ah Hoon?" she asked Lester. She had never heard him speak that name before.

"It's just something I'm working over." She knew that Lester was superstitious about letting anyone read anything of his until he was done with it. He felt that the act of its being read would trigger something in his mind that said that the work was done; it had been read; it was over. Apparently the story of Ah Hoon fell into that category because "something I'm working over" was his stock response to questions about his writing.

Monk was kicking at the pot sticker under the table. He made contact and it skittered slickly across the tiled floor.

"Go get that!" Ham was imperious, assuming his father's mantle of control.

"You get it," Monk said with defiance.

"That's all right," Lester said. "I'll get it."

He stood up. Monk looked enviously at his height and said, "I bet if you had a son he'd be taller than you."

Lester smiled and tousled the boy's hair. "You're probably right." He walked toward the pot sticker.

"Are you ever going to have some boys?" Monk asked Norma.

She felt her lips purse for a moment. Both boys looked at her, earnest and eager for a response. She looked at Lester as he sauntered across the restaurant and felt something break in her chest. His whole life revolved around creating stories for boys, and he would never have his own to share them with. She realized a truth about the rest of her life. She smiled at the boys, to reassure them. "No," she said. "I don't think so."

They looked disappointed.

The front door slammed open. The sound startled her, and she reflexively choked back the tears which she had been verging upon. As she turned her head to look, she saw Lester in mid-bend toward the pot sticker, and Mr. Yee speaking with the old man at the front table.

"Hey!"

It was the fat cop they had seen harassing the fishmonger earlier in the day. His face was overly pink and oily, as if he had been drinking. He swaggered through the door, his silvery, greedy eyes swiveling around. She saw Ham grow tense and wary, and Monk quickly slid off his chair and slid up to her side, under her protective arm.

"I heard there was some street fighting outside earlier and one of them punks was from here. Come on, Yee. Give it up. You speakee English better'n any other Chink down here."

"I don't know what you mean," Yee said politely. "A man fell down outside. That is all."

The old man at the table continued to eat, oblivious, while the younger man glared at the cop. Yee placed a hand innocently upon his shoulder as if to reassure him. From the creases which appeared in the man's jacket, Norma could see that he was actually applying pressure. She realized that he was keeping the man seated, and she wondered what exactly the young man was capable of. "There was no fighting here."

The cop had already lost interest in Yee and was casting his gaze around the room. His eyes lighted upon the pail of money. "That's some collection you're raising there, Yee. Church building?"

"It's the fund for the defense of Beijing," Yee replied.

He reached his hand into the pail and it came out with a fistful of bills. "Think of me as the *auxiliary* defense league."

The young man at the table brushed Yee's hand aside as if it were a stray branch and leapt to his feet with a shout. Yee barked at him.

The cop broke into a big grin. "Your friend sure looks like he could be the kind to start a rumble in the street." He reached in and pocketed another handful. "Anybody want to change their story here?" He reached in again. The rustling of the paper bills made the change scratch unpleasantly on the bottom of the pail. "I didn't think so."

"That money is for widows and orphans." For the first time the cop seemed to notice the presence of white people and he seemed to be especially surprised that the woman had just snapped at him.

"Lady, this is between me and the Chinee," he snapped at her. But his voice wavered.

Lester took a step toward him. Norma tried to stand too, but Monk held her fast. She pulled the little boy closer. She could feel his heart pounding against her side.

"Like she said, the money is for widows and orphans. And you ain't either. I want your name and badge number."

The cop took a step closer. "You're so tough, why don't you tell me your name."

"My name," Lester said, "is Kenneth Robeson. I want you to put that money back before I report you to your superiors and the mayor's office and the papers."

"Okay, Robeson, let some of that steam out of your collar." The cop was nervous. He hadn't expected to be challenged, and certainly not by a white man who loomed over him. "Look, I'm putting it back." He twisted back to dump the money in the pail.

"All of it," Lester commanded.

"Sure," said the cop. Then he suddenly charged at Lester, drawing his truncheon from a ring around his belt.

Norma gasped. Lester didn't move a muscle. The cop raised his arm and was opening his mouth to say something or yell something when his whole attitude changed in an heartbeat. His eyes opened wide in fear and he seemed to lose control of his legs, which flew out from under him. His arms flailed around; his club knocked into his mouth. Off balance and moving fast, he crashed to the floor, his head banging, then bouncing, off the tiles.

Norma looked down. Mashed onto the sole of the cop's shoe at the tail end of a long and greasy skid mark was a slick residue of cabbage and pork and dough, the sad fate of the lost pot sticker. There was a sudden quiet in the restaurant. Even the cooks in the kitchen stopped cooking and came to the door. Lester bent down over the moaning cop. "Can you hear me?"

The cop shook his head from side to side.

"Okay. I have your badge number now. I want you to stay out of this restaurant forever, do you hear me? Leave the Yees alone. Or so help me I will be hanging your badge over my mantle by spring. Hear me?"

The cop nodded.

"And I want you to act more decently to the Chinese folk on your beat. Treat 'em nice."

"Les . . . Kenneth," said Norma. "It's enough."

"Okay." He turned to the cop. "Do you want me to call an ambulance?"

The cop shook his head. He crawled to his hands and knees and staggered to his feet. He had his hand over his head. He fumbled toward the door.

"Remember what I said. You won't come back here, right?"

The cop nodded.

Norma watched as Lester remained motionless as the cop staggered into the night. Lester slid the tip of his shoe across the slick floor streak of squashed pot sticker.

"Boys, when it comes to pot stickers or dumplings," he said, with a wink to Monk and Ham, "I gotta tell ya, I'm coming down on the side of the pot stickers."

Episode Fifteen

It was summer in the Year of the Monkey. The solstice had passed a few weeks before and the days were long and hot. The men fighting and dying were hidden by the dust of the battle.

Blood streamed down the blade of Mei's *pudau* and onto the wooden hilt. It was warm and his fingers stuck to it. He had lost sight of Xueling and Zuolin soon after the charge. Now he fought on only to reach the river. The river was life.

Troops loyal to Beijing had ambushed Zhang Zuolin's army as they prepared to cross the river. It was a preemptive strike, intended to keep the warlord from bringing the war to the gates of the Forbidden City itself. The surprise attack was a desperate attempt to catch Zhang's army while they were still spread in a line, unable to create formations quickly.

Fortunately, Mei's own division was only several miles west on a parallel course, preparing to ford the river at a different point. Messengers reached him within an hour of the ambush.

Though it was not his first battle, he was already coming to be known as the Dragon of Terror and Peril, but Mei's heart had pounded fearfully in his chest as they crested the hill above the fray. Down the hill in the small valley soldiers swarmed like ants and he could not see if his adopted father had survived the attack, if men he knew had fallen. He felt as if he would scream for the battle that was lost. At last the signal had been given and they had raced out of the trees to the attackers' unprotected rear flank.

The surprise worked. Mei and his men had plunged into the mass of confused and terrified soldiers like a shark cutting into a school of fish. The entire rear of the Beijing army collapsed in an instant from a unified organism of destruction into individual cells of fear. The traitorous ambushers were trapped between pincer claws. Mei's brother, Xueling, had led his cavalry toward the river after the charge in order to seal off retreat. That position would now be fortified. That was where safety lay.

Mei felt as if his body had never performed as strongly before and never would again. His horse had been cut out from under him at the height of the charge, its front legs sheared away at the joints. He had miraculously landed on his feet in the midst of his enemies. Slashing and blocking as he had practiced so many times, he made men fall before him. The straps of his armor bit like razors into his back. He knew he had to reach the river and Xueling. His blade was dulling from impact. It bit deeply into the side of a man, grating on rib, and fastening deeply into the spine. He threw his foot against the man's body to dislodge him from the weapon.

Something hit him with the force of a mountain falling. The chest of a runaway horse. He curled into a ball as he fell and the hooves fell harmlessly about him before the horse galloped off. He could die here now, he knew. A sword could fall, a spear could pierce; he had played his part. Men had fallen at his hand.

He heard the sound of his death rushing toward him. It was as horns calling above the din. Slowly he brought himself to his knees. He could hear water now and smell the moss. All around the battlefield men stood. Zuolin's men, Xueling's men, the men of the Northern Lands, his men. A cheer was rising. Hands grabbed him and helped him up. A face he recollected was speaking to him. He knew the man, he realized, one of his own soldiers. He was speaking with great excitement. Mei waited patiently for his words to make sense and suddenly they did.

"Beijing is taken!" the man shouted. He was a peasant, such as Mei himself had been once. This man's lowly life could have been his. Instead, while this man would return to his village and his rice paddy tomorrow, Mei would ride with his adopted father and his adopted brother into the great city of Beijing. "The enemy runs! We are victorious! China is united!"

Mei looked back. His own path toward the river was visible as a line of corpses fallen as bamboo is knocked aside by a bear moving through a forest. He had reached the river.

Episode Sixteen

"You know, it's almost not as heavy as you would think a coffin would be."

Someday, Gibson thought, how he and Hubbard and a perfect stranger ended up carrying Lovecraft's casket through the dismal rain and icy mud at the Swan Point Cemetery to the Phillips family plot might make a funny story.

Someday.

Right now he was having too hard a time keeping his feet from sliding out from under him to think about a story.

"You think there's a latch on this thing?" the stranger wheezed. Gibson hoped he was not about to burst into one of his coughing fits. Not now. Not while supporting his share of the casket. "He's not . . . Nothing can flop out, right?"

"You feel anything shifting inside?" Hubbard snarled. "Just keep it steady."

Might.

Gibson would have to begin the story when the stranger suddenly woke up coughing and gasping in the back pew of the Providence Chapel during Lovecraft's service and nearly startled him and Hubbard to death. It was easy to be scared in the small chapel because even though it was day, the sky was dark, and for some reason the shabby chapel had lost its power. Until the stranger made his abrupt appearance Gibson and Hubbard had been the only guests in the dark, dark, very dark chapel, listening to the ancient minister evoke the prophets. Fortunately the stove had kept the room warm.

Actually, the story really would have to start with Hubbard falling asleep, Gibson thought, as he slipped on a patch of grass and heard Hubbard curse quietly behind him. "Sorry," he said, winded.

"You all right?" If Hubbard was half the writer he was, then he probably exercised about half as much. And half of nothing is . . .

Hubbard had fallen asleep and the church had been empty.

That's where it should start. The service had started with only him and Hubbard in attendance. Then the mustachioed stranger with the high forehead had awakened, coughing. But before that, the minister had begun the service. That was about the time Hubbard had fallen asleep, after muttering something about organized religion being a crutch for the weak-minded.

He was coughing again now.

"Pal, how about you? Are you all right?" Gibson asked him. He stopped, acting as if the coughing had interrupted his progress. In fact, he was grateful for the break. "You been coughing up oysters all afternoon."

The man inhaled, nodded, and began coughing again. The other two men juggled the coffin against his spasm. The stranger was much taller than Gibson, and the burden of the coffin tilted unfairly toward Gibson. Fortunately, nothing shifted inside.

"Lung damage," the man wheezed. "Tuberculosis."

"Now?" demanded Hubbard, leaning away.

The man shook his head. Gibson could see exhaustion in the dark circles under his eyes. He seemed young, probably around Hubbard's age, but he had put some miles on his lanky frame. He had the weary, defeated look of so many American men his age who had finally lost hope but hadn't yet slid into despair. He cleared his throat with a mighty effort and regained control of his breathing. "It hit me a few years ago when I was in the navy. Had to retire and move to California. Nice and dry there."

"Retire?" Hubbard asked. "What're you? Forty?"

"Thirty." Gibson could believe it if one gave the man the benefit of imagining him with a sleep, a shave, and a haircut.

Hubbard appraised him for a moment. "Retired," he finally said. "Well done."

The stranger shrugged. "Welcome to Easy Street."

"I'm ready whenever you are," Gibson said. His arms were aching and his fingers, already stiff from a night of typing, were beginning to go numb. He knew they were going to ache too much for him to write tonight. Oh well, he could work on Blackstone's magic trick.

"Right," the stranger said. He wore workman's clothes—dungarees, a sweater, and a Salvation Army–issue peacoat.

"Okay," Hubbard grunted. They continued their slog toward the wrought-iron gate and the few plots beyond. "Aren't your friends and family supposed to be your pallbearers?" Hubbard complained.

"He was kind of a hermit. Lived with his aunts. Then one died. So, just an aunt. I wonder why she's not here." Gibson had half-feared and half-hoped that Sonia would make an appearance, but she hadn't. It made him feel worse for Howard. "At least somebody he knew showed up, though. Right?" He indicated the stranger.

"To be honest, I don't even know who we're burying," the stranger said.

Gibson stopped and stared at him. "Then who the hell are you?"

"I helped dig the grave."

"You're a grave digger?"

"Well, I'm not *the* grave digger. I dug this grave. Look. I'm stuck in Providence, which is a strange land. I needed some cash. One thing I've learned is that graves always gotta be dug. Once we get this fella planted, I get fifty bucks, which gets me down to New York City."

"What's in New York for you?" Hubbard wanted to know.

"Not my ex-wife."

"Ah." Hubbard seemed skeptical.

They moved through the gate and set the coffin with a thud upon the slats over the grave. They all massaged their hands.

"At least it has stopped raining," said the stranger. Gibson nodded in agreement, although the skies were still dark and foamy. Along the path they had taken, the ancient minister was slowly approaching.

Hubbard groaned and rotated his shoulder in its socket a few times. "I specifically became a writer to avoid working," he said, grinning at Gibson.

"You're a writer?" the stranger asked.

"As a matter of fact, I am," he replied. "Ron Hubbard."

The stranger shook his head apologetically. Gibson noted that even in his destitute position he carried himself with the rigid dignity and force of a military officer.

"Ever read *Adventure Magazine* or *Two-Fisted Tales*?"

The stranger nodded and shrugged at the same time. "Sorry, pal. Never heard of you. Ever write for *Astounding Stories?* I read that."

"Great," Hubbard sighed. "Look. You heard of *The Shadow*?"

"Sure. Everybody knows *The Shadow.* You write *that*?"

"No. He does."

"Seriously?" the stranger asked. "You're Maxwell Grant?"

Gibson ground out his cigarette. "Now there's a name you'll never find in the Irish sports pages. I'm Walter Gibson. Maxwell Grant's a nom de plume." He held out his hand and the stranger shook it. His grip was firm and steady. This man was no rummy or hophead, Gibson decided. Gibson waited for a few seconds after releasing his hand. The man seemed disinclined to provide any more information. "So what's your name, pal?"

"Driftwood," he said, without hesitation. "Otis Driftwood."

Gibson smiled and was about to speak when Hubbard butted in. "I know that name! Are you a writer?"

"Naw, I'm in high society. Can't you tell?"

"Yes," Gibson said. "You're obviously an opera lover."

Driftwood gave him a sly smile. "I'm kind of trying to keep a low profile these days. Trying to keep out of the funny pages, if you know what I mean."

"G-men?" Hubbard asked. "Revenuers?"

Driftwood shook his head. "Business associates," he said. "Like I said before, I was in the navy. I was a gunnery officer out of Annapolis. I got TB.

"I'm from Missouri originally, but the hospital the navy discharged me to was in Arizona because it was hot and dry. After I recovered enough, I decided to move on west to California. Another fella who mustered out with me, a marine, said he knew of a silver concern in the San Jacinto mountains and wanted to stake a claim. But he needed some partners to help him finance it and work the mine. Well, I had a little discharge money, and some disability money coming to me. Plus I can squeeze a nickel till the buffalo shits.

"We went to work. The high mountain air was good for me. I mean, it was really hell at first. Like trying to suck air through a straw. But it really helped build my lungs and my strength back up. Turns out I wasn't the only investor, though. My partner had dug up some real unsavory types in Los Angeles, gangsters or what have you. This was before we had headed up into the mountains. I don't know why he went to them. I think maybe he owed them some money from some gambling debt, which maybe was why he had ducked into the marines in the first place. I don't know. I sure as hell didn't know about any of that.

"I learned quick and in a few weeks I was running the operation onsite. Y'know how silver is mined? It's not like panning for gold dust or crushing it out of rock. It's really difficult. First you dig through the rock looking for the kind of ore that just might, I say, might, contain silver. Then, if you've been lucky enough to find it, that mined ore gets crushed and mixed with water into a slurry. Then you wash that over amalgamation tables which are coated with mercury. The silver sticks to the tablets while everything else—the tailing, it's called—gets sluiced off into the river. So it's not exactly like pulling big hunks of silver out of the ground. It's slow going and the returns are small at first, but eventually the silver starts accumulating.

"At first I guess they started harassing my partner because the mine wasn't paying off. Then it wasn't paying off fast enough. Then it turned out that it was going to pay off big-time. One week we banked fifty dollars in silver. The next week, nothing. A week later we banked ten grand!"

Hubbard stared at him with wide eyes. Driftwood nodded.

"That's right. And it looked like that was going to be just the tip of the iceberg. Boys, there I am. I am thinking that I have got it made in the shade. My ship was come in. I am going to be living the life of Riley from here on in. I guess my partner felt the same way because he telegraphed his associates to tell them of the great days a-coming.

"I was in the pit when he drove up. I could hear him talking to my partner. My partner starts putting up a stink and this is where I hear the whole story for the first time. My new associate wanted the mine. Not just my partner's share. My share too. The whole tamale. So I started climbing out of the pit, figuring I'm going to add a little muscle to the mix, turn this fella around and tell him where to get off. Well, I didn't even get to dust myself off before I noticed what he had brought as a bargaining chip. A Thompson sub. Ever seen what a machine gun can do to a man at close range?"

The two men shook their heads.

Driftwood ran a hand over his weary face. "It chews a man up. I took a few steps right back into the pit. The man lobbed a few spits of lead after me but it's dark down there and there are places to hide. Finally the sun went down and I made it out of the pit and into the mountains, dodging wildcats and rattlesnakes the whole way."

"Jesus," said Gibson. "How long ago was this?"

"About three months ago," Driftwood said. "I took it as a sign that it was a good time to see the rest of the country that wasn't particularly California. Been shacking up in Hoovertowns. I got rolled in Boston. I haven't shaved in a week and I'd give a tooth to make it with a woman.

I'm diggin' graves in the middle of winter and I ain't a silver tycoon. But I am alive."

"Keep sinking lower and next thing you'll probably be a pulp writer," Gibson joked.

"You don't suppose this fella's looking for you?" Hubbard asked. "Seems like he got what he wanted."

"That's what I'm hoping. I just figure to keep my head down for a little while longer. Never really been to New York, so that's kind of where I'm headed."

"That's where we're from," Hubbard said.

"Not from here?"

"No," Gibson said. "Came up for this. He was a writer too, like us. And a friend of mine."

"That's good. It's good to have friends," Driftwood said. "If I had died in those mountains my friends wouldn't have even known it, let alone made it to the funeral. I think you owe it to your friends to at least let them come to your funeral. You think working in a graveyard has made me a little bleak? You know, I actually used to do a bit of writing myself."

Gibson nodded. "Really?" Everyone was a writer, he had found. The quickest way to find out about somebody was to ask him about his novel. Everyone was always writing one, or about to.

"I used to write the newsletter for EPIC—End Poverty In California."

"You're a red?" Hubbard blurted.

"A socialist," the stranger countered with indignant defensiveness. "If Upton Sinclair had won that election, California would have been leading this country out of this Depression this very day."

"As if the New Deal isn't bad enough," Hubbard replied. "Now why not just give abandoned factories to a pack of poor people and let 'em try to make whatever they want?"

"Production for use is so much greater than that."

"Speaking of product," Gibson said, looking down, "nice hole."

"Thanks. It gets easier when the torches thaw it out."

Hubbard wouldn't drop the subject. "All I know is no one is giving me a free typewriter or free paper to do *my* work! And I've been as poor as poor can get," he said. He put his hand on the casket as he shifted his weight out of a muddy spot.

"Gentlemen," the old minister croaked as he shuffled through the gate. "We are all there is."

"Isn't Howard's aunt coming?" Gibson asked.

Gibson looked down at the headstone, which leaned against a tree, already prepared. He lifted the wet muslin from the cover to read the inscription. Under Howard's name and birth date, and the blank spot that would be filled with the date of his death, was a simple epitaph:

I am Providence.

"Unfortunately the cold weather has restricted Miss Gamwell to her home," said the minister, "but she has invited all the attendees to her house for a small reception."

Gibson looked at all the attendees and they both shrugged and nodded. "Sure," he said.

"Then let's begin, shall we?"

Then, without warning, Hubbard slipped and fell into the muddy grave with a graceless thud, and Gibson suddenly knew he had his ending.

Episode Seventeen

Zhang Mei strode angrily down the street and the citizens cleared a path for him. He was a fearsome sight, tall in his officer's uniform with his saber smacking heavily against his thigh. He only hoped someone would stumble into him; then he would take up his sword and vent his rage upon that unfortunate, clumsy soul.

He hated Beijing. It was filthy. It stank. Rats and dogs ran with carefree abandon through streets that were slick with the grease and refuse which overflowed from the open *benjo* ditches. The constant smoky aroma of cooking horse flesh hung thickly in the air. The people were eating horses because the supply of pork and beef from the countryside was thin and constant harassment by pirates and foreigners such as the Japanese had made the seas dangerous for the fishermen.

He hated the Beijing bureaucrats who swarmed over the palace. Their life's work was self-preservation; many of the ministers and counselors had survived the regime changes of the past two decades, steadily accruing power for themselves until no gate could be opened or dish served without their say-so. To Zuolin's face they were respectful and obsequious, agreeing with every decision, flattering every thought. They showed him all consideration due to the ruler of the various coalition factions occupying Beijing: his own men from the Northern Lands, the western provincials and Christians, even representatives of the popular Dr. Sun Yat-sen's Imperialists from the South. Yet behind his back they schemed and plotted and undermined him at every move.

His adopted father, accustomed to a martial life, seemed to accept their pledges to execute his orders without question. This was Mi-Ying's province, and the thieving diplomat seemed to pull as many strings behind the courtyard as Zuolin did upon it. Mei's dismayed warnings to Zuolin and Xueling about Mi-Ying had been waved off—Mi-Ying's actions were considered sacrifices necessary to attempting to bring order to China. If Mei had been emperor, he thought, these diplomats, even the Americans, but especially all the Chinese ones such as Mi-Ying, would learn to fear him before being put to death. Fear was the only way to control them.

He passed under the Gate of Supreme Harmony, glaring back at the bronze lions guarding it, and marched across the square to Wenyuang, the Imperial Library. This was the heart of the bureaucracy. He had nearly as much contempt for the bureaucrats as he had for the diplomats. Of all the bureaucrats he hated, the one he most despised was Lu Zhi, the librarian who controlled the Sikuquanshu, the Four Treasures of Knowledge, the Encyclopedia of the Universe—what Mei most wanted access to in all of Beijing. The peace had brought him time to pursue knowledge beyond what his brother found useful. What he could learn from the Sikuquanshu! If only Lu Zhi would bend to his will!

Although the librarian was neither the most powerful bureaucrat nor the most subservient, something in Lu Zhi's nature disturbed Mei greatly and kept him from peace. He entered the vast building, the scrolls and paintings lost upon him in his wrath. Today he would settle the score with at least one of the irritating civil servants.

He found Lu Zhi in contemplation of a new book in the publishing gallery. The sight made him quiver. His hand fell to the hilt of his sword.

"Lu Zhi," he called. His blood was rising. The battle was engaged.

Lu Zhi turned. "Master Zhang?" His visit was unexpected.

"You have driven me mad," he said to her. She was the most exquisite sight he had ever laid eyes on. "I have come to ask you to be my wife."

And, in another Year of the Rat, she said, "Of course."

Episode Eighteen

"Is it me?" Hubbard rubbed his hands on his arms. "Or is it colder in here than it was outside?"

"No," replied Gibson through teeth he was clenching to keep from chattering. "Aunt Annie's house is cold as hell!"

"Fellas," said Driftwood in a low voice. "She's coming back."

Annie Phillips Gamwell, the last of Howard's kin, lived alone at 66 College Street in a dilapidated Victorian house on a block that wouldn't have seemed out of place in Red Hook, Gibson noted with sad irony. The street itself was heavily trafficked and irritatingly noisy. An ice delivery truck was parked across the street from the Gamwell house, and the cars and cabs that wanted to pass it had to pull into the opposite lane, honking loudly and rudely as they did.

The withered old lady had invited them into her foyer and then left them standing there, shivering, as she wandered off down the dark hallway to put the kettle on for tea. Evidently she must have thought they had followed her, for she had begun a conversation with them in the kitchen which she continued as she came out of the dark corridor toward them.

"The Phillips plot has been in that cemetery for generations. It's traditional for anyone of our line, or anyone who married into it, to be buried there. Although his father isn't," she said dismissively. "Howard's surname may have been Lovecraft but he was a Phillips as far as we've always been concerned. So we're glad to have him home where he belongs." Her eyes looked up, as if following a thought that had drifted away from her. When she found it, she spoke again. "Howard was deathly afraid of being buried. He thought he might wake up while he was down there. Would you men take a drink in the parlor?"

"Oh, no, Miss Gamwell," said Gibson. "We just stopped by to pay our respects. We don't want to trouble you anymore."

"Please," she insisted. "You've all come so far, from New York City! And then being out in the cold and rain like that." She pointed to the parlor again. "Please help yourself. I hear the teakettle whistling."

"I don't hear . . . ," Hubbard started to say, but Driftwood gave him a gentle poke in the ribs. Gibson looked at the other two men and nodded. He didn't know about them but he really wanted a drink. Several, in fact. "Thank you," he said after they nodded in resigned approbation.

She creaked back into the gloomy passage, her black dress merging into the darkness so her silver head seemed to float by itself in the air. It reminded Gibson of the old school of French theatrical magic where assistants—dressed completely in black on a black stage, making them nearly invisible to the audience—would lift objects at the command of a sorcerer. To the awed spectators it appeared as if the objects were levitating. *Magie noire.* It was the foundation of the illusory ability of The Shadow to move through the pervasive darkness of the criminal underworld so effectively. Black magic is real, he thought. Not pulp.

As she completed her vanishing act, the men entered the shabby parlor. The heavy drapes were drawn against the gray day. Gibson went to a dusty liquor cabinet and poured some bourbon out of a heavy decanter into three glasses. His fingers left marks on the grimy crystal.

"Well, I didn't hear any teakettle," Hubbard complained.

"She's an old woman, Hubbard. Cut her a little slack," Gibson replied.

"I don't think anyone's been in this room for years," said Driftwood as he took a glass. "Between the damp outside and the dust in here, this town is gonna kill my lungs."

Gibson picked up a telegram which sat on the coffee table. It had been sent from Chicago. MY CONDOLENCES STOP SONIA. The simple expression, devoid of any emotion, made him feel sadder for Lovecraft than had any part of the service. He set the telegram down.

"This has been one hell of a strange day," said Hubbard. "You know, I have a crazy aunt, and her house always smells like ammonia too. Ammonia and lavender sachet. I always wonder where the smell comes from."

"I don't know if it's the cool air or what," said Driftwood, "but I got the feeling we're being watched."

"Well, if we learned anything today," said Hubbard, "it's that there ain't nobody interested in Lovecraft but us."

Gibson poured himself a second drink to keep the first one from growing lonely.

"Listen," said Hubbard. Gibson turned his attention to the creaks and sighs of the old house. There was a distant murmur of a low voice. "She's talking to herself. Must be hard to suddenly be all alone."

Her distant and muted voice suddenly broke off. The house seemed incredibly still. They could hear floorboards groan outside the parlor. Gibson suddenly found his heart racing. He looked at Driftwood, who, in spite of the cold, had broken into a sweat. Hubbard's normally florid face had suddenly gone pale. What are we afraid of? Gibson thought. What if what turned the corner wasn't an old, grieving woman but one of Lovecraft's ancient and horrible things from beyond space and time and human comprehension?

"Tea biscuits?"

Gibson exhaled with relief. The other two men shifted their weight, visibly relaxing. Gibson felt the tension leak out of him as suddenly as it had come upon him. He had a recollection of Lovecraft's Brooklyn home as having the same dread atmosphere. He thought of how much vibrant effort Sonia had put in to dispel the gloom with bright furniture and clothes and light, never realizing that perhaps the murk was Howard's own atmosphere.

"No thanks," he said. The other men politely accepted, each taking a handful. Driftwood especially seemed hungry. She placed the tray on a small end table. They stood looking uncomfortably at each other for a long moment.

"I knew your nephew in New York," said Gibson finally. "And his wife too. Does she know about Howard?"

"Of course she knows," the woman said crossly. "She wasn't much of a wife to him in life, so why should she care that he's dead?"

She rubbed her hands together as she spoke. The gesture appeared miserly but Gibson saw her wincing as she tried to work some relief into her joints.

"Miss Gamwell, it seems a bit cold in here. Do you need some help with your heat?" Driftwood asked. "We could build a fire or check your boiler—is it in the cellar?"

"No!" she exclaimed.

"It'll only take us a few moments."

"We like it cold," she insisted.

He looked down at the pattern on the rug, embarrassed for her.

Hubbard said, "I'll have another one of those biscuits, if you don't mind." He reached over toward the end table but stayed his hand for a moment before picking up an object which lay to the side of the cookie tray instead. "Hey, Walter," he said. "The Shadow's been here!" He tossed Gibson a small shiny item.

"You're right! It's a Shadow decoder ring." He smiled at the object in his hand. It was a cheap tin device that used a simple type of code called a substitution cipher. A disk of alphabet letters rotated around an inner ring of identical letters. All a kid needed to know to decode a jumble of letters was the offset key—3, for example—and whether to turn the wheel to the left or right. If the first letter in a jumble was A, then turning the A three clicks to the right placed it over D, which would be the actual first letter. "Julius Caesar invented this code."

"But did he invent the salad?" Driftwood cracked.

"Latin's not hard enough, he had to put it into a code?" Hubbard shuddered. "I hated Latin."

"That was one of Howard's gewgaws," the old lady said. "You can have it if you'd like."

"Oh, that's okay," said Gibson. "I've got a shoebox full." He held out the ring to her but she refused to release her hands and take it. After a moment he put it down on the table.

"I guess we should be going," he said. "Thank you for the drinks." She stepped aside to let them pass and they headed into the hallway. Gibson reached for the doorknob.

"Thanks," added Driftwood. "I'm sorry about your nephew's death. Cancer is awful."

"Cancer!" the woman scoffed. "Howard was murdered."

"I'm sorry?" Gibson stopped turning the doorknob. His hand began to tremble. He felt as if he were back onstage with Litzka. "How do you mean, 'murdered'? I thought he had stomach cancer."

"I mean murdered as in somebody done him in. Killed him, deliberately."

"Who?" Hubbard challenged.

"Mr. Jeffords. He owns the Providence Medical Lab, where Howard worked. I saw him at the hospital when Howard died. That ugly, bald man was choking Howard and then he ran off and Howard died. And I know why he won't leave the Medical Lab again. Because he has what Howard has. Had."

"What do the police say? Have you talked with them?"

"Bosh! The police. The only thing more corrupt in Providence than our politicians is our police. Jeffords is a rich man. That's who the police listen to. When I called the police, they talked to the doctor and I know he told them I was a senile old woman and not to believe me and that Howard was dying from stomach cancer. That's Providence for you; only thing that gets more sleep than its dead is its police. But he was murdered. I saw it."

"Why would someone do that?" Driftwood asked.

"Because something happened at the lab. Something that made him ill. And he was going to tell people. But then he was murdered."

Something bumped in the cellar, startling the men.

"What was that?" asked Hubbard.

"Rats in the walls," she said. She put her hand to her throat and toyed with her thin strand of pearls. "I'm sorry, gentlemen. I'm afraid I'm just a very overwrought old woman and it's a difficult time."

"Of course," said Gibson.

She turned and looked back down the dark hallway again. "I know your coming today means a lot to Howard," she said finally.

"You sure there's nothing we can do for you?" Driftwood asked with concern. "It's very cold in here."

She shook her head. "Thank you. Thank you for coming."

Gibson was going to ask her more, but she turned abruptly and walked down the corridor, disappearing into the gloom.

Hubbard looked at the two of them. "Brother, I wish your train could drop us off right at the front door of the White Horse Tavern. We get back, that's where I'm heading. I feel like it's going to take a month of drinking there to get this out of my system."

Driftwood nodded. "I hear that."

Gibson opened the door and the three men moved out to the porch. The yellow Checker Cab they had come in was idling at curbside while its driver smoked a cigarette. The skies were still gray and lowering. Gibson closed the door behind them. He shook his head. "Howard was afraid of his own shadow," he said. "I can't imagine him getting involved enough in anything where someone would want to kill him."

"What exactly did he do at the Providence Medical Lab?" Driftwood asked.

"Ghostwriter. Turning all that science jargon into English. Not exactly the stuff conspiracies are made of." He pulled out his pocket watch. "It's four o'clock," he said to Hubbard. "The train's not pulling out until eleven-thirty. Want to meet me there at eleven?"

"Okay." Hubbard seemed a little uncertain. "I thought you guys might want to grab a bite to eat or a couple of beers."

"Can't," Gibson said. "I've got just enough time to drop in on an old friend."

Driftwood grinned. "A girl in every port."

"Something like that." Gibson smiled back every bit as broadly. "You want the cab?"

"I'm on foot," said Driftwood. "I'm off to find a soup kitchen."

"I saw a pub about a block back," said Hubbard. "How about that beer?"

"You're buyin'?"

Hubbard winced. "Sure," he said. "Come on. I'll meet you at the train."

"Right." Gibson held out his hand to Driftwood. "Otis, it was nice to meet you. When you get down to the Empire City, look me up. I'll either be at Street & Smith or, as Ron said, boozin' it up at the White Horse."

"A pleasure, Walter." Driftwood shook his hand.

Gibson climbed into the cab and watched the two men walk down the sidewalk. He looked back at the house. He knew what Driftwood had meant when he described the sensation of being watched. Even now, outside the house, Gibson thought he saw the parlor window curtain sway as if stirred by some vague, unnatural breath.

"Where to?" The cabbie was uninterested.

Gibson rubbed his hands together. They were still chilled but the cab was warm and it felt great to get some heat. He felt sorry for the lonely old woman and wondered how she would ever manage. What became of people like her, he wondered. How did people cope with being abandoned?

Robert would know. Why not just ask him?

The thought hit him like a sledgehammer to the stomach. An old woman must understand that loved ones are taken. A wife might understand that a husband could go. What would a young son know? His son. Robert. An emptiness beyond knowing?

The driver cleared his throat.

"You know where the Providence Medical Lab is?" Gibson said.

Issue 3:

The Night Watchman

Episode Nineteen

THE DOOR to the Pullman flew open with a crash and Walter Gibson, his suit torn, his hair wildly disheveled, slumped wearily against the doorjamb.

"Jesus, Walter! I guess her husband got home early, huh?" Hubbard said, putting his scotch down and rising from his club chair as Gibson dragged himself into the train car.

"I hope you got in a few good licks yourself!" Otis, in the other chair, stood too, while Chester moved swiftly to Gibson's side to help him aboard.

"Whew, that's some smell," Hubbard's happy commentary continued. "What'd you do? Fall into an outhouse?" He put a handkerchief over his mouth. "I ever tell you about the time I did just that thing . . ."

Chester helped Gibson peel off his torn jacket. Driftwood snatched a cloth napkin and poured a few ice cubes from the ice bucket into it. He wrapped it up and gave it to Gibson, who put it against his bruised and bloodied nose.

"What happened, Mr. Gibson?" Chester was worried. "Someone try to roll you?"

Gibson flopped down in his club chair, grateful for the cool pack against his face. His head was throbbing. In fact, his whole body ached. Driftwood poured him a drink, which he accepted. The three men gazed at him with concern.

"I, uh, invited Otis to hitch a ride down to New York with us. I hope that's copacetic?" Hubbard looked like a puppy who had piddled on an heirloom rug.

Gibson nodded. He was actually happy to see some friendly faces. He inhaled the alcohol's fumes through his nose, trying to get rid of his own stench, which seemed to be adhering to his nasal membranes. He wasn't usually one for gulping booze, but tonight he poured the contents of the glass down his throat and felt it explode in his stomach. At that moment, with a whistle and a lurch, the train began to move. Just in time, he thought. Providence was going to kill me if I didn't leave.

"Mr. Gibson?"

"I'm all right, Chester," he said. "I could use a bite to eat, though." He wasn't hungry at all, but he didn't want the men hovering over him like a bunch of nursemaids. Chester nodded and moved to the end of the car where a small galley stood, and began to poke around in the cabinets. Gibson knew he was all ears.

Driftwood removed the ruined jacket from the banquette and sat down. "Brother Walter," he said. "I bet you got some story to tell us!"

"Well," he said, "I took the cab to the waterfront."

"There must be someplace in Providence that's nice," Gibson had said to himself as he got out of the Checker. "I just haven't seen it yet."

The cab drove away from the lab as soon as he had paid his fare, its driver insisting that the train yard was close enough for Gibson to walk to and that he had a wife and a Sunday roast to get home to. The wind that blew in from the harbor was so cold it made his cheekbones ache, and he turned his face into his shoulder to try to shield it. He had been cold all day and it was wearing him out; even the brief trip in the cab hadn't been enough to allow the warmth to penetrate the chill which seemed to have settled deep within him.

It suddenly occurred to him to curse Lester Dent. In a way it was really that big hick's fault that he found himself here, investigating the mystery of a murder that probably hadn't even happened. If Dent was serious, as Hubbard had told him, about finding an ending to the Sweet Flower War story, he would have it over Gibson forever. Lester had been right in that, at the least, he should have had some sort of ending for the Sweet Flower story. Even though he had just been telling the story to Hubbard, it had been lazy of him not to take the time to come up with one. Being caught without an ending offended his pride as a onetime journalist, to not mention as the best-selling pulp author in America. He just couldn't possibly tell another story without an ending at the White Horse or the Knickerbocker. People would say he had gone soft.

He looked around. His cabbie had told him that this was where the Providence Medical Lab could be found, but all he could see were long, low, windowless buildings which fronted the stinking inlet. He went to the doors of several buildings but found no signs, no markings, save for street numbers. He rubbed his hands together and blew on them for warmth. He looked up and down the street. Where there was a wharf, there were longshoremen, and where there were longshoremen, there was a tavern, and where there was a tavern, there was information. Gibson located the blinking neon Beverwyck Breweries sign within moments. Waterfront bars always seemed immune to Sunday blue laws. He turned up the collar of his jacket, thrust his hands deep into his pockets, and walked briskly to the tavern.

At first he thought that maybe a fire had swept through the establishment and that the owners had simply swept up a little, restocked the icebox, and opened for business. On second thought he decided they hadn't swept up. The room was long and narrow. The bar, which ran the entire length, cut into nearly half the room, leaving only enough space for a few tables at the back. Otherwise, the few men who were here perched on stools. Their weather-beaten faces turned to look at him in a single motion. He couldn't have been more unwelcome if he had suddenly walked into any one of their living rooms.

The bartender gave him an appraising eye, which told Gibson that he had been pegged for an easy mark. Gibson ordered a pilsner from him and leaned against the bar. The radio was tuned to a hockey game over the CBC from Montreal: the Canadiens against the New York Rangers. He looked at his watch. Moments from now in New York, Orson would begin broadcasting this week's episode of *The Shadow.* He thought how well it might go over in this crowd to ask the bartender to change stations. Maybe not so well.

"You lost?" The voice was deep and salted with New England air. He hadn't even been served his drink and it had started.

Gibson looked at the wharf rat and his pal. The bigger man who had spoken was older and toothless, weathered like a mast of spruce. The little man next to him had several more teeth, and the cord of muscles in his neck twisted down to the top of his shoulders like huge snakes. Gibson looked quickly from one to the other, trying to figure out which was the dumb one and which was the dangerous one; these types usually ran in pairs. In this case it looked as if they were both dangerous. Their eyes glittered with a certain kind of wanton amoral lunacy. There were few crimes these men could commit and not escape from on the next boat sailing.

"In town for a funeral," he said. He had found through his early years as a reporter in Philadelphia that the easiest way to stay out of trouble in a situation like this was to be straightforward and unpresumptuous; common ground would eventually appear.

"There ain't no cemeteries around here," the big one said in a thick Oyrish brogue. "What was it? A burial at sea."

Funny, Gibson thought, from all the hair he would have pegged him as Russian. "You're right," he said, "the funeral wasn't around here. But the man who died worked around here at the Providence Medical Lab. Know where that is?" The little man blinked in surprise while the other one seemed to scrutinize him more closely.

The bartender set his drink down in front of him. "Shove off, fellas," he said. "Let the man drink to his friend in peace. It's the Lord's day, after all."

The two men looked at each other and shrugged. The little one pulled down his wool cap to just above his eyebrows. "We was catching the next tide anyways," he growled to the bartender. He put a hand on Gibson's shoulder. Gibson could feel the power of a life spent stowing loads and hauling sheets in his grip. He looked at the hand out of the corner of his eye. It was so covered with scars and tattoos that it was impossible to tell whether any original flesh was left. He could see an ink drawing of a severed head, dripping blood from its neck. The knife that did the cranium in was stuck gratuitously from temple to temple, to indicate that beheading wasn't enough. The man drew close and Gibson could smell the liquor on his breath. He tried to keep his breathing easy and his gaze level.

"Keep a weather eye out for the night watchman," he growled.

"Who's that?"

"Ask 'im," he said and tilted his head down the bar. Gibson did not take his eyes from the man's face to look; he'd be damned if he'd turn away from him for even an instant. Finally, the wharf rat released his shoulder, and he and his hairy Irish friend swaggered into the encroaching evening. A few moments passed and the bar wound back up to normal speed like a clock after its chimes have been struck.

Gibson motioned for the bartender to draw close. "Who's the night watchman?"

The bartender concentrated on polishing his glass. "Ignorant sailors," he said, moving away.

Gibson choked down a swallow of his thin beer and looked around. There was an old man sitting at the far end of the bar. Gibson met his eyes briefly. A moment later and the old man was at his side, settling onto a stool. "Want to know about the night watchman, so?" he asked. Gibson acted as if that thought had never crossed his mind before.

"I guess."

The old man cleared his throat to indicate how dry he was. Gibson nodded at the bartender, who filled a glass from a cask of rum. Gibson watched the old man's Adam's apple bob up and down as he threw down the liquid. It seemed to be the part of his body that functioned the best; certainly the blossoms spreading across his nose and face spoke to certain inadequacies of the liver and kidneys and blood, not to mention spleen and gallbladder and probably stomach. His retching cough completed the picture of health.

"It's why we all been getting off the waterfront afore the sun goes down of late, so?" Gibson wasn't certain if a response was needed; he kept his expression open. "Eve'y night walkin' the docks, swingin' his lantern. They says they found something on Harmony Isle and brought it back and he's come to find it."

"Found what?" Gibson whispered conspiratorially.

The old man leaned in. His breath was about the worst thing Gibson had smelled since leaving Philadelphia. "A curse."

"Was this something they brought back to the lab with them?"

The old man shrugged. He looked out toward the warehouses. Gibson tried to follow his gaze. Between the warehouses he could see the light reflecting off the surface of the inky black harbor. In the distance he could see a dock to which a long, low boat was made fast. A fog was coming in with the wind and the opposite shores were disappearing in the gloom.

"They used to have Indian sacrifices on that island, did you know that? For hundreds of years them savages would paddle out there and make sacrifices to their heathen gods. Human sacrifices. I heard of stone altars still got markings on 'em and each corner points to the four corners of the compass. The magnetic compass! Now you tell me how them redskins knew about that, I ask you."

Gibson shrugged and the old man continued. "Four good men shipped to Harmony Isle. Went out on the *Zephyr.* A few nights later, the *Zephyr* came back, but not the crew. A few weeks after that and the night watchman begins walking up an' down these here docks in the dead of night, scarin' off decent souls."

"Did the night watchman kill the crew of the *Zephyr*?"

"Goddammit, don' you understand nothin'?" His voice rose. "I told you about the curse!" He emphasized the point by smacking his palm down, rattling the bottles.

"Hey!" the bartender shouted at Gibson. "Can it!"

"Look, I'm sorry," Gibson said.

"I don't give a rat's ass!" exclaimed the bartender. "We like things quiet here. Now get the hell out before I beat ya!" His eyes were bulging. The old man began mewling that he had no place else to go. "Out!"

"Sure." Gibson tossed a few bucks on the bar and backed out into the night. No one seemed inclined to follow him and the vicinity appeared as abandoned as before. He could hear the foghorns in the distance, and the lapping of the water against the pilings, and the distant clanging of channel buoys. To the south the train whistle blew. He pulled the belt on his overcoat tight and put his hat on. He took a deep breath of cool, damp, fish-scented air and looked around. The fog drew eerie coronas from the yellow street lamps, which in this part of town were still powered by gas.

The Shadow's menacing laughter caressed his spine. He leaped around in near terror. It emanated from the bar. How about that, he thought. He had fans up here, or at least The Shadow did. It never occurred to him before to ask himself why The Shadow laughed. Gibson knew when he laughed, of course. Both in his mags and on the radio the laughter signaled the audience that The Shadow was about to strike. It was meant to drive fear into a criminal's heart, to let the evildoer know that the weed of crime he had tended had yielded bitter fruit, to mock his feeble plans. The laughter faded into the mist but left Gibson feeling far colder than the winter night.

The train whistled again. He felt he ought to start walking toward it. But then again, that boat was just tied up out there on the dock. And no one was around. Not even the night watchman. Or any watchman, for that matter. And since he hadn't been able to pry the location of the lab out of anybody, at least he could still investigate something. Anyway, there was almost no chance at all that a quick examination in the near dark would yield any information. Almost.

The fog was coming in thick and fast now, and the sun had completely set. The auras around the lamps had a physically solid look to them now, as if they were pale yellow globes with candlelit centers one could harvest.

The wharf was part of a wooden boardwalk which ran behind the warehouses and connected buildings as far as he could see in either direction. Through the mist he could see dim lights of long jetties which jutted out at intervals from the boardwalk. The *Zephyr* was tied up at the end of its dock; the tide was low and its railings bumped against the boards. The transport boat was nearly seventy feet in length and fifteen wide at the beam. He guessed it drew about seven feet. Light waves rocked it gently.

He walked toward it, his footfalls tapping hollowly on the wood. The scents of salt foam and creosote filled his nostrils. The fog grew thicker and thicker as he drew closer.

The boat had begun its life as a fishing trawler on its way to being a runabout. Its cockpit was lofty and protected, its prow wide and high. There was plenty of room on the rear deck for cargo or for men to work. Gibson looked the boat up and down and shook his head. He clambered aboard and peered into the hold, where only gear was stowed. The deck boards creaked under his weight.

He opened the door to the cockpit and entered the small, glass-enclosed cabin. It felt great to be out of the wind for a few moments. He ran his hands through his hair, thinking he must be out of his mind. What was he doing on this boat? It was Providence, that was all. Dead writers, crazy aunts, superstitious drunks—a terrible environment for an imagination like his. All he had to do was get back home to New York where it was normal and when people went to a funeral that was the end of the story, not the beginning.

He looked at the navigation station. There was a spyglass, and a stack of charts with a compass and a protractor arranged upon it. He walked over and examined the yellowed chart at the top of the stack. It displayed the section of Long Island Sound somewhat south and west of the boat's current position. There were endless handwritten notations on the chart, the markings of voyages undertaken, then forgotten, overwritten, crossed over with lines from other voyages. He looked up from the chart to the window and tried to imagine his chart to his voyages, his markings.

Gibson froze. Someone else was on the boardwalk.

He picked up the small telescope and put it to his eye.

"What'd you see?" Hubbard asked.

He took a bite out of the steak sandwich Chester had cooked up for him. Moments ago he hadn't been hungry, but now it seemed he had never been so hungry in his life. He swallowed and looked at the three men.

"I saw The Shadow."

Episode Twenty

He couldn't imagine anything more beautiful than their son. Not the dawn mist rising blue on the distant Thousand Lotuses Mountain, not the eight ancient treasures in Yunguang Cave, nor the waves breaking at Golden Stone Beach.

Zhang Mei named him Shaozu, a name which meant that he brought honor to his ancestors. He had his mother's green eyes, brilliantly aware of his surroundings even at birth, and a smile which must have come from Mei's father, for it was neither his nor his wife's. Only Mei could bring out the biggest, widest smile on Shaozu's face, sometimes by tickling him, or throwing him high into the air; sometimes by merely smiling at him first.

Mei knew Xueling and his brothers thought it unseemly for him to spend so much time with the boy. Until a boy was five or six—in other words, old enough to begin to learn to ride and fight—his upbringing was best left to the one who stays at home and the women of her family. But Mei couldn't help himself. His brothers had always had a father; they had never known what it was like to be alone in the world. At play with his son he felt as if his father was finally with him and at peace within him. Zuolin, his adopted father, seemed to understand. He too loved the new baby.

In the morning the governess would bring the slumbering boy to them and he would lie between Mei and Lu Zhi, and Mei would admire his long lashes and chubby fingers and breathe in his scent, and he would know that his son was his destiny. He wanted to grow old for his son so he would be able to offer him wisdom and comfort the many days of his life. He wanted to watch his son grow strong and confident and become a scholar, perhaps, like his mother. But not a warrior.

He waited for the baby to awaken so he could listen to Lu Zhi tell them both the legend of the time the Monkey King created a contest between the Wind God and the Sun God which neither could win (the Monkey King was so clever!) and so both had to live among men. Later, as he watched his son sleep, he would puzzle over the enigma that was his nation: how to bring it peace, how to rule it? He did not want his son to die young, even for glory. He wanted a rich and safe life for him.

He wanted the wars to end.

Episode Twenty-One

GIBSON COULD feel his blood roaring through his arteries. A breathless dread seized his chest. This was no painting or vision or story. This was neither longshoreman, nor the effects of bad beer, nor even the dismal atmosphere of Providence. As certain as he was of the fear that gnawed at his spine, he was certain that he was in the presence of his Shadow.

It was the way his Shadow coalesced out of the night, standing in the open doorway of one of the low warehouses, absorbing the dim light from the space beyond. A great black overcoat swirled around him and blended into the darkness, blurring the distinction between where the night ended and he began. His nose was neither as long nor as hawklike as Gibson had imagined it to be. But the eyes: Gibson had described the eyes perfectly—lethal, spectral, glittering. That the man was an Asian was little more than a mild surprise. For years Gibson had written that "Ying Ko" was the name the denizens of Chinatown called The Shadow when he moved among them. It had never meant anything to him before; it was merely a bit of exotic embellishment. But here on the docks of Providence The Shadow had revealed another layer of his identity to Gibson: beyond Lamont Cranston, beyond Kent Allard, he was Ying Ko. He was Chinese.

He sees me, Gibson thought, and his breath caught in his chest. Then he realized that the man was only peering into the mist and the fear which had gripped him began to ease. An instant later the shadowy figure spun around and swept smoothly into the building, his coat filling the door frame with blackness before it closed altogether.

Gibson sat down heavily in the pilot's chair. He wanted a cigarette but he knew any light from a match might give him away. He thought about how close he'd just come to being apprehended and his hands shook. When he thought of the man's piercing gaze, the chill set in and he could not warm himself enough to be rid of it.

The first time The Shadow had appeared to him was on the night he had left his home, his wife, and his son. He had felt as if someone were following as he walked down the street away from his house, felt eyes upon him. He had found a room in a cheap hotel near the Main Line and watched the trains go by. Despair was a yawning black pit which devoured everything he might have been able to feel. He had wondered what it would feel like to throw himself under the train wheels.

He had tried for so long to explain to his wife why he felt compelled to move to New York to be a writer, until that night when there were no more explanations. Nothing he had said had motivated her one bit; she did not want to leave Philadelphia. There hadn't been a fight that night, like all the others; he had just nodded after her refusal and walked out. He had been so mad at her that it wasn't until afterward that he realized he had also walked out on Robert. In his anger, he wanted his boy's sadness to make her feel even more guilty.

Sometime during that night (and afterward he was never quite sure if it was while he was awake or sleeping) the shadows had coalesced into a human shape. He had felt the sensation of a watchful presence again, as he had walking down the street earlier. And all of a sudden there was something in the shadows, whispering promises he couldn't quite make out. When, a week later in their office at Street & Smith in New York,

Nanovic and Ralston had asked him if he had any ideas about how to turn the host of the *Detective Story Hour* radio show into a book, he suddenly understood those promises and was able to say that yes, he knew what to do: he would open his story with a man on a bridge in despair and with the dark figure which emerges from the shadows to save him.

He heard the train whistle again, far away and lonely, reminding him of another train and another time. He'd had enough. It was time to stop pretending there was a story here and go home to New York. He hadn't known Lovecraft well enough, really, to waste an entire weekend coming to his funeral, and Lovecraft certainly wouldn't have come down for his had the roles been reversed. But being away meant he wouldn't have time to talk with Litzka. That's what he needed to do. Talk with her. Maybe there was time to straighten things out with Litzka. Hell, he didn't even know what the tour schedule was. For all he knew the show was already packing up.

He knew this feeling of not wanting to go home. He had felt it before. It was the feeling that had driven him from Miami to seek out Silver Springs. It was what had kept his feet walking forward that night when he had left Charlotte. And Robert. And Philadelphia. Only now he didn't really have a home to avoid. Sure, he had an apartment. In a hotel. He could pack that up and be on the road in a day. But where would that get him? Just to another waterfront in another town. One thing he knew was that running around Providence pretending to be a reporter again was only a waste of time. Altogether this was turning out to be a completely fruitless trip. He realized with deep satisfaction that he wanted to go home.

He stepped out of the cabin and onto the deck. Perhaps he should write a sea tale, like Joseph Conrad. He didn't know as much about ocean-faring life as he would like; maybe this would inspire him to research the field a little more deeply. He could buy a boat. Or just take this one. Throw off the lines and head for the horizon. A warm horizon. He would call for Litzka when he arrived at Bora-Bora or Fiji and, maybe, she would come. He sighed. When he stepped off the boat, his little adventure would be over.

He clambered up the rope ladder and reached the dock. He carried with him the sensation of the boat, bobbing on the waves. He looked toward the warehouse that the man had emerged from; its door was closed once more. He had to pass it to reach the alley which led to the street that ran in the direction of the train station. He put his hands in his pockets and kept his head down, to try to give the appearance of someone who was just taking a nighttime waterfront stroll on the boardwalk, should anyone happen to notice him. He stopped near the door and tried to keep his head from turning. He couldn't resist a look. There, under a buzzer, was a small brass sign which read Providence Medical Laboratory. Found it, he thought. He listened at the door but heard no sound from within. He put his hand on the doorknob. The train whistle blew again. He pulled his hand from the knob and began walking briskly up the alley.

The blow to his head knocked him to his knees. As the red stars cleared from his eyes he saw two pairs of scuffed work boots through the blur.

"Hey, Shorty! I warned you to keep a weather eye open for trouble, din't I?" he heard the wharf rat growl.

One of the pairs of boots disappeared. A moment later a strong hand gripped his wrist, twisted his arm up behind his back. His head was yanked back. There was a cold knife at his throat. He could feel hands rifling through his jacket, looking for his wallet. They would do well, he thought; he had over a hundred dollars on him. The worth of his life. If only he had seen it coming, he thought. If only he had had a fighting chance.

"Got it!" he heard the wharf rat tell his pal, excitedly.

"The picture," Gibson gasped.

"What?"

"The picture of my son! Give it to me. It's all I have!"

"You want this?"

Gibson's head was yanked back and he could see the picture of Robert, taken when he was six.

"You ain't gonna need it where you're goin'," was the reply. "Cut his throat and drop him in the bay."

He felt the pressure of the blade on his throat suddenly grow. He wanted to see the picture one more time but it had been removed from his view.

He heard a sharp but distinct crack behind him. The pressure on his neck suddenly disappeared but some tremendous force threw him, prostrate, to the wood boardwalk. He tried to move away and ended up rolling across the boards.

The big man fell to the ground with a thud where Gibson had been a moment before. Gibson looked up. The wharf rat was held by his neck in the grip of the black-clad man Gibson had mistaken for The Shadow. His companion was groggily drawing himself to his knees. Then he took off, running toward the lights of Providence.

Gibson's wallet dropped from the wharf rat's hand and fell to the boardwalk. The Chinese man's speed and power were incredible. Gibson watched, astonished, as an instant later he had lifted the wharf rat into the air and thrown him neatly into the bay. Gibson could hear him splashing and coughing in the cold water. The mysterious man reached down and picked up Robert's photograph, which lay near Gibson's wallet. He looked at the picture for a long time and his hard, dark eyes grew even more narrow. Gibson pulled himself up to a sitting position, rubbing his head as the man approached. Suddenly his hand flicked out; Robert's photo pinched between two fingers. Gibson took it from him.

"Thanks," he said. His voice was raw and hoarse.

The man nodded back at him. He seemed on the verge of saying something—Gibson wondered if he even spoke English—but instead he drew his coat tightly about him and in a moment he had disappeared into the night. Gibson could hear the man's footsteps fading away as he staggered to his feet. Then he was alone on the boardwalk. The splashing of the wharf rat had stopped. He had either found his way to shore or drowned. Gibson didn't really care either way. The side of his head was throbbing. He slipped the photo into his wallet and tucked it back into his pocket. Not that it mattered to him now, but the money was still in the wallet as well.

The door to the Providence Medical Lab was open. A wedge of light broke through the fog. Gibson felt the warm flow of blood against his face and on his throat. He needed to appraise his wounds, and a medical lab could provide any first aid supplies he might need.

"So you had to go inside?" Driftwood said.

"I didn't really have a choice," Gibson said. He polished off the sandwich. "For all I knew I was bleeding to death. There was no way I was going to make it back to the train. No way at all. At the least I could find a phone to call for help."

The train's rhythm was soothing and he put his feet up on the footstool. Of course he hadn't told them about his thoughts of Litzka, or his doubts. It was his story and he told it the way he wanted to.

"How did you know he wasn't going to do you in?" Driftwood wanted to know.

He massaged his sore shoulder. He couldn't describe what he had seen in the man's eyes. "I just knew."

"So you went inside?"

"Yes, I did. Though now I wish to God that I hadn't."

Episode Twenty-Two

ZHANG MEI mixed the powdered herbs thoroughly into the soup. The soup and the powders needed each other to work properly. Eaten by itself, the soup would only nourish. Taken by themselves, the herbs would only cause diarrhea. But the powder, combined with the right amount of dog meat and a certain type of bean, would create distress in the eater's belly and soon after, death. It was a technique he had learned from a monk who had been brought to Shenyang Palace when they were young to teach them these secret arts. Xueling had had no stomach for it. Zhang Mei had turned out to be an excellent student in this, as he was in all the ways of death. It had been the monk who explained that one who had complete mastery over an art was known as a dragon and that Zhang Mei was the Dragon of Terror and Peril. Zhang Mei took no pleasure in his talent or his title; he was only pleased that he was able to serve his adopted father to the best of his abilities.

He wished that this soup would be fed to Chiang Kai-shek, the general of Dr. Sun Yat-sen's Nationalist Kuomintang troops. The little general was brusque and dismissive to his adopted father's face. But the general had ridden out that very morning to join his troops in an expedition against a small force deep in the western lands who called themselves Communists but were in reality colonial tools of their Russian masters. It was just as well that he had left. Dr. Sun Yat-sen was a popular man in Beijing. If both he and his general were to die on the same night, it would be apparent to all that their deaths were assassinations. Zhang Zuolin was playing a dangerous game. The battles had not ended. They had only become much, much smaller.

The secret meeting with Dr. Sun Yat-sen was at Zuolin's invitation. The doctor's Army of the South had grown powerful and fearsome, driven by officers, including Chiang Kai-shek, created at his own unique military academy. It had recently become apparent that he only had to give the word and the army could crush the combined forces of Zhang and his old allies.

And yet, the word was never given. Dr. Sun Yat-sen perceived greater threats from abroad: Russians, through the Communist insurgents, and the antagonistic militarization of the Japanese. He claimed to hold his army back to defend only against these predicted conflicts. However, the threat of his war machinery was enough to cause the members of Beijing's ruling council to consider offering the doctor the opportunity to rule over them all—before he killed them in battle—and by extension over China. This new position would see him elevated over even Zuolin. This point was what Zuolin had offered to discuss with the doctor in the secret meeting.

Mei instructed the servant on the position of the soup bowls before the guests. The man said he understood and he shuffled out of the room. He would taste each of the soups in front of the men to vouch for their purity. It would only make him ill much later in the evening, out of the sight of the true targets.

Mei paced the quiet halls. Few in the building knew of the meeting. Mei felt anxious, and not about whether the poison would work or whether his adopted father's plan would unfurl properly. Something else was gnawing at him.

He heard voices from a waiting room and walked silently toward it. On the other side was Mi-Ying, the diplomat. He was discussing shipping permission with one of the diplomats from the Japanese consulate. It seemed as if there were more Japanese in the palace some days than Chinese. Their tone was warm, nearly brotherly in nature. Mi-Ying was offering promises of influence, most beyond his grasp.

Zhang Mei swept the curtain aside, startling both men. Mi-Ying stood without even a formal greeting and looked at him levelly. Zhang Mei glared back. "This is not the night for diplomatic fornication," he said.

"My lord! We are only conducting the business of state," Mi-Ying protested. "My only interests are China's interests."

Zhang Mei had no rejoinder. He had not actually interrupted anything duplicitous and all the men knew it. He had only succeeded in embarrassing himself, and perhaps clarifying the enmity of Mi-Ying.

Zhang Mei let the curtain fall and strode away. He chewed his upper lip while the nagging feeling grew into a solid thought. He had heard the rumors: that were Dr. Sun Yat-sen to bring his army to bear in a new civil war, Zuolin would draw on Japanese clout. He couldn't imagine that Zuolin would call on such a devil for power, but at the same time he knew that there was no force in China that could stand up to Dr. Sun Yat-sen and his general, the little Chiang Kai-shek. What deals had Zuolin made with the Japanese?

Perhaps Dr. Sun Yat-sen was right. Perhaps the greatest threat to China lay within and without at the same time. Perhaps he was right. He would like to speak with the well-educated old man and perhaps discuss such matters with him. But it would never happen.

By now, the soup Zhang Mei prepared had been set before him.

Episode Twenty-Three

"THE DOOR to the lab was hanging open," Gibson continued his story. "It squeaked quietly on rusty hinges as it swung to and fro in the soft breeze. The slight sound carried up and down the lonely boardwalk. Other than the lapping waves of the rising tide against the pilings, everything was still. I took a deep breath and went in.

"Turns out I should have held that breath. The stink of the lab hit me first. It was thick and oily, like the garbage in the alley behind a fishmonger's. The smell of fish makes me retch anyway, so this was infinitely worse. I fumbled for one of my silks and put it over my nose and mouth, which helped a little bit. At least I could breathe."

"Silks?" Driftwood looked curious.

"I'm always carrying a couple of magic tricks on me just in case."

"In case what?"

"In case I need to perform a magic trick."

"Oh."

"I looked around. There were a few lights on. Mostly in the back. This place is long and low, like a warehouse. Most of the space is open, but starting about two-thirds of the way back, there are stairs up to the second floor, where all the offices are.

"I took a few steps in. It was a wide aisle. On either side were long rows and rows of metal shelves which held jars and bottles of all different shapes and sizes and full of a variety of powders and liquids. Then there were medical cabinets full of specimens. One shelf was just full of jars, the size of the jar of olives that the White Horse keeps under its bar, and each jar was filled with eyeballs suspended in a solution, all just staring at me. One jar had all brown eyeballs. One had all hazel eyeballs. One was full of blue eyeballs.

"I don't know how long the place has been in business, but it seems like quite a while. Maybe twenty or thirty years. Lot of old military surplus chemicals in old containers on those shelves. Pretty clear that they buy old stuff from Uncle Sam and sell it along.

"Through the shelves I could see a lab space in the middle of the building. As I walked toward it my shoes started crunching through glass. There were broken jars everywhere. Several shelves had been knocked over and their contents had spilled all over the floor. These are heavy, heavy shelves and cabinets and when they were stocked up they must have been very difficult to budge. As I drew closer to the lab I could see that even more of them were knocked back from the core. It reminded me of a daisy which had opened, with the lab as its hub of florets and the rows and rows of fallen cabinets flung out from that as its rays. It was like coming upon the scene of a bomb blast. But there was no crater.

"Once I got to the center of my strange blossom I realized that, in fact, my instincts had been right. There had been some kind of detonation in the building. At the epicenter of the flower lay a rusty hundred-gallon drum, probably about four feet high and two feet in diameter. I know the type. The army uses them to transport everything liquid, from gasoline to chicken soup. When I was stuck in the mud of St. Mihiel at the end of the Great War, we used empty ones just like it for latrines and campfires sometimes. Like all the others, this had once been a military-issue drab olive color. But it was so old that much of the paint had stripped off, exposing its rusted skin. It rested on its side; a rupture along its seam had violently flayed the metal open so it looked like the curled-back lips of an open mouth. This was the source of the energy which had thrown the lab into disarray.

"You know how smells can bring back stronger memories than almost anything else? I had lowered my silk for a moment and another smell hit me which brought back more military memories from my days in France. None of those memories, or smells, are particularly pleasant, but this was one smell I hoped I would never remember again as long as I lived. It was the smell you discover coming upon a battlefield a day or so after the fight at the height of summer. It meant there were dead bodies there.

"There were seven dead men on the floor. They wore white lab coats and were stacked neatly against one another in a line. Their bodies were frozen in contortion; their backs were arched and their arms were curled up. In one man's twisted hand was an unlit cigarette, clenched between his fingers. Death must have come suddenly. Their faces were hollow, leathery, desiccated. They looked for all the world like dead roaches left in a nest after an exterminator's visit. It took me right back to the battlefields.

"Aunt Annie was right that something bad had happened here. I slowly approached the canister. It was empty and bone-dry. The area around it was covered with a fine, gray powder, about the granularity of flash powder. Do you know that stuff? No? I have some in that cabinet I can show you later. Just imagine gray flour. It was light enough to puff out from under my shoes as I took steps. I wanted to see if I could find out this drum's story. There was probably a stencil on it somewhere, so I looked. Believe me, I was careful not to touch it. I found what was left of the stencil just below the ruptured seam. I recognized the typeset: Property of the U.S. Army. Sealed on March 4, 1917. Over twenty years old.

"I have seen some horrible ways to kill people in war, but the gases were by far the most horrible. By the end of the war there were some pretty strange chemicals being used on the field. It was as if the French, the Krauts, and the Americans all knew that the war was ending and they wanted to try out all their different toys before the grown-ups took them away. On the other hand, each side was so desperate to score decisively that they were willing to throw everything they had at each other. You see atrocities toward the end of a war that you could never see at any other point. The smell of rotten lemons, the withered and dried-out postures of these scientists, brought memories back to me I wish I'd never acquired. I have seen this horrible gas used before.

"I've seen it with my own eyes before. My division was supposed to rendezvous with a supply truck hauling some, but the truck must have hit a ditch or trench because it went off the road. I drew patrol with some buddies and we had to go after it. What we found was a scene remarkably similar to the one I found in the lab. Three men were dead. Two poor sons of bitches who lived we brought back to base, but they died on the way. The other—Private Woods from Oklahoma—well. We brought him back, but what the gas did to him was worse. The MPs took him away. We heard stories about what happened to him, but I always thought they were pulp."

He paused and finished his drink. The swaying of the car was relaxing him, finally. "Hard to believe, I know. But bear with me because it gets stranger. I heard someone crying. Crying in the lab.

"The sobs were soft and broke my heart. Like the sound of a child crying at its mother's funeral. They came from near the staircase which led from the first floor to the second. I called out, 'Who's there?' And, 'Is anyone there?' After I spoke, the sound stopped completely, though I thought I heard the scrape of hasty footfalls. My heart was pounding again. But I went toward the direction the sounds had come from instead of away.

"There was another dead man on the staircase. Unlike the scientists, this man wore a suit. He had obviously been dying from exposure, and slowly. His skin was hollowed out and thin, but his tie had been knotted this morning. But it wasn't the gas which had killed him. His blood, which was everywhere, was still wet. It was the long, thin blade plunged deep into his chest which seemed to have done him in. The hilt of the blade was carved wood with jade inlays. Chinese craftsmanship."

"Jeffords?" Driftwood asked.

"Yeah," Gibson nodded. "He was ugly and bald."

"But why would the Chinaman kill him?" Hubbard questioned.

"I don't know. Maybe he expected to find more than just a bunch of dead men there."

"Like what?"

"More gas."

Driftwood chewed his lip as Gibson continued. "There was someone behind me. You only need to be attacked from behind once in a night to be a little sensitive about a sneaking presence. I spun around.

"What was left of the man who stood there was a massive, shambling wreck. Oily folds of greenish skin hung from its outstretched arms. Shreds of a shirt and tattered pants hung from it in a parody of decency. The top of its head had flattened and drooped back as if the skull had softened and lengthened. Its eyes were wide and terrifying and a sickening slurping sound issued from the gaping maw that should have been a mouth. I realized that the liquid which flowed from its eyes was tears. In its hand it held a hanging lantern.

"I had found the night watchman.

"I don't know how much faculty the man had had before his exposure to the gas. I think he may have been feeble to begin with. Whatever his previous mental state had been, there was no reasoning with him now. His blind fury and grief had reduced him to trembling.

"The night watchman pointed at the body on the stairs and tried to speak. Its mouth encircled a word that I could barely distinguish.

"'Daddy,' I realized it spoke.

"I tried to reason with it. I shook my head to indicate that I had had no part in this. But the motion only seemed to snap it out of its stupor. It lurched toward me. I tried to dodge but I slipped in the blood and fell to the staircase. I could feel the hot, slimy hands fumbling to get a grip on my neck. There was tremendous strength in the grip. He won't just choke me, I realized. He was going to completely crush my throat.

"The night watchman stank like a tidal pool at low tide, like rotting crustaceans and seaweed. I felt an electric stab of fear bolt from my stomach and spread into my body: panic was setting in. I twisted and at the same time pushed against the creature's bulk. It slipped on some of the blood and stumbled back toward the lab. At least I could breathe. The creature regained its balance.

"I put my hands out to push myself up as it charged toward me. I felt the knife in the corpse's chest. I seized it and pulled it from the torso. It was heavy, and well balanced. The night watchman was nearly upon me."

He stopped speaking and rubbed his right hand. No one spoke for quite a while. Driftwood arched a skeptical eyebrow. Hubbard cleared his throat and in a high, nervous voice said, "This is pulp, right, Walter? Not real."

Gibson flexed his hand a few times, watching it critically as if it needed to explain how it ended up at the end of his arm. "Anyway," he told them at last, "I lived to tell the tale."

Episode Twenty-Four

HE RODE unescorted to the frontier, the far western lands, as an emissary of Zuolin. Dr. Sun Yat-sen's death had not led to the collapse of the Kuomintang Nationalists as Zuolin had predicted. General Chiang Kai-shek was emerging as their leader and he was making it clear that he would use the mighty Army of the South against Zuolin rather than keep it sheathed awaiting an outside invasion as his predecessor had.

Zhang Mei was sent to the west to meet with the young leader of the revolutionary Communists, to persuade him to ally with Zuolin against the general. Another alliance, as with the Japanese, that Zhang Mei had deep misgivings about.

He had met the professor once before, at the library, early during the occupation of Beijing. The professor was not a bureaucrat; he was a scholar and Lu Zhi thought highly of him. Only a few years older than Mei, he had fought the civil wars, although on which side it was unclear. He had a fierce mind and a penetrating gaze. More importantly he had the adoration of a growing number of the restless peasants in the countryside.

Zhang Mei and the professor took jasmine tea and soft cakes filled with red bean paste under a grove of willow trees near a spring in the late afternoon as the heat of the day waned. Mei studied the man's face and sensed that he was even more powerful and self-possessed than he had been in Beijing. Although his Communist force was small—Zuolin's spies estimated that he had the ability to raise only a thousand to two thousand men-at-arms—his reputation was growing among the farmers and villagers and others who toiled for the landlords.

"Zhang Zuolin believes in your cause," Mei began. The words felt empty, as if they were the platitudes that might fall from the mouth of Mi-Ying. "He believes General Chiang means to destroy us both."

"Zuolin is a bandit," the scholar said, "and he has increased the influence of the Japanese within China to the extent that they now see our land as a colony. You know this to be true. Your true feelings toward your father's advisers are known."

"That may be," Mei replied, "but as long as China is weak, Japan will be a power here. If General Chiang launches a war against the northern provinces, the chaos will only create more opportunity for foreigners of all kinds. Not just the Japanese but the British and French as well. Even the Americans."

The professor shrugged. "Perhaps the next war will be a just war," he said. "Perhaps the chaos it will create will sweep away old obstacles—the landlords, the bureaucrats, the merchant class, the corrupt, the imperialists. Even the warlords. Then the heel would be lifted from the throat of China's sons. This would be a just war. I see disappointment in your eyes. This is not the expression you hoped to take back to your master?"

"It is not what I hoped to hear, that is true," Mei said. "But not for my father. For me. I seek to end the wars."

"Through a political solution?"

He nodded.

"War can only be abolished by war."

"Wars!" Mei spat. "Zuolin has been a warrior his entire life and while he is fortunate to have survived, he knows no other way than war. I and my brothers have been trained as warriors, ensuring that the legacy of war will survive yet another generation. I would like my son to know another way, perhaps a scholar's way such as the one you chose. Or an artist's. I do not wish to perpetuate the warrior line."

"Do you not think that the farmer wishes any more for his son? Or that the laborer any more for his? You feel the weight of the oppression of your circumstances. Does any man not feel it just as keenly? The wars you seek to end will only be eliminated through progress. Progress itself is a war, and the struggle against it is a war as well. Do you understand the inevitability of war yet?"

"I do not accept it, Professor."

"Only when men are free of class will wars end. That may happen in our lifetime. This choice is for men like you and me to make. A revolution to purge the body politic and end wars is within our grasp. Politics is war and war is politics and the only difference is the amount of blood spilled." He paused and grimaced slightly with distaste. "Just as some would wish that diplomatic negotiations can be resolved with an assassination. Do you understand?"

They sat in silence for a great while. The spring gurgled and bubbled. Mei thought that if the spring had consciousness it would think as the professor did, that as the water carved a path through the rock, it was unaware that in mere miles it would be swallowed by the vast waters of the mighty river which it fed into. In this same way would the professor be devoured by the greater armies of Chiang's Kuomintang. Mei understood the professor's true meaning about the inevitability of war. The professor would have no alliance with Zhang Zuolin. Perhaps he had already allied himself with Chiang. Perhaps not. Perhaps he would simply wait, growing stronger out here in China's farthest reaches, until either Zhang or Chiang was victorious but weakened. Then he would make his move.

"You could stay, you know," the professor said, at last. "A dragon is always necessary in war."

Mei stood and dusted himself off. Then he ceremoniously bowed to the little man, who also stood. He knew at this moment that there were archers, with bows pulled, just out of sight, waiting for a gesture to strike and bring him down. For the third time in his life he prepared for his immediate death. The professor kept his arms stiffly at his side.

"Professor Mao, my wife sends her respect," he said, "and you have mine as well."

The professor flinched slightly at the mention of his wife. He nodded his head. "Lu Zhi is a rare woman," he said after some consideration. "Her perceptions of the tales of universal balance are unique. She has done well to marry you and bear you a son. Take my greetings back to her as well."

He gestured and Mei prepared for the stabbing pierce of the arrows. The thought of his son and the sound of the spring brought him peace.

Instead, Mei's horse was brought to him, and he rode out immediately, unprovisioned. As he rode, he sensed the arrows of the archers upon his back day and night until he reached the border of the province.

Episode Twenty-Five

WALTER COULD feel the night watchman's clammy, moldering hands around his windpipe, crushing it. He could feel the hilt of the knife shudder as the lethal blade sank through muscle, tissue, and veins. He could feel the hot spurt of blood on his hand. He could hear the creature calling out one last time for its father.

He sat up in his bunk. The train had stopped moving. Early dawn light crept through the wood slats of the blinds. He heard snoring from the guest compartments, Driftwood in one and Hubbard in another. His traveling companions had turned in soon after the conclusion of his story, for what else could be said? He wondered what Driftwood thought of him; his piercing dark eyes were intelligent and quizzical. He hadn't spoken much during the story of the night watchman. He seemed like a straight-up guy, but Gibson wondered who he really was and where he had come from.

For a moment he thought that the police had stopped the train and would be swarming in to question him. But some distant angry car horns reassured him that he was back in New York.

He had tried to sleep but it had been difficult. He had always been prone to nightmares, and living through one had made it hard to tell where his day had ended and his slumber began. He had spent the late hours of the ride at his magic work desk concentrating on spring-loaded strikers.

He lay back for a few moments. Maybe the question he should have asked Hubbard that night in the White Horse was really where does pulp end and reality begin, not the other way around. His world seemed twisted out of sorts. His life reminded him of one of those awkward first attempts at sound pictures a few years back; the moving image would often lose synchronization with the sound recording so that the actors' voices would trail the movement of their lips just enough to be noticeable and irritating. That's how he felt now. A few seconds behind his own action.

His body was sore and aching, not only from the various bruises and scrapes but from the actual exertion which had begun with carrying the coffin. He was a writer, after all, and not given to exercising much.

He could smell coffee. He got up and padded across the small chamber to the door and opened it. Chester had placed a carafe outside his door, along with some eggs and toast. He brought the tray inside and set it on the bunk. He drank his first cup, black, staring at the window. He finished his second cup after washing up and had emptied the carafe by the time he was dressed.

He stepped into the main cabin and walked over to his writing desk. He looked at the manuscript. It wasn't his best work, by a long shot. But it was probably good enough, and, more importantly, it was done. Nanovic would always prefer to have a poorly written book in on time than a late masterpiece. He drew out a brown envelope and dropped the pages into it.

He heard the galley door open. "Everything all right, Mr. Gibson?"

"I could use another year of sleep, Chester," he said. "And I already gotta get a move on. This book's gotta be dropped off."

"I called Manny as soon as we got in, so he's waiting for you. You want me to drop your luggage off later?"

"Thanks. That'd be a help." He saw the issue of *Bronzeman* and picked it up. "Congratulations, by the way."

Chester beamed. "Thank you, Mr. Gibson. I've been using your typewriter."

"I would hope so. Mind if I take this with me so I can read it?"

"Oh no, sir. That'd be real fine."

"What's it about?"

"It's about the fire. Only I turned it into a story so it wasn't so real, y'know?"

Gibson nodded. A few years ago several prisoners at the Ohio State Penitentiary had set some paint cans on fire hoping to escape during the commotion. Instead, the fire quickly spread out of control. Men were trapped in cells that wouldn't open. The guards had no evacuation strategy. The building was over a hundred years old and stuffed to twice its capacity with poor saps, most of whom had been caught by the circumstances of the Depression. Over 320 men died in the space of an hour. Many of the men who survived, including Chester, had been given an early parole. It was still no compensation for his scars.

"I'll give it a good read." Gibson folded the magazine into his coat pocket. "Just keep writing, keep writing," he offered.

"I will."

Gibson went to the door and opened it. "Listen," he said. "If those two want breakfast or anything, help them out. And if Mr. Driftwood, the new guy, wants to stay onboard a night or two before he gets straightened out, let him know he's welcome to. It's not going back to the yard until next week."

"Yes, sir. Are you still planning on going to Miami next month?"

"I'll let you know."

He stepped off the train into the chill of the clear morning air. The train yard was slowly coming to life; the shouts of teamsters and railmen mixed with the low rumble of the big engines and the occasional squeal of metal grinding against metal. He saw Manny's Checker Cab and the big heavyset man eating dunkers behind the wheel.

Manny knew his way around the city as if a map of its entire road network had been tattooed upon the back of his eyelids. In addition to his flawless, instinctive sense of direction, he seemed to be related to one half of the city and on a first-name basis with the other half. To Walter, who was originally from Philadelphia but wrote about New York, Manny was a library on wheels. It didn't matter that his knowledge was sometimes suspect; what mattered was the accent of authority he gave it. He had given Gibson a lift home once and had easily drawn out who he was and what he did. Gibson had given the man a couple of signed mags for his kids and the man was eternally grateful. From that point on, whenever he had the chance, he acted as Gibson's self-appointed chauffeur. All he had to hear over his radio was that Walter needed a lift, and there he'd be. No one else was allowed to pick him up, even if it meant that Gibson sometimes had to wait a little longer.

Manny tossed him a wave and started his engine. Gibson waved back. He stopped and stretched his sore arms over his head. The air was brisk but it was warmer than it had been in Providence. He took a deep breath of Gotham air and began to feel better. His Pullman was still hitched to the longer passenger train and people were disembarking. Suddenly Gibson froze.

He saw The Shadow again.

The Chinese man was in New York. As he stepped off the passenger car, his eyes swept the train yard like a wind that could blow dust from its every corner. Gibson stepped back between the train cars, hoping the long early shadows would conceal him so he could watch. It worked. Not noticing him, the Chinese man began to walk toward the parking lot. He parted the small crowd with what seemed to be a palpable emanation of energy. People moved out of his way without realizing they were doing so. Gibson began to follow him. The man walked with assurance; once he was certain of his surroundings, he gave them no other thought and never looked back to see Gibson.

The dark character slid smoothly into the back seat of the cab parked in front of Manny's. Gibson could see his hawklike profile framed in the window. The car headed toward the street and Gibson realized there was no way he could make it across the yard in time to get to Manny's cab in order to follow. But he had to know about this Chinese stranger who had saved his life but probably ended Jeffords's. The story had not ended with the death of the night watchman. The true ending to the story was about to turn onto the avenue.

He gave Manny a whistle and when the cabbie looked at him, Gibson ran his hand back and forth across his hat brim a number of times. Then he pointed to the departing cab. Manny nodded. Gibson watched him plop his cigar between his thick lips, and a moment later the cab spun out of the yard, gravel spitting away as the wheels dug in for traction.

Gibson rubbed the stubble of his chin thoughtfully for a moment. Every bone in his body ached to follow them. He broke out his pack of Chesterfields and lit his first cigarette of the day. The Chinese man hadn't seen him. He was positive of that. He wondered what could have brought this man to New York, and as his mind began trying to draw connections from Providence, trying to create a story, he looked for another cab. He would have loved to follow them, but the brown envelope in his hand was growing hot. No matter how much this new story begged to be told, the fact of the matter was that he still had a manuscript to deliver.

Besides, Manny had understood the meaning of his signal. While Gibson was a Phillies man, Manny was a Brooklyn Dodgers fan. During the summer his radio was locked on to Ebbets Field. Gibson's signal, the rubbing of the hat brim, was a classic Casey Stengel command to his pitcher, Van Lingle Mungo, when a man at first was preparing to steal second.

Keep your eye on the runner.

Episode Twenty-Six

CHINA WAS shattered.

All the previous wars Mei had fought in were mere squalls to the typhoon which engulfed the land from mountain to sea, and from border to border. It touched all lives. It was as if the concept of peace had been vanquished from life and memory. His son learned riding and swordplay from soldier masters as he had, and spoke of winning battles as eagerly as he had. He was only six.

Loyalties changed as often as the tides. Chiang had been ejected from the Kuomintang but had regained control. Chiang and the professor's Communists had briefly allied, but that alliance had fallen apart when Russian meddling in the affairs of the Communists surfaced.

Across the countryside Communist rebellions increased in ferocity and nipped at the flanks of the Kuomintang. One of Chiang's generals formed an army of his own and brought it against Chiang in Nanking with help from British and American warships. Mei found the shifting political landscape dizzying, as complicated as the beautiful game of chess that the Russian diplomats had once enjoyed so ferociously in the courtyards of Shenyang Palace.

Zuolin himself now commanded an army of a million men. He joked that he longed for the days when he rode with only two hundred warriors at his side. Mei had seen the burning campfires of six hundred thousand of those troops turn a valley at night into a lake of fire. Battles had been fought at forlorn places with names such as Xuzhou, Lincheng, Jiujiang, Xuehuashan Mountain, and Longtan. Yet still Chiang's Kuomintang pounded back at them with relentless force. And now, at last, Zuolin was retreating from Beijing.

The Japanese had landed troops at Jinan. Mi-Ying had assured him that they were only securing their vital national interests, but the old warlord saw what Mei had warned him of for so long: the Japanese were establishing a beachhead in order to pave the way for an invasion one day should the civil war weaken the Chinese to the point where that opportunity would present itself. Zuolin ended his alliance with the Japanese and Mi-Ying, who stayed behind in Beijing to await his next master. Or his fate. Without Japanese support, Zuolin's position as the ruler of China was untenable.

"We will return to Manchuria, the land of our fathers," the warlord told his sons. "Let them have this sewer. Behind the protection of our mountains and walls we will wait and grow stronger, and when they are weak we shall come again. We are not leaving China. China is with us."

Lu Zhi sobbed at the thought of leaving her beloved library behind. Beijing had been her home all her life and leaving grieved her. His son was eager to ride the train and see his grandfather's great palace. Mei had assured him that it was not only more beautiful than Beijing's but cleaner. The boy's eyes had glittered eagerly in the lamplight at bedtime as Mei described the wondrous things he would see in Lianoning: the caves they would explore, the mountains they would climb, the surf they would swim in, the kites they would fly, the birds they would catch, the deer they would hunt. Until the early morning when he had ridden out in preparation for the retreat, he and his wife had lain together and known love.

His men were certain that Shenyang City was secure. Some Communists had been executed and the families of the remaining Japanese were taken to the port for deportation. Flags of joy for the return of the Emperor of the Northern Lands hung from doorways and trees and flew from rooftops.

On the morning of their arrival he took a train from Shenyang Palace to Huanggudun Station on the far outskirts of the city. He had decided to surprise his wife and son by meeting them here and joining them for the remainder of the journey instead of waiting for them to arrive. Even weary Zuolin would be pleased to see him. His son loved trains. He had an elaborate collection of American tin miniatures which he spent hours with. He thought the metal dragons the most incredible inventions, and most of all Mei wanted to share in at least a part of his son's thrill in riding one.

There was a small crowd at the station hoping to catch a glimpse of their leader. The bees hung in the air much as they had a morning long ago in a distant copse at the far end of a rice paddy. He brushed the soot from his clothes; on his trip from the palace, the train windows had been open to let the fresh summer morning air in. He heard the distant whistle of the train announcing that it was clearing the final mountain pass several miles away, and his heart leapt. He could feel his Shaozu's arms around his neck, taste Lu Zhi's lips. On the horizon, a thin gray cloud of smoke mixed with steam appeared above the trees.

There was a face in the crowd, turning quickly from him as if to avoid his eyes. Mei moved his head to catch a better glimpse. The man was furtive. Mei pushed toward him, calling for assistance from his detail. The man broke into a run at the sound of his voice. Mei recognized him. Mi-Ying. There is no reason for him to be in Shenyang, Mei thought, and at the same moment he knew, of course there is.

The explosion threw great chunks of the train into the sky. They ascended so gracefully, so slowly through black ash that they almost appeared like dry leaves driven before the wild wind. Then the sound reached his ears, a mighty roar, and the power that lifted those sections of the train revealed itself. At the station people began to murmur, then scream.

He leapt upon a horse and rode in the direction of the noise and the fire. It wasn't what he thought, he told himself. It wasn't the right train, he prayed. Shaozu was special, he knew, favored by the gods. And the gods would protect him.

The woods were aflame. Great pieces of shrapnel lay in craters, smoldering. He tried to drive his horse through the flames to the twisted wreckage beyond, but there was no approach. The horse was not a soldier's mount and responded to the command with fear. It bucked and reared and threw its rider. As he fell through the air like another piece of debris, Mei knew that the bomb had been placed with devastating precision for maximum impact.

They were all dead, was his last thought as his head hit the earth. And he knew it was true.

Episode Twenty-Seven

"WHERE THE hell is The Shadow?" Orson Welles's voice boomed through the movie theater. His ribbing cracked through Gibson's headache like an anarchist's brick through a government office window. "Is he even in this piece of crap? It's called *The Shadow Strikes.* Where's the goddamn Shadow and when in hell is he going to strike?"

The pain in Walter's head had been growing steadily since his leaving the train yard. A long morning of defending his book to Nanovic hadn't helped anything either. Nanovic must have gotten a good night's sleep because he had torn into Gibson's writing as if the formula for writing these stories was so simple that anyone but Walter B. Gibson could write them. He knew that Nanovic sometimes did that when he wanted to feel more like a writer and less like a glorified proofreader. Since the appearance of Kent Allard and the debacle which had followed, Nanovic had taken great pains to drag a fine-tooth comb across each page, questioning Gibson's every word choice. He was taking great pains to see that nothing like that was ever going to happen again.

After the meeting Gibson had placed a call to the Providence police department and told them he suspected some kind of dustup at the medical lab down by the docks. There had been a long silence at the other end, and then the voice said, "So?"

"Don't you think you ought to look into it?" he had asked.

"It's looked into," the voice replied. "What's your name?"

Gibson had hung up. Seemed like old Aunt Annie had been right again regarding the competence, if not the outright complicity, of the Providence police force.

He had met Welles for lunch at the Automat. Welles had grumpily complained about how he wanted to go to Reuben's for one of their eponymous sandwiches: corned beef, sauerkraut, Swiss cheese, and Russian dressing toasted under the broiler. But too many magicians lunched there. Reuben's was very popular with the crowd who patronized Tannen's Magic Shop. Guys like Tommy Hanlon Jr., who worked with Orson at his theater; Herman Hanson, who had understudied Thurston and was so good at impersonating him that when the master had suddenly died of a stroke during an intermission last year, Hanson had taken the stage for the second act and anyone in the audience would have sworn that he had seen Thurston; and Joe Kavalier, a quiet artist who had a fascination with Harry Houdini and prodded Gibson for an anecdote every time they came together. Welles knew all those fellows as well. He was a proficient amateur magician and admired their talent. He constantly pushed Walter to star in his own show. Walter always retorted that he'd star in a show when Orson started writing pulps.

Gibson could not face too much scrutiny from the brotherhood. Not as long as he was having an affair with one of its members' wives. The group prided itself on its closely held age-old secrets, so it was hard to keep a secret from them. He knew that there were already whispers.

He'd had to explain this situation to Welles to get him to stop grumbling so peevishly about the sandwich that Gibson had so cruelly deprived him of. Fortunately the only thing which improved the young man's mood more than food was gossip, and the storm clouds of despair which had overshadowed his normally exuberant and optimistic nature had parted instantly.

"You're breaking up a marriage?" Welles had asked, conspiratorially. "And she's fifteen years younger than you? I must meet this Salome!"

"I'm not breaking up a marriage," Gibson had replied. "And if you think I'm too old for her, he's nearly sixty! He married her young to lock her up. And now he's loaning her to Blackstone anyway."

"Well, it's obvious she has her type. You've got to admit that. Let's say she likes her men somewhat experienced, shall we? Wasn't she the bird who used to have a chicken act?"

"Still does. But she's moved on to mind reading now and retired China Boy except for the kids. She's a hell of a mentalist too, I gotta tell ya. She picked a few things out of my head I didn't know I had up there."

"What happened to the chicken?"

"You're in the theater district a lot. Keep your eyes peeled. If you see a beautiful girl wearing a big floppy hat and carrying a basket with a black rooster's head sticking out of it, that's my gal."

"I shall look for nothing else." He had plunked another nickel in one of the cases and removed a second slice of apple pie. "Where do you think this can go, Wally, my friend? Do you think she'll leave him? And think about this: do you really want her to? What would you do with her if you had her? Hm?"

"I want her," Gibson had said without hesitation. "No. I don't know. I want to see her. That's all. If that means that I'm in love with her, I don't know. I just want to go get her."

"So go get her."

"It's Monday. The theater's dark today and she's not at her hotel. I sent her a telegram, though. Told her I want to see her again."

"Then you must make her leave him and damn the consequences. And by God, make sure she brings that chicken."

"She won't. She just won't. Have you ever been out with a married woman?"

"Of course! Married women are the most in need of someone to love and admire them. Single women get that from every man. Married women get it from none."

He hadn't told Welles about the Providence experience. It was an easy topic to avoid. Welles had wanted to hear gossip about Blackstone's opening night party, which had been at Mamma Leone's, the au courant Broadway restaurant where patrons could fish for their dinner from a trout-filled brook or converse with Mamma's horse, which lived in its own special stable with Dutch doors that opened onto a vast dining room.

They had finished their lunch and made their way to the movie palace to catch this week's chapter, the fifth, of the two-reeler serial adventure adaptation. Walter had written the first draft of *The Shadow Strikes* last October and sent it off to the Alexander brothers at Grand National Pictures in Hollywood. Welles and Gibson had eagerly sought out the serials for the past few weeks to see how their character had made the transition to the screen. Changes had been made.

Welles's level of concern about the quality of the film was well placed; like Gibson, he had a vested interest in the character of The Shadow. Welles was starring as the voices of The Shadow and Lamont Cranston on the wildly popular weekly radio adaptation of Walter's mag. A successful Shadow serial would create even more demand from which Gibson and Welles could profit. On the other hand, nobody wanted to be associated with a flop. Welles had made two significant contributions to the legend of The Shadow (three, if you took into account that he gave voice and life to an enigma). He had introduced a new character, Margot Lane, The Shadow's faithful friend and companion, to banter with The Shadow on his adventures and to give him somebody to rescue from time to time. The Street & Smith policy toward women in *The Shadow* may have been for Walter to stop writing about them at the knees and start again at the neck, but Welles wanted something a little sexier and he got it. Welles had also conferred upon The Shadow the power of invisibility; on his show the avenger became a frightening voice from the ether which surrounded criminals and audiences alike through the mystical ability to cloud men's minds. When Gibson, who spent long hours writing radio scripts with Welles, had initially and loudly questioned whether an audience would accept the trick of invisibility, the young man had earned his eternal respect by replying confidently, "If radio listeners will believe in a ventriloquist act they can't see, they'll believe even more in invisibility!" Gibson wrote it that way for the radio, and Welles was right—the audiences ate it up. But The Shadow would never be invisible in his mag. Not as long as he wrote it. In his mags The Shadow would always be there, if a person only knew where to look.

Despite the radio broadcasts' tremendous success, the sponsor, Blue Coal, was threatening to pull out because it found Welles and his versatile troupe, the Mercury Theatre on the Air, too difficult to work with. They often missed deadlines and refused to allow the coal-mining executives to comment on scripts. The network had assured Welles, and Street & Smith, that the Goodyear Tire Company had expressed sponsorship interest and was waiting in the wings. Should Blue Coal drop out, The Shadow would soon be cautioning drivers about the evils of driving on wet roads with unsafe tires.

"There's no Shadow in this movie!" Welles was nearly standing. Fortunately the theater was nearly empty. The Shadow as a movie character was a bust. Without the spectacle of Welles's invisibility angle, or the detailed nightscape moods of Walter's stories, what was it about? Just another detective story. On the screen, the former silent picture star Rod La Rocque, mostly famous for being Vilma Banky's husband, poked around one of the phoniest mansions they had ever seen, occasionally running into someone he suspected of embezzling eleven million dollars. "When does he become The Shadow?"

"Maybe next episode?" Gibson said, hopefully. "I know I wrote him in."

"Don't they listen to the radio? They don't even get Cranston's name right! They keep calling LaRoque Granston. Don't they read the magazines? Didn't they read the script?"

"As I recall I think they started production before my script was in."

"Don't they know what they have here? Don't they know what The

Shadow is? You know what it is, what the thing is? They don't have any respect for him. They think he's just a pulp." Welles dropped down, irked, in his seat. He shifted uncomfortably in his seat a few times and then he leaned over to Gibson. "Want to know how I'd make a Shadow movie if they gave me a chance?"

"Not a play?" Gibson asked. Welles had a brilliant imagination and a true knack for creating amazing stage scenes. Last June his *Voodoo Macbeth,* a Federal Theatre Project–WPA production, had created a bona fide New York craze. It was the event which put 125th Street on the A-train map for many white downtowners. The fashions inspired by the production could still be seen on the mannequins in the windows of Fifth Avenue eight months later. Walter had seen the production twice at the Lafayette and once at the Adelphia and been completely transported to another world. In those theaters, the rhythms of the islands had come to life and destiny moved through the fetid, steamy jungle Welles had realized in the middle of civilization. Welles had used Shakespeare to penetrate the heart of darkness. The production had made him the toast of the town. He was a sensation.

When the curtain had risen on that show, and on him, he was twenty-two years old.

"No," was the reply, "a movie. A real movie."

Walter squirmed again as Rod La Rocque lumbered through a phony fight scene. "Let's hear it."

"It will be dark," Orson began softly, in the deep performance voice he used for The Shadow. "It will be dark. Perhaps the darkest movie ever made. Light will barely penetrate the mists and darkness and when a shaft of life breaks through, it is only to shine for a moment on a brief moment of good which is to be snuffed out when it fades. Moonlight illuminates a sleeping baby. In the darkness she disappears. A man smokes a cigarette beneath a fading street lamp. When it flickers out he is mugged with a blackjack. This is the black world through which The Shadow moves.

"It doesn't matter what the story is. What matters is the world. I would have The Shadow, or some part of him, in almost every shot. Somewhere. In the background, you might see a hint of his cloak, or the brim of his hat or the glint of his eyes. I'd set the story entirely in the criminal underworld. The villains would be the protagonists and The Shadow would be their antagonist. He's a force of nature. He coalesces around evil the way clouds come together along a cold front to form a thunderstorm. His glee at being summoned again, at being needed, at being alive is what makes him laugh. It's his thunder, and his actions are his lightning. My Shadow movie would be about the panic and fear he creates in the minds of the black-hearted.

"In this film, the darkness is something real, unconsciously shared and connected throughout all of humanity. It's the darkness that we all share, that you've personified, given a name. The Shadow is the champion of despair. He is a trickster unleashed by the evil that men do to restore balance. It's as if the act of evil deeds cracks the mantle of humankind and what bubbles up through the new crevasses, like a spring, is The Shadow. He can't be unleashed until the crime is committed, but once it has been, he is the opposite reaction to the criminal's action."

"But doesn't that make him part villain too?"

Welles thought about that for a moment. "Yes. Yes, of course he is! It takes a villain to know a villain, right? In some ways, the villain is even closer to him than the hero. Without the villain he wouldn't exist, wouldn't bubble up, as I was saying. He'd certainly have no purpose even if he did. The villain taps down directly into the liquid well of darkness, the sanctorum of The Shadow, and steals from him that which he safeguards, violence and fear. The Shadow manifests himself through the righteous, all his faithful agents, to retrieve what was his to begin with, that part of himself which was stolen, and to restore universal harmony."

Gibson almost blurted out that he had seen The Shadow, nearly told Welles about Providence. But Welles was a hard man to interrupt.

Welles shrugged. "The only good characters I'd present would be the agents of The Shadow—Harry Vincent, Margot Lane, Shrevnitz, the working stiffs who would be exploited by the criminal element if it weren't for him. In fact, I'd want the audience to suspect each of them—the cabbies, the construction joes, the fruit vendors, and the doormen—of being The Shadow. The audience expects Lamont Cranston to be The Shadow, so that's one place where I'd throw them off. Cranston, or Allard, what have you, he's just another agent in the end, doing The Shadow's bidding, spying on the underworld, bringing him information. The Shadow's agents are the tools through which The Shadow acts and he uses them to change the villain's world, manipulate his destiny, moving them like chess pieces, forcing the villain to react and react and react, each time thinking that he's defeated The Shadow only to find that another agent has become The Shadow and is challenging him again and again, trapping him in an illusion of mirrors, until that villain's fate is inescapable. And that fate is, of course, his doom.

"I'd never use a straight cut when The Shadow was in action. Everything would be done in dissolves so the images flow into each other. I'd pick the craziest angles I could shoot so that the audience would feel like the criminals, off balance and operating outside of normal conventions. Movies are about the interplay between light and dark, black and white. And so is The Shadow."

"Well, it's an awful lot to draw out of some pulp mags."

"It's all about the lie. The big lie. That's what our audiences want from us, Walter. From you and me they want the big lie. They want the big stories about the great things. Not for us the little tales of simple people. We have to tell the big lie. The bigger the better. As far as I can tell, the best way to lie is to use film. Everything about it is a lie. The script is a lie the writer tells, which the actor speaks, lying to convince you that the words are his. The cameraman uses light and angles to lie about how good that actor looks. Then the editor takes all the lies, picks the best ones, and stitches them together into one great lie from beginning to end. But in spite of all that, when it's done right, somehow it becomes something quite like the truth. That's what I want to do. But," he added wistfully, "you know the joke, right? How many Broadway directors they say it takes to change a lightbulb?"

"I don't know."

"Ten. One to do it, and nine to tell each other how they would have done it better."

They sat in silence for a few moments as Rod faced menace from a gun-wielding thug. They both sighed at the same time as the cliff-hanger came to an end.

"Hey! There's a one-reeler cartoon, *Hawaiian Holiday,* after the newsreel," Orson said as the Movietone logo splashed across the screen. "Want to stick around? I love Walt Disney."

"Really?"

"Absolutely. He is certifiably the only genius working in Hollywood today."

"I knew him in France during the war. Skinny kid. Drove an ambulance. Who knew?"

"I can't wait to see what he does with *Snow White. Variety* says it'll ruin him; they say people won't go see a feature cartoon. But I'd bet any amount that they will if Disney makes it. It's amazing to me that the man is able to craft such a personal artistic statement in an art form that requires so much anonymous collaboration."

"I don't really follow the kids' stuff too much."

"Yeah, that's right. I forgot you're a *serious* writer. And how is your great American novel coming along anyhow?"

"I'll let you know when I start it."

"Too busy writing good to write great."

"Which reminds me, I've got another script to get to you. Interested in a paper caper? A powerful news tycoon is murdered and only The Shadow can solve it."

"Interesting. But hold that thought. Stick around and I'll show you what I'm talking about."

Gibson looked at his watch. "All right," he said, "let's see what we shall see." He lit a cigarette. The silver light cut through the smoke. Suddenly the newsreel, which had been running, caught his attention.

Thunderous howitzer cannons blasted an unseen enemy. "Dateline: China! General Chiang Kai-shek, leader of the Nationalist army, has ended the civil war against Mao's Communist rebel army in the greater interest of expelling the advancing Japanese army, whose devastating invasion of the Manchurian provinces continues."

The narrator's delivery was spitfire fast over spectacular battle footage of the brave and bold Chinese fighters. They crawled through mud or manned 37mm artillery guns. "The generalissimo came late to this conclusion, and only after being kidnapped by a faction of officers within his own troops led by General Zhang Xueling."

The shot changed from weapons of war to one of a group of Chinese men in uniform. They posed stiffly, as if for a still photograph, looking all the more foolish for trying to remain motionless before the lens of a motion picture camera.

"General Chiang Kai-shek was persuaded to embrace the cause of Chinese unity at the home of General Zhang's brother and closest political adviser, Zhang Mei. Sources claim that Zhang Mei, known as the Dragon of Terror and Peril, could himself lead the Chinese government at some future time."

Gibson's hands began to tremble. He instantly recognized the eyes of the intense dark man standing behind the soldiers. It was his Shadow, the Chinese stranger. He was the only man in the group whose very stillness seemed to reflect who he was, not what he wanted the camera to commemorate.

"Subsequent to the kidnapping, while all the plotters of the conspiracy have been rounded up, the general's brother, the inscrutable Zhang Mei, has escaped into the shadows of war! Current whereabouts? Unknown."

Stunned, he felt stuck in his seat. The cartoon began and Welles immediately began chortling, then laughing.

The Shadow's laugh.

Walter sprang from his chair, not unlike his companion had when the serial had begun.

"What about the cartoon?" Orson shouted.

"I can't stay!" Gibson hollered back as he ran up the aisle toward the exit. "I've got to find a cab!"

Episode Twenty-Eight

"DEAR BROTHER," Xueling said to him, "Manchuria needs you now. I need you now."

Snow was falling. Xueling was visiting Mei in the small house he had claimed near the outskirts of Shenyang, far from the palace. Mei scratched his hands through the long beard he had grown during his mourning.

He could see his brother's eyes moving from him to the object behind him. Some time ago Zhang Mei had sent soldiers back to his home village and had them retrieve the statue of the god whose priest he had once pretended to be. He had wanted to show his wife and son something of his childhood, and this hollow old statue was the only tangible memory he could provide them. Of course, Lu Zhi thought it silly and had banished it to a far corner of her garden. Still, he'd had artisans restore its golden glory. When he had moved from that house, the statue was all he had asked to accompany him.

"I have nothing more to give to Manchuria," he replied. "Nor to China. I have given all."

"I have lost my father, as well," Xueling reminded him.

Mei nodded but did not reply. He brushed a minute speck of incense ash from his black silk robe. "I wear the black robes of the old monk who taught us in our youth. Do you remember he once told us that in order to wear the white robes of healing, one must first wear the black robes of destruction?"

"You will find Mi-Ying someday," Xueling said. He knew Mei had been scouring the countryside on the trail of the traitor. His quest had yielded no fruit, no relief.

"I believe he has fled to the south." Mei nodded. "I will follow him there."

"I have decided to strike my father's colors," Xueling said, suddenly. "I have made this decision with the advice of my brothers."

This, at last, distracted Mei from his concerns.

Xueling continued, "The men of Manchuria are brave and determined, but General Chiang's army will overwhelm us in the end. I will order my father's colors struck at sunset tomorrow and at dawn the next day we will raise the flag of the Republic of China. Henceforth, I will be the commander in chief of the Manchurian border. It is peace. Of a kind."

"A peace with those who have killed my family? What kind of peace is this?"

"A peace that will unite China."

"I believe we should fight on forever!" Mei spat, his voice dripping with bitterness. "Hit them harder, and harder, and harder!"

"Even if many more sons and wives and fathers die?" Xueling asked with surprising tenderness. "Even if the Han race be wiped from the face of the earth?"

"Yes!" Mei felt a murderous rage sweep over him. He dashed his weapons rack to the floor. "How can I swear loyalty to a man whose heart I want to rip out?"

Xueling gestured to an aide who stood nearby, who quickly left through the door. There came the sound of low voices in the small courtyard beyond. "I thought, as we all did, that General Chiang was behind the assassination. However, one who represents interests other than China's has recently come to me with new information."

The aide reentered the small room with another man. He was white and wore the uniform of an American officer.

"This is Captain Towers of the United States," Xueling introduced the man, who bowed deeply and formally. He bore himself alertly and carried the demeanor of a warrior. "He has been attached to diplomatic relations in many other countries. He has recently brought intelligence to me of conspiracies which sought this assassination to push us over the precipice into a great civil war. Then, like vultures, the plotters would pick apart the corpse of the land. He has helped me turn away from that fall for the good of China. Now you will see who Mi-Ying's merciless allies in this conspiracy are." He turned and looked at the young captain, who stood ramrod straight. "Who has caused the death of our father? Of this man's wife and son?"

The aide began to translate haltingly to Towers but the man cut him off with a wave of his hand. Towers's eyes met Mei's and his strong gaze did not waver for an instant.

"Japan," Captain Towers, the American officer, said in Chinese. "The Japanese."

Episode Twenty-Nine

"SO, THIS is where it gets interestin', 'cause this is where I lost him," Manny said, hitting the brakes with enough force to bounce Gibson forward against the dashboard.

"You lost him?"

Unfazed and unmoved, the cabbie chewed on his unlit cigar stub. "Wanna know what happened then?"

Gibson sat back in his seat. "Hell, yes!"

It had taken Manny's dispatcher several hours to track him down. During this suspenseful wait Gibson had managed to convince himself that something unfortunate had happened to his affable friend. In the end, however, the familiar cab had squealed to a stop in front of his hotel. The trip down the West Side had taken only minutes. Manny had just stopped his cab by the newsstand on the Ninth Avenue IRT elevated tracks at Sixteenth Street. A young man was hawking afternoon editions of the *New York Post.* The light from the setting sun was sliced into neat slivers by the massive ironwork trestle overhead.

Manny leaned on the horn. At the sound the paperboy stopped hectoring the commuters and, with a smile of recognition, ran to the open window on the driver's side.

"What's up, Manny?" He was a teenager, of slight build and with dark eyes. His fingers, gripping the ledge of the door, were long and thin. The hair under his gray cap was a dark mop of brown curls and his eyes were wide and street-wary.

"Mr. Gibson, this here's Kurtzberg."

"Hiya, mister." The kid shook his hand.

"Hello."

"He plays stickball with my kid out in Sunnyside. So here's what's what. I follow your fella to here and then the cab stops and he gets out. He's heading for the elevated and I want to keep an eye on him but if I leave my cab behind I'll get fired. I'm on call, my dispatcher's barkin' at me. Nothin' I can do. So I think fast. I look over and I seen Jakey selling his papers right here on that corner. I give him da sign, and as sure as Bob's your uncle, he's up the El after him. Even jumps the turnstile."

"That's right." The kid nodded.

"Where'd he go?" Gibson asked.

"Just up to Thirty-fourth Street near the post office," the teen replied. "I followed him off the train, and down at the entrance there's this guy waiting for him with a car. But he ain't Chinese. He's American. Kind of an older guy, older than you even, with short silver hair. I tried to get close enough to hear them talking, but I couldn't do it. Whatever the Chinese man tells this guy really ticks him off something fierce. He starts pounding on the roof of the car. Then the Chinese man tells him something that completely turns him around, makes him laugh. They get into the car.

"Now I can't follow him on foot and I ain't got no cab fare. But I see a pal of mine, Stanley Leiber, who works at his cousin's husband's newsstand up there."

"That's one of Martin Goodman's stands," Manny said.

"Yeah, I know him," Walter said. "Also prints *Stag Magazine,* right?"

"He's got a string of newsstands. Real bona fide operation." Jakey continued his story. "Stan's also a part-time Movietone news runner, a guy who rides his motorcycle to the site of a news story. The cameraman gives him the film and then he beats the devil through traffic back to the lab to get the film processed so it can get onto movie screens before *The March of Time.* He says it's kinda like bein' on the pony express," he added somewhat wistfully. "Plus he makes some good scratch."

"Forget it, kiddo," Manny said, "I ain't talkin' your pop into getting' you no motorbike. Them things are a menace."

"Anyway, I tells him to keep his eye on the runner and he sets off after 'em and that's the last I seen him."

"Great work, kiddo. I'll see you at the next game." Manny slipped him a few bucks and put the car into gear and they raced up Eighth Avenue toward the post office district.

The car squealed to a stop at the newsstand, its racks bursting with titles, an Indian scout leaning against one wall.

"Hey-ho, Stan the man," Manny hollered at the young man sitting on a stack of magazines before the stand. The young man, about the same age as Jakey, and just as gangly, nodded and rose stiffly. His face bore a fresh bruise, his fingers were dark with oil stains, and he walked with a limp over to the cab.

"Jesus, pal! Somebody rough you up?"

"Nah, Manny," the young man said, defiantly, spitting on the sidewalk. "I got hit by a tuna."

"How's that again?" Gibson asked. The kid appraised him coolly.

"'S'all right," Manny reassured him. "He's the one calling the plays."

The kid spat again. "I followed that car all the way downtown. You know the Fulton Fish Market, by the water there?"

Both men nodded.

"That's where I got hit by a tuna. Some son of a bitch thrown it from a stall to a truck and the sucker smacked right into me. Forty-pounder, easy. Laid me right out on Peck Slip. Knocked the chain off my dang bike. Took me hours to get her running again. A crime too, 'cause I missed the drop from London out at Idlewild."

"Damn," Gibson sighed and sat back in his seat.

"Game called," Manny grumbled.

"Naw," Stanley seemed offended. "We got a pulp stand down there. Big Sammy the Boxer works it. You'll know him when you see him, a huge grizzled piece of meat with a face that looks like a pile of broken brick. I gave him the signal. He hitched a ride on the back of a fish truck which was heading in the same direction."

After slapping Stanley a few bucks to help him recoup the loss of the London drop, they left midtown and sped toward the waterfront. He was in it now, Gibson thought, grinning at the exhilaration of it all. The story was coming. He could feel the sense of urgent, unstoppable momentum rising up within, the same sensation he experienced when it all went well, the writing, as it went on the train when he had opened up the throttle and let the words out. He rubbed his hands—his fingers were throbbing—then leaned forward to watch the buildings flash by as the Brooklyn Bridge grew large.

Within moments they were in the midst of the Fulton Fish Market. The smell of fish permeated the car, even with the windows closed. Most of the buyers were already in business, bidding on and then distributing to local restaurants and fishmongers the day's fresh catch being brought in from the sea. They found the plug-ugly pugilist, just as Stanley had described him, sipping a last whiskey of the day in his newsstand next to the tavern that sat behind the open-air fish stalls. Two drinks later and they were back in the cab heading farther south, into the financial district, the only part of New York that could truly be considered abandoned at night.

Manny pulled the car to a stop in front of an office building. It was indistinguishable from hundreds of other New York office buildings. Six or seven stories high, no ornamentation. "This was where Sammy the Boxer followed them to."

Gibson could see lights on in the lobby and a pair of uniformed security guards inside. "Do you feel that?" he asked Manny. "The vibration?"

"Mm-hmm. Subway."

Gibson shook his head. "No. There's a rhythm to it. You catch the same sensation in the Street & Smith building. I think there's a printing press down below us. Probably in the basement. It may even extend under the sidewalk."

"What're they printing?"

"I don't know," Gibson said and then pointed to the end of the block. "But I do know how we can find out." They headed to the dilapidated newsstand on the corner. A German shepherd barked at them as they arrived.

"Easy, killer," Gibson said to the alert hound. "Sammy the Boxer sent us."

An old man in a battered fedora rubbed the nape of the dog's neck. It sat back on its haunches. The old man squinted at them. At least one eye seemed to. The other eye was long since gone.

"Yeah," he grunted with a phlegmatic rattle.

Gibson folded a bill into the tin cup the man left out for change. "You, uh, keep your eye on the runner?"

"What do you think?"

"Hey, mac," Manny said, impatiently, "you know what goes on in that building back there?"

"Well," the old man said, "if you'd asked me that this morning I'd have said I didn't know. But since Sammy told me to watch the runners and they seemed particularly interested in it, I got a customer who's a rocketeer to find out for me."

"What's a rocketeer?"

"The post office guys that operate everything coming and going through the pneumatic tubes are called rocketeers. Okay, all the post offices in the city are connected by pneumatic tubes, thirty miles of 'em or more, with cylinders about this long"—he held out his hands to indicate a span of about two feet—"that go whizzing through them all day and all night. My rocketeer wrote down his question and put it in the tube at the Church Street office and it shot up to Times Square. Then it went to the Ansonia station, then on and on to the Planetarium office, the Cathedral office, and the Morningside office, before it finally gets to the Manhattanville station on a Hundred and Twenty-fifth Street, where someone who finally knows something about the building works. Two hours later, my rocketeer's back with the answer. Ain't the modern age great?" He unfolded a crumpled piece of paper. "That building there is the American Bank Note Company. Ever hear of it?"

Gibson shook his head.

"No? They print up money for other countries. It's a foreign currency mint."

Gibson pushed the now insistently nuzzling dog away from his crotch. "Did they go inside?"

"Nope. After a little while of looking it over and talking, the car drove off. I couldn't follow that."

"Of course not." Gibson grimaced with disappointment, feeling the trail of pursuit suddenly grow cold.

"Not the car. No. But that big Chinaman, he left on foot."

"Tell me you sent your dog after him, right?"

"Hell no! Shep minds the store. I followed him," he pointed north, toward Chinatown. "Went down an alley on Doyers. The door with the red light over it."

"You know," Manny said to him as they climbed back in the car, "a red light in Chinatown? That means opium."

"I know."

Manny turned the cab into the twisted net of Chinatown streets. He pulled up in front of an alley. At the back of the alley was a door. The red lightbulb flickered weakly in the darkness.

"This fella. He owe you money?"

"Nope."

"You owe him money?"

"Uh-uh."

"Then what's he to you? What do you want with him?"

"He's got the ending to my story."

He opened the cab door, stepped out, closed the door. and leaned in through the window, placing some bills in his hand. Manny would find out later that Gibson had slipped him a hundred bucks.

"You sure you want to go in there?"

Gibson shrugged. "You know, it probably won't even be the worst place I've been in this week."

"You want I should stick around?"

"No. I might be a while."

"Some game, huh?"

"Yeah," he replied, "sure was. Really kept our eye on the runner."

He watched the cab drive away. After a night spent calling on what felt like half of New York he suddenly was all alone. He looked down the long alley to the dark door. Extra innings, he told himself, and headed toward it, his footfalls echoing softly.

"*Fook yuen? Fook yuen?*" the smoke peddler called as Gibson slipped him money to enter. He had been in opium dens before, and this was an opulent example of one. Men lying on red silk pads on pallets on the floor behind carved screens were being tended to by a few men with pipes. The thick, richly sweet smoke hung low in the air. Several musicians played odd stringed instruments, a slow, meandering melody that sounded to Gibson like the memory of a brook in spring. An ancient staircase to the left vanished into the darkness upstairs. "*Fook yuen?*" the man asked again, trying to tug him toward a low couch.

Gibson shook his head. He held up a hand for caution and slowly reached into his jacket, pulling out the long, lethal knife which he had found in the corpse of Jeffords. He presented it, hilt first, to the little man, who seemed gnarled right to the tips of his tinted, curved fingernails.

The sleek peddler's eyes narrowed cagily. Gibson stared back at him. The men slipped away behind some curtains for a few moments. Then he returned, and the knife was gone. The man drew back the curtains. Gibson could see a simple iron spiral staircase leading up into darkness. Another Chinese man was guarding it; this man did not look like the smoke peddlers, who were shifty and cowed. He stood proud and alert. Gibson placed him for a soldier. He approached the man and attempted to stare him down as well. This man wasn't going for it. After several moments he smirked at Gibson and turned and climbed the staircase. Gibson followed.

The staircase opened onto a landing. Another Chinese man was guarding the door. This man appeared to have had his jaw broken recently. It was swollen and purplish and pushed about an inch too far to its right. A red bandana was wound tightly around his head. The pain must have been significant but he stoically held his post. The first man spoke to him. Through his clenched jaw the second man uttered a sound which could have been a chuckle. Then he opened the door.

Gibson instantly recognized where he was. It's the backstage of a theater, he thought. Indeed, the flies and drapes and boards were still intact, though covered with dust. The front of the stage was blocked by a great tattered backdrop. Seen in reverse, it appeared to be a Chinese temple scene. There was even a statue in front of it; he could see its shadow on the painted muslin.

There were stacks of long crates which were much cleaner, much newer, and the footprints and slide paths surrounding them showed that they had been placed here recently, probably by the small group of Chinese men who were right now sitting or leaning on them and looking at him. Some of them cleaned their knives. Some of them cleaned their guns. All of them glared at him.

"Zhang Mei," he said loudly. "I want to speak with Zhang Mei."

A voice rolled toward him from the shadows behind them; it was deep and melodious and fluidly inflected. It was a voice Welles would have admired. "Who are you?" it asked of him, simply.

"I'm your biographer." It just came to him. There was long pause.

"Who are you?" The voice was more quizzical now.

Gibson took a few steps closer to the Chinese group. He still couldn't see the speaker. He now stood in the midst of the Chinese. "I am a writer. I write for the pulp magazines. Popular stories."

"Who are you?"

"I am Walter Gibson. The man from the docks in Providence. You saved my life."

"Who are you?"

"My writing name is Maxwell Grant. I am the best-selling writer in this country." His eyes were adjusting to the new, darker wing of the stage. He could make out a black figure now. "You have reached out your hand from your land and touched this land. Already your name is known here. But not your life's story."

"My life speaks for itself," the shape said.

Gibson knew that he had been dismissed. He felt the men behind him begin to stir. It would only be another second before a knife slid between his ribs, or a thin metal thread was pulled tightly around his throat.

"Al Capone!" he exclaimed. "You've heard of Al Capone."

Even for a man from the other side of the world, that legendary name still had resonance. It gave the men creeping up behind him pause. The black shape before him shifted, and he realized that the man he had been speaking with had had his back turned to him the whole time. The figure stepped into the dim light and Gibson could see that this was indeed the man he'd been looking for. His eyes were glittering and hard but there was something in them that Gibson recognized. Something that again gave him the feeling that he might be looking into the eyes of his own creation.

"I was his biographer. And when he dies, his story will live on. He gave me what I wanted and I gave him what he wanted."

"What is that?"

"Immortality."

Zhang Mei smiled. It was a dead, mirthless smile. But it wasn't menacing. Gibson had simply amused him to the extent that he was able to be amused.

"If you stay you cannot leave without it being my will. I may never will it so."

"I know."

"And you will have to write fast, then. For my story is long and our time is brief."

"Well," Gibson said with some modesty, "in addition to being the best-selling writer in America, I'm also the fastest."

Zhang Mei nodded and the men fell back with soldierly ease and went about their crate-shifting exercise. Gibson took out his notebook and pencil. Gibson noticed that Zhang Mei had a delicate teacup filled with steaming tea and he wrote down that detail, accompanied by a note that the tea smelled like jasmine. Zhang Mei took a sip of the tea. "Well then, biographer, where should I begin?"

"Start with your parents," Walter said, already writing his lead sentence. "Who were they? What were they like?"

"I never knew my father," Zhang Mei said. He thought for a moment longer and then he spoke, and as he spoke, Gibson wrote. "The man who would be my father was a Manchu and he rode from the west, from the Nulu'erhu Mountains, across the windswept, snowy plains of the Lianoning Province, behind Zhang Zuolin, the warlord."

Issue 4:
Hell Gate

Episode Thirty

SHE COULDN'T sleep. Lester didn't seem to have the same problem. He was slumbering away in their bed. His snoring managed to be reassuring and irritating at the same time. She left the room and padded down the hallway to the living room to get another book from the shelf. Other books, which she had been poring over in an attempt to find some history of her statue, were strewn across the living room. It would require some explanation, she realized, as the room hadn't looked like this when Lester had fallen asleep only hours ago.

They had been making love since their return from Chinatown the night before. She had thought they would be too tired, or overwhelmed, for passion, but in fact it was just the opposite. They stayed in bed and ate leftover Chinese food and made love over and over. It was the first time since sometime before the pregnancy ended. It was as if the excitement had ignited her need for him.

She added several of Lester's research books to her of-interest pile and then her hand fell upon a German travel guide. Slowly she pulled the book down. The book fell open to the page she knew it would: the crease in the spine was permanent. She looked at the photo of the palace of Ludwig II, the mad king of Bavaria. Deep under his castle nestled high in the Alps was rumored to be a treasure guarded by a hall of mirrors so devious and fantastic that it could make someone mad within hours. This book had been in her purse last year in Switzerland. It had been the book she referred to when she begged Lester to take her just a little bit over the border, only twenty miles. She had even spoken with some locals and knew of an unpatrolled border crossing they could drive their little Citroën over. Lester hadn't wanted to, but he did it.

She closed the book and put it back on the shelf. What the book didn't say was that the palace had been turned into a Nazi troop bivouac. Books could be useless like that.

She spent some time cleaning up the books, putting them away. There were no answers to be found in them. No treasure clues.

She climbed back into bed. She could still hear the ringing voice of the young Nazi soldier who approached them as she leaped out of the car. She could hear Lester urgently asking her to get back in. Why had she stubbornly argued with him?

She lay back and curled up against him, pressing hard into his body, resting her leg over his, laying her head on his chest, rousing him. He wrapped his arms about her and kissed her forehead. "I think we're going to miss church tomorrow. Today. We'll go next week."

"Mm-hm." She toyed with the hairs on his chest. There were a few gray ones she hadn't noticed before. "Why did you tell that cop your name was Kenneth Robeson?"

"Did I do that?"

"Mm-hmm."

"Really? I don't remember that. I guess I felt more like Kenneth Robeson than Lester Dent."

She could almost hear him thinking about the events at the restaurant, reliving them.

"I nearly got you killed twice."

"Not bad for your first time out."

"Don't joke about it," she insisted. "I get us in trouble."

"I'm not joking." He sat up. "Can't we go out to dinner at our favorite restaurant and not have an adventure? You went into the theater without me. You mouthed off to that cop. It wasn't quite as bad as getting us chased over the Alps with the entire German army shooting at us. But it was close."

"Why don't you stop me?"

"Because you're a hard woman to say no to." She rolled away from him onto her other side and was quiet for a while.

"I always get us into these things and you have to get us out. Don't you get mad at me for it?"

She heard him exhale in frustration. "Maybe you're just the kind of person that things like this happen to. You know, some people have good luck, some people have bad luck, some people have money luck or romance luck. Maybe you've got adventure luck and these things find you. And one of these times your adventure luck is going to run out and I'm not going to be able to save you, because you don't let me protect you."

"I thought you did a pretty swell job in Chinatown."

"It could have gone the other way on a dime."

"There are things you can't protect me from, Lester. There have been and there will be."

"I'm aware of that. But at least I feel that in some ways, I'm a good counterbalance to your adventure luck. I have a touch of protection luck. But only a touch. In the hospital, for example," he went on. "Turns out you and I have the same blood type and I could give you a transfusion. But I couldn't protect you from losing the baby."

"You're right," she sniffled and then blew her nose on what she thought was rough for a handkerchief, but was really soft when it turned out to be a sock.

"So okay," she said. "I'll try to watch out for my adventure luck. I love you too much."

"I love you too," he said, and she wondered if he had heard her and understood her. It occurred to her that married people use "I love you" to convey a variety of meanings from "I'm sorry" to "I'm right, but . . ." to "This is great" to "I'll do exactly what you say from this day on." She thought he might be reading that very interpretation into her expression, when what she really had meant by "I love you" was that he was her man. But her emphasis had slipped at the last moment.

"I love you too," she said, meaning that they didn't have to continue their conversation right now. She knew the doctors had told Lester that she would never be able to carry a baby to term, and that he wanted to talk about what that meant for their life together. Lester may have finally been able to get her to leave the apartment, and that was a big step in the right direction, but she wasn't ready to talk about their never having a child together. She rolled over and looked up, trying to distinguish his features in the dark. She helped him glide a hand up her side to her breast, sliding her thigh against his. She parted her lips and kissed him.

The night after crossing the border back into Switzerland, they had made love the same way as they did now. She couldn't smell him or hear his voice, not to mention look at him, without wanting to be enveloped by him. She could remember the way she felt when they had exited the Citroën and had seen the angry, punctured metal in the bonnet, torn through by the machine gun's bullets.

It was a month after their return from Europe, after the day in Bavaria and the nights in the Alps, that they had discovered she was pregnant for what would be the last time.

Episode Thirty-One

LIGHT BROKE apart through the Rose Window and scattered in dappled fragments of color across Norma's hymnal.

The pastor read from the Gospel of John, "Jesus said to Nicodemus, 'Most assuredly, I say to you, unless one is born again, he cannot see the kingdom of God.'"

Holy Trinity Church was a Gothic structure on Central Park West. It was far bigger than the small Lutheran church she and Lester had attended back in La Plata, and sometimes she felt overwhelmed by its great presence: the elegance of the triptych of Christ rising behind the alabaster altar, the Louis Tiffany stained-glass windows, but especially the great pipe organ. Their old church had had a donated upright piano which had been lovingly tuned once a month. Holy Trinity incorporated much more music into its services than her old church had, and she loved that.

"Nicodemus said to Him, 'How can a man be born when he is old? Can he enter a second time into his mother's womb and be born?'" She watched Lester's fingers tap silently against his thighs, writing another book or transcribing the pastor's sermon, she wasn't sure which. He didn't like church very much but he dutifully went along with her every Sunday. During a very busy period it could be the only time during a week that he stopped moving. He stifled a yawn. Almost.

"And Jesus answered, 'Most assuredly, I say to you, unless one is born of water and the Spirit, he cannot enter the kingdom of God. That which is born of the flesh is flesh, and that which is born of the Spirit is spirit. Do not marvel that I said to you, "You must be born again." The wind blows where it wishes, and you hear the sound of it, but cannot tell where it comes from and where it goes. So is everyone who is born of the Spirit.'"

The organist began to play and she looked down at the words on her page: "Come, Oh, Come, Thou Quickening Spirit." She felt Lester touch her hand and she smiled at him as he intertwined his fingers with hers. He was too shy to sing out loud, even in a great mass of people, but he enjoyed listening to her sing. The hymn brought tears to her eyes.

On the steps she and Lester stopped to shake the pastor's hand and thank him for the sermon. As they parted, a voice called out to them, "Excuse me!" They stopped and saw a couple, their age, a few steps up from them. A little boy in his Sunday suit held on tightly to his mother's hand. Norma recognized both the mother and the son. The mother was new to the city and their church. Her husband had died and she had moved up from somewhere in the South to live with her sister. Norma could see that the little boy held something tightly in his hand. "We're so sorry to bother you, Mr. Dent," the mother said. "But last week one of the boys in Sunday school told him that you were a writer. Would you mind . . . ?" She helped the little boy take a step toward them. He unfurled the object in his hand. It was the latest *Doc Savage* issue. "He's such a big fan."

Lester grinned. "Of course," he said. He pulled a pen from his pocket and took the magazine from the little boy's hand. "*The Sea Angel.* One of my very favorites. What's your name, son?"

"Bruce," said the little boy.

"Okay, Bruce." Lester scribbled down a quick message on the cover. "For Bruce—Remember to strive every moment of your life to make yourself better and better, that all may profit by it. —Kenneth Robeson." Then he wrote, in parentheses, "Lester Dent." He handed the book back to the wide-eyed youth. "That's the first sentence of the Doc Savage oath," he said gently. "Do you know the other lines?"

The little boy nodded. "By heart," he said and quickly rattled off all four lines of the oath so it sounded like one long sentence: "Let me strive every moment of my life to make myself better and better, that all may profit by it; let me think of the right, and lend all my assistance to those who need it, with no regard for anything but justice; let me be considerate of my country, of my fellow citizens and my associates in everything I say and do; let me take what comes with a smile, without loss of courage; let me do right to all and wrong no man."

Norma and Lester burst into proud laughter and Lester tousled the boy's hair. The child's mother thanked them profusely, embarrassing Lester. Then she politely pulled her little boy away.

They stood alone on the steps; all the other churchgoers had moved on to the rest of their Sunday. The pastor closed the doors to the church. A strong wind rustled the bare trees across the street in Central Park. Norma sighed and Lester put his arm around her.

"I'm getting better about it," she said. "I really am." She meant it. In the past week as she had put aside Dutch Schultz and turned to researching the golden statue she had seen in the theater, she had had to admit to herself that she just wasn't feeling as bad.

"I know," he said with a reassuring pat on her hand. "Come on and let's walk over to the Tavern on the Green. I'll buy you a Manhattan."

She nodded and they began to walk.

The Chinese men seemed to appear out of nowhere (although afterward she would recall that they had been lurking on the outskirts of her awareness all morning) and surrounded them before they knew it.

"What the hell?" Lester said loudly. It appeared neither of the men spoke English. They were dressed in suits. The man in charge nodded his head politely toward a sedan, which Norma now realized had been idling in front of the church as they had come out. For a moment she thought that this was her retribution for breaking into the theater, until she suddenly recognized him. She felt Lester's arm begin to slide from her body.

"Wait," she said to him. "This man works for Mr. Yee. He's his cook!"

The man nodded, recognizing Yee's name, and gestured at the car.

"Is something wrong? Has something happened to Monk and Ham?"

The man gestured again to the car. She looked at Lester. He shrugged. "I don't like it," he said.

"I'm going."

"Then so am I."

They climbed into the back seat of the Buick. The two men slipped into the front seat and they pulled away from the curb.

They drove downtown. Lester and Norma tried various ways to communicate with the men but were met only with patient smiles. Finally they gave up and watched the city pass by their window. In no time they were entering Chinatown. Norma could see the tall pagoda roof of the bank on Canal Street. The car pulled to a halt in front of a building she recognized as one that Lester had pointed out to her last week.

"It's the Hip Sing Association," he said to her.

The two men got out of the car and opened the passenger doors. Lester and Norma stepped out. It was as busy as any day in Chinatown. They were escorted into the building.

Inside the small lobby stood Mr. Yee. He was elegantly dressed in a white Chinese jacket and pants. Instead of buttons the jacket had toggles made of knotted silk which slipped through loops. The lobby was festooned with regal decorations in advance of the upcoming unity parade which was to end here with a great feast.

"Yee," said Lester, "we're being kidnapped!"

"Oh, no!" Yee said, looking surprised. "My cooks refuse to learn English."

"Is everything all right?" Norma wanted to know. "Are Monk and Ham all right?"

"Yes," he said. "I'm very sorry to have upset you like this. This is a very special day." He snapped at the cook in a burst of spitfire Chinese which Norma figured probably translated along the lines of ". . . or at least it was supposed to be until you ruined it!"

"Why?" asked Lester.

"Because I am repaying my debt to you."

"What debt? You don't owe me anything."

"You have been my friends for many years and you stood up against that policeman. He came in this week and actually put money into the China fund. For this I am so grateful and as a Hip Sing man I am able to show my gratitude by welcoming you into the brotherhood as my brother." He looked at Norma. "I'm sorry the Hip Sing does not extend the same honor to women, but you will understand that my appreciation flows from your husband to you as well."

"Really?" She felt a little stab of disappointment.

"Yee," said Lester, "I don't know about this."

She took his arm with both hands. "My husband is honored by this." She turned her smile from one man to the other. "We both are."

"I didn't know that a white man could join the Hip Sing." Lester was still hesitant.

"On occasion and only to a certain degree," he replied, smiling at how well his surprise was playing out after all. "For example, you will never be called upon to marry a dead man's wife or return his bones to China. Will you follow me upstairs?" As he spoke he handed Lester clothes similar to his. "You will put these on when we enter the temple."

"Temple?"

"You will see."

The building had several floors. The doors on every floor were closed to them. The stairs were wide—a dozen men could easily stand shoulder to shoulder on the staircase—and the ceilings were tall. The air was fragrant with aromatic incense. The walls were lined with photographs and newspaper articles depicting the history of Chinese in America. Norma saw images of men working on the great railways, huddling together in alleys, gambling in saloons.

They reached the landing before the last staircase and at last saw another man. A Chinese warrior stood, bare-chested, at the top of the stairs. He had both hands on the hilt of a sword with the biggest blade Norma had ever seen. The point of the sword rested on the floor. They looked up at the man and he looked down at them.

"Mr. Yee," Lester asked, "is there any pain involved in becoming your brother?"

He shook his head. "No," he said. Then he added, "Just death."

"What?"

"It is merely a ritual death."

"Is that a better kind than regular death?"

Yee led Lester up the stairs. "Please lower your head when I tell you to. But quickly." Lester stood in front of the guard, who raised the broadsword to his shoulder like a batter.

"Now!"

The sword passed cleanly, with a whisper, over Lester's bowed head. Norma breathed a sigh of relief. The guard smiled at them both.

"Death is the necessary step on the road to enlightenment. Come," urged Mr. Yee, "Mock Sai Wing awaits."

"Who's that?" Lester asked.

"My uncle. He is a very important man. Your newspapers sometimes refer to him as Mock Duck," Yee said, with a proud smile. Norma made a mental note to remind herself to ask Lester why that name had caused him to stammer and go pale.

The guard opened the large double doors and led the two men under the arch into the joss house, a temple on the top floor of the building. It was as if a treasure chest had been opened in front of her eyes. Light streamed into the room from all sides through floor-to-ceiling windows. Red banners hung from the ceiling and posters decorated the pillars holding up the vaulted ceiling. There was a large statue of Buddha at the far end of the room and incense burned before it, filling the air with the smell of jasmine. Norma counted a dozen men in the room. They were all dressed, as Mr. Yee was, in elegant white silk pajamas. The men broke apart and formed two lines as

Norma and Lester entered. At the far end of the gauntlet they had formed stood an aged man. Norma recognized him as the old man who had been dining in the restaurant with them.

Lester looked around. There was nowhere for him to be modest, so he disrobed and dressed in full view of the other men.

"That's some scar on your uncle's neck," she said to Mr. Yee.

"Many years ago an assassin came right up to him in the street and shot him at point-blank range. And yet he survived. There is an old Chinese joke about Chinese men being bad shots. Not funny. But true."

Lester turned, dressed in black silk.

"Very good. Black is the color of destruction. After you are destroyed you will then be given the white clothes of healing."

"Okay."

"They will ask you many questions and I will translate and then help you respond. Are you ready to stand before Shen Yi, the Sun-God, and receive his arrows?"

"Ritual arrows, right?"

"Yes."

"I am."

Mr. Yee indicated that it was time for Norma to leave. Frustrated, she took a few steps back, letting the guard close the heavy, carved doors. She stepped up and put her eye to the seam and found she was still able to watch. Lester's eyes were sparkling with delight as he was escorted to the head of the gauntlet. Mr. Yee left him there and walked around to join his uncle at the end of the line. The men raised swords. As Lester walked down the line, each man lowered his sword and gently tapped Lester against the back of his neck. Norma breathed a sigh of relief as he reached the end and the last man. Then the two lines of men closed ranks behind him, blocking him from her view. She could see the top of his head nodding solemnly and hear his deep voice repeating Mr. Yee's soft responses. But she couldn't make out any details.

She was put out. She and Lester were partners in so many things they did. She wasn't used to being sidelined and didn't appreciate having the strictures of five thousand years of culture applied to her. She was pleased that Lester would have a new experience, but she wished she were having it with him. So it wasn't so much that she was bored or indifferent but more that she was a little jealous when she turned away from the ceremony for a few moments to look at the wall of old photographs behind her.

Many of the photos were of men who must have been members and the places they came from. One photograph in particular caught her attention. She recognized it as San Francisco's Chinatown, reduced to rubble in the aftermath of the great earthquake.

Her self-pitying indignation was swept away by a great thrill at the sight. Sitting placidly, untouched amidst the devastation, as if the walls of the surrounding temple had collapsed directly outward only to reveal it and the devastation as far as the eye could see, was her golden statue. As small as it was in the picture, it still leered horrendously at her. The delicious tingles of discovery swept down from the crown of her head. She wanted it. She wanted to go back to the theater and bring the world to see it. She wanted to grab Lester and show him, but he was in the middle of drinking some symbolic blood. At least, she hoped it was symbolic.

The ceremony ended with a great "*Ho!*" resounding from the room, which Mr. Yee later told her translated as "Good!" The great doors opened and she was invited to enter. Lester was beaming with pride. The men surrounded him and clapped him on the back. He changed back into his church clothes. Then, as a single mass sweeping her husband along, the men headed downstairs to celebrate.

Norma motioned for Mr. Yee and when he came to her she showed him the picture.

"What's that?" she asked.

"That is Tai Yi Jiu Ku Tian Cun," he replied. "The Judge of the Dead. The highest ruler in hell. He is carried forth by ten monks who represent the ten Lords of Death. Upon death all souls must appear before Tai Yi and be judged."

"Well, that Tai Yi," she said, unable to say the rest of the Chinese words, "that's the statue I found in the theater. I guess I didn't describe it well enough for you. That's my treasure."

He pursed his lips for a moment. "He is not a treasure to be found. He is an omen of great death and destruction. He is not something you should ever hope to see for real in your lifetime. He judges men and gods alike."

"Well, of course. I'd never want to see him for real. He sounds very unpleasant. But I'm talking about this statue, not the real god. This is a statue made of gold. Like this one in this picture of San Francisco thirty years ago. I'm sure of it. I'd love to take another look. I'd just love to! To just know."

His gentle dark eyes grew cloudy with worry for her. "You must not go back to the theater. You must not look for Tai Yi. Tai Yi comes when there is misery and sorrow and troubles, and many dead to judge. Look closer at the picture, Mrs. Dent. You say it is just a statue. How would you know a god if you met one?"

Episode Thirty-Two

"Dear Editor,'" The Flash read to Driftwood from the latest issue of *Astounding Stories*, "'This is to notify you of the official commencement of the Iowa City Science Fiction Advancement League at the Iowa University Law School. We wish to express our utmost appreciation to the publishers of *Astounding Stories* for the creation of such a worthwhile literary genre, adding many hours of enjoyment to the average Iowa law student's hectic life. The ICSFAL consists of seven full-time members—six students and one faculty member. In particular we wish to stress our admiration for the scope and detail of John Campbell's essays on the latest knowledge of the solar system. They are accurate and exciting and full of insight into OUR UNIVERSE NOW. Your articles show that good science writing can be as entertaining as good science fiction writing. Also, we are an organization wishing to grow and support science fiction, *our* fiction, and we are looking for new members in the Iowa City area who wish to join us or like-minded organizations across the country who share our mission and would like to establish larger communications. For us the living, I am, Randolph Farmer, Iowa Law Commons, Iowa City.'

"And there's three other science fiction club announcements just like it." He tossed the latest issue of *Astounding Stories* onto the table, where it began soaking up the dribbles of beer. "I'm telling you, Otis, there's a real gold mine in this science fiction. Something huge is happening here. It's bigger than Walter Gibson money or even Edgar Rice Burroughs money. I'm talking about publisher money. Tycoon money. A law student doesn't have time to scratch his own ass or chase girls, but he finds time to get a group together in a dormitory basement and spend an evening talking about rockets to the moon?"

"They're crazy?" Driftwood suggested. He picked up the magazine and thumbed through it. He had been staying at The Flash's hotel. The Flash had fronted him some cash until his disability checks were forwarded from California. The Flash didn't know exactly why he was trusting this stranger (after all, what kind of name was Otis Driftwood?) but he had taken a liking to the fellow and wanted to lend a hand up. Driftwood was a caustically cynical and suspicious son of a bitch, but he was funny and The Flash (who wasn't funny at all but admired people who were) enjoyed his company. After a morning spent writing he had gathered up Driftwood and hit the newsstand for the latest issue; then they had made their way to the White Horse for Dutch courage.

The brutal cold spell which had followed them down from Providence had lifted somewhat, though the warmth of the fireplace was still welcome. Few people had drifted in this afternoon: two boys barely old enough to drink were rifling through some papers in an open portfolio at the bar, and a tired drunk, whose head was slumped down on his chest, was drowsing near the drafting door.

"In the beginning was Hugo Gernsback and he begat *Amazing Stories.*" The Flash sighed wistfully. "Now there's a guy who could have had it all. What he must take to bed with him at night!"

"What happened?"

"He saw it all coming and he reached for the brass ring and missed it, that's all. Old Hugo was the ed on *Amazing Stories* and he saw that the mags that sold the best were the ones that had a science fiction story in them. Usually it was just a Welles or Verne reprint, but every month he'd have some new stuff. Well, a competitor to *Amazing Stories* was *Wonder Stories,* and it was on the verge of folding. Old Hugo scraped together every dime he had and he bought out the old *Wonder Stories* title and he started to publish mainly science fiction stories and it really took off.

"Then he started the SFL, the Science Fiction League, and sold club charters through the magazine. He made money off the stationery and stamps and pins and membership dues. So he's building something akin to the Boy Scouts, y'know? A nationwide network of fans who communicate with each other through his magazine and take their marching orders from him.

"Now the thing you gotta realize about the fans is that there are two types. There's the group that'll read science fiction and other stuff as well, but then there's this core group that takes it so seriously they won't read anything else. And you better get the science part right or you're going to be hearing it. And the core members in different cities start communicating with each other through the letters column and they're complaining that the mag isn't publishing their kind of stories, don't feel like they're being taken seriously enough, don't have enough of a voice in the rules or the charter of this club, and they revolt!

"Some of the core fans in Brooklyn announce the formation of the International Scientific Association, the ISA, a completely fan-run organization. Now old Hugo should have just let them have their moment in the sun and it would have faded away, probably. But instead he treated them as if they were important and he announced, in print, that they were officially expelled from the SFL. This turns them into revolutionary heroes in the eyes of the other core fans, right?

"Well, in protest, all these clubs start rejecting the SFL and *Wonder Stories.* This means money out of Hugo's pocket. So he has to sell the magazine to keep the club going. But what he doesn't realize is that without the mag he's got no way to talk to its members. He got shut out and the fans took over."

"Amen, brother!"

"Hear me out! Science fiction magazines are the only mags on the newsstands today where the sales numbers go up every month! So when I say there's big money to be made in this science fiction writing game, I mean there's big money there, Otis. It's virgin territory. That's what John Campbell believes. And I do too. I have high hopes of using science fiction to smash my name into history so violently that it will take a legendary form. I am going to write science fiction stories until my fingers drop off. And I tell you what. It's gonna make me rich."

"From writing?" Otis sipped his beer. "How many rich writers do you know? I guess a fella could do all right peddling hokum, but I don't know about rich. And speaking of hokum and malarkey, do you think he's full of crap?"

The Flash was confused. "Campbell?"

"No. Gibson."

"About what?"

"About the night watchman. Was that some bullshit?"

"Well, it does seem a *little* pulp."

"A little? I don't know, brother. Chinese murderers, and poison gas, and monsters?"

The Flash hesitated. He felt he had to defend Gibson. This guy, this stranger, had no idea what Gibson was really about. Not the way The Flash did. Who was this Otis Driftwood, anyway, to doubt a great pulp writer like Walter Gibson? If Gibson said there had been a chemical incident at the Providence Medical Lab, then a fella had to believe him, right?

"Well," he replied, drawing his words out in a hesitant manner, "real or pulp, I guess it doesn't matter. It's a hell of a story and I wish I had dibs on it."

"Sure, but . . ."

"I'm going to get the next round," The Flash interrupted, because obviously Driftwood wasn't going to and he didn't want to keep arguing about Gibson. He shook the kinks out of his legs and strolled over to the bar. Was it possible that Gibson was still tweaking him the way he had tweaked him with that Sweet Flower story? He leaned against the bar and ordered.

While he waited for the bartender to draw his beers, he looked over the shoulder of the two teens going through their portfolio.

"Funny pages?" he asked them.

"Kind of," said one. It came out *kaand uf.*

"Sort of," said the other. It came out *sert ef.*

"You boys are from Chicago, right?"

They nodded.

"We're trying to sell a comic book story," one of them said. He had jet-black hair. "Comic books are the next big thing. We came all the way in for a meeting with some publishers."

"We got turned down," the other one said.

"We got another meeting tomorrow," the first one said, none too optimistically.

The Flash looked over their shoulders. As far as he could tell it was a comic strip, even though there were a lot more panels on the page. The crude drawings seemed to show a muscular strongman in circus tights chasing some crooks. "Is he actually wearing a cape?"

The boys nodded.

The Flash shrugged and paid for the beers. "Seems to me as long as people can buy a book full of words and stories by real writers they ain't gonna want to pay the same price for a book of pictures," he said. "People like to read, boys. It's the most popular form of entertainment there is! If the movies and radio haven't got people to stop reading books, then nothing will. And by the way, at least Alex Raymond's stuff looks good."

Feeling pleased with himself for defending his chosen profession so vigilantly (but aware that he had just taken out his anxiety about Gibson and Driftwood on these two poor saps), he left them there and sauntered back to the table. He plunked Driftwood's beer down in front of him.

He was just settling back into his seat when the old drunk from across the room lurched up to their table.

"Aw, come on!" The Flash said. "What are you drinking? You smell like ammonia!"

"Hey, bub!" Driftwood asked the man. "You all right?"

The man wasn't as old as The Flash had thought he was at first. But if it were possible for a man to be a human shipwreck, then The Flash was looking at one. He was thin, thinner even than Driftwood. His skin was waxy and jaundiced, and The Flash was nearly certain that he could see the veins underneath.

"I used to be a writer," the man said. His jaw seemed locked in an unsettling position while his lips continued to move. This made it appear as if his voice was not cooperating with the movements of his mouth. The Flash had never seen anything quite like it before. Certainly not from any rummy. "I'm a writer."

"Of course you are. Everybody is," Driftwood said. "Have a seat here, brother, I'm gonna buy you a drink and you're gonna tell us a story." The Flash wished that Driftwood wouldn't encourage the stranger; he was getting an unsettling feeling about him. But Driftwood seemed to really enjoy the whole my-down-and-out-comrade routine, and The Flash could tell that he was getting earnest about speaking with the drunk. The bar was empty at the moment. The two boys from Chicago had packed up and left as soon as The Flash had finished speaking with them. The bartender was outside arguing with a shopkeeper from next door about a truck which had been blocking his store for two days. The bartender was maintaining that he'd had no delivery scheduled.

The man eased himself slowly into a chair. "Hot in here," he said. "Too hot."

"Because of the fireplace," The Flash pointed out sarcastically, really hoping now that the man would move along.

Driftwood shot him a look he wouldn't have expected from a man who owed him as many beers as he did. Then Driftwood looked back at the rummy and said, "You all right, friend?" His tone was genuine; he was concerned. But there was no response except the man's slow breathing. After a moment Driftwood shrugged, stood, and said, "I'm going to hit the head. When I come back we'll get this guy to the hospital."

The man seemed to be catching Driftwood's comment on an echo, lifting his head to watch him depart after a long moment of distracted thought. Hubbard smelled ammonia again. And something else. What was that other scent? Then it suddenly hit The Flash where he had smelled this before, this combination of ammonia and lavender.

"Christ in a handcar!" The Flash would have leapt out of his chair if the man's hand hadn't reached out and curled tightly around his wrist. His clutch was ice-cold. "You're a Christ almighty dead man!"

The thin gray man attempted to smile; at least the skin around his lips folded back to reveal some teeth. "Almost," he whispered.

"How? How? How?" The Flash's heart was pounding.

"Cool air. Ammonia. Certain elements, military elements, which help maintain the viability of life without life. It came to me, lurking in the shadows of my dreams. It's my own new science. Bionecrology. What do you think? I'm thinking of endowing a chair at Providence College. If I had left any money." He tried to laugh; it sounded like a cat retching.

"This is impossible. We buried you," The Flash said.

"You came to my house. You talked with my aunt. I heard one of you say you came here. So I've been waiting." His head drooped to his chest momentarily and when, with great effort, it rose back up, it hung to his right and stayed there, awkwardly. "It's too hot," he said almost apologetically. "Watched you all at my aunt's house but couldn't talk. Wasn't sufficiently reanimated."

The Flash looked on in disgust as a thin black fluid dribbled down the back of the hand still gripping his arm. He clapped his hand over the bony wrist. He instantly realized there was no pulse. And yet he could not remove himself from the clasp. When he pulled his hand away there were bits of flesh clinging to it. The Flash asked in horrified amazement, "Are you rotting?"

The man's body jerked with a spasm. He put his hands with their long spidery fingers on the table to steady himself. "Is Walter Gibson coming? I wanted to see him. I tried to call him." He looked up at them with a pathetically desperate and haunted look in his eyes. A piece of flesh tore free of his cheek, and an eyeball began to sink into its socket. The Flash could see the revealed muscle contracting. It began to turn gray even as he looked. The Flash shook his head and the other man managed an expression that resembled sadness.

"What happened?" Hubbard asked. "Tell me about the lab. Tell me what happened. Tell me about the gas."

"The gas. That's why I'm here." He seemed to draw some energy from rediscovering his mission. "In its day it was so new that it wasn't even given a name. It was just known as 'the gas,' or sometimes 'that shit.' It's only effective as a gas for a very short time. It's extremely volatile in its liquid form, which makes it doubly effective as a gas and an explosive, so even though it dissipates quickly, it covers a lot of ground before. Reaches a lot of troops. In its gaseous state you definitely have to inhale it for it to kill you. It might burn your skin a little, but the gas won't kill you if you don't breathe it in. If you do get a full lungful, it kills you fast. So fast you end up looking like you froze where you were. That's the best death you can hope for.

"Say you're a little farther back from the gas when it's released and don't inhale it at full strength. It will still kill you, but instead of fast and painful, it's slow and even more painful. It'll make you wish you had just taken a deeper breath. Days, or even weeks. All the liquid is slowly drawn out of your organs as you dehydrate from within. Your skin turns transparent and you can practically see the muscles and veins beneath. Through it all, you never lose your mental acuities. Your mind stays as sharp as ever, which is how you want it as your body melts like a candle from the inside out. That's what happened to me.

"But it's while it's in the liquid state that it is particularly horrifying. It seems that there is something about its nature, when it's concentrated into that form, that really lets it get into a person in a horrible way. Only a small amount coming in contact with the skin seems to drive directly toward the central nervous system. Your mind goes before your body does. Imagine the worst case of rabies madness you've ever seen in a dog transferred to a man. There was a watchman at the lab; I fear for his soul."

"Where did the gas come from?"

The man nodded in his dreamlike way. "Colonel Towers came to us one evening just after the new year with a discovery he had made in some old army files. A record of a weapon lost and forgotten over twenty years ago."

"Who's Colonel Towers?"

"A frightening man, Colonel Towers. There must be men like him in every army throughout history—the kind of soldier the army can't do without but fears one day will turn against it. The kind of officer who leads a coup. A Caesar. A Cromwell. Extremely erudite and well traveled. I know he speaks a dozen languages and there hasn't been a war on this globe in the past thirty years, no matter how far-flung, that he hasn't observed on behalf of his masters. He journeys wherever the winds of war are blowing. He's an instigator and a meddler. He doesn't really have a command, but neither does he seem to be commanded. He's a man to be regarded with respect, even though he may be of the most villainous nature. A man like Towers needs to be at war, needs a war of his own. I believe that is what he has sought all these years. That's what led him to discover the gas. And its whereabouts.

"Harmony Isle. A little outcropping of Perdition on earth. Towers and Jeffords hired the *Zephyr* and went. I think Towers must have already known the power that was within his grasp and he began to erase his tracks even at that moment, for when they returned, the crew, good local men I had grown up with and worked with, had been left behind. Jeffords insisted there had been an accident. But I think they were abandoned there. It was left to us—the few researchers at the lab, myself, Towers, Jeffords, and the night watchman—to bring the deadly cargo into the lab. Into our lives. Back into the world.

"Jeffords and his crew worked diligently around the clock. Towers wanted a neutralizing agent, an antidote. Some key which would allow him to open his demon box safely. Meanwhile, he would leave for long stretches at a time. Finally, several weeks ago, I transcribed the fruitful results of the research. A formula. We had discovered Towers's key.

"I've seen that at the moments of greatest triumph in life, the moments of greatest disaster are not far behind. The metal drum that the chemical was transported in was old and had been rusted by its exposure to salt air. The researchers had taken great care to remove only the amount they needed to work with, so that it needed to be touched only when absolutely necessary. But still, as they say, accidents happen. And then I saw why Towers wanted this abomination. I saw firsthand, in an instant, what it could do."

He coughed, unable to clear the rattle from his throat. "Afterward, when I realized I had time to live, I destroyed every bit of our work. I thought that would be enough to stop Towers. That without the neutralizing agent he would be unable to use it. I thought it was enough and I thought I could do more. But I should have known better. And I was so afraid. Of dying." He tried to laugh and it turned into a seizure which convulsed his body, and he doubled over, his head hitting the table. He brought himself upright, the skin peeling away from his skull where it had impacted upon the wood. The black fluid streamed down his face.

"What can I do?" Hubbard asked.

The man slid The Flash's magazine around to him. "Never got published here," he wheezed. "Barely ever got published. Not leaving much behind." He picked up a pen and scribbled something on its cover. He set the pen down. "My last story," he said. "Get this to Walter Gibson. He'll get it to someone who can stop Towers before he uses more of the gas. I know he will."

He collapsed on the table with a moist thud.

"Holy hell! What happened?" Driftwood was back. The Flash felt barely able to breathe. One by one he lifted the dead man's fingers from his arm until he was finally able to remove the hand.

"Is he dead?" Driftwood asked. Driftwood reached out and gave the bony shoulder a shove. He nodded at The Flash.

"Goddammit!" exclaimed the bartender, bursting into the room. "Some ass drove an ice truck all the way down here from Providence and then just abandoned it in front for two friggin' days." He looked at them. "What the hell's going on here? Is that guy dying in here? People can't die in here. We'll get a reputation!"

"Relax, Pete," said The Flash to the bartender. He picked up the magazine, looking for meaning in the last words the man had written. But all he could see scrawled was cockeyed gibberish. "If it means anything to you, he didn't really die here."

Episode Thirty-Three

THE URGENT pounding at the door startled her.

She had been reading a letter to Kenneth Robeson from a little boy in Beavercreek, Ohio, who was nine years old. He had just read his first issue of *Doc Savage* and had fallen in love with it. This little boy wanted to be a writer when he grew up, just like Kenneth. Norma answered all of Lester's fan mail. She had a stack to her left and they were all similar to the one she had been reading. As she had reread the letter she heard the young boy's voice speaking of his hopes and dreams for a meaningful life of excitement and adventure as embodied by Doc Savage. These were Lester's boys. She had wondered if he ever really knew what an important part of these lives he had become. But she knew when it came down to it that no one understood better than he.

When she opened the door, there stood two young men she didn't recognize. One of them was short and stocky and had a loose mop of curly red hair on the top of his head. The other was tall and slender and handsome with deep, dark eyes. The redhead was wild-eyed, as if he had just come from an exciting ball game. The other man kept his eyes down and seemed uncomfortable.

"Lester," she called, and the sound of typing stopped. "You have company."

"Well. That is some story, fellas," Lester said at last, looking up from his coffee and giving Norma a sly uplifted eyebrow. "It ends like it should, with the cops taking a body away."

"It's not my story," Otis said. The two men sat across from the Dents at their comfortable little kitchen table, which had once belonged to Norma's grandmother. He seemed reluctant to speak and she gave him a smile of encouragement. "Ron's the one saying he's who he says he was. Maybe he's just been hiding out in Providence this whole time while Gibson's gas was killin' him slowly, but before it did he came down to New York. Don't I know that it's easy enough to go underground. And that it's easy enough to go crazy while you're doing it. All I know is some poor son of a bitch died in a bar, pardon my French, ma'am."

"That's all right," she replied. "I'm fluent."

Lester cleared his throat. "And you haven't found Mr. Gibson?" He rose and went to the bookshelf while they answered.

They shook their heads simultaneously. It was almost comical how perfectly they were matched, she thought. Like Laurel and Hardy except that Otis was much better looking than Stan Laurel. More like Leslie Howard. But together they were quite a pair.

"Absolutely not, Mr. Dent. Absolutely not. We actually tried to find him, but we haven't had any luck. We've been to his apartment and the doorman said he hasn't been there in days," Ron said. "And Nanovic told us that he missed a couple of story meetings for the first time. We went by his train. We can't find him."

"If this is something Walter Gibson is involved in," Norma said crossly, "then we want no part of it." She folded her arms defiantly and looked at the two men. "His is not a welcome presence in my home."

"I . . . I'm sorry, Mrs. Dent." Otis looked at Hubbard. "I thought you said they were friends."

The word made Norma laugh. "A friend? Walter Gibson? I can

think of a lot of things that Walter is, but a friend is not one of them! Do you know that he nearly ruined us once?"

"Look, Mr. and Mrs. Dent, I'm really sorry about all this." Otis lit a cigarette. His hands were trembling. "I don't really know Mr. Gibson. But it seems to me that whenever his name comes up, it's always in relation to something that's almost impossible to believe."

"Hey!" Hubbard sat up.

"Listen, brother. I wasn't there for the night watchman. I wasn't there for any of the talk you had with that rummy, and that's what I'm calling him, 'cause that's what he was. I do know, however, when I came back he was dead. But for all I know everything else is just a big lie."

"Or a pack of lies?" Lester asked, still at the bookcase. He held a large chart book of northeastern waters and was thumbing through the index.

"Exactly!" affirmed Otis with satisfaction.

"Well. In the absence of Mr. Gibson, one way to find out whether this is pulp or real would be to find Harmony Isle."

"Uh . . ." Otis seemed confused. "Okay."

"But there is no Harmony Isle in Long Island Sound." Lester studied a page closely.

"Are you sure?" Ron said, sounding disappointed.

"Well, this is a pretty comprehensive survey of the coast from Nova Scotia down to the Outer Banks. There is no Harmony Isle."

"Damn!" Ron slammed his hand down, rattling the coffee cups on the kitchen table.

"Nope. Like I said. No Harmony Isle." Lester said, shooting Norma a sly grin. "But there is a Haimoni Isle." He put the chart on the table and pointed to a tiny isle between Long Island and Connecticut. "*Haimoni* sounds a good bit like *Harmony* when you think about it. Doesn't it?"

Both men nodded. "When you put that New England accent behind it, it could," Otis said begrudgingly. Norma found herself wishing that she could introduce him to some of her friends back in La Plata. The unmarried ones.

Lester thumbed quickly through another book and found what he was looking for. "Haimoni. I thought it rang a bell." He snapped the book shut. "The Haimoni Indians lived in hut villages along the coast of Connecticut thousands of years before the Pequot and Quinnipiac tribes took over the area. Haimoni Isle was the site of their sacred stone. It was an altar upon which their shaman would perform ritual human sacrifices to the fishing spirits.

"According to legend, a shaman once refused to sacrifice the woman he loved upon the altar. That night a storm raised the waters so high that they tipped the stone on its side. The entire tribe was swept away in the flood. Long after they vanished, the legend of the Haimoni Stone lived on and the other Indian tribes considered it a cursed place. Evil."

"Oh," said Driftwood, "*that* Haimoni Isle!"

Norma took up the chart and studied it. She traced her finger toward the little speck on the map and she could see her fingernail quiver as she did. "We should go," she heard herself blurt out. The men turned to look at her. "We should go there."

"Norma, it's the middle of the night in the dead of winter."

"It's the only way to know for sure."

"But isn't this Mr. Gibson's problem?"

"Oh, to hell with Mr. Gibson! What could he possibly know that we don't know? Don't you want to go see? I want to go see."

"It's an easy trip from Providence," said Lester. "Not so easy from New York. The *Albatross* is docked at Seventy-second Street. She'd have to be brought around the bottom of Manhattan and up the East River to get into the sound. If the winds prevail from the southeast it could take a day and a night's sail just to get there. And that's if I get her through Hell Gate in one piece."

"Mr. Dent," Otis said in a reassuring tone. Norma found herself resenting his earnest charm because she found it so hard to resist. "I am an Annapolis graduate and a retired officer of the U.S. Navy. There's no vessel I can't sail and no sea I can't sail her through."

"Now you want to go?" Lester asked.

"I'm gonna wait for you to come back and tell me another story?

Maybe this one will be about Atlantis! No. I'm going to see for myself what's pulp and what's real."

"I'm sorry," said Ron with a nervous note in his voice. "Did you say something about something being called Hell Gate? You're actually considering sailing a boat through something called Hell Gate to get to a cursed Indian island? Maybe it's just because I'm a pulp writer, but does any part of this sound like it might be a bad idea?"

"Come on, Hubbard!" Otis replied. "Weren't you the one telling about all your great sailing voyages on the USS *Nitro,* from Shanghai to Guam to Hawaii to Seattle on a three-masted corvette? From lookout to first mate too. Never saw a man rise that fast in the U.S. Navy. So I'm going to let you have the helm."

"I'm skipper," Dent muttered, "that's my decision."

"I recommend L. Ron Hubbard for the helm, skipper," Otis said.

"Sure," Lester grunted.

"No, wait!" Ron jumped up. His face was deep red. "I can sail. I can. That particular trip that, that there, my parents paid for."

"It was a cruise?" Driftwood was shocked.

"Of a serious nature. And there were times when I performed a mate's duties, bringing the coffee to the deck in the morning. And I did get to go up to the crow's nest several times in calm seas as long as there was a sailor already up there." He chewed on his finger. "I was fourteen."

"You made it sound like it was a year or two ago."

"He's young at heart," Norma rushed to his defense. Otis smiled and for her sake decided to stop haranguing Hubbard, for the time being.

Lester, still concerned, asked Ron, "You do have a boat, right? You do sail a boat?"

"I day-sail a sixteen-footer."

"Then you're on winches."

Ron's face was still red. Norma noticed that Ron was so mad at his companion that he couldn't bring himself to look at Otis. Otis, appearing self-satisfied, pretended not to notice. She made a small show of pouring a fresh cup of coffee for him, adding sugar lumps and stirring it for him. When Otis rattled his cup for coffee, she left the pot at the side of the table and he had to cross Ron to get it.

Thump! Lester put his index finger heavily down on the map at the point where the East River merged into the Long Island Sound. "This is Hell Gate," he said. "You see the East River is not really a river. It's a tidal estuary. So it doesn't really flow so much as it just sloshes back and forth like soup in a bowl. This spot right here is where the edge of the estuary flowing back and forth one way meets the currents of the sound flowing crosswise against it, which causes the water depth to change unpredictably. Which only matters because there are shallows and rocks which can sometimes spring up and slash a ship's hull open. Meanwhile the wind is bringing additional pressure to bear on the irregular currents and sometimes opens a whirlpool. Hell Gate is an open water cemetery. In 1904 the steam ferry *General Slocum* on a Lutheran picnic outing caught fire and became trapped in the swirling waters of Hell Gate. Over a thousand women and children went down right there in broad daylight in full view of Manhattan, Queens, and the Bronx. An entire New York neighborhood was destroyed in a single moment." He tapped the ashes out of his pipe and gazed into the empty bowl for a moment.

Norma took his other hand. "We've been through Hell Gate before. Several times. Just the two of us."

"Not at night with ice on the water." He rose and put the chart back on the bookcase.

She took a cigarette from Otis's open pack and lit it. The two young men both looked at her with surprise. Evidently they hadn't been prepared for Lester Dent's wife to show much interest in their goings-on. Am I up for another adventure? she thought to herself. No, was the answer. No. Don't leave the house. Don't leave your safe cave. There are grocery lists to prepare and biscuits to cook. You don't need adventure to make Lester look at you the way you used to like him to. She rose and went to his side and spoke comfortingly to him.

"We'll have two more able-bodied seamen. We might find some proof, and then what a story you'll have!"

"And if not?"

"Then at the least we'll have had a bit of an adventure."

"I thought you didn't want any more adventures."

Wrong, she countered in her head. I need adventure to make myself look at me the way I used to like to. "This will hardly be an adventure. More like an outing."

"Okay." He nodded but he still looked gravely concerned.

She gave him a quick kiss. "Ain't adventure luck the goddamnedest thing?"

Episode Thirty-Four

"Is it always this rough?" Hubbard hollered back from the bow of the *Albatross.* He was lying on his belly with his head hanging over the deck above the water and shining a light into the foam below.

"Are you kidding?" Driftwood yelled back from the helm, the wheel ever so slightly under his hand. "This is some of the best sailing weather I've ever seen."

"Keep that torch on the water," Dent roared from belowdecks where he was reading charts. "It's the only way we'll see the rocks coming."

Hubbard whipped the beam of light back onto the water. "And icebergs!" he shouted.

"Ice drifts!" Dent bellowed. "There are no icebergs on the East River!"

Driftwood smiled as he imagined what Hubbard was muttering to himself. From what he had seen of the man in the little time he had spent with him over the past week, Hubbard considered himself quite the dashing adventurer, so it was amusing to see how high-strung he turned out to be in what was admittedly a tense situation. The man could handle himself around a boat, though; Driftwood had to give him credit for that.

He felt great. The wind was brisk and smacked his face like the northern Atlantic waters he had sailed only a few years before. The *Albatross* was a beautiful ketch: a forty-foot blue-water sailer with a clipper's prow, which he adored on a boat. They had reefed in the jib and the mainsail, and with a little help from a sturdy engine she sliced through the East River at a handsome twelve knots with barely a groan from her solid planks as she heeled to port. Chunks of ice flowed by at a distance on either side.

"It's four a.m.," Mrs. Dent said. She stood next to Driftwood in the open, the collar on her oilskin turned up. Her cheeks were flushed with windchill and excitement. Her blond hair spilled out from under her black wool cap. Under the pretense of thoroughly checking his sail trim, he snuck looks at her. She was a damn beautiful lady, he thought. She had those steel-gray eyes he loved in a woman, and the beautiful breasts he loved even more. She was tall, and from what he had seen she had some pair of legs as well.

Between the silver mine and his time on the run, he hadn't given much thought to women; that wasn't his style in general. But now being this close to one who was as pretty as Mrs. Dent was really distracting. Fortunately he had the upcoming Hell Gate to keep his mind focused. Not to mention Mr. Dent.

But did she have to have that low, come-hither voice as well? "You know there's a fortune in treasure right below us?"

"Hm?"

"The *General Slocum*'s only one of many ships that went down here. In 1780 the British war frigate the HMS *Hussar,* a privateer, sank here. Not only was she carrying the gold and silver for the payroll of the British troops in America during the Revolutionary War, but on the crossing she had seized one French ship and two American ships and taken their wealth. Then she had rendezvoused with another British treasure ship and its contents were transferred to her as well because her ribs were considerably stronger. She was supposed to deliver this fortune to the payroll office on Cherry Street. But upon entering the East River, her captain received intelligence that two French frigates were hot on her tail.

"The ship was too weighed down to make it back into open water, so the captain decided to sail into the sound and seek the protection of the British forts and fleets which were stationed there. On her way through Hell Gate she hit a rock and sank like solid gold stone. No one's ever been able to recover even a farthing, but they say that in today's market the value of the treasure would easily be over one hundred million dollars. Only there's no way to get at it." She sighed and looked longingly down into the deep, dark water. "Can you imagine? All that treasure is probably less than sixty feet away."

"When you talk about treasure you get some look in your eyes," he managed. "A glow." He suddenly felt like he was falling in love. It was the best part of a romance, that falling. He tried out one of his most charming smiles on her as he slipped the wheel a few degrees against the deceptive currents. "You come alive."

"Thank you, Mr. Driftwood." She smiled back, but her smile did not seem to acknowledge the magic of his smile.

Driftwood. He hated lying to these nice people about who he was, hiding his identity like Paul Muni in *I Am a Fugitive from a Chain Gang.* He'd love to tell Norma all about himself, see how he measured up in her eyes against her husband. But he was scared. That's what it came down to. Fear. He didn't believe that these three people could betray him to a murderous gangster back in California; it wasn't about them. It was about never letting his guard down, not even for a moment.

"Don't we need an expert up here?" Hubbard shouted back.

"Just keep her in the main channel for now," Dent answered, already sounding distracted. This was followed by a brief racket.

"Lester?" Norma called.

"I'm okay."

"I'm sure you are. What are you doing?"

"Getting some gear together."

"I don't believe you'll need your metal detector out here."

"We might."

"I don't think so. Now how about coming up and helping out like you said you would?"

"In a minute."

Otis caught her amused, affectionate smile and felt a spike of jealousy stab up through him. He was suddenly glad Lester was below. He gently pinched the boat up a couple of degrees and saw what he had been looking for.

"Wake!" he called and the boat bobbed roughly over some small waves smacked back from the shoreline. He heard a crash from below, as of pots and pans clattering from cabinets, and an oath from Lester. The sudden list upset Norma's balance, causing her to pivot and slide against him. He caught her and steadied her, feeling a hint of her body through the heavy fabric.

"Watch those waves, sailor!" It sounded like Lester was extracting himself from whatever mess had been made.

"Aye aye, Cap'n," Driftwood called back, sounding as seriously innocent as he could. Norma secured her footing, though she remained close enough that he could sense her warmth, and he returned his hand to the wheel. "Sorry about that," he said, sincerely. "Little rough out tonight."

"Does your wife know where you are tonight?" she suddenly asked him, touching the tanned ring finger on his left hand, right below the knuckle. It would be years before the sallowness of that thin band of flesh disappeared completely.

Her directness caught him off balance just as his ship maneuver had, he hoped, caught her. Her eyes, which had seemed so placid and reflective moments ago, now snapped with electricity, focused on him. He felt as if he were the sole focus of her world, and his mouth went dry. When she arched a curious eyebrow, his resolutions about exposing himself vanished. He would answer any question she asked. He'd even give up his name. If she'd ask.

"Actually, I'm divorced," he said. "My former wife went crazy."

"Most men say that about their wives."

"Yeah, well, mine really did. I'll give you the address of the asylum."

She blinked and he searched her eyes for any new meaning, empathy, compassion, comfort. The cold air was playing hell with his weak lungs and made his chest ache. He cleared his throat. "It all happened while I was away in the navy. She didn't come out of the basement for weeks. They had to break the door down to get to her. Her parents wanted to help more than I could, and she responded to them better than to me. We found a judge who could divorce us so they could have more control over her care. You probably think that makes me a real heel."

"Oh, no," she said. He was hoping she'd put a hand on his, but she didn't. Well, there was time. Since they were obviously on a snipe hunt, he could look forward to a long and leisurely sail with lots of easy time to talk with the missus while her mister was playing Wolf Larsen.

"Anyway, she's better now, I hear. She's been out of the hospital for about a year. But she's never forgiven me for the divorce. And I think she never will."

"Ahoy, Ron!" Dent interrupted from deep in the vessel, thumping on the cabin ceiling.

"Try and give us a little more warning on those wakes, Otis, all right? Some of us get banged around more than others." Norma said it slowly and softly. Driftwood could feel her gaze on him drift away, but he felt that she hadn't yet decided what to make of him. But she had called him Otis. The next conversation he had with her would be about her marriage, and he already knew where to start: how could someone as graceful as she be married to such a great lumbering ox and an obvious coward to boot? She'd had to practically drag him out tonight, when anyone who truly loved her would have risen to the challenge in a moment, inspiring her passions and arousing her spirits.

"What? What?" Ron's voice was thin and strained.

"You know how you were asking on the way to the marina whether I had any tricks to writing pulps?"

"Sure. But . . ."

"I've got a little thing I call the master plot." Lester poked his head out of the cabin vent. It was a little like watching a cuckoo pop out of a clock. Driftwood focused on a smokestack on the Queens side of the river. "It's a formula, a blueprint for any yarn. It's guaranteed, surefire, bulletproof, works every time, and you're on the boat to prove it." Then he dropped back below.

"Oh, you don't have to go into that right this minute."

"First." Lester was moving back and forth, and with each trip he piled more gear onto the deck. As he moved, his voice faded, then grew louder in a rhythm which ran with the surge of the sea. "You need to come up with a different murder method for your villain, a different thing for the villain to be seeking, an exotic locale, and a menace which hangs like a cloud over your hero."

"No, really! Les!"

"In the first line or as near thereto as possible, introduce your hero and swat him with a fistful. Just shovel that grief onto him. Something the hero has to cope with, like an incredibly difficult physical conflict."

"Like a huge God-blasted ship?" Hubbard practically screamed. "Right in goddamn front of us! Is that enough of an incredibly difficult physical conflict for you?"

Lester dropped his gear and sprang swiftly to the forestay. Hubbard clumsily used the sheets to steady himself as he met Dent there. Driftwood stood tense at the wheel, years of naval training filling him with the preparation to instantly execute an incoming order from his senior officer.

The freighter was black, and running without lights. She rose up out of the murky waters like an ancient leviathan risen to the surface for a great gasp of air. Driftwood now realized that he had been sensing the thrumming of her engines for some little while as it had grown closer, without knowing what it was. "Her helmsman can't see us!" From where he stood, the other ship appeared motionless in the water. Which meant that they were on a collision course.

"Ship ho!" Dent called. "Ship ho!" Even his deep voice seemed overwhelmed by the dark ship. There was no response. Hubbard shouted and waved his flashlight at the ship, to no effect.

"I'll get on the radio," Norma said to Driftwood and started below.

"Don't bother," he replied, and she paused. "Not enough time," he said with a shrug.

"Come about!" Dent was moving quickly aft toward the rigging, Hubbard following on the port side.

"Coming about," Driftwood rolled the wheel over, feeling the sensation of the rudder flexing against the boat's motion. The *Albatross* skidded in the current like a sled which had hit an ice pond at the bottom of a steep snowy hill. The slope of the deck pitched over a few degrees and the bow began to head to starboard. Dent finished wrapping his sheet around the winch. Then he slid across the cabin roof to Hubbard's side. He grabbed a gaff stick. "Hubbard," he shouted. "Get behind me." Hubbard moved behind Lester. "Get ready to fend off!"

"What do you mean?"

"I mean that if that ship gets too close we're going to have to use this stick to push away from her. Here, grab the end."

"Against that?"

Lester resolutely braced himself. Holding the long shaft, prepared to plunge it against the side of the rising blackness, he appeared to Driftwood like a harpooner of old preparing to strike boldly against some giant, wrathful whale. The freighter was less than its own length out. Hubbard's flashlight beam played upon her prow; streaks of rust and age had not entirely corroded away the letters stenciled there years before: *Star of Baltimore.*

"Ready!" Dent shouted to them all.

Driftwood realized that none of them, not even Norma, were wearing life vests. He could now see the motion of the freighter; the rushing gap between them was closing. Its great black hull loomed over them. Dwarfed into insignificance by its massiveness, Hubbard instinctively stepped back from the rail. Driftwood hung on to the wheel, fighting the turbulence as the *Albatross* thumped heavily into the *Star of Baltimore*'s bow wake. The sailboat shook from stem to stern; he heard the contents belowdecks slide across the galley floor.

Dent stabbed the gaff at the black hull, and as it made contact, he braced himself against the cabin. Driftwood slid the throttle of the weak engine up as high as it would go and felt the *Albatross* surge in response. The gap between the two vessels, measurable in inches, held steady. He had to keep the stern from sliding into the *Star of Baltimore* as the bow turned away. A foot of space opened between the two boats. The metal hook on the end of the gaff caught hold of something and was ripped from Lester's grip. Two feet. Norma grabbed Otis's arm. With a glance he could see that she was watching the action unfold with pure carnal delight; her eyes glittered even more brightly than when she had spoken of treasure. Three feet. As the gaff slid past him, dangling in the air, he could see that the hook had snagged the latch on the watertight hull door. Dent had speared his Leviathan.

They cleared the stern and skittered across the last of the foam and turmoil churned up by the ship's big prop. To Driftwood, the impact of the final heavy bounce seemed right beneath his feet; at the same instant he felt the throttle go lifeless in his hand, the steady vibration suddenly ceasing. He looked behind him, to starboard; almost as quickly as the ship of mystery had appeared out of the elemental darkness, she had allowed herself to be swallowed back up into it. Almost simultaneously with its disappearance, he felt the currents settle as they made the transition from the murky, icebound waters of the East River to the calm waters of Long Island Sound.

He felt warm, soft lips against his cheek. The flush was gone from Norma's face; she was ashen, but the intensity of her eyes was still stirring.

"Good job," she said.

He nodded. She took one of his cigarettes from his jacket pocket, lit it, and handed it to him. He shook his head. His hands were stuck to the wheel. She stuck the cigarette between his lips and he inhaled deeply.

"Damn Sunday drivers," he muttered grimly. She smiled, just as grim. "I think I killed the engine."

"It's okay."

"Do we go back?"

She shook her head. "No."

Hubbard sat heavily on the cabin roof. "It was the ghost of the *General Slocum,* right?"

Dent stood above him, leaning against the mainmast for support, and staring at the wide, long wake of the vanished vessel. "That reminds me. The most important writing tip of all?" He turned his eyes toward the east, the sound. He lit up his pipe and grinned. "Avoid monotony."

Episode Thirty-Five

LIFE ON the water had its own rhythm, which they became a part of easily.

Lester and Hubbard spent time below with the engine, but while it was not leaking fuel, and the bilge pump was functioning properly, its silence remained beyond their ability to divine without dry-docking the vessel and giving it careful attention. They both suspected the jamming of a piston; perhaps one of the rods had snapped as the boat had been tossed about. Nevertheless, the wind was strong and steady and they forged ahead through a day that was bright and clear. Dead reckoning and the sighting of landmarks along the Connecticut coast to confirm their location on the chart came easily to all of them, confirming their steady progress throughout the day.

In a bleary fog at the end of her noon shift, when she should have curled up in the warm spot Lester had recently vacated, Norma laid out roast beef, a beefsteak tomato, lettuce, mustard, mayonnaise, and home-baked bread which she had brought from the apartment. One thing marriage had taught her was that there were few things a man better liked to be in control of, and few things that gave him a greater sense of control, than the creation of his own sandwich. She set the platter aside on the galley table and set about refreshing the coffee. Then, feeling a little more in control herself, she climbed into their bunk.

As she lay between consciousness and sleep she could hear the men above discussing airplanes; Lester loved to fly and Hubbard was claming to be an accomplished pilot who had flown on expeditions over China, India, and Tibet.

"You look really good for your age," she heard Otis crack wise. "It'd take most men forty or fifty years to do all the things you say you've done."

Dent roared with laughter while Ron protested the veracity of his claims. As the young man, who did seem prone to exaggerating, launched into a detailed biography of his life, she heard someone come down the ladder. Moments later, Lester crept quietly into the cabin and slipped under the sheets to lie next to her. She could feel the cold air flowing off his body and she pressed against him to give him warmth.

"Getting any sleep?" he whispered.

"Sure," she said. "Sounds like the boys are getting a little testy. They may not get their milk and cookies later."

"What about me?" he asked, snuggling closer.

"No," she said, slapping his thigh lightly. "Because then you'll just want to sleep through your watch."

When she went on deck later for her shift, Ron was sulking. She began talking to him about his children and soon his dark clouds began to dissipate. His mood became downright giddy when, several watches later, he was the first to lay eyes on their destination.

The small island rose out of the fog to meet them in the gathering gloom of nightfall. Its shores were high and rocky. Here and there they could see trees clinging to the top of the sea cliffs.

"It looks as if there's a deepwater mooring on the windward side." Lester said, looking up from the charts. Otis turned the wheel appropriately while Ron let out the sails.

Norma kept her eyes on the water looking for rocks. The water was black, with a prismatic oily sheen glistening on top. "There's a dock," she shouted. The wood was old and untended, and there were planks missing, but it was obvious from the length and width of the dock that it had been built to support large, oceangoing vessels. Without an engine to help they had to retry their approach under sail several times before Hubbard was finally able to leap to the dock and make the spring lines fast. Night had fallen heavily across the sound by the time Norma finally set foot upon the creaking wood of the dock. She could see the lights from distant dwellings twinkling far across the water, beckoning her to come out of the lonely cold and back to the warmth of home.

The rocky shore blocked the wind and all became silent and motionless. A dank stink of decay rose from the ground, as if seaweed and more had been washing into the isle's rocky crevices for hundreds of years and rotting. Upon everything was a haze of oppression, a miasma of the unreal and the grotesque. The large, bare rocks which formed the isle swept up in odd angles away from the waterline, until some fifty yards above and ahead of them the party could see the twisted shapes of small, ugly, leafless trees which struggled to survive here.

"Stygian," said Ron.

"Cimmerian," Otis agreed.

"Like Skull Island in miniature."

Norma saw Lester tuck his pistol into his coat pocket and realized that this was what he had been rummaging for earlier.

"Got one of those for me?" Otis asked.

Lester shook his head. "Sorry. Let's go." He led them down the short way to the end of the dock, where the wood met the outcropping. "Look at all these fresh scrapes," he said. "Someone's been here recently."

"A lot of fellas by the look of it," Ron added.

Carved into the rocks was a smooth, narrow path which ran quickly uphill and disappeared in a small grove of those gnarled trees. They set off up the steep, moss-lined trail, their flashlight beams looking nearly solid in the dank mist. The trees in the grove were low and withered, their branches spread out just above the explorers' heads and occasionally snagging the taller men, Lester and Otis. At one point, Lester held them up and urged silence. They each strained to hear what he had heard, but if there had been a sound, it was not repeated. They clambered on.

"Hey, Otis," Norma heard Ron whisper nervously, "who's your favorite writer?"

She could hear the tension in Otis's voice as well. "Can we close the writing salon for the time being?" he snapped. "This place is giving me the willies."

"Sure," said Ron. "Not a problem. You can all keep playing the heroes. I'm still just a pulp writer." She could hear him muttering a list of writers to himself, as if summoning them and the spirit of their tales to ward off the dangers of this night. "Of course, Jack London sets the standard for all of us. Hemingway? Honestly, I don't get the big deal. He couldn't handle real pulp. The Brits? Kipling, Doyle, and Conrad. Stevenson and Wells. Are the Brits better at pulp than we are? Maugham. Did I say that right? How do you say *Maugham,* really? Is it with an f sound or an h or is the gh completely silent?"

He grew silent as they crested the top of the hill and the path leveled out. The trees were sparse up here and craggy boulders jutted up from the gray ashy dirt. They could see the ocean on all sides from this vantage point.

"I can see the Empire State Building." She pointed out the distant light to Lester. "It looks like a star on the horizon."

"I wonder what's worse when it comes down to it?" Hubbard's nervous monologue began again. "Is a bandit worse than a brigand? Is a crook more dangerous than a thief? Why do we have more words for *villain* than *hero?*"

At the entrance to the clearing was a rusted chain-link fence clinging vaguely to leaning ground posts. The remains of an old gate hung desperately to a pole. Otis swung his flashlight around the clearing. The fence had once encircled its perimeter.

Lester lifted a rectangular piece of metal which lay to the side of the path and flipped it over: PROPERTY U.S. DEPT. OF THE ARMY. NO TRES-

PASSING. The small date stenciled at the bottom of the sign read August 1918.

"I'd hate to be the private that got assigned this sentry post," Otis said.

"I think they forgot about this place," Lester replied, tossing the sign back to where he had picked it up.

"There's something up ahead." Norma pointed her flashlight.

They walked past the gate toward the low structure. Concrete walls on three sides rose only as high as their waists. There was a wide cement staircase beginning at the top of the open fourth side and descending a short way into the earth, where it was stopped by a metal door. The door hung ajar several inches, exposing only darkness.

"An underground depot," Otis explained. "Looks like Uncle Sam wanted this sealed up but good."

Lester pulled the gun from his coat pocket. When the others gave him raised eyebrows, he shrugged back. "Better safe than sorry," he said. He took Norma's flashlight in his other hand and descended the steps. He reached the floor and nudged the door open with his forearm. Then he shone the flashlight inside.

"It's a room," he told them. "A big storeroom. A big empty storeroom. Wait a sec. There's something in the corner."

"Lester?" Norma called, but he had already entered the bunker. There was a long moment of silence and then she heard him swear, something he never did. He came out a moment later and leaned heavily against the doorjamb. She started to slip past him to see for herself but he grabbed her roughly and held her.

"Bodies," he said, shaking his head. "About a dozen dead men. Sailors by the looks of 'em." He looked up at the other men. She felt him suddenly stiffen and stare at a point behind her. She spun around and couldn't contain the horrified gasp which leapt from her throat.

There were two of them, appearing from behind the scrub trees which lined the path. Their eyes had a cunning, merciless, brutish glint but without a glimmer of human intelligence. Each of them had sallow skin glistening with oily liquid oozing from the broken pustules covering their face and hands. Clinging to each of them were the scraps and remnants of peacoats, wool sweaters, dungarees; one of them still had a knit cap clapped loosely to his head.

"The sailors from the *Zephyr*!" Driftwood whispered through his gritted teeth. "That's why Towers marooned them. They're contaminated exactly like the night watchman."

"So now you believe him?" Hubbard whispered.

"Hell, yeah."

Lester has the gun, Norma thought. We'll be all right. She saw him start to leap up the stairs while at the same time another creature materialized from the rocks overhanging the door to the bunker, arms outstretched. In an instant the contaminated sailor had its arms around Dent and they tumbled against the steps, the pistol flung forcefully from Dent's hand. Ron and Otis had intercepted their attackers and each now grappled furiously with an opponent.

A fourth slavering monster appeared from behind a rock pile and flung itself at Norma. Its moist hands closed around her throat. She grabbed its wrists and her fingers sank into the soft flesh without effect. All the man's teeth were gone and she could see the bloody gums in its gaping mouth centered in its horrible black beard. Its breath smelled of rancid fish.

She tumbled back under the force of its weight and landed heavily on her back. The impact knocked the wind out of her and she began to struggle, desperate to get the creature off her so she could catch her breath. She clawed at its face with her fingernails and it pushed away from her in pain. The texture of its face reminded her of the yellow wax beans she had prepared as a little girl. Gasping, she pulled herself to her feet. Looking around quickly, she could see that Ron and Otis were on the ground. She couldn't see Lester but she could hear the sound of his fight by the bunker door. The creature which had attacked her jumped in front of her, enraged. On its face were bloody stripes left by her fingernails. She saw a blur at the bunker wall, yet another man. Her small party was now outnumbered.

Her attacker sprang at her with a howl at the same instant that a sharp crack rang through the night, echoing off the rocks. The creature seemed to suddenly curl in midair, its trajectory changing. As it flopped heavily to the ground, Norma stared dumbly at it. Blood spurted with each beat of a weakening heart from a hole which had cratered open in the side of the beast's head. The shocking sound of three more successive blasts made her tear her gaze away from the twitching corpse, and she looked up to see Otis and Ron pushing dead creatures off them.

"Lester!" She ran to the bunker and nearly tumbled down the stairs trying to help him. He was leaning against one of the concrete walls trying to catch his breath. The biggest creature, by far, had attacked him. His shirt was ripped open and his chest was scraped and bloodied beneath it. He threw an arm around her and she kissed his face. The creature who had attacked him lay in a heap at his feet. Chunks of its brains were leaving bloody tracks as they dripped down the heavy door.

"Thank God you got to the gun!" she said.

"No," he said. "He did."

She looked up to the top of the wall, to the fifth creature she had seen out of the corner of her eye rushing to join the fracas. He stood on the rim of the wall, the smoking pistol hanging with easy familiarity in his right hand. The wind swept his long duster around him while the moon behind him bathed him in its silvery glow. The man pushed his battered ten-gallon hat back on his head, revealing a handsome young face ringed by long, loose blond hair. He seemed as untouched by any old military chemicals as the island trees themselves were untouched by the color green.

"Ain't those boys full of some fiendish shit?" No doubt, he was a Texan in drawl and swagger. "I sure am glad y'all decided to show up." He twirled the pistol back and forth expertly on his finger the way she'd seen only expert rodeo shooters back in La Plata do. "I'm even gladder y'all decided to bring a pistol along. Even if it is kind of small."

"You're glad!" she exclaimed.

"You folks mind if I ask if y'all got any grub?" His grin was bright and charming. "There ain't nuthin' to eat out here 'cept fish. An' I hate fish."

Episode Thirty-Six

"THANK YOU, ma'am," the cowboy said as she handed him another opened tin of William Underwood's deviled ham. He had already scooped the meat out of four other cans and he proceeded to do the same to this one.

Otis and Ron were on deck piloting the yacht back into the sound as the sun came up. The strong wind continued to hold steady. Lester sat across from the man. Norma guessed him to be about the same age as the boys on deck, somewhere in his twenties.

"You're a long way from home, aren't you, friend?" Lester asked.

"Not as far as I been," he replied. "Once I gave up prizefightin' and caught a ship out of New Orleans, I been to Rio de Janeiro, Capetown, Fiji, Marrakesh, Singapore, Borneo, Egypt, Zanzibar, Panama. Not bad for a cowhand from North Dakota. An' it's a damn sight better 'n being punched in the face."

He tore a hunk of bread from the loaf and chewed it greedily. She poured them all some fresh coffee. Then she took the pot on deck and freshened Ron and Otis's cups as well.

"We're making good time," Otis said to her from behind the wheel. His left eye was swollen shut from the attack. The skin on the back of

Ron's knuckles was scraped off where he had tried to hit one creature. "We should be back around midnight." Otis winked at her reassuringly. Even after having taken a beating, he still had it in him to flirt with her.

She rewarded his efforts with a tired smile. "That's good," she said. "Either of you want some more Bayer?" The day was breaking in scarlet streaks across the sky.

They both nodded and she handed them the bottle. Ron chewed his dry. "The stranger giving up anything useful yet? Like a name?"

"Lew," she said, then paused at the stairs. "Actually what he calls himself is 'Lew No-Less-No-More,' so we're just calling him Lew."

"I don't trust him," Otis said, crossly.

"He saved our lives. Those things would have killed us."

"I'd almost put mine down," Otis said with a shrug.

"You're just jealous that he got to rescue us and Mrs. Dent," Ron said, gleeful.

"Can't you work on the engine again?" Otis asked, giving the throttle his undivided attention.

Below, she took her seat next to Lester. The cowboy nodded at her and continued his story. The pace of his eating had slowed to dabbing at the juices at the bottom of the tin with his finger. "Ever been to Formosa?"

"No."

"It's a Chinese island out there in the Pacific. Nothin' but fish markets and skeeters. We put in there about three months ago. Had to run the Japanese blockade to do it, so it was really some tough going. Docked in Keelung harbor and unloaded some cargo. Guns. Weapons. That whole side of the world's at war but you wouldn't know it back here so much, I 'spect.

"Then, after a few days of doing what sailors do in port, we took on some passengers. Chinese men. About two dozen or so of the meanest cusses you ever saw. Bastards each and every one of 'em. Stayed belowdecks the whole trip back, smokin' butts, playin' cards, fightin', cookin' up food that smelled like manure, and prayin' to this big ugly statue of a god which they brung with 'em. Wasn't the first time we smuggled human souls from one place to another. I ain't proud of that, but it's true.

"There was one American came aboard with 'em. Army fella. He's the one what seemed to have the arrangement with the captain. He didn't stay below with them others. He took quarters with the captain and the mate. Spoke fluent Chinese. He put off in Honolulu with one of the Chinese. Big fella. Seemed to be the boss of all the others. I drove 'em to the airport where they had a plane, and some other men, waiting to take them stateside. Seems like they were in more of a hurry than what our boat could provide for. One of the things that went with 'em was that unholy statue. I was glad for that.

"We headed on through the canal after that, and most days, even though it was infernal hot, you wouldn't even know there were men down below. They got real quiet once them others left. Just did their business real quiet. To be honest, I near forgot about 'em. We all did."

He drank some coffee and continued, "A few nights ago we sighted the Montauk lighthouse and come around the point at dawn on the tide. Late in the day we put in at Crap Island. Then he takes us straightaway up the path to the storeroom. Now as you saw from the looks of the place, there ain't been nobody set foot there in a generation. But Cap'n had the key to that door from that army guy. I got it now, along with all the other keys to the ship. Cap'n throws open the door. 'That's our cargo, lads,' he says. 'Let's get it aboard.'

"That bunker was full of fifty-gallon metal drums. Those eggs were older than dirt. Rusty old tins full of some liquid. There were about three hundred of 'em, all told. And that's what we did all night was haul them drums down the hill to the hold.

"I was ashore with half a dozen of my shipmates when we heard the shootin' start. Quick as a stuck bull those Chinese had taken over the ship. They killed the men that were aboard. They had all the guns. They opened fire on us and drove us up the hill and there was nothing we could do. We watched them steal our boat. Our home. It's a strange feeling to be marooned on a deserted island within sight of New York City. Only, as it turns out, the island wasn't really deserted after all.

"All the time we were loadin' the drums I kept feeling we were being watched. Soon after the ship was away, a man appeared on the beach. We hailed him from the bluff and asked where he was from. 'Providence,' was all he shouted back. We ran down the beach to him thinkin' that he must be a fisherman and must have a boat. But when we got closer to him we could tell that he wasn't exactly all right. And then his three friends came out of the scrub and ambushed us. We headed back up the hill to the bunker but I was the only one what made it all the way."

He idly set one of the empty tins spinning on edge. "I couldn't very well leave my buddies out there, even though they were dead. They wouldn't have left me behind. So I started sneakin' out and draggin' 'em one by one back to the bunker."

"Wasn't that dangerous?" Norma asked.

"Otherwise I would have been bored to death. Once you knew they were out there it was easy to keep away from them. I tried a time or two to sneak up on 'em and kill a couple but that didn't happen either. I couldn't kill them and they couldn't kill me and we left each other alone for a day or so. It was just the surprise of 'em that got my cap'n and mates killed. Schooly Pete. Crooks. Sammy the Smoker. Hey Tony. Q. And Irving. Good men. I wish I could have done more for 'em. I ain't never spoke a bad word about a man because o' his race but if I ever get my hands on any one of those Chinese sons of bitches there'll be hell to pay."

His hands were rough and coarse from years of hard labor and sport. He drummed his fingers on the table. "I missed you all comin' along 'cause I was on the far side thinkin' about whether or not I was desperate enough to paddle a log across to Connecticut."

"Glad you didn't have to find out," Lester said.

"Oh, I coulda done it. I just wouldn't a been happy about it." He yawned. "Y'all don't mind if I stretch out for a few moments and get some shut-eye, do you? I haven't slept good in days."

Lester and Norma left him in their cabin and went up on deck, where they told the story to Ron and Otis. The rest of the trip was uneventful as they nursed their bruises. Their new passenger slumbered blissfully through the day into the night. Ron examined some of Lester's electronic inventions and the two of them discussed engineering plans. Otis tried to speak to Norma several times but she wasn't feeling very communicative. By the coming of night they had cleared Hell Gate and were once again on the East River.

Norma was seated on a lazarette and Lester had the wheel as they sailed between Manhattan and the southern shoals of Blackwell's Island near the abandoned smallpox asylum known as the Renwick Ruin. "I haven't felt wind this cold since Wyoming," he said. He hardly ever spoke about his boyhood. But she knew about Wyoming. She took his hand. She knew what he meant: he hadn't felt a cold wind like that since he was a boy standing on the plains looking for his mother and father to return home from their nearest neighbor, who lived over a dozen miles away. The closest town was twenty miles away. His parents were on horseback and the journey could take hours. His little horse had died a few weeks before. In the deep grip of a plains winter his father would not let him ride behind either of his parents. Two horses meant two riders. And so he had to stay behind and wait. He had no brothers or sisters. He was eight years old and alone on the plains.

Lester had been six when his father had taken it into his head to become a farmer. The three members of the Dent family had driven a horse-drawn covered wagon from Missouri to their home in Wyoming. His recollections of his father were of a presence that always seemed to be disappointed in him. His father seemed disappointed that Lester couldn't do more to help, disappointed that Lester's mother insisted on schooling him instead of letting him help out more in the fields, disappointed that the little boy was afraid at night, disappointed that the boy disappeared to play alone for hours at a time.

The thick white snow surrounded the little Dent farmhouse. Night had fallen. Lester's parents had not returned. In two years he had become accustomed to being alone, having adventures all his own under the vast blue sky. In two years he had played with children his own age exactly four times on visits to town. But this night was different. Now the wind howled around the house and his parents were not home. He fed himself and lighted all the lamps even though he knew his father would disapprove of wasting the oil. He built a fire too. A big one. Again, he knew his father would raise Cain over the wasted wood. But he was bound to upset his father somehow or another and the fire kept him company.

He could read, of course; there were plenty of books. His mother made certain of that. But he didn't feel like reading. He felt like playing with a friend. He was lonely. He was always so lonely. So he decided to make up a friend, and this one wouldn't disappear when they were done playing. He took a pencil stub from his tin and the notepad he used to practice his cursive in, and he began to write. It was a story about a man named Jayse who sailed a ship around the world with his many friends, including his best friend, a gorilla named Mr. Harry C. Lees. At the end of the story they rescued a beautiful woman from a monster in a faraway jungle. He called it "The Voyage of the Gossamer Goose!" It was his first story and it took him all night and part of the next day to finish it. As he wrote the last sentence, he heard his mother calling to him. He saw his father's face cloud as he entered the house. But the boy stood tall and held his father's glare until the old man had broken it off, sensing a new courage in his son. Young Lester felt braver than ever before, for he knew he now had friends who would never leave him alone again on a vast and abandoned wintry plain.

Four years after he had written "The Voyage of the Gossamer Goose!"—a period in which he had played with other children exactly ten times—his father had given up on the ranch and dragged them back to La Plata. Only Lester had managed to harvest anything from that hard land. Tucked into a case that had once carried farm tools, which now lay broken and scattered across the plains, were several dozen lined tablets filled with Lester's best friends—Jayse, Mr. Harry C. Lees, and many, many others.

Norma stood and slipped her arms around him, snuggling up to him. "I don't ever want you to be that cold again," she said.

The other men came up on deck. Otis was trying to pry the origins of Ron's given name, Lafayette, out of him. The cowboy stretched, and the kinks cracking out of his body were audible. He stopped when he saw the skyline and whistled. "That is just about the most beautiful sight I ever did see," he said breathlessly.

"Yeah," Ron said. "It does look good from far away or high above. It's only when you get down in it that it turns ugly."

"Looks mighty fine to me."

"Can you imagine trying to explain New York to a Borneo wild man or an Australian Aborigine or a man from a thousand years ago? Where would you start to describe a skyscraper? Or the lights? Or the millions of people?"

"I'll be damned!" This burst from Otis, who was the only person onboard not gazing at Manhattan. He had turned his attention to the piers of Brooklyn. It took them a moment to realize that he wasn't involved in Ron's history. "That's the ship that nearly ran us down!"

The ship was berthed at an otherwise deserted Brooklyn pier. Her stern was facing them. Her heavy prow had shattered the ice choking the slip as she had docked. They could see the deck crane swinging over the dock and crew activity onboard. They were close enough to see a few men walking along the pier.

"That's her," Lew cried. Norma saw a white fury overcome him. "That's the *Star of Baltimore.* That's my ship!" He gripped the backstay.

"Toss me my binoculars," Lester said to Norma. He looked through the glasses while Otis took the wheel. "Keep your heading." The *Albatross* shuddered as a thick slab of ice careened off her side. Lester rubbed the frost off the glasses and took another look. "Well, I'll be superamalgamated. They're all Chinese all right, just as Lew said."

On the wooden pier Norma could see a cloth-covered military supply truck. Men were unloading heavy boxes from it onto a pallet on the pier, while other men motioned for the deck crane's big lifting chain to be lowered. Other men scurried up and down the thin gangplank.

"Sons of bitches!" Lew snapped, and before they realized his intentions he had flung himself over the railing into the small tender.

"What are you doing?" Otis shouted.

"What's it look like? I'm gettin' my boat back."

"You're gonna get yourself killed."

"Ya think I'm a fool? I know what I'm doin'!" He jangled his captain's keys at them defiantly. "I'm gonna hog-tie the engine so she can't go nowhere 'fore I call the Coast Guard. I know that ship better'n anybody. They'll never know I'm there."

"You can't do something like that by yourself," Norma told him.

"Mrs. Dent's right," Lester said. "I'll go with you." His face was set with the familiar Dent determination. "If I don't he's just going try something stupid like running across the ice," he said to her, grimly.

"You're protecting him now?" she asked.

"I'm gonna try. He's got adventure luck worse than even you."

"Lester, for God's sake, stay here. Stay with me. Or let me come. What about our deal?"

He gave her a rueful half-smile. It was the look of broken promises. "You can make it up to me. I know you'll think of something."

"Lew," she called. "If you go, my husband's going to go with you, and he could die if he goes with you."

"Mr. Dent, sir," the cowboy said as he pulled the tarp from the Evinrude and primed it, "your missus would like you to stay back."

"Well, Lew," said Lester, sliding into the tender. The little boat tottered and bobbed under his weight. "Let me tell you why you need my help. That's a two-stroke engine there. Makes a noise like a band saw. If you use that you may as well send them a card with your name on it that says you'll be dropping by. You want on that boat, you're gonna have to row for it. You'll find oars under your seat." He looked up at Norma. "I just gotta try and keep him alive."

She nodded. "Okay."

Moments later, the knot untied, Lester let the line slip through his fingers as if trying to hold on to the *Albatross,* and Norma, a little bit longer. Finally he tossed the rope and Hubbard caught its wet coils deftly. Lester took up the tiller as the cowboy threw his back into the deep strokes needed to move the boat ahead. Lester turned his eyes forward, away from Norma's toward their new direction. He never looked back.

Issue 5:
The Judge of the Dead

Episode Thirty-Seven

"What do you want?" Walter Gibson asked The Shadow.

"To live," The Shadow replied. "To survive."

"How?"

The only answer was laughter.

Walter Gibson woke up on the floor of the truck. It was moving again. He thought they were still in Manhattan but he couldn't tell for sure; the canvas flap covering the back of the truck had been pulled tightly shut. His head was throbbing from the blow that had knocked him unconscious. It must have been the butt of a gun. He looked up at the Chinese soldiers holding tightly to the benches on either side of truck. The son of a bitch with the busted jaw smirked mercilessly at him. Of course, Gibson thought, if he had to be honest with himself, being popped in the head with the butt of a machine gun wasn't the only reason his head was hurting. The opium probably had something to do with it as well.

It turned out that he liked opium.

He thought of some of the euphemisms his fellow writers had used for the process of ingesting it over the years. Smoke eating. Chasing the dragon. Banging the gong. They could call it whatever they preferred; for Gibson it was a little like kissing heaven.

The peddlers in the den under the theater had known when to administer just the right amount so as to prevent the excruciating headaches which would occur if too much time elapsed between doses. Since he had entered Zhang Mei's circle, warm hours had passed in languid hazy dreams of serenity and universal vision. Food became unnecessary and unwanted. Sips of tea quenched the parched throat. Random fleeting thoughts became great prophecies, and the slightest musings took on profound significance. During periods of lucidity he would scribble madly in his notebook, desperate to be able to recall the vast enlightenments which came upon him, keenly aware of Samuel Coleridge's opium-driven experience of images "rising up before him" and the crushing loss of his mystical masterpiece, *Kubla Khan,* erased under the burden of sober reality.

At other times Gibson would lie on his back and stare at the ceiling and try to picture Howard Lovecraft's face, but he couldn't remember exact details, even though the drug allowed him to recall so many more obscure faces from his past with impressive precision. He attempted to communicate telepathically with Sonia Lovecraft but he never received an answer. Helplessly he would find himself hallucinating that he was Lovecraft, buried in the cold earth of Providence, his eyes gummed shut, his fingernails and hair growing, his body frozen, waiting for the warmth of spring to begin the horrors of decomposition. His dry mouth, sewn closed, begged to cry out for justice. When these hallucinations ended he would swear not to take another puff of the sweet smoke. But only the smoke itself had the power to cloud those visions from his mind.

Sometimes he would hear laughter, but not the cruel, portentous laughter of The Shadow. Robert's laughter, the peals of joy of an excited young boy. It was years of laughter, years he had missed, and he realized that it wasn't laughter, not Robert's laughter at all, but his own sobs. He had other conversations with The Shadow, who warned him that the disloyalty of an agent would not be tolerated. He was not laughing. Then The Shadow's face would melt into that of Zhang Mei, who would take an adjoining divan and continue with the story of his life. During these sessions Gibson would rouse himself to something resembling full functionality and diligently interview and transcribe the man's words.

Late one night Zhang Mei led him up the stairs onto the stage of the theater above. In the center of the stage stood a terrible statue, carved from wood and covered with gold. It was very old, Zhang Mei explained, and had traveled as far as he had. He gave it an affectionate pat, which echoed hollowly inside. Its face was fearsome and Gibson realized that the statue's cold eyes followed him around the stage, as alive as those in one of Rozen's paintings. Only this statue wasn't a simulacrum of The Shadow; it resembled nothing more than Rozen's recurrent Death visage. "I am the only priest he has left," Zhang Mei informed him, and Gibson nodded and said he understood. "I give him my breath, which is his judgment."

At other times a strange American soldier, Colonel Towers, would appear and their sphere of intimacy would be burst. Gibson was possessive about his companion and felt that Towers had an untoward influence on him. Upon the occasions of his visits, Towers and Zhang would depart the theater, leaving Gibson in the opium den beneath it. When Towers was around, Zhang was considerably crueler toward Gibson, as well as to his own men who had accompanied him from Hawaii. "I am, as your expression goes, waiting for my ship to come in," was his disdainful answer to Gibson's eventual query about his excursions.

Towers made it clear that he didn't trust Gibson, but he knew that there was no way Gibson could escape the opium den unless Zhang gave the word. There were smoke men ready to plunge knives into him in an instant. From their mysterious outings Zhang would return alone hours later, angered and frustrated. Until his rages passed, Gibson would remain silent and investigate the deep inner workings of his own being. He spent a lot of time thinking about Litzka. He had begun to realize that the chances of his seeing her again were growing slim.

Late on the night before the one that found him in the back of a truck, he had walked with Zhang through Chinatown. The streets had been cleaned and festooned with decorations in preparation for an upcoming parade. Zhang and Gibson seemed to pass invisibly by the small clusters of people. Gibson never caught anyone looking at the tall dark Chinese man and the short white man at his side; they slid by as if they were shadows.

Bright red banners hung from the lampposts. Posters proclaiming solidarity with brothers and sisters back in China were hung in store windows. The mood in the streets was celebratory, in spite of the recent news which described defeat after defeat of the Chinese army at the hands of the Japanese. Though the fall of Beijing appeared imminent, the weekend's festival would be a show of support for the homeland.

"The kidnapping was my plan," Zhang told Gibson, as they stood before posters declaring support for General Chiang Kai-shek, "to force the general to unite with Professor Mao against the Japanese. Chiang is smart. He quickly agreed to come to an understanding with the Communists and focus the fight against the Japanese. But he demanded that Xueling and I exile ourselves from China in order that he would not have to fear another threat from us.

"I laughed at him. We were in the position of power. China was ours to save. But my brother agreed to the terms of his prisoner. No matter what I said, his mind would not be swayed. I made an attempt to kill Chiang, but he stayed my hand. I begged, pleaded, threatened; his path was set. He did not want to lead the army. He did not want the future of China to rest upon his shoulders. For him, the wars were truly over. Let it rest on mine, I said to him, but again, no. You understand I could have killed my brother then? But I did not. Instead, I did what Zhang Zuolin himself would have done. I retreated. And I formed a new alliance. With Colonel Towers.

"Xueling had already exiled himself to Hawaii by the time I was prepared to leave. He took with him men who were loyal to me, who would wait for me. When I last saw the shores of China, it was a day not unlike this, cold and raining. I was on a ship bound for Formosa. I watched the horizon until the land disappeared. I was leaving behind the bodies of my wife and my son with no one to pay them honor or light the candles and incense for them. And I had been unable to avenge them upon Mi-Ying. I wept openly for all which I had lost beyond the horizon.

"It is good that the general now recognizes Japan as the true enemy and fights with Professor Mao instead of against. But the time for victory slips away. There is not enough leadership. The Japanese war machine is mighty. There is not enough money for food or for arms."

He stopped and fingered one of the red flyers taped to a lamppost. "My friend, Colonel Towers, came to me in Taipei when all seemed lost. He knew of a way to defeat the Japanese. He knew where money could be found to supply an army. He knew of a weapon which could drive them from our shores forever." He tore the flyer from the post. "He brought me hope when there was none."

Gibson looked at the photo printed above the Chinese text. He recognized General Chiang Kai-shek but the man next to the general meant nothing to him. He said as much to Zhang, who nodded.

"Of course. Why should you know the face of the consul general? Why should you know his name? He is of no importance to anyone but himself. A mere diplomat." He snatched the paper back, crumpled it up, and threw it into the gutter, where it unfurled slowly in the water from the melting snow. He added his own spit to the swirl. Then he began to walk again.

"What's in it for Towers?" Gibson asked.

They turned the corner back to the street which led to the theater and to the opium den at the end of the alley. "Colonel Towers is a complicated man. He speaks Chinese like I speak English. We have taught each other much. Like many men, Colonel Towers dreams of being a wealthy man. A powerful man. The kind of man who can influence the course of history. Though he may be an American, he is a true citizen of the world and his ambitions do not obligate him to remain in America. He will be content to be wealthy wherever his wealth finds him."

"Will you make him wealthy?"

"If he can deliver to me the power of my destiny, which I believe he can, then it will be within my power to do this for him. Yes."

A canvas-covered military truck had parked in front of the theater. The driver leapt out of the truck upon seeing Zhang and fell to his knees. Tears streamed down his sea-worn, weather-beaten face. Zhang fell upon him and the two men embraced and spoke rapidly to each other in their own tongue. Gibson was momentarily forgotten. For a moment the thought occurred to him, *Run!* He could disappear into the city. But he stood still and watched. He had never seen Zhang happy and he found it fascinating. He almost felt as if he shared in the man's joy.

Soon they were inside and the warmth of the drug filled his being once more with hallucinations of merciless Chinese statues, the red eyes of The Shadow, and the lost laughter of a little boy who loved trains.

The activity lasted all day long. He heard scraping and bumping upstairs in the theater, big objects being slid across the floor. Men came and went. Zhang barked orders. Men responded. The sounds of commotion upstairs blurred into those from the street—the preparations for the parade. Finally, at the coming of night, he was roused from his stupor by Zhang. Gibson's vision took a while to come into focus.

"Come with me, my biographer," Zhang Mei snapped, impatient at Gibson's groggy ineptitude. "There is another chapter to be written tonight." A pure formidable energy emanated from Zhang, and Gibson could see in his bearing the warrior who had slain so many men single-handedly at the battle of the river, who had led troops into battle under the banner of Zhang Zuolin. He knew in an instant that his secret sharer was gone forever. Zhang's men hustled Gibson out toward the back of the truck. One of the men flipped down the rear gate of the trunk, while another swept back the canvas cargo door.

"Jesus Christ!"

Two rusty old canisters—identical to the one he had found in the Providence Medical Lab, right down to their weathered army stencils—were lashed tightly to the bed of the truck. Hands propelled him up and on, the momentum knocking him against one of the drums. He scrambled away from them and picked himself up. The rest of Zhang's company clambered in after him. They were solemn and resolute, and they eyed him with stern silence. On the floor was an open crate of machine guns. Another held cartridges for those guns. A third box remained closed. The last man aboard dropped the canvas over the back.

He heard Zhang's voice outside.

"Zhang Mei," he cried, "Zhang Mei! What are you doing?"

But there was no reply. Moments later he heard both doors of the cab slam shut and the engine roar to life.

He had no sense of where they were when the truck finally came to a stop. The men seemed restless, but they made no move to exit. Gibson felt a rumbling sensation vibrating against his tailbone on the bench where he was seated. It was a familiar sensation and for a strange moment he thought they had parked by the loading dock of the Street & Smith building. But the instant he had that thought, it introduced another which told him exactly where they were. The American Bank Note Company lay on the other side of the canvas wall.

The gate of the truck was carefully and quietly lowered and the men filed off. One man remained in the truck with his gun in Gibson's ribs. There was a crisp, efficient order to the distribution of guns and ammo. The third case was opened and gas masks were pulled from it. Each man put one on. Gibson stared as one of the two drums was carefully lowered to the street by anxious men. The masks gave them an insect-like appearance, with bug eyes and a drumlike proboscis hanging down to their chests.

"Zhang Mei? What's happening?" he said loudly. The men looked at him. Zhang Mei gave him a disdainful glare. He felt the muzzle of the gun poke his ribs, hard, and his heart began to race. Three men picked up the drum and ran with it to the front door of the building, and he knew the guards were done for unless he did something. "Hey!" he shouted, trying to warn the men inside. "Hey!" The guards in the lobby stirred.

He felt something explode off the back of his head, and he sank to his hands and knees, bolt of pains radiating through his body like the energy waves broadcasting from the RKO Studios' theatrical emblem. For a moment he thought he had been shot, but he realized that he had been cocked with a rifle butt. Nausea overcame him and through blurred vision he saw one of the men use an implement to rip the stopper from the drum. The guards were rising now; they looked startled. One of the Chinese men took a sledgehammer to the glass door, smashing it.

White gas blew from the hole in the drum like a whale's plume, and Gibson remembered the pressure it was under. The men rolled the drum through the shattered glass. In an instant the lobby was filled with white, billowing clouds which swallowed up the guards. With the glass gone Gibson could hear their coughing screams of wretched agony. The sound lasted only a moment. They had been given no time to raise the alarm. Anyone else in the building, especially in the floors below as the gas sank, would also be dead within moments.

The drum exhausted its pressurized contents rapidly. While the lobby was still full of poison, Zhang Mei barked a command and the men followed him inside. The gas spilled out of the lobby and onto the sidewalk toward Gibson. He felt for his glasses—one lens was broken. Half blind, he dragged himself to his feet. The man who had hit him kept the gun trained on him in a way which let him know that he would not be given a second chance. The gas stayed low, like a heavy mist, and soon the truck was surrounded. Gibson snatched a gas mask from the crate and held it to his face.

The gas swirled around his feet but rose no higher and soon it began to evaporate into the air. Suddenly he felt the vibration stop. The printing presses had been turned off.

After a lengthy period of inactivity the men emerged from the lobby. Still wearing their masks, they looked like ants pouring out of an anthill. They carried case upon case, which they stacked upon pallets in the truck. The addition of the cases made the truck sink under their combined weight.

"Years ago the ruling coalition in Beijing, under my adopted father, placed an order for new currency from this place. It was bought and paid for by the Chinese people." Zhang Mei was speaking up to Gibson from the curb. His voice was flattened by the mask. "When the coalition collapsed, it became unclear to whom this money should be released. Many claimed ownership, but none could prove it. And so here it has rested these many years."

"No receipt. No money. Holy Christ," Gibson murmured. "It's the greatest lost Chinese laundry ticket joke in the history of the world."

"And here is your punch line: Your government can never admit that this money has been taken. To do so would destroy all that is left of its global economic integrity."

"How much money?"

"Enough to win a war. Enough to rebuild an empire after its invaders have been repelled. Enough to avenge my family. Enough to seat a new emperor in Beijing—one who will bring peace to China."

"But how much?"

"Seven hundred and fifty million dollars," Zhang replied. "Tomorrow night, after we celebrate with our brothers, we shall begin our journey home. Colonel Towers has arranged it so that we will not be pursued by your coast guard or navy."

The engine rumbled to life and the men climbed back on board, considerably more cramped. Zhang disappeared from Gibson's view in the commotion of moving soldiers. That's when Gibson made his break for it. He lunged for the rear gate, hoping to take advantage of the confusion.

That must have been about the time the rifle butt hit him for a second time, because the RKO antenna in his head began broadcasting pain again, and he lost consciousness. Now as he lay on the floor, looking up, he felt the truck incline gently and heard the sound of tires rumbling over wooden planks. It was the sensation any New Yorker, especially a Dodgers fan who took cabs out to Ebbets Field, knew well. They were leaving Manhattan by way of the Brooklyn Bridge.

EPISODE THIRTY-EIGHT

AS THE tiny boat carried Lester and the cowboy farther away and closer to the black ship, The Flash turned to Driftwood and said, "I would have bet money that if anybody had gone overboard tonight, it would have been you."

"Me too," he muttered through his clenched teeth.

"All right," Mrs. Dent said, as the current swiftly drew the launch through the ice floes behind the freighter. "We're going to have to circle back and get them when they come back." She pointed to a wide expanse of black water, free of ice, in the distance. "We can come about in the waters between Red Hook and Governors Island."

"Sure," Driftwood replied as she went below. "Maybe they'll pick up some beer and steak from the galley on the way back. Invite some of those nice fellas on the dock to come back for a cookout."

"Why don't you take it easy, Driftwood? That's the lady's husband out there."

"And he's not coming back," he replied darkly.

The Flash felt his blood rise. "This whole trip you've been calling me a liar to my face, trying to pick a fight with the cowboy, and putting the make on Mr. Dent's missus. Now, I introduced you to them and they're nice people and I feel responsible, so show a little respect."

"You have to admit you've spun some yarns."

"I'm sure when you start telling Mrs. Dent the truth behind your whoppers, she's completely going to throw her husband over for your skinny, weak-lunged, hoboing, grave-digging ass. Send me an invite to the wedding. I'll bring something from Tiffany. Meanwhile, we got a boat to sail and you're at the helm, so sail already."

In a subdued voice Driftwood asked The Flash to let out some sail so they could pick up some speed. The Flash did what he was told for Mrs. Dent's sake, but he was tired of taking orders and tired of being on the boat.

He picked up the binoculars and could see the two men forging their way across the Stygian scene, the blocks of ice, some as small as a dime, others as big as a flat house, adding chill impediments to their progress. Below him he could hear Mrs. Dent as she tried to raise the Coast Guard, but the radio issued only static. She emerged, frustration clearly showing on her face. He handed her the binoculars.

The little boat made its way along the starboard side of the freighter to a hatch just above the waterline. It was identical to the one on the port side which had hooked Lester's gaff. "He said he had the keys," she said. A moment or two later and the hatch was open, the two men vanishing into the bowels of the ship. She lowered the binoculars and smiled slightly. The tone of her voice and the steely glare in her eyes made The Flash think that, for a while at least, Lester would probably be safer aboard the ship. She tossed the binoculars back to him and went below again.

"Coast Guard! Coast Guard! Come in, please. This is the *Albatross.* Come in, please! Coast Guard. Coast Guard? Come in. Do you copy?"

"Copy that," the radio finally crackled to life, as she fiddled with the squelch, "This is the Coast Guard. Go ahead. Over." The voice was young. The Flash imagined that the radio operator was one of his readers.

"I'm reporting a hijacked ship at the pier just south of the Brooklyn

Bridge. The ship is named the *Star of Baltimore.* There are lives in danger. Do you copy?"

"Copy that, *Albatross.*" The radio sputtered again and an icy voice, nearly metallic in timbre, interrupted the conversation.

"Attention, Coast Guard." The new speaker commanded attention. Speaking softly, but with a power that caused Mrs. Dent to adjust the volume, the new voice said, "This is Colonel Towers. Do you copy?"

"Yes, sir!" The young man responded with fear and respect.

"Do you recognize my authority in this matter?"

Colonel Towers. The Flash looked at Driftwood, who acknowledged his shock with a nod and a grimace.

"Yes, sir, Colonel Towers, sir. I am fully aware of your standing orders. There is no ship. Repeat. There is no ship. Over."

"Good, sailor. Good work."

"Coast Guard!" Mrs. Dent pleaded. "Listen to me. The ship is named the *Star of Baltimore.*"

The Flash looked out across the water to Governors Island, the headquarters of the United States Coast Guard's Atlantic fleet. He imagined the young signalman at his station. He chose a window in a building and decided that was where the young man was. Stu was his name, he decided. Stu, from Nantucket, who had grown up on the coastal shores of his island. Stu was one of his fans. Stu would help.

"Attention, *Albatross,*" Stu spoke at long last. "There is no vessel registered as the *Star of Baltimore.* This channel is for emergency use only. If you persist in your hoax your ship will be impounded and you will be prosecuted to the full extent of United States maritime law."

"No! Please! You have to help!"

"Coast Guard, Governors Island Station, out!"

Damn you, Stu, The Flash thought angrily. The next time I write a coward who shoots men in the back, he's going to have your name. The radio remained silent.

Mrs. Dent came up from the cabin. Her jaw was clenched and roses of fury blushed her cheeks. She took a deep breath.

"It's gonna be close," Driftwood said. The Flash turned and watched the blackness which indicated open water rapidly approach. "Sure wish we'd fixed the motor."

"You up for this?" The Flash asked him. His eyes were trying to factor in a dozen different potential hazards at once.

"It'd be easier with an engine."

"Well, we don't have one," Mrs. Dent snapped at him. "And if you don't feel like you're up to it, just step aside and let me do it."

"That's okay," Driftwood said, cowed. "I can do it."

The Flash looked into the frigid, swirling waters. Once, fishing as a boy in the early Montana spring, he had slipped in the mud and fallen into the Missouri River. The runoff from the winter snow had been colder than anything he could have imagined. His head slipped only briefly beneath the surface of the water but his breath had been snatched away from him by the cold. His diaphragm would not expand even as he struggled to inhale, and panic had set in almost immediately. The stabbing of a thousand chilling needles in his flesh, the vicious, ruthlessly gripping current, turned him into a violent thrashing animal, a wolf with its paw in a trap. All he knew, had ever known, would ever know, was that this cold death was so fast, so powerful, so overwhelming. Only his clawing hand, reaching for a low-hanging branch, had secured his rescue. Only the feeling of his hand on that branch, that security, had restored his reason, had allowed his rib cage to expand with air in spite of the water's viselike grip.

He knew exactly what it would feel like to die in the water.

"Ready to come about?" Otis asked. His voice was thin and tight.

"Ready!" Mrs. Dent stood ready to cast her sheet off.

The Flash grabbed the handle and prepared to coil his sheet around the winch when the sail was tossed free. "Ready to come about!" he shouted.

"Coming about!"

The boat heeled over in the opposite direction and The Flash braced himself against the cabin. He felt a solid thump as ice cracked against the hull. They were right up against the ice shelf.

"We're aground!" he shouted. "We're on the ice!"

"I know!" Driftwood grunted, wrestling with the wheel. "I know!"

From his angle he could see only ice below. The boat scraped against it with a crackling shriek. He secured his lines and the sails filled with wind, the *Albatross* trembling as it ground against the outer edge of the ice.

"Get ready to jump to the ice!" he yelled to Mrs. Dent.

"No!" She shook her head. "She'll make it. You hear me?" she hollered to Driftwood. "She can make it!"

Suddenly the *Albatross* shook with a thud as it knifed back into the water, free of the ice and heading back up the channel. The Flash sank against the cabin to catch his breath. Mrs. Dent reached for, and he gave over, the binoculars. She looked for a long time and he peered at the ship, following her gaze. He thought he saw the blur of a figure ducking behind a vent at the front of the ship, near the cabins, but he couldn't be sure. She swore and lowered the glasses. He took one look at her face and knew something terrible had happened.

"What?" he asked.

"It's Lester," she said. "He and the cowboy are up on deck."

Episode Thirty-Nine

GIBSON HEARD the sound of lapping water. He had been concentrating so hard on making the pain in his head go away that it took him a few moments to realize the truck had stopped moving and the engine had been shut off. Zhang Mei's men filed off the truck as before, unconcerned with the prostrate white man.

He staggered to his feet, using the bench for support. Through the cargo flap he could see glimpses of Manhattan across the water. He parted the canvas and looked out. The truck had backed down a large wooden pier, much greater than the one he had explored in Providence. He made his way cautiously off the truck. To his right loomed the Brooklyn Bridge. To his left a great black ship—blacker even than the putrid water beneath its hull, a ship old and carrying the scars of decades of battle against the sea and elements—soared high above him. There were still more Chinese men on board the ship, speaking excitedly with their comrades on the dock as they lowered a gangplank down. Zhang Mei led the ascent, embracing the men on the ship as he reached the deck.

Gibson began to back away, hoping to steal off down the dock, but a hand shoved him forward. It was his old friend, the soldier with the busted jaw. Overhead, the deck crane had been brought roaring to life. Its arm swung out over the truck and the operator slowly lowered the hook at the end of the steel cable toward the truck. Men helped guide the heavy hook inside the cargo truck, where the hook was fastened to the chains binding the crates of money to the first pallet. Then, with men shouting directions, the operator began to winch back, soldiers inside the truck guiding the pallet out as the slack went out of the cable, then the pallet swung free and began to rise. The first load of lost Chinese loot began its journey home.

Gibson's escort forced him on toward and up the gangplank. He heard the sound of grinding gears and saw that the great doors to the hold in the center of the ship were being winched open and the pallet was being lowered into its depths. Zhang Mei watched from the edge of the hold, arms crossed in satisfaction. Gibson was allowed to sit on a crate and smoke. The men worked efficiently and quickly, but even so, Gibson grew weary.

Finally Zhang Mei beckoned to him. He rose and walked to the hold, wary of the yawning opening. "America is a young country," Zhang Mei said, "but one thing they have become better at than anyone else is the art of killing."

Far below them, arranged like neat little clusters of eggs in a country farmer's stall, were dozens upon dozens of the ancient army drums. Thousands of gallons of malevolent death waiting to be spilled across distant battlefields.

"You can't use this," Gibson said, horrified. "It's obscene."

"Once wives and children become the targets of war, that word loses its relevance. I will use this gas to drive the Japanese from every inch of the Middle Kingdom, then I shall take what's left of it and bring it to their shores. By the time the summer flowers bloom beyond the walls of Shenyang Palace the war will be over. And I will once more be able to lay those same flowers upon the graves of my wife and my son." He leaned in close to Gibson and whispered his final thought before sweeping away from Gibson's side and vanishing down the gangway.

Walter Gibson felt the weight of his life upon his shoulders and was unable to move. The shouts of men and the grinding of the crane gears receded along with his sense of the rest of the world. He knew that he was about to die and suddenly all he craved was the sight of one more dawn.

Across the great distance that seemed to separate his unmoored mind from reality he heard a sharp crack, as if some ice on the river were breaking up. He looked up and saw the engineer operating the crane stagger from his cab, a hand against his bloody face. Something seemed to strike him and he fell back against the control levers. The arm of the crane suddenly dropped down with tremendous speed, crashing against the deck with tremendous force; he could feel the entire boat shudder. The pallet that had been dangling near the hold opening fell to the deck, then was yanked with great force by the falling crane across the deck. It skidded away from where he stood and smashed into the gangplank, dislodging and shattering it. Together, the pallet of heavy cases and what was left of the gangplank toppled to the pier, exploding through the wood into the water. The cable, still attached to the pallet, was drawn taut before snapping; it sailed into the air with the crack of a whip, then fell across the ship. The recoil of the cable springing back was enough to send several heavy iron beams that had been part of the crane structure hurtling into the hold. Fascinated, horrified, Gibson watched as the debris slammed into a bundle of canisters, crushing them like tin cans.

The men below never had a chance. He looked down into hell. Gas jetted out through the hold in a horrifyingly wide spray. Great feathery plumes spurted up into the night sky, then fell back to become part of the roiling gray mass, devouring the luckless men trying to escape it. It spread to fill the floor of the hold and then rose up, like a tub filling with water. So quickly, he thought. The sight of onrushing doom was paralyzing; he was rooted to the deck.

Robert. I'm sorry.

For a moment the turmoil below seemed to coalesce into a giant form in which he could see the rage of The Shadow, his Shadow, his dark angel of retribution, sweeping up toward him, eyes ablaze with wrath. The mass spilled out onto the deck, flowing over his shoes.

Litzka. I'll try to hold my breath for you.

He felt the impact of a body slamming into his side. The impact lifted him off his feet, knocked the wind from his lungs. He had the dizzying sensation of motion, of being swept down the deck by a great force, of arms around him. Someone was dragging him. A man. Not The Shadow. The gas poured across the deck toward him. He was at the bow. How had he arrived here? There was a thunder in his ears.

Then he felt himself being lifted up against the rail. His mind finally seemed to uncloud and he looked at the man forcing him up.

"Dent?" he said, amazed, and then began the long fall into the black abyss.

The pain he felt was immense beyond measure. It was as if all the pain he had ever felt in his life had revisited him all at once. As a writer, he never believed that words could fail him, yet this was a pain beyond describing in any sense that could be conveyed to another person.

It was a complete and resounding agony.

Episode Forty

THE FLASH could never have imagined that bodies could fall so fast.

"Oh my God," Mrs. Dent cried. "They're in the water!"

The midsection of the *Star of Baltimore* disappeared beneath the thick, lethal fog billowing from its hold. A light breeze stirred the gas to starboard; it flowed heavily over the side almost like a liquid, sizzling away as it made contact with the seawater. Behind the ship Lester's head emerged; then, within a moment or two, the form of the other man he had thrown over the ship's bow appeared several yards from him.

"Is that the cowboy?" Driftwood yelled to them.

"I can't tell," The Flash hollered back.

Dent swam to the limp form as the current pulled them both away from the freighter and the roiling gas.

"Get them," Mrs. Dent commanded to the both of them. Driftwood angled the *Albatross* to intercept, while The Flash grabbed the life ring. Suddenly they heard a low roar, like a bow being drawn along a bass fiddle.

"What's that?" The Flash yelled. "What's that sound?"

"That," Driftwood said in a choked, hoarse voice, "is the sound of a machine gun."

With the excitement on the ship The Flash had forgotten about the men on the dock. A half dozen or so men stood there now, amidst the gangplank wreckage and the debris from the pallets. The air around them was alive with fluttering slips of paper. A man in a long black coat stood in their midst towering over the other men. While the men on the dock pointed at Dent in the water, this man stood still with his face turned away, looking back at the ship. Another one of the Chinese men gripped a machine gun and fired bursts into the water. Lester struck out against the water with one hand while supporting the other man.

"No way in hell am I going near those machine guns!" Driftwood's face was white, drained of blood.

"You have to! That's my husband up there."

Driftwood kept his eyes focused on the water in front of him. The Flash realized that Driftwood was terrified. Beyond terrified. He was panicking. He slid down the deck to the helm as the sails began to luff.

"It's all in your head."

"Get away from me." Driftwood looked at him angrily. He was almost beyond reasoning with. "You ever stare down a machine gun? I'm not dying that way."

"It's just in your mind. You need to get control of it. Get your monkeys in order."

"Monkeys?" The seeming randomness of simians' being introduced into the conversation caught the edge of his attention. Just as The Flash had intended.

"The monkeys in your head. The ones that are running in a million different directions. You gotta get them running in one direction. That way!"

Driftwood pushed him roughly away. The Flash slipped to the deck by Mrs. Dent's feet. He pulled himself up and looked at Driftwood, who was staring at the dock. At last he looked up and met The Flash's eyes. For a long moment The Flash couldn't tell (and afterward he was never sure) whether Driftwood at that moment was completely sane or completely insane. A sardonic smile twisted across Driftwood's face, making his mustache twitch. "Monkeys!" He gave the wheel a tremendous spin; the sound of the spoke smacking into his hand when he finally stopped it sounded like wood cracking. The sails filled again with a steady breeze. The Flash felt the *Albatross* heel again. He slid to the other side of the deck as the boat swung around toward the *Star of Baltimore.*

"What the hell! If we're gonna die, we're gonna die!" Driftwood shouted as the sail snapped across the boat. "That's what my monkeys are telling me!" He barked out a laugh. The Flash's side was aching where he had fallen against the hold door. He rubbed it. Driftwood looked at The Flash. "All monkeys reporting for duty."

"Good."

Driftwood made a quizzical face, his eyes rolling up. "Hey! You little bastards better clean up your crap when you're done."

As the yacht drew near to Dent, the wind changed again and what was left of the gas began to flow the other way, toward the dock. It dribbled down the side of the ship and the Chinese men broke and ran, clambering over the wreckage and shattered planks to reach the truck. Finally, the tall man in the long coat turned around and looked out to the river. He was Chinese, his face fierce and strong. His eyes glittered like carved obsidian, and The Flash could feel his rage radiating across the water toward them. Thin tendrils of gas crept across the dock toward his feet. At last he broke his gaze and spun rapidly away. He moved with the athletic deftness of an animal across the broken pier, leaping aboard the truck as it roared down the pier and into the night.

The last of the gas dissipated across the waters and a strange silence fell across the river, the stillness of a big city on its way to dawn. Not a pure silence. A silence that vibrated with life and energy in a single, inaudibly low tone.

Lester struggled feebly as Otis expertly brought them alongside the hull. Hubbard threw the life ring out to Dent's upstretched hand, and within minutes the two men were finally back on the *Albatross.* Norma threw herself against Lester, feeling the cold water soak into her jacket. He was shivering uncontrollably and his lips were blue. Ron emerged from belowdecks with blankets and she wrapped Lester as he sat on the deck. He grinned at her.

"Don't try that Dent smile on me," she said. "I am not in the mood for charm." Slips of paper about the size of dollars bills were plastered against his hair. She was not gentle about slapping them off; in fact they seemed to require the extra effort. "You just had to go up on the deck of that ship, didn't you? Protection luck, my ass."

He tried to look sorry. He tilted his head so his eyes looked even guiltier. "If it makes you feel any better, you can cross jumping off a ship into icy water off my list of things to do before I die," he managed, through chattering teeth.

In rapid succession she slapped the last few pieces of paper from his head. "You're an idiot. You'd just better hope you got a good story out of it, that's all I have to say. 'Cause that one might cost you. It might cost you some toes. It might cost you a marriage."

Ron hurried up from below with some more blankets.

"Who is that?" Norma asked Ron as he covered the second man.

"That's Walter Gibson. He writes The Shadow."

"I know what Walter Gibson writes, thank you, Ron," she said icily, snatching a blanket from him and wrapping it around her husband.

"We're taking on some serious water. I'm going to tie us up to the dock," Otis said. "Before we sink," he added.

"Okay," Ron answered, standing to prepare the dock lines. "It looks clear."

"Ahoy below!" A voice hailed them. Standing on the bow of the *Star of Baltimore* and looking down at them with a curiously worried expression was Lew, the cowboy. "Everyone all right?"

"Appears to be the case," Otis shouted back. "How'd you stay alive?"

"I can tell which way the wind blows, pard. Gas heads that way," he pointed starboard, "I heads this way." He pointed to the prow. "It's all evaporated now."

"Get down and help us tie up."

"Sure," Lew called back. "I reckon everyone's dead up here. How're them fellas?"

"Little cold. Little wet. Little closer to a divorce."

Lew found some cargo netting, tossed it over the side and scrambled down to the wrecked dock.

After some careful negotiation they managed to get the yacht into what Otis and Ron agreed was a safe berth. Lester emerged from below in a dry set of clothes and was able to lend a hand. He had stuffed as much sailcloth as he possibly could into the crack in the hull, stopping the flow of water for the time being.

Upon stepping foot on the dock, Ron eagerly scooped up a fistful of paper. "Chinese money," he said, examining it. "Worthless." He flung it away, exasperated. "Just my luck. When money finally falls from the sky it's useless to me."

"What the hell happened up there?" Driftwood demanded. "I thought you were just gonna disable the engine."

"It was my fault" Lew replied. "I just wanted a look up top. The crane operator, he saw me. He shot first." He tossed Lester his pistol back. "Thanks for the loan."

"We need to get Mr. Gibson to a hospital," Norma said.

"No," a weak voice said. She turned around. Gibson was sitting up. He coughed. "Just take me home."

"You need a doctor."

"Mrs. Dent, right?"

She nodded. "Please?"

"Well, Mrs. Dent," he said with a cough, "I'm either gonna die or not and there's not a thing any doctor can do. Just take me home and I'll find out."

"Mr. Gibson," she began, "there's something I've always wanted to say to you if ever we met. You are a damned piehead!"

"Mrs. Dent, I've never heard it put exactly that way before but that sounds about right."

"Fine. Now we'll take you home."

"Hold on a split second," said the cowboy, "I'm afraid this is where we say adios."

"You're not coming?" Lester asked.

"This here is my ship. I lost her once but I ain't losin' her again. I'm staying with the old girl until the police come by. Somebody needs to tell 'em this story. Might as well be me."

"Okay. Otis, would you mind staying with the *Albatross* until I get back?" Lester asked.

"Can't Hubbard do it?" Driftwood asked.

"Why me?" Hubbard said. "It's not like you've got to be anywhere. And you know her so well, now."

"Fine. I'll do it."

"Hey," said the cowboy, twirling the pistol. "I'm all out here. Got any more bullets?"

Lester shook his head. "I never thought I'd need more than six."

Norma approached the young man and hugged him gratefully. "Thank you," she told him. "You never did tell me your last name. So we can look out for you."

The man hung his head bashfully. "Aw, ma'am," he said, "it's kind of embarrassin'."

"Don't be silly. Tell me."

He whispered it softly into her ear and she smiled and laughed and kissed him on the cheek. "I love it. I absolutely love it."

"You think?"

"Absolutely. Much prettier than Dent!"

As she helped Lester and Walter change into warm clothes below she could hear Otis and Ron up on deck. They had discovered what was left of a bottle of Lester's Cuban rum and were already spinning their recent adventure into tales, as if they hadn't been at each other's throat only a half hour before. There were things she would just never understand about men.

They disembarked and moved around the gaping hole in the pier, Ron and Lester supporting an unsteady Walter. Soon they were able to hail a wandering cab on Joralemon Street and were on their way back over the Brooklyn Bridge and into the city. Through the suspension cables they could see the two boats and the smashed pier in the distance. Then they lost sight of them altogether.

"Walter," Lester finally asked, simply, "what the hell happened?"

Walter Gibson stared back at him and life seemed to come back into his eyes. "Let me tell you a story. You can decide what's real and what's pulp."

Episode Forty-One

He hadn't given them every detail. For instance he didn't tell them about his surprising fondness for opium, or about having seen The Shadow in gas. It was his story and he told them what they needed to know.

"What'd he say to you?" Lester asked, as the cab pulled to a stop before the Hotel Des Artistes. "I saw Zhang Mei whisper something to you before he left you to die. What did he say?"

Gibson rubbed the palm of his hand across his chin, feeling the growing stubble. He gave a little snort. "He said that perhaps I wasn't a biographer of great enough stature for his story after all. He felt he needed to find Ernest Hemingway. Can you believe that he said that to me? Me?"

"Well," said Norma, even as Lester tried to shush her, "he is a well-regarded author."

Gibson looked mortally offended. "I could outwrite Ernest Hemingway any day of the week. Name the weapon. Spikes and stone? Clay tablets and straw? Pen quill and parchment? Hell, straight bourbon and blarney, and I will tell the story straight and clear over Ernest any day of the week in any land under any weather. 'A Clean, Well-Lighted

Place,' my ass! Try that against 'I Rode the Black Ship of Death with the Dragon of Terror and Peril!' Huh!" A coughing fit ended his grand speech. As he caught his breath, weakened by the exertion, they helped him out of the cab. The crisp night air and the feeling of Manhattan *firma,* known to all, far and wide, as the most stable land in all the world, the rock that will be there for you to walk on, to run on, to chase after another pair of feet running away from you on, to ride the subway through, to fall on, to sleep on if you're desperate, slip on, spill on, urinate on, spit on—to feel his feet stake their claim seemed to imbue him with the ability to draw himself to his full, and expansive, five-foot-eight-inch height. He looked at his three concerned companions and, sweeping his arms up and to the sides, proclaimed grandly, "Anyway, I have lived to tell the tale." The exertion made him cough hard enough that they all had to turn away. "For a little while."

The first thing Norma noticed when the doors opened on his hallway was the chicken. It was a healthy representative of the species and it fixed a suspicious eye upon the four people in the elevator. She felt that it demanded a response from her so she greeted it with a casual "Hello," as if she were used to stepping off big-city elevators and being greeted by chickens every day of the week and twice on Sundays. The bird clucked at her. Then there was a shriek from one end of the hall and a beautiful young woman had rushed past them and thrown her arms around Mr. Gibson. Norma had never given any thought to Mr. Gibson's private life and she found herself surprised that such a stylish and attractive young woman might be Mrs. Gibson. Norma had seen her hairdo in *Harper's Bazaar* only last month.

"I knew that something had happened," she said to him, kissing his face. "I knew it. I knew it!"

"He needs to lie down," Norma said to her; the young woman nodded back, and in that gesture, polite though it was, she let Norma know that she would now be tending to Walter.

She led them through the open door into Mr. Gibson's apartment, which was large and full of books and magazines and magical apparatus. The chicken followed them in. Framed posters of Houdini, Blackstone, Porter Hardeen, and others were hung on the walls. The young woman opened another door for them and then followed them into the bedroom. Lester and Ron lay Mr. Gibson gently on the bed. His body was limp and his eyes remained closed. Unconscious or asleep or somewhere in between—Norma couldn't tell which.

"I'm going to get him some water." The young woman swept out of the room. Her motions and movements were light and graceful.

"What do we do now?" Lester asked Norma. Even though he was speaking as softly as he could, his voice bounced around the room. Hubbard leaned over to hear the answer. "He lives or dies and we wait and pray and try to help out his wife."

"Oh, he's not married," Hubbard said discreetly, as if he was surprised that they didn't know this.

"Who is she?"

"Well, from what he told me on the way up to Providence, she's some kind of trouble."

"Ah," she said. "Should we keep an eye on her?"

Hubbard looked down at his feet, a little embarrassed.

"A different kind of trouble," Lester said with a faint smile.

The young woman came into the room again with a bowl of water and a washcloth. The two men excused themselves from the bedroom, Lester to get some coffee brewing and Ron to slip out and get some Bromo. The two women went about stripping Gibson and making him comfortable.

Norma was reconsidering all the thoughts and feelings she had let build up inside her about Walter Gibson over the years. In her mind he had taken on the bearing of a giant, because of the way he had loomed over her and Lester. It was shocking now to see how short he was. She carefully placed his glasses on the credenza next to the bed. She looked around his room. It was clean and the furniture was well chosen. Walter Gibson was short, and wore glasses, and lived in a nice apartment like theirs, and someone seemed to care for him. He was not some malevolent villain bent on destroying the Dents. He was just a writer. A man.

"My name's Norma Dent," Norma introduced herself.

The young woman tucked the sheet under Walter's chin, then tucked a wayward lock of hair behind her ear. "I'm Litzka. Do you think we should call a doctor?"

"He won't have one. I didn't know Mr. Gibson was married," Norma said, indicating the ring on Litzka's finger.

"He's not," she replied, returning Norma's quizzical gaze coolly. "I am."

"Oh."

"Well, he's not going to die. I won't let him." Litzka sat on the edge of the bed and rubbed his arm with her hand. Then she took his hand in hers. He opened his eyes and saw her. He smiled, slipped his hand from hers, tenderly touched her cheek, and retucked that lock of hair, then put his hand back in hers again.

"Hi."

"Hi," she answered. "I missed you."

"I missed you too."

"What happened?"

"I got myself into a little trouble." He closed his eyes and sank back upon the pillows. His breathing was shallow but even and some proper color had returned to his face. "I'm sorry I acted like such a"—he smiled—"a damned piehead."

"So am I," Litzka replied.

"Well, you're here now."

"I am."

Norma left her caressing Walter's hand and slipped out as quietly as she could. Lester drowsed on the sofa. The chicken scratched at the magazine on the floor. Ron had had it in his coat pocket and had tossed it onto the sofa when they arrived. Lester must have knocked it to the floor. Norma thought Ron might not appreciate having his magazine scratched up by a chicken, so she shooed it away and picked it up. On the cover of the *Astounding Tales* magazine yet another tentacled beast menaced a lingerie-wearing damsel. Someone had taken a pen to the cover and scrawled some letters but they appeared to her to be gibberish: GZXUVG HKRRGJUTTG VRAY/SOTAY NEUYIEGSOTK.

She sat down, feeling rather helpless, on the sofa, and thankfully, Lester wrapped a comforting arm around her. She settled in against him and closed her eyes, still holding the magazine.

Ron came in a while later with a big blue bottle of Bromo Seltzer and a *New York Post.* While he and Lester exchanged their stories of the events, he prowled around the apartment looking at the magic equipment and giving the chicken a wide berth. Eventually he picked up a wicked-looking dagger. It had a curved golden hilt and the long blade comprised three sides forming a triangle, each one having a razor edge. He pressed the point gingerly into the palm of his hand.

"That was a gift Harry Houdini gave to me when he returned from Egypt," Mr. Gibson said from the doorway. He had put on an undershirt and a fresh pair of pants. He coughed but held himself up. Litzka stood anxiously behind him.

"Is it magic? Does it retract or something?" Ron still pressed the point into his hand.

"No. It's just very, very sharp." Hubbard had just come to the same conclusion and put the knife back quickly.

"You know, I always wondered how he escaped from jail cells when he was naked." Ron remarked, stanching the blood flowing from the tiny cut in the palm of his hand.

"Easy. He'd take a lock pick kit. Like this." Gibson picked up several small, thin strips of metal. "He'd roll it in soft wax until it formed a pellet. Then he'd stick it up his ass. Enter the jail cell, and abracadabra! Magic!"

"Glamorous," Ron muttered with a disillusioned tone.

"You should be resting, Mr. Gibson," Norma said.

"Please, call me Walter. Or Walt. Wally even."

"Walter, then."

"And there'll be plenty of time for resting," he said, with a cough. He looked at Lester. "I could hear you telling what happened on the *Star of Baltimore.* It's got a good ending. You save my life." He stepped unsteadily into the room. "As long as we're on the subject of endings I'd like to give another story a new and better ending. I'd like to apologize about *The Golden Vulture.* I guess it comes as no surprise to you that after I read it, I had Nanovic squash it. It was not my finest moment. I was afraid of losing The Shadow. If it's any consolation, I did it because it was obvious you were a natural pulp man and you had written such a great pulp."

"It really wasn't a good Shadow story," Lester replied. "Too much story and not enough atmosphere." Norma could see no trace of the anger which Lester had held for Mr. Gibson.

"Still, I'm sorry."

"It's all right, Walter," Norma said, turning to look at the weary man. "*The Golden Vulture* did have a happy ending for us. It led Lester to Doc Savage." She was suddenly distracted by a tug on the paper in her hand. The chicken was pecking again at the mag cover.

"China Boy!" Litzka admonished him and he turned sheepishly. "He knows better."

"That's my mag," Ron noted. "I got it from Lovecraft."

"Lovecraft?" Walter looked shaken to hear that name.

"Long story," Ron answered. "He tried to write something on it but it's just garbage. I couldn't read his writing when he was alive and I guess I can't figure it out when he's dead either."

"Let me see that." Norma handed the magazine to Walter. He looked at it for a moment and then his face lit up.

"Code," he chuckled. "It's my code." Gibson eased himself into the armchair. "But without the offset number I can't decode it."

"Offset number?" Norma felt a thrill stab through her.

"It's the number which tells you how many letters to move forward in the alphabet to find the correctly corresponding letter. There's no point in writing something in code if nobody else has the key. How'd you get this?"

Ron started to tell him the tale of the dead man who came to the White Horse Tavern. Norma picked up the mag while Walter and Litzka listened incredulously.

"Well," Norma said as Walter reached the point where Lovecraft began to melt, "this monster has seven tentacles drooping from his face. Couldn't that be the key? Seven?"

"Seven?"

"I'm pretty good at finding treasure clues," she said proudly.

Gibson rifled through an end table drawer and came up with a pencil and something which looked suspiciously to her like a decoder ring. "Read the letters to me." He went to work fiddling with the ring as she read and scribbling on a notepad, stopping occasionally to cough violently. Finally he looked up at her, eyes gleaming. "Atropa belladonna plus/minus hyoscyamine."

"That sounds like some sort of compound," Ron said with a tone of indifference. He had been reading the paper while they worked and now he looked up. Norma wasn't certain but she thought he was a little sore that he hadn't been the one to figure out the code. "You'd need a chemist to know for sure."

"Maybe it's an antidote for the gas?" Norma said.

"Good boy! Good China Boy! See Walter? China Boy loves you! He's trying to help." Litzka picked up the chicken and hugged it while it clucked contentedly in her arms.

"Anyone know a chemist?" Gibson asked.

"Sure," Ron replied, turning another page of the paper his nose was buried in. "We all do."

"What?"

"Dr. Smith. He's one of us. He's a pulpateer." He realized that they were all staring at him. "What? You don't like the word *pulpateer?* I just made it up."

"No," Walter said as slowly and as patiently as he could manage. "I want you to find Doc Smith!"

Episode Forty-Two

"Is it just me?" the cowboy asked Driftwood. "Or is Mrs. Dent one helluva damn fine dame?" They were standing on the stern of the *Star of Baltimore* watching the sun come up over the East River.

Driftwood felt a surge of possessive jealousy. "Yeah. She's all right." He had taken a strong dislike to the cowboy and didn't like his speaking about Norma in that way.

"Shoot. Just all right! I'll say. First of all, those stems of hers are dynamite. And could you imagine waking up with those gray eyes looking at you from across the pillow? Or running your hands through that hair? I do love the blondes, y'know."

"Hey, I think she's spoken for, so why don't you just step off that high horse you're on about her and let someone else have a ch—I mean leave her to her husband. I saw her first anyway."

"Hell, I know she's spoken for, pard. What I want to know is where can I find one just like her that ain't spoken for. I been at sea a long time and marooned on a desert island. I'm ready for a real woman. A mate of mine told me about a cathouse down in Chinatown," he added in a slyly conspiratorial tone. "Y'know, after once the police get here."

"You were marooned for how long? A few days?"

"I wrote a poem for her." The cowboy lit a cigar stub he had found on the dock. "'On the sea is a memory of dreams that have gone. Of oceans of sorrow and fathoms of fair hair.' What do you think?"

"Seems a little personal."

"I think she kinda likes me too," he added. "Something in the way she comes in real close to talk to you, y'know?"

"Well, since you shot up the *Star of Baltimore* we'll never know, will we?"

"I could say the same about you cracking up her boat, pard."

"None of that would have happened if you'd stayed on it."

Driftwood was relieved to hear automobile tires rumbling along the planks of the dock. "I think the cavalry's arrived."

He walked to the wreckage of the gangplank, leaving the cowboy at the stern.

"The cops sure do drive nice cars up here, don't they?" the cowboy called to him.

The sedan was one of the most elegant cars Driftwood had ever seen. As it stopped, five men climbed out and stood upon the dock.

"There's good news," the cowboy said. "Somebody sent in the marines."

"That's U.S. Army," Driftwood said, feeling his old friend, that sinking feeling, clutch at him. "And that *ain't* good news."

The other men drew their sidearms. The last man out of the car was an officer; Driftwood recognized authority when he saw it, even when it wore a non-issue overcoat. The man wore his silver hair in a crew cut. His skin was nearly brown from years spent in tropical climes. He picked up a piece of paper and crumpled it. He flipped his head up, his gunmetal eyes blazing at them from under his furrowed eyebrows. In an instant Driftwood realized that he knew exactly what the man's voice would sound like. He had heard it over the radio of the *Albatross* less than an hour ago.

"Run!" he shouted at the cowboy.

The cowboy had good preservation instincts. Not needing further prompting, he dashed down the deck. Driftwood last saw him scurry into an exhaust vent. He swiveled his head around. The crashed crane on the deck made it impossible to advance to the bow. Driftwood turned and saw the hold behind him. The only way out was in. He leapt into the opening, landed on a crate, and using the crate and drums as steps down, he moved quickly to the floor of the hold.

Trying to ignore the disturbing sight of the contorted dead men on the floor, he scanned the four walls looking for an exit. A metal watertight door was set into the wall opposite his position. Far away. He heard the soldiers clambering up the cargo net. Damn, he thought, damn me for not pulling that up when I had the chance. He snatched up a fire axe. It gave him a momentary sense of power which faded into futility when he realized how useless it actually was. The soldiers had guns.

He sprinted across the floor hoping to reach the hatch door, leaping over the corpses, feeling vulnerable and exposed to the great sky above. He reached the door and threw back the metal bar which held it fast. The room was dimly illuminated by a thin beam of light from the window in the hatch of the far end of the room which seemed to lead to a corridor. He took a step into the room, then saw something that chilled his blood. He forgot all about the armed soldiers above and froze instantly.

Not all the Chinese sailors had been killed when the bullet punctured the drum. A handful of them had made it this far and managed to swing the door shut behind them. But they had been just a little too slow. One of them swung its head around to look at him now. The skin of its face had pooled around its jaw like melted wax from a candle, pulling clumps of matted hair down along with it. Drool mixed with blood foamed from its toothless maw. They must have been hit with a liquid burst of the chemical before it became a gas.

With a guttural howl, the creature threw itself at him, while the others, alerted to his presence, followed on its heels. He stumbled back into the hold, swinging the door shut as he did so. He threw the fastening bolt. He felt the creature slam into the door and saw its enraged face through the glass as it tried to gnaw its way through the porthole.

Homicidal soldiers on deck and slavering monsters below. Scylla or

Charybdis, he thought. The lady or the tiger. Okay, put a plan together. I could . . .

"Down below! Hold it right there! Don't move or I'll shoot."

One of the soldiers had Driftwood in his sights. Without hesitating Driftwood raised the axe over his head. The nadir of its trajectory was the top of a one of the barrels. "Anyone moves and I'll split one of these eggs wide open!" he shouted. "Have you seen what this shit can do? Look around. You won't have time to piss yourselves."

"Hold your fire!"

"Hey, son? " He heard another voice. It was kind and fatherly and concerned. "Hey! Can you hear me?"

"Yes," he replied. He kept his arms raised and tense and his eyes focused on the drum.

"My name is Colonel Towers," the voice continued.

"I know who you are."

"No one needs to get hurt here."

"I couldn't agree more."

"Why don't you tell me what happened here."

"Well, Colonel, it all started when I followed a white rabbit down this hole."

"That's very funny," said the colonel.

"Yes, sir. It just keeps getting curiouser and curiouser."

"Your arms getting tired there, friend?"

"No, sir. I could do this all day."

"I'm sure it won't come to that. I can tell by the way you call me 'sir' that you've seen service duty. What branch?"

"I'm part of the Fredonia Freedom Fighters."

"We're not going to get very far if you don't start cooperating."

"I don't really feel the need for cooperating, Colonel. I just want to get out of this alive."

"All right, then. Now we've found something we both want. I'll let you off this boat if you just step away and let me have my cargo."

"Can't do that, sir."

"Why not, friend?"

"Driftwood. Otis P. Driftwood. Lieutenant Driftwood."

"Okay. Why not, Lieutenant Driftwood?"

He could feel sweat trickling down the back of his neck and his palms were getting slick. He was back in the silver mine again. Only this time there was no cover and the man with the gun knew where he was. "Because we both know that this gunk is supremely deadly and we wouldn't want it to fall into the wrong hands."

"Lieutenant Driftwood, those barrels were forgotten about when you were still in short pants in whatever backwater you come from."

"So it's okay to give 'em to the Chinese to use against the Japanese?"

"This weapon will end a conflict and save tens of thousands of lives."

"Or it could escalate that conflict and cost hundreds of thousands more. Only not just soldiers. Innocent women and children. Either way, if these canisters are opened, more people die. If I can stop you from letting that happen, I will." He heard footsteps clattering on the other side of the wall and realized that the colonel had sent men into the ship. They would reach the outer hold door soon.

The colonel, stalling for time, sat down on the edge of the crane. "I first heard about this chemical more than a dozen years ago from one of its creators, an old officer much like myself who felt like confessing. I assured him of his absolution. In spite of what he told me, it was incredibly difficult to find. No one seemed to know where it had wound up. If I could have pursued it full-time, then I might have found it in half the time. As you can see, I've got a job.

"But I kept coming back to it. Found a journal notation here. A chart there. But no antidote. Never an antidote. So once I found it, even though I knew where it was, I had to wait and see if an antidote could be developed. I got so damn close, but that asshole Jeffords up in Providence could fuck up a free lunch! You know one of his morons actually burnt the antidote?"

"Guess you can't use it, right? So we can all go home, right?"

Towers barked a short, cruel laugh. "Hell no! I was thinking about it all wrong. I just decided I didn't need an antidote after all. First we are gonna use it against the Japanese. And then we're gonna use it against the renegade Chinese to bring them in line. And if a few Chinese soldiers get killed in the cross fire, who's gonna even care what happens on that side of the world? They've got scientists in China too. They can figure this stuff out. Make more of it. I can see us sailing into Tokyo Bay with a shipload of this stuff and conquering Japan without firing a shot. Who knows after that?"

"Russia's just a steppe away."

Towers laughed. "But I'm not a warmonger. I want peace. It's going to be hard to enjoy a vast fortune if I'm constantly at war."

Driftwood shifted his weight.

"The police aren't going to show up to save you, you know. No matter what happens out here, my connections will keep them from showing up. I pulled in all my favors. Dug up all my best threats. Looks like you pulled a very long watch. Bet you'd like a cigarette?"

"Yeah. I'm dyin' for one. What happens to you if this goes up in smoke, Colonel? What's the army going to do to you when they find out about this?"

"There's still time to put all this right," was the reply. "This ship will sail. It may not be carrying as much money as we had hoped. But it will still tip the entire balance of power in the Pacific. In my favor."

Driftwood heard a clang from beyond the door and then there were screams, and a single shot was fired.

"What's that?" Colonel Towers asked. "What's going on?" His confident tone wavered.

"Your boys just met some more of your boys," Driftwood said. "You should be very proud. It's a family reunion."

The shrill scream of a man in terror penetrated thinly through the heavy door. A spurt of crimson blood jetted thickly across the porthole glass. Then the sounds stopped.

Towers raised his gun and clicked back the hammer. "Okay, Groucho, I've had enough of you."

"The name's Driftwood."

"And I saw *A Night at the Opera* too!"

"Yeah? Remember the scene where Margaret Dumont falls off the patio into the pool?"

"No."

"Too bad. Because you might have remembered that she didn't fall, she was pushed."

The colonel's flat expression registered a touch of exasperation as he made certain of his aim. That was the look that Driftwood never forgot, the way he remembered Towers forever, because the man's expression never changed even as the cowboy broke a wooden plank across his back. The pistol dribbled from his fingers and he took a step forward, then stumbled over the edge, his body twisting as he fell. He crashed heavily onto the crates above Driftwood's head. The sound of the impact was so sickening that Driftwood was actually surprised when he heard the man begin to groan.

Driftwood lowered his aching arms. "Jesus Christ! Am I glad to see you."

"Yeah." The cowboy grinned as he threw down a rope. "I figured you'd be dead by now."

The bitter end of the rope fell in front of Driftwood. The muscles in his arms screamed as he picked it up. "My arms are kind of deadwood."

Towers continued to moan.

"Wrap it around your forearms and I'll pull you up."

Driftwood listened and watched, feeling helpless, as Lew dragged a block and tackle across the deck and hung it from a twisted piece of the crane wreckage. He began to loop the rope through the pulley.

Driftwood looked down from the figure of the cowboy to see Colonel Towers scrambling over the edge of the crates toward him, his face a moist, shapeless, bloody mess. Except for the eyes. The eyes were gleaming with fury and murder. The colonel skidded down the stack of crates, the rough wood edges tearing cloth and flesh from his body.

The rope still felt slack. Behind him Driftwood heard the pounding on the hold door suddenly increase as if the creatures on the other side had suddenly grown more frantic.

Somehow Towers landed on his feet on the floor of the hold, and staggered with clumsy determination toward Driftwood, what was left of his teeth now gritted and showing as his lips peeled back. He raised his hands toward Driftwood not as if he were going to punch him, but as if he were going to claw him apart, rip his throat and his eyes out, dig out his heart and his bowels.

"Damn me," Driftwood muttered to himself.

His arms were yanked up abruptly, and the pain snapped through his body with the force of a whip. His feet were leaving the ground. He felt the rush of air as Towers leaped for him and missed, and then he was several feet above the colonel and still levitating. A look of desperate frustration snarled across Towers's face, and Driftwood knew that this man would never stop coming for him. His eyes never leaving Driftwood's, Towers put his hand on the hold latch. Driftwood could hear nothing on the other side.

"I wouldn't," he cautioned Towers.

"I'll meet you on deck," the man snarled back. The latch slammed back and he threw open the door.

Driftwood caught a glimpse of the room beyond the hatch, gore and viscera as in a butcher's shop. He would never eat a rare steak again. He saw Towers freeze in the doorway. Then the colonel turned and ran back into the hold. Driftwood watched him scramble madly upon a pallet of gas-filled barrels in the center of the hold. His quick glimpse of a rush of creatures slithering and mashing their way into the hold was suddenly obliterated by the brilliant sunlight as his head was raised above the level of the hold.

Driftwood grabbed at the deck and Lew helped him roll over onto his back. He lay on the deck, breathing deeply. The warm sun was shining on his face and he could hear seagulls crying in the air. The sea air smelled delicious. The pain was receding from his arms and he was alive. He began to chuckle, helplessly.

"What is it?" the cowboy asked. "Why are you laughin'? Damn it! What's so funny, Otis?"

"Bob!" He shouted into the cool morning air, "My name's Bob! I'm Bob again. Bob. Bob. Bob!" Then the laughter came on again and it all seemed so sublimely ridiculous. He couldn't stop laughing or saying his name; to say it now seemed so simple and so funny. *Bob.* It was the funniest sound in the universe. In a little while, the sheer giddiness of it left him and he was able to speak again. "It feels so good just to hear my own name again after so many months of lying about it. Bob. My name's Bob Heinlein, Lew."

"Pleased to meet ya, Bob."

"Yeah. Yeah. Likewise." The deck metal felt cool against his back. It felt good. Everything felt good again. "I didn't think I was gonna get out of that hole alive. I feel like I've been in that hole a very long time."

The cowboy nodded.

Heinlein sat up, slowly. "I don't think I've ever felt so good in all my life." He smiled and drank in the feeling. "There's only one thing that could make me feel any better, y'know?"

"A woman." The cowboy nodded again.

"Or two." He closed his eyes and tried to imagine it.

"Well, Bob. There was that little place down in Chinatown I was mentioning earlier."

He opened his eyes. "What about him?" The sounds of Towers trying to kick the creatures off the barrels had reached his ears. He thought about looking into the pit to see what exactly was happening, but he knew he didn't need to see exactly what was happening. The creatures would be swiping at Towers like lions in a zoo trying to pull a carcass from a meat hook.

"I reckon he might have other things on his mind than a few loose women."

"Throw me a rope," they heard him scream.

"Sorry, Colonel," Driftwood said, as he rose to his feet, in a voice far too low for the colonel to hear. "I think your ship has finally sailed."

Towers began to scream as the two men climbed down the cargo netting. By the time they reached what was left of the dock, the screams had turned to distant gurgles. And as they gingerly picked their way across the wrecked boards to safety, silence fell upon the *Star of Baltimore.*

Episode Forty-Three

"THERE WAS death afoot in the darkness.

"The eerie fog still gripped Chinatown and the red flag of war still flew from the top of the highest building. And while the cops and the On Leong tong had placed men all around the old hotel to protect Ah Hoon, what they forgot to watch was the rooftops," Lester Dent told Walter Gibson. "Two Hip Sing men made their way furtively across the roofs, from one building to another. They stayed low because the fireworks were illuminating the sky and they didn't want to be caught in the glare.

"Their meticulous trip took them several hours and it was early in the morning when they finally arrived at the building next door to the old hotel, the one with the windowless wall. Seven floors below them, on the opposite side of the gap, Ah Hoon sweated out the night. They had carried an old wooden chair with them and when they reached the building's ledge, they tied some rope around it. Then one of the men tied the other man into the chair. He looped the rope around the chimney and lowered him down the wall.

"Remember, there was only about a three-foot gap between the buildings, and a lethal abyss waited below, so the man in the chair had one helluva lousy ride. When he finally reached the level of the window, he pulled out a rifle that he had carried with him and rested the barrel on the windowsill so that that the bullet wouldn't shatter the glass. The little comic must have heard that small sound, that frightening tap. He sat up in his bed and slowly looked to the window. His eyes met those of the man dangling beyond the glass and he recognized his assassin. What he saw was Mock Duck, bound to a chair and dangling precariously outside his window like a side of Peking pork ribs in the window of a Chinese chop suey shop. Ah Hoon knew that Death had found him, but the sight of his once-feared antagonist's face covered with flop sweat and glowing red from the tightness of the ropes, his clothes torn from the bouncing scrapes against the walls and his eyes wild from the terrors of the descent, was too much for the comedian. He showed his approval for the comedic efforts on his behalf the only way he knew how. He began to laugh.

"As Ah Hoon broke into his first peal of laughter an enormous skyrocket exploded overhead. The blast from its charge rattled the windows of buildings for blocks and its glittering flames drew all eyes. Under the cover of its storm and stress, Mock Duck pulled the trigger. The look of astonishment the police found on Ah Hoon's face the next morning was the look of a man who found his own death ridiculously funny. Which is an appropriate epitaph for a comic.

"That one shot was all it took to end the reign of the On Leong tong and bring victory to the Hip Sing. The On Leong were crushed, demoralized. That one shot ended the Sweet Flower War and signaled the ascendancy of the Hip Sing. By noon of that day, as the menacing mist dissipated, the flag of war was lowered, and to this day it has never flown over Chinatown again.

"And that," Kenneth Robeson told Maxwell Grant, "is the story as I got it direct from the horse's or, in this case, the Duck's mouth."

Even as he sat across the dining room table from Lester Dent, Walter Gibson could feel his body craving opium. The coughing fits were killing his chest, and his throat was raw. He didn't want to worry them, especially Litzka, but he was struggling to keep his words from slurring and his hands from shaking. Every time he closed his eyes he instantly envisioned the gas roiling up at him. Still, his mind felt more alert than it had in months, and he had the sensation that a weight had been lifted from his shoulders.

Smith's wife had informed them that the writer had already left but that he breakfasted every morning at a coffee shop in the vicinity of his doughnut laboratory—in order, she said, to see what doughnuts people favored. Hubbard had been dispatched to scour the area. While they waited for him to call, the conversation had turned to writing. Walter actually found it pleasant to have a conversation with Lester Dent. Dent was the only other writer in the pulp game who could understand the kind of pressure Gibson operated under.

"How much do you hate not being able to use your own name on *Doc*?" Gibson asked.

"Almost as much as I hate not being paid a percentage of the sales. John Nanovic showed me a list of house names to choose from and said take it or leave it. I picked Kenneth Robeson because it sounded rugged and adventurous, yet vaguely cosmopolitan," Lester told him. "What about you?"

"I came up with Maxwell Grant from two friends of mine. One was Maxwell Holden, who had just retired from vaudeville to open a magic shop in New York. He had a hand shadow act in which he formed life-size silhouettes that moved across a screen. My other friend was U. F. Grant, of Pittsfield, Massachusetts, who invented an illusion used by the Great Blackstone in which he walks away from his own shadow, leaving it behind in full view.

"Since these were both devices that I intended to attribute to The Shadow in his role as an avenger, I felt that the pen name of Maxwell Grant would be appropriate, so I appropriated it." He sipped his coffee.

"There's something I've been wanting to ask you," Dent said. "Why did you mess with success?"

"Hmm?"

"The Allard thing? Why mess with your formula?"

Gibson thought for a moment. He hadn't been able to answer the question for Welles or Rozen. He looked at his fingers. "I wanted to try and find out who The Shadow really was," he said at last.

Dent leaned in. "And?"

"Only The Shadow knows."

Norma came out of Gibson's bedroom, having changed into the clothes Lester had brought from the boat: a brown skirt with a cream-colored blouse. She had refreshed herself with a shower. Gibson appraised her quickly, hoping her husband wasn't watching him. Old Lester had done all right for himself, that much was for sure.

He heard a cough. Litzka was curled up on the sofa reading Hubbard's *Post.* He saw her eyes flit from him to Norma. "Feeling better?"

"Much. Anything in the paper?"

"Nothing about the Bank Note building. Nothing on the radio either. You'd think something like that would at least be on the radio."

"Towers," said Gibson, simply. The two women agreed.

"Avenger," murmured Dent. "Now that's a good word. Avenger. *The Avenger.* I've been thinking of a new character who is a master of disguise, which is my favorite pulp trick. I have this image of this gray face, stone gray, like a dead man's. Instead of using makeup, he'd actually be able to mold his face to look like the person he wanted to impersonate. And the only way his villains would know he wasn't who they thought he was is that he is incapable of showing emotions."

"As if the nerves of his face didn't work?"

"Exactly. Because maybe some bad guy did something to him to make him that way. Only he can't keep up the disguise for very long. Just long enough to get into trouble or penetrate a group and find out evil plans. Everything else he'd have to handle with other skills. And his role would be a kind of an avenger for those who have nowhere else to turn."

"That sounds like a character Street & Smith could get behind. You should talk to Nanovic."

"Who knows?" Lester shrugged the suggestion off. "There just never seems to be enough time to write everything that needs to be written. I mean, sure, I could write *The Avenger.* But if I'm writing that, then I'm not writing something meaningful. Something great."

"*Doc Savage* is great pulp. You shouldn't put yourself down."

"Yeah, but it's not important."

"To who? To a bunch of ivory-tower longhairs? To the fellas that run the slicks? To hell with them and the horses they rode in on! I read *Doc Savage.* It's obvious how much you love writing it. You shouldn't be embarrassed about it."

"You read *Doc Savage?*"

"Of course I do. The only way to stay number one is to know what number two is doing."

"Yeah. I feel the same way about *The Shadow.*"

Gibson smiled at him. Dent pulled out his pipe and his tobacco pouch. When he unzipped the pouch, water sloshed out of it and onto the coffee table. "Damn! Sorry."

"Don't worry about it. In case you haven't noticed, the contents of this apartment include a chicken. A little water's not going to hurt anything."

"I don't suppose you have any pipe tobacco?"

"No. Just cigarettes."

Dent shook his head. "I'm a pipe man."

"Well, there's a smoke shop about five blocks down on the west side of the street. They should open in about fifteen minutes."

After Dent left, Litzka helped Gibson drink a little more Bromo Seltzer; it soothed his headache. "You know, that's the longest conversation I've ever had with Lester."

"Well, he's not much of a talker around people he doesn't know very well," Norma said, sitting down and picking up Lester's unfinished coffee. Litzka flipped to the theater section. "He didn't grow up around people, and they can make him nervous."

"What do you mean, 'he didn't grow up around people'?"

"He had a lonely life growing up. I can't imagine a lonelier life for a little boy and it makes my heart ache.

"Sometimes I see it in his eyes when he doesn't know I'm watching him, that faraway look like he's back out there in the middle of nowhere, alone and friendless and looking over the horizon and wondering if he'll ever escape there. It's one of the reasons he loves New York City so much; he likes to be surrounded by people. He likes the constant noise and the commotion and the sense that he can't ever really be alone here, no matter what."

"My family was a part of Philadelphia society," Gibson said. "There were always parties to go to and people around."

"But you looked at the horizon too," she said, "or you wouldn't be here doing what you're doing."

He nodded. "I guess you're right."

"What do you think Zhang Mei's going to do with the gas?"

"I have no idea."

"You said there was one drum of gas left on the truck that was never put aboard the ship. What do you think he'll do with it?"

"Like I said, I don't know."

"You spent all that time with him writing about him. Think about him as if he's one of your characters."

"My characters aren't usually that deep."

"Maybe he's not either. Maybe you just wrote him that way. What would he be after if he were your character?"

"Revenge. He'd seek revenge. If he couldn't strike back at the Japanese, he'd try to find a way to strike back at Mi-Ying. But he's ten thousand miles away back in China. It'd be just as hard to get back at him as it would be to get back at the Japanese. But that's what I'd have my character do, anyway."

"Ming!" Litzka suddenly interrupted, looking up in surprise from the *Post.*

"What?" Gibson asked.

"Ming, right? You said Ming?"

"Mi-Ying."

"That's what I said," she snapped. She flipped back a few pages and then held out the newspaper. "The New York Chinese consul general's name is Mi-Ying."

Gibson scanned the small article. He smacked his forehead the way Norma had seen Lester do time and time again. He put the paper on the table. She could see one man whom the paper identified as General Chiang Kai-shek standing next to another man, Mi-Ying. "This is the same photo on the poster that Zhang Mei showed me. That's why he said he would be celebrating with his brothers. If Mi-Ying is going to be there, Zhang Mei will be there as well."

"Revenge?" Norma asked.

"Revenge," he nodded. "He doesn't care about anyone in Chinatown. Barely thinks they're real people, let alone real Chinese. If he has to open that drum of gas to get his revenge, he'll do it. But he'll want to see Mi-Ying's face when he dies."

"What happens to Chinatown if he lets the gas out?" Litzka nervously toyed with China Boy's feathers.

"Oh, my God!" Norma stood up. "Mr. Yee will be there. He's throwing a banquet for his Hip Sing Association. And he'll have Monk and Ham with him."

"Who's that?" Litzka asked.

"Friends. Children. My dumplings."

Norma grabbed the telephone but the operator was unable to connect her with Mr. Yee's restaurant or anyone who spoke English at the Hip Sing Association, and the police were lazily indifferent to her warning about a gas attack in Chinatown. "I'm going down there," she said resolutely, hanging up. "I have to warn them."

"Why don't you wait for Lester?" Gibson said to her.

"I'll be all right," she said. "I'll be back before he is."

"Let me get dressed," he insisted. "I'll come with you." He heard his front door close as soon as he left the room.

The elevator took forever to work its way back up to his hallway. The building was coming to life in the morning and people got on at almost every floor. Finally it opened on the lobby and he got out. He rushed outside and saw Lester Dent sauntering down the sidewalk, puffing contentedly on his pipe.

"Hey." Lester grinned at him. "What are you doing up?"

Quickly Gibson filled him in. Dent's face clouded over and he threw his pipe aside. A family wagon was pulling away from the curb and Gibson watched in astonishment as Dent sprang upon its running board as he had had Doc Savage do a hundred times over. The little boy in the back seat looked through the window at him in naked amazement.

"Chinatown!" Dent loudly commanded and the driver complied by hitting the accelerator like Barney Oldfield. The momentum was too much for Dent. He was flung from the car and landed in a sprawling heap in the middle of the road. Amused, Gibson ran to help him up as the car rounded the corner and disappeared from view, presumably still heading toward Chinatown.

"Okay," he said, helping Dent up. "Looks like you found another thing that only happens in the pulps."

Episode Forty-Four

THE WALL of noise was deafening.

"A Chinese festival can last for days!" Dent shouted to Gibson over the furious storm of firecrackers. "Not like American parades at all!"

"I've been to Chinatown before, Dent!"

The festival had started at dawn; streets were closed to traffic and the cabbie had been forced to let them off at Grand Street. The day was warming quickly. The sidewalks were thronged with revelers. In the streets, two-man lion dancers from one association squared off against a longer, dozen-man dragon costume from another, while men bearing wooden drums hung from straps on their necks beat the tempo. Bottle rockets blasted into the sky and exploded over their heads. Men waved boards plastered with solemn photos of General Chiang Kai-shek, and children shouted Chinese chants of solidarity with their brothers back home. Exotic aromas from a hundred kitchens filled the air like a haze.

The gate was still down at Mr. Yee's restaurant and no amount of pounding seemed to rouse anyone from within. An old woman suddenly appeared by Lester's side. He looked down into her wrinkled face. She spoke to him but he didn't understand. Then she pointed away down toward Mott Street and Hip Sing territory. Lester grimly noted that the woman had no fingers on either hand; she gestured with a scarred knuckle-stub while she yammered urgently in Chinese.

They forced their way up the sidewalk toward the Hip Sing Association building. Lester plowed through the mass of people; his sheer bulk relative to the smaller people all around him made his progress almost unstoppable. At the same time he had never felt so powerless. He kept looking for that glint of golden hair which would be Norma, but there were no blondes on the streets of Chinatown today.

Gibson was out of breath. His face was gray and sweat poured profusely down it. He kept pace without complaining, but Dent had seen him stagger loosely once or twice as he was clipped by the elbows or shoulders of bystanders.

"You okay?" Dent asked at one point.

Gibson nodded. But he knew what the staggers meant. Exposure to that shit.

They entered the Hip Sing Association building. The men inside were formally dressed in suits or traditional Chinese silk robes. Dent recognized a man as one of those who had attended his induction and he rushed to him. The man's English was poor but Dent pantomimed and stressed the names he wanted to communicate. Was Mr. Yee here? No. Had a woman come by to find him? Yes. Where had she gone? The man smiled but could only shrug, helpless.

Suddenly something was tugging at Dent's pants and he heard a voice squeaking, "Mr. Doc! Mr. Doc!"

He looked down and there was little Ham. Monk came running up to join them.

"Hey, boys! Where's your father?"

"He's shopping," said Monk. "Mrs. Doc was here," he added as a matter of fact.

"She was. Was she with your father?"

Ham shook his head. "No. But she was looking for him. We told her that he was coming back. Then she told us not to go anywhere and she left."

"Where did she go?"

The two boys took a sullen, silent stance. They had done something wrong.

"You didn't stay here, did you?"

Ham nodded as the confession was pried out of him.

"Did you follow her?"

The little boy nodded again.

"Where did she go?"

Ham looked to his older brother. "She went to the old theater," Ham said, guiltily, at last. "She tried to go inside. But some big men came out instead and took her."

"Damn."

"You know where she went?" Gibson wanted to know.

Lester turned to Gibson. "Her and her goddamned treasure. And I'm the one who's supposed to give up adventures?" He turned to the dumplings. "Boys, this time I'm very serious. I want you to stay here. Tell your father where I went. I promise you, you won't get in trouble." He looked at Walter. "Coming?"

"Hell yes!"

They left the worried boys behind and forged back into the confusing mass before Gibson was fully able to catch his breath. They pushed their way to Doyers Street, which, being off the parade route, was not in as much turmoil. Lester burst into a sprint and arrived at the front door of the theater. He threw his weight against the heavy boards but they wouldn't budge. He turned to call for help from Gibson.

Gibson was standing, helplessly, at the head of the alley. He seemed forlorn. "There's another way in," he said, flatly. Lester joined him and they looked down the long, dark alley. A red lantern hung over a door at the end of the pathway.

The opium den was dark and appeared abandoned as they entered. "This is the place?" Lester asked Gibson.

He nodded. "Yeah. This is the place."

There was a soft rattle from the darkness; it was the gentle sound of beaded curtains being moved. Dent's eyes fell upon three men who stood in the shadows. Dent was positive they hadn't been there the moment before. It was if he had simply blinked, and in the instant in which his eyes were closed, they had appeared out of thin air. Each held a long sliver of curled steel. One of the men hissed at him through clenched teeth. Dent recognized him. It was the man he had knocked to the street during the last trip to Chinatown. The glare in his eyes showed that he was ready to settle the score. He hissed at Dent again.

Dent suddenly found himself wishing he had brought the gun from the *Albatross.* Even empty it might have menaced his attacker. For all his close scrapes he had never been much of a fistfighter and he knew his chances against this knife-wielding fiend were low. His eyes swept around for something, anything, which could be used as a weapon. But the flimsy opium pipes lying near the abandoned daises were the only possible objects at hand. The man made a threatening gesture at him. Then he grinned maliciously and raised his knife.

Walter Gibson suddenly stepped forward, in front of Dent, and held out his hands, palms toward the men. A brilliant burst of fire seemed to explode in the air just before his fingertips. The lethal attacker staggered back, blinded. The other two men drew back. Gibson thrust his hands forward again and another fireball exploded in the room, closer to them. Sparks showered upon the man who had threatened to attack Dent, and curls of flame appeared on his shirt. He dropped his knife and began pounding at them with the palms of his hands even as they spread.

"Go!" Gibson shouted at Dent. With a nod of his head he indicated the staircase to Dent's left. Dent raced up. He heard another *whoosh* and felt the heat of another one of Gibson's miraculous fire bursts. He heard a man screaming. He hoped it wasn't Walter. Then he was at the top of the staircase and entering the back of the theater.

Spots caused by the bursts of flame danced before his eyes. It took him a few moments to clear his vision and scan the stage, which was barren except for fallen bolts of aged stage cloth and the spiderweb tangles of theatrical rope which swooped up and down through the rigging. His eyes fell on one of the bundles and he realized in a moment of pure horror that it wasn't a pile of velvet. It was his wife.

She was motionless. He fell to her side. Her arms were raised over her head and a rope bound them together at the wrists. The taut rope ascended into the rafters.

"Norma?"

Her chest rose and fell but he couldn't rouse her. He patted her cheeks but there was no reaction. He felt panic rise up in him. He slipped a hand under her head and felt something warm and wet. He pulled his hand away and stared dumbly at the blood. He felt again; the lump at the base of her skull felt as large as an egg to him. Somebody had clobbered her good.

He smelled smoke and looked back; it was billowing out from the wings. He struggled with the knot but the rope was thick and the knot was fiendish. He looked around for something to cut it, but the stage was devoid of anything that could be used. He tried tugging at it, but it was fastened securely up above. He tried again with the knot; he couldn't even begin to figure out where the end was. Her wrists were chafed and scraped and her fingertips were pale blue. He pulled on the rope as hard as he could.

"You're just making it tighter."

Gibson was at Dent's side. He was breathing heavily but his eyes blazed with excitement. He squatted beside her and his fingers flew over the knots like the wings of a dove. Dent sat back on his haunches and felt her wrist; her pulse was weak and fluttery. Smoke was filling the theater.

"I think I set the place on fire," Gibson muttered.

"I don't think anyone'll care."

Suddenly the ropes fell in loose coils from her wrists and Gibson sat back with a triumphant gleam on his face. "*The Complete Guide to Knots and How to Tie Them* by Walter B. Gibson. It's still in print. You should pick up a copy."

"I will." Dent scooped Norma up. Her body was amazingly light and frighteningly limp. "Her treasure's gone," he said.

"You're right," Gibson sounded surprised. "There was a statue here yesterday."

Dent turned to the wings and the staircase, but smoke poured out of the staircase as though it were a chimney. He heard a metallic clank on the stairs and the warrior with the busted jaw stepped out of the smoke. He had ripped off his jacket and shirt. Dent and Gibson could see the fresh burns on his torso. He let an object fall to the floor. Lester recognized the metal tip of the whip chain as it hit the boards with a heavy thud.

"Any more magic tricks up your sleeves?" Dent said.

"What do you want, a grand finale?" Gibson asked.

"Got one?"

"I might."

The man unfurled the long coils of chain, slowly dragging their length through his hands. He sneered at Dent and Gibson, a desperate, enraged expression.

Dent heard a loud crash from the middle of the auditorium. A section of wood floor exploded back in a cloud of dust. The building's collapsing, he thought. An instant later a familiar face and shoulders appeared in the new hole in the floor, emerging from the dust cloud the trapdoor had stirred up like a genie rising from a bottle.

"Yee!" Dent shouted.

"This way!" Yee replied urgently. "Chinatown tunnels!"

Dent turned back to Gibson, who had bravely stepped between him and the chain-wielding man. Gibson nodded at him.

Dent said, "I'll meet you at the Hip Sing building."

"Don't be late."

"I've never missed a deadline in my life."

Dent took the small flight of side steps down to the house floor. He gently lowered Norma down to the arms of Mr. Yee, who vanished with her into the dark tunnel. The dry boards of the stage burst into flames and any path back to Gibson was cut off. Dent jumped into the passageway.

Lester made his way through the darkness following the bobbing flame he could see ahead of him in the distance. The air was fetid and the smell of smoke followed him. His feet splashed through dank, cold water that smelled of street refuse. He had to keep his head low; he found this out after running heavily into a low rafter. Above him he heard the thudding sound of the celebration as he traveled along. Periodically he would hear an encouraging shout from Mr. Yee, which kept him from choosing the wrong way at any number of intersections which cropped up along the way.

In time he saw a ladder at the end of the tunnel, rushing toward him as he ran. The hatch above it was open and light poured down in a distinct shaft. He scrambled up the steps and found himself suddenly surrounded by helpful hands and concerned Chinese faces. He felt little bodies embracing him.

"Thanks, boys," he said to the dumplings, giving Ham a reassuring hug. He was in the basement of the Hip Sing Association building.

Norma lay on the floor, still comatose, as he disentangled himself from the two boys. "She's been hit in the head," he said to Mr. Yee. "She needs a doctor."

"Follow me," his friend said.

Lester gently hoisted her up again and followed Mr. Yee up the flights of stairs to the joss house. The room was full of men, Dent noted at once. They stood at the windows watching the parade pass below them. The room was elegantly and elaborately decorated for the celebration, with red and gold banners and money gathered by the good people of Chinatown and prepared in chests to be delivered to the Chinese consulate. Mock Duck sat in a carved wooden chair and another distinguished man sat in a chair next to him. This man was being subserviently tended to by the man Mock Duck had been having dinner with the night Lester and Norma had come to the restaurant from the theater.

Mr. Yee quietly pulled a man from the crowd at the window. The man came to Dent and examined Norma's head. He clucked his tongue in worry and then he indicated that Dent should carry her body to a room hidden behind a sliding screen.

They laid her out on a small table and gently rolled her on her side. The man examined her more closely. He took a silk cloth and folded it a number of times and then placed it against her head. It instantly began turning red with blood. He placed Dent's hand on the cloth and indicated the severe amount of pressure he wanted him to apply. Then he turned and picked up a collection of small needles which lay on a red pillow. As he transferred the collection to the table he spoke to Mr. Yee.

Mr. Yee placed a comforting hand on Dent's arm. "He wants you to know there is much blood flowing to this injury which may be swelling the brain. He is going to try to decrease the swelling and slow the blood. He wants to know if you understand about Chinese medicine and acupuncture."

"A little. I've read about it. But I've never seen it."

"He says we must get started right away. The needles will not hurt her. He is a very good healer. He is the very best in America. Can you trust his skill?"

Lester thought for a moment of trying to carry Norma through Chinatown to find a hospital. There would be blocks and blocks filled with people. No ambulance could possibly get through in time. "You are my Hip Sing brother," Lester Dent said at last. "I can trust this man's skill if you say I should."

Mr. Yee gave a single nod to the healer. Then he pulled Lester aside so the man could work. The dumplings circulated around their knees, nervously. Dent rubbed Ham's hair.

"Yee?" he asked. "Who's that man by your uncle. The VIP?"

"Him? He is an important diplomat. He is the consul general. His name is Mi-Ying."

Episode Forty-Five

THE WHIRLING chain of death was mesmerizing.

The warrior spun it around with such force that it fanned away the smoke attempting to engulf him. Yet Gibson was amazed at how conservative his motions were; there was no waste of energy as he methodically built up the speed of the tip and plotted its trajectory toward Gibson's heart. This was going to be a kill that he wanted to savor.

The floorboards beneath Gibson's feet groaned as he took several wary steps back; the supports beneath them were being devoured by the growing conflagration in the den below. The man with the chain calmly adjusted his position. Gibson knew he was being toyed with. He could feel the temperature rising in the room. Glowing embers drifted up between the cracks and gaps of the planks. The whole world was going up in flames. The stage floor threatened to crack open beneath him; hell awaited below.

He shook his hands to unhinge the magical apparatus he had spent the train ride from Providence working on. From his left hand fell the squeezable pouch of flash powder, now empty. Attached to his other wrist was a modified mousetrap; the mechanism was turned on its side and reattached to a metal cuff; flint and rock were fastened to the striking mechanism. It took only a quick flick from the left hand to reset it while the audience's vision was still bedazzled and distracted by the previous explosion. Now the contraption seemed stuck to him. Maybe his sweat had glued it to his skin. He wondered what Blackstone would say about how his magic had been put to use. He would probably say something like "Rest in peace, Walter Gibson."

He coughed, and the metal spike whizzed past his moving head, tearing through a muslin flat depicting a mountain of rice paddy terraces. The blackest smoke seeped up from below and as the killer yanked back on his chain, pulling the spike free, the room grew dark, the only light coming up in thin shafts from below. Terrific, Gibson thought, now I can't even see him.

If I can't see him, he can't see me.

He slipped through the gap the whip chain had just created in the mountains and ducked. The spike punched through the muslin again, above his head, tearing another hole. Gibson heard the man cough; the smoke was growing thicker. He leaped over a row of seats and ran for cover behind the gates of an Imperial palace, a rotting wood frame of forced perspective. He heard the spike bite at the wood of the seats he had just rolled over. The killer had truly lost sight of him. He produced a scarf and held it to his mouth and nose, filtering out as much of the smoke as he could. Floorboards creaked wearily: the man was hunting for him, moving in his direction. Smoke continued to seep up into the room.

Beyond the gates where he now hid, a tattered silk scrim hung loosely from bamboo poles. Dyed upon it were the faded shapes of a court of powerful Chinese gods. The delicate fabric would have seemed nearly invisible when lit from behind. But when lights were focused on it from the front of the stage, it would have become as opaque as a wall and the images of the gods would have magically appeared, startling the audience caught under their watchful, judging gaze. In the dim orange glow of flames and sparks licking up through the stage boards, the gods flickered in and out of existence. Behind the scrim lay the brick wall and beyond it lay the dark shapes of other set pieces. On the other side of those relics was the back of the house where the doors to the street would be.

As quietly as he could while still moving, Gibson slid from behind the palace gate to the scrim, his back against the wall. He moved by inches, his hand still holding the cloth to his face, until he was behind the first deity, a thunder-faced ogre. He tried to relax his heaving chest as Houdini had once shown him. The sensation of being exposed was terrifying to his instincts; he forced himself to suppress the fear. It was one thing to know intellectually that he was concealed; it was another thing to believe it without actually being on the other side to see the proof.

He could see the killer clearly. The man stood only several yards away, fanning away the smoke that clouded his vision. He had coiled his whip chain up around his arm and the spike extended like a fang from his fist. He turned to and fro, wildly searching for a sign of his prey, snarling in near-animal frustration, surrendering to his instincts when Gibson would not.

A shower of sparks burst up through the stage. As the killer spun to look, Gibson slid farther down the wall, taking his place behind a goddess who stood holding the oceans in one hand and a ship in the other. He stifled a cough and the killer, unsure of his ears, swung his head in Gibson's direction. The man's eyes fell upon the scrim as a section of the upstage planks surrendered to the flames devouring it from below in a great crash, flames bursting through in an excited rush to fill its vacuum. The killer, staring right at Gibson, became a silhouette against the flaring light. Gibson held perfectly still, not even breathing lest he stir the silk and destroy the illusion. He looked through the eyes of the goddess, abandoning his visual focus, letting his sight grow soft, seeing it all at once so nothing could surprise him. He felt his flesh become the brick of the wall at his back, flowing out and finding purchase in the infinite crevasses like moss on a rock. He willed his mind to give no indication of its presence and as the light from the burning stage fell upon the scrim, he became invisible, the shadow of the gods.

His killer took several steps closer and cast a skeptical eye on the mural he must be seeing quite clearly on his side. Gibson was so close he could see the man's shaking hands, the tears pouring from his rage-red eyes, the black smoke smudges drawn across his face. The man spat on one of the gods. Evidently some grudges run deeper than others, Gibson thought. As the man moved to the goddess, Gibson could see through her eyes how the man admired in her form the perfection of his race. Gibson forced himself to be cold, to have no emotion about the man, the god, or their communication. With a rending squeal, the stage collapsed completely, and Gibson could feel the tremendous heat from below roil up with volcanic fury. For sure, it filled the stage with enough light to guarantee the illusion the scrim provided. His killer leaned forward to look into the goddess's eyes. Gibson's eyes were an inch away. Slowly his killer leaned in and tenderly kissed the painted mouth of the goddess. His lips were as close to Gibson's as a whisper. As he finally stepped away to take in the spectacle of the destruction of the stage, the inferno from below was raising the final curtain on Death.

The floorboards began to crack in a centerline rift, falling to the left or right, wherever their attachments were strongest. Gibson could see the backdrop of a small rural village being devoured in flames. His killer staggered back as the building shook, then raced to the other side of the room as if he had heard or sighted Gibson there. He struck several times but only succeeded in impaling a weary old wicker mannequin.

Total clarity came to Gibson. The building would be devoured within minutes: no infant spark could ask for better tinder than what it could find here. The exit lay ahead. With his killer distracted, he ran. The floorboards were shifting, losing solidity, but weirdly seemed more alive and true to their natural origin. As they rattled and clattered against one another, they became strange leaves rustling together on a flat tree, or a windswept field of long grass. He sprinted through a simple family hut, all the furnishings still set around the feasting table through intricate, patient layers of bas-relief paint. He heard a shout behind him and the rattle of chain. He leaped over a train track and knocked a hollow bookcase filled with hollow books out of his way. A cinder fell on his shoulder and he slapped a hand back against the pain. He felt the metal sliding away and realized that the fire he felt wasn't from the flame. The spike had only glanced off him but had flayed his shoulder blade open.

The impact made him stumble. He fell with his back against the wall and slid to his knees.

The whip chain spun again. He held up his forearm to shield his face and the spike drove into it with a stunning impact. The warrior grinned savagely. Gibson returned the grin. The killer gave the chain a tremendous pull with both hands, attempting to rip Gibson's arm out or fling him halfway to him. Gibson's sleeve burst open as if it had exploded. And the metal band which held the fireball device that he hadn't been able to release earlier released because of the spike embedded in the locking mechanism, and it flew back toward his killer, striking his forehead. Blood foamed forth immediately. Blackstone had always told him a secret to an old carny geek trick, "Lot of blood vessels up there. Small cut—lots of blood." Gibson could remember to tell him now, "Big cut—much more blood."

Gibson slid back up the wall. He checked out his wrist. It would be bruised, but the tip of the spike hadn't broken through the armband. He heard his killer scream at him and saw the spike flying toward him again. He slid to the left and it struck the brick to the right of his head, showering brick dust into his face. The floorboards began to collapse down the center of the room, a blazing chasm opening up between his killer and him. The spike came again and slid back again. And then again. He couldn't even see his killer now; he could only sense the angry dart seeking him out. A plaster of paris golden mountain blocked his progress finally. He fell back against the wall and something snagged the back of his jacket, pinning him.

A gulf of fire opened between the two men; it opened like a seam tearing to reveal a blasted vision. His killer launched his dart up into a beam, where it bit deeply; then he swung across the flaming chasm, landing ten feet away from Walter. He yanked on the chain, unable to free it. He smirked: his next tug would.

Gibson, struggling to free himself from the object that had hooked him from behind, found his hand upon a doorknob. He uttered a silent prayer to his goddess and gave it a twist. It opened out and he flung himself backward against it. Bright light fell upon his face and he hit the sidewalk. He instantly raised his head to prepare for the final attack.

His killer screamed and jumped into the air, grabbing the chain with two hands, hoping to let his falling weight drag it free. At the same moment the opening of the door allowed a huge rush of oxygen-rich air to sweep in to replenish the rapidly dwindling supply. Gibson actually felt the rush of the wind. The flames leaping through the gap behind his killer suddenly roared with renewed, violent vigor. In midair as this happened, the man's spike pulled free and he dropped into the center of a swirling whirlwind of fire. This horror lasted but a moment as the impact of his landing sent him crashing, with a shriek, through the crumbling boards into the roasting inferno below.

Gibson pushed himself quickly to his knees. "Holy Christ!" Suddenly from below, he saw a glint of an object flying up. The spike was driven deeply into the balcony rafter. Gibson didn't want to, but he looked down into the canyon of hell. He saw the man engulfed in flame climb his chain. One hand after another, while he screamed until his vocal cords burned away. Gibson rose to his feet. And still his killer tried, a trembling hand reaching for the wood plank, fingertips gripping. With a snap, the burning links of the chain fell apart and the man disappeared forever from view.

Gibson began to cough and it was several moments before he successfully spat, belched, vomited, and expectorated the smoke out of his lungs. He produced another silk, a clean one, and wiped the tears from his eyes.

"Walter?" He was still too close to the dark smoke and shadows of the building to see the figure in the alley. He took a step forward, into the light.

"How'd you find me?" he gasped.

"What did I warn you about falling for a psychic?" Her lips found his and she whispered, "I will always be able to find you."

When he opened his eyes finally and finished drinking her in, they ran from the alley and the burning theater and the opium den. Across the street he recognized the smug smiling face of Lafayette Ron Hubbard. Already he could hear the distant wail of the approaching fire engine. They reached the street and turned and walked casually away from the fire, which was beginning to attract onlookers from the nearby parade.

"I guess you couldn't find Smith?" he asked Hubbard.

"Oh, no," Hubbard said, and pointed out a stout man examining a window full of roasted duck. "He's already thinking about lunch." Smith heard Hubbard's sharp whistle and dashed over.

Walter shook Smith's hand. "Elmer, good to see you."

"I whipped up a little something for you," he said.

He pulled a mason jar of clear liquid from the brown paper bag he carried. "It's a decoction of deadly nightshade," he said, handing the jar to Gibson.

"Bottoms up!" Hubbard said proudly.

"Deadly nightshade?"

"Atropa belladona," Smith said. "Atropine. I think I made atropine. At least I hope I did. Or something like it. It's a nerve agent counter-agent. You're supposed to inject it into your thigh, but I think this solution will have an effect if you drink it. I think. I mean, I don't know. I'm not a medical doctor; I'm just a chemist. My father wanted me to be a doctor, but I don't like the sight of blood."

Gibson fumbled with the clasp. His fingers were trembling. He handed it to Litzka. "I need help."

She opened it and held it up to his mouth. He took a deep swallow. "Tastes like vanilla," he said, "and rum." The doc puffed visibly. "Best doughnut I ever drank, Smith. How long should it take this stuff to work?"

"If it works?" Smith looked worried. "It should be pretty quick. If it doesn't, well, from the looks of you that could be pretty quick too."

They reached the top of the block. The exuberance of the parade would have shamed any self-respecting Irishman's Saint Patrick's Day spectacle. The parade was pouring through the street like a raging river with the Hip Sing building as its terminus. One after another, the bands, dragons, dancers, dogs, marchers, drummers, and fighters would reach the building and put on their finest performances for the dignitaries who watched from its great windows, open to the mild morning to keep the crowded room from growing too hot. Then they would melt into the crowd or be invited in as the men on the top floor indicated.

"Is that the ugliest goddamn float you've ever seen?" Hubbard asked them.

The platform was borne by six men, three on a side, shouldering two poles which ran through rings along its side. The men wore black hooded robes which hid their faces. A seventh man, dressed the same but free from the burden of carrying the statue, led the small procession. The cheering crowds shrank back from it as it approached, growing quiet as if in fear.

Gibson recognized the fearsome statue instantly. He had seen its grotesque visage when it sat upon the stage of the theater and glowered at him. He knew with certainty that the draped platform upon which its throne was perched was big enough to conceal a fifty-gallon drum.

The crowd silently parted as the seven men and their deadly burden entered the doors of the Hip Sing building.

"Stay here!" Gibson ordered the others. Then he began to run, pushing his way through the crowds which were beginning to congregate at the entrance to the building. The whole tenor of the crowd had changed from one of celebration to one of agitation. Gibson burst into the lobby, breathless. It was filled with revelers partaking of the vast feast. Several men, Hip Sing guards, came toward him, trying to wave him out. He barked Zhang Mei's name at them. They didn't seem to know it, but the forceful repetition of a Chinese name seemed to give them pause, as if the strange white man did have some claim to be here. He heard sounds from the staircase and bounded up them as quickly as he could.

He flew up the stairs, feeling revitalized. Smith was right. The antidote seemed to be working quickly. A large dragon costume—there must have been fifteen men inside—was swirling down the stairs toward him. He came face-to-face with the dragon. It snorted in his face and shook its whiskers. He could see the eyes of a young man peering at him through the dark opening of the beast's mouth. He put his face into the gaping maw and snorted back. The head of the dragon took a side step to the wall and the rest of the body flowed along, following its lead.

He reached the top floor, where large double doors stood open onto another world. As he walked through the opening, he felt as if he were entering an ancient court in Imperial China. The traditional costumes, the creaking tables loaded with food, the rich smells of incense, the regal decorations all combined to transport him away from New York. He revised his first impression: he felt as if he were entering a temple, a shrine, inhabited by living Chinese gods.

The crowd in the room applauded the entrance of the statue. Most of the men in the room were standing in a wide circle at the windows, which gave a panoramic view of the Manhattan skyline. This left a clearing in the center of the room for the performers to make their obeisance. At the far end of the room, opposite the doors through which Gibson was entering, was a raised dais upon which sat a number of distinguished elderly men. They all wore formal Chinese garb except for one man, who sat in the middle seat of honor. He wore a Brooks Brothers suit and a bored expression on his sour face.

The hooded men drew past the center of the room, proceeding directly to the raised platform. Expectant eyes fell upon it as the assembly waited to see what its performance tribute could possibly be. The room grew silent as the sense of expectation grew, as well as a growing sense of dread perhaps inspired by the appearance of the statue or the suspenseful, stately pace of its bearers.

The hooded leader drew to a stop before the dais. He raised his hand and the other robed figures slowly lowered their heavy burden to the floor. The leader bowed low before the man in the suit. The man replied with an indifferent wave.

"Zhang Mei!" Gibson shouted across the quieting room. "Wait."

The hood of the leader turned to look at him. From the shadows beneath its folds, Gibson thought he could see Zhang Mei's eyes, gleaming with triumph.

Zhang Mei revealed himself. There were soft murmurs from the crowd, but the strongest reaction came from the dais as the man in the American suit suddenly attempted to stand. His face had turned as white as the silk clothes the other men wore. He stumbled to his knees, begging, pleading, groveling for mercy.

Zhang Mei spoke something, savagely, to him in Chinese. Then, in a fluid movement that surprised everyone with its speed, he snatched the great sword from the hand of the Judge of the Dead, swung it through the air in a great arc of golden light, and struck the head from the man who had killed his Lu Zhi and little Shaozu.

Episode Forty-Six

LITZKA SHRIEKED.

Mi-Ying's head fell at the base of the statue. Gibson saw its mouth open in surprise and its eyes blink in astonishment as its body took a step forward. Its hands clawed at its neck, from which a great streaming jet of blood spattered the men rushing to exit the stage. The body staggered limply off the stage and collapsed, still, at Zhang Mei's feet.

Gibson had heard the clatter on the steps behind him and he knew without looking that Litzka and Hubbard and Smith had followed him after all. He grimaced to himself, wishing that for once, just once, she had listened to him.

Outside Gibson could hear the roar of the oblivious throng as the revels in the street picked up frenzy. It was just past midday; in Chinese terms this meant the festivities had only just begun. Another parade was wending its way down the street full of entirely new participants.

With surprise he noted Lester Dent emerging into the doorway of a recessed alcove in the room. Dent's shirt was torn and soaked with large blossoms of blood; his face seemed drained of emotion. It was gray, claylike, expressionless. So, we're all here at the last, Gibson thought sadly. He nodded his head at Dent. Dent looked at him with dead eyes, as if the emotional nerves behind them had been severed, and slowly shook his head.

Zhang Mei took a step upon the platform and turned to face the assemblage. Mi-Ying's blood streamed down his face. The men who had sat upon the dais leapt away from the stricken diplomat and the sword-wielding madman. Zhang swung the sword toward the base of the statue, slicing away the curtains to reveal the old military-issue drum under the squatting statue. He cried out, harshly, in Chinese and what he said stilled the panicked room. His men moved quickly to bring the drum out from under the platform.

He spoke to his men again and they fell upon the baskets of money which had been placed at the feet of Mi-Ying. These they bore back and placed under the statue where the gas drum had been.

"A thief!" Gibson heard his own voice. He stepped into the room. "After all this, you're a common thief?" Gibson asked Zhang Mei, approaching slowly.

"If Mi-Ying were to take this money, none of it would ever reach China. With me, it will."

Gibson took a few more steps. "Last night you were the champion of China. Now you're stealing from her weakest people. Is this where the dream ends? Is this the destiny of your father?"

"I have no father," Zhang replied. "I am the Judge of the Dead."

"What about your dreams for peace?" Gibson was close enough now to see the man's mad eyes glittering. Out of the corner of his eye he saw movement. Dent was taking a few steps.

"This will bring peace to all who suffer upon the Golden Mountain."

An old Chinese man, a scarred veteran who had been sitting next to Mi-Ying, barked at Zhang Mei, who turned around. The old man was someone of obvious status in the community. Zhang Mei heeded his voice with a respectful stare.

Gibson took a few more steps. Dent did too.

The conversation rapidly grew heated. The old man's tone turned scolding and the younger man's turned sarcastic. The old man made a surprising move; with a graceful jump he flew onto the stage and attempted to strike Zhang Mei with a flurry of blows unlike anything Gibson had seen before. His fists were deftly parried and the old man was quickly knocked aside. Dent rushed to help him. When Dent looked up, the point of the great golden sword was level with his eyes. Blood dripped down the blade and fell upon the old man's wispy beard.

"Who are you?" Zhang Mei asked Dent.

"I am the husband of the wife you murdered today at the old theater." Dent's voice was as dead as his eyes.

Zhang Mei nodded. His eyes filled with something close to remorse. "I am sorry. She was unexpected. My men were defending me."

Gibson spoke. "So in the end, you are no different from Mi-Ying. A killer of children." He pointed to a pair of frightened children clinging to a man near the alcove Dent had emerged from. "And wives."

"In the end we are different because I am alive while he is dead." Zhang coughed.

Dent helped the old man to his feet. Gibson stepped before the drum. Zhang Mei stood on the riser on the other side of it. The tip of the sword suddenly flicked in Gibson's direction. He looked up the shaft to the man holding it.

Gibson swallowed hard. The edge was level with his throat. "You should have asked me to figure out this ending for you. As it is, I don't think your ending is going to work."

"What ending would you write?"

"Well, let's see. You've taken a room full of people hostage with a drum of deadly gas. You and your men have come in contact with the gas. Coughing is a sign of gas exposure." He had Zhang's full attention. Zhang lowered the sword, resting its tip on the lid of the drum. "Your ship is out of commission. Your patron is missing in action. Every person in this room wants you dead. The only plan that really matters to you, revenge, has gone off spectacularly well. Escape seems nearly impossible.

"But there is an ending and it coincides with the ending of your life's work. You wanted to bring peace. Well, you have. You have brought peace to the souls of your wife and your child. There is little more for you to do.

"I want you to know that I've figured out how your story ends."

Zhang tilted his head, curious. "Immortality?" he offered, caustically.

"Eternity."

Dent threw his arms around Zhang Mei. While Gibson spoke, Dent had maneuvered slowly behind the warrior. Zhang Mei was unprepared for an attack from someone of Lester's size. Dent locked his hands around his own wrists. Zhang's arms were pinned in front of him. They still held the hilt of the sword. Its point still rested on the top of the metal drum.

The room seemed to surge forward as men prepared to run to Dent's assistance. Zhang Mei's body was trembling. His face was growing red, as was Dent's. Zhang Mei continued to look at Gibson.

"You are right," he said through his clenched jaw.

Instead of struggling, he suddenly let himself fall forward, drawing his weight and Dent's down upon the sword. With a shriek, the sword plunged through the lid of the drum. Lester was thrown from Zhang Mei by the force of the impact and he landed heavily on his back on the floor.

Gibson heard the venomous hiss of the gas before he saw thin jets of it bursting out from underneath Zhang Mei.

"Run!" he yelled. His cry galvanized the room. Men began streaming for the exits. There was a flurry of combat in the confusion as Hip Sing men fell upon Zhang's monks, dragging them along.

Zhang Mei, placing his hands on either side of the drum upon which his chest was centered, hoisted himself up with a jerk. Blood streamed from the gaping wound beneath his torso where the hilt had gouged into the tissue and muscle of the tender abdomen. He staggered back against the platform, gasping for air.

The sword trembled against the pressure of the gas within the drum. Thin plumes feathered out around the neat incision. Gibson clapped his hands over the moist hilt, keeping the sword plugging the hole. He could feel the turmoil within the canister. It was like trying to hold back a tornado. In that moment he suddenly was able to recall Lovecraft's face quite distinctly.

"Dent! I don't think I can hold it!"

Lester gripped the hilt above his hands. Sweat streamed down both of their faces.

"Just hold it till the room's empty," Gibson spat.

Dent nodded ever so slightly, every ounce of his will concentrated upon the sword.

"Let me strive every moment of my life to make myself better and better," he muttered through gritted teeth, "that all may profit by it."

"What are you saying?" Gibson asked. The phrase sounded familiar.

Dent raised his voice so Gibson could hear. Out of the corner of his eye he saw a Chinese man emerge from the alcove carrying Norma, limp, in his arms. Outside he could hear screams and shouts as the panicked people from the Hip Sing building hit the street.

"Let me think of the right, and lend all my assistance to those who need it."

Dent was invoking the Doc Savage oath. Gibson felt a ridiculous grin spread helplessly across his face as he began to speak along with Lester. "Let me be considerate of my country, of my fellow citizens, and my associates in everything I say and do."

Dent grinned back. "Let me take what comes with a smile, without loss of courage."

A breeze swept through the room. Although the windows were open, from where Gibson stood it appeared as if the gusts came from the statue itself, as if they issued from between its carnivorous jaws. As if it were breathing. Wind, he thought, wind would be good.

The room was empty except for himself, Dent, and the corpses of the adversaries. "Go!"

"You sure?"

Gibson nodded at the gas. "I've already taken my hit. Find Hubbard. He's got the antidote."

"Okay. On the count of three. One . . . two . . . three!"

He let go and Gibson felt the full force of the gas again under his control. It was a desperate, live thing that wanted only to escape.

"Try to get everyone back," he said. "I'll hold it as long as I can!"

Dent patted him firmly on the back. The sensation was reassuring but in the end there was nothing more to say. Gibson listened to Dent's footsteps fade down the staircase. The wind had picked up now. That statue is really screaming at me, he thought. The breath of judgment.

Suddenly Gibson felt the sword jump with a new force. Zhang's hands gripped the hilt and Gibson was face-to-face with him. The two of them stood nearly nose to nose glaring at one another, the sword vibrating between them. Gibson looked deep into those dark eyes and in those eyes, at the end, he saw their fate.

"Let me do right to all and wrong no man." He grunted out the rest of the oath. Zhang Mei's teeth curled back in something resembling a cruel smile. Gibson realized that he was not fighting Zhang Mei, that the man had added his muscle and sinew, the fiber of his being, to the attempt to keep the sword in its deadly scabbard.

The poisonous vapors began spilling out in plumes from the edges of the puncture. Both the men were trembling at the effort. Gibson could feel the sword shaking and Zhang Mei's hands straining on top of his.

Gibson grinned back. Their predicament was untenable but there was something humorous about its very futility. He realized something about The Shadow that he had never understood before: sometimes The Shadow laughed because laughing in the face of Death was the only revenge against Death that a man could have. Laughter was as life-affirming, as hopeful, as spiteful toward Death as having a child. Zhang Mei seemed to understand something similar at the same instant.

"Always time to learn something new," Gibson suggested, as more gas spurted out. They each shifted their weight to try to keep the sword in.

"Yes," Zhang Mei chuckled and nodded.

"Let me strive every moment of my life to make myself better and better," he began, and Zhang Mei repeated after him, "that all may profit by it."

And then the men suddenly found themselves at the mercy of their own overwhelming laughter as the billowing white clouds of death enshrouded them both.

Episode Forty-Seven

"HOW MUCH of that antidote do you have?" he yelled to Smith. The stout little man, sweating profusely, was being towed down the stairs by Gibson's young woman. She seemed to have no hesitation about throwing an elbow jab to keep the men around her moving. Of course Smith had every reason to be scared. There was enough gas in that canister to wipe out all of Chinatown and a good section of downtown New York as well. From the window of the temple he had been able to see City Hall (he hoped the mayor was enjoying his lunch; it might be his last), Trinity Church, and the financial district, all within the cruel grasp of the poison. It was going to be a bad day for everyone south of the Hip Sing building.

He expected the gas to roil over him at any moment, but it still hadn't as he reached the next landing down. God, he thought, if you get me out of this, I promise I'll never abuse adverbs again. As if in mocking response, the man next to him on the stairs stumbled into him at full tilt. The force of the impact knocked him out of the streaming mass of humanity and onto the landing. He struggled to keep his balance but momentum did not favor him. Then his feet lost the sensation of being on the floor, he was tipping over, and he slid into an ornate screen arranged on the landing. The knock to the top of his head made it feel as if his vertebrae were collapsing into one another. Luckily his shoulder absorbed most of the impact.

After several moments of grimacing through the flare of pain, not moving, not even breathing, he opened his eyes. As he struggled to refocus, he saw a Chinese man bearing Mrs. Dent in his arms gliding smoothly down the stairs past him. At the sight of her he felt his heart breaking. Her left arm bounced lifelessly. She didn't deserve this. None of them did. But especially not her. She had been so nice to him, taken a special interest in him on the *Albatross.*

The man carrying Norma seemed to be the last person out of the temple, other than Gibson and Dent. He thought he could hear their voices in conversation, but as his senses weren't functioning properly, he couldn't seem to bring them into focus. In much the same way he was almost able to absorb what appeared to be an impossible sight, lurking in the corner of the landing. He tried to blink it away, or process it as something, anything, else. Statues. Paintings. Memories. Then, through the blazing hurt, a sort of clarity descended and what had seemed impossible a moment before became horrifyingly real.

The two young Chinese boys were terrified. The younger one, whose dark eyes were wide and fearful, held tightly to the older one. It reminded him of the way an organ grinder's monkey would cling to its master. Together they were kneeling, huddled as far back on the landing as they could go. If he hadn't fallen, no one would have seen them. He pulled himself to a sitting position as quickly as he could.

"I fell down," the younger one said.

"So did I," he replied. He struggled to his feet and snatched the little one and tucked him under his arm. He clapped his hand around the other one's wrist and helped him. The stairs were empty. Carrying one, pulling the other, he began to run.

The Flash.

In all his life he had never wished so much that he could live up to his nickname as he did right now. He'd give anything to become truly fast. He'd give up his dreams, his hopes, his wishes, his ambition, his talent, his skill, his imagination, if he could just get these boys out of the building. The flights seemed endless. He didn't remember all these steps. At one landing he dropped the older boy's arm so he could hoist the little one over his shoulder. His shoulders and head ached. He didn't want to die. He just wanted to go home to his wife. How could such a little kid weigh so much? He wasn't fast enough. The Flash wasn't going to be fast enough.

They burst out onto the empty sidewalk and the brilliant daylight stunned him. The crowd, composed of paradegoers and evacuated guests, had re-formed on the sidewalk opposite the Hip Sing building. Exhausted, he lowered the little boy from his shoulder. The older boy grabbed the younger and the two scampered across the street, vanishing into the crowd.

He couldn't take another step. If this is where the gas took him, then so be it. He had done all he could hope to do, all he had wanted to do. He sat down heavily on the curb and lifted his head straight up and back. High above him, he could see the temple floor, the silk curtains fluttering in the breeze wafting through open windows.

"Hubbard!"

He wasn't The Flash anymore.

"Hey! Ron!"

The Flash hadn't run those steps carrying those boys. He had.

"Lafayette! Hey! Ron Hubbard!"

L. Ron Hubbard heard his name. Dazed, he looked around. Two dark figures loomed over him; with the sun in his eyes he couldn't see them. Not the Chinese boys. Bigger. Men. Strong hands were gripping him, pulling him, dragging him across the street, away from the Hip Sing Association. They entered the building's shadow, and he could see his rescuers, finally. Driftwood and the cowboy helped him to his feet.

"How did you find me?" he asked them as he steadied himself and caught his breath. As he waited for an answer he began to explore the painful parts of his body, looking for blood or extruding bone, both of which he was sure he would find but neither of which he did. Both men seemed pleased to see him, to the point of genuine self-satisfaction. "What are you doing here?"

"Just had a bite of Chinese," Driftwood said, stifling a yawn.

"Best I ever et," the cowboy added. "What brings you here?"

"That shit!" he said, throwing an indicating thumb back over his shoulder.

"Aw, son of a bitch!" the cowboy said. "I seen about enough of that."

Litzka pushed through the crowd to join them, with Smith panting along behind her. Hubbard patted Smith on the back.

"Nice to see you alive," he whispered to the chemist.

Smith nodded gratefully, gasping for air. In his shaking hand he still held the half-full mason jar of decoction of belladonna, the liquid swirling around and around.

Hubbard turned to see Lester Dent standing in the doorway of the Hip Sing Association, blinking back the sunlight. Hubbard watched him scan the crowd until his eyes fell upon what he was looking for. Then Dent dashed into the street in their direction but to the right. Hubbard turned to see where the man was headed. "Oh, God."

With the assistance of two other men, the Chinese man who had carried Norma past him on the staircase was gently attempting to slide her motionless body into the back seat of an automobile. Hubbard could see instantly that any attempt they made to get her to a hospital was going to be blocked by the crowds thronging the street. With Norma in the car, another Chinese man in the driver's seat began honking the horn, pulling away from the curb. Hubbard began running to catch up to Dent, with Driftwood and the cowboy in pursuit. This time he felt fast.

The trio was steps behind Dent as he reached the car and banged on the trunk. It stopped and he threw open the rear door. Hubbard, Driftwood, and Lew ran to the front of the car, shouting and pushing people to move. All eyes were affixed to the top of the Hip Sing building; few people even acknowledged Hubbard.

Driftwood, realizing the problem, turned to him in frustration. "We're never going to get out of here."

Hubbard spun around, ready to yell at the driver to just gun the engine, when he stopped short. The door was still open and Norma Dent lay half on the seat and half in Lester Dent's arms, her blond hair spilling down to gently touch the cobblestones. The skin on her cheeks was shockingly white. He could only stare at her still, calm face.

A great and terrible murmur swept through the crowd. They all turned to look up at the top floor of the Hip Sing Association building. A cloud of white gas spilled out of the windows like a wave crashing against a rocky cliff. It spread across the sky, blocking out the light of the sun and casting a shadow over the crowd below. Wispy tendrils, pulled by gravity, began to descend.

"Son of a bitch." This Hubbard said almost in unison with the cowboy. For a moment he almost thought that somehow, in the roar of the gas, he could hear the sound of laughter, of men laughing as hard as they could, but that could only have been a strange echo because in moments it had vanished.

They all felt the wind at the same instant. It seemed to rush from the building, or from above it. It was a massive, gasping breath of air, as if the great throng, exhaling as one, had created it. It was a merciless, pitiless wind, colder than any he had ever felt in New York. It swirled skyward, sweeping up the lethal cloud.

Slowly, the deadly gas began to rise into the sky, dissipating, dispersing. The tendrils were whisked away. The wind was stiff and steady. The supply of gas within the temple seemed to reach its end. Shafts of light began to penetrate the cloud. Its solidity began to drift away in wisps. At last the sun broke through and the white haze vanished. There was a long moment of silence and then people in the crowd began to cheer with joy.

Hubbard looked at the building. The doorway was dark. Then a solitary figure emerged from the darkness into the light. It was Walter Gibson. In his hand he held the golden sword, which he tossed onto the ground with a clanging ring which echoed up and down the quiet street. The look on his face was triumphant and defiant. Hubbard knew from that look that no one else would emerge from the doorway alive. Gibson's girl burst from the crowd and dashed across the street into Gibson's arms. He caught her up in a kiss so passionate and intimate that Hubbard had to look away. Moments later they came to where Lester sat holding Norma.

"Lester?" Gibson asked, softly.

"There weren't going to be any more adventures." Dent rubbed his cheek against Norma's, nuzzling. "You promised." The others slowly gathered around the pair but it was as if they weren't there. Gibson gently placed his hand on Dent's back.

Hubbard felt the sadness well up in his throat and his eyes grow wet. Norma had seemed more alive than any woman he had ever known. Somehow this seemed impossible. He looked at her again.

Almost imperceptibly her eyelids fluttered. Then they opened. "Lester?"

With a great sob of relief, he lifted her head higher.

"Are you mad at me? Why do you look so worried?" she asked. Dent lowered his lips to hers and kissed her tenderly. She brought her hand up to his face. "Did you see I found my treasure?"

He smiled and nodded, holding her tight. She wound her arms around his neck and he helped her out of the car. As they came to their feet, Hubbard made sure that both Dents took a hearty sip from Smith's mason jar. Then he stepped back as they kissed.

A great, joyous sense of giddy relief sweep through Hubbard. He looked at Driftwood and the cowboy. They were experiencing it too. The color even seemed to be returning to Smith's cheeks. Litzka was embracing Gibson and sobbing almost inconsolably in her delight while a grateful and relieved look of thanksgiving spread across his face.

One by one Hubbard committed them all to his memory; then he took them all in at once, a great vivid tableau of a moment he was living in that he wanted never to forget. After everything he had been through with them, this is what he didn't want to see end. His friends had survived.

There was a rustle and the two little boys emerged from the crowd.

As the Chinese man who had carried Norma clapped his hands in delight, they ran straight into the arms of Lester Dent. That's gratitude for you, Hubbard thought; it's not like he saved their lives or anything.

"What's the matter with everyone?" Norma Dent asked her husband as he lowered her feet to the pavement. "At a loss for words?"

Episode Forty-Eight

A WARM, early May breeze scattered the few remaining leaves left on the ground from the previous autumn and gently stirred the airport's wind sock as Walter Gibson stepped out of Manny's cab and onto the tarmac of Floyd Bennett Field. The dew was still sticking to the grass and he shielded his eyes from the bright morning sun, looking for the small plane.

Lester Dent and an engineer were inspecting the engine on the closed-cabin Beechcraft. Dent beamed when he caught sight of Gibson. The big man jumped lightly off the stepladder, ducked under the plane, and came toward Gibson, wiping oil from his hands onto his jumpsuit.

"Gonna name this one the *Albatross II*?" Gibson called out as he walked toward it. The wind kept threatening to pull the light objects under his arm away. "Keep tempting the fates?"

Dent shook his head. "Picked another name for him."

"Him?"

"Figured if ships are female, this fella's gotta be a male. Like it?"

"He's impressive. Heroic." He shook Lester's hand. "You're really moving back to Missouri?"

"I've got a contract for four more years of *Doc*, at least. Hopefully I can find more time to write some stories for the glossies. And maybe I can finally get around to writing a real bestseller."

"I hope you do. How about the Sweet Flower mystery? After all, you sure earned the right. You found out how it ended."

"I told you that night back at the White Horse, those literary bestsellers need to be chock-full of metaphors, analogies, and irony, and there's none of that in this story. It's too simple."

Gibson nodded. They watched the wind stir the flags near the hangars.

"You didn't have to come out to see us off," Lester said quietly.

"Sure I did," he replied, before being hit in the side by a heavy yet soft object. The impact of Norma's embrace nearly lifted him off the ground.

"Walter!" she cried, planting a kiss on his cheek.

"All packed up?" he replied, and she nodded. "New York's not going to be the same without you."

"I know," Norma said. "But I promised Lester fewer adventures."

"But if there's a Chinatown in La Plata, I'd steer clear."

"Actually"—Dent cleared his throat and gestured at the plane—"we're taking a little Chinatown with us."

"Hurry up!" cried little Ham as he leaned halfway out of the cockpit's open window. "I could walk there faster!"

His brother pulled him back inside to safety. Mr. Yee gave them an apologetic wave from inside the plane, as fathers will when their sons have embarrassed them. Gibson smiled and waved back.

"We're going to help him open La Plata's first Chinese restaurant. Norma thinks his pot stickers are a treasure worth sharing back home."

"Dumplings," she corrected him. "How is Litzka?"

"She's on the road again. Somewhere on the West Coast. I probably won't see her until the fall. If I see her again. If she comes back, I mean."

"Maybe things will work out in the future. That's what the future's for, right?"

"That's what she says. And if you can't believe a psychic when it comes to the future, who can you believe?"

She squeezed his hand. "Then trust her."

He smiled. "I wanted you to have a few things before you left. That's one of the reasons I came out here." He handed Dent a mag. "It's the next issue of *The Shadow.* With everything that happened I kind of fell behind on my writing, so I asked Nanovic to run this one."

Dent took it. He looked at it for a long moment, and when he finally spoke, his voice was thick with emotion, *"The Golden Vulture!"* He was glowing as he handed the magazine to Norma.

"Hot off the presses. And there's something else too. Since I didn't have to write this month's episode of *The Shadow* I was able to throw our idea to Nanovic. And he loved it!" He drew the board from under his arm and proudly peeled back the brown covering paper so the Dents could see it. "Says it might even get him to forget about the Kent Allard incident."

They recognized Rozen's signature flourishes on the painting immediately: a dead-faced man, wielding pistols, emerging amidst a swirl of gas pouring from the mouth of a hideously alive, golden Chinese statue. Gibson chose not to tell them that his descriptions of the hero to George Rozen had been based on the look he had seen on Lester Dent's face that one horrible moment in the temple. "Meet Street & Smith's newest hero. The Avenger!"

"It's remarkable," Norma said.

"So this is where it all winds up," Lester said, studying the painting. "In the pulps."

"Where it should stay."

Lester nodded.

"Nanovic says he'll run it. But only if we both write it. He wants us to switch off. I can write it one month and you can write it the next. If you've got the time."

Dent looked at Norma. "He'll find the time," she said, with enthusiasm. Her eyes moved from the painting to the last mag rolled up in Gibson's hand. "What's that? Another surprise?"

"Sort of. Yes." He gave a wave back to the cab and after a moment a little boy stepped out. He came slowly across the tarmac toward them. "Kind of a favor, actually."

Norma slipped her hand into Dent's as the little boy approached. He must have been about nine years old.

"This is my son, Robert." Gibson said, putting a hand on the boy's shoulder. "His mother agreed that he could spend this summer with me in New York. He's a huge *Doc Savage* fan. He was wondering if he could get your autograph."

"Hi, Robert," Dent said warmly. "Would you like Kenneth Robeson's autograph?"

The little boy shook his hand, shyly. Then he turned to his father. "Doesn't Lester Dent write *Doc Savage*?"

"That's right," Lester Dent said. "Kenneth Robeson is Lester Dent. That's me."

He autographed the first-ever issue of *Doc Savage* for the boy and handed it back.

"Thanks," Robert said, and as he read the inscription, his face lit up.

"He looks just like you," Norma said to Walter.

"You think so?"

"Those Gibson boys are handsome."

"Looks like you've got a good tailwind today," Gibson said as the wind ruffled his hair.

"Should be a quick flight," Norma replied. "If we don't stop for any adventures along the way."

"You never know," said Lester. "Adventures have a way of stopping for us."

Gibson took Robert's hand as they stepped from the airstrip to the grass. Dent slammed the door shut and Gibson laughed when he saw that *Doc 1* was stenciled in dramatic letters across the hatch. Robert clutched his newest possession tightly against his chest. Gibson rested his arm across the boy's shoulder. It felt good.

"Where's the pilot?" Robert asked him.

"Look," he said.

Norma and Lester took their seats in the cockpit—pilot and copilot. He and Robert waved and the Dents saluted them. Then Norma turned her attention to the control panel, and a few moments later, the engine roared to life. Before the turning of the plane blocked them from view, Walter caught one last glimpse of Norma speaking excitedly to her husband and pointing out something in the distance. Lester, as always, was nodding his big head in complete agreement.

With a thunderous roar the plane sped away from them and lifted gracefully into the air. Soon it was a speck in the sky, no bigger than the nearest gull as it grew closer to the clouds.

"Hungry?" Walter asked Robert.

His son nodded.

"Let's go get some lunch. I've got a story to tell you."

He looked back once, but the Dents had gone over the horizon.

"So did Zhang Mei say anything to you before he died?" asked the man they still called Otis P. Driftwood, even though they now knew his name was Bob Heinlein.

Gibson raised a forkful of steak to his mouth. "Who says he died?" he asked, and then bit into the beef. The expressions on the faces of his dining companions were ones never to forget. Driftwood and Robert, his son, were intrigued, but Hubbard looked astonished. He was glad that the two young men had been able to come to Rosoff's and meet his son. He felt a certain sadness as he realized that his circle of new friends, which had seemed so large so recently, was suddenly dwindling away. The Dents were now gone. Lew, the poet cowboy, had hopped a train to Baton Rouge in search of the ship's company's paymaster after having been evicted from the captain's quarters aboard the *Star of Baltimore* when the Department of the Navy had seized it. He felt he was owed quite a good bit of money for his services as acting captain of the vessel and he was "aimin' to collec'." Dent had made certain to retrieve his pistol before the young man had embarked upon this quest.

Driftwood would also be leaving New York in the next few days. Yesterday he had read in the newspaper that the man who had tried to take over his silver mine, the man who had killed his partner and forced him into a fugitive's secretive life, had been found shot to death in a coffee shop in Los Angeles. The cops had arrested a luckless gangster as the gunman. When pressed about what his future held, Driftwood joked that he might run for a congressional district seat that had opened up back home. Or he might become a writer. Whichever promised the most money and least work.

"You're saying he didn't die." Hubbard gaped. "But I was there."

"Were you?"

"Hell, I was! I saw the whole thing!"

"Yet you admit you don't even know what happened to Zhang Mei."

"To hell with that!" Heinlein challenged. "Did he die or didn't he?"

"How does it end?" Robert was wide-eyed and spellbound.

A vision briefly appeared before Gibson's eyes: Zhang Mei's darkly sparkling eyes vanishing behind soft enveloping veils of white gas spilling out of the canister. He could still feel the man's hands as they slipped from the sword hilt. "How do you want it to end?"

"What's the question here? Zhang Mei's dead!" cried out Hubbard.

"His lifeless body lay at the feet of the Judge of the Dead, his hand still reaching out to help contain the deadly gas, frozen forever in his final redemptive act. That's definitely one ending. But is it the right one?"

"Malarkey!" Hubbard muttered.

"Did you see his corpse? I seem to recall that you and Driftwood and Lew headed straight for the nearest tavern long before the cops started investigating. So if you didn't even check to make sure he was dead, how can you be so sure what end he came to? But if you need an ending, I'll give you an ending."

The two men set their forks down. Robert, however, continued to eat his club sandwich. Gibson felt his fingers twitch. He thought for a moment about dramatizing his story with a magic trick and then thought better of it. He would let it speak for itself.

"Zhang Mei's hands were ripped from the sword by the pressure of the escaping gas. He staggered back, surrounded by the poison, desperately holding his breath. This was enough to keep him from being fully exposed. He tried to find his biographer in the gas, but the man either had died or was lost in the haze. He plunged through the miasma toward the temple door. His head was swimming from lack of oxygen as he flung himself down the top flight of stairs and away from danger.

"He reached the lobby of the building. Outside there were Hip Sing men and On Leong men and American police. He didn't know what had happened to Towers but it was obvious that Towers had failed; whether the colonel had betrayed him, had died, or had been captured was irrelevant. What was relevant was that Zhang Mei was completely alone, a foreigner in a foreign land. But his skill was always survival. He looked around, knowing there is always a path to salvation, that there is always a way to the safety of the river. He spied the door to the basement, the stairs leading down, and rushed forward, the black fabric of the judge's robe swirling around him. In the basement he discovered that the secret hatch to the Chinatown tunnels was still open. He leapt into the opening. But it was too late. The gas had poisoned him after all, and though he struggled on as mightily as any man could, he died as the sewage swallowed him up."

"Suitably tragic," Heinlein said.

"What's the matter, Robert?" Gibson asked his son, who seemed downcast.

"It's sad."

"Most tragedy is," Heinlein replied. "And this is a villain we're talking about."

"But," Robert insisted, "he was only a villain because of what Mi-Ying did to him." He looked at Gibson. "And he was your friend, even though he did bad things. He was your friend, right?"

"So you think he deserves a better ending?"

The boy nodded.

"Good. Because there is another ending."

"There can't be," Hubbard insisted.

"There is. With the dank waters washing away the worst of the poison, Zhang Mei makes his escape into the vast network of twisted tunnels which worm their way under Chinatown. He disappears into the gloom, rats swirling around his ankles, a hundred secret doors to safety awaiting him. A hundred chances. A hundred destinies. A hundred new stories. A hundred endings."

"Is that the real ending?" Robert asked. "He's alive?"

"If you want it to be, then let's say it is. Zhang Mei lives to strike again!"

"Careful, Robert," Heinlein cautioned the kid with a wise smile. "Take any story a writer tells you with a grain of salt. Even if he's your father. Especially if he's your father!"

"I don't care if it's real or not. I just like the story now." Robert said, sure of himself.

"What I really want to know," said Hubbard, "is who's got dibs on it?"

"What?" Gibson asked.

"It! This story! Our story. It's bigger and better than the Sweet Flower story, by far!"

Gibson smiled at the redheaded writer. Even Hubbard might soon be leaving New York. He and his wife had been exchanging letters of reconciliation and Gibson knew how he missed his children. If he did leave, Gibson would definitely miss him.

"Why don't you write it, Ron? Hell, I'll even give you a title. How about *The Murder of the Shudder Man*? Or *The Terrors of Providence? The Trials of the Tong*? Or *Marooned on Tomb Island*? Or *The Heinous Heist.* Maybe even *The Pulp Heroes.* Lots of titles. Lots of stories. Pick one."

"Yeah, but those aren't my stories. They're yours. I can't tell those."

"They're not all mine. Some of them are Dent's. One of them belongs to Lovecraft, but he's dead. As far as we know."

"Well, I guess I could tell *The Tale of the Dead Man."*

"I was there for that too," Heinlein spoke up. "It could be my story. If I were a writer. And *The Long Watch on the Ship of Doom* is definitely mine. Definitely. For that one I just might have to become a writer."

"What happened in Chinatown was just the ending to a lot of other stories," Gibson said, looking at Hubbard. "There's lots of things that happened to us that we'll never tell each other. For example, if I tried to write about how you saved those boys' lives, I'd get it wrong. I wouldn't get your details right. The personal details, the things you were thinking, the way you were feeling. You know, the messy true things that only slow down a great pulp. Am I right?"

"Can I just use my imagination? Make stuff up? I am a writer, after all."

"There's a difference between a lie and a story," Heinlein said softly.

Gibson nodded. "Oh, you could try to tell *The Chinatown Death Cloud Peril*, but between the pack of lies you think is the truth and the truths you'll never know about, you'll be as lost as Zhang Mei in the forgotten tunnels under the streets. Unsure of which tunnel leads to freedom, you'll splash through the wet darkness, fumbling for light, hoping the path you're on is the right one, only to find yourself facing more dead ends than endings, the doors sealed shut by time and inertia and the dread that people have of the creatures that lie behind those doors."

"Do you think Zhang Mei is still down there?" Robert asked, his brows furrowed as he tried to imagine the fate that befell the adopted son of the warlord. "Do you think that he never came up from the tunnels? Maybe he decided that he was safe down there. That no one would ever look for him. And that's another ending, right, Dad? Maybe?"

"Maybe," said Gibson, and ran a reassuring hand through his son's hair. It felt just like his own. "'Maybe' is how all writers, even pulp writers, begin their stories."

His mind suddenly raced back to that day in Chinatown as they all stood together, sharing in the joy that they were all alive and, more than that, triumphant. He remembered the way he had lowered his face from the clear sky to the ground, bowing his head in thanks. He recalled the ancient grating he had noticed set in the cobblestones. He thought of the shudder that had gripped his body as he caught a glimpse, only a glimpse, of a dark and familiar face sagely gazing up at him from below the surface of the earth. If he closed his eyes momentarily he could still see the complicated look sparkling in the eyes—the rage, the fear, the loss, the knowledge, the triumph. After that, all he could recall was Litzka, warmly pressing her firm body against his, and the distant fading echoes of footsteps splashing away into dark shadows. Afterward he wasn't sure whether he had seen something or not. He told himself he would never be sure. But he was sure.

He stood up and reached into his coat for his wallet. His belly felt full of good food and beer, and a fine feeling of contentment settled over him. Spring was in the air, he would be seeing Litzka soon enough, he felt good, and he felt like writing. "Maybe Zhang Mei will remain down there, lost and lurking forever in the catacombs as the world above him marches on and remembers him only as a phantasm they think they hear below their feet at night when the city is quiet. The master of his subterranean sanctum." Robert stood up too and began putting on his jacket. Norma Dent was right, Robert did look just like him. "At any rate, my friends, my advice is to stay out of those tunnels. Because in the end you never know what you'll find or who you'll meet down there."

"Well, at least promise me that you'll never write it," Hubbard said.

"It's not my story either. I may use it. But I'll never write it. I promise you."

Gibson tossed enough money down on the table to cover all their meals, plus a little extra. "Why don't you fellas have a quick one in honor of Howard Lovecraft before you go. On me."

"You have to go?" Hubbard asked him.

"Yep." He shook their hands. "Gonna take my boy up to the top of the Empire State Building to see where King Kong fell. Then I've got to get cracking on a new story. I'm feeling mighty inspired; the presses never stop and I'm already behind." Walter Gibson grinned at his friends. "These things don't write themselves, you know."

Epilogue

THE PULP Era ended.

The big presses finally stopped running, turned off by wartime paper shortages while the mags themselves were physically torn from the newsstands by Mayor La Guardia's garbage enforcers. The controversy metastasized from New York, and decency and morality oozed across the nation like black tar and old blood. Attentions and imaginations drifted elsewhere, to war, to comics and movies. And then only attentions were left to drift to television. The pulps, the pages where American myths had been born, were gone.

But some shadows of the era live on.

Why tell my story now? Survival. Emperors, like heroes, villains, people, myths, and even eras, can be forgotten. Obscurity is the true death of them, of us all. Does it matter whether my story is true or not? Not if in the end it means I won't be forgotten. The Pulp Era is dead. Long live the Pulp Era.

The people. They matter almost as much as I do.

Lester and Norma Dent returned to La Plata, where Lester continued to write Doc Savage and Avenger novels for many years. He and Norma started a thriving business in aerial photography and ran a small fleet of planes. It took him eleven more years before he was published in the glossies. In the intervening years he bought a big car with DOC 1 on the license place and patrolled his town with a big dog at his side. Their dreams for a child of their own were never to be fulfilled.

China was devastated by the war against the Japanese, although the alliance of Chiang Kai-shek and Mao held together for the duration. In the end Mao was able to seize control of China. Zhang Xueling, while hailed as a hero by the Communist Party, was forced to spend the rest of his life in exile in Hawaii, considered too much of a threat to the movement that his actions had inadvertently saved.

Dutch Schultz's treasure has never been recovered. Today it would probably be worth as much as fifty million dollars. Neither has the gold of the HMS *Hussar* been recovered from the bottom of the East River. Its value today could be as much as a billion dollars. Both are a gift from me to you. But be aware that the weed of crime bears bitter fruit. Crime does not pay.

Mock Duck died in 1943 of natural causes. So the stories say.

For years, until the tunnels were finally sealed up for good, people who were superstitious spoke of the demon who prowled under the cobblestones of Chinatown. Such people cut a wide berth around sewer grates, manhole covers, and cellar doors, while those few who weren't superstitious heard only the unsettling nighttime keenings and scrablings of lost cats and large rats echoing up from beneath the streets. Today only a few can even remember the tales of the demon, or describe his horrible laughter.

Robert Heinlein ran in, but lost, that election. So he became a writer too. Politics' loss is literature's gain. In the end he may have been the best writer of the lot, and he was the first science fiction writer to regularly write for the slicks and to make the bestseller lists.

Howard Lovecraft was far more widely read after his final death. Fans of his formed a small press to distribute his books, which have been in circulation ever since. The creatures which haunted his imagination continue to bubble up into the imaginations of others, like a virus of mythology.

Ron Hubbard did Lovecraft's postmortem career one better. He died a few years ago but somehow manages to keep writing bestsellers. He created more than a mythology; he created a philosophy which became a religion. I truly salute his initiative in this effort.

Neither Orson Welles nor anyone else has ever made a good movie out of *The Shadow* or *Doc Savage.* And no one ever will.

My last faithful friend and companion, Walter Gibson, wrote over three hundred Shadow novels, and as if that weren't enough his contributions to the art and science of magic have placed all magicians of subsequent generations in his debt. He married Litzka, who was the great love of his life, after a suitable period in which she mourned the loss of Maurice Raymond (whom she had always loved and whom she tended until the end). They lived and wrote together about magic until the end of Gibson's life. She was the first woman inducted into the Magic Hall of Fame by the Society of American Magicians. They loved each other dearly.

I may have driven Gibson mad from time to time, but don't all the best faithful companions do that? And I was faithful to him. I do believe he returned the favor to me, as you have now seen. His mouth formed the words around my breath. I have been mute for so long without him. But now there is you.

How do I alone know the path of the tunnels, through all the dark places, to doors which lead to the right endings? And how am I able to see into the hearts of all my agents and know, finally, what stories, real or otherwise, lurk there? You have read my tale. You know.

You are my agent, my new faithful friend and companion.

Listen and you will hear me laughing and you will know I am coming.

I will always be right behind you.

Especially at night, when you will not be able to see me in the darkness.

You will hear me laughing not because you are evil and not because we are about to die but because I have you now, my dear reader, and because sometimes I just have to laugh.

THE END

Acknowledgments

IN ADDITION to the voluminous works of Maxwell Grant and Kenneth Robeson, three books have fueled my imagination for over twenty-five years: *Doc Savage: His Apocalyptic Life,* by Philip José Farmer; *The Duende History of* The Shadow Magazine, by Will Murray; and *The Shadow Scrapbook,* by Walter B. Gibson himself. Other works that helped me tell this tale include *Pulp Art,* by Robert Lesser; Spider Robinson's introduction to *For Us, the Living,* by Robert A. Heinlein; *The Immortal Storm,* by Sam Moskowitz; *Man of Magic and Mystery: A Guide to the Work of Walter B. Gibson,* by J. Randolph Cox; *Walter B. Gibson and The Shadow,* by Thomas J. Shimeld; *Lester Dent: The Man, His Craft and His Market,* by M. Martin McCarey-Laird; *I. Asimov* and *In Memory Yet Green,* by Isaac Asimov; *The Futurians,* by Damon Knight; *Lost Gold & Buried Treasure,* by Kevin D. Randle; *L. Ron Hubbard, Messiah or Madman?,* by Bent Corydon and L. Ron Hubbard Jr.; *Bigger Than Life,* by Marilyn Cannaday; *Shudder Pulps: A History of the Weird Menace Magazines of the 1930s,* by Robert Kenneth Jones; *The Great Pulp Heroes,* by Don Hutchison; *The Hatchet Men,* by Richard H. Dillon; *The Encyclopedia of Science Fiction,* by John Clute and Peter Nicholls; *The Encyclopedia of American Crime,* by Carl Sifakis; *Tea That*

Burns: A Family Memoir of Chinatown, by Bruce Edward Hall; *Bare-Faced Messiah,* by Russell Miller; *H. P. Lovecraft: A Biography,* by L. Sprague de Camp; the *Mock Duck/Blood of the Rooster* series by Jay Maeder for the *New York Daily News;* and *Fortean Times Magazine.* I made many online trips to Syracuse University Library's Street & Smith's Preservation and Access Project, to ThePulp.Net, HMSHussar.com, Wikipedia.org, Zoetrope.com, Writers.net, and to the site by Ah Xiang, UglyChinese.org.

Thank you to Tony Spina of Tannen's Magic for playing Walter Gibson for me once, for the gift of Norgil, and for telling me a few stories about the man you once described to me as your "best friend." Thank you also to Forrest J. Ackerman, for opening the Ackermansion and telling me some stories. My gratitude also to Robert Lesser, Mark Halegua and the Gotham Pulp Collectors Club, Tom Johnson, the Popular Publications archive at the New York Public Library, and Robert Weinberg. Of friends I must first mention the beautiful minds of Tracy Fullerton and Anton Salaks for their insights. Jennifer Levesque, thanks for opening the door. From one draft to another, Sam Hutchins, James Graham, Richard Siegmeister, Peter Bock, and Barry Crooks were the best of supportive friends, and Jerry Quartley always brought great wine. Thanks also to Chris Wickland, Charles Ardai, Albino Marsetti, and Judith Zissman for their encouragement. For early advice I turned to the generosity of Heather Swain and Kevin Smokler. I would also like to express my appreciation to the talented people it is my pleasure to work with every day at R/GA—Bob Greenberg, John Antinori, Nicole Victor, Chapin Clark, Ted Metcalfe, Ken Hamm, and Mae Flordeliza—for their forbearance.

Susan Golomb, my agent, I cannot say thank you enough to express how much I really mean it. Thanks also to your loyal and trusted sidekicks, especially Jon Mozes, but Kim Goldstein and Casey Panell as well. Geoff Kloske, my editor, thanks for joining me in the adventure and pointing out the perils and pitfalls. A heartfelt thank you goes to David Rosenthal. And to Jackie Seow, thanks for the great cover. Also at Simon & Schuster my deepest appreciation goes to Victoria Meyer,

Elizabeth Hayes, Tracy Guest, Kathleen Maloy, and Laura Perciasepe for all their hard work. And a special thank-you to Marysue Rucci.

Ed and Giulia Herbst, thanks for all the support and meatballs. Jason and Andrea, love always. Mom, thanks for the late-bloomer gene that finally bloomed. And Dad, in 1976 when I was ten, you introduced me to the Doc Savage and the Shadow you knew back in 1936 when you were ten. It was great to catch up with them again. Thanks.

About the Author

Paul Malmont works in advertising. He lives in Brooklyn with his wife and two boys. This is his first book.

Mars

Mars

THE LURE OF THE RED PLANET

William Sheehan &
Stephen James O'Meara

59 John Glenn Drive
Amherst, New York 14228-2197

To our favorite Martians:
Debb and Donna,
Brendan and Ryan

Published 2001 by Prometheus Books

Inquiries should be addressed to
Prometheus Books
59 John Glenn Drive
Amherst, New York 14228–2197
VOICE: 716–691–0133, ext. 207
FAX: 716–564–2711
WWW.PROMETHEUSBOOKS.COM

05 04 03 02 01 5 4 3 2 1

Library of Congress Cataloging-in-Publication Data

Sheehan, William, 1954–
Mars : the lure of the red planet / William Sheehan and Stephen James O'Meara.
p. cm.
Includes bibliographical references and index.
ISBN 1–57392–900–X (alk. paper)
1. Mars (Planet) I. O'Meara, Stephen James, 1956– II. Title.

QB641 .S4838 2001
523.43—dc21 00–067358

Printed in Canada on acid-free paper

Contents

Part II. A Swelling Orb

Part III. The Mars of Romance

Part IV. Marsfall

Part V. The Abode of Life?

Preface

In the early days Mars was a "wandering star," one of five mystical bodies that followed an invisible path through the heavens in a most puzzling way. About every two years the ruddy "star" would flare into angry brilliance, change direction as it did so, then return on course before fading into safe and distant obscurity. Its erratic motions mimicked the mood swings of the sky's whimsical deities. Its pulsing light mirrored the rise and fall of human emotion. Little wonder, then, that Mars commanded such a prominent place in early thought. Like a mountain seen from afar, it formed a distant backdrop to human activity. But along with the march of history, Mars came to loom ever larger in our view. In our own time, it has become a mountain all but filling it. If there is something to this mountain analogy, then the mountain Mars begs to be explored.

"Every high mountain," writes Daniel Boorstin, "was idolized by people who lived in its shadow; the Hindus had their High Places, the Himalayas; the Japanese had their Fujiyama, and the Greeks their Olympus, 'never swept by the winds nor touched by the snow . . . where the gods could taste of happiness forever.' "[1] A generation ago we had the Moon. Now we have Mars.

Frontier and mountain, Mars looms as an affront to man's attempt to conquer nature. Of course, man can no more conquer nature than he can a world.

But in the theater of the human spirit, "to conquer" means to triumph, to achieve some lofty goal. Sir Edmund Hillary and Tenzing Norgay triumphed when they surmounted Everest. America triumphed when Neil Armstrong set foot on the Moon. What will be the next giant leap for humankind? As we stand on the pinnacle of mountain Earth and look across the great gulf of space at mountain Mars, do we see our next frontier? It is human nature to explore, to give thought to the mysteries of the universe. By exploring we expand the limits of our understanding.

That is why Mars now lurks in our consciousness like a talisman or an Aboriginal totem, part of an endless vision that unites men and nature. Mars is these things—and more. For ages, to know Mars has been to know, or to come to know, ourselves.

And so it was 3,000 years ago that astrologers believed that Mars and its fellow wanderers could affect human destiny. They used the positions and meetings of planets to predict events on Earth and the ways of human affairs. But when the planets wandered off course—as inevitably they always did—the astrologers lost confidence in their predictions, and humans began to doubt their ability to achieve mastery over their world. The effort to understand the motions of Mars ultimately led to a new philosophy of thought, a new understanding of our place in the universe. We learned that the action of gravity and the laws of nature, not magic, governed planetary motion. Freed from the puppet strings of astrology, skywatchers began to look upon Mars as the key to understanding the clockwork mechanism of our universe.

With the advent of the telescope, Mars became another world, as round and complete as our own. Here was new terra incognita, uncharted land fertile with opportunities for discovery. Adventurers without ever leaving their observing chairs or moving from the eyepieces of their telescopes set out across interplanetary space, on expeditions as exciting as the navigations of Columbus or Magellan. They scanned a globe that seemed to show continents and oceans, a world more like our own than any other in the solar system.

Nineteenth-century astronomers brought Mars to life. They found tantalizing evidence for a network of artificial canals that seemed to crisscross the planet's surface. Visions of a noble but dying Martian civilization haunted the dreams of astronomers. But with each advance in telescopic technique, the water that filled the sea-basins conjured up by early observers proceeded to dwindle (until at last it had become a mere trace) and the theory of Martian canals ceased to "hold water."

By the mid-1950s, astronomers had turned their attention fully away from Martians and toward the more scientific endeavor of understanding the planet's geology and meteorology. A decade later we received our first clear images of the Martian surface: it was a desolate, cratered, violently wind-swept world devoid of signatures of life. The surface of Mars proved to be actually much drier than the most arid deserts of the Earth, its atmosphere thin and toxic.

But in 1971 the *Mariner 9* spacecraft revealed that the now desiccated Martian soil had once been dissected by outflow channels and inundated by flash floods. Suddenly there was a new hope: during at least the first billion years or so of its planetary career, Mars was warmer and wetter than it is now. So the mysteries of Mars continue their allure. Gullies seen on Martian cliffs and crater walls in high-resolution images from the *Mars Global Surveyor* spacecraft suggested the possibility that water has seeped onto the surface in the recent past. The relative freshness of these features may indicate that liquid water exists in some areas at depths of less than 500 meters (1,640 feet) beneath the surface of Mars.

These findings lead us to the all-important question: was Mars once the abode of life? Might there be microbial life there today?

Are we alone in the universe? Clearly we can only answer this question by coming to terms with this world beyond our own. And so Mars becomes not only a world of deserts and unexplored territories—a vast wilderness with a surface area equal to that of all the continents of the Earth combined—but an untamed intellectual frontier. It is a region untenanted and waiting to be claimed and challenged by our ideas.

Meanwhile, Mars is, as historian William Hickley Prescott wrote of the conquest of Mexico, "the most poetic subject ever offered to the pen of the historian."[2] The trailblazers who have led us to Mars have had various sources for their obsessions with the planet. Their obsessions, in turn, have contributed to our ongoing fascination. Some of the Mars-intoxicated ones were heroic figures; others were flawed, though their grand romantic visions often proved to be more inspiring than the truths of narrower minds. All were pioneers, dreaming of a brave new world that was disclosed to their eyes long before they or anyone else could arrive bodily. And so it is that we continue to explore Mars in our hearts and minds, until, one day, we remove Mars from the imagination and make it real.

William Sheehan	Stephen James O'Meara
Willmar, Minnesota	Volcano, Hawaii

Acknowledgments

The authors would like to thank the following for their particular help: Dr. William Baum of the University of Washington; Dr. Victor Baker of the University of Arizona for providing information about J Harlen Bretz and the Channeled Scabland debate; Dr. Michael J. Crowe of the University of Notre Dame; Dr. Steven J. Dick of the United States Naval Observatory; Dr. Audouin Dollfus of the Observatoire de Paris; Dr. William K. Hartmann of the Planetary Science Institute, Tucson, and the University of Hawaii, for discussions especially about the colors of Mars and for writing an early draft of what became chapter 14; Dr. Owen Gingerich of Harvard University, Dr. Nick Hoffman of La Trobe University, Australia; Dr. Donald E. Osterbrock for discussions of W. W. Campbell's spectroscopic observations of Mars and for help in obtaining Campbell's spectrographs of Mars and the Moon, also to Dr. Joseph S. Miller of the Lick Observatory for permission to reproduce the same; Dr. Stephen Larson of the Lunar and Planetary Laboratory, Tucson, Arizona, for CCD images of Mars at the 1988 opposition; Robert Naeye, editor of *Mercury*; E. Myles Standish of the Jet Propulsion Laboratory for calculating the closest approaches of Mars between 3000 B.C.E. and 3000 C.E.; David Graham and Dr. Richard McKim of the British Astronomical Association; Helen Horstmann of the Lowell Observatory; Dorothy Schaumberg of the Mary Lea Shane archives of the Lick Observatory; Larry Webster of the Mt. Wilson Observatory; Imelda Joson of *Sky & Telescope* for her help in photo research; Gregg Dinderman for creating the diagrams in this book; Daniel W. E. Green for his help in the Harvard Observatory archives; and David Levy and Wendee Levy for the use of their book collection. Executive Editor Linda Greenspan Regan was particularly kind in the encouragement department and we appreciate her comments, editing, and suggestions. And finally we would like to thank our loving wives, Deborah Sheehan and Donna O'Meara, for providing us with valuable insight and inspiration—and for enduring the loneliness that accompanies such literary journeys. All have made our mission to explore Mars a spiritual success.

Part I
Pale Red Dot

1 Lilac Dawn

The rosy-fingered dawn appeared, the early-born.

—Homer, *The Iliad*

July 4, 1997. We were back. Twenty-one years after we established our first human outpost on Mars with the *Viking 1* lander, fifteen years after we received our last transmission from that mechanical pioneer, a hopeful emissary from our planet hurtled out of the bleak Martian sky at more than 26,000 kilometers per hour (16,000 miles per hour) and headed straight for the ground 130 kilometers (81 miles) below. It was

2:55 A.M. Local Mars Time, and the end of a seven-month-long journey was just minutes away.

Back on Earth, mission specialists at Cal Tech's Jet Propulsion Laboratory (JPL) in Pasadena, California, braced themselves for impact; in five minutes *Mars Pathfinder* would smash into the red and rocky soil at 80 km/hr (50 mi/hr) . . . they hoped. The final minutes passed in nervous anticipation. It was like watching a skydiver jump out of a plane and waiting for the parachute to open. Although no one likes to say it, interplanetary travel has its risks; failure is not an option, though it's a possibility.

The last mission to Mars was a bust. In August 1993, *Mars Observer*, a billion-dollar-baby with a $22 million camera and a host of other expensive instruments designed to help us understand the history, geology, and space environment of Mars, died of a ruptured aneurysm in a fuel line just before the spacecraft entered orbit. The death of *Mars Observer* ended twelve years of hard work and countless scientific dreams. No one wanted to see *Pathfinder* repeat that dismal performance.

In the wake of the *Mars Observer* disaster, NASA's chief, Dan Goldin, adopted a new slogan: "smaller, faster, better, cheaper." *Mars Pathfinder* was advertised as the first of a new wave of inexpensive, quick-turnaround missions that, it was hoped, would revivify the American Mars Program. In all it cost only $280 million to fly. A masterpiece of miniaturization, it was built largely with off-the-shelf components. Three triangular petals covered with solar cells powered the landers; one of them housed a weather station equipped with windsocks and a thermometer. The base between the petals had a mast which could hoist a camera 1.5 meters (5 feet) above the ground and thereby furnish a human's-eye view of the Martian terrain.

The lander also carried a rover, called *Sojourner*, after Sojourner Truth, an ex-slave who became a leader of black emancipation and women's suffrage in nineteenth-century America. (Valerie Ambroise, a twelve-year-old from Connecticut, suggested that name in a winning essay, which was submitted to a contest sponsored by JPL and The Planetary Society; students were asked to name the rover after a heroine who had blazed a trail for humanity. Thus, *Sojourner* became the first American spacecraft named for a woman.) The toy-sized buggy measured 0.6 meters (2 feet) long and 0.3 meters (1 foot) high. It had six steel wheels that could roll independently over the Martian surface. A tiny microprocessor "brain" gave it roughly the intellectual capacity of an insect. If it arrived safely, *Sojourner* would become the first automated vehicle to roam another planet (not, however, the first to roam another world; in the early 1970s the Soviet Russians had successfully deployed similar landers, the Lunokhods, on the Moon, and used them to carry out sample-return missions.)

Unlike other Mars landers, *Pathfinder* would bypass the complicated and costly orbit-and-descent choreography usually employed and instead make a beeline for the planet's surface—parachutes and retrorockets would slow the craft until a system of gas bags inflated and allowed the lander to bounce to a stop. On paper, *Pathfinder*'s purpose was to get something—anything—to land on Mars. "After [that]," project scientist Matthew Golombek said, "whatever we did was pretty much considered gravy."

But in the hearts of the millions of earthlings who were also watching, waiting, and hoping (by the end of the first day, Americans would log 40 million hits on NASA's *Pathfinder* Web pages, 500 million by the end of the month), *Pathfinder*'s journey to Mars symbolized the latest American Dream. In truth, scientists and lay persons alike all wanted the gravy. More than any other planet beyond Earth, Mars alone has had the power to pique the human imagination, to cause us to ponder the possibility that we may not be alone in the universe, that planets with life—no matter how small or faceless—may be as abundant as the number of stars overhead.

Mars has offered us that hope for more than two centuries. But not until *Mariner 9* orbited the planet in 1971 did the real Mars come into focus. The spacecraft's unprecedented images showed us a world with features much like those on our own planet, features that displayed legible marks of historical change. Seasons of ice ages had scarred the landscapes around the planet's icy polar caps. Sand dunes attested to the incessant action of wind erosion and deposition. There were signs of great geological upheavals, like shield volcanoes—towering mountains built by episodic outpourings of molten lava; some of these volcanoes soared 22,860 meters (75,000 feet) into the thin Martian air, more than twice the height of the loftiest mountains on Earth. There were networks of canyons, with one so vast it rips across one-sixth of the planet's circumference, thereby dwarfing even the Grand Canyon of Arizona. But above all we saw for the first time evidence of ancient flood-plains and dry river valleys. One of them, Ares Vallis, an ancient flood channel near the planet's equator, was *Mars Pathfinder*'s final destination.

The area had been identified as one of the most intriguing places on the planet, where possibly massive floods had once raged across the surface. If true, evidence would be forthcoming. As Ambroise concluded her essay, "*Sojourner* will travel around Mars bringing back the truth."

But first the craft had to arrive safely. And not everyone was so sure it would. In the months leading up to impact, JPL's Tony Spear had been haunted by dreams of *Pathfinder* smashing into a thousand pieces and ruining the mission's chance for success.

When *Pathfinder* penetrated the upper atmosphere of Mars, it sped like a missile toward the ground with a descent angle of only 13.9°, just shallow enough to keep it from burning up as a meteor (a protective shell and heat shield, whose efficiency proved worthy on previous Mars missions, also helped). Two minutes into its fiery descent, *Pathfinder* dropped from 130 kilometers (81 miles) to 9 kilometers (6 miles) above the planet's surface. A parachute billowed open, slowing the craft's speed to 1,336 km/hr (830 mi/hr). One hundred seconds from impact, the heat shield was jettisoned. Eighty seconds from impact, a tether lowered the lander 20 meters (65 feet) from its protective shell; this maneuver would safeguard the lander from the braking rockets when they fired. Thirty-two seconds from impact, the lander, now traveling at 241 km/hr (150 mi/hr), turned on its ground-detection radar system. Ten seconds from impact, a bulbous panoply of air bags made of Vectran (a bullet-proof vest material) inflated to surround the craft. Six seconds: the braking rockets fired 304 meters (1,000 feet) above the surface. Four seconds: the tether was cut, and *Pathfinder*, nestled within its airbags, smashed into the surface at 3 A.M. Mars Time. But the journey was not over. The force of the impact sent the craft bouncing 15 meters (50 feet) back into the air. *Pathfinder* bounced more than 15 times in the first minute, before it rolled end over end for another minute and a half until—not quite a mile from where it had first touched down on Mars—it settled in a safe and secure resting place. By sheer chance it happened to roll over into an upright position, thus eliminating the need for a planned righting maneuver.

From the surface of Mars, *Pathfinder* beamed a faint but hopeful "Hello." The message was borne on radio waves across 191 million kilometers (119 million miles) of space to the morning-star Earth. *Pathfinder* had reached its destination, well within the planned 97 × 193 kilometer (60 × 120 mile) landing ellipse. After deflating its airbags and unfolding its three solar panels, *Pathfinder* triumphantly raised its weather mast and windsocks. Shortly after 2:00 P.M. Pacific Daylight Time, the Sun crested over the horizon of Mars and activated *Pathfinder*'s solar cells, enabling its stereoscopic camera to click open and take its first picture of its new environment. The mission specialists back at JPL were not disappointed: displayed before them in wall-sized wonder were the black solar panels atop *Pathfinder*'s open petals, deflated air bags, and a waiting *Sojourner* ready to roll down its ramp onto the lone and level sands of Mars, beneath the butterscotch skies of a clear Martian morning.

What captured the scientists' eyes lay beyond, and presumably around, the lander, for *Pathfinder*'s camera was looking out upon a rocky expanse unlike any that had ever been seen on Mars before. The images showed that the craft had landed among a field of gently sloping dunes sculpted by winds and littered with rocks ranging in size from a few millimeters to boulders several meters across. The most common size was from a few centimeters to about 20 centimeters (8 inches). "We wanted rocks," Golombek said, "and we got rocks." Ares Vallis was supposed to be a geological wonderland, and it was.

Donna Shirley, the thirty-five-year-old aerospace engineer in charge of managing the Mars Exploration Program at JPL that had built *Sojourner*, was especially intrigued by an area southwest of the lander, where "rocks were crammed together over 30 percent of the surface." The rounded rocks in this plot of Martian real estate, dubbed the Rock Garden, lay on the far wall of a trough and were stacked and slanted to the northwest, like books on a shelf. The consensus swelled unanimously: "The area," Golombek said, "shows the effect of catastrophic flooding." Torrents of water, perhaps having a volume equal to that of all the Great Lakes combined, had washed down the valley from the southeast, carved the trough, and deposited the boulders. "In a typical flood like this on Earth," Golombek explained, "we would expect to see big rocks deposited during the first rush of water. Then, as the water volume and speed lessen, we see dust and smaller particles deposited around the rocks."

Welcome to Mars. This photomosaic was taken by the *Mars Pathfinder* camera on July 4, 1997, between 4:00-4:30 P.M. Pacific Daylight Time. The foreground is dominated by the lander, newly renamed the Sagan Memorial Station after the late Dr. Carl Sagan. All three petals have been fully deployed. Upon one of the petals is the *Sojourner* rover in its stowed position. The terrain of the Ares Vallis region of Mars is in the background. NASA

Indeed, much of the landing area was powdered with the silt-fine red drift materials so ubiquitous on the Martian surface. Sandbars tailed leeward of some of the rocks, which displayed all manner of shapes, sizes, colors, and textures. Some rocks appeared to have flattened forms and sharp edges, suggesting they might have been tossed there from an impact crater—perhaps from the one whose rim was visible as a low knob in the distance, only 2.25 kilometers (1.4 miles) away—or from an unseen volcano. Other rocks displayed a layered structure suggestive of sedimentary origin—meaning it was created by debris laid down horizontally by the action of rivers, lakes, glaciers, or wind. Many of the rocks exhibited interesting textures; about half had long flutes on their surfaces that were probably carved by windborne particles. Other rocks were pitted, suggesting they were formed from the exsolution of fluids from volcanic rock, the weathering away of soft minerals within the harder rock, or erosion by the wind. Then again, perhaps the sockets had contained pebbles within conglomerate rocks, like puddingstone on Earth.

To make identifying the rocks easier, the scientists quickly began naming them. "Within hours," Shirley recalls, "scientists were jostling for position in front of wall-sized prints of the lander's pictures and demanding to name the rocks. The crush was so great that one young scientist was given the policing job. He would put a sticky note with the selected name onto the picture. Squash, Half Dome, Wedge, Cradle, and Flat Top got stickies. Stimpy and Ren were named after cartoon characters, and there was even a Scooby Doo, a flat white area which later proved to be more likely a dried up mud puddle than a rock." A pair of mountains, the Twin Peaks (named after the popular David Lynch television series) loomed over the horizon, along with gullies, drift deposits, and terraces fashioned, presumably, by repeated episodes of flooding. Even the lander was renamed:

Map of rocks named at the *Mars Pathfinder* landing site. NASA

NASA christened it the Sagan Memorial Station, in honor of Carl Sagan, the late great doyen of planetary studies and science popularizer, who had died in December 1996.

Sojourner's deployment was delayed for two reasons. First, the lander and *Sojourner* had trouble communicating. Apparently, the problem was caused by a temperature difference between the modem in the rover and the modem in the lander. "If the temperatures were different the [modem] frequencies were different," Shirley explains, "and they couldn't communicate." The other, though not unforeseen, problem was that one of the landing airbags crumpled against the petal the rover was to slide down. This forced mission controllers to carry out an extra maneuver. Just before sunset on Sol 1,* they sent a command to the *Pathfinder* to lift one of its petals 45°. With the petal tilted, the lander was reoriented, the airbag further retracted, and the petal reextended. Although it took longer than expected to deploy the rover, this wasn't really a problem, because there wasn't any real deadline for getting the rover off the lander. Just before the fast-sinking Earth set below the horizon of Ares Vallis, moments ahead of the Sun, and severed the communications link with ground control, *Pathfinder* captured an image showing that the maneuver had succeeded. Though part of the airbag still drooped over the petal, there was room enough for the rover to roll down the ramp.

As the Sun dipped toward the west-northwest horizon, the surface of Mars began to cool; the atmospheric pressure dropped, and the atmospheric temperature plummeted as heat rushed off the surface and radiated into space. Thin waifs of icy clouds reflected the dying embers of the Sun. A pink twilight gave way to the cold black expanse of night with Venus burning in the west and the summer Milky Way raining down a multitudinous starlight.

---

*Sol 1 was the first day on Mars, where 1 Sol = 24 hours, 39 minutes, 35 seconds, the synodic rotation period of Mars (the rotation period relative to the Sun). By comparison, the sidereal rotation—the rotation relative to the stars—is 24 hours, 37 minutes, 23 seconds.

Mars Pathfinder captured this image of the Sun ready to set on sol 24 at about 4 P.M. Local Mars Time. (NASA)

The temperature differences between day and night on Mars are both wild and extreme. Because the atmosphere of Mars is about 140 times thinner than the Earth's, a separate temperature regime exists between ground level and approximately 1.5 meters (5 feet) from the surface of the planet. At the hottest point in the daytime, a person standing on the surface would feel the ground beneath his feet a comfortable 47° C (65° F) but the top of his head would be chilled at –9° C (15° F). This is because the thin Martian atmosphere lets most of the sunlight pass through unimpeded to the surface where it is absorbed. Daytime high temperatures are usually much higher for the ground than for the air. "An extreme example," explains JPL's Mike Mellon, "might be walking on the sidewalk or a beach, barefoot on a hot summer day. The air is hot, but the ground is much hotter and you could even burn your feet." At its coldest point during the night, the Martian surface dips to a frigid –90 C (–130° F) while the atmosphere 1.5 meters (5 feet) above is only –19° C (–105° F). Come morning, the Sun warms the surface and heat rises in eddies as clouds blow in from the northeast.

July 5, 1997. The radio link was restored on Sol 2, and *Sojourner* glided down the ramp to begin its epic trek across the Ares Vallis flood plain. (Once the rover moved off the petal, the communication's link functioned as expected.) Its maximum speed was only 46 meters per hour (150 feet per hour)—about the speed of a tortoise. Built-in gyroscopes equipped it with a primitive vestibular system to prevent it from toppling over as it explored nearby boulders. Five laser beams helped it "feel" its way, in blindman's-bluff fashion, across the surface. *Sojourner*'s progress across the flood plain, traced in the thin tracks it left in the rust-red Martian soil, was recorded by the cameras of the fabric-draped Sagan Memorial Station.

As *Sojourner* explored, the skies overhead presented an intense, ever-

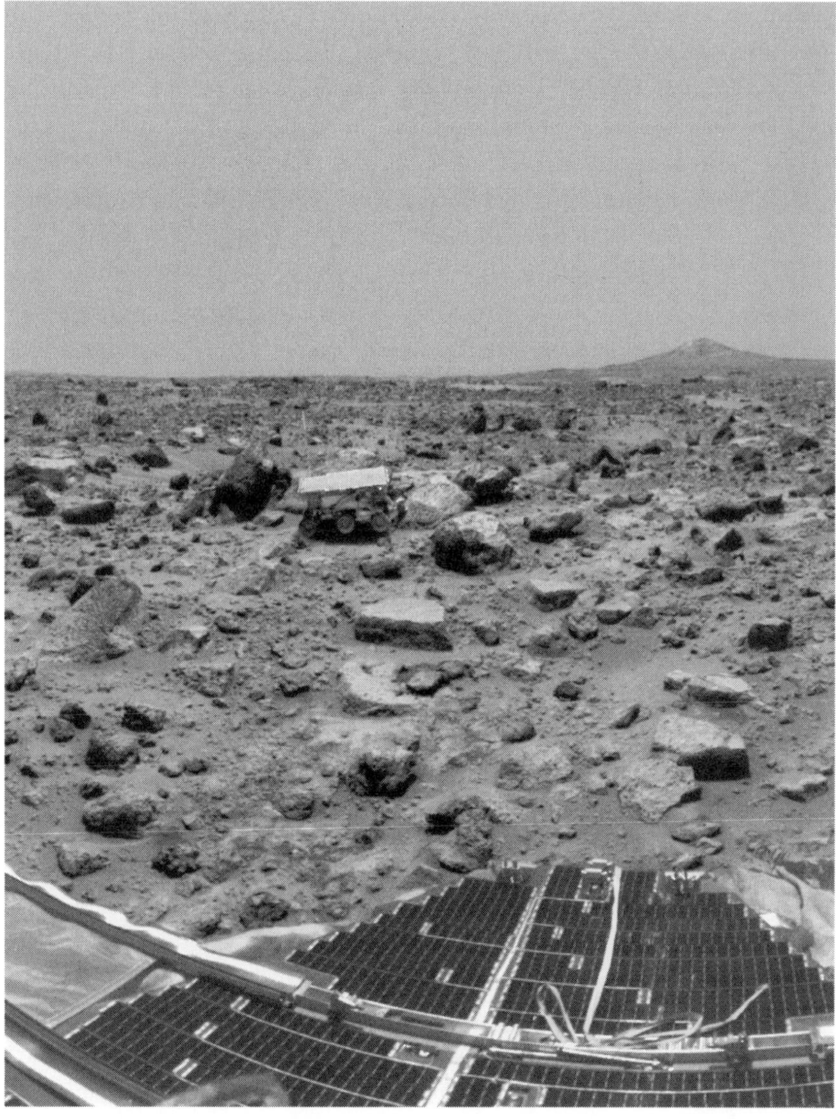

Sojourner enters the Rock Garden and meets a rock named Moe. The view is to the southwest, with the Carl Sagan Memorial Station in the foreground and South Twin Peak on the horizon about 1 kilometer (1/2 mile) from the lander. (NASA)

changing panorama. Despite the stratospheric thinness of the atmosphere, it had been known, ever since the *Viking 1* landing in 1976, that the Martian skies were remarkably bright ("like the skies over Los Angeles on a smoggy day," one *Viking* scientist had quipped). Early in the *Viking* mission, their color had at first been rendered in evocatively Earth-like blue. In the end it was decided it was no true-blue, only the product of our having too long drunk to intoxication the idea of an Earth-like Mars. Later images were recalibrated with greater sophistication to a more Martian appearing salmon-pink (brownish-orange might have been still more accurate). Because the cold Martian atmosphere is so thin, common sense requires the sky to appear dark. But it isn't. It's bright. That's because the atmosphere of Mars—95 percent carbon dioxide, 3 percent nitrogen, and traces of oxygen, argon, carbon monoxide, and water vapor—is seeded with micron-sized dust particles, which extend to altitudes of 30 kilometers (19 miles). By Sol 16, predawn images from Ares Vallis showed thin wisps of water-ice clouds in violet skies. The clouds, 16 kilometers (10 miles) high, floated across the video screen from the northeast, wafted by winds blowing at 24 km/hr (15 mi/hr). Another intriguing picture showed the tiny Martian moon Deimos suspended in the sky—the first time a Martian moon had ever been captured from the surface of the planet.

The Martian sunrises were grand Homeric stirrings: glorious bursts of color and light in a white sky tinged with the faintest hint of blue. They were majestic lilac- rather than rosy-fingered affairs. The Sun, as seen from Mars, was noticeably smaller than as seen from the Earth—which was hardly surprising, since the planet is one and a half times the distance of the Earth from the Sun. As the Sun climbed higher above the horizon the wispy evanescent water-ice cirrus clouds burned off. By noon they had vanished without a trace, and the dusty skies had turned to murky brownish-orange—the strange skies of a strange rust-red world.

Sunsets were events of breathtaking grandeur as darkness and repose settled once more upon the lonely plains of Ares Vallis. The feeble glow of twilight faded to dark and muddy brown; the brown gave way to violet, the violet to eerie blue (the blue color was produced by the same process of forward-scattering of blue light by fine dust particles that on rare occasions causes blue moons and blue suns on Earth). The fading blue of the sunset gave way at last to the vast and unfathomable solitude of the night, as the landscape became a realm dark and mysterious, haunted, perhaps, by howling Martian ghosts. A realm just as mysterious to us now as the red dot of the planet wandering in the inky skies of night was to humanity's first skywatchers.

2

Mars in the Solar System

Now while the great thoughts of space and eternity fill me I will measure myself by them, And now touch'd with the lives of other globes arrived as far long as those of the earth or waiting to arrive, or pass'd on further than those of the earth, I henceforth no more ignore them than I ignore my own life.

—Walt Whitman,
"Night on the Prairies"

In the popular mind, Mars has always been a world apart, fixing attention as has no other. Admittedly, in the universe as a whole, it is a rather insignificant body—as, for that matter, is the Earth itself. Mars is but a tiny pinprick in the vast fabric of space-time, a mere mote in the solar beam. Whatever interest inheres in it lies in that which concerns us most nearly—the presence, or possible presence, of life, that odd but extraordinarily versatile phenomenon that has appeared in the almost diaphanous skim-layer of our own planetary globe and, it seems reasonable to suppose, has likely appeared elsewhere on some of the multitudinous globes that fill this immense and awesome universe. Perhaps on Mars.

Life, wonderful life, the magician that has brought forth so many wonders, has developed its greatest conjurer's trick thus far—the brain. Creatures that possess it in highly developed form alone can ponder their place in the wider scheme of things, raise the question of their own significance instead of shuffling along mindlessly, uncomprehendingly, between oblivions.

Mars has long been of particular interest in this stirring intellectual adventure. To understand its special significance, it is useful at least briefly to consider the rest of the worlds of the solar system.

The map of the solar system divides naturally into two parts: the inner part consists of the small rocky worlds Mercury, Venus, Earth, and Mars, which formed inside the gas-vaporization zone of the swirling primordial nebula from which the Sun and planets emerged four and a half billion years ago; the outer part is ruled by the massive gas giants, Jupiter, Saturn, Uranus, and Neptune. These two parts of the solar system—inner rocky worlds, outer gas giants—are separated by a zone of rocky debris, the asteroid belt, which contains remnants of a would-be planet disrupted from forming because of proximity to massive Jupiter and its strong gravitational pull.

Mercury is the innermost of the planets from the Sun.* It is a small planet, only slightly larger than the Moon. Quite likely it started out with a rapid rotation, but this was efficiently slowed by the pull of the powerful solar tides; the planet now rotates only once every fifty-eight Earth days—exactly two-thirds of its period of revolution around the Sun. So far Mercury has been visited by only one spacecraft, *Mariner 10* in 1974, which sent back pictures showing that its surface was heavily battered by meteorites during the early history of the solar system. Unlike the Moon, it has a large iron core and a weak but detectable magnetic field. It is almost entirely

*During the nineteenth century, it was believed—because of an unexplained drift of the perihelion of Mercury's orbit—that a planet even closer to the Sun than Mercury might exist. Its existence was affirmed by the greatest mathematical astronomer of the day, Urbain J. J. Le Verrier of France; there were even a few fugitive sightings—for instance, a supposed transit of the planet across the Sun was reported by a physician-amateur astronomer, Edmond Lescarbault, in March 1859—and it was even given a name, Vulcan. But later and more careful searches failed to show it, while the motions it was invoked to account for were explained away by Albert Einstein's general theory of relativity. There is no longer any reason to believe in it, and it has now joined the ranks of the Loch Ness monster.

devoid of an atmosphere, but—and this was quite unexpected—it seems to have water-ice caps near the poles. They were even predicted by an amateur astronomer, V. A. Firsoff, in the early 1970s, though no one paid any attention at the time. They were "officially" discovered by radar astronomers in 1991.

Because of its similarity to the Earth in size and mass, the next planet outward from the Sun was long known as the Earth's twin. This is Venus—the bright Morning and Evening Star of our skies. A shroud of dense and highly reflective clouds accounts for its great apparent brilliance. The clouds are laced with sulfuric acid, which drizzles incessantly from the sky toward the surface. The atmosphere is massive in the extreme—its surface pressure is ninety times that of the Earth—and consists mainly of carbon dioxide. It sloshes around like a liquid ocean.

Because of the "runaway greenhouse effect," the atmosphere acts as a heat-trap of sinister efficiency, and conditions at the Venusian surface are hellish in the extreme. The ground temperature reaches 477° C (890° F), so lavas and molten metals are the only liquids able to survive there. Though the planet has a slow rotation period (247 days in the "wrong" direction; i.e., retrograde to the direction of the Earth's rotation), the atmospheric circulation effectively spreads the heat around, so oddly enough, there is almost no temperature differential between the day and night sides. In the 1970s and 1980s, several Russian spacecraft succeeded in penetrating the clouds and landing on the surface (because of the stifling thickness of the atmosphere, no parachutes were needed; instead, landing there was more like settling a bathyscaphe on the floor of the ocean!). The images they returned showed reddened landscapes of flattened volcanic rocks. More recently, the entire surface has been mapped in exquisite detail by the orbiting American radar-equipped spacecraft, *Magellan.* It proves to be a predominantly volcanic landscape characterized by lava flows, canyons, and magnificent shield volcanoes. There are also some well-preserved impact craters.

After the searing conditions of Venus, it is a relief to come to the Earth. It is sometimes referred to as a "water world"—aptly enough, since it is the only planet in the solar system where liquid water is stable on the surface. It is quite possible that wherever there is liquid water on a planet, life follows as an inevitable detail. Certainly life is ubiquitous on Earth—as ubiquitous as rust is on Mars—and thrives in even the most extreme conditions. Thermophilic bacteria are found near deep-water thermal vents in the deep ocean, algae flourish under the Antarctic ice cap.

Like the other planets, the Earth suffered the massive bombardment that took place during the early history of the solar system. Some of the impactors were of planetary dimensions. It is now almost certain that four and a half billion years ago a body the size of Mars (or perhaps somewhat larger) struck the Earth. The resulting ring of debris quickly reaccreted into the Earth's companion, the Moon.

Though void and lifeless itself—a crater-pocked wilderness—the Moon has played an indispensable role in the epic of life on Earth. It has had a moderating effect on the Earth's climate, since its presence acts as a massive counterweight to stabilize the Earth's spin-axis, which remains tilted to within about one-degree of its present value, $23\frac{1}{2}°$ to the plane of its orbit. (On Mars, which does not have a large Moon, the spin-axis precesses wildly over geologic time, producing extreme gyrations of climate.) The impact that formed the Moon was a tangential blow, and gave the Earth its rapid rotation—originally the period was only five hours; however, the tidal braking of the Moon has gradually slowed it to its present value. The energy imparted by the giant impact may have given the Earth enough internal heat to support the development of plate tectonics—something that never got started on moonless Venus. It may also have blasted away enough of the Earth's early volcanically enriched atmosphere to allow the Earth's surface temperature to drop below the boiling point of water. Thus, instead of a hell-hole like Venus, the Earth has evolved into a comparative Eden among the planets. Without the Moon, it is probable that complex lifeforms would never have been able to develop. It may well be no Moon, no man.

We pass over Mars for the time being. Beyond it lies the belt of the asteroids—fragments of planetary debris, but quite interesting in their own right. Some, such as the 934-kilometer- (560-mile-) wide Ceres, are large enough to have gathered gravitationally into small globes. The smaller ones, such as Eros, targeted by the *NEAR-Shoemaker* spacecraft that made a close fly-by in February 2000, are of markedly irregular shape.

Beyond the asteroid belt lies Jupiter, the mightiest and most majestic world of the solar system. It contains over a thousand times the volume of the Earth and 318 times the mass. It formed in the region of the solar system far enough from the Sun to have captured a large amount of gas, and probably acquired close to its present mass within only the first 100 million years of the solar system's history, before the primordial nebula dispersed. Jupiter consists of a small rocky core surrounded by a huge gaseous envelope (made up mainly hydrogen and helium). In a telescope, it does not show a solid surface; only its cloudy upper atmosphere is visible.

Jupiter is surrounded by a dim ring, a family of natural satellites, and four large moons, including Io, which, as the two *Voyager* spacecraft found during their encounters in 1979 and 1980, is continually worked upon by massive tides from the giant planet; the flexing and shuffling of its interior generates heat and causes it to be the most volcanically active world in the solar system. Indeed, it appears to be in a state of continual eruption. Another moon photographed by the *Voyagers* was Europa, a mysterious world almost entirely lacking in impact features; it appeared quite as smooth as a billiard ball, and was covered with strange lineations—undoubtedly cracks in the ice. It has now been more carefully studied by the Galileo spacecraft, which entered Jovian orbit at the end of 1995. There is no doubt its surface is made up of water-ice, in some places cracked and crazed, in others chaotically jumbled. Such features strongly suggest the existence of an underlying liquid-water ocean. Admittedly, the surface of Europa is intensely cold—at –168° C (–270° F), it makes the coldest temperature ever recorded on Earth, –89° C (–128° F), seem almost balmy. However, warmer conditions prevail under the ice, and may be comparable, perhaps, to those found on the Earth beneath the Antarctic ice cap where, as noted earlier, colonies of algae thrive. After Mars, Europa seems the next most likely place in the solar system to look for extraterrestrial life.

Jupiter itself may have a closer connection to our very existence than its aloof majesty in our night-sky would suggest. With its massive gravitational field, it has played the part of a gigantic vacuum-cleaner to sweep the outer solar system clear of wandering debris. There is no doubt that it and its system of satellites have shielded us from many a cometary stray that might otherwise have ventured into the inner solar system and smashed into the Earth. The frequency of mass extinctions on the Earth has thus been reduced to the level where higher forms of life have been able to gain a foothold. The giant planet's ability to capture cometary wayfarers was strikingly demonstrated in July 1994, when fragments of the Shoemaker-Levy 9 comet impacted in the planet's southern hemisphere. The fragments exploded 100 to 200 kilometers (60 to 120 miles) above Jupiter's visible cloud deck, leaving vast clouds of fine debris—effectively, flattened comet-corpses—suspended high in the Jovian stratosphere. For a few weeks dark bruise-like spots were distinctly visible even in small telescopes—a fascinating sight—but they were soon blown into tattered fragments by the east-west Jovian winds; by late September 1994 all that was left of them was a diffuse band of dusky material smeared throughout the impact zone.

Saturn is another gas giant like Jupiter, its mass 95 times that of the Earth. It is notable for its magnificent system of rings—the orbiting remnants of one or more broken-up moons. The complex gravitational structures in the rings, including resonance gaps and spiral-density waves, were unsuspected before *Voyagers 1* and *2* passed by the planet in the early 1980s.

The largest of Saturn's many moons, Titan, is comparable in size to the planet Mercury, and has an atmosphere with a surface pressure 60 percent greater than that of the Earth. It consists mostly of nitrogen, mixed with methane, ethane, and other hydrocarbons that at high altitudes are dissociated by sunlight into a thick orangish-brown smog. The smog prevents sunlight from reaching the surface and blunts the greenhouse warming by methane and other gases—as a result, Titan's atmosphere is an inefficient heat trap, and the temperature at the surface registers a chill –180° C (–292° F). Infrared observations with the Hubble Space Telescope have shown that below the clouds the surface may well be covered with lakes of liquid ethane.

Beyond Saturn are two more ringed giant planets, Uranus and Neptune. In composition they contain a much higher proportion of water than Jupiter and Saturn—this is only to be expected given the greater distance at which they formed in the solar nebula. Uranus is unusual in that its spin-axis lies in the plane of its orbit, so that it alternately points one of its poles or its equatorial region toward the Sun. Its "seasons" are thus decidedly bizarre, with each lasting for twenty-one Earth years. Neptune has a more normal spin-axis, but its magnetic field is just as deranged as that of Uranus. Both planets were possibly toppled by giant impactors early in their histories. They were visited by *Voyager 2*: Uranus in 1986, Neptune in 1989.

Like Jupiter and Saturn, Uranus and Neptune have large retinues of satellites. The most interesting of the lot is probably Neptune's chief moon, Triton. It is an intensely frigid world, with a surface temperature of –235° C

(–391° F), not far above absolute zero (–273° C or –459° F); it is thus even colder than Pluto. Even so, the surface is not entirely inactive; when frozen nitrogen encasing the surface is periodically exposed to intervals of direct sunlight, the nitrogen warms above its boiling point and produces geyser-like plumes ejecting gases and embedded organic materials at explosive speeds. Instead of being locked in a perpetual deep-freeze, Triton has a surprising vitality. Also, it has been undergoing gradual—and so far unexplained—warming in recent years.

We come finally to Pluto, discovered by Clyde Tombaugh at Lowell Observatory in 1930. It is less than 2,250 kilometers (1,400 miles) across, and hence much smaller than the Moon. Pluto has a large companion, Charon, about half its own size, which was discovered as recently as 1978. The surface of Pluto has been mapped using the Hubble Space Telescope, and shows bright polar caps consisting, presumably, of nitrogen-ice intermingled with small amounts of methane and carbon monoxide. There are also various dark patches, possibly exposures of bare rock or smears of hydrocarbons formed by ultraviolet irradiation of methane. Charon lacks Pluto's bright polar caps and is a more uniform and duskier grey. Both of these worlds consist largely of rocky materials. (Pluto's density is twice that of water, meaning it is made up of half rock and half ice.) They thus differ significantly in composition from other satellites of the outer solar system that are found to consist mainly of water-ice.

For a long time it has been suspected that Pluto does not, properly speaking, deserve to be considered a true planet at all. It is certainly true that—while unique in size—it is only the charter member of a group of similar bodies that orbit in the frigid zone beyond Neptune. These make up the Kuiper Belt, consisting of debris left over from the formation of the solar system. After Pluto-Charon, the next of the Kuiper-belt objects was not found until 1992. Several score are now known; there may well be 70,000 with diameters of 100 kilometers (60 miles) or more. The largest are 800 or 900 kilometers (500 or 560 miles) across, making them roughly the size of the asteroid Ceres. Some of the most interesting objects are "plutinos"—like Pluto itself, they are "captured" in 2:3 resonance orbits with Neptune.

The Kuiper belt is thought to be the main source of the short-period comets, which have been jarred loose by the giant planets (especially Jupiter) into orbits taking them into the inner solar system. The most famous example is Halley's comet, which returns to the inner solar system about once every seventy-five years; its last appearance, a disappointing one since the geometry for viewing it from the Earth was almost as unfavorable as can be, was in 1986, but it is due back again—though again unfavorably displayed—in 2061. Beyond the Kuiper belt are the still deeper regions of space that are the source of the long-period comets (those with orbital periods of more than 200 years). These are spread in a vast dandelion-head haze known as the Oort Cloud, which ranges out to distances of 20,000 to 200,000 times that from the Earth to the Sun and defines the utmost reach of the Sun's gravitational sway. These primordial comets, of which there must be at least a hundred billion, have existed in deep-freeze so far out that the Sun itself appears as no more than an unusually brilliant star. Now and then a few of them in the outer part of the cloud are jostled loose by the gravitational attraction of other stars passing the Sun and travel in highly elongated paths toward the inner solar system. Examples of such long-period comets include the best comets of recent memory, Hyakutake, which made one of the closest approaches of the Earth of any comet in recent history in spring 1996, and Hale-Bopp, which put on a brave show only a year later.

The Sun itself is a typical Main-Sequence star; there is very little remarkable about it, apart from the fact that it is a solitary star (most of the stars have stellar companions and belong to binary or multiple-star systems). As observed from far out in space, the Sun would reveal the presence of its planetary retinue—or at least of Jupiter—by its wobbling back and forth through a distance of 643,720 kilometers (400,000 miles), a distance equal to its own radius, in a period of twelve years. More careful measures would also betray the existence of Saturn and the other planets—a tangled gravitational weave. By using this technique, astronomers from the Earth have now succeeded in identifying extra-solar planets. The first, companions of the star 51 Pegasi, were discovered only in 1995, but now there are scores of them known—indeed, they seem virtually limitless.

By putting things into the wider cosmic perspective, we have, after all, only been begging the question: among all these planets, all these moons, all these realms of fascination—why Mars?

The obvious answer is that Mars represents, so far as we know, the closest analogy to the Earth. Though an arid desert now and unable to support liquid water on its surface—its atmosphere is too thin—Mars once had raging rivers and perhaps extensive oceans. Its climate was once as temperate as that of the Earth. If so, it might have been the abode of life—of primitive life, at any rate, bacterial life—relics of which, some scientists believe, have been identified already in the famous Martian meteorite ALH84001 (of which more later).

Furthermore, Mars is the next—and in reality, the only reasonable—destination for human exploration in space. The Moon was only a leap away. Reaching it required little more than a Columbus-like mad-dash across the Atlantic of interplanetary space. Mars poses a far more formidable challenge; it will be reached only by a much bolder and more arduous expedition, more like Magellan's circumnavigation of the globe.

We dare not underestimate the hardship. Perhaps it will be the most difficult thing that humans have ever attempted. But it is within reach, and all who believe in our future as a spacefaring species desperately need such a destination.

3
Wanderers and Wonderers

Wonder is the seed of knowledge.

—Francis Bacon,
The Advancement of Knowledge

Often when setting out on a path into the future, it is best to begin by reflecting upon the trail that has already been trodden. We begin our account of the human romance with Mars with the fires that cast their flickering shadows in the deep forest, with the old songs that still haunt us—songs learned by campfires in the dim infancy of the human race. Some of them were learned when our mammalian ancestors were small creatures crouching in the shadows of tree-ferns, perhaps even earlier.

We begin when Mars was a half-terrifying, half-fascinating red coal burning in the darkness, a drop of curdled blood in the night sky. We begin when Mars did not have one name, but many names: *Nirgal*, *Mangala*, *Auqakuh*, *Harmakhis*, when it was first perceived as a strange denizen among other stars, a wanderer as we were wanderers. As we still are wanderers.

The Wanderers

Three and a half million years ago, on the dry Laetoli plain of northern Tanzania, in East Africa, three hominids—creatures belonging to a species known as the australopithecines, walking erect on feet like ours, with brain capacities larger than a chimpanzee's—crossed a volcanic plain and forged a 23-meter (75-foot) trail of footprints. One of them paused and turned left for a moment, before continuing north. "This motion, so intensely human, transcends time," wrote Mary Leakey, who uncovered the footprints with a dental pick and brush in 1978. "A remote ancestor . . . experienced a moment of doubt."[1]

These footprints across the volcanic plains of East Africa were of a family of creatures that would one day leave their footprints upon the volcanic plains of the Moon and track their robotic emissaries across the soil of Mars.

Long before, in the jungles of the Jurassic, back when the dinosaurs still ruled the Earth, the ancestors of the Laetoli walkers had been small, rodentlike mammals, forced to climb into the trees for food, shelter, and refuge. Over millions of years, in response to selective pressures, they evolved into more specialized creatures, with long agile arms, grasping fingers, and opposable thumbs. Instead of the sideways-directed sight characteristic of rodents, they acquired forward-directed sight, which provided them with the sharpest images in the central part of the visual field. In time they also acquired stereoscopic vision, or depth perception—a marked advantage allowing these graceful creatures, with superb eye-hand coordination and an intuitive grasp of Newtonian gravitation, to judge distances accurately in their death-defying leaps and "break" the camouflage of their prey that were only too well concealed to monocular vision. Early on, these primitive primates must have resembled the lemurs of Madagascar or the tarsiers of Malaysia; later they gave rise to the large families of monkeys, whose rowdy bands still shriek and cavort in the tropical forests of the world.

Apart from the obvious advantages, there were disadvantages, too, with forward-facing eyes—the most important being that the creatures that possessed them were deprived of the nearly panoramic view of other mammals, which made them more vulnerable to attacks from behind. It is possible that this led them to abandon the solitary ways of most primitive mammals for a more social existence, in which the eyes of many could compensate for the restricted visual field of the individual. This may have led to the first experiments in social cooperation and in the production of the vocalizations with which primates alert one another to the encroachment of predators.[2]

For some reason—an environmental cataclysm of some kind, possibly the geological disruptions that opened up the Great Rift Valley of East Africa—some of these creatures abandoned their arboreal homes and set out for the open savannahs.

On the savannahs, bipedalism conferred a distinct advantage. Though its attainment cannot have been easy—requiring, as it did, structural modifications in the anatomy of the pelvis and the foot—it was well worth the trouble, and led, somewhere between four and six million years ago, to the line of the australopithecines branching off from the other apes. By standing upright, these creatures were better able to track their prey and to see and avoid their enemies in the tall grass; even more important, their hands were free to manipulate tools, such as crude stone hammers and blades, and—taking the longer view—their eyes, lifted toward heaven instead of rooting in the ground, were able to contemplate the wonder-world of stars.

Tool-making—the invention of technology—allowed the early hominids to exploit carcasses left behind by other predators and, instead of feeding on a heavily vegetarian diet, to shift to the energy-rich, high-fat diet their human descendants still favor today. This change in dietary habits not only preceded the expansion of the brain, it was probably a prerequisite to it, since larger, more voracious brains require more energy. Whatever the precise mechanisms involved, from the chimp brains of the early australopithecines, the hominid brain began a tremendous growth spurt two million years ago when the first tools began to be used, resulting in a doubling of brain size by the time our ancestors had reached the more advanced *Homo erectus* stage about one and a half million years ago. *Homo erectus* was the Promethean species which discovered the use of fire.

The possessors of these better brains long led a wandering, nomadic existence. Thriving on hunting and gathering, they migrated from place to place as dictated by the changing seasons and the fluctuating food supply. So attachment to hearth was always transient. On the other hand, the urge to wander—the itch to set out for strange lands, to leave the settled and the familiar for the next stretch of open savannah—must have conferred selective advantage on those individuals and groups who possessed it in heartiest measure—those with the keenest sense of adventure in their bones, or with the power to lead their tribes fearlessly into the realms of the unknown.

It may be that wide prospects already stirred something elemental in these hominid ancestors, who by two million years ago had spread from their origins in East Africa to as far as China and Indonesia. Leaving the dark and close forests for the open savannahs and broad skies gave birth to a yearning for the frontier. Thus, the first stirrings of the indomitable spirit of exploration, the one that draws us irresistibly now to Mars, seems to have grown hand in hand with the increased capacity of the hominid brain for technology—and with the ability to dream a future for itself.

During the last half million years or so of hominid evolution, the human brain has continued its phenomenal growth, from the roughly 450 cubic centimeter capacity of the early ancestral days to the 1500 cc capacity of today. In addition to increased brain size, there have been changes in the brain's organization, with dramatic growth taking place in the frontal and temporal lobes, including the areas now implicated in speech. The shape of the skull has changed, becoming less apelike and more human, with a shorter distance from the back of the mouth to the spinal column making for a shorter mouth; the larynx descended, the tongue became rooted in the throat—all preconditions for a rapid and versatile speech.

Sometime before 200,000 years ago, the hominid line divided; one branch led on to *Homo sapiens*, the other to *Homo neanderthalensis*. Only sometime between 130,000 and 100,000 years ago does *Homo sapiens* emerge in the fossil record in central Africa. By about 73,000 years ago members of our species had migrated out of Africa and spearheaded their way into Asia and—apparently by sailing rafts from Indonesia—as far as Australia, while only about 51,000 years ago did the first wave of migration reach from the Middle East into Europe.[3]

For tens of thousands of years, members of *Homo sapiens* inhabited some areas of the Middle East and Europe alongside their Neanderthal cousins. Bizarre as it may seem, *Homo sapiens* did not then dominate the Earth; there were two distinct human species, coexisting with one another.

Europe was then in the grip of an Ice Age; its more northerly and central parts were in the throes of a harsh glacial climate probably not much different from that experienced at the present time by northern Scandinavia. Because of the low temperatures and heavy snowfall, significant tree growth disappeared from all except the most southerly parts of Europe; the trees being replaced by large areas of open tundra and steppes. These landscapes provided ideal conditions for cold-adapted herd animals—reindeer, wild horses, steppe bison, mammoths, and wooly rhinoceroses. On the regular migration trails of these animals between summer and winter pastures, at largely predictable periods of the year, humans of the Upper Paleolithic established their settlements in order to carry out "intercept" hunting.

At this moment—with the Ice Age at its height—humans of the Upper Paleolithic, with apparently dramatic suddenness, began to use their brains in a remarkably different way. Though the anatomical changes needed for speech had been in place (for *Homo sapiens*) probably by 150,000 years ago, only now—about 40,000 years ago—did signs of complex language begin to proliferate. Now—and suddenly—we are confronted with the first archaeological documentation for a marked representational ability. Our ancestors began to draw what they saw. These were not mere sketches either, but a remarkable efflorescence. In the famous cave of Lascaux, the recently explored Chauvet Cave in France, and other sites in southern Europe, there is evidence of a surprisingly vigorous and sophisticated culture. Prior to this time art could not be produced and the flint tools used by humans showed little variation; now, with a dramatic abruptness that is almost magical, we have fluent, effortlessly drawn, well-proportioned animal figures.[4]

The balance now began to tip decisively in favor of *Homo sapiens* and against the Neanderthals. The latter may have even recognized, at least dimly, the power of the revolution they were witnessing, as shown by the plodding attempts they made to imitate some of its innovations such as new types of tools. But they could not really participate in it. Their brains were as large as ours and they were capable of doing stone-knapping. They hunted cooperatively often in close quarters with their prey, following the migration routes of the herds. They did all this, but they do not seem to have been capable of speech. Certainly they do not seem to have had that quintessentially human capacity—the power of symbolic thought. Hence, as Ian Tattersall has noted, "Art, symbols, music, notation, language, feelings of mystery, mastery of diverse materials and sheer cleverness: all these attributes, and more, were foreign to the Neanderthals and are native to us."[5] By 30,000 years ago—when the unknown artists of Chavuet cave and Lascaux began to set to work—the Neanderthals, a distinct human species, vanished. It would be only too easy to believe—given the well-known propensity of *Homo sapiens* for war—that they were ruthlessly wiped out. A more positive view might suggest that it was *Homo sapiens'* greater aptitude for social cooperation rather than ferocity that proved the decisive factor; they succeeded in domesticating wolves—in effect, bonding with them, making them members of their extended families—and the alliance would have given them a marked advantage in hunting over the less sociable and dogless Neanderthals. But it is at least possible, given their lower fertility and less energy-efficient body types, that the Neanderthals simply petered out. The important point is that our species—*Homo sapiens*—now became the lone human species on the planet, beginning its remarkable if sometimes violent and bloody struggle to understand and dominate nature—as well as to understand and dominate members of its own kind—a rise that would lead after some thirty millennia from cave art to the dream of missions to Mars.

The Wonderers

Up until now, astronomy can hardly have been said to have existed, not even the impulse for it, unless the interest of humans in the sky predated the emergence of the capacity for symbolic thought. But presumably the oldest science had been born by the time humans began to leave the first traces of their thoughts in their cave paintings—those outline drawings in ocher, charcoal, and natural pigments that represented the great beasts of the Ice Age, antelopes, bison, oxen, and horses, and also wooly mammoths, which man himself hunted to extinction. Man, the hunter, enters the pictures only in the margins; he is rudely sketched in as a small stick figure, less developed than the animals he draws. (It is as if even in his own esteem he still filled only a corner of the world dominated by the beasts, of which he still stood in awe.) By representing their forms, he hoped, perhaps, in some magic way to acquire power over them.

The realms of the sky must also have seemed like the walls of a great and mysterious cavern, to be filled with images of hidden fears and desires. And the night was to be feared, for that was when our ancestors were most vulnerable to nocturnal predators. Detection of movement was essential to survival. Perhaps the same tactic was applied to watching the "animals" in the heavens. Primitive man would certainly have noticed the motion of the Moon among the stars and of the stars' motion across the darkened mouth of his cave. To understand what he saw—roving points of light—he began to group the stars into patterns. Presumably the earliest sky-pictures took the same forms that adorn his caves—the forms of animals. "The sense organs receive patterns of energy," explains Cambridge University psychologist R. L. Gregory, "but we seldom see patterns: we see objects. A pattern is a relatively meaningless arrangement of marks, but objects have a host of characteristics beyond their sensory features. They have pasts and futures; they change and influence each other, and have hidden aspects which emerge under different conditions."[6]

The oldest constellation of all may have been Ursa Major—the Great Bear. It was known as the Bear both to the North American Indian tribes and to the nomads of Siberia, suggesting that when tribes crossed the land bridge across the Bering Straits the celestial bear crossed with them. Since the Bering Strait opened some 15,000 years ago, the Great Bear must be at least that old—but it is probably much older.[7] It may well stand as a starry petroglyph from the time when the cave paintings of Spain and France were being painted, after the last glacial period began and the endless snows and long winters and rasping sheets of ice pushed downward from the north and covered even the mountains of Europe in snowdrifts like the now largely buried mountains of Antarctica. At this time humans retreated to caves, as did bears, the closest living things to themselves in their manner of cave living, their appearance, and their habits. Another ancient constellation was based around the V-shaped Hyades cluster, with its ruddy star Aldebaran; it has been known since at least late Neolithic times as Taurus, the Bull.

Cave drawing of a red bull surrounded by stick figures of men. The artwork appears in the Museum of Anatolian Civilizations in Ankara, Turkey. © Stephen James O'Meara.

We can only guess that Mars, too, must have awakened the curiosity of those Ice Age humans. Unfortunately, we know nothing of the details; the human discovery of Mars is buried in the snowy wastes of prehistory. We do know that Mars was a part of the Australian Aborigines' Dreamtime—a vision from a time beyond memory, a mystical part of the culture that has been handed down by legends, songs, and dance for more than 40,000 years. The Aborigines' view of the cosmos is based in their concept of a distant past when their Spirit Ancestors created the world. To the Aborigines—some of whom lived in the red soil of the desolate Outback, a place more like Mars than almost any other place on Earth—Mars was *Waijungari*, a newly initiated man who, in ceremony, was covered with red ocher. One day, to escape the wrath of a jealous hunter, Waijungari threw his spear into the sky and, when it stuck, used it to climb into the heavens, where we see him today.[8]

The Aborigines had an impressive knowledge of the night sky. They differentiated between the stars' nightly and annual movements. And from these motions they devised a complex seasonal calendar, using star brightness and color as important identifiers. Interestingly, the primitive Aborigines identified the V-shaped Hyades cluster as a row of red girls—daughters of the conspicuous red star Aldebaran—and a row of tjilkera (white) girls.[9] The Aboriginal recognition of the stars and their movements allows us to confidently extrapolate the discovery of Mars and the other planets to that remote time when the starry She-bear and the Bull first began to haunt the imagination of our Paleolithic ancestors. That Mars could have had an influence on primitive man seems indisputable, considering that its sight has even caused alarm in relatively recent times (as in August 1719, when its brilliancy was such as to cause a panic in parts of Europe).

As the indomitable march of time pressed forward, more star patterns (objects) became clear in the night—according to Russian historian Alex A. Gurshtein, some as early as 16,000 B.C.E., a time so remote that the phenomenon of the precession of the equinoxes, the slow drift of constellations due to a wobble of the Earth, would have made the brilliant Deneb, in the constellation Cygnus the Swan, the pole star, instead of Polaris which holds the position at the present time. (Curiously, Deneb is now the pole star of Mars, whose axial tilt is similar to the Earth's). The Sumer-Akkadians of that remote period (inhabitants of the Fertile Crescent in Mesopotamia) seem to have divided the heavens into upper (airborne), middle (earthborne), and lower (aquatic) realms. Among their airborne star groups was the storm-demon of the Panther-griffin (our Cygnus) and the Great Swallow (our Pegasus, the Winged Horse). By the sixth millennium B.C.E., the path of the Sun among the stars—the ecliptic—was identified, and the first quartet of constellations of the Zodiac were being defined—the constellations now referred to as Gemini, the Twins; Virgo, the Virgin (but originally perhaps a Mother-goddess associated with fertility); Sagittarius, the Centaur (a hunter on a horse with a bow in his hands); and Pisces, the Fish.[10]

The planets, of course, walked along the ecliptic. The Egyptians from the time when the Pyramids were being built described a group of northern constellations centered on *Meskhetyu*, the bull's thigh (the Big Dipper), which consisted of the circumpolar stars that never set below the horizon from Egypt—the "Imperishable Ones." The signs of the Zodiac and the planets, by contrast, with their endless movement around the sky, were the "Unwearying Ones." The Egyptians already singled out Mars from the rest of the starry host, referring to it as *Har dacher*, the Red One, and also as *sekhed-et-em-khet-ket*, he who moves backward.

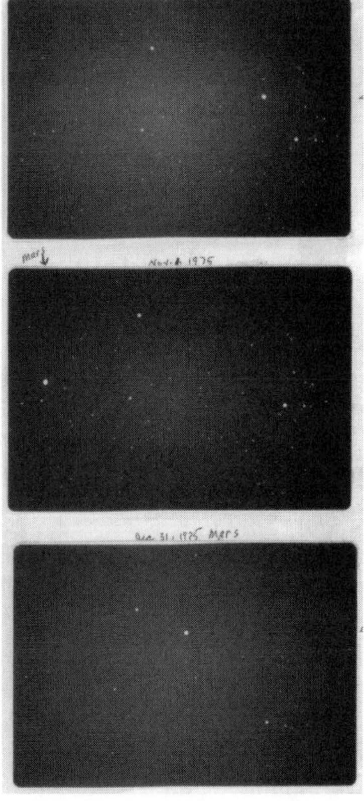

Retrograde motion of Mars among stars of Taurus the Bull. The V-shaped Hyades cluster with brilliant Aldebaran appear at the right of each photo. ©William Sheehan, 1975.

A tablet found at Nineveh, in Babylon, dating to about 1700 B.C.E., shows that the motions of the planet Venus—worshiped as *Ishtar*, goddess of love and fertility, sister-star to the Moon—were already followed with keen attention. The Sun, Moon, and Venus were set apart, forming a heavenly triad ranking above the rest of the starry host. Even after Babylon was conquered by Assyria, Venus remained the center of an important cult, since the Assyrians largely adopted the pantheon of Babylonian gods. The Assyrians were, moreover, preoccupied with astrological affairs; even more than the Babylonians had been, they were enchanted by the strangely compelling and still potent idea that the motions, positions, and brightnesses of the heavenly bodies in some unfathomable way controlled human destiny. "Astrology connected the life of man so closely with the heavens," wrote historian Anton Pannekoek, "that the stars and their wanderings began to occupy an important place in his thoughts and activities; it was his destiny that the luminous gods wove in those wonderful orbits. Now that his eyes had been opened and his interest awakened, man grew more and more conversant with the course of the planets."[11]

The Babylonians and the Assyrians used the celestial phenomena to try to forecast terrestrial events. The planets, which wandered among the background stars, "in the most unexpected ways, sometimes standing still or reversing their courses, sometimes combining among themselves or with the bright stars into ever-changing configurations," became the interpreters. "They seemed like living beings spontaneously roaming through the starry landscape, and they increasingly became the chief object of the Babylonian priests' attention. They were the stars of the great gods who ruled the world."[12] There was Jupiter, the Star of Marduk—the Babylonians called it *Umanpa-udda*, or *Sagmegar*, and regarded it as a lucky star, as it was also in the Vedic astrology of India. There were also *Ninib* (Saturn) and *Nebo* (Mercury).

But in some ways Mars was the most compelling. To the Babylonians it was *Nirgal*—the Star of Death; in India, it was *Angakara*—the burning coal. In the Far East it was known as the "fire star"—*Huoxing* in China, *Kasei* in Japan. In ancient Greece, it was Ares, for the blood-drenched god of war. Today, we call the planet by its Roman name, Mars. (The origin of this name is uncertain. Its root may be *mar* or *mas*, which, some argue, signifies the generative force. Others offer mar in the sense of "to shine," implying that Mars may at first have been a solar divinity. The most ancient forms of the name are Maurs and Mavors.)

From very early times, the planet's ruddy cast, which reminded people of the color of a drop of blood, gave it an ominous aura. As the great nineteenth-century astronomy writer Camille Flammarion put it: "Unfortunate Mars! What evil fairy presided at his birth? From antiquity, all curses seem to have fallen upon him. He is the god of war and carnage, the protector of armies, the inspirer of hatred among the peoples, it is he who pours out the blood of humanity in hecatombs of the nations."[13] We now know, of course, that the reason for Mars's reddish color is indeed the same as that for the reddish color of a drop of blood. When ferrous iron (Fe^{3+}) in Mars's soil combines with oxygen, it turns to ferric iron (Fe^{2+}), more popularly known as rust—this is the same chemical reaction that occurs in the hemoglobin molecule. Mars is, quite literally, blood-red.

But Mars was not always the god of war, at least not in Rome, where the earliest symbolic portrayals were tied in with fertility and agriculture. It appears that Mars carried the same connotation as ruddy Aldebaran, in the Bull, for in ancient Roman times Mars was Silvanus, the god of vegetation and fertility; he presided over the prosperity of cattle and protected agriculture. Silvanus evolved into Gradivus (from *grandisri*, "to become big, to grow"), the God of Spring, and was honored in the festivals of the Amarvalia, celebrated in Rome each May 29. His warrior functions came only after his title Gradivus was corrupted into the verb *gradi*, "to march," and Gradivus became a foot-soldier by the name of Mars, then ultimately the god of battles. (In Greece, he was Ares, the god of war.) Mars, then, metamorphosed into different forms corresponding to the successive conditions of the Roman citizen, first a farmer, then a bloody conqueror.

Mars—the Red One. Certainly the reddish cast of Mars is easily noticeable with the naked-eye. Its redness can be striking—though it is not equally so to all observers. The varying degree of intensity of Mars's redness is real, a consequence of the eccentricity of the planet's orbit. Mars is as much as fifty times brighter when it is nearest to us than it is at its greatest distance. When Mars is at its brightest, it shines with a wheat-colored hue; when it is at its faintest, it appears as a blood-red spark. So we can see the "two successive conditions of the Roman citizen" symbolized in the color of Mars as the planet waxes and wanes throughout our nights.

The existence of a poetic tradition involving Mars's color suggests it likely provoked a strong emotional response in the nomads of the savannahs, the Egyptians, the Persians, and the Greeks. For that matter, there can be no doubt that red is a special color; it is especially reactive on our nervous systems.

Indeed, as primitive vocabularies grow to describe colors, the first color they include after black and white is red. It is the last part of color vision to disappear in cases of brain damage, and is also the first to come back during recovery. It is an ambiguous stimulus; red signals danger, as in the eyes and body of some poisonous tree frog, but it is also a sexual attractant.[14] From the red star Aldebaran (the eye of the Bull) we get the familiar phrase "seeing red." Flowers use it to attract insects, while cosmetic makers (and restaurateurs) know its ability to command attention and heighten sensual arousal.

Red seizes our attention; its very ambiguity forces us to linger on to decide whether to approach or withdraw. Mars, by virtue of its color alone, must have seized the attention of stargazers from time immemorial, catapulting them into inescapable fantasies. If it had been some other color, it might not have so commanded our attention for so many centuries nor given rise to so much myth, longing, and speculation. We do have a deep visceral and emotional response to the redness of Mars.

Once it had seized their attention, Mars had other tricks to play on the early stargazers. The Babylonians and Assyrians realized that there was something special about the times when the planets we now know as Mars, Jupiter, and Saturn appear opposite the Sun in the sky. Like the Moon at full, they all then glow with their greatest brilliance. Rising at sunset and setting at sunrise, they sail mightily on the high seas of the night. Mars, being the most rapidly moving of the outer planets, is the most flamboyant in calling attention to these wanderings. Its usual motion among the stars is from west to east. Around the time of opposition to the Sun, just about the time it reaches its peak brightness, it stops, reverses direction, and moves "retrograde" for a time; then it stops again and resumes its usual motion from west to east. (Thus, the Egyptians' old epithet for the planet—he who moves backward.) After completing a loop, Mars's light grows gradually feebler as it approaches and finally passes behind the Sun. No one has better described these apparent peregrinations among the stars than the German astronomer Johannes Kepler: "It was apparent that the three superior planets, Saturn, Jupiter, and Mars, attune their motions to the proximity to the Sun. For when the Sun approaches them they move forward and are swifter than usual, and when the Sun comes to the sign [of the zodiac] opposite the planets they retrace with crablike steps the road they have just covered. Between these two times they become stationary. . . . At the same time, it was clear to the eye that the planets appear large when retrograde, and small when anticipating the coming of the Sun with a swift and direct motion."[15] Whenever the intensity and color of Mars changes it seems especially ominous. Thus, as recorded in one Assyrian text: "Mars is visible in Duzu; it is dim. When Mars culminates and becomes brilliant, the king of Elam will die. When the god Nirgal in its disappearing grows smaller, like the stars of heaven is very indistinct, he will have mercy on Akkad. . . . When Mars is dim, it is lucky; when bright unlucky." Says another text: "Mars has entered the precincts of Allul [Cancer]. This is not counted as an omen. It did not stay, it did not wait, it did not rest; speedily it went forth."[16] From such texts we can deduce that the Assyrians were intimately familiar with the schizophrenic changes in Mars's motion. They also recorded its frightening rises to fiery prominence and, after its anger had been appeased, its descents back to obscurity.

So Mars had already begun its rise to the forefront and vantage of human consciousness by early in the first millennium before Christ, when war-mongering Assyrian kings with names like Tiglath-phileser, Shalmaneser, Sargon, Sennacherib, Asarheddon, and Ashurbanipal sat on the then-most powerful throne in the world and paid special heed to this blood-curdling, martial star. In an age when it was taken for granted that the planets controlled human destiny, Mars—now a burning coal, now a fading ember; now moving forward, now falling backward with crablike steps—was something alive and powerful. Even then it unmistakably cast its allure on the minds of men. They worshiped, feared, and wondered.

4

The Untrackable Star

Their wandering course now high, now low, then hid,
Progressive, retrograde, or standing still.
—John Milton,
Paradise Lost

Our view of history has tended to be, and tends still to be, profoundly Eurocentric. It is skewed to the Mediterranean, the chain of inland seas lying between Africa, Asia, and Europe, a body of water that occupies only .5 percent of the surface area of the globe. The reason, of course, is that the Mediterranean (meaning "inner sea" in Greek) was the center of the Greek world, and it was among the

Greeks that a stirring revolution of thought began in about the sixth century B.C.E. "They did not," writes classical scholar Bruno Snell, "by means of a mental equipment already at their disposal, merely map out new subjects for discussion, such as the sciences and philosophy. They discovered the human mind."[1] This discovery of the human mind was undoubtedly the most fateful in all human history, the most fateful of all those that would one day lead on to Mars.

The Greeks were celebrated as skillful sailors. Despite their reputation, however, they were always uncomfortable sailing in the open sea. Even the Black Sea, marking the easternmost limit of their "inner sea," filled them with extreme trepidation. According to Greek myth, the Argonauts had been the first to open it up to navigation—no mean achievement, and one for which they would be regarded forevermore as heroes and demigods.

A legendary son of one of the Argonauts, Odysseus was celebrated as the first man to explore the western part of the inner sea. Following the sack of Troy—a successful raid by Greek marauders on Asia Minor—he broke away from the rest of the fleet, who were satisfied to follow the usual course of Greek sailors returning home by way of Lesbos and thereby carefully avoiding the open sea by hugging the coast and remaining always within sight of land. Instead, Odysseus, perhaps intent on doing some more plundering before returning home, veered off for the city of the Cicones, in the northern Aegean. It was a fateful decision, for after leaving the city of the Cicones and sailing on through the islands of the Cyclades, his ship was (as Homer says) swept by a strong gale past Cytherea at the southern tip of Greece and blown further and further from land into the unexplored waters of the western Mediterranean. He thus became "the first who ever burst into that silent sea."

After nine days of being lashed by the wind, Odysseus and his crew reached the Land of the Lotus-eaters. To Homer, the far reaches of Mediterranean geography were still shrouded in mystery: they were enchanted, fairy lands. Even Italy was unknown. From the Land of the Lotus-eaters, Odysseus—realizing he had drifted far south of Greece—steered his course by the Bear, "which alone among the stars never partakes in the baths of the Ocean." The myth does not say whether he also noticed a reddish star that from time to time grew more glaring until it became one of the brightest of all the starry host. But we like to imagine that he had seen it glowering in baleful eminence high above the Trojan watchtowers, foretelling the doom of the city when the shadows of the fires of the Greek campfires had trembled on the walls. Mars was itself a kind of Odysseus-wanderer of the starry realms, its hands reddened with Trojan princes' blood or besotted with gore from Polyphemos's eye; it was a restless adventurer in the seas of night.

Odysseus sailed on to adventures in the Cave of the Cyclopes, the Island of the Winds, the Land of the Laestrygonians, Circe's Island, the Island of the Sun-God. Oddly but fittingly, all of these names—through the circuitous routes of poetic invention and scientific discovery—have found their way onto the map of Mars.

In Odysseus's journeys, he encountered no other ships. The wider Mediterranean was still a realm unexplored by the Greeks. Of course later Greek sailors again ventured into the strange seas that Odysseus had opened up, though they never did develop much of a taste for open water. In doing so they removed some of these places from the category of myth and placed them securely into that of reality. The Ionian Greeks of Phocaea (on what is now the Turkish mainland, along the Gulf of Izmir) colonized the Tyrrhenian basin as far as Sicily, Tartessian mariners (from the part of the Iberian peninsula now known as Andalusia) dared to venture beyond the once-fearsome Pillars of Hercules (Gilbralter).[2] Each time the boundaries of the known world were exceeded, the frontier of the unknown slipped beyond the farthest outpost or the most extreme landfall and the view of the larger world expanded accordingly—this same expansion of territory and thought is what would one day, far in the future, lead our thoughts to the exploration of Mars.

By the sixth century B.C.E., the Greeks' explorations of their Mediterranean world had brought them into contact with many new countries and peoples, peoples who held different views from themselves about the Earth and the sky. These encounters made the Greeks more receptive to new ideas, and led them to begin to distance themselves, at least temporarily, from astrology. They also encouraged them to blaze new trails leading away from their ancestral worship of the gods of Mt. Olympus.

As they were the first to venture far beyond the known boundaries of the Earth, the Greeks—especially the Ionians, those who lived in the islands of the Ionian Sea and in the cities that flourished along the Greek-colonized coast of Turkey—became the first humans to try to look at the heavens with a yearning to understand it through logical inquiry rather than through the eyes of superstition, a concept that may have been first proposed by Thales of Miletus (c. 624–547 B.C.E.). Thus, to understand Mars, they first had to determine what it is, then why it is, and finally how it got to be that way.

A first important discovery came from Pythagoras of Samos (c. 570– 500 B.C.E.), who seems to have taught that the Earth is a sphere, an idea later extended to the other celestial bodies. If the Earth is a sphere, and the sky is a sphere (and even the Greeks of Homer's time believed in the dome of the sky), how then do the stars move across the heavens? After a few philosophical foibles, the truth suddenly emerged with Heracleides of Pontus, who proposed that the Earth simply rotates in a west to east direction on its axis. Unfortunately, Heracleides' great idea was dropped (even though we know it it to be true today) because other powerful minds argued that if the Earth were spinning, a body thrown up into the air would simply be left behind. But a more compelling argument was that Heracleides' theory did not explain the motions of the planets. As seen from Earth, the planets usually move in an west to east direction around the sky, and that fits the theory. But sometimes the planets reach a stationary point and reverse direction; meanwhile, the stars remain unaffected by these motions. How can that be? In the case of Mars, the planet would later on reach yet another stationary point, then resume its usual west to east advance. How can so many independent motions be explained by the Earth simply turning on its axis?

As if this were not bad enough, there are at least two different types of planetary motions that need to be explained: Mercury and Venus have one type of motion, Mars, Jupiter, and Saturn display the other. Mercury and Venus rise above the horizon and fall back down (over the course of weeks or months, respectively), rather like stones tossed into the air. They never venture far from the Sun (Mercury never more than 28° from it, and Venus never more than 48°), so they are never seen in the deep dark night. These planets perform their dance either in the evening or in the morning. That is why since ancient times, they have been known as either evening or morning stars. Pythagoras, however, was the first to propose that the evening and morning appearances of these oscillating "stars" might be explained by having them travel in circular orbits. It was a bold step that provided some kind of comprehensible structure to the universe. Mars, Jupiter, and Saturn sailed across the midnight skies with the zig-zagging motions of Mars described above. But Jupiter and Saturn moved with agonizing slowness. If the ancients saw Jupiter in the constellation Scorpius, they had to follow it for twelve years before they saw it return to the same place in the sky; if it were Saturn, the planet would take nearly thirty years to complete its circuit.

That is why Mars stood out so clearly from the rest of the planets. Only Mars pranced across the entire sky every two years with a dynamic grandeur and grace, performing a striking backward loop, like Odysseus's ship being blown off course. At times Mars moves half the Moon's apparent diameter every night, so its motion against the background stars is easy to notice. Its red color also makes it stand out, as we noted earlier, and it undergoes a fifty-fold variation in brightness. The movement of Mars also has a rhythm, and Pythagoras sought to explain it in terms of the harmony of music. Indeed, his school tried to ascribe all natural happenings in terms of numbers and ratios. As Aristotle wrote of the Pythagoreans, "They assumed that the elements of numbers were the elements of all things, and that the whole heavens were harmony and number."[3] The Pythagoreans, by the way, also believed that life existed on other worlds, and that the Moon was a mirror of the Earth. Some of the Pythagoreans, among them Philolaos, taught that the earthly appearance of the Moon was due to its being inhabited by animals and by plants, "like those on our earth, only greater and more beautiful; for the animals on it are fifteen times as powerful, not having any sort of excrement, and their day is fifteen times as long as ours."[4]

The Ionian philosophers were the first men to reason boldly about the structure of the universe, but unfortunately their reason sometimes led them astray. Almost all of them began with two concepts that to them were self-evident: (1) the Earth is the center of the universe and (2) all the heavenly bodies must move uniformly in circular paths (the circle was the perfect form, and surely nothing short of perfection could be allowed in the divine heavens). One of the most famous of all philosophers was Plato (427–347 B.C.E.), an Athenian and student of Socrates and the teacher of Aristotle. He founded a school in Athens in 387 B.C.E., called the Academy, over whose entrance were these words: "Let no one enter here who knows no geometry." Plato believed that *ideas*, not the things we see, were the true reality. And since the real world is perfect, pure, and eternal, it can only be experienced by the mind. What then were the planets but imperfect and temporary phenomena, admittedly "more beautiful and perfect than anything else that is visible . . . yet far inferior to [the things] which are true." Blood-red Mars was not only temporary and imperfect; it also lacked purity, because purity cannot be stained.

But Plato saw angels in the architecture of the heavens. The imperfect planets, he argued, occupied independent transparent spheres (circular, invisible, and thus perfect). The spheres were made of pure crystal and each was centered on the Earth. Of course, to conform with his theory of perfection, all celestial motion had to be circular, and all astronomical bodies had to be spherical; so Mars, suddenly, had a shape. In Plato's model, the Moon occupied the first sphere outward from Earth, followed by the Sun, Mercury, Venus, Mars, Jupiter, Saturn, and finally all the stars. Aristotle would later provide proof that the planets lie at different distances: "Yet these planets are farther from the [Earth] and thus nearer to [the Moon] as observation has itself revealed. For we have seen the moon, half-full, pass beneath the planet Mars, which vanished on its shadow side and came forth by the bright and shining part."

It is almost a cliche of art historians that the architecture of the Greeks was dominated by, and developed by simple addition to, their basic structure, the lintel spanning two columns. "Starting from simplest wooden forms," writes art-historian William R. Ivins Jr., "the Greek architects at an early date effected a transformation of these forms into stone, but thereafter apparently contented themselves with the introduction of linear subtleties and applied ornament into the roughly standardized shape. . . . I have never heard that the Greeks were either lacking in curiosity or averse to new fashions, but, if I may so express it, Greek building remained in the realm of simple addition."[5] In their planetary theories, the Greeks would also proceed, in effect, by simple addition. Instead of inventing fundamentally new schemes, they were satisfied to tinker with the same basic pattern until they had perfected it as far as possible. In the case of architecture, some believe that they ultimately achieved, in the words of Ernest Renan, "la perfaite beauté." Their planetary theories, on the other hand, became pure Rococo, overly elaborate manifestations of the creative (overworked?) mind.

In the fourth century B.C.E., Plato introduced his theory of the heavens to his pupil Eudoxus of Cnidus and assigned him to work out mathematically how the movements of the planets might be explained by an arrangement of nested spheres. On this basis, indeed, Eudoxus succeeded in producing an ingenious model, the first theoretical explanation ever offered to account for the retrograde movements of Mars. He supposed that Mars moved in a circle upon a circle as if it were a small wheel pinned to the rim of a larger wheel. Furthermore, he tilted the axis of the sphere of Mars so that it was not parallel to the axis of the sphere of the sky, though the two axes remained connected to each other like a compass in a gimbal. Eudoxus did not believe that these spheres had any real or physical existence—he saw them as no more than mathematical devices to explain the physical motions. Aristotle, however, took them literally, and created his own model of planetary motion consisting of an elaborate system of fifty five nested spheres. Although Eudoxus's model explained to some degree of accuracy the retrograde behavior of Mars, it did not explain why the planet varied in brightness (why, if the planet was centered on the Earth, should Mars's brightness vary at all?).

A later Greek—Aristarchus of Samos—suggested a radical solution: displace the Earth from the center of the universe by making it an ordinary planet rotating on its axis once every twenty-four hours (as Heracleides of Pontus had suggested) and circling the Sun once every 365 days. He arrived at this idea—a rudimentary form of the heliocentric system—by 250 B.C.E. Unfortunately, we know too little about the man who was the first to see through what Philip Morrison has called "the master illusion of all illusions": the apparent movement of the whole heavens around the Earth every twenty-four hours due to the rotation of the Earth on its axis. Aristarchus was also the first to recognize that the apparent backward loop-the-loop of Mars was another illusion, reflecting the fact that we reside on a moving, not a stationary, platform: the planets not only move against the velvet curtain of the night while we, in the audience, watch silent and motionless, but we ourselves are part of the moving planetary stage-machinery.

Alas, Aristarchus's idea, like Heracleides', attracted scant attention at the time. "Why," William Stahl asks in his entry on Aristarchus in the *Dictionary of Scientific Biography*, "did the Greeks develop a heliocentric hypothesis and then let it fall by the wayside?" It may be that the Greeks even of Aristarchus's time realized that the theory did not fit all the observed facts. For instance, the Earth's seasons are of uneven lengths. How could this be if the Earth were in a circular orbit about the Sun? Any solution to this problem, it seemed, would mar the beautiful symmetry and simplicity of the heliocentric picture.

For whatever reason, the emphasis of the later Greeks was to be less on breathtaking speculative leaps than on careful observations and rigorous mathematical demonstrations. They opted for such an approach perhaps because they were no longer as interested in the questions which interest us and seem to have interested Aristarchus and the other Ionian philosophers, questions about the true structure of the universe. In the end, the Ionian philosophers had failed to realize their bold dream; they had failed to explain, to the satisfaction of all, the workings of the universe on logical principles. For their less adventurous successors, the movements of the planets among the stars were of concern mainly in the belief that they would allow them to detect heavenly influences upon the Earth. Astronomy thus became once more accessory to a subject that seemed to have far more important implications—astrology.

The successors of Aristarchus preferred to keep the Earth at the center of their system—perhaps in large part because that is the obvious place for it if one's preoccupations are chiefly astrological, according with the belief that the positions of the planets relative to the stars as seen from Earth determined the destiny of man. They continued to try to capture the apparent movements of Mars by making it move on a small circle attached to a larger one—the intricate system of epicycles. In fairness, it must be admitted that the epicycle solution will indeed produce loops in Mars's path at just the times of its oppositions to the Sun; however, in order to account for the different sizes of loops observed at different points around the zodiac, the more subtle astronomers—notably, Hipparchus of Rhodes, who lived in the second century B.C.E.—had to offset the main circle from its center on the Earth. When even that wouldn't do, his successors had to introduce still other complications. Pliny, the Roman writer who approached the volcano Vesuvius too closely and perished during its eruption in 79 C.E., summed up the mounting frustrations of astronomers from Hipparchus's day to his own by referring to Mars simply as *inobservibile sidus*—the untrackable star.

The last of the ancient tinkerers with the theory of Mars's motion—the last, in fact, to make any fundamental improvements for some fourteen centuries—was Claudius Ptolemy, who lived at Alexandria, Egypt, in the second century C.E. In Ptolemy's day, Alexandria was still the site of the magnificent library founded by Ptolemy Soter, one of the generals who had divided the empire of the city's founder, Alexander the Great, after the latter's premature death in 323 B.C.E. It was in a province of the farflung Roman empire, the empire of the Antonines: of Hadrian, Antoninus Pius, and Marcus Aurelius. The historian Gibbon, in a famous passage of *The Decline and Fall of the Roman Empire*, described this era as unquestionably the period in the history of the world "during which the condition of the human race was most happy and prosperous." Ptolemy was the greatest astronomer of this ostensibly golden age.

He was an encylopaedist, employed on colossal projects, and concerned with vast things. In the Middle Ages his reputation was chiefly founded on his *Geography*, a work that has now been largely forgotten. (A pity!) Although he drew on the writings of earlier geographers, such as Eratosthenes, who is best remembered as the first to make an accurate measure of the circumference of the Earth, his real contribution was "the scientific, quantitative spirit."[6] He contributed methods for projecting the surface of the spherical Earth onto a flat surface such as parchment, and recognized the need for a map-grid indicating latitudes and longitudes. He himself published latitudes and longitudes for eight thousand places in the then known world. His most serious mistake was to follow Strabo instead of Eratosthenes in his estimate of the length of a degree (80 kilometers [50 miles] instead of 113 kilometers [70 miles]). Thus he greatly misjudged the circumference of the Earth (he put it at 28,967 kilometers [18,000 miles] instead of 40,232 kilometers [25,000 miles]), and coupled with his mistake of extending Asia far beyond its true dimensions, this "had the effect of grossly reducing the extent of the unknown parts of the world between the eastern tip of Asia and the western tip of Europe."[7] The result would be that Ptolemy's work had the effect of hastening the European encounter with the New World.

Ptolemy worked out his astronomy in a book bearing the Greek title ἡ μεγίστη [syntaxis] (the "Great Syntaxis," to distinguish it from a lesser collection of astronomical writings; the title was later corrupted by the Arabs who added the definite article to make it *Al-majisti*—the *Almagest*, the Greatest). It remained the supreme authority on the subject for centuries, wherever Greek culture and learning survived. Ptolemy was more an assimilator and a perfecter of the existing system than a bold innovator—

in fact, such a successful assimilator that the technical details of the works of his predecessors have not survived. He was the last of a distinguished line of Greek technicians, a consummate craftsman of the almighty circle. Ptolemy brought the Earth-centered model of planetary motion to such a seeming state of perfection (it was still wrong) that it remained unchallenged for a thousand years. He did not, as is sometimes alleged, irresponsibly pile circles on circles in his planetary theories. His model of planetary motion was precise enough for predicting where the planets would be at some later time (as long as it wasn't too far in the future, because that's when the predictions became less reliable). Thus, he does not deserve his reputation as an uninspired jobber who produced "a crank machine."

He was especially pleased with his theory for Mars, which was indeed ingenious, and solved a problem that "had defeated Hipparchus as well as Eudoxus before him, and by 135 C.E. could be considered the outstanding unsolved problem of astronomy."[8] He made Mars travel on a small circle (epicycle) that moved around the Earth on a larger circle (the deferent). As the epicycle turned, a point on its rim followed a looped path swinging in toward the center of the deferent, before moving outward again in reverse, just as called for to explain the retrograde motion of the planet. This wasn't Ptolemy's only problem, however; another was that Mars's motion around its orbit was nonuniform—when it comes to opposition in Capricorn/Aquarius, it travels almost twice as fast as when on the other side of its orbit in Cancer/Leo. In order to account for this variation, Ptolemy made his deferent circle slightly off center from the Earth. Now he had the speed of Mars's motion right and, with the Earth off center of the Martian orbit, he could also account for the planet's notorious variations in brightness. However, the size of the retrograde loops failed to agree with what was observed. At last Ptolemy proposed a radical solution—he made Mars move uniformly not around the center of the deferent but around another point, called the equant; it was located at a point equal and opposite from the Earth along the line through the center of the deferent, and it worked beautifully—though it did, of course, breach the rule of uniform circular motions.

Ptolemy's theory also made the radius of Mars's epicycle parallel to that of the Earth-Sun radius. By means of this arrangement, he ensured that the retrograde loop of Mars would always occur when Mars is at opposition (in the opposite direction from the Sun). His model was certainly an elegant

The Ptolemaic System

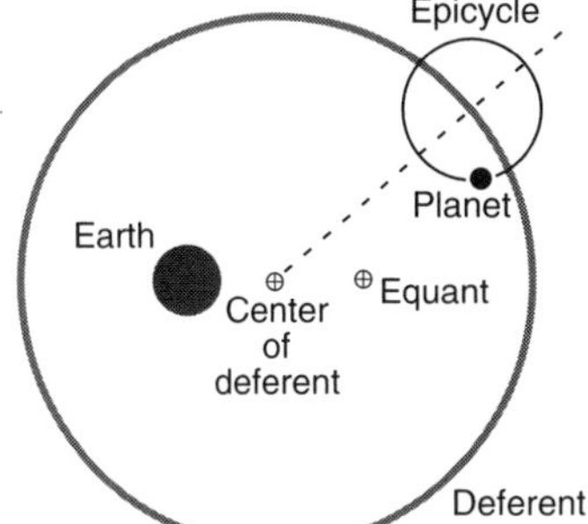

Retrograde Motion in the Ptolemaic System

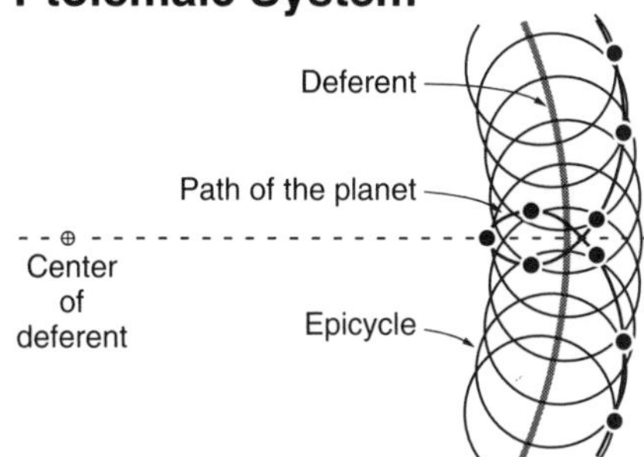

piece of work, and elated Ptolemy so much that he did not hesitate to apply it to the rest of the planets. He once wrote, "When I trace the windings to and fro of the heavenly bodies, I take my fill of ambrosia, food of the gods."

There is an evocative wooden sculpture of Ptolemy in the Cathedral of Ulm: eyes closed, a faint smile on his face, he holds an armillary sphere in one hand while pointing casually upward toward the heavens with the fingers of the other. It is a picture of smugness and complacency—the face of an astronomer so satisfied with the completeness of his theory that he no longer bothers to look into the heavens. Perhaps he really was as smug and complacent as this, a blinkered supporter of the status quo; certainly he was not primarily an observer. Still, on the whole, he deserves our sympathy rather than our contempt. It is fair to judge him only according to the time in which he lived.

That time, golden as it might seem by outward appearances (and as it appeared to Gibbon) was an era of *pax Romana*, of Roman peace. But the age of the Antonines was also an age of exhaustion and world-weariness. Its prevailing outlook was well summed up in the gloomy meditations of the Roman emperor and Stoic philosopher Marcus Aurelius (c. 121–180 C.E.) with their profound note of resignation: "Everything harmonizes with me which is harmonious with thee, O Universe!" Under the Antonines, slavery, the blight of the ancient world, was as rampant as ever; the splendor of the cities existed for a very small minority of the population, while the great majority lived in unimaginable poverty and squalor. Much of Italy was no longer under cultivation, making Rome desperately—and precariously—dependent on the provinces for grain. Superstitious cults and astrology were popular, but by its very nature astrology is a religion of fatalism, and more than any other factor "made Fate a terrible and crushing power such as we can scarcely believe."[9]

Since "men looked to the past for what was best; the future, they felt, would be at best a weariness, and at worst a horror,"[10] it is not surprising that Ptolemy's efforts should have been directed more toward perfecting the traditions of the past than toward breaking new ground. He was a traditionalist in religion and in physics—and, presumably, in politics. He believed that the planets were divine, and accepted without demur the standard arguments against the mobility of the Earth. He never questioned the widespread belief in astrology, or doubted the grim determinism with which it shackled the human mind. Indeed, he wrote a book, long known as the "astrologer's bible," in which he espoused notions that must already have been cliche in his own time and are still often enough repeated by astrologers in ours (for instance, he said that for love-matches planetary "trines" and "sextiles" are harmonious while "squares" and "oppositions" are disharmonious). The separation of his astrology and his astronomy into separate books has tended to obscure his singleness of purpose. Clearly, if the motions of the planets could not be accurately computed, the astrological premise—that this knowledge could in turn be used to forecast events of importance in terrestrial affairs—could not be relied upon. Since what is important in astrology is practical knowledge of how to calculate the positions of the planets and not knowledge of the ultimate structure of the universe—if epicycles and eccentrics, despite their artificiality, served that purpose, and in Ptolemy's hands they did so, admirably—then that was enough. It was sufficient to know that the world ran (almost) according to the astronomers' tables.

By the time Ptolemy died—probably in the last quarter of the second century C.E.; his last observation was made in 151 C.E.—happiness had largely departed from the ancient world. Despite Marcus Aurelius's own admirable personal qualities and his stoic fortitude, he presided over a realm beset by a series of unmitigated calamities. There were floods and famines in Italy, earthquakes in Asia. The emperor himself spent much of his time on the empire's frontiers, fighting defensive wars against the Parthians in the east and the Germans in the north. His successors of the next century watched with increasing alarm the encroaching dangers and raced to keep them at bay by building defenses from the Veneto to Milan. Rome itself was surrounded with massive walls and fortifications. Instead of marking the farthest limits of the imagination in its indomitable struggle with the unknown, the word "frontier" acquired the meaning it still has in Europe—"the sharp edge of sovereignty, a line to stop at not an area inviting entrance."[11] It was the outermost wall of fortifications on a verge of fear.

Inevitably, shells of dogma also hardened to encase the human mind. Science, whose seed had first been planted in Ionia in the sixth century B.C.E. and had branched and prospered for centuries, had petered out into its apparently final twig in Ptolemy's complicated clockwork. Then, like a species bound for extinction or a flickering candle blown by the wind, its impulse seemed to have exhausted itself. Fortunately it did not vanish altogether; in spite of the double destruction of the library of Alexandria—once by Christian fanatics, and again by the Muslim ruler Caliph Omar—some of the best of the works of ancient learning survived, including copies of the works of Ptolemy. Eventually they would be translated into Arabic. In this form, the living-fossils of Ptolemy's geography and of his planetary system with its orb-in-orb elaboration and intricate complexity survived to reach later generations and to produce a reawakening, a second birth, of science.

During all this time—more than a thousand years—Mars traced the prescribed workings of its Ptolemaic machinery. Instead of a world, it became a mere set of complicated gears, dropping far back into the remote curtain of the sky well beyond the retreating frontier of the human intellect. It was then not a realm to arouse the human imagination, but a remote, inaccessible, pale red dot.

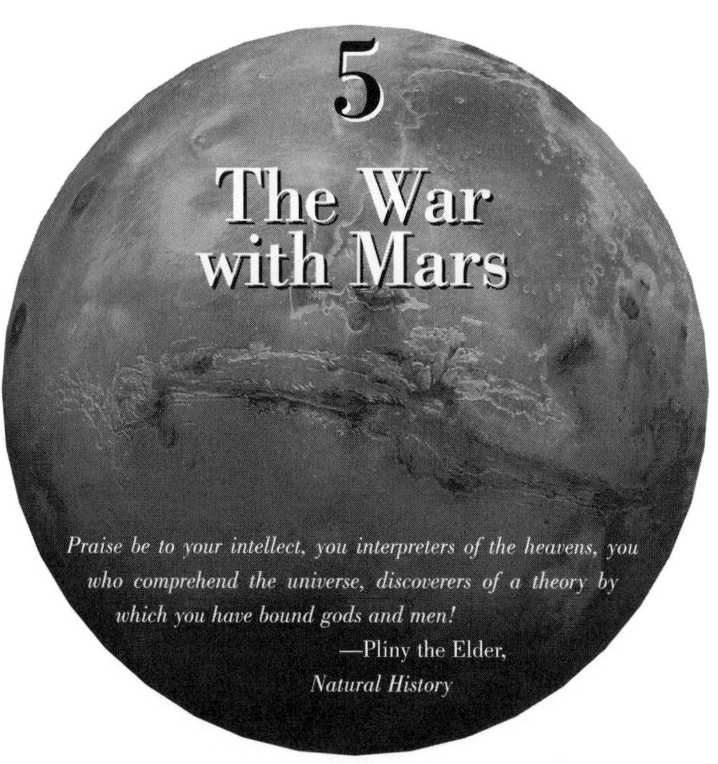

5 The War with Mars

Praise be to your intellect, you interpreters of the heavens, you who comprehend the universe, discoverers of a theory by which you have bound gods and men!

—Pliny the Elder, *Natural History*

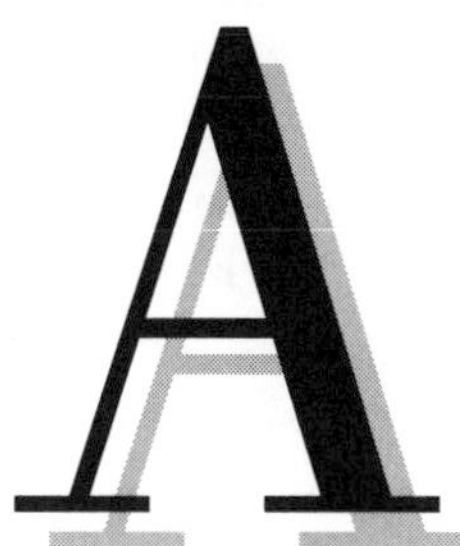

A copy of Ptolemy's *Geography*, in Greek, was brought from Constantinople to Florence in 1400 and translated into Latin. Thereafter numerous manuscripts, sometimes accompanied by maps based on Ptolemy, were circulating in Western Europe. In some of these maps subequatorial Africa was joined up to Asia on the northeast, to form a great southern land mass enclosing the Indian

Ocean and the China Sea as a kind of inland lake. Thus, it seemed that it would be impossible to reach India by sea. Meanwhile, the inland route to Asia followed by the Venetian Marco Polo in the thirteenth century had become unreliable after its safe paths were cut off by the disruption of the Mongol Empire.

Though a sea route to the Far East was always something devoutly to be desired, it remained inconceivable until Ptolemy's map was revised and the purported obstacle of the great southern land mass ("Terra Incognita") was removed. Already by the mid-fifteenth century, a few maps, including the celebrated "planisphere" of Fra Mauro (1459), had separated Africa from Asia. They encouraged a few travelers who hazarded passages to India by crossing Egypt overland, then sailing along the Red Sea and across the Arabian Sea to promote the idea that the rich spice islands of the East might be more easily and reliably reached by sailing right around Africa.

Nowhere did these ideas fall on more fertile ground than in Portugal. On the western edge of the Iberian peninsula, with no ports on the inland sea of the Mediterranean, Portugal faced westward into the Atlantic and southward toward the unfathomed continent of Africa. King John I's third son, prince Henry, had led a crusade in 1415 against Gibraltar, during which his imagination had been fired by the wealth in pepper, cinnamon, cloves, and ginger, tapestries, Oriental rugs, gold, silver, and jewels that had been brought there by caravans from sub-Saharan Africa in the south and from the Indies in the east. When his father refused to authorize another crusade against Gibraltar, he left the court at Lisbon sulking. A man of monkish disposition, he retreated among the sea gulls, establishing himself in a fortress vantaged on beetling cliffs at Cape Saint Vincent, the southwestern tip of Europe, then the extremest verge of the watery unknown. In ancient times it had been known as *Promentorium Sacrum*—the Sacred Promontory (a name corrupted by the Portuguese to Sagres). For forty years, "in the first modern enterprise of exploring, from that spot he sent out an unbroken series of voyages into the unknown. . . . There he applied the zeal and energy of the crusader to the modern exploring enterprise."[1] His dream was to find a sea route around Africa to the East. In the process he and his sailors replaced the caricature maps of the ancients with accurately drawn outlines of hitherto unknown coasts; replaced the clumsy astrolabe, used by medieval navigators to work out their latitudes, with the handier cross-staff; and replaced, too, the heavy trading vessels then in use—square-rigged barcas or Venetian carracks—with the lighter, swifter caravel. The caravel was the *Mars Pathfinder* of Prince Henry's day.

Into the unknown seas along the unexplored coast of Africa, Henry hurled caravel after caravel—no less than fifteen expeditions between 1424 and 1434. They reached as far as Cape Bojador, on the bulge of Africa, then beat their way back; they dared not plumb beyond. The wild and forlorn cape seemed the end of the world, at least the end of the habitable world; there seemed to be only deserts and deserted coastlines beyond. One of Henry's captains told the prince that Cape Bojador was in fact impassable. But Henry was undaunted; he simply increased the reward for a successful venture. The same captain set out again. This time he doubled the Cape, "and found the lands beyond quite contrary to what he, like others, had expected." The way was now opened to further explorations, and Henry proceeded to eke out knowledge of the rest of the coastline of Africa.

Denis Dias would round Cape Verde, the western tip of Africa, in 1445. After Henry's death in 1460, the Portuguese mariners continued their incremental explorations of the African coast, and in 1488—just four years after an obscure Genoese navigator named Christopher Columbus came to Lisbon to promote his scheme of reaching the Indies by sailing west—Bartholomeu Dias, driven by storm around the southern tip of Africa, anchored his ships in Mossel Bay. His achievement was followed by the even greater endeavor of Vasco da Gama, who sailed four ships from Lisbon harbor in July 1497, rounded the Cape, and reached Calicut on the southeastern coast of the Indian peninsula in May of the following year. Two of da Gama's ships, the square-rigger *San Gabriel* and the caravel *Berrio*, carrying a handful of survivors of a crew decimated by scurvy, returned to Lisbon harbor in mid-September 1499. There could no longer be any doubt—the *mappa munda* of Ptolemy was incorrect. There was no *Terra Incognita*; it had vanished from the map, to be replaced by the first seafaring route to the Indies.

During those fateful years when Portuguese navigators were tacking around Africa for the Indies, Nicolaus Copernicus was enrolled as a student of canon law at the University of Bologna. Analogous to the assault on Ptolemy's map of the Earth that the Portuguese had accomplished, Copernicus would begin the assault on Ptolemy's equally flawed map of the heavens. In doing so, he would round an equally formidable Cape Bojodor of the human mind.

Copernicus had been born in 1473, at Torun (now in Poland), on the river Vistula. When he was eighteen his uncle, Lucas Watzelrode, a Catholic bishop, sent him to Cracow to begin the study of the liberal arts, the first step toward a career of service in the church. His uncle's efforts to obtain for him a sinecure as canon in Frauenburg Cathedral were at first unsuccessful. But Copernicus was not a young man in a hurry; he was only too happy to continue his education in Italy, taking courses in canon law and medicine. Later he would serve for a time as his uncle's personal physician. Only with the bishop's death in 1512 did Copernicus at long last take up residence in Frauenburg Cathedral (according to tradition, in the northwest tower of the wall).

The voyages of the Portuguese had proved the fallibility of the ancients in geography. Ptolemy had made mistakes in his map of the Earth; why not, then, in his map of the heavens? Taking his time, long in maturing—he was already almost forty—Copernicus came to Frauenburg as a man with an idea that would set the world in motion.

He now sat down to write a short sketch (the *Commentoriolus*—little commentary) of a new planetary theory, based on the proposition that the Earth—instead of being the center of the universe—is an ordinary planet, in orbit around the Sun. No doubt he had been thinking on the subject for a number of years. It is possible that he had groped his way to a full-fledged heliocentric system through a hybrid system that initially incorporated both heliocentric and geocentric elements.[2]

We know that Copernicus's chief objection to Ptolemy was his introduction of the equant, whereby the Greek astronomer had tacitly abandoned the requirements that the Earth be at the center of the universe and that the planets keep to a uniform circular motion. For Ptolemy, the only thing that mattered was to produce a machine for calculating—i.e., predicting—the motions of the planets. Whether the planet moved around the Earth or around some other point did not so much matter. To Copernicus, however, it did matter; he saw clearly that the equant—a mere mathematical point—could not have a real physical significance, and instead of attempting to produce a mere calculating device, Copernicus aimed at something far grander—the discovery of nothing less than the true struc-

Nicolaus Copernicus (1473–1543). Portrait hangs in the halls of Harvard College Observatory. © Stephen James O'Meara.

ture of the universe. From his perspective, Ptolemy's scheme "seemed neither sufficiently absolute nor sufficiently pleasing to the mind."

Seventeen hundred years earlier, a heliocentric system had dawned on Aristarchus; now Copernicus rediscovered it. The new formulation was indeed what he had hoped it would be, a glimpse of the true structure of the universe— it was more aesthetic, more gratifying, more pure than Ptolemy's system. As he would later write:

> In the middle of everything is the sun. For in this most beautiful temple, who would place this lamp in another or better position than that from which it can light up the whole thing at the same time? For, the sun is not inappropriately called by some people the lantern of the universe, its mind by others, and its ruler by still others. [Hermes] the Thrice Greatest labels it a visible god, and Sophocles' Electra, the all-seeing. Thus indeed, as though seated on a royal throne, the sun governs the family of planets revolving around it.[3]

As soon as the Sun instead of the Earth was properly enthroned as the center of the system, the fact became no less apparent to Copernicus than

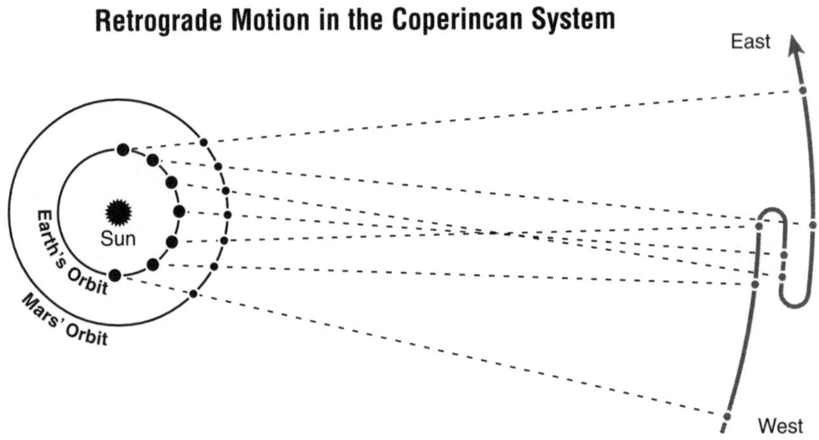

it had been to Aristarchus that the retrograde movements of the planets—and those of Mars in particular—are only illusions, reflections of the Earth's motion in its orbit around the Sun. In order to account for these, Ptolemy had had to introduce the first and largest epicycle into each of his planetary theories; now, with a single stroke, they were swept away. It was also possible to understand why the retrograde loops always occurred when the planet stood in opposition to the Sun, a coincidence that had never made sense in Ptolemy's scheme.

Of course, the most straightforward heliocentric model, in which the planets travel around the Sun in simple circles, fails to account for the motions of the planets in detail. The times between oppositions are not exactly equal, while the successive retrograde loops made by the planets are also irregular. Like the Greeks, Copernicus was unable to conceive of any motion other than circular for a planet, and so had no choice but to bring back the complicated machinery of eccentric and epicycle, orb in orb.

For thirty years Copernicus sat in his tower puzzling over the complications of his theory. At last he was ready to publish. His great book, *de Revolutionibus orbium caelestium* (the revolutions of the celestial orbs), appeared in 1543, with the imprimatur of the ranking officials in the Catholic church and with a noble dedication written by Copernicus to Pope Paul III. By now Copernicus was an old man, seriously ill; indeed, the first copies of his great book did not reach him until he was on his death bed.

The theory produced a violent reaction. Martin Luther, for instance, objected that the heliocentric theory seemed to contradict certain passages in the Bible (such as Joshua's command, "Sun stand thou still") and called Copernicus a "fool who would overturn the science of astronomy." But resistance to the theory was not based on theological considerations alone; though some astronomers embraced it, others were frankly skeptical—notably, Tycho Brahe, the leading astronomer in the generation after Copernicus.

Tycho was an entirely different sort of man from Copernicus. While Copernicus had been first and foremost a theoretician—he made only a few observations himself, and claimed for them no great degree of accuracy—Tycho was above all an observer, one of the greatest who ever lived.

Tycho Brahe was born in 1546, three years after Copernicus died. Adopted at birth by a well-to-do uncle, Jørgen Brahe, Tycho was early destined for a career in statecraft. At age sixteen he went to the University of Copenhagen to study law. While there, on August 21, 1560, Tycho witnessed a partial eclipse of the Sun; it changed the direction of his life. The date of the eclipse had been predicted long before by astronomers, and Tycho, as his early biographer Pierre Gassendi wrote, "thought of it as divine that men could know the motions of the stars so accurately that they could long before foretell their places and relative positions."[4] Almost at once he acquired a copy of Ptolemy's *Almagest* and enthusiastically worked his way through it. His uncle, who regarded these studies as an absolute waste of time, sent Tycho from Denmark to the University of Leipzig, along with a tutor named Vedel. Vedel's task was to make sure that Tycho kept his nose in his law books. However, Tycho was nothing if not strong-willed; he studied law during the day, but at night, while Vedel was asleep, he continued to steal out beneath the stars.

On August 17, 1563, he watched a most unusual tryst between Jupiter and Saturn. They were so close together as to be almost indistinguishable. It was an impressive sight, but when he checked, he found that Ptolemy's tables had erred in their prediction of the date of the event by a full month, while even those based on Copernicus were off by several days. To Tycho these were outrageous errors—after all, it had been the accuracy of its predictions that had first attracted him to astronomy in the first place. Thus, when only sixteen years old, "his eyes were opened to the great fact, which seems to us so simple to grasp, but which had escaped the attention of all European observers before him, that only through a steadily pursued course

Tycho Brahe (1546–1601). From the 1655 edition of *Tychonis Brahei Equitis Dani* by Petro Gassendo (Pierre Gassendi). Book courtesy Owen Gingerich. Photo © Stephen James O'Meara.

of observations would it be possible to obtain a better insight into the motions of the planets."[5] Soon after the conjunction of Jupiter and Saturn, Jørgen died, and there was no longer anything standing in Tycho's way.

From Leipzig, Tycho moved to Wittenberg and then to Rostock (where he famously lost his nose in a duel; it was fought not over a woman but a mathematical point over which Tycho and his fellow combatant had disagreed. Tycho promptly had the missing member replaced with an artificial nose of copper and silver). He moved again, to Basle and to Augsburg. All the while he was collecting the best instruments available for making accurate astronomical observations. When he could not find instruments good enough, he designed his own, and was especially proud of a brass and oak quadrant thirty-eight feet in diameter. At the age of twenty-six, his education complete, he returned to Denmark, settling briefly on the family estate at Knudstrup. But he was soon bored with the life of a Danish nobleman, spent among "horses, dogs and luxury." He aimed for something higher—a life of the mind. Again he moved, this time to Herrevad, the estate of another wealthy uncle, Steen Bille, who alone among his relatives approved of his scientific tastes and who dabbled in alchemy himself.

On November 11, 1572, when returning from Steen Bille's alchemical laboratory to supper, Tycho noticed a brilliant star near the familiar W asterism in the constellation Cassiopeia. The star, nearly overhead, shone as bright as Venus, and was visible in broad daylight. It remained conspicuous for a time, then began to fade, but during the period when it was visible, Tycho with his instruments was able to show that it was exceedingly remote—to all intents and purposes located in the sphere of the "fixed stars." He promptly wrote a book about the star, *De Nova Stella*, which made him famous and brought an offer from the Danish king Frederik II that he could not refuse—the grant of the island of Hven (a name that Tycho always insisted meant "the island of Venus") in the Baltic between Elsinor and Copenhagen. There, above the white cliffs rising from the sea, Tycho built the most magnificent observatory of his age—Uraniborg, the Castle of the Heavens. The architecture was baroque, with an onion dome and cylindrical towers within which Tycho set up a gallery of his instruments (every one had open sights, since they were meant to be used with the naked eye; the telescope, after all, had not yet been invented). Tycho, who always regarded his astronomical work as a form of divine worship, never observed without first putting on his most luxurious robes. He was like a priest in star-studded vestments.

His mature—that is, as he put it, his "virile, precise and absolutely certain"—observations began in 1580. He set out to produce a new star catalog, much more accurate than those of Hipparchus and Ptolemy; he also carried out important studies of the motions of the Sun and the Moon. But from the beginning his "astrologically-directed mind" was preoccupied chiefly with the planets, so it is not surprising that planet observations made up the largest share of his work at Uraniborg. Mars in particular—the planet most obstreperous in its defiance of eccentric and epicycle, orb in orb—drew his attention. He observed every opposition from 1580 onward. But other astronomers also observed Mars's oppositions. Tycho, more diligent than they, kept Mars under careful scrutiny at other times. Thus, the breakthrough of his observations was not based on precision alone, but also on continuity of record.

In 1583, Tycho noted that near opposition Mars was moving retrograde at a rate of nearly a half degree every day. This proved that the planet could approach much nearer to the Earth than the Sun, which was possible in the Copernican system, but impossible in the Ptolemaic. Nevertheless, Tycho still could not bring himself to accept the ideas of Copernicus, and instead adopted a compromise position—the Tychonic system—in which the Earth remained at the center of the universe. The planets circled the Sun, while the Sun in turn moved around the Earth.

The 1595 opposition of Mars was the last Tycho observed at Hven. After twenty years, the lord of Uraniborg had worn out his welcome. He certainly treated his long-suffering tenants scandalously (his taxes were all for the good of astronomy, admittedly, but this cannot have meant much to the abused tenants who were forced to pay them). For all that, he must have cut a striking figure: haughty and aristocratic in bearing, with a bald head, cool, sharp, unsympathetic eyes, and a red handlebar mustache. After Frederik's death the Danish court saw fit to cut off his funds. In 1597, Tycho left Hven in a huff, taking along with him his cache of observations and the most portable of of his instruments. His first destination was Germany, but soon afterward, at the invitation of the Holy Roman Emperor Rudolph II, he moved yet again, to Prague, in Bohemia.

Europe was then being convulsed by religious wars between Protestants and Catholics. In 1600 Tycho was joined by a victim of this warfare, a young

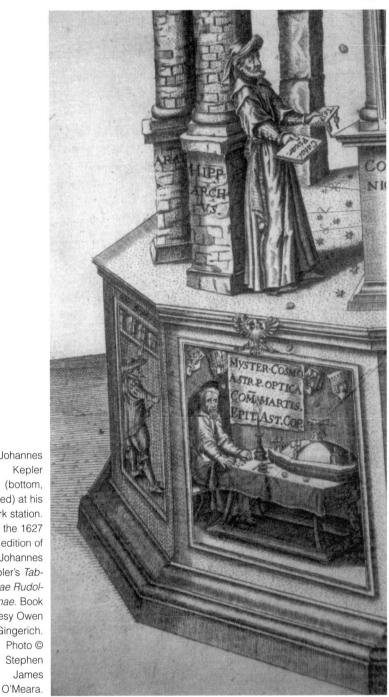

Johannes Kepler (bottom, seated) at his work station. From the 1627 edition of Johannes Kepler's *Tabulae Rudolphinae.* Book courtesy Owen Gingerich. Photo © Stephen James O'Meara.

Protestant mathematician, Johannes Kepler, who had been expelled from his position as mathematician at Graz, Austria, because his religion was different from that of the Catholic Archduke, Ferdinand. Kepler's childhood had been poor and unhappy—"not spoiled," as his biographer Max Caspar put it, "by any parental love."[6] His father was a brutal self-centered man who narrowly escaped the gallows, abandoned his family, and must have come to a bad end. His mother was placed on trial as a witch. Johannes himself was a sickly, mangy youngster—"doglike," as he put it in a candid self-horoscope. But he was a serious scholar and a gifted mathematician, and—perhaps as a way of compensating for the horrors of his mange-eaten and chaotic childhood—he dreamed as the Greeks had dreamed of the rationality and intelligibility of the world. He hoped to discover the mathematical harmonies of the universe. Perhaps, he thought, the ratios of the orbits of the planets could be expressed in terms of the harmonics of music, or their orbits constrained within the geometric forms of the five regular solids (the subject of his first book, the *Mysterium Cosmographicum*).

Apart from being a brilliant theoretician in contrast to Tycho who was first and foremost an observer, Kepler, ever since his student days, had been a confirmed Copernican. As soon as he arrived in Prague, he found Tycho and another assistant, Christian Severinus (or Longomontanus, as he styled himself), at work on the theory of the motions of Mars. Tycho assigned Kepler to the same monumental task.

But Tycho was not about to open his observing books to his untried assistant. He confided only certain observations on a "need to know" basis. Kepler complained: "Tycho gave me no opportunity to share in his experiences. He would only, in the course of a meal and in between other matters mention, as if in passing, today the figure of the apogee of one planet, tomorrow the nodes of another. . . . Tycho possesses the best observations and consequently, as it were, the material for the erection of a new structure; he has also workers and everything else which one might desire. He lacks only the architect who would put all this to use."[7] Kepler had arrived in Prague depressed and physically ill; he was under great strain, unable to tolerate the confusion of Tycho's household. There were violent quarrels, in which the fault—surprisingly, given Tycho's difficult personality—seems to have been mainly Kepler's. He admitted he behaved at times like a "mad dog," perhaps out of frustration. In June 1600, Kepler had finally come to the end of his mental and emotional resources, and returned to Graz with no certain plans for the future. He probably intended to stay there. However, as soon as he arrived he found the Protestant Seminary was in the process of being closed down. There was nowhere else to go (briefly, he even considered studying to become a physician). At last he resigned himself to his fate. His best prospect was to return to Tycho, and so in October 1600 he made his way back to Prague. ("If God is concerned with astronomy," he wrote, "which piety desires me to believe, then I hope I shall achieve something . . . for I see how God let me be bound with Tycho through an unalterable fate and did not let me be separated from him by the most oppressive hardships").[8]

When Kepler arrived back in Prague in September 1601, he felt greatly refreshed; moreover, Tycho had only a month to live. After attending a drinking party from which he was too polite (or proud) to excuse himself in order to relieve his bladder, he developed a bladder obstruction, from which he died on October 24 (in his delirium, as he lay dying, he kept repeating over and over again these words: "Let me not seem to have lived in vain"). Kepler now took possession of Tycho's observations (there still lay ahead of him a long fight with Tycho's heirs over their ultimate fate). Able to work more or less freely, he turned to Mars with a passion.

In Tycho's records, the observations of Mars of more than twenty years were scattered through many pages. Kepler's task was to bring order into the confusion and to try to use them as the basis for forming a theory of Mars's motions. Through backbreaking calculations he was able to establish that no circular orbit could possibly account for the motions of Mars. Next he used the observations, in whose accuracy Kepler had absolute faith, to show that Mars's positions in its orbit always fell slightly inside where they would have been if its orbit were circular. Thus, the orbit had to be an oval of some kind; perhaps it was egg-shaped. (If only, he confided to a friend, the orbit were the mathematically simplest oval, the ellipse, he could simply look up its mathematical properties in the texts of Greek geometers such as Archimedes and Apollonius.)

Kepler found his calculations greatly simplified by his discovery that the line connecting Mars and the Sun sweeps out equal areas in equal times—in other words, Mars travels fastest when it is nearest the Sun, slowest when it is farthest away. Known as Kepler's second law of planetary motion, this was, in fact, the first discovered. Still, the main result—the precise shape of the Martian orbit—seemed as elusive as ever.

After taking a year off in which he sought relaxation in researching optics, Kepler returned to his "war with Mars" in early 1604. He decided to use Tycho's observations to plot the planet's positions in its orbit at twenty-two different points. At last the great realization dawned upon him: "I awoke," he declared, "as from a sleep." On Easter 1605, he made his immortal discovery: the orbit of Mars really is a true ellipse, with the Sun at one focus.

Kepler realized that what was true of Mars must hold true of the other planets: they, too, must follow elliptical paths. Only now he saw how fortunate he had been in starting with Mars. Had he worked from Tycho's observations of any other planet, he would never have made his discovery. Apart from Mercury, the most difficult to observe because of its proximity to the Sun, Mars's orbit departs more from circularity than any of the planets known in Kepler's time—indeed, its orbit is the only one eccentric enough for the fact to have been revealed by Tycho's observations. Had Kepler begun, say, with Venus, whose orbit is almost perfectly circular, the solution would certainly have escaped him. "I therefore," he reflected, "again think it to have happened by divine arrangement, that I arrived at the same time in which [Tycho] was intent upon Mars, whose motions provide the only possible access to the hidden secrets of astronomy, without which we would remain forever ignorant."[9]

The rest of Kepler's life was full of trials. Flush with his success with Mars, he appealed to Rudolph II for funds to extend his work from Mars to the other planets. But Rudolph, chronically short of funds, did not have the money to fight all his battles on Earth, much less to wage planetary warfare. Even the money to publish Kepler's book in which he announced his discovery of the elliptical orbit of Mars was not immediately forthcoming, and it did not appear until 1609. Kepler's salary was continually in arrears, and he was often obliged to appear at court and appeal for it. At the end of 1610 his first wife came down with fever, suffered seizures, and finally died, and that same year he lost his six-year-old son to smallpox. By 1612 Rudolph was dead, and Prague itself had become a battleground. Kepler fled to Linz, Austria. In spite of all, he continued his laborious studies, and in 1619 announced the discovery of a formula (his so-called harmonic law) linking the periods of the planets to their distances from the Sun. With this formula, Kepler had found the key to working out the scale of the solar system.

In 1626, Linz itself came under siege, and Kepler was forced to flee again, eventually finding refuge at the court of the general-in-chief of the armies of the Holy Roman Empire, Albrecht von Wallenstein (for whom Kepler had once cast a horoscope) at his newly formed Duchy of Sagan, in Silesia. He worked on as ever and published his long-awaited tables of the motions of the planets, named the *Rudolfine Tables* in loyalty to his deceased patron. But as always his wages were badly in arrears. At last, in October 1630 he set out on a trip from Sagan to Regensburg, hoping to confer with the then-emperor about yet another possible residence, but the trip proved too much for him, and after a short illness he died, on November 15, 1630.

He wrote for his epitaph: "Once I measured the heavens, now I measure the earth's shadows." The cemetery in which he was buried was destroyed during the Thirty Years' War. But his true epitaph consists of his three immortal laws of planetary motion.

During his troubled life, Kepler once wrote, "It seems to me as though the world only now is beginning to live, or rather rush madly about." His life spanned a time of religious intolerance marked by the violence of the Thirty Years' War, which nearly wrecked Germany. But he lived also in an age of promise and achievement that witnessed the plays of Shakespeare, the founding of the first permanent settlements in the New World, and the invention of the "perpicillum," or telescope as it was soon to be renamed, with which Galileo Galilei, Paduan professor of mathematics, observed the heavens during the very year that Kepler published his timeless discovery of the elliptic shape of the Martian orbit.

Of this telescope, Kepler himself later exclaimed: "O you much knowing tube, more precious than any sceptre. He who holds you in his right hand, is he not appointed king or master over the work of God!"[10]

Kepler dreamt of even more illustrious times, in which men would teach themselves to fly. By this means they might even reach the Moon or the other planets: "Ships and sails proper for the heavenly air should be fashioned. Then there will also be people, who do not shrink from the dreary vastness of space."[11] Of course such sails and ships remained centuries off, but Kepler's wide-ranging imagination conceived of them.

When they finally came, those sails and ships would follow elliptical paths around the Sun, and on approaching the Moon or a planet would be swung into elliptical paths around them. For the laws of spaceflight are also Kepler's laws. The open road to Mars was paved by the mind of Johannes Kepler from a dingy little room in Prague.

Part II

A Swelling Orb

6
The Sails of Imagination

At last his Sail-broad Vans
He spreads for flight, and in the surging smoke
Uplifted spurns the ground, thence many a League
As in a cloudy Chair ascending rides
Audacious....

—John Milton,
Paradise Lost

The Europe of the Middle Ages was static, confining, oppressive. There were well-defined social classes; the population pressed hard on the means of subsistence.[1] Ptolemy's universe was also close, confining, and oppressive. But Ptolemy himself had inadvertently contributed to the overthrow of that world and that universe. He had grossly underestimated the size of the Earth. That underestimate encouraged the dreams of a Genoese mariner—a man with the fanatic eyes of an intense faith, who devoted all his energy and will to one of the most visionary and counterintuitive ideas in history (another had been Copernicus's idea that the Earth traveled around the Sun). Instead of hugging the coast of Africa and painstakingly crawling his way around it to the Indies as the Portuguese were doing, he thought he saw a more direct route to the Indies across the Atlantic. He would sail west—into the sunset—to reach the East.

The man, Christopher Columbus, imagined that the distance from the Canaries to Japan was as little as the actual distance from the Canaries to the West Indies. Thus—by his calculation—the Azores, which had been reached by Genoese navigators a century before Prince Henry's time, were a third of the way to Japan. Columbus began by pleading his case to the Portuguese at the court in Lisbon. They politely but firmly turned him down, since they had already committed themselves to reaching the Indies by way of Africa. He next turned to the Spanish court of Isabella and Ferdinand. For a long time there was no response. At last even his patience was exhausted; he was on the verge of leaving for the French court of Charles VII when the keeper of the privy purse pointed out to Isabella that the funds necessary to equip such an expedition would cost no more than a week's entertainment of a foreign prince (by the same token, the *Mars Pathfinder* cost the American taxpayer about $0.50 a year over a four-year period). This put things into perspective: Isabella saw the light, at long last Columbus had his fleet—the *Nina*, the *Pinta*, and the *Santa Maria*. The rest is history.

The discovery of a New World—vast continents of virtually inexhaustible wealth—brought a windfall to Spain, in whose employ Columbus had sailed. The European extroverts who reached the Great Frontier inaugurated one of the most memorable adventures of modern times, an event thus far unique in the history of the world. Columbus had blundered onto something of even greater worth than the luxuries of the Indies. "With the discovery of [the Caribbean] sea and its lands the whole tight medieval world became unsettled. Appear now lands and people that the Bible knew not of."[2] Columbus's discovery, writes Walter Prescott Webb, "was the miracle which changed everything, which threw open a vast prospect beyond human comprehension. Even now, after four hundred years, we can still grasp what that new world must have meant to the Europeans who first experienced it: new forests, new soil, new streams; new silences and new immensities." What had been revealed was "inherently a vast body of wealth without proprietors . . . an empty land five to six times the size of western Europe, a land whose resources had not been exploited."[3]

In the first place, the wealth seized on was the most portable. Gold beyond the wildest dreams of avarice, seized by the *conquistadores*, Cortés in Mexico and Pizarro in Peru, was returned in avalanches, looted (in the name of Spain and the Catholic religion) from the native Aztecs and the Incas, then loaded onto Spanish galleons for transport back to the Old World. Later came other riches: coffee and tobacco from South America, sugar from the West Indies. Spain benefited first of all the countries of Europe from the great economic boom following Columbus's landfall in the New World—by 1560, wages there stood very high in comparison with those in England and France. The boom in England did not begin until 1573, following the return of Francis Drake's third voyage on the *Golden Hind*. Instead of bringing gold and silver from the source, from Mexico and Peru, as the Spaniards had done, Drake, with the financial backing of syndicates and companies in England, seized Spanish treasure-ships and began to unload their bullion upon England. "The years 1575 to 1620 were," wrote the celebrated English economist John Maynard Keynes, "the palmy days of profit—one of the greatest 'bull' movements ever known."[4]

The palmy days of profit put so much money into circulation that national banking institutions were soon needed. The first of these was the Dutch Bank of Amsterdam, founded in 1609—the same year Kepler published his discovery of the elliptic shape of the orbit of Mars.

Yet another boom began that same year, a boom as consequential in the realm of ideas as Columbus's landfalls in the realm of material wealth. Reports from Holland reached Galileo Galilei, a professor of mathematics at Padua, in the Republic of Venice, of an invention made there by means of which "visible objects, though very distant from the eye of the observer, were seen distinctly as if nearby." Galileo managed to work out the principles of the invention for himself. By arranging two spectacle lenses in a lead tube, he put together a crude telescope magnifying distant objects by a factor of 3X. By the end of the year he had managed to produce a much better instrument magnifying 20X. Realizing it would give an overwhelming advantage to speculators on the Rialto by allowing ships to be recognized at great distances before they came to harbor—a form of insider-trading—he at first dreamed of the commercial uses of the telescope, and went about Venice showing it off to the Doge, senators, and other notables from atop the highest campaniles. But Galileo was also a scientist, and it was not long before he realized the tremendous possibilities the telescope had opened up for pure research.

On the evening of November 30, 1609, he turned his 20X telescope toward the four-day old Moon. He was not the first to observe the Moon through a telescope; England's Thomas Harriot, intimate friend of the dashing Sir Walter Raleigh, had already done so the previous July, and had even gone so far as to produce a crude sketch. However, Harriot had been largely uncomprehending of the image presented to him by his "trunke," as he called it. It was Galileo who first claimed the lunar landscapes for the imagination.

Galileo showed that the surface of the Moon was rough and uneven, full of great cavities and mountains. By January 1610, he had discovered the four largest satellites of Jupiter, and had made a critical series of observations of Venus revealing its moonlike phases. In the Ptolemaic scheme, only the crescent phase was possible; however, as Galileo found, Venus also passed—as implied by the Copernican theory—through half, gibbous, and full. He wrote a book, *Sidereus Nuncius* (Starry Messenger), announcing his discoveries. Published in March 1610, it created a sensation. Sir William Lower of Wales, an early experimenter with telescopes and erewhile correspondent of Harriot, had fumbled for a way to come to terms with the confusing telescopic images he had been seeing. Now everything began to fall into place. "Me thinkes," he wrote to Harriot, "my diligent Galileus hath done more . . . than Magellane in openinge the streights to the South Sea or the dutchmen that were eaten by beares in Nova Zembla. I am sure with more ease and safetie to him self and more pleasure to me."[5] Lower was far from alone in being stirred with a sense of the great possibilities offered by an *otro mundo*—another New World—in the Moon, a world whose shores might one day prove as reachable and perhaps even more portentous than those on which Columbus had made his fateful landfall. Hitherto navigators had always been confined to the two-dimensional surface of the Earth. With the telescope, another dimension—the vertical—was opened for exploration. Equipped with "optic tubes" or "trunkes," astronomers could throw their eyes plumb-upward into the heavens, their minds following in hot pursuit after them.

Here, for aught anyone could say to the contrary, there were "new lands and new peoples that the Bible knew not of." There might be new forests, new soil, new streams, new silences; there certainly were new immensities. Kepler wrote an excited response to Galileo's work, a *Conversation with the Starry Messenger*: "There will certainly be no lack of human pioneers when we have mastered the art of flight. Who could have thought that navigation across the vast ocean is less dangerous and quieter than in the narrow, threatening gulfs of the Adriatic, or the Baltic, or the British straits? Let us create vessels and sails adjusted to the heavenly ether, and there will be plenty of people unafraid of the empty wastes. In the meantime, we shall prepare, for the brave sky-travellers, maps of the celestial bodies—I shall do it for the Moon, you, Galileo, for Jupiter."[6]

But the New World in the Moon could be reached more safely—and certainly more immediately—by discoverers armed with telescopes. For the next three and a half centuries, the "optic tube" would remain the best means of transport across interplanetary space—though admittedly the feeble optics of the early instruments would have to be augmented by the brain-directed sight of the observers spreading widely, to adapt a phrase of the poet John Milton, "the sail-broad vans" of the imagination. In the case of the nearby Moon, observers found a wealth of detail and could embark Columbus-like on voyages in which the wish was father to the thought. They discovered—or believed they had discovered—hints of "another world of men and sensitive creatures, with cities and palaces." Mars was another matter. It was going to be a harder nut to crack. For one thing, it was far away. At even the most favorable opposition, it never approaches closer than 140 times the Moon's distance. Second, Mars is small. We know that it is only 6,780 kilometers (4,213 miles) across, only half the Earth's diameter (and slightly less than twice the Moon's diameter). These factors conspire to ensure that Mars's disk never gets larger than $\frac{1}{100}$ the Moon's diameter—and in fact, its apparent size is scarcely larger than a medium-sized lunar crater. The same telescopes that showed so much on the Moon showed of Mars little more than a tiny orb of light. The planet was effectively beyond the reach of the earliest telescopic reconnaisances.

As early as 1610, Galileo had trained his telescope on Mars, but at the time it lay near the Sun, at almost its greatest distance from the Earth. As a confirmed Copernican since 1597, Galileo knew that Mars moves around the Sun outside the orbit of the Earth. That being the case, it could never show a crescent phase as Venus does, but it ought sometimes to show a gibbous phase, most marked whenever the Earth lay at its greatest angular distance from the Sun as seen from Mars. Then Mars's phase resembles that of the Moon three or four days from full. Galileo strained to make out the gibbous phase, but in his small telescope even the small disk was barely visible, and he had to augment his view with his imagination—as he wrote to Father Benedetto Castelli, one of his former pupils, on December 30, 1610: "I ought not to claim that I can see the phases of Mars; however, unless I am deceiving myself, I believe I have already seen that it is not perfectly round."[7]

Better views of Mars awaited better telescopes, more sea-worthy caravels with which imaginatively to challenge the daunting seas of interplanetary space. The "optick tubes" Galileo used employed a convex lens as the objective and a concave lens as the eyepiece, and were badly impaired by chromatic aberration, a blur of color produced whenever light passes through a simple lens. In effect, the lens acts as a prism, and all bright objects are surrounded with a haze of prismatic splendors. In addition, Galileo's telescopes had an inconveniently narrow field of view—it was difficult for him even to center it on the Moon. Kepler later proposed (though he never built) a much improved telescope design in which a convex lens was used for the eyepiece instead of a concave lens. This had the advantage of producing a wider field of view—though at the cost of inverting the image (henceforth Mars would appear in telescopic views made from the Northern Hemisphere of the Earth with south at the top and north at the bottom).

A telescope built according to Kepler's design was used by a Jesuit astronomer, Christoph Scheiner, as early as 1617. Yet another was employed by Francesco Fontana, a Neapolitan lawyer, who in 1636 produced a sketch of Mars showing a dark pill-shaped spot in the center of its disk (unfortunately, as he recorded a similar spot on nearly featureless Venus, there can be no doubt that it was only an optical defect of his telescope). On Christmas Eve 1644, Father Bartoli, a Jesuit at Naples, recorded two patches on the "lower part" of the Martian disk (he believed that future observers would see them better "if God so willed")—these seem to have been the first genuine surface features ever recorded on the surface of

Mars. Other patches were glimpsed in 1651 and 1653 by two other Jesuits of the Collegio Romano in Rome, Giambattista Riccioli and Francesco Grimaldi. These men had even better views in 1655, when Mars presented under the unusually favorable circumstances of a perihelic opposition.

A word should be said here about the best times for observing Mars. In general, this will be around the time of opposition, since the Earth and Mars then approach each other on the same side of their orbits from the Sun. However, not all oppositions are created equal. Because the orbits of the Earth and Mars are not perfectly circular and Mars's orbit in particular is markedly eccentric, the distance between the two planets at a given opposition will vary depending primarily on where Mars happens to lie in its orbit. Should it happen to lie at the point where it is nearest to the Sun—perihelion—then the separation between the Earth and Mars may be as little as 56 million kilometers (35 million miles); if Mars is at its greatest distance from the Sun—aphelion—the separation may be as much as 101 million kilometers (63 million miles). After an opposition occurs, another follows at an interval of some two years, two months—the interval needed for Mars, in its stern chase, to catch up with the faster-moving Earth. Since this period is slightly longer than a Martian year, successive oppositions are displaced at different points around the Martian orbit, and the most favorable oppositions—the perihelic ones—recur at intervals of fifteen or seventeen years.

At the present historical epoch, perihelic oppositions always occur in late August or early September, since the Earth passes the point in space near Mars's perihelion in late August each year. The perihelion point is located in the direction of the stars of Aquarius. The Earth passes Mars's aphelion, located in the direction of the stars of Leo, in late February.

At a perihelic opposition, the apparent size of the disk of Mars can reach 25".1; at aphelic oppositions, only 13".8.* For obvious reasons, the great Martian years of discovery have usually coincided with the years of its perihelic oppositions.

At the perihelic opposition of 1655—only the third to occur since the invention of the telescope; the others had passed unavailingly in 1625 and 1640—the credit went to Fathers Riccioli and Grimaldi, but only because

*The apparent size of a celestial object is an angular measure of its dimensions against the celestial sphere. The units of angular measure are degrees (s), arc minutes ('), and arc seconds ("): 1s = $\frac{1}{360}$ of a circle; 1' = $\frac{1}{60}$ of a degree, and 1" + $\frac{1}{60}$ of an arc minute. The full Moon measures $\frac{1}{2}$s in apparent diameter, or 30' (1,800"), which is 72 times larger than Mars at its best perihelic opposition.

the greatest observer of that era, Christiaan Huygens of Holland, seems to have been otherwise occupied until well past the date of opposition, by which time Mars had receded far from the Earth. Using a telescope with a 5-centimeter (2-inch) lens and 3.2-meter (10.5-foot) focal length, with which he had discovered Saturn's largest moon (Titan) the previous March, Huygens was able to record nothing more than a "sombre band." The view was so discouraging, in fact, that he did not return to Mars again until 1659. On November 28, at 7 P.M., he turned his telescope toward the planet, which was then near a better-than-average (but not a perihelic) opposition and showed a disk 17.3" across. There were various patches on the disk, and in particular a V-shaped marking showed up well enough for Huygens to make a sketch. This drawing, Percival Lowell later wrote, was "the first drawing of Mars worthy of the name." To anyone with the least knowledge of Mars, the marking shown therein is immediately recognizable—it is the most prominent dark area on the planet, now known as Syrtis Major, though for a long time it bore the more descriptive name of Hourglass Sea. When Huygens again viewed the planet on the evening of December 1, he found that the same marking had returned to very nearly the same place on the disk. He therefore noted in his journal: "The rotation of Mars, like that of the Earth, seems to have a period of 24 hours." A stubborn fact had finally been seized on about the physical condition of Mars.

Huygens's main competitor for the glorious spoils to be won with the telescope was Giovanni Domenico Cassini, a native of Italy who moved to France at the invitation of Louis XIV to become the chief astronomer at the new Paris Observatory. According to Camille Flammarion, he was "by temperament much more Italian than French." Indeed, he seems to have been a thoroughly Baroque figure—colorful, excitable, above all possessed of a remarkable penchant for making discoveries that appealed to the vanity and imagination of the monarch the citizens of Paris called "le Grand." In the courtyard outside the architecturally fine building of the Paris Observatory, the work of Claude Perrault, the same architect who had designed the colonnade of the Louvre, Cassini set up long telescopes of his own, including 5.2-meter- (17-foot-) and 10.4-meter- (34-foot-) long instruments built by the noted Roman instrument-maker Giuseppe Campani. He used them to discover two new Saturnian satellites, and in 1684, with 30.5-meter and 42-meter (100-foot and 136-foot) telescopes mounted atop an old wooden water tower which Cassini

Christiaan Huygens (1629–1695). From an engraving by Edelnick appearing in A. V. Schweiger-Lerchenfeld's *Atlas der Himmelskunde*, 1898.

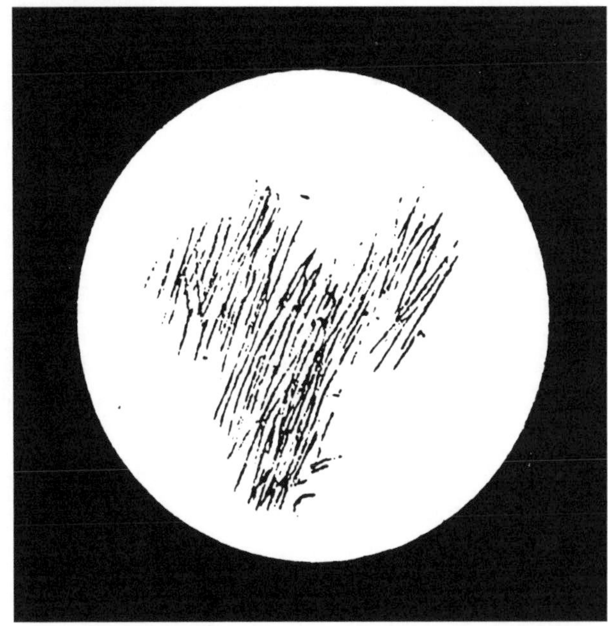

This drawing of Mars by Huygens on November 28, 1659, shows a V-shaped marking. It is the earliest known showing identifiable features. Percival Lowell would later call it "the first drawing of Mars worthy of the name." From Camille Flammarion, "La Planète Mars," vol. 1.

Paris Observatory. (Courtesy David Graham)

had transported to the observatory, he added two more. Cassini called the lot of them, with a flourish of his cap to the Crown, the "Louisian stars."

As early as 1666, Cassini had made out some of the Martian surface patches—this despite the fact that the opposition, which took place on March 19, 1666, was an aphelic one. His drawings are primitive: the spots, represented in some drawings in the form of a dumbbell, are not easy to reconcile with those actually known to exist on the planet. They cannot, however, have been illusory, since Cassini noted their slow drift across the disk. Moreover, he found that after a period of 36 or 37 days they returned to precisely the same positions at the same hour of the night. This led him to refine the rotation period of Mars to 24 hours, 40 minutes.

Huygens, meanwhile, remained active. Despite being a Protestant, he had spent several years in Paris at the invitation of Louis XIV. However, in the 1680s Protestants were increasingly being persecuted in France, and Huygens returned to Holland. There he and his brother Constantyn began to experiment with ever longer and more powerful telescopes. The objective lens was mounted on a ball and socket joint that could be moved up and down a tall pole. The instrument was aimed by pulling on a wire connecting the objective lens and the eyepiece assembly, which the observer held in his hands while resting his arms on a moveable wooden support. These gossamer tubeless instruments were all but immune to buffeting by the wind, but protracted work must have sorely tested the observer's patience. Huygens employed "aerial" telescopes of 37.4, 51.8, and 64 meters (123, 170, and 210 foot) focal length at his country estate of Hofjwick (near The Hague), and observed Mars right up to its aphelic opposition of February 1694—a year before his death.

Though astronomy had by then made tremendous strides, results regarding Mars were disappointing. There were various dark and light patches, whose nature could only be guessed. (Cassini, as early as 1666, had tentatively suggested they might be counterparts to the various features of our own globe, in other words, oceans and lands. The oceans, he wrote, would presumably be dark, since water absorbs sunlight; the continents would appear light.) The length of the Martian day was known—it was a little longer than ours. But that was all. When, in 1686, Bernard le Bovier de Fontenelle of France published a charming book, *Entretiens sur la pluralité des mondes* (Conversations on the plurality of worlds), in which he felt justified in speculating in detail about the possible inhabitants of the Moon, Mercury, and Venus, he devoted only two bland sentences to Mars: "Mars has nothing curious that I know of; its days are not quite an hour longer than ours, and its years the value of two of ours. It's smaller than the Earth, it sees the Sun a little less large and bright than we see it; in sum, Mars isn't worth the trouble of stopping there."[8]

Fontenelle's book inspired a competing work from Huygens, *Kosmotheoros* (Theories of the Cosmos). It did not appear until 1698, three years after Huygens's death. Huygens maintained that all the planets must have their own forms of life, since otherwise "we should sink them below the Earth in Beauty and Dignity; a thing that no Reason will permit." Mars, he noted, because of its greater distance from the Sun, must be cooler than the Earth; its rotation period, established from the movements of its spots, was similar to that of the Earth, and its axis only slightly inclined to the plane of its orbit, so that the inhabitants enjoyed seasons less extreme than ours.

At the end of the seventeenth century, Mars, in even the best telescopes, was nothing more than a small disk, variegated with a few spots of uncertain duration. At the moment it was almost too little for even the sail-broad vans of the imagination to make headway.

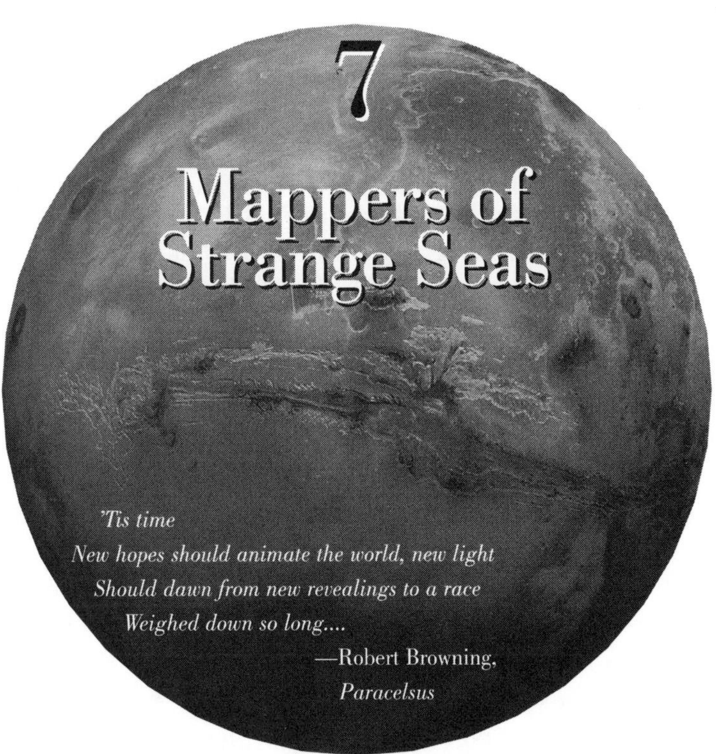

7

Mappers of Strange Seas

'Tis time
New hopes should animate the world, new light
Should dawn from new revealings to a race
Weighed down so long....
—Robert Browning,
Paracelsus

From the pale red dot in the night sky, which was all it had been since earliest times, Mars, with the invention of the telescope, expanded into a tiny disk, the image of a world at first too remote to be clearly visualized. In Galileo's telescope magnifying 20X, it would have appeared, even at the most favorable opposition, only about the size of a pea viewed from a distance of 4 meters (13 feet). In the aerial telescopes of Huygens and Cassini, which bore useful magnifications of about 100X, its image grew to the apparent size of a pea viewed from half a meter (1.6 feet).

As better telescopes gave clearer images of Mars, it was as if the planet were being viewed from ever closer points in space. In effect the telescope became a space-faring machine. Observers like Huygens and Cassini, who squinted to make out detail from the eyepiece-end of their instruments, were in a real sense the first spacefarers to Mars.

Huygens died in 1695. Cassini lived on until 1712; by then, like the aged Galileo, he had become blind. His nephew, Giacomo Filippo Maraldi, carried out the best work on Mars of the next generation, with the 10.3-meter (34-foot) telescope at the Paris Observatory. At the perihelic opposition of 1704, Maraldi made out a dark band on the planet's disk. The band contained a small bump that he used as a "marker point" for timing the planet's rotation period. However, for a few nights—September 4 to 10—the bump was invisible. According to Richard McKim, Mars Section Director of the British Astronomical Association, the reason for its invisibility may have been the presence of a dust storm in this region, which are observed from time to time on the planet. If so, it was by almost two centuries the first observation of a Martian dust storm ever made.[1]

At the perihelic opposition of 1719, Maraldi again made useful observations of the planet, making the first careful study of the white spots at the poles. During the winter, the spot at the south pole grew much larger than its northern counterpart. Moreover, it visibly traced a small circle as Mars rotated, proving that its position must be slightly offset from, or eccentric to, the pole. Thus, Maraldi concluded, the point of most intense cold must be some distance from the pole of the axis of rotation, as is also the case on Earth. (We now know that Maraldi was quite right: according to *Mars Global Surveyor* measurements, the point where the cap's elevation is greatest is different from the pole by some 250 kilometers [155 miles].) Not only did the southern white spot grow to greater size but, Maraldi noted, its shrinkage was much more rapid and complete, and in August and September 1719 the patch—whatever it was—vanished altogether. Evidently it was made up of material that underwent physical changes of some kind, though Maraldi did not hazard a guess as to just what kind of material this might be.

That was left to William Herschel, who was undoubtedly the greatest observational astronomer of the eighteenth century. He was born in Hanover, Germany, in 1738, and trained as a professional musician. As a young man he left Germany and sought his fortune in the England of the Hanoverian Georges, settling in Bath, where he became the organist in the Octagon Chapel and took up astronomy as a hobby. On hiring an aerial telescope and being dissatisfied with its performance, Herschel put his energies into developing a different sort of instrument—the reflector, which had been introduced by Isaac Newton in 1672. Since it uses a mirror instead of a lens to gather light, it effectively avoids the problem of false color. In due course he set up a 2.1-meter (7-foot) reflector (at the time the convention was to refer to telescopes by their lengths rather than their apertures as is now the case) in the south-facing garden in back of his house at Bath, and used it to observe Mars at the opposition of 1777.

Herschel confirmed Maraldi's studies of the polar caps and made the obvious suggestion that they were most probably made up of water-ice. In his own words: "If . . . we find that the globe we inhabit has its polar regions frozen and covered with mountains of ice and snow, that only partly melt when alternately exposed to the Sun, I may well be permitted to surmise that the same causes may probably have the same effect on the globe of Mars; that the bright polar spots are owing to the vivid reflection of light from frozen regions; and that the reduction of those spots is to be ascribed to their being exposed to the Sun." Herschel further established that Mars's axis of rotation was only slightly more tilted than the Earth's, which meant its seasons must be like ours—though naturally, given the fact that its year is more than twice as long, correspondingly longer—and he concluded the inhabitants "probably enjoy a situation in many respects similar to ours."[2] Here is the first unequivocal statement of Mars's likeness to the Earth. With this statement Herschel finally opened, full-wide, the sailbroad vans of the imagination.

In the 1830s, the first map of the planet's markings appeared—the work of two Berlin amateurs, Wilhelm Beer and Johann Mädler, who used a 9.5-centimeter (3.75-inch) refractor fashioned by the noted Bavarian optician Joseph von Fraunhofer. In contrast to the refractors of the seventeenth century, which had used a simple lens, theirs was an achromatic refractor, built around a compound lens—one component of crown glass, the other of flint glass, and so designed to make the chromatic aberration of the one lens cancel out that of the other over a large part of the visual spectrum. The image of Mars in such an instrument was beautifully sharp and well-defined, and Beer and Mädler could routinely use magnifications of 185X on the planet. Effectively, the planet swam in their eyepiece as large and detailed as if it were being viewed from less than the distance from the Earth to the Moon.

Beer and Mädler made out a small round patch, "hanging as if from an undulating ribbon." It lay only 8° south of the equator, and they used it as a reference point in making precise timings of Mars's rotation (in the end, they came up with a figure of 24 hours, 37 minutes, 23.7 seconds, which has been scarcely improved upon to this day). When they came to draw their map, they used this feature as the zero meridian—the Martian Greenwich—a precedent that has been followed by all later astronomers.

At the opposition of 1858, Mars was extensively observed by the Jesuit astronomer, Angelo Secchi, director of the observatory of the Collegio Romano in Rome. He used a 24-centimeter (9.5-inch) refractor, with magnifying powers of 300–400X. In one of his first observations, on May 7, 1858, he described "a large triangular patch, blue in color." This was the well-known Hourglass Sea, but Secchi gave it a different name—the "Atlantic Canale." He commented that "it seemed to play the role of the Atlantic which, on Earth, separates the Old Continent from the New." (Here let us solemnly note the first occurrence of the fateful term "canale," which was later to prove so consequential in the history of Martian studies.) Later Secchi referred to the same feature as the "Blue Scorpion"—an apt description of its appearance at the time. With hindsight we can recognize the first record of the seasonal phenomenon of the Syrtis Major Blue Cloud, of which more later.

Secchi was impressed with the great variety in the tints of the Martian features, and made a brave attempt—given the vexsome nature of the Martian color scheme, which would continue to challenge astronomers for more than a century—at rendering the planet in pastels. He found the dark areas surrounding the polar caps "ashen-colored"; the other dark areas appeared generally bluish, though with an occasional hint of green. He regarded the dark areas as seas and the light areas as continents, and even went so far as to write, "The existence of seas and continents . . . has been conclusively proved."[3]

As better telescopes became available, more and more detail on Mars became visible. It was soon shown, for instance, that the small round patch of Beer and Mädler was actually a pointed tongue—an observational feat achieved by the English amateur Warren De La Rue using a 33-centimeter (13-inch) reflector in 1856. Beyond that, it was a forked tongue, as was recognized by another English observer, the Rev. William Rutter Dawes, with a 20-centimeter (8-inch) refractor in 1864–65.[4] Dawes was an exceptionally keen-sighted individual (at least at the eyepiece of the telescope; however, he suffered from myopia so severe that without his eyeglasses he was quite incapable of recognizing his wife if he passed her on the street! Of course, the telescopic image can always be focused so as to suit the observer—which is why it is always advisable for wearers of glasses to remove them before attempting to look through a telescope). The remarkable quality of Dawes's drawings of Mars inspired a prolific astronomy writer, Richard Anthony Proctor, to use them as the basis of a map, which first appeared in 1867. It is noteworthy in containing the first attempt to name the various Martian features (on their map, Beer and Mädler had merely designated the features with arabic letters). Proctor's scheme was straightforward in principle; he gave the names of various observers of Mars to the different features, which—following Secchi's confident assertion—were regarded as seas and continents. Thus, the spot chosen by Beer and Mädler for the zero of longitudes on Mars became, following Dawes's resolution of it into a pronged feature, "Dawes's forked bay." Other features included De La Rue Ocean, Maraldi Sea, Dawes Ocean, Cassini Land. Unfortunately, Proctor was too chauvinistic in naming a disproportionate number of features after his own countrymen (Dawes alone was associated with no less than six different features), which made it all but inevitable that the whole scheme would eventually be overthrown, as indeed it was only a few years later.

Thus far the history of Martian exploration has been closely intertwined with the optical improvement of the telescope. Reflectors in the eighteenth century were joined, by the early nineteenth, by achromatic refractors such as those made by Fraunhofer and his successors. These instruments largely overcame the problem of color blurring which had put such severe limits on the efforts of earlier observers.

However, there was one barrier that astronomers were unable to surmount, even in principle. They were unable to escape the limits to their seeing imposed by the wave nature of light.

Since light is a wave—a fundamental fact of nature that Christiaan Huygens himself had done much to elucidate in the seventeenth century—whenever light from a point source, say, from a star, passes through an aperture, the image produced is not a point but a small disk surrounded by a series of dark and light bands (known as interference rings). It is this image that one actually examines with the eyepiece. In similar fashion, a planet's surface can be thought of as consisting of innumerable light and dark points, so that the image formed in the telescope is effectively a mosaic of tiny diffraction-patterns. The overlapping diffraction patterns produce an overall blurring of the surface detail. Blowing up the image beyond a certain point will, therefore, only magnify confusion. (Though the analogy is not quite exact, it is a little like the case of a picture produced by newsprint—magnifying it beyond a certain point only reveals the individual dots and does not reveal more detail.)

The limits to the resolving power of a telescope set by diffraction are invincible. In fact, the only real remedy is to increase the aperture, since the larger the aperture, the smaller the diffraction disk and the more compact the surrounding rings. With his 20-centimeter (8-inch) refractor, Dawes, at the opposition of 1864–65, generally employed a magnifying power of 258X. This was not a particularly good opposition—the greatest apparent diameter attained by the planet was only 17".3. With 258X, Dawes saw the planet a little sharper than the Moon appears as seen with the naked-eye. At such a distance, it was beginning to show tantalizing detail—it is clear that Dawes's telescope, eye and brain were close to realizing the limits of diffraction. One could only imagine what the view would be with a still larger instrument.

Larger instruments were soon being built—though their builders rarely took into account the steadiness of the atmospheres above their telescopes, and so placed them in such chronically unfavorable locales as Newcastle upon Tyne, in north England (where the 63.5-centimeter (25-inch) Newall refractor was set up in 1869), or "foggy bottom," the malarial flats along the Potomac River in Washington, D.C. (where the 66-centimeter [26-inch] Clark refractor of the U.S. Naval Observatory was set up in 1875). The users of such instruments were often foiled by blurring due to unsteady air. Since a larger telescope takes in larger and stronger areas of atmospheric turbulence, in general a small instrument operating in good atmospheric conditions will surpass a large one operating in bad conditions. Indeed, it is rare that the atmosphere of the Earth allows an aperture of much more than 40 centimeters (16 inches) to be used to advantage visually on Mars.

Now, indeed, we enter upon a new era. By the mid-nineteenth century telescopes had reached the point in their development where atmosphere—the medium of air above the telescope—began to assume the role of the most critical limiting factor to what was revealed on the surface of Mars. Trans-atlantic mariners such as Columbus had learned to take advantage of favorable winds. Avoiding the rough and monstrous heaving North Atlantic, they steered their caravels across the glassy seas of the northeasterly trades. Henceforth the mariners of interplanetary space—at least the most savvy of them—would likewise set out in search of calmer seas of air. Avoiding the turbulent mid-latitude jet stream of the "roaring forties," they would increasingly turn to places—far mountain and lonely desert—where the atmosphere formed more stable layers above the telescope, places where the quavering jelly-like image of Mars might grow as sharp as a steel-engraving and reveal a host of magical details.

8

"A Less Difficult and Bloody Conquest"

Through a round opening I saw some of the beautiful things which heaven bears, and thence we came forth, to see again the stars.

—Dante, *Inferno*

Christopher Columbus's voyage of discovery in 1492 was arguably the most important and epoch-making voyage in human history. The most important and epoch-making voyage in the exploration of Mars has not yet been made—it will take place sometime in the twenty-first century, possibly when the first spacecraft brings back soil from Mars containing living microorganisms or rocks containing

Giovanni Virginio Schiaparelli (1835–1910). (Courtesy *Sky & Telescope* archives)

indisputable evidence of fossil life; or perhaps later, when the first humans arrive on the planet. But arguably the most important and epoch-making voyage of discovery ever made in the telescopic era was embarked upon by the Italian astronomer Giovanni Virginio Schiaparelli, at the grand perihelic opposition of September 1877. Schiaparelli certainly made the most ambitious exploration of Mars up to that time. It was he who put Mars on the map—both literally and figuratively.

Indeed, the analogy between these two illustrious Italian navigators of formidable seas—the one sailing his caravels across the Atlantic, the other projecting his eye and mind across interplanetary space—was not missed even during Schiaparelli's lifetime. In dedicating *Mars and Its Canals*, his magnum opus on the red planet, to Schiaparelli, Percival Lowell wrote, "To Schiaparelli, the republic of science owes a new and vast domain. His genius first detected those strange new markings on the Martian disk which have proved a portal to all that has since been seen. . . . He made there voyage after voyage, much as Columbus did on Earth, with even less of recognition from home."[1] And yet in contrast to Columbus, who had dedicated years in his single-minded quest to find a passage west to the Indies, Schiaparelli's interest in Mars was slow in developing. Before he burst upon the Martian scene in 1877, he had made but a single sketch of the planet (in 1862). His career had given no indication that he was about to emerge as the greatest Mars observer up to his time and one of the greatest of all time.

Schiaparelli was born in Savigliano, in the Piedmont region of northern Italy, in 1835. He was educated in the local schools there and at the University of Turin, from which he graduated with a degree in architecture and hydraulic engineering.* But his real passion was always for astronomy. After a brief stint as a school teacher in Turin, he was awarded a stipend from the Piedmontese government to receive training at two of the greatest European observatories of the day, at Berlin and Pulkova (in Russia). He returned to Italy on receiving an appointment as *secondo astronomo* to Francesco Carlini at the old observatory of Brera in Milan.

The observatory had been founded by the versatile Slovenian Jesuit astronomer Roger Boscovich in 1760, as part of the Jesuit college established in the Spanish Palazzo of Brera.† When Schiaparelli first came here, Milan was a first-rate site for astronomical studies—the skies of Lombardy were famously blue, the clouds of industrial smoke and smog had not yet begun to gather, as now, in an oppressive cope over the city. Unfortunately, the observatory had no telescope larger than 10 centimeters (4 inches) of aperture. (It is necessary to point out that Italy was still very much a backward country in the mid-nineteenth century; its economy was tied to agriculture, and four out of every five citizens were illiterate.) In taking a job at such an ill-equipped institution, many men would have seen their careers languish. But Schiaparelli saw opportunity instead of despair. His country was experiencing heady days; his native Piedmont had led the struggle for Italian independence (a brother, Eugenio, had died from wounds suffered in the battles of San Martino and Solferino fought in June 1859 against Austria). Garibaldi and the *Risorgimento* had triumphed, and on March 14, 1861, the king of Piedmont and Sardinia, Vittorio Emanuele II, would assume the throne of the united Kingdom of Italy. Almost at that very moment, de Gasparis, at Naples, had discovered the first asteroid from Italian soil—in a patriotic gesture he had named it *Ausonia*, a poetic name for Italy. Only six weeks later, Schiaparelli, with the 10-centimeter (4-inch) telescope, discovered another asteroid,

---

*Schiaparelli knew in intimate detail how canals and their systems of locks worked.

†Author Sheehan visited Brera in 1975, a year before *Viking 1* landed on Mars. Entering the Palazzo from the *Via Brera*, he passed through a colonnaded square arrayed with copies of classical sculptures—nymphs and heroes, gods and goddesses. By means of a stairway just beyond a niche occupied by a marble Patroclus dying in the arms of Menelaus, he progressed, Dante-like, "to the stars." Brera today is an art academy, and the old observatory is only a library and archive, but the 22-centimeter (8.6-inch) Merz refractor has been recently refurbished and is once more being used. It remains in its old dome on the roof of the Brera Palace, near the center of the great city of Milan, where it has stood for well over a century.

Esperia—Hope (but the name also recalled that with which the ancient Greeks had referred to Italy, *Hesper*—West).

A year later Carlini died, and Schiaparelli, at the age of only twenty-seven, became director of the observatory. He immediately drew up an ambitious plan for its reform, which called for—above all else—a large telescope. The Ministers of education and finance, Giovanni Lanza and Quintino Sella (the latter, like Schiaparelli, educated as an engineer at the University of Turin) approved his application for a 22-centimeter (8.6-inch) refractor, to be built by Fraunhofer's successor, Merz of Monaco. But the instrument would be long in coming. Vittorio Emanuele II had other priorities. Spending money lavishly to pay off mistresses and to maintain his palaces and villas, most of which he never visited, he had no interest whatever in the sciences or the arts—Lord Clarendon, the British foreign secretary, regarded him as "an imbecile." While waiting for his telescope, Schiaparelli, ever resourceful, set to work with pencil-and-paper, and by 1866 had succeeded in forging a link between comets and meteors—an immortal work in which he showed that the Perseid meteors of August follow the same orbit as the bright Swift-Tuttle Comet, which had appeared in 1862. His result has stood the test of time; for this achievement he was awarded the prestigious Lalande prize of the French Academy of Sciences in 1868.

By then, Vittorio Emanuele II was secretly pledging to involve Italy in the Franco-Prussian War (on the French side). The Italian army was hardly strong enough to defend the Italian frontier, much less to enter into a suicidal fight with mighty Prussia. Fortunately, Vittorio Emanuele's ministers recognized this, and succeeded—though by the narrowest of margins—in keeping Italy out of the war. These ministers deserve at least a grateful footnote in the story of Mars. If they had not succeeded in opposing Vittorio Emanuele's plans, Italy would certainly have been crushed with France in the war with Prussia. There would been no money for telescopes, and Schiaparelli's pathbreaking studies of Mars would never have taken place. The world would never have adopted those romantic names that he later introduced on his map of the planet, and to this day we might still be using names such as Fontana Land and Beer Sea.

At last, in 1874, Schiaparelli's telescope was installed on the roof of the Brera Observatory, and he began to use it in making routine measurements of double stars. He was still faithfully engaged in this work in the summer of 1877—without plans, apparently, to make any special study of Mars.

That September, Mars was due to come to one of its perihelic oppositions, when it approaches within only 56 million kilometers (35 million miles) of the Earth. Already in August, the American astronomer Asaph Hall had announced the discovery of the two tiny satellites of Mars, Phobos and Deimos, with the 66-centimeter (26-inch) refractor at the U.S. Naval Observatory in Washington, D.C., then the most powerful telescope in the world. And there were other important studies underway. Nathaniel Green, an amateur astronomer and professional portrait artist who at one time had given lessons in painting to Queen Victoria, observed Mars with a 33-centimeter (13-inch) Newtonian reflector from the island of Madeira, in the Atlantic off the coast of Morocco.[2] He drew up a map, and noted brightenings at the limb and terminator of Mars—evidently the first observations of the morning and evening limb-clouds (the same cirrus ice-crystal horsetails that would later feature prominently in images from the *Mars Pathfinder*).

In August, at the very moment Hall was tracking his satellites, Schiaparelli was busy with the routine work of measuring double stars with the 22-centimeter (8.6-inch) Merz refractor. In his observing log, his references to Mars that month are almost casual. On August 13, after completing his double star measures for the night, he made the following entry at 3:30 A.M.: "Very handsome Zodiacal light rising in lenticular form directly toward the Pleiades. I see the Gegenschein (a faint glow opposite the Sun) 15 to 18 degrees west of Mars."[3] There is no further mention of the planet until August 23, when there was an eclipse of the Moon.

One can well imagine the magic of that night: the Moon, in eclipse, turning blood-red, with Mars nearby glowing like an ember in the sky. A dark, olive-skinned figure, with sharp penetrating black eyes, rolls open the shutter of his turret-like dome. He is a man of classic moderation, careful to abstain from coffee, tobacco, and spirits. He is neither nervous nor apathetic. Seeking a temporary diversion from the eclipse, he swings his telescope toward Mars. What floats into the field of view is wonderfully *enchanté*: a beautiful Fabergé egg of a planet, a salmon disk streaked here and there with patches of rust- or cinnamon-brown. His first vision is confused. "I must admit," he wrote afterward, "on comparing the aspect of the planet before me in the telescope with the recently published maps, this first attempt did not seem very encouraging."[4] But his interest had been stirred. He makes a first sketch, and resolves to turn to Mars again. So he

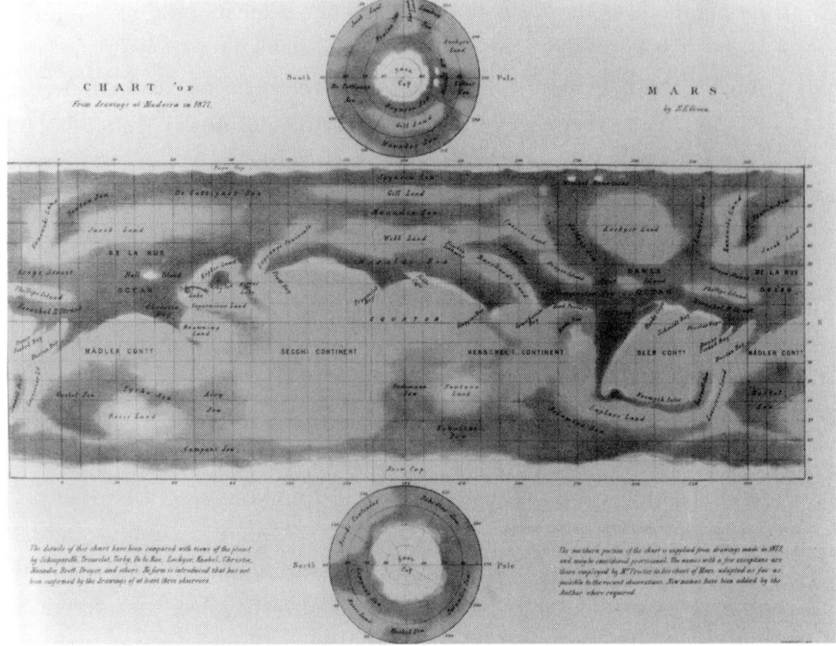

Nathaniel Green's map of Mars, 1877. (William Sheehan collection)

does, on August 28. His sketch that night shows the markings beginning to gather into recognizable shapes. In his observing book, page by page and night by night, he records his progress in learning to see.

By September 12, 1877, a week past Mars's opposition, Schiaparelli had decided upon nothing less than an all-out observing campaign that would lead to a new map of the planet. Unlike his predecessors, he started with a series of measures made with a micrometer of the longitudes and latitudes of a number of points on the Martian surface—sixty-two fixed points on the surface, representing those that were most distinct and easily recognizable. These points formed a network of precision, a reference frame within which he could capture the rest of the details by sketching them in directly at the eyepiece.

What Schiaparelli set out to produce was an *areography*, a geography of Mars. This was to be distinguished, following the method of classical geographers such as Ptolemy, from a *chorography* of the planet, which was being produced at the same opposition by Nathaniel Green. Ptolemy had written:

> Geography is a representation in picture of the whole known world. It differs from Chorography in that Chorography . . . treats more fully the particulars of . . . the smallest conceivable localities, such as harbors, farms, villages, river courses, and such like. Geography looks at the position rather than the quality, noting the relation of distances everywhere, and emulating the art of painting only in some of its major descriptions. Chorography needs an artist, and no one presents it right unless he is an artist. Geography does not call for the same requirements, as any one, by means of lines and plain notations can fix positions and draw general outlines. Chorography does not have need of mathematics, which is an important part of Geography.[5]

In his map, Schiaparelli did make some effort to render the relative intensities of the hues in the areas known as seas; in the continental areas, he admitted, "the gradations are too delicate." But recording the relative intensities was secondary to his main purpose, which was to fix as exactly as possible the *places* of the main features on the map of Mars.

The apparent diameter of the Martian disk loomed largest in August and September (reaching a maximum of 25"). However, this period served Schiaparelli only for a broad reconnaissance. The "most delicate explorations" were not carried out until October, when he enjoyed some nights of superb seeing. Thus on October 2, 1877, on a disk of only 16"—which with his usual magnifying power of 322X enlarged Mars into an orb almost three times as large as the Moon as seen with the naked-eye—he enjoyed "moments of more perfect telescopic vision than before or since," during which he made out the tiny "inland lake" he named Juventae Fons—the Fountain of Youth.

Moments such as these allowed him to use to advantage the full resolving power of the Merz refractor. The sheer richness of the details forced him to abandon the hitherto standard maps of the planet—not only Proctor's rough chart, but another, only marginally better, just published by the French astronomer Camille Flammarion. He found, for instance, that the bright landmasses Proctor had depicted as the four main continents of Mars were broken into a multitude of islands; several of Proctor's seas had disappeared or else had shrunk into insignificance (Main Sea, Dawes Sea), while still other seas had apparently opened up. "In order to avoid misunderstandings and mistakes," he explained, "I had to create a special

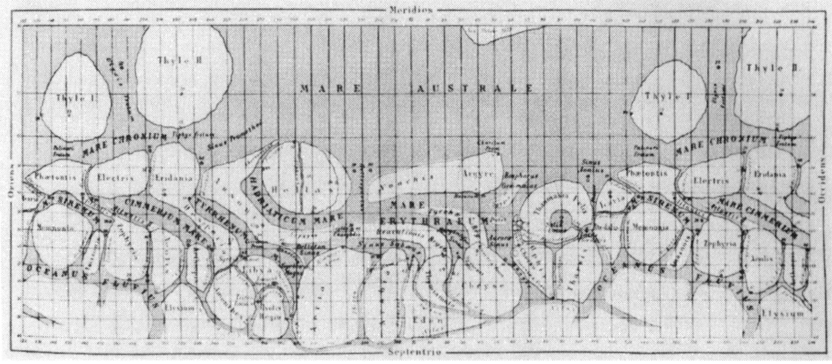

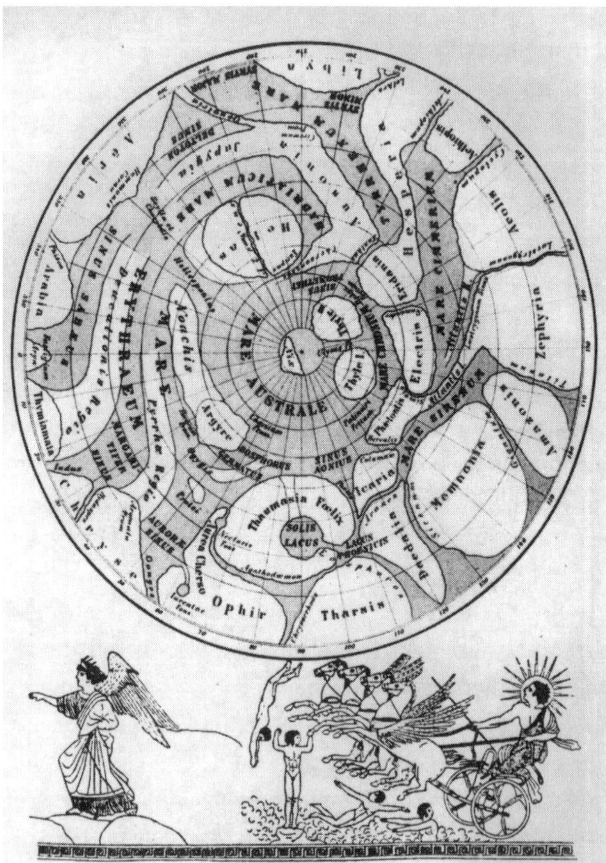

Top: Schiaparelli's map of Mars. *Bottom:* Schiaparelli's map of south polar region of Mars supplied with a portion of an ancient vase painting (illustrating Schiaparelli's intimate knowledge of and love for the classics). (William Sheehan collection)

nomenclature, which served my particular purpose. This nomenclature, devised while I was laboring at the telescope, is probably not without many shortcomings, but I have retained it in my memoir only because it has the advantage of describing perfectly everything I have seen."[7] As a scholar steeped in the classics—a man who unbent his mind by writing verses in Latin hexameters—Schiaparelli derived most of his names from Homer, Herodotus, and the Bible.

Later he provided an account of the invention of his scheme of Martian nomenclature in a letter to an old friend, Otto Struve, of the Pulkova Observatory: "At first I counted on using the names of Proctor; but his map (and also, to some extent, the more recent one by Flammarion) is so poor, that I wasted much time simply trying to orient myself. Finally, as I found it more and more necessary to record my observations quickly, and wished to avoid any chance of ambiguity, I began to populate my sketches with names from the Odyssey; then I added others from the Argonauts, and so on, until I had produced a hodge-podge of mythical and poetic geography. This explains the curious and disordered arrangement you will find there."[8]

By early November 1877, Schiaparelli had completed his first series of observations and had drawn up a map of the southern hemisphere of Mars—the map destined to serve as the template molding all future perceptions of the planet. He followed with a descriptive *Memoria Prima* (First Memoir), which appeared in 1878.* Schiaparelli introduced his study with a determination of the position of the axis of rotation, the first prerequisite to the mathematical methods of areography; he presented a table listing the coordinates of his sixty-two fundamental points, including the zero of areographic longitude. (He called it *Fastigium Aryn*, the Vertex or Dome of Aryn—a place, according to Arab cosmographers, situated at the exact midpoint between the eastern and western limits of the Earth. The position was the same Mädler had earlier chosen for the origin of longitudes on Mars.)

On the whole, Schiaparelli regarded the bright areas of Mars as continents, the dark areas as seas. Other regions, which were half-tones compared to the main features, he suspected of being shallow seas or marshes.

---

*For some strange reason, it was not translated into English for over a century. In 1994 author Sheehan decided to remedy the deficiency. His translation was published by the Association of Lunar and Planetary Observers: G. V. Schiaparelli, *Astronomical and Physical Observations of the Axis of Rotation and the Topography of the Planet Mars: First Memoir, 1877–1878* (San Francisco: A.L.P.O. Monograph Number 5).

"In general," he wrote, "the configurations seen posed such a clear analogy to those of the terrestrial map that it is doubtful whether any other class of names would have been preferable. Do not brevity and clarity also induce us to use such words as *island, isthmus, strait, channel, peninsula, cape*, etc.? . . . In order to avoid prejudice regarding the nature of the features on the planet, these names may be regarded, if one wishes, as a mere artifice."[9]

The ancient Greek founder of physical geography, Dicaearchus, had drawn a line through the middle of his map of the Mediterranean world running from the pillars of Hercules in the west to the Taurus mountains in the east. This line Dicaearchus had called the "Great Diaphragm." Schiaparelli drew a similar line on Mars running between the belt of dark markings to the south and the lighter regions to the north. The main dark areas were given the names of bodies of water of the ancient Mediterranean world. The Sea of Sirens and the Sea of the Cimmerians were magically inspired by Homer's *Odyssey*; the land of Ausonia (Italy) was separated from Libya by the Tyrrhenian Sea. Other places included Hellas (Greece), Chryse, Tharsis, and Elysium—names that have since grown rich in Martian lore. Indeed, though his names were at first resisted, especially by Nathaniel Green and other English observers who remained partial to Proctor's scheme, by the 1890s they had been adopted by all the main observers of the planet, and they remain the basis of the system still in use today.

In addition to his map of the planet's surface, Schiaparelli also provided full descriptions of the Martian polar regions, which he compared with those of the Earth revealed during the most recent polar explorations:

> On the Earth, the snowy masses are proportionately a good deal larger than those of Mars. Though with us the arctic snows can, and indeed do, retreat as far as the 84° parallel in the summer . . . in other directions they remain unaffected throughout the summer as far as the 62° parallel, as is the case in the southernmost parts of Greenland. In the winter, a vast area of the Earth is covered with snow, to below the 45° parallel. On Mars, the area of the winter snows would be judged small in comparison with the Earth . . . but it is certain that in summer the polar snow dwindles to a very small area indeed. . . . The southern snows during the 1877 epoch were eccentric with respect to the planet's pole, and were more extensive in one part than the opposite. In November they contracted so far as to

> leave exposed the pole of the planet, something which probably never happens on the Earth.[10]

Schiaparelli's 1877 map of Mars, bearing names so rich with nostalgia and so apt to appeal to human emotions, was the first to include the strange linear features that he referred to as *canali*. In Italian, the term can mean either natural channels or artificial canals. As earlier noted, it had already been applied by the Italian astronomer Angelo Secchi to a feature on the surface of Mars (Schiaparelli's Syrtis Major) as long ago as 1858. But between the time Secchi introduced the term and Schiaparelli reintroduced it to Martian nomenclature, canals and canal-building had risen to the forefront of human consciousness. After all, it was an era in which great canals were being built—the greatest of all thus far being the Suez, completed in 1869, which turned into a reality the long-dreamed of connection between the Mediterranean and the Indian Ocean and rendered unnecessary the round-the-southern-cape of Africa route of Vasco da Gama. Its success made its designer, the French engineer de Lesseps, dream of an even greater engineering feat—the construction of a canal across Panama, which would link the Atlantic to the Pacific. At a time when canals were viewed as among the hallmarks of an advanced civilization, it was all but inevitable that Schiaparelli's term "canale" would be translated as "canal," a term that carried with it connotations of artificiality unintended by its progenitor.

The story of the canals of Mars is a fascinating one, and bears out science-fiction writer Ray Bradbury's observation: "It's part of the nature of man to start with romance and build to reality."[11] No discussion of Mars could possibly be complete without mentioning the canals. Certainly they will forever have a special place in Martian lore, and they have contributed enormously to the complex motivations leading to the exploration of the planet.

Schiaparelli's first glimpses of the *canali*—or canals, as we shall henceforth call them, without apology and without quotation marks—were obtained during the fine nights of October 1877, while he was busy making his observations for his map of the planet. In the moments of atmospheric calm which he sometimes enjoyed that month, "it seemed as if a veil were removed from the surface of the planet, which appeared like a complex embroidery of many colors. But such was the minuteness of these details, and so short the duration of their visibility, that it was not possible to form a stable and sure impression of the thin lines and minute spots therein revealed."[12]

It was obvious from the start that Schiaparelli himself believed these thin lines and minute spots were natural features. Indeed, he often used the word *fiume* (river) as a synonym for *canale*. Schiaparelli first announced their discovery in a letter to Otto Struve, November 23, 1877: "What I find most remarkable is the complicated system of dark lines (or *canals*), running into the various seas which girdle the whole planet. There is a great deal of difficulty in the measures, but I can't believe they would be so distinct unless they were at least 50 or 60 kilometers (31 or 38 miles) in width. Beyond that, it is clear that, to our eyes at least, the map is similar to that of the Earth, with continents and islands. And yet one cannot speak properly of continents, since all of them are subdivided into a great number of islands."[13]

Schiaparelli observed Mars extensively at the next opposition, in November 1879. The seeing at times surpassed even the best moments of 1877—"the image in the field of the eyepiece looked like a painting, absolutely steady and of indescribable beauty," he wrote to Struve.[14] Schiaparelli obtained micrometric measures of 114 points on the surface, including, on November 10, 1879, a small whitish patch (only half a second of arc across) in the Tharsis region. He named it Nix Olympica—the Snows of Olympus—and noted that it was frequently the site of whitish veils. He also announced that some of the dark areas had changed since 1877. Most notably, Syrtis Major had apparently invaded some of the neighboring bright area of Libya. Schiaparelli assumed that the shallow sea in this region had overflowed into the adjoining lands. As for the canals, they were represented as finer and more regular than they had been on the 1877 map, and one of them even showed up double—the Nilus, located between the dark patches Lunae Lacus and Ceraunius. "To see it as two tracks regular, uniform in appearance, and exactly parallel, came as a great shock," Schiaparelli wrote. This was the first instance of a *gemination*, a bizarre process that seemed to affect at least some of the canals.

Schiaparelli's map of 1879 was more naturalistic than the diagram-like effort of 1877. He tried to represent as lines, he wrote, "those forms which actually do have such an appearance in the telescope, and with gentle gradations of tone those which consist of diffuse shades." Compared to the broad winding appearance he had given them in 1877, his canals now appeared uncannily regular, as straight or curving sharp lines. At succeeding oppositions—in 1881, 1884, 1886, 1888, and 1890—Schiaparelli launched expedition after expedition, unfurling his telescopic sails upon the sometimes treacherous seas of interplanetary space. Like Henry the Navigator who from his rugged promontory at Sagres had sent caravel after caravel ever farther around the horn of Africa, Schiaparelli, from his tower in Milan, had commenced the "first organized enterprise" into the unknown world of Mars.

His maps of the planet show the canals ever more rectilinear, ever more suggestive of a system; they travel without bends or irregularities—an aspect which, he insisted, "has not been exaggerated in my drawings."

Beginning with the winter opposition of 1881–82, Schiaparelli observed more and more instances where canals, formerly single, began to appear in the form of parallel tracks on the surface—his so-called geminations. None of the canals had been so affected in late 1881; however, double canals began to show up, and with appalling frequency, in January and February 1882. Thus Schiaparelli wrote, "I passed from surprise to surprise. On January 21, I discovered the doubling of the [canal] Orontes, the Euphrates, the Phison, and the Ganges. . . . On the 29th I ascertained that of the Gehon. On February 3 the Thoth and the Phta were doubled."

At first Schiaparelli himself was baffled, and strongly suspected optical causes such as eye fatigue or double vision (strabismus). However, after carrying out careful experiments, he concluded that the geminations were quite real—they reflected some process actually occurring on the surface of Mars. Admittedly, he had no idea just what this might be. He did suggest, however, that the geminations were apparently seasonal.

For a while, Schiaparelli had his visions of the canals all to himself, and among the leading observers of Mars, none saw the planet as he did. (In part, this may have been a result of the peculiarities of Schiaparelli's vision; see "A Color-Blind Astronomer" sidebar). British observers—and especially the astronomer-artist Nathaniel Green, his rival mapper at the 1877 opposition—were openly critical. However, Schiaparelli remained confident and above the fray. "The most curious part of the affair," he confided to his favorite correspondent on Martian matters, the Belgian astronomer François J. C. Terby, "is that some of the objects of which Mr. Green *denies* the existence have been seen splendidly with low powers and without going to Madeira. I think that in the present case, before he speaks of *illusions*, he ought to wait until he has a chance to study my results."[15]

A Color-Blind Astronomer

Color-blindness is a remarkably common phenomenon. It is estimated that 10 percent of males have vision that is markedly color-deficient. The significance of this is that, since the color-blind individual's wavelength-discrimination is not as good as a normal person's, he will see as identical many colors which others see as different.

There are various forms of color-blindness (more precisely, color-defectiveness). The most common involve a confusion of reds and greens. Those so afflicted cannot discriminate reds, oranges, yellows, and many greens on the basis of color—if they distinguish them at all, it is only on the basis of differences in brightness.

Perhaps the most famous example of color blindness in the astronomical literature is that of the Viennese astronomer C. L. von Littrow. In 1835, Littrow claimed, from an inspection of the notebooks of the Jesuit astronomer Maximilian Hell, that the latter had altered data pertaining to his observations of the 1769 transit of Venus (a rare event in which the planet appears as a black spot in passage across the disk of the Sun). In part, Littrow's accusation was based on his finding that in many places in the manuscript, data had been erased, with the changes apparently entered in ink of a slightly different color. A half century later the Canadian-born astronomer Simon Newcomb, during a visit to the Vienna Observatory, reexamined Hell's notebooks and found that the erasures and corrections had been made at the time of writing, not afterward, and that the the "ink of a different color" was merely ink over an erasure. It turned out that Littrow suffered from color blindness—he was unable to distinguish the orange tint of Aldebaran from that of the whitest star. Newcomb concluded: "For half a century the astronomical world had based an impression on the innocent but mistaken evidence of a color-blind man respecting the tints of ink in a manuscript."

In the same way, during the 1870s and 1880s, the astronomical world based its impression on the appearance of Mars largely on the evidence of a color-blind man respecting the tints of the planet's surface features.

Schiaparelli, too, suffered from red-green color blindness (technically, he was a deuteronope), making it difficult for him to distinguish gradations of these hues (he once declared that for him "the general appearance of the planet . . . was almost that of a chiaroscuro made with Chinese ink upon a general bright background"). In some ways this was an unfortunate handicap for a Mars observer, inasmuch as Mars is a planet of subtle colors. Through a large telescope—in which the disk expands to fill the eye—subtle color contrasts are enhanced for the normal observer, "with wavelength perception being shifted nonlinearly away from the center of the visible spectrum: dim orange-yellow turns darker orange (i.e., brown), and faint yellow becomes olive green." The salmon-colored Martian desert begins to appear nuanced with patches of yellow, russet-brown, rust, vermillion; the seas appear blue- or green-tinted. Unfortunately, the color-blind observer remains oblivious to all this rich palette of colors (some illusory!—see Appendix B: The Colors of Mars)—he can only distinguish color differences by variations in brightness.

In other respects, however, Schiaparelli's color-blindness gave him a decided advantage, for color-blind observers can be much more sensitive to contrasts than "normals." E. M. Antoniadi, one of the greatest critics of the canals in later years, acknowledged "the unrivaled acuteness" of the Italian observer, which allowed him to discover, "under a symbolic, geometrical form . . . the minor irregular shadings variegating the Martian surface."*

It is only too certain that Schiaparelli's color-blindness must account in large part for the idiosyncratic nature of his representations of Mars—the hardness of his outlines, his tendency to build up his map in terms of lines (the boundaries of intensity differences). These characteristics of his maps were strikingly evident to the first

*That color-blind individuals possess superior vision, at least for certain types of observations, is attested by at least one other case known to me. According to Donald Osterbrock, Lick Observatory astronomer Nick Mayall was color blind, "and he believed that it made his eyes more sensitive to faint light, so he could find and observe fainter stars, nebulae and galaxies than other astronomers with normal eyesight. Certainly when I visited him at the Crossley reflector [at Lick] one night around 1955, he was taking a spectrum of an object that was too faint for me to see, though he evidently could see it well and the spectrum (a multi-hour exposure) was a good one when he developed it the next day." Several other astronomers have told me that color blind observers can see fainter objects at night than those with normal eyes.—W.S.

observers confronted by them. Thus, Charles E. Burton in 1879 remarked regarding the canals, "It is possible that some of these lines may be the boundaries of faint tones of shade," while Nathaniel Green—a gifted artist as well as observer—accused Schiaparelli of turning "soft and indefinite pieces of shading into clear, sharp lines." That the explanation for the difference between Schiaparelli's map and Green's might be founded in differences in their eyesight was hinted at by a noted British observer, the Rev. T. W. Webb, who wrote, "Green, an accomplished master of form and color, has given a portrait . . . the Italian professor, on the other hand, inconvenienced by colour-blindness, but of micrometric vision . . . has plotted a sharply-outlined chart."

Beauty is in the eye of the beholder; so, evidently, are planetary surface features. Schiaparelli's niece Elsa Schiaparelli went on to become a famous fashion-designer, while her color-blind uncle introduced a new fashion into the study of Mars.

Imitation is the highest form of flattery. The astronomer at the eyepiece of the telescope is not immune, but as Percival Lowell once observed, "Fashion is as potent here as elsewhere." A generation of more or less suggestible observers—with normal color vision, but brought up on Schiaparelli's drawings and charts—went on to see Mars in terms of the same hard sharp outlines and canals that he saw, thus creating the "Martian canal furor" of the 1890s.

In Italy, at least, Schiaparelli was a hero, and carried all before him. Vittorio Emmanuele II had died in January 1878, shortly before the publication of Schiaparelli's first Mars memoir. That April, Schiaparelli gave a lecture on Mars before the Academy of the Lynxes in Rome (an elite body to which Galileo Galilei had once belonged), attended by ministers of the Kingdom of Italy, where he made such a strong impression that an encore performance was scheduled at the Quirinal Palace before Vittorio Emmanuele's successor, King Humberto I, and Queen Margherita. The gist of his talk was that everything he had accomplished had been done with only a modest telescope; what might he do with a really powerful instrument, like the 63.5-centimeter (25-inch) Newall refractor at Newcastle upon Tyne or the 66-centimeter (26-inch) refractor at the U.S. Naval Observatory in Washington? Italy was alive with patriotic sentiment, and the new king and his intelligent and cultured queen proved to be warmly enthusiastic. They emphatically recommended to the ministers the acquisition of a larger telescope. The result was a 48-centimeter (19-inch) Merz-Repsold refractor was installed at the observatory—renamed the Royal Observatory of Brera—in 1886.

The first confirmation of the canals by professional astronomers did not take place until that same year, 1886, when Henri Perrotin and his assistant Louis Thollon of the Nice Observatory (on the French Riviera) succeeded in making out a few of the canals. Schiaparelli was far in the forefront of Martian research—and he knew it. He wrote to Terby that he had begun the exploration of "a New World, this world of Mars . . . which we must conquer little by little. It will be a less difficult and bloody conquest than the exploits of Cortés and Pizarro."[16]

From perhaps ten observers seriously occupied with the planet in 1886, there were scores of observers of the planet at the next opposition in 1888—including several at the Lick Observatory (Mt. Hamilton, California), who were using the recently unveiled 91-centimeter (36-inch) refractor, easily the most powerful telescope in the world. Though the Lick observers did not begin their studies until well past opposition, they did succeed in glimpsing a few of the canals. Other highlights of the 1888 opposition included Terby's discovery of bright projections at the terminator of the planet. Were they Martian signal lights, or only high-altitude clouds glinting in the sunlight? Terby had more difficulty confirming the gemination of one of the canals about which Schiaparelli had put him on the *qui vive*. (S: "I am alerting you—assuming this is even necessary—that we have a gemination so beautiful that I believe you will finally see it without difficulty. The long track of the Euphrates is presented exactly as it is shown here." T: "I must thank you for your letter . . . alerting me to the gemination of the Euphrates. . . . As you requested, I made every effort to succeed in this observation; yesterday, June 2, I had some particularly favorable conditions—favorable enough to allow, I should have thought, some decisive finding. . . . But I didn't see the Euphrates, despite the most sustained attention."[17]) However, Schiaparelli urged him not to lose heart:

> Do not become discouraged. . . . It may be that the inability to make out such details has been owing to the state of your atmosphere; it may be you

Schiaparelli at the eyepiece of the 48-centimeter (19-inch) Merz-Repsold refractor. (Courtesy Luigi Prestinenza)

will be more successful tomorrow or the next day. It sometimes happens that the images here appear perfectly steady, and yet one still sees very little: a kind of veil seems to be thrown over the disk, for no apparent reason. . . . I will give you a striking example: I believed I saw the planet well on May 9, 25, and 27. . . . But I was unprepared for the joy I experi-

Dome of the 38-centimeter (15-inch) refractor of the Nice Observatory, used by Perrotin and Thollon to obtain the first confirmatory observations of the Schiaparellian canals in 1886. (William Sheehan collection)

enced on June 2 and 4, when for the first time I began to understand the true power of a 19-inch [48-centimeter] aperture on Mars. The memorable nights of 1879–80 and 1882 returned again. I had those wonderful images as exquisite as a steel engraving, and reveled in the magic of the details.[18]

By the early 1890s, interest in the planet had become worldwide, and was approaching hysteria proportions in August 1892 when the planet made its closest approach since 1877. It was greatly stimulated by the pre-opposition publication of a massive résumé of Martian research, *La Planète Mars*, by the French astronomer and writer Camille Flammarion—a work which is still invaluable today. Flammarion had his own private observatory at Juvisy-sur-Orge, located some 48 kilometers (30 miles) outside Paris and dedicated, "like a temple," to the planet Mars and to the proposition that it might be an inhabited world.

By the time Mars came to be most favorably placed for observation, scores of telescopes were turned in its direction, including the great Lick refractor in southern California (the Lick astronomers, who succeeded in making out a few canals, had failed in their bid to entice Schiaparelli on an all-expenses paid trip from Milan to Mt. Hamilton for the purpose of observing Mars; he had pleaded ill health). Even the Lick observers were upstaged, however, by results from the southern hemisphere, where Mars was much higher in the sky. Harvard astronomer William H. Pickering, using a 33-centimeter (13-inch) refractor at Arequipa, a site high in the Peruvian Andes, announced dramatically: "Many so-called canals exist upon the planet, substantially as drawn by Professor Schiaparelli." Pickering did not, however, make out any of the geminations. Pickering also reported the discovery of numerous "small lakes" on Mars, and confirmed not only Terby's bright projections at the limb of the planet but recorded others at the terminator as well—clouds they were, he concluded, suspended at an altitude of some 32 kilometers (20 miles) above the surface, which made them loftier than those of the Earth (a result, he pointed out, that was entirely consistent with the planet's smaller mass and lower surface gravity).

By 1892 Schiaparelli's results were winning general acceptance. The discoverer himself had so far been satisfied to present his observations in a series of rather technical memoirs, and had rigorously avoided speculating about the nature of the canals. But in 1893, in a widely reprinted paper, "The Planet Mars," he finally broke his silence. The canals, he had always believed—and still believed—were most likely natural features of the geology of the planet:

> The network formed by these was probably determined in its origin in the geological state of the planet, and has come to be slowly elaborated in the course of centuries. It is not necessary to suppose them the work of intelligent beings, and notwithstanding the almost geometrical appearance of

> all of their system, we are now inclined to believe them to be produced by the evolution of the planet, just as on the Earth we have the English Channel and the Channel of Mozambique.[20]

It was not Schiaparelli's own preferred explanation, but the possibility he mentioned only to shy away from—that the canals were the work of intelligent beings—that was to capture the imagination of an American abroad and lead to the most obsessive study of the planet so far attempted. In 1892, this American, Percival Lowell, had carried a 15-centimeter (6-inch) telescope to Tokyo, and was apparently intending to do little more than a bit of casual observing. As late as October 1893 he was thinking of spending Easter 1894 on holiday in Seville. But then a book—Flammarion's *La Planète Mars*—fell into his hands. It was a momentous event that would change the whole course of Martian studies.

Mars
Excerpt of a poem by Percival Lowell

One voyage there is I fain would take
While yet a man in mortal make;
Voyage beyond the compassed bound
Of our own Earth's returning round:
Voyage whose shining goal by day
From stupid stare lies hid away
Amid the sun-dimmed depths of space. . . .
But when staid night reclaims her sphere
And the beshadowed atmosphere
Its shutters to sight once more unbars,
Letting the universe appear
With all its wonder-world of stars,
My far-off goal draws strangely near,
Luring imagination on,
Beckoning body to be gone —
To ruddy-Earthed, blue-oceaned Mars.

* * *

So like yet so unlike our Earth
The face of that planet that had its birth
From our parent sun into space to be whirled
A separate individual world
Aeons before our Earth began,
Then being smaller aged more fast,
Disclosing now to us as we scan
The tell-tale traits of an older past;
Surface through which half the oceans have sunk,
Their once broad bosoms already shrunk
To gourd-shaped straits whose gaining strand
Foretells the time now close at hand
When the last vestiges of seas
Shall be swallowed in its cavities,
And Mars like our Moon through space shall roll
One waterless waste from pole to pole,
A planet corpse, whence has sped the soul.

Already far on with advancing age,
Has it passed its life-bearing stage?
And has that spirit already fled
From that planet of war, once doubtless rife
With myriad forms of happy life
Waging natural selection's strife—
But are the survivors themselves all dead?
Or is Mars yet inhabited?

9

Lowell's Mars

The mind can make substance, and people planets of its own with beings brighter than have been.

—Lord Byron,
"The Dream"

In Japan, Percival Lowell is still regarded as one of the hundred most important men of the twentieth century. This is more for his diplomatic role in and authorship of books about the Far East than for his thinking about Mars. One might quibble over his being so ranked, but there can be no doubt whatever that he belongs on anyone's short list of the most important figures in the history of Mars. From 1894, when he

Percival Lowell's favorite portrait with his signature. (Yerkes Observatory)

founded an observatory to study the red planet, to his death in 1916, Lowell masterfully shaped public opinion about Mars, which he seeded with fertile myths. Historian William Graves Hoyt's assessment of him is certainly correct: "Of all the men who through history who have posed questions and proposed answers about Mars, the most influential and by all odds the most controversial was Percival Lowell."[1]

Percival Lowell was born in Boston on March 13, 1855, scion of one of the oldest, wealthiest, and most distinguished families in America (according to the well-known toast, "And this is good old Boston,/ The home of the bean and the cod,/ Where Lowells talk only to Cabots,/ and Cabots talk only to God"). He was as patrician as they come, his blood the bluest of the blue. He looked the aristocrat so perfectly with his sharp commanding eyes, thick moustache, bald pate, and impeccable dress that in several European books of the period 1910 to 1914 his portrait is actually captioned "Sir Percival Lowell," despite the fact that he is clearly identified as an American.[2]

An ancestor, Percival Lowle, had left the English port of Bristol at the advanced age of sixty-seven and followed John Winthrop to America in 1638, soon after the arrival of the Mayflower and still during Galileo's lifetime. The astronomer's great-great uncle, Francis Cabot Lowell, had built the first cotton mill in New England and had established the family fortune in textiles to which his grandfather John Amory Lowell and his father Augustus Lowell had both added hugely. (By the time of Percival's birth, a collateral branch of the family—which included the poet James Russell Lowell, great-granduncle of the modern poet Robert Lowell—had become leading abolitionists. There is some irony in this, given that slavery had largely come to flourish in the South because of the cotton plantations which had so long fed the Lowell looms and made their fortunes.)

Percival's father, Augustus, was "a man of such strong self-assertion that many people found him repellent."[3] An imperious, cool, and rather conventional-thinking businessman, he was a pillar of Brahmin society and a leading exemplar of bourgeois productivity. Percival's mother, Katherine Lawrence Lowell—who had also descended from one of the leading "cotton" families in Boston and could boast a comparably distinguished lineage, since her father, Abbott Lawrence, had served as minister to the Court of St. James's—seems to have been conventionally subservient to her husband but transferred her needs for emotional intimacy to her eldest son. This may, as Percival Lowell's most consummate biographer David Strauss has suggested, have produced (unconscious) resentment on the part of the father, weakened his eldest son's identification with him, and contributed to Percival's later rejection of the expected role of firstborn and his rebellion against the conventional role and values into which he was being reared. Certainly, to the extent one can glean attitudes from existing letters, Percival's willful struggles with his father contrast with his deep emotional involvement with his mother, to whom he would continue writing, on an almost daily basis, whether from India, Japan, or Arizona, for the rest of her life, while her correspondence with him usually begins "My darling Percy." The following—written as he left Boston in August 1894, after a brief visit during which he first developed his theory of life on Mars—conveys some of the tone of her usual address where he was concerned: "I watched you till you had quite gone last evening and my heart was in my throat. I love you so my darling. . . . You [are] the person I love best on earth."[4]

As his business prospered Augustus bought a mansion in Brookline, which he called "Sevenels" because there were seven Lowells living there. In addition to Percival and his parents, the household consisted of younger brother Abbott Lawrence, who would later become the president of Harvard, and three sisters; the youngest, Amy, was referred to by the family as "the postscript," and would become a cigar-toting, avant-garde poet. The landscapes of Sevenels were, as Amy later described, "so cunningly cut by paths and with the trees so artfully disposed that one can wander happily among them and almost believe that one is walking in a real wood."[5] As a child of privilege, and growing up in a family where the values of the mind were always strongly encouraged, Percival was educated in the best private schools at home and abroad; by the age of ten he had learned French, and at eleven he composed passable Latin hexameters on the loss of a toy boat. His lifelong interest in astronomy was also early awakened—his first conscious memory was of Comet Donati of 1858, of which he later wrote, "I can see yet a small boy half way up a turning staircase gazing with all his soul into the evening sky where the stranger stood."[6] In his teens, Percival set up a 5.7-centimeter (2.25-inch) refractor in the cupola of Sevenels, and used it, as he later recalled, "to study Mars with as keen interest as I do now."[7]

Lowell continued his formal education at Harvard, where he was influenced by a book that—significantly—his mother had purchased for him in his freshman year, Richard Anthony Proctor's *Saturn and Its System*. It contained a popular exposition of British mathematical physicist James Clerk Maxwell's theory that Saturn's rings were an aggregation of small satellites. Proctor made the further point that the Saturnian system was analogous to the nebula from which, according to the nebular hypothesis of the eighteenth-century French mathematical astronomer Pierre Simon de Laplace, the solar system itself had formed. As a freshman, Lowell also embraced Darwinian evolution, in defiance of his father who adamantly opposed it, and he became an ardent disciple of British philosopher Herbert Spencer, who taught the doctrine of cosmic evolution, the notion that matter must progress, in Spencer's often quoted phrase, "from an indefinite, incoherent homogeneity to a definite, coherent heterogeneity." Lowell would later attempt to fit Eastern and Western societies into a similar Spencerian evolutionary scheme, and would end by trying to understand the planets in terms of the same sweeping generalization of homogeneity to heterogeneity, in which Mars was assumed to occupy an older, more evolved, and thus more advanced, position than the Earth.

Though intellectually Lowell developed early and discovered the themes that were to shape the lifelong categories of his thought—already, as his part in the commencement exercises at Harvard in 1876, he spoke on the nebular hypothesis—in other respects he was less precocious; he long remained emotionally vulnerable and uncertain of the direction of his career. After graduating from Harvard and making the obligatory European Grand Tour (as far as Syria), he returned to Boston and at first attempted to fulfill his father's expectations for the eldest son of a respectable Brahmin family, serving as head of a cotton mill and managing trusts and electric companies as an investment banker. However, he found himself increasingly frustrated and bored. He was unhappy with Boston's puritanical and repressive society, which he described as "the most austere . . . the world has ever known"; he was also profoundly dissatisfied with his conventional upper-class role. After six years of business and a romantic crisis in which he broke off—apparently in a panic—an engagement to an unidentified Brahmin woman (as early as 1877, he had confided to a friend "one needs to take every precaution before he throws away his independence")[8] he bailed out and booked passage to Japan. With Percival abdicating, his younger brother Lawrence was left to assume the responsibilities traditionally upheld by the firstborn, taking over his father's role managing investments and supporting cultural institutions in Boston such as the Lowell Institute, in which he succeeded Augustus as Sole Trustee.)

The immediate stimulus for Lowell's interest in Japan was a series of lectures given in 1882 at the Lowell Institute by zoologist Edward Sylvester Morse, a crusader for preserving traditional Japanese culture in the face of rapid modernization. Like Percival Lowell's cousin, Boston physician William Sturgis Bigelow, who called the lectures "the turning point of my life" and accompanied Morse to Japan on his return trip, Lowell saw Japan as a way of resolving his psychological crisis. For Bigelow, the trip to Japan ended a long period of depression and aimlessness.[9] He embraced esoteric Buddhism, which at least temporarily gave him a feeling of peace and a sense of purpose that he had lacked in Boston society. Lowell always remained a more ambivalent expatriate. In 1883 he rented a sumptuous house in Tokyo and hired Japanese servants. At first he enthusiastically found everyone in Japan "a poet"; however, he soon grew frustrated with what he perceived as Oriental lethargy and lack of application. "The far eastern peoples," he wrote, "might aptly be described as impossible peoples. The impossibility of obtaining anything like exact information is only equalled by the impossibility of getting anything done." Despite his strong attraction to Japanese art and gardens, his romantic impulse for the Far East was increasingly tempered by his irritation at what he considered the inefficiency and irrationality of a premodern people.[10] In the most intellectually important of four books he wrote about the Orient, *The Soul of the Far East* (1888), Lowell offered the Eurocentric theory that the Oriental personality (in contrast to the Western and especially the American) was immature and unevolved. It was distinguished by what he described as a quality of impersonalism. (Significantly—in an obituary for Augustus—he would later describe his father with the same term, "impersonal.") Comparing a class-conscious, closed, feudalistic society, similar to that of Europe in the Middle Ages, with a young, individualistic, aggressive society whose psychology, ideas, and institutions bore the indelible stamp of the frontier experience and of the incredible resources a new continent was providing for economic development, Lowell confused cause and effect and came to the unjustifiable conclusion that it was intrinsic to the Oriental character not to value individual expression, work, and efficiency as much as restless Americans such as Lowell himself valued them.

As Lowell's infatuation with the Far East began to wane, his mind returned increasingly to his boyhood interest in astronomy. On his last trip to Japan in 1892, he shipped out with him a 15-centimeter (6-inch) refractor, with which he observed Saturn from his Tokyo residence.

Lowell, a self-described man "of many minds and many moods," seemed just then to have been going into what would be described as a "hypomanic" state, perhaps not unlike the one his ancestor Percival Lowle had experienced before setting out from Bristol. (According to the current handbook of diagnoses published by the American Psychiatric Association, *DSM IV*, the symptoms of hypomania include "elevated expansive mood, high energy and physical restlessness, decreased need for sleep, and sharpened and unusually creative thinking."[11])

Lowell wasted no time. For generations *Occasionem cognosce*—seize your opportunity—had been the family motto, and Lowell, always determined to live life to the fullest, attempted to be true to it. Though prior to his departure from Tokyo he had written to a friend that he was considering an Easter jaunt to Seville in the spring of 1894, he was suddenly possessed of a much more grandiose ambition. His imagination was fired by Flammarion's *La Planète Mars*, which he received as a gift at Christmas 1893 and immediately devoured. Henceforth Mars became an all-consuming interest, not to say obsession. Above all Lowell was captivated by the compelling idea that Mars might be a living world. Whereas the East had beckoned him earlier with its sense of fascinating strangeness, Mars surpassed even Korea and Japan with its extraterrestrial exoticism.

The idea that Mars might be a living world had been enthusiastically supported by Flammarion, who had gone so far as to write: "We may hope that, because the world Mars is older than ours, humankind there will be more advanced and wiser."[12] The same idea had also been endorsed, in at least a qualified sense, by Schiaparelli, who in the 1880s had recorded changes in the dark markings on the planet leading him to exclaim: "The planet is not a desert of arid rocks. *It lives!*"[13] Even before he set eye to eyepiece, Lowell wrote a poem, that has never been published, apart from the excerpt which stands at the beginning of this chapter, recording the impact of Flammarion's writings. Later, but still before he had actually made a close study of the red planet, he gave a talk to the Boston Scientific Society in which he declared that in the canals of Mars "we are looking upon the result of the work of some sort of intelligent beings. . . . The amazing blue network on Mars hints that one planet besides our own is actually inhabited now."[14]

Almost at once—during mid-January 1894—Lowell sought contact with William H. Pickering, a member of another patrician family who had grown up nearby on Boston's Beacon Street.[15] As early as 1890, Lowell and Pickering had been corresponding about Mars. Pickering, by virtue of elder brother Edward's being director of the Harvard College Observatory, had been placed in charge of the Harvard Observatory observing station at Arequipa, high in the pure air of the Peruvian Andes, in which capacity he had made and published some of the most widely discussed observations of Mars at its previous opposition in 1892. It was only natural for Lowell to want to join forces with him. Pickering was also available just then; due to financial mismanagement and his director-brother's disapproval of his sensationalistic claims about Mars (for example, his announcement of having discovered a large number of "small lakes" on the planet), he had been dismissed from his Arequipa position. In January 1894 he was adrift and uncertain about his future.

Lowell invited Pickering and his young assistant, Andrew Ellicott Douglass, to join him in a bold scientific expedition for the purpose of studying the red planet and the possibility that it might be the abode of life at its forthcoming (October 1894) opposition. Lowell was thirty-nine—an advanced age for turning to a new career, but much younger than his namesake ancestor had been when he left Bristol for the New World. He was neither as old as Columbus when he set his westward course for the Indies nor as old as Schiaparelli when he took up the study of Mars. But then, when one is as well-connected and as wealthy as a Lowell, it is never too late to take up a new career in pursuit of one's heart's desire.

Not everyone welcomed Lowell's initiative. Charles W. Eliot, president of Harvard, wrote to Edward Pickering saying that Lowell was an "unreasonable person" and "a man without good judgment." Another Bostonian, Seth Carlo Chandler Jr., suggested (in confidence to Lick Observatory director Edward S. Holden) that Lowell "had not selected the right kind of companions for his astronomical picnic. . . . What he needed was some young, well-equipped astro-physicist (I mean with the education & the mental qualifications of a scientific man), sound and conservative, to sit on his coat-tails and keep him down to business, and prevent wild flights of fancy. . . . He was well-warned before he started . . . but expressed unbounded confidence in his ability to keep W. H. P[ickering] under his thumb, as he put it."[16]

Perhaps there was something passionate and inspired but also unbalanced and impetuous about Lowell's decision. It recalls his earlier decision to throw away his career in the investment trade for a trip to the Far East. Psychiatrist Anthony Storr has said of Winston Churchill, "had he been a stable and equable man, he could never have inspired the nation. In 1940, when all the odds were against Britain, a leader of sober judgement might well have concluded that we were finished."[17] The same may be said of Percival Lowell in late 1893 and early 1894. Had he then been an entirely stable and equable man, he would never have set out to build an observatory in the passionate quest for life on Mars.

Having decided to build an observatory and wanting the best place for it—for Lowell realized, as many others had not, that the quality of air above the telescope is as important for the kind of exacting observations he had in mind as the telescope itself—Lowell sent Douglass west with the 15-centimeter (6-inch) refractor he had carried to Japan to test seeing at various sites in the Arizona Territory. In mid-April, from Douglass's reports, Lowell selected Flagstaff. At 2,000 meters (7,000) feet it was the most elevated of the sites studied and conveniently located on a line of the Atlantic and Pacific railroad (soon afterward amalgamated into the Atchison, Topeka and Santa Fe, of which Lowell would become a director). It also—as Douglass often quipped in later years—had the best saloons. The components of a dome designed by Pickering were shipped west, along with two borrowed telescopes of 30.5-centimeter and 46-centimeter (12-inch and 18-inch) apertures (the latter was nearly the same aperture as the larger of the two telescopes used by Schiaparelli in Milan). The exact site chosen for the observatory was on a low hill west of town—Mars Hill, as it is still known today. By working at white-heat, Pickering and Douglass had everything in readiness—telescopes mounted piggyback inside Pickering's pre-fab dome which had yet to receive its canvas covering—when Lowell arrived on May 28, 1894. (He faithfully announced his arrival in a letter to his mother: "Here on the day. . . . Ready . . . for Arizonian virgin view.") The most ambitious observing campaign on Mars ever undertaken up to that time was about to begin.

Mars Hill, with dome of 61-centimeter (24-inch) refractor, as it looked in about 1930, when Clyde Tombaugh discovered the ninth planet, Pluto. (Lowell Observatory)

It was a portentous moment. The Frontier of the American West had opened with the English settlement at Jamestown, Virginia, in 1607, during the lifetime of Percival Lowell's ancestor. It had officially closed with the Oklahoma land rush in 1890, the last grab of free land offered by the U.S. Government in the continental United States. Now the slow but inevitable movement of Europeans on a broad front from the Atlantic to the Pacific was complete. In 1893, a young professor of history at the University of Wisconsin, Frederick Jackson Turner, provided the frontier with its first philosopher; his "The Frontier in American History," the "single most influential piece of historical writing ever done in the United States,"[18] argued that "the existence of an area of free land, its continuous recession, and the advance of American settlement westward, explain American development."[19] Now, a year after Turner had given his brilliant distillation of the meaning of the frontier experience, at a new settlement in the Southwest along the farthest verge of that farflung frontier on the beetling edge of a fir-crowned mesa, Percival Lowell, expatriate Boston Brahmin and disillusioned Orientalist, was pointing to a farther outpost destined to become a new West of the Imagination: it was decidedly a frontier of the far future, for even from Arizona, from Lowell's thin-aired eyrie, Mars was a far-westering world.

Lowell's observing logbook records his first impressions with the 46-centimeter (18-inch) telescope. On June 1, 1894, Mars was still four months from opposition. Inconveniently placed before the dawn, it had to be sought by early risers at 3 o'clock in the morning, appearing then as a small gibbous in the great blue circle of the eyepiece. Even so far away, its disk tantalized and rewarded scrutiny. "Southern Sea at end first and Hourglass Sea about equally intense," Pickering noted, to which Lowell added, "Terminator shaded, limb sharp and mist-covered forked-bay vanishes like river in desert."[20] Lowell's use of the term *desert* is remarkable, and suggests that Lowell's imagination may already have been captured by the stark Arizona deserts located south of the fir-covered mesa on which he had built his observatory. Certainly there is no doubt that his imagination was later stirred by such vistas.

The dark areas of the southern hemisphere of Mars appeared to Lowell as "chiefly blue-green." After a month of observing the tantalizingly small disk, Lowell returned to Boston. He did not return to the observatory again until late August.

He had been impressed almost from the outset with the lack of contrast in the Martian markings, which made him suspect that what earlier observers had taken for seas were in fact ghost-seas—dried-up basins. This view of them was confirmed when Pickering, equipped with an instrument he called his polariscope, failed to detect the telltale polarization of light due to water. Mars, then, was evidently a much drier planet than earlier observers had represented it. Clearly there was no blue Martian Mediterranean to be navigated by Martian men. The Schiaparellian map which had so beautifully invoked the romantic image of the classical world had all been based on a deceptive surmise. But if the dark areas were not seas, what were they? Lowell's observations increasingly suggested an answer.

When Lowell had first observed Mars, early spring had held sway in the southern hemisphere of the planet, then tilted toward Earth; it was May on Mars, and the markings stretched in a broad, dark belt unbroken from the Hourglass Sea (Syrtis Major) to the Columns of Hercules. The polar cap was beginning to melt, and as it did so it became surrounded by a dark-blue band, which Lowell regarded as a temporary polar sea. With the cap's melting, changes ensued in the appearance of the whole Martian globe. By August, the uniform dark belt in the southern hemisphere was broken by the return of a lighter-colored peninsula—Hesperia on Schiaparelli's map. Following its reappearance, "the lighter areas in the southern latitudes extended and grew lighter in tint, while the dark areas proportionately decreased in size and became fainter in color."[21] Lowell left for Boston a second time in September and returned to Flagstaff again in October and November only to find the markings even more faded. "The whole amount of the blue-green upon it had diminished, and that of the orange ocher had proportionately increased," he wrote. "Mars looked more Martian in November than he had in June."[22]

In these subtle changes of tint and coloring, Lowell thought he could trace the effects of water transport on the growth of vegetation—leaves and grasses —across the surface of Mars. This, then, was his first important finding. He concluded that the Martian seas were not seas at all but vast tracts of vegetation. "If the polar sea were . . . to descend in a vast freshet toward the equator such are the appearances the freshet might be expected to present. As the water progressed farther and farther north the regions it left behind would gradually dry up, and from having appeared greenish-blue would take on an arid reddish-yellow tint; precisely what is observed to take place."[23]

Again, "we find that in June, 1894, it was May on Mars, while in November it was August. Here, then, we see that if the blue-green tint were due to vegetation, that blue-green color should have been most pronounced at the earlier date, since then the vegetation would have been most luxuriant, and should then have changed to ocher as the crops got into their sere and yellow leaf. And these tints were the very ones observed, and observed in this very order. The blue-green on the one hand, therefore, and the ocher on the other are perfectly explicable on the supposition of a Martian vegetation."[24]

From the first, Lowell had been on the look-out for the canals. In June, they were scarcely evident, apart from some particularly broad ones, and Lowell recorded his evident disappointment in his observing logbook: "With the best will in the world, I can see no canals." Was it possible his expedition to the Arizona Territory had been for naught? However, he kept up his nightly vigils and—aided by Mars's diminishing distance and, no doubt, by the power of hypnotic suggestion, for there were no doubt potent psychological forces also at work here[25]—by August they had become a blooming presence on the disk. His logbook now contained entries such as:

Suspected multitudinous canals.
Network of canals. General effect quite like Schiaparelli's globe.

There they were, along with tiny dark spots (Pickering's "lakes") which partook in the same changes affecting the rest of the disk; changes not so much of size as of color. The "lakes" deepened and became richer in hue, which to Lowell's mind contributed the essential clue to what they were. Not lakes at all, they were rather like Flagstaff itself, a verdant spot on the verge of a desert. "When we put all these facts together," he wrote, "the presence of the spots at the junctions of the canals, their apparent invariability [in] size, their seasonal darkening, and last but not least the resemblance of the great equatorial regions of Mars to the deserts of our Earth, one solution instantly suggests itself of their character, to wit: that they are oases in the midst of that desert." And he continued, "Here then we have an end and reason for the existence of the canals and the most natural conceivable one—namely that the canals are constructed for the express purpose of fertilizing the oases. . . . And just such inference of design is in keeping with the curiously systematic arrangement of the canals themselves. . . . The whole system is trigonometric to a degree."[26]

The straightness of the canals (their traveling along geodesic lines, the shortest distance between two points on the planet's surface) could mean only one thing. They were artificial. This was not an unreasonable conclusion. One of the first things stressed in art schools has always been that nature never draws a straight line (a principle abundantly borne out by the astronauts' views of the Earth from orbit. Story Musgrave, veteran of six Earth-orbital flights in the Space Shuttle, mentioned to one of the authors [W.S.]: "Nature never makes a straight line; every time you see a straight line that's humanity at work. Nature likes curves, humans like straight lines"). Given the existence of a network of linear markings like the canals of Mars, Lowell's deduction was not only logical but inescapable: they must be the handiwork of denizens of the planet.

This, then, was Lowell's theory: Mars, being a smaller world, had evolved more rapidly than the Earth; it had already lost much of its water-supply, and was well on its way to utter desiccation. To survive, its inhabitants had to build a vast system of irrigation canals to transport precious water from the melting polar caps, where most of the water on the planet was locked up, to the equatorial regions. These were the very system of canals that Schiaparelli had first described in 1877.

Lowell arrived at this interpretation in Boston in the summer of 1894.

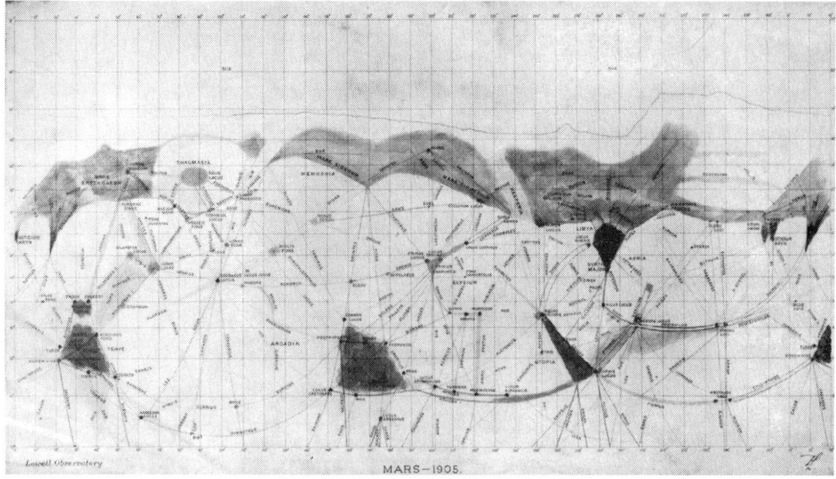

Lowell's 1905 map of Mars showing the canals in their fullest development. (Lowell Observatory)

He had observed Mars for just a month. He would hold tenaciously to this view, like a Sophoclean tragic hero, until the end of his life. He proceeded to unleash his ideas on a fascinated public in a series of articles, written in a manic flurry of literary activity, in *Popular Astronomy* and the *Atlantic Monthly*, then presented them in a packed series of lectures at Boston's Huntington Hall in February 1895. The public was, of course, enthralled by Lowell's theory, and almost equally so by Lowell himself. A multimillionaire at a time when that still meant something and, at the age of forty, a bachelor (the most eligible, by some accounts, in Boston), Lowell on his return from Arizona could sometimes be clearly seen in the window of the house he purchased on Beacon Hill's West Cedar Street. "His handsome head was to be seen vis-à-vis the *Boston Evening Transcript* beneath a life-sized plaster Venus similar to those that infest the Athenaeum. Visibility was perfect, for the shade was always raised to the very top of the window as if to admit no impediment to a message from Mars."[27] Between appearances in his window, Lowell worked hard at his first book on the red planet, *Mars*—based largely on his *Popular Astronomy* articles, it appeared in December 1895 just as he was about to depart for Europe to consult with his fellow Mars enthusiasts, Flammarion and Schiaparelli. (Flammarion, as expected, found Lowell's theory "of the highest interest, though certainly controversial,"[28] while Schiaparelli, older and wiser, was more guarded. He confided to his Belgian colleague François Terby: "It is certain that Lowell commands superior means to any hitherto employed on Mars. If his perseverance and enthusiasm do not desert him, he will make considerable contributions to areography; on the other hand, he needs more experience, and must rein in his imagination."[29]

In the conclusion to *Mars*, Lowell conjured up an evocative vision of life on a planet slowly but surely dying of thirst—a fate that, though in the long run inevitable, was in the short run being magnificently resisted by the efforts of the large-brained and peaceable race that had built the canals:

> The evidence of handicraft, if such it be, points to a highly intelligent mind behind it. Irrigation, unscientifically conducted, would not give us such truly wonderful mathematical fitness in the several parts to the whole as we there behold. A mind of no mean order would seem to have provided over the system we see,—a mind certainly of considerably more comprehensiveness than that which presides over the various departments of our own public works. Party politics, at all events, have had no part in them; for the system is planet wide. Quite possibly, such Martian folk are possessed of inventions of which we have not dreamed, and with them electrophones and kinetoscopes are things of a bygone past, preserved with veneration in museums as relics of the clumsy contrivances of the simple childhood of the race. Certainly what we see hints at the existence of beings who are in advance of, not behind us, in the journey of life.[30]

On the whole, it seems probable that Lowell had originally planned only a single expedition to the Arizona Territory to study Mars. His success in 1894 made him resolve on a series of expeditions to favorable climates for the purpose. He returned the borrowed 46-centimeter (18-inch) refractor he had used in 1894 to Pennsylvania's Flower Observatory (later Flower and Cook Observatory)* and from his portly pocketbook he funded a new telescope—a 61-centimeter (24-inch) refractor fashioned by famed telescope-maker Alvan Graham Clark—and set out for Tacubaya, near Mexico City,

*After many years of service, it was shipped to Mt. John Observatory on the South Island of New Zealand. Unfortunately, it was never set up there. During a year's sabbatical in New Zealand, author Sheehan caught up with it in Christchurch—the 46-centimeter (18-inch) objective was in a crate in the Physics and Astronomy Department at Canterbury University, the tube and mounting, dusty but otherwise no worse for the wear, in the Yaldhurst Transport Museum.

where he hoped to obtain observations of Mars at its next opposition, on December 1, 1896. He arrived before Mars was well-placed, and diverted himself by tackling other planets with the telescope. On Mercury he made out a maze of linear markings even Schiaparelli professed to find "terrifying," while on Venus he claimed to make out a series of spokelike markings quite unlike anything seen elsewhere; their appearance led him to the surprising conclusion that the planet did not have the substantial veiling of cloud generally believed in by students of the planet and unleashed a flurry of criticism of the utmost ferocity from other astronomers.

Pickering had departed after the 1894 opposition, but Douglass and several new assistants, including Lowell's secretary Wrexie Leonard, helped him study Mars extensively from Tacubaya. In the end Lowell decided the conditions in Mexico were no better than those in Flagstaff. By spring 1897 he was once more intent on moving his observatory—possibly to Algeria. In the end, he decided to return to Flagstaff again.

For three years Lowell had been under constant strain. Now at last his health gave way, and he collapsed into depression. He spent six months trying to recuperate in his West Cedar Street home, before attempting to take the train back to Flagstaff; however, he made it only as far as Chicago before he collapsed again. Overwork must have contributed to his breakdown, but other factors may also have been involved, including the death of his strongest supporter—his mother—at the end of 1895, closely followed by the hostile reception given by professional astronomers to his work on Mars and especially Venus. Lowell's most recent biographer, David Strauss, has suggested that all his life Lowell showed a "strong commitment to personal independence"; it had led him to diverge from his father in the matter of a career, to break off an earlier engagement, and to seek his fulfillment in unorthodox careers such as a writer on matters Oriental and now a planetary astronomer. But in the matter of Venus he had not only departed from conventional views about the planet, he had gone off 180 degrees from them; while nearly every astronomer of the day was convinced that Venus was surrounded with highly reflective clouds, Lowell was seeing a spiderweb structure—radial lines and spokes emanating from "a certain center." This had brought him into irreconcilable conflict with the rest of the astronomical community and all but guaranteed that he would be perceived as an outcast (leading professional astronomers, George Ellery Hale and

The 61-centimeter (24-inch) refractor of Lowell Observatory as it looks today. ©Stephen James O'Meara.

Percival Lowell drawing artificial planet disks at the eyepiece of the 61-centimeter (24-inch) refractor, late 1890s. (Lowell Observatory)

James Keeler, to refuse any longer to take his contributions for their newly founded *Astrophysical Journal*). As Strauss has suggested, "Assuming that at some level Lowell took this criticism to heart, he must have been gripped by a sense of paralysis as he thought about continuing the work." The questions raised about his work may also have reenergized the longstanding struggle with his father. As T. J. Jackson Lears has suggested, "The stringent demands of the modern achievement ethos had been intensified for Lowell by his father's insistence on accomplishment 'of real significance.' A virtually unattainable paternal ideal, embodied in a father who was difficult if not impossible to please, may ultimately have contributed to the breakdown of the striving son."[31]

Regardless of the reasons for his nervous collapse, Lowell was assigned by his doctor to a "rest cure" in his father's house on Commonwealth Avenue, where he remained for several months in 1897; he next went to Bermuda in the company of his doctor, and spent from the fall of 1898 to the spring of 1899 in a New York hotel where he was nursed by his secretary Miss Wrexie Leonard. After the turn of the century, he traveled to the French Riviera and joined Boston astronomer David Peck Todd for an eclipse in Algeria. All in all, his illness would put him out of commission, astronomically, for four long years.

By the time Lowell recovered, he had largely succeeded in reorganizing his psyche, and when he returned to Flagstaff in spring 1901, he did so with a will. Lears notes that henceforth he became "a model of punctuality, order, and productivity." He was determined to make his observatory a permanent institution and to tackle the problems of planetary astronomy in a more quantitative (that is, presumably, in a more scientifically exacting) manner. To his continuing program of visual observations of the planets, he added ambitious investigations utilizing the spectroscope, a still relatively novel instrument used to analyze light from the planets and stars, which he hoped would lead to unambiguous determinations of the rotation of Venus and the presence of water vapor on Mars. He also experimented with photography to objectively record the canals. He fired Douglass, who during his illness had become an outspoken critic of the spokes of Venus and the canals of Mars, and added several new assistants, including Vesto Melvin Slipher, an Indiana native, who would lead Lowell's spectroscopic campaign and later make the most important discovery ever made at Lowell's observatory—the red shifts of what were then called white nebulae, including the spirals, which furnished the first evidence of the general expansion of the universe. Increasingly, too, Lowell became absorbed in a taxing mathematical investigation of the motion of Uranus, hoping to extract the probable position in the sky of a planet beyond the orbit of Neptune (a trans-Neptunian planet, or "Planet X"). This pursuit was rivaled only by his fascination with Mars itself as the most absorbing obsession of his later years.

Lowell did not return to Flagstaff until a month after the unfavorable Martian opposition of 1901, so his results there were correspondingly limited; but at the opposition of 1903 he obtained most of the observational material that formed the basis of his magnum opus on Mars, *Mars and Its Canals* (1906). With his assistants concentrating on spectroscopy and photography, Lowell carried out most of the visual work on the planet, which covered from the end of January through the end of July, including a stretch of forty-six consecutive nights in April and May when he was able to observe the planet without a break. Most of the time he used a diaphragm to stop down the aperture of the 61-centimeter (24-inch) refractor to 41 centimeters (16 inches) or so—he found this gave the best definition of the planet's markings—and with magnifications of 310 and 400X, he made hundreds of drawings showing the gossamer filaments of the canals. One sensational result was the detection, in late May, of a large projection at the terminator of Mars; first noted by V. M. Slipher, who immediately called Lowell to the eyepiece, it appeared "ocher orange" in color and Lowell interpreted it—correctly—as a dust cloud. Most of Lowell's attention at this opposition was devoted to Martian seasonal phenomena and included the recording of color changes in Mare Erythraeum—a Martian dark area that seemed to turn from blue-green to chocolate-brown as the Martian autumn gave way to deep winter—and the compiling of graphs he called "cartouches" which were alleged to show the progressive development of individual canals as a function of Martian dates and latitudes. These observations were made in an attempt to document the "wave of color" or "wave of darkening" that swept alternately from the planet's poles. Lowell regarded these changes as evidence of the spring quickening of vegetative growth along the banks of the canals. He reaffirmed his belief that these changes furnished proof-positive of the existence on Mars of an advanced civilization. "That Mars is inhabited by beings of some sort or other we may consider as certain as it is uncertain what those beings may be," he wrote.[32]

Also in that busy year 1903, Lowell trained his telescope once more on Venus and saw the same spoke-like markings leering back at him that he had seen in 1896–97. And at the same time he made a very determined attempt to resolve his problems with Venus in another sphere as well—still unmarried, he made a (rejected) proposal of marriage to a Miss Struthers. After this rejection, he consoled himself in his diary: "And so I go back to my only solace. Work. Alone! Yes, always alone, though I had hoped for the opposite. . . . Perhaps that I may make a success; my own life is such a dismal failure."[33]

To work Lowell went, and at work he continued for the rest of his life—pausing only for the occasional European trip and to finally marry, in 1908, when he was fifty three, a Boston neighbor, interior decorator, and real estate entrepreneur Constance Savage Keith, from whom he had earlier bought his Beacon Hill house. (She was as much an eccentric as he, and for years after his death she continued to wear mourning black and hold séances in which she tried to contact his spirit. She also tied up his estate in a long drawn-out lawsuit that in the end left the Lowell Observatory famously broke.)

During the 1900s and 1910s, the observatory on Mars Hill became Lowell's whole life. On the heels of *Mars and Its Canals*, he published *Mars as the Abode of Life* (1908), based on his Lowell Institute lectures of 1906. In general more technical than his earlier books, it nevertheless contains some passages of unforgettable Lowellian prose:

> To let one's thoughts dwell on these Martian Saharas is gradually to enter into the spirit of the spot, and so to gain comprehension of what the essence of Mars consists. . . . In our survey of Mars . . . we behold the saddening picture of a world athirst, where, as in our own Saharas, water is the one thing needful, and yet where by nature it cannot be got. But one line of salvation is open to it, and that lies in the periodic unlocking of the remnant of water that each year gathers as snow and ice about its poles. . . .[35]
>
> The struggle for existence in their planet's decrepitude and decay would tend to evolve intelligence to cope with circumstances growing momentarily more and more adverse. But, furthermore, the solidarity that the conditions prescribed would conduce to a breadth of understanding sufficient to utilize it. Intercommuncation over the whole globe is made not only possible, but obligatory. This would lead to the easier spreading over it of some dominant creature,—especially were this being of an advanced order of intellect,—able to rise above its bodily limitations to amelioration of the conditions through the exercise of mind. . . .[36]
>
> Thus, not only do the observations we have scanned lead to the con-

> clusion that Mars at this moment is inhabited, but they land us at the further one that these denizens are of an order whose acquaintance was worth the making. Whether we ever shall come to converse with them in any more instant way is a question upon which science at present has no data to provide. More important to us is the fact that they exist, made all the more interesting by their precedence of us in the path of evolution. . . .
>
> A sadder interest attaches to such existence: that it is, cosmically speaking, soon to pass away. To our eventual descendants life on Mars will no longer be something to scan and interpret. It will have lapsed beyond the hope of study or recall. Thus to us it takes on an added glamour from the fact that it has not long to last. For the process that brought it to its present pass must go on to the bitter end, until the last spark of Martian life goes out. The drying up of the planet is certain to proceed until its surface can support no life at all. Slowly but surely time will snuff it out. When the last ember is thus extinguished, the planet will roll a dead world through space, its evolutionary career forever ended.[37]

The Evolution of Worlds (1909) followed, based on lectures Lowell delivered at MIT in 1908. It developed further Lowell's ideas about the evolution of worlds—the subject matter of the new science of planetology, as Lowell called it, in which he envisaged a progression from youthful worlds such as Jupiter (which retained enough of the heat of its formation to radiate its own heat), through middle-aged worlds such as the Earth and Mars, to cold dead worlds like Mercury and the Moon. Admittedly, this work had less popular appeal than his earlier work—Mars was mentioned only in passing, only a paragraph was devoted to it. The questions that now engaged him did not excite the public as had his earlier announcement of the existence of life on Mars, and—despite the steady accumulation of circumstantial evidence supporting his views—in the end he failed to produce final incontrovertible proof of those sensational claims.

"Lowell certainly does delight in his canals of Mars," a friend visiting him at his observatory noted. Mars remained his chief passion, and Lowell's gusto, his zest for life, his enthusiasm and exhaustless energy remained very much in evidence during these years of continuing endeavor. And yet there was also a lurking melancholy. Above all he was disappointed and embittered by the failure of his views to gain currency among scientists. A particularly vigorous attack on the reality of canals had been launched by astronomers at the opposition of 1909 (we shall say more about this reaction to Lowell's work later), while even old Schiaparelli expressed skepticism toward the exfoliating network of gossamer lines with which Lowell had garbed the surface of Mars: "The enormous quantity of detail that one can easily recognize on your drawings does not exist on the planet, at least this is my present opinion," the Italian astronomer wrote to Lowell in his last communication with him on the subject.[38]

More and more Lowell saw himself as the persecuted pioneer. Alluding to the ferocious criticism to which he had been subjected, he compared himself to Darwin during a lecture tour he gave in the fall of 1916. "Little discoveries are not received in this hostile manner," he declared. "It is only the great ones that are." To a friend he commented that he didn't get the recognition he deserved because "he didn't have an average mind."[39]

On November 12, 1916, he died at Flagstaff, of a massive intracerebral hemorrhage. At the age of only sixty-one, depressed and discouraged by the attacks on his Martian theory and by the failure of his ambitious search for "Planet X" beyond Neptune, he was prematurely aged. In his belief in the existence of Martian life, he remained, however, unshaken to the end. Nor did his influence wane or the causes he championed end with his death. It has been aptly said that "great men have two lives; one which occurs while they work on this earth; a second which begins at the day of their death and continues as long as their ideas and conceptions remain powerful."[40] For the next half century—at least until the *Mariner 4* spacecraft bypassed the planet—Lowell's views of Martian conditions, the lingering romance of the intelligent canal-builders, would dominate the debate about the planet. Mars would remain, even in Lowell's absence, Lowellian.

10 La Grande Lunette

The method of scientific investigation is nothing but the expression of the necessary mode of working of the human mind.

—Thomas Henry Huxley, *Our Knowledge of the Causes of the Phenomena of Organic Nature*, 1863

The early telescopic observers interpreted images of planets in terms of the one they already knew—the Earth. At first, when the images were small, they conceived them in terms of the whole Earth. Thus, Mars's dark and light areas were sorted into oceans and continents. As telescopes grew larger and revealed ever more detail, astronomers' interpretations became more refined, and their descriptions began to take on the coloring of certain terrestrial landscapes—painted deserts, distant mountains, corn fields—often those within view of their own observatories.

At one time the globes of the planets had been regarded as smooth, perfect, almost as if they had been fashioned with a lathe; only later did it become clear that the apparent smoothness was merely an effect of remote perspective. No less than the Earth did these other worlds have their share of irregularities—mountains, rugged surfaces—as Galileo had first demonstrated with his small telescope and the Moon. But whereas the Moon can be seen well under conditions of low Sun illumination, when the irregularities of its surface are cast into high relief by shadows along the terminator, Mars never shows a phase more extreme than the gibbous the Moon shows three or four days from full. Near opposition, its features are presented under the nearly direct illumination of a high Sun, and the observer is roughly in the same position as someone looking out over the Grand Canyon under the intense glare of high noon:

> During the long, hot summer days, when the sun is high, the phenomenal features of the scenery are robbed of most of their grandeur, and cannot or do not wholly reveal to the observer the realities which render them so instructive and interesting. There are few middle tones of light and shade. The effects of foreshortening are excessive, almost beyond belief, and produce the strangest deceptions. Masses which are widely separated seem to be superposed or continuous. Lines and surfaces, which extend towards us at an acute angle with the radius of vision, are warped around until they seem to cross it at a right angle. Grand fronts, which ought to show depth and varying distance, become flat and are troubled with false perspective. . . . Even the colors are ruined. The glaring face of the wall, where the light falls full upon it, wears a scorched, overbaked, discharged look.[1]

The circumstances of the observing geometry—together with the fact that Mars has an atmosphere that tends to conceal any defects in the planet's outline—have long contributed to the belief that Mars was a world nearly devoid of significant elevations, a globe flat and monotonous in the extreme. (This, by the way, was a necessary prerequisite to the belief in canal-builders; the canals in their courses, after all, deviated hardly at all from perfect straightness—as Lowell had said, they were trigonometric to a degree—which suggested that their builders had not needed to work around obstacles.)

Despite the generally washed-out appearance of the Martian disk, like a distant Grand Canyon seen at high noon, in a large enough telescope it begins—at least for those having imaginations working that way—to evoke a sense of true geology. Sir John Herschel, William's son, a famous astronomer and geologist himself, was one of the first to invoke an explicit comparison between the contours of the Martian disk and the landscapes of Earth. He found something in the planet's ruddy hue that reminded him of the Old Red Sandstone outcrops of Scotland. And Percival Lowell, by no means immune to the deceptions of glaring midday illumination that made Mars look flat and troubled with false perspective, saw in it the likeness of the Painted Desert near his observatory at Flagstaff:

> The resemblance of its lambent saffron to the telescopic tints of the Martian globe is strikingly impressive. Far forest and still farther desert are transmuted by distance into mere washes of color, the one robin's-egg blue, the other roseate ochre, and so bathed, both, in the flood of sunshine from out of a cloudless burnished sky that their tints rival those of a fire-opal. None otherwise do the Martian colors stand out upon the disk at the far end of the journey down the telescope's tube. Even in its mottlings the one expanse recalls the other.

At the same opposition at which Lowell cut his teeth as a Martian observer, that of 1894, another astronomer, Edward Emerson Barnard, was prospecting from the eyepiece of the great 91-centimeter (36-inch) refractor at Mt. Hamilton. After a long dispute with his director, Edward S. Holden, Barnard had finally obtained rights to the telescope every Friday night, and early in September 1894 he used it to obtain some of the most impressive views of Mars ever obtained up to his time. Thus, on the night of September 2-3 he entered into his observing notebook: "There is a vast amount of detail. . . . I however have failed to see any of Schiaparelli's canals as narrow straight lines. In the region of some of the canals near Lacus Solis there are details—some of a streaky nature but they are broad and diffused and irregular and under the best conditions could never be taken for the so called canals."

A week later Barnard had another chance at Mars. Syrtis Major was

E. E. Barnard and signature. (William Sheehan collection)

coming into view, and Barnard found it a mass of irregularities, confiding his impressions in a letter he wrote next day to U.S. Naval Observatory astronomer Simon Newcomb: "I have been watching and drawing the surface of Mars. It is wonderfully full of detail. There is certainly no question about there being mountains and large greatly elevated plateaus. To save my soul I can't believe in the canals as Schiaparelli draws them." In order to convey some sense of what had been revealed to him, Barnard could do no better than picture to Newcomb the mountainous landscapes of the Coast Range near the observatory on Mt. Hamilton:

> Under the best conditions these dark regions, which are always shown with smaller telescopes as of nearly uniform shade, broke up into a vast

The 91.4-centimeter (36-inch) refractor of the Lick Observatory. (Photo by authors)

> amount of very fine details. I hardly know how to describe the appearance of these "seas" under these conditions [but] from what I know of the appearance of the country about Mount Hamilton as seen from the observatory, I can't imagine that, as viewed from a very great elevation, this region, broken by canyon and slope and ridge, would look just like the surface of these Martian "seas."

Now that we have close-up views of this hemisphere of Mars, we can see that Barnard was indeed correct—the surface here is broken up in much the manner he described. Instead of a large sea or dried-up seabottom as earlier observers had imagined, Syrtis Major is, in fact, a vast elevated plateau, sloping off on either side and covered with dark materials originating in a low-relief shield volcano lying within its vast rolling expanse. The southern part of Syrtis Major is streaked and mottled due to wind action, and there are also extensive dune fields.

With Barnard's observations, we enter upon a new era in the study of Mars. The planet appeared to him not only in distant perspective, as to all previous observers; instead it began to show details, individual landscapes, hints of surface relief. Barnard's observations contain, in contrast to the

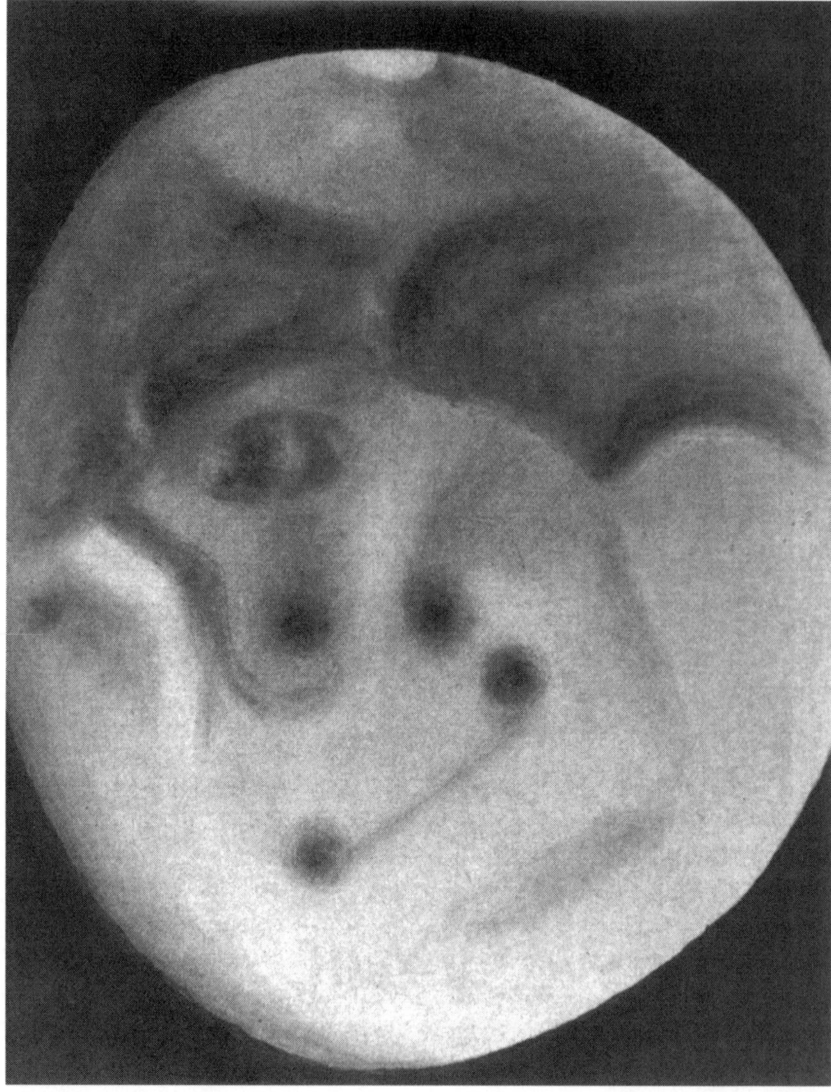

Barnard's view of Mars with the Lick refractor, September 2, 1894. How unlike Lowell's views at the same time. (Yerkes Observatory)

noonday view of the Grand Canyon described above, something of the falling away of deception and false perspective as occurs when the Grand Canyon's fronts are viewed in the later afternoon:

> As the sun declines there comes a revival. The half-tones at length appear, bringing into relief the component masses; the amphitheaters recede into suggestive distances . . . and the whole cliff arouses from lethargy and erects itself in grandeur and power, as if conscious of its own majesty. . . . But the great gala-days of the cliffs are those when sunshine and storm are waging an even battle. . . . Then the truth appears and all deceptions are exposed. Their real grandeur, their true forms, and a just sense of their relations are at last fairly presented, so that the mind can grasp them. And they are very grand—even sublime.[2]

Barnard glimpsed something of this in 1894 with the great refractor on its majestic eyrie on Mt. Hamilton. More than any man before him, he captured the truth about the Martian surface: its grandeur, its true forms, a sense of their relations.

The next man to have a vision of the reality of the Martian surface—to see something of its geology, rather than only its far-flung planetary disk—was Eugène Michael Antoniadi, "an architect by training and an astronomer by genius."[3] Antoniadi emerged from the mists of obscurity around the turn of the twentieth century to become one of the most vocal opponents of Lowellian dogma. During a burgeoning career at Meudon Observatory (just outside Paris), he stood in broad-chested defiance against Lowell's canal theory, offering astronomers new ways to see the Martian surface. Just as Mars had its rivals among the stars (the angry red stars Aldebaran, Antares, Betelgeuse), so, too, did Lowell among his colleagues. But only Antoniadi was as insistent and aggressive about his views as was Lowell. No matter how much correspondence passed between the two great observers, neither man could be swayed from his beliefs; they went to their graves with fists still shaking in the air. In the end, Antoniadi's meticulous observations of the red planet would rise to the forefront of Martian studies to preserve the integrity and propel the advancement of planetary science.

Eugène Antoniadi, the son of Michel and Photini, was born on March 1, 1870, in Constantinople (now Istanbul). Antoniadi was a common name among the Istanbul-born Greeks, and little is known of the family's early history apart from one anecdote, which the authors gleaned from the noted French planetary astronomer Henri Camichel. When Antoniadi was six, the Ottoman sultan Abdülaziz died. Young Antoniadi said he was glad of it. His father responded: "Don't be glad; the next will be worse." He was right; the

E. M. Antoniadi on the *Norse King,* awaiting departure on an eclipse expedition to Norway in 1896. (Courtesy Richard McKim and Council of the British Astronomical Association)

next was Abdülaziz's mentally deranged brother Murad V, who was deposed after only three months.

Eugène was likely raised in affluence, for "the Greeks in Constantinople . . . enjoyed wealth and privilege."[4] His lifestyle in later years certainly suggests he had an inheritance of some kind, for he worked for little money yet lived and traveled in comfort. An undated portrait from his youth, but perhaps from about the time of Abdülaziz's death, shows us a composed and tender child with a slender nose, gentle lips, and handsome brows; his hair is slightly tussled, and his eyes appear soft and open, like those of a poet or an artist, but they also possess a focused intensity—the kind of visual sharpness one expects to see in the eyes of a savant. His passion for astronomy and art were well established by the time he was seventeen. Antoniadi had set up a 7.6-centimeter (3-inch) telescope in Constantinople and at Prinkipo, an island in the Sea of Marmara, and began rendering his impressions of sunspots, Jupiter, Saturn, and Mars, "revealing . . . an observer endowed with an unusually acute and sensitive vision, and a gifted draughtsman."[5]

What first turned Antoniadi's eyes skyward and kindled a flame in his heart for astronomy is unknown. The catalyst could have been the spectacular apparition of Comet Tebbutt in 1881, whose head burned with the intensity of a planet and whose tail stretched across the sky for 40 Moon diameters.[6] The ability of bright comets to arouse public interest in astronomy is well documented, and the effect has changed little to this day. Even Antoniadi's fellow Martian aficionados (Lowell and Barnard) were first inspired by comets. Lowell, as we have seen, remembered Donati's comet, which appeared when he was three—it was one of his first memories.[7] Barnard recalled, "When I was very small I saw a comet; and I have a vague remembrance that the neighbors spoke of this comet as having something to do with the terrible war that was then desolating the South."[8]

The appearance of a great comet sailing above Constantinople must have had an emotional impact on Antoniadi and his countrymen. Perhaps it seemed a portent of impending disaster. After all, Antoniadi grew up during the long and bloody decline of the Ottoman empire. In 1878 his parents' homeland had declared war with Turkey. This declaration followed on the heels of a costly war between Turkey and Russia, which had plunged the Ottoman empire into financial and political distress. Although the Greeks in Constantinople had been protected since the days of Mahomet the Conqueror, the horrors of history are hard to relinquish; what Greek or Turk still living in those days could forget the great revolt of 1821, in which Greeks had murdered almost every Moslem (some eight thousand men, women, and children in all) in major towns like Navarini and Tripolitza? The Turks in Constantinople had demanded instant revenge, executing some of the leading Greeks, including the Greek Patriarch, Gregorios, and murdering thousands of ordinary Greeks. The Sultan of the time had made no attempt to stop these excesses, which lasted on both sides for nearly four years.

Meanwhile, in Europe, astronomers could still watch the heavens scintillate with visions of beauty and peace. Even as Turkey was battling Russia in 1877, Schiaparelli in Milan was experiencing "moments of absolute atmospheric calm," under which conditions he had discovered the famed canals of Mars, the very features that would inspire Percival Lowell to envision his advanced race of peaceful Martians. "Party politics," Lowell would write in his classic work *Mars*, "at all events, have had no part in them. . . . Certainly what we see hints at the existence of beings who are in advance of, not behind us, in the journey of life."[9] Like the sudden appearance of a Great Comet, Mars and its inhabitants captured the public's attention. "Like the savage who fears nothing so much as a strange man," Lowell continued, "like Crusoe who grows pale at the sight of footprints not his own, the civilized thinker instinctively turns to thought of mind other than the one he himself knows."

Like Lowell's civilized thinker, Antoniadi turned his thoughts away from the savage horrors of his homeland to enjoy the serenity of Mars through his telescope. He might have indulged his passion by reading Percy Gregg's science-fiction classic *Across the Zodiac,* a two-volume novel about a trip to Mars—a planet with pale green skies and orange foliage. Certainly he would have devoured the works of the great French astronomy writer Camille Flammarion, whose sought-after book *Astronomie populaire,* published in 1880, sold 130,000 copies. It was Flammarion who fathered the amateur astronomy movement in France by founding the Société Astronomique de France in 1877 and the journal *l'Astronomie* in 1882. Under Abdülaziz, Turkey had cultivated close relations with both France and Britain, and Antoniadi had acquired a firm command of both French and English. Also—like Schiaparelli—he loved to read the classics, which of course he could translate from the original Greek.

The condition of the Ottoman empire became deplorable in 1889 when an Italian anarchist assassinated Empress Elizabeth of Austria on Turkish soil. The event preceded Sultan Abdülhamid II's decision to organize and direct a ruthless plan of extermination against Armenians; the massacred millions soon added their blood to the already red-tainted Turkish soil, and the Sultan became known in Europe as the Red Sultan. "It is impossible to give an idea of the state of things," a Moslem wrote to the British Consul, Sir Alfred Billiotti. "Tyrannized over, robbed, and driven from their lands by Government officials and *agas*, Moslems as well as Christians shed tears of blood. The aspect of the country is desolate."[10]

Antoniadi had staged an escape from his homeland (intentionally or not) by making his mark on the astronomical community abroad. He published papers in English in the journal of the Liverpool Astronomical Society. In 1890 he become an original member of the British Astronomical Association (BAA), and he joined the ranks of Flammarion's Société Astronomique de France a year later. Some of his observations were published in Flammarion's *Bulletin* and four of his Mars renderings, attesting to his marvelous powers of draftsmanship, appeared in the first Mars *Memoir* of the BAA.[11] These achievements positioned him on the same stage with some of the world's greatest planetary observers. Moreover, they captured the eye of Flammarion himself. The result was that Antoniadi came to France. It is not known who made the first overture. Possibly Antoniadi, in eagerness to leave Constantinople, first inquired of Flammarion about the availability of employment, but it is also possible that Flammarion made the offer after seeing Antoniadi's superb Mars drawings. Regardless, Antoniadi, much like Lowell, was prepared to seize his opportunity (*Occasionem cognosce*). He now cast his eye toward Europe, where new telescopic explorations of Mars (explorations as great as any on Earth) were fast underway. Indeed, Schiaparelli's discovery of the canals in 1877 had opened new portals to the imagination, while his new scheme of naming features on Mars after old geography and its associated mythology had Lowell praising him as the "Columbus of a new planetary world."[12]

At this moment Antoniadi was, as a portrait obtained in Constantinople shortly before his departure for France shows, an upright and handsome young man of twenty-three sporting a neatly waxed moustache; his lips look tight and his eyes peer out with restrained excitement. After his arrival in France, Flammarion employed him as an assistant at his Juvisy Observatory, equipped with a 24-centimeter (9.5-inch) Bardou refractor. It was located at Juvisy-sur-Orge, near the village of La Cour de France, some 30 kilometers (19 miles) by rail south of Paris. Here Flammarion had received as the bequest of an admirer an eighteenth-century chateau—complete with stables, servants' quarters, and a parklike setting. It was a site rich in historic associations; the kings of France had rested here on their journeys between Paris and Fountainbleau, and here, too, on March 30, 1814, l'Empereur Napoleon had first learned of the capitulation of Paris, an event that marked the downfall of his empire. (Later, after his return to power for the

Juvisy Observatory. (Courtesy Richard McKim)

Hundred Days and his final defeat at Waterloo, Napoleon, in bitter exile on St. Helena, would present a romanticized version of his career to an attentive British ship's surgeon, Barry Edward O'Meara [a distant relative of author O'Meara], the author of *A Voice from St. Helena.*)

In 1892, Flammarion had just published *La Planète Mars et ses conditions d'habitabilité,* the work that had so fired Lowell's imagination. At the prime of his powers, Flammarion regarded himself as the world's leading expert on Mars. Antoniadi must have found the small bearded Frenchman with a tidal wave of hair parted down the middle—whose fantastic visions about the red planet had stirred public opinion across the globe—a stimulating *tour de force.* But Antoniadi, too, was a man of solid foundation. Like Flammarion he was a self-assured visionary who sought truth in his astronomical endeavors. Both shared a love of Mars and a curiosity about life beyond Earth. No planet had offered them more promise than Mars of discovering the truth about humanity's place in the cosmos.

Mars must have long held an important place in Antoniadi's heart, for not only was it a possible abode for civilized life, but it carried the names of familiar places—names that hailed from his beloved classical mythology. Thanks to Schiaparelli's new nomenclature, Antoniadi could enjoy his love of the classics through his observations of Mars. To reach the observatory, Antoniadi would have to travel from his home in Paris to Juvisy and climb the stairs of the tower to avoid having to pass through Flammarion's private quarters. As the young man peered into the eyepiece of the Bardou refractor and looked upon that ruddy world with powers he had yet to realize, a new landscape unfolded before his eye.

Before he arrived at Juvisy, Antoniadi had used only a 11.4-centimeter (4.5-inch) Mailhut refractor. Now he was looking at Mars with a telescope with twice the aperture and four times the light-gathering power. Here were places, clearly seen, with names "whose sounds awakened such pleasant memories." Here was Hellas (Greece), home to his parents and the center of the world to those long gone. Here was Elysium, the abode of the blessed at the western bounds of the Earth—described by Homer in his *Odyssey* as a place where there is no snow, "no heavy storm, nor even rain, but ever does Ocean send up blasts of the shrill-blowing Zephyrus/West Wind." The planet's yellow-ocher plains dominated the disk, where he could see in the north Arcadia, named for a mountainous and inaccessible region in southern Greece, where "rural Acadians kept the old, untainted customs with their healthy strength and cheerfulness."[13] And Tempe, named after the charming Peneios valley south of Mount Olympus, "which in poetic language has become the embodiment for every beautiful valley area." In a sense when Antoniadi looked at Mars he was looking at his ancestral home projected across the corridors of space onto a globe that in every way seemed to mimic Earth. He peered at that world as any Martian would the Earth—with an unbridled yearning to understand. Schiaparelli had effectively refashioned Mars with a set of romantic and wistfully evocative names, whose power was not to be lost on the human capacity to yearn after lost paradises and conjure up nostalgic visions. And Antoniadi relished it.

What was this strange new world? Were there oceans, forests, and intelligent life? Antoniadi was curious but not grounded in any firm belief; he was on an adventure of exploration—the truth would have to reveal itself. Flammarion, however, certainly believed in Martians: "Being probably more advanced than ourselves in its planetary age, Martian humanity is most likely more reasonable and is not mixed up with the littleness of frontiers, dialects, customs, national rivalries. . . ."[14] Already a year before Antoniadi arrived at Juvisy, Flammarion, familiar with the experiments of

Edison, suggested that the natural magnetism of the Earth might be harnessed to propagate sounds across space in an attempt to communicate with the Martians. "It would be difficult for a human species to be less intelligent than ours," he added, "because we do not know how to behave and three-quarters of our resources are employed for feeding soldiers."

For a modest salary of 300 francs a month, Antoniadi worked diligently eight hours a day, six days a week, day and night. Under the ebullient Frenchman's employ, Antoniadi's contributions to planetary science indeed blossomed, though Antoniadi probably looked at the situation differently—it was his presence and work that benefited the name of Flammarion and his observatory. In 1896 he became the director of the Mars Section of the British Astronomical Association and was made a Fellow of the Royal Astronomical Society in 1899.

Under Flammarion, Antoniadi's drawings of Mars were aesthetically superior versions of the canal-filled renderings of Schiaparelli and Lowell. Indeed, Antoniadi collaborated with Flammarion on creating several canal-filled maps of the planet. At this time Antoniadi was convinced (perhaps at Flammarion's suggestion) of the canals' existence. Gradually, however, Antoniadi began to have doubts about the reality of the canals. As early as 1896–97, only the second opposition he observed at Juvisy, he found them "very difficult objects, visible only by rare glimpses," and added that but for "Prof. Schiaparelli's wonderful discoveries, and the fore-knowledge that 'the canals are there,' " he claimed he would have missed three-quarters of those he recorded on his chart of the planet. As a gifted artist as well as an astronomer, Antoniadi was well aware of the truth of something described by the great English artist and art critic John Ruskin as the "law of mystery": "the law, namely, that nothing is ever seen perfectly, but only by fragments, and under various conditions of obscurity."[15] Of course, Flammarion was also a gifted artist and astronomer, but in Antoniadi's view, his objectivity was blinded by his imagination. In a perfect world, men of science would, by definition, be open to new ideas; after all, science is the exploration of knowledge with no final truth. That Antoniadi would even question the reality of the canals under Flammarion's employ, however, proved fatal to their relationship. How could two men of solid ego and opposing opinion work pastorally under one dome?

Antoniadi struck a precarious balance by accepting that the linear markings existed as a visual phenomenon but not necessarily as true fur-

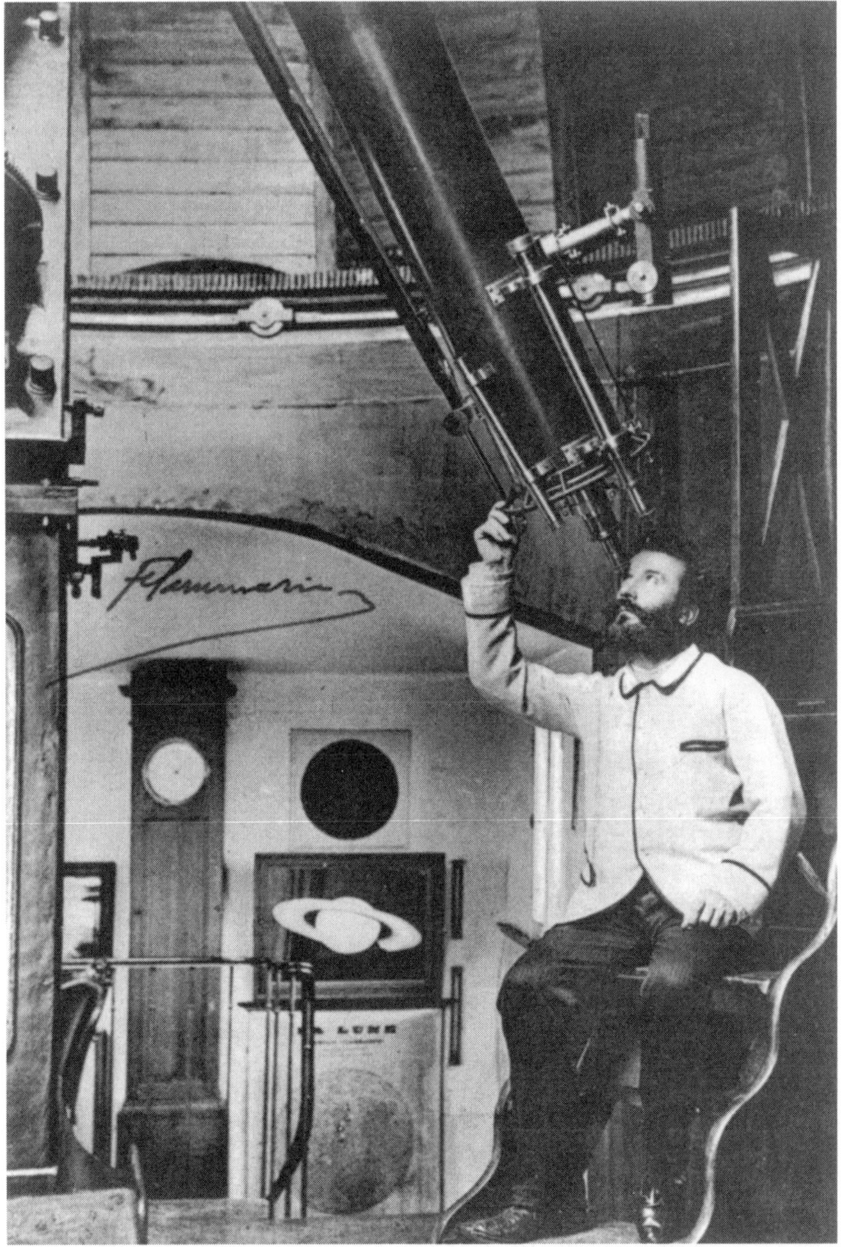

Camille Flammarion behind the eyepiece of the 24-centimeter (9-inch) Bardou refractor at his Juvisy Observatory. (Mary Lea Shane archives of the Lick Observatory)

rows on the planet. In his report on the observations of Mars of 1896–97, he found it prudent to throw out the work of at least one embarrassingly prolific canal enthusiast, C. Roberts, who despite using only a 16-centimeter (6.5-inch) reflector recorded no less than 134 canals on his highly stylized drawings. And when he summarized the observations from 1898–99, Antoniadi included this cautionary comment: "Notwithstanding the natural skepticism of many scientific men, every opposition brings with it its own contingent of confirmations of Schiaparelli's discovery of linear markings, apparently furrowing the surface of the planet Mars. The difference between objective and subjective in the daedelian phenomena presented by these appearances will be the work of future generations. But the value of the great Italian results will be everlasting."

Antoniadi's doubts about the canals increased still further in 1902, when he finally characterized his position as "agnostic." His attitude had also grown sarcastic, and his health had begun to fail—long, cold nights at the telescope, coupled with long hours at the office (not to mention the deteriorating conditions in his relationship with Flammarion) added to a growing frailty of his mind and body. Some of his complaints, at least, were psychosomatic. The English astronomer Edward Maunder's wife, Annie, complained that Antoniadi worried too much. "Poor M. Antoniadi," she confided to a colleague in August 1900. "He is a first-class observer, but I think he has imbibed in Paris a little of the French touchiness." Then in December she revealed that "M. Antoniadi has decided to become an Englishman. . . . He says he could not stand M. Flammarion any longer."[16] Indeed, by 1902 Antoniadi had felt the need to go his own way. He resigned his position under Flammarion, and at the same time he published a chart of Mars from which he carefully excluded all trace of the canals.

On the brighter side, Antoniadi had just married Katharine Sevastupulo, a member of one of the leading families in Paris's Greek community; like Eugene, Katherine was born in Turkey and seems to have had independent means. In any case, the marriage was good for Antoniadi, because his health soon began to improve. "He seems stronger and less sensitive," Annie Maunder wrote in February 1903, "and with a much keener sense of humour. He hopes to come and live in England some time—and how he does hate the French!"[17] Although Antoniadi briefly flirted with becoming an Englishman, he decided at last to remain in

France; he and Katharine found an apartment on the Rue Jouffroy, in one of the most expensive districts in Paris, and there they remained for many years. As his compatriot Audouin Dollfus later explained, the man did not really hate France, for he was a "*grand admirateur de la culture française*."

For several years Antoniadi gave up much of his astronomical work, instead concentrating on an intensive study of the architecture of the Mosque of Saint Sophia in Constantinople; an endeavor that eventually led to the publication of a three-volume work on the subject (*Atlas of the Mosque of St. Sophia,* 1907). Antoniadi received special permission to pursue this "formidable labour" from none other than the "Red" Sultan, Abdülhamid II himself.

Once Antoniadi finished his work on the Mosque, he returned his gaze skyward, for Mars beckoned. In 1909 he knew the red planet would make one of its closest approaches to Earth, sweeping within 58 million kilometers (36 million miles). If ever there were a time to seek irrefutable evidence for the existence or nonexistence of the Martian canals, this would be it. To help Antoniadi toward this end, Henri Deslandres, the director of the Meudon Observatory, placed the 83-centimeter (32.7-inch) *Grande Lunette*—then, as now, the largest refractor in Europe, and the third largest in the world—at his disposal for the favorable opposition. So once again Antoniadi appeared on the astronomical stage, this time to play the greatest role of his life.

Even before he received the invitation to observe at Meudon, Antoniadi had been studying Mars with his own 22-centimeter (8.5-inch) reflector. In August, he found the markings on the planet unusually pale, as if covered with a pale lemony haze. On August 12, "it was nearly impossible to see patches normally as dark as the Mare Tyrrhenum, Syrtis Major, and the Sinus Sabaeus! It was truly a unique spectacle. On the following days Mare Cimmerium began to be lightly obscured, and the yellow cloud . . . covered almost the whole of the planet." As we now know, Mars was then in the throes of a planetwide dust storm—the first such event ever observed. The planet's atmosphere gradually cleared during later August and September; fortunately it was almost completely clear—apart from a "brass-coloured veil" that remained in suspension over Hellas—by the time Antoniadi began his work at Meudon.[18]

On September 20, 1909, Antoniadi had his first and best night with the great refractor. His experience can almost be described as spiritual, for it

Meudon Observatory. (Stephen O'Meara collection)

would change his view of Mars forever. Just being at Meudon must have humbled the great man. It was here, in Meudon—this picturesque Paris suburb on the south bank of the Seine—that the nineteenth-century impressionist painters Manet and Renoir and the sculptor Rodin all had their studios. The dome that houses *La Grande Lunette* is gothic. Built on the foundations of a seventeenth-century castle, badly damaged by the Prussians during the Siege of Paris in 1871, it rises on the edge of a high terrace that slips unimpeded to the Meudon Park below, from which one enjoys a splendid panoramic view of the city of Paris, including the Eiffel Tower, shrunk with distant perspective to the size of a thumb held at arm's length. At night, the silhouette of the 18-meter (60-foot) dome would have stood out boldly against the heavens, like a cathedral's grand cupola against the stars. If Antoniadi arrived through the western entrance, he would have passed through a colonnade reflecting the traditions of ancient Greek architecture, which could only have warmed his spirit with haunting memories of his beloved classics. His heart probably did warm with anticipation as he approached the doors leading to the venerable telescope, for what grandeur and elegance awaited him. The *Grande Lunette* is a masterpiece of glass and steel—a twin leviathan built by the Henry brothers, Paul and Prosper, consisting of a 83-centimeter (32.7-inch) visual telescope coupled with a 62-centimeter (24.4-inch) photographic refractor. Both telescopes share a single tube 16 meters (52.5 feet) long. This impressive empress of the air is mounted on a steel pier that stands 24 meters (80 feet) above the earth. To gain access to the eyepiece, the observer had to walk across the hard wooden floor, listening to his hollow footsteps echo under the massive dome, until he reached a long platform that raised and lowered on a system of giant rails and pulleys. Riding the platform off the floor, he would have seen only a long vertical strip of starlight through the dome's narrow slit as the business end of *La Grande Lunette* approached. Darkness would have swallowed everything else around him. And when the platform stopped, Antoniadi would have looked out from that lofty perch and seen the telescope's lengthy tube pointing to Mars bleeding in the black night. If he was true to his nature, the man would not have rushed to the eyepiece. Like an artist studying a canvass for the first time, or an explorer looking into the distance at a mountain he must climb, he would have taken a moment to reflect upon that mountain Mars to "make him realize / The mountain he was climbing had the slant," to quote Robert Frost.[19]

Mars through the great refractor would have been dazzling. Compared to Flammarion's 23-centimeter (9-inch) telescope, the *Grande Lunette* was 3.5 times larger in aperture but had 12 times the light-gathering power. Mars in the eyepiece at the telescope's usual magnification—Antoniadi thought 320X best—loomed nearly three times the diameter of the full Moon seen with the unaided eye. But planets seen through large telescopes are more susceptible than through small telescopes to turbulence in Earth's constantly moving atmosphere; astronomers call this turbulence "seeing," and Antoniadi measured it on a scale from I ("glorious") to V ("appalling").

Understanding the concept of "seeing" is integral to understanding the canal controversy, so it is necessary to explore this further.

The reason a large telescope is more susceptible to "seeing" than a small telescope is simple: A large telescope collects light from a larger area of sky than a small telescope, so there's more turbulence to see. During moments of "perfect seeing," a planet will appear rock steady and details on its surface will resolve into sharply defined shapes. In "bad seeing," the planetary image will move erratically—it will shimmer, blur, distort, or

La Grand Lunette. (Stephen O'Meara collection)

enlarge—creating spurious details on the disk. A terrestrial analogy of bad seeing would be, say, looking at a bird seen above the hot pavement on a summer's day or through the turbulent air rising above a barbecue grill.

The state of Earth's atmosphere governs the resolving power of a telescope or its ability to see fine details like the canals on Mars. Theoretically, the larger the aperture, the greater the resolving power. So larger telescopes can see finer details than smaller telescopes. The difference is akin to seeing the arm of a man verses the individual hairs, pores, and freckles on its skin. Unfortunately, the atmosphere rarely remains stable long enough to allow large telescopes to reach their theoretical limits of resolution. That's why planetary observers have had to accustom themselves to spending long hours behind the eyepiece, waiting through long periods of bad seeing in hopes of a fleeting moment or two of perfect seeing that will bring the image into crystal clarity. If the atmosphere cooperates, a skilled planetary observer, through fits and starts, can capture details on a planet at or near the telescope's theoretical limit of resolution. This patient manner of observing best exemplifies the method practiced by Antoniadi and Barnard.

Another way an astronomer can turn a night of bad seeing into a night of good, or at least tolerable, seeing is to "stop down" the telescope. This is achieved by making a mask with a hole smaller than the diameter of the lens and placing it over the lens. In essence, the astronomer is "switching" telescopes, substituting for one with large aperture another of smaller aperture while keeping the focal length of the instrument the same. By doing so he sacrifices resolving power for steadiness. Unlike Antoniadi and Barnard, Percival Lowell preferred to stop down his 61-centimeter (24-inch) telescope, usually to 30 or 46 centimeters (12 or 18 inches). The difference in observing styles may seem perfunctory, a simple matter of prerogative. But the issue was the outrageous arrow fired in letters across the Atlantic that Antoniadi and Lowell used in vain to wound one another during the great canal controversy.

The volley began shortly before Antoniadi started work with the *Grande Lunette*. In a letter to Lowell, Antoniadi informed the great champion of the canals that he was about to embark on his visual journey to Mars with the great refractor. By return post, Lowell offered this advice: "I am glad that you are to use the Meudon refractor but remember that you will have to [stop] it down to get the finest details. Even here we find 12 to 18 inches [30 to 46 centimeters] the best sizes."

Before this letter arrived, however, Antoniadi had already trained the *Grand Lunette* on Mars. From the terrace at Meudon, because of the sheer drop to the Meudon Park below, the seeing is generally very good for objects east of the meridian. To the west, there is no such drop, and air currents from the ground exert more deleterious effects, with the result that the seeing often deteriorates rapidly as objects climb into the sky. But on the night of September 20—with Mars a red coal burning close to a nearly full Moon in the sky—a temperature inversion occurred over Paris; the air had arranged itself into stratified layers. The lower layer of air over Meudon was a settled claim and the seeing fantastically still. Peering into the eyepiece, Antoniadi could hardly believe his eyes. He experienced something akin to an astronomical miracle, for the image of Mars remained "glorious" for two hours:[20] "The first glance cast at the planet on September 20 was a revelation," he wrote. "The planet appeared covered with a vast and incredible amount of detail held steadily, all natural and logical, irregular and chequered, from which geometry was conspicuous by its complete absence." A "maze of complex markings" covered the south part of Syrtis Major, which was then approaching the central meridian; the deserts of Libya and Hesperia appeared shaded, while Mare Tyrrhenum looked "like a leopard skin." Antoniadi described the land between Syrtis Major and Hellas as being "like a green meadow, sprinkled with tiny white spots of various sizes, and diversified with darker or lighter shades of green."

Five days after these breathtaking views of the planet, Antoniadi wrote excitedly to W. H. Wesley, secretary of England's Royal Astronomical Society: "I have seen Mars more detailed than ever, and I pronounce the general configuration of the planet to be very irregular, and shaded with markings of every degree of darkness. Mars appeared in the giant telescope very much like the Moon, or even like the aspect of the Earth's surface such as I saw it in 1900 from a balloon at a great height (12,000 feet)."

Antoniadi continued to observe and draw the planet but never again would see the planet with the same clarity as on that marvelous night. "We had only two really good nights at Meudon," he later wrote to Barnard, "and two or three others more or less satisfactory." But the observations procured on these nights were more than enough to convince him of the illusory nature of the canals. "By utilizing the best moments," he continued, "I managed to resolve almost one-third of the 'canals' into . . . larger components."

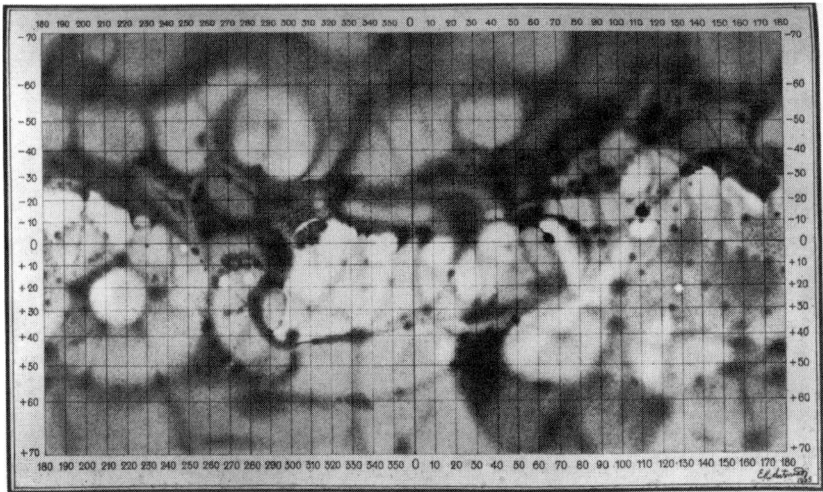

Antoniadi's great map of Mars, 1930. (Courtesy Audouin Dollfus)

On October 9, three days after he had another night of "excellent definition," Antoniadi fired off yet another excited letter. This time it went to Lowell. The letter started off full of praise: "I am extremely indebted to you for your letter of the 26th . . . and, above all, for the marvelous photographs you are taking of the planet Mars. . . . The photograph of Juventae Fons, with its two minute 'canals', *is the greatest example* ever obtained in planetary photography, and is an achievement above praise." He then offered Lowell four of his drawings obtained with the *Grand Lunette.* Each was a visual thrust from Antoniadi's sword—none of the drawings showed canals, but where there would have been canals in Lowell's representations, Antoniadi instead showed a series of disconnected patches. He added: "The tremendous difficulty was not to see the detail, but accurately to *represent* it. Here, my experience in drawing proved of immense assistance, as, after my excitement at the bewildering amount of detail visible was over, I sat down and drew correctly, both with regard to form and intensity, all the markings visible. . . . However, one third of the minute features I could not draw; the task being above my means."

Perhaps as a gesture to sooth the exuberant tone of his letter, Antoniadi offered as a postscript, "Any differences between our drawings must be due to clouds on Mars." He can hardly have believed this, however.

Antoniadi's letter must have come as a shock to Lowell, who had been observing the red planet now for thirteen years with the 61-centimeter (24-inch) refractor at Flagstaff. In those thirteen years, Lowell had formed a "religion" based on his unshakable belief in the canals and on the need to stop down a telescope's aperture to gain resolution. Now here was a letter from an observer Lowell likely considered as a callow youth—in fact, Antoniadi, at thirty-nine, was the same age Lowell had been when he founded his observatory on Mars Hill—who after only two weeks of observing was challenging the foundations of Lowell's beliefs.

Lowell offered a pointed response: "This is the great danger with a large aperture—a seeming superbness of image when in fact there is a fine imperceptible blurring which transforms the detail really continuous into apparent patches. . . . This subject we have carefully investigated here and all of our observers recognize it." Lowell did not forget to return Antoniadi's parry, and he did so by enclosing some of his own Mars drawings, complete with the canals as continuous lines. But this was not Lowell's final thrust, for the great canalist added this rather perverse remark: "The one [drawing] you marked tremulous definition strikes me as the best. It is capital." This one drawing, needless to say, was the only one that showed canals. The others, which had shown the planet as it had looked in "moderate," "splendid," and "glorious" seeing, he dismissed as "not so well defined."

Although Antoniadi remained respectful, even deferential, to Lowell in his correspondence, we see a certain arrogance in his report of the 1909 apparition to the British Astronomical Association, where he scoffs at drawings showing canals, declaring, "It is high time that evidence of this kind should be pronounced worthless; and but for such uncertain data, usually obtained with inferior telescopes, there would never have been a question of the canals on Mars." Although Antoniadi conceded that he, too, had seen "the fleeting apparition of hideous straight lines" on Mars even with the Meudon refractor, he explained that the lines were visible only when the seeing conditions deteriorated. And in a letter to Wesley dated October 30, Antoniadi concluded, "the spider's webs of Mars are doomed to become a myth of the past."

Antoniadi did not ignore Lowell's response, however. In his reply to Lowell, he politely but firmly disagreed:

> You have a great advantage in your *splendid* atmosphere, an advantage which requires no proof. In 1909 I had the advantage of *separating* power.

> I understand from your letter that you consider my knotted Mare Tyrrhenum as due to blurring; but I beg to call your attention to the fact that I was holding steadily this knotted structure; and that two days ago, I found this particular knotted appearance confirmed by photography. . . . I am glad to say that photography shows Mars in 1909 as I saw him. . . . I base all my ideas of Mars on what I saw myself at Meudon; and as I have not seen any geometrical canal network, I am inclined to consider it as an optical symbol of a more complex structure of the Martian deserts, whose appearance is quite irregular to my eye. . . . Do you think that your telescope, stopped to 12 or 15 inches, can really be considered to have a separating power comparable to an aperture of 33 inches . . . ? I would never stop down a perfect object glass.

Antoniadi closed his letter with a plea: "I hope you will excuse some differences of opinion I may have. We both work honestly for the discovery of truth; and we are both eager to accept the truth, even at the hands of a scientific foe, if necessary."

Needless to say, Lowell's opinion of Mars could not be changed—not by Antoniadi who saw no canals with the Meudon 84-centimeter (33-inch) telescope, nor by Barnard who had seen none with the Lick 91.4-centimeter (36-inch) refractor in 1894, nor any through the Yerkes 1-meter (40-inch) refractor in 1909, nor by George Ellery Hale who observed Mars in 1909 with the Mount Wilson 1.5-meter (60-inch) reflector, then the most powerful telescope in use in the world. Hale wrote that while he had been "able to see a vast amount of intricate detail," he found "no trace of narrow straight lines or geometrical structures." But it was Antoniadi who became the most vigorous advocate of the crushing superiority of large telescopes for visual planetary work. In a letter dated December 11, 1909, he summarized his thoughts to Barnard:

> My general conclusions on the "canals" are:
>
> I. That the true appearance of the planet's surface is a natural one;
>
> II. That the geometrical network of Dr. Lowell is entirely non-existent; and
>
> III. That the so-called "canals" of Schiaparelli (and Schiaparelli only) do have some objective basis,—in this sense, that they are the optical products of very complex and irregular natural duskiness, sporadically scattered all over the Martian surface.

> I am quite sure of all this, so that I fail to see the possibility of ever changing from such a position. It would almost be absurd to speak of true canals on Mars. If such exist, they will forever remain invisible to us.

Although Barnard, Hale, and others were quick to praise Antoniadi's work, the canal controversy was prolonged well into the next decades. "The chief trouble with Antoniadi," Lowell said privately, "is that he is a man without knowledge of how to observe." Thanks to the passage of time, we can now say with confidence that Antoniadi did indeed know how to observe—we can compare his drawings of Mars with CCD images of the planet, which show as nothing else the remarkable powers of his eye-hand coordination—and there is no arguing with his conclusions about the canals. In all fairness to Lowell, however, many skillful observers have supported his practice of diaphragming large lenses to get the best match to the seeing—though the superiority of large instruments seems to be, based on our own experience, less a matter of the separating power emphasized by Antoniadi and more a matter of increasing the saturation of the delicately hued features that mottle the Martian disk; the larger the aperture, the purer the colors and hence the more magnificent and stunning the view.

Antoniadi resigned from the British Astronomical Association and surrendered his directorship of the Mars Section in 1911. He returned to Meudon as an unpaid observer in 1924, the year that Mars made its closest approach to the Earth in the twentieth century. Although Lowell had passed from the scene, the canal controversy hadn't. Not only was Lowell's staff at Flagstaff, especially pioneer planetary photographer Earl C. Slipher, carrying the torch for the canals, but a distinguished Lick Observatory astronomer, Robert J. Trumpler, had viewed Lowell's canals with the same instrument Barnard had used in 1894. It cannot be denied, he wrote, "that the better defined canals show a strange directness of line; mostly, but not always straight nor following a great circle, they are at least always smooth continuous lines without break unless an oasis or intersection with another canal is met."[21] Though views of the canals with large instruments were hardly common, they did occur often enough to keep the controversy boiling right into the spacecraft era (see "The Canals of Mars" sidebar). Illusion they may have been, but a compelling illusion, at times even to the most experienced and best equipped observers.

Antoniadi remained undistracted. In 1930 he published a comprehen-

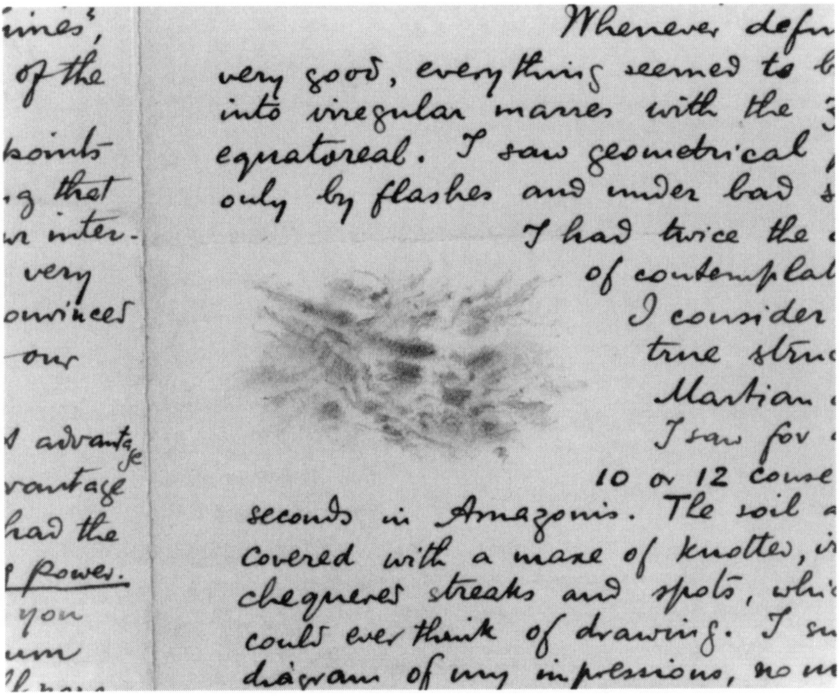

Antoniadi's impressionistic sketch of detail in the Amazonis desert. (Lowell Observatory)

sive summary of his Martian work, *Le Planète Mars*, an impressive publication in which he presents a series of comparative drawings of the planet, all executed in meticulous stipple style, which shows the canals resolved into vague, variously shaded, but distinctly separate features. But the heart of the book is Antoniadi's corrected, updated, and systematized scheme of Schiaparelli's nomenclature for the planet's topography. His background in classical literature made him the perfect man for the task; in all the book includes 560 names complete with summaries of each feature's observational history. "This [book]," writes William Graves Hoyt "combined with later photographic work with large telescopes at prime locations tended to reduce the canal controversy, if not the question of Martian life, to the status of an historical curiosity."[22]

By reading Antoniadi's book and his 1909 report "On the Possibility of explaining on a Geomorphic Basis the Phenomenon presented by the Planet Mars," we get our first glimpse of a canal-less Mars. "We thus see in the so-called 'canals' a work of Nature, not of Intellect," Antoniadi said,

The Canals of Mars

During much of the period of human fascination with Mars, discussion centered on the canals. It is now obvious that they do not exist; but if they do not exist, why did so many observers report seeing them—and why do some observers continue to see them to this very day?

The principal reason is that the human eye, for all its many fine qualities, did not evolve principally in order to study fine detail on small planetary disks. It evolved for survival. The eye is primarily adapted to emphasize contrasts at boundaries and edges, which makes it extraordinarily sensitive to lines. Almost any rough alignment of splotches will trigger its linear detection features. Thus, there is some truth to Antoniadi's claim that, under higher resolving power or better seeing conditions, the canal-covered networks of Schiaparelli, if not Lowell—Antoniadi was always less generous to Lowell—gave way to "winding, irregular knotted streaks, or broad irregular bands, or groups of complex shadings, or isolated dusky spots, or jagged edges of half-tones."

Antoniadi's drawings of the planet convey these impressions beautifully. They are, indeed, the renderings of an impressionist—someone who believed that the underlying reality of Mars was better represented by dots or dashes of paint than by the rule and compass of the draftsman. He was the Manet or Renoir of Mars. Now that we have CCD images and Hubble Space Telescope images showing the real Mars, we can judge his representations against the reality. We can now judge that he was indeed a gifted observer and artist; and yet in a way his impressionism turns out to be just as stylized as the Schiaparellian and Lowellian diagrams. Though uncannily accurate in his depiction of broad features, when it comes to the finer details he, too, includes much that is illusory. In particular, many of the knotted, irregular, checkered streaks and spots filling his drawings of the Martian deserts do not exist; they seem to be quite as illusory as most of the spidery Lowellian lines. Apparently, people tend to "see" detail down to the limit of their vision, whether it is present in the image or not!

And what, then, were those lines so obsessively depicted by Lowell? Not quite figments of his imagination. They seem to have had a basis in reality in the odd irregular dusky splotch or series of dots each individually below the threshold of vision. With the eye stretched to its limits, these fragmentary details were enough to stimulate the hairtrigger linear-detection capabilities mentioned above and were registered in consciousness as lines.

The Martian canals are undoubtedly the most famous illusion in all astronomy. Even now, and knowing better as we do, they can sometimes appear—in startling Lowellian moments—with all the conviction of truth. And it is simply not true, as is sometimes alleged, that large instruments fail to show them. Consider the following comments by Larry Webster, a skilled observer who for many years has been in charge of observing at one of the solar towers on Mt. Wilson:

"Now I have my own story about Mars and its—ahem!—'canals.' I've seen them myself. Now before you start writing up the papers to have me committed to Las Encinas, let me explain. When I first came to the observatory, I worked for about nine months on the 100-inch [2.5-meter] telescope as a night assistant. At that time I really didn't know much about astronomy, let alone the history of astronomy, but I did know there were no such things as canals on Mars. When the seeing at the 100-inch is good, it can be very good—in fact, it can be extraordinary! During my nine-month position there were several times when the seeing was sub-arc second. During times like these the astronomer using the telescope would often drop his or her observing program to do just what you or I would want to do, that is go looking around at neat stuff. Among the objects I remember seeing during these times were the dwarf companion of Sirius, Saturn's moon Titan as a perfectly round orange disk, and one of the inner ring gaps of Saturn perfectly well-defined where normally one would not see it at all. Anyway, one night in late 1981 or early 1982, when I was no longer working on the 100-inch, the seeing was again extraordinary. Roger and Rita Griffin were using the telescope at the Coudé focus, and a few employees of the observatory, including myself, just happened to be outside the dome. Roger saw us from the catwalk and called us all down into the Coudé room to have a look around. Since Mars was up, he decided to go for it. With the perfect seeing conditions, 100-inch aperture, and 254-foot [77-meter] focal length, it was glorious! I remember the motionless disk as being reddish-orange with dark green patches on it, and one could also easily see one clear white polar patch. But here is the really interesting part: As I looked at the image of Mars floating in the eyepiece, I saw what seemed to be very thin straight lines crisscrossing all over the surface between those dark patches! They would come and go, but they really were there. Being something of a novice in this business of visual planetary observing, I was reluctant to call serious attention to what I had seen to the others in the room. However, I do remember saying something like: "Wow, the seeing is so good, I can see the canals!" Whereupon everyone chuckled. (They didn't know how serious I was, and I didn't push the issue.) I did bring it up later a few times during dinner at the Monastery, but I was hesitant to insist on what I had

"the spots relieving the gloom of a wilderness, and not the Titanic productions of supernatural beings. To account for their various phenomena, we need only invoke the natural agencies of vegetation, water, cloud, and inevitable differences of colour in a desert region."

Antoniadi's Mars was a natural world. Indeed, through his eyes we get our first glimpse since Barnard's of the planet's soil, which "appears covered with a maze of knotted, irregular, chequered streaks and spots."[23] For the first time a man had grasped the true character of the Martian deserts. In a desert known as Amazonis he saw the surface "diversified with the faintest imaginable dusky areas, and marbled with irregular, undulating filaments, the representation of which was evidently beyond the powers of any artist. There was nothing geometrical in all this, nothing artificial, the whole appearance having something overwhelmingly natural about it." Antoniadi, even with his remarkable artistic skill, despaired of recording all these details, but he did provide Lowell an impressionistic sketch of what he had seen. There is a striking similarity between this sketch and the *Mariner 9* and *Viking* imagery, which shows that Antoniadi had indeed recorded the real structure of the surface of this part of the planet.

With the spiderweb network of canals dusted off the globe, to his satisfaction at least, Antoniadi focused his attention on trying to decipher the planet's speckled patterns and changing colors. His work became the bud seen, and if anyone else saw the canals that night, they didn't mention it either.

"For almost twenty years I wondered about that night and what I observed. Was I imagining these straight lines? Was I predisposed and then imagined them? Was there some sort of optical phenomenon going on? Finally, I happened across an interesting paper by one of the old Mt. Wilson astronomers, Edison Pettit, entitled 'The Canals of Mars,' in which he describes how on one night when the seeing conditions were just right and he was using a 6-inch [15-centimeter] refractor, he observed the 'canals' on Mars! Now I have much more respect for Schiaparelli, Lowell, and others who reported seeing lines on the surface of Mars. There is no doubt in my mind that under the right conditions straight lines crisscrossing the planet's disk will be seen!"

of a new branch of science—the study of comparative geology on the so-called terrestrial planets. By comparing the colors he saw in certain features on Mars with those he saw in the landscapes on Earth, he tried to deduce their nature. Of the sands of Mars, Antoniadi had no doubt, especially in those regions that wore a reddish hue, small parts of Thaumasia, Aethiopis, and "some of the southern islands of smoky vermilion color—[these] do seem to be deserts." "The continental wildernesses of the planet," he said, "occupy an area almost ten times larger than that of our Sahara together with the deserts of Libya and Nubia."[24] Indeed, the whole surface of Mars, as we now know, is littered with dunes. Some of the red soil he attributed to volcanic origin. Although he never witnessed signs of volcanic activity, he believed the "frequent and cindery aspect of the red land" and the yellow atmospheric clouds were manifestations of it. Even today we have never witnessed volcanic activity on Mars, but we do know the red rocks of its surface are due to oxidized iron in basaltic lavas. And some of the channels (discovered by Schiaparelli and confirmed by Antoniadi) can be identified in spacecraft images as true canyons. Even Antoniadi's observations of the Martian atmosphere touch upon post-spacecraft era reality: "Winds are feeble, whitish clouds inconsistent and transparent; but on the other hand there will be more yellow clouds than are found above terrestrial deserts." He talks of cirrus clouds, of Martian snows in the polar regions, and of the porosity of the rocks and a gradual flowing of waters into the interior of the planet: "But even if there cannot be much water on the surface, this does not preclude the possibility of any water on Mars." How profound that statement seems now that we know water has indeed rushed across the Martian surface in the past, and may still leak out, from time to time, from underground sources.

Of course, Antoniadi was not infallible. For instance, although he did not believe that the dark areas (maria) were seas (for there was, he pointed out, no solar specular reflection in them), he remained true to the Lowellian orthodoxy in believing them to be tracts of vegetation, whose color changed with the seasons. And though he disputed the canals, he did not rule out the possibility of intelligent Martian life, at least in the past history of the planet:

> The observations of clouds at considerable heights shows that though the atmosphere of Mars is very thin, it is still able to hold ice needles or water droplets in suspension—or even particles of dust. Therefore the atmosphere does not seem to be too rarefied for living things. . . . In this connection we must bear in mind that the people of Tibet have no difficulty in breathing in an atmosphere twice as rarefied as ours. If, then, we consider also life's marvelous power of adaptation, one of the aims of the Creator of the Universe, we can see that the presence of animals or even human beings on Mars is far from improbable. . . . However, it seems that advanced life must have been confined to the past, when there was more water on Mars than there is now; today we can expect nothing more than vegetation around the vast red wilderness of the planet.[25]

Antoniadi continued to use the great Meudon refractor until his death on February 10, 1944, from "an incurable complaint," which may have been heart disease. (Curiously, his death preceded by only a few months that of Abdülmecid II, the last caliph and crown prince of the Ottoman dynasty of Turkey, who had been living in exile in Paris since 1924.) France was under German occupation, and Antoniadi, whose apartment was near the *Arc de Triomphe,* no doubt witnessed many of the daily formal parades, where a jackbooted company of the Wehrmacht in full regalia would march beneath the *Arc de Triomphe*, to the accompaniment of a band playing the march "Precious Glory." He did not live to see the liberation of Paris by the Allies in August 1944.

In the end, he had become an anachronistic figure, his outlook more in tune with the nineteenth century than the twentieth. "My aversion to XXth century speculation," he once wrote, "and its infectious breath, is founded on the impossible 4th-dimensional spatial theories of Einstein; on [the] accurate enumeration, by Eddington, of the particles composing the universe, the number of whose suns and worlds will eternally remain an insolvable mystery. . . . Perhaps the most important discovery of Jeans is that St. Paul's cathedral contains as many flies as the universe's stars and planets."[26] As an old man living in an occupied city, with his health failing, Antoniadi became depressed, and before he died seems have taken all his records on Mars and destroyed them. With that gesture we end another curious legacy—one of a man whose only ambition in life was, as he had written to Barnard in 1913, "to defend the truth and write nothing susceptible of being overthrown."

His greatest triumph had been to remove from Mars the mask of illusory canals and to reveal instead the solid bedrock and shifting sands of the planet's true topography.

Part III

The Mars of Romance

11

Invaders from Mars

A credulous mind . . . finds most delight in believing strange things, and the stranger they are the easier they pass with him; but never regards those that are plain and feasible, for every man can believe such.

—Samuel Butler,
Characters (1667–1669)

“Few western wonders are more inspiring than the beauties of an Arizona moonlit landscape; the silvered mountains in the distance, the strange lights and shadows upon hog back and arroyo, and the grotesque details of the stiff, yet beautiful cacti form a picture at once enchanting and inspiring; as though one were catching for the first time a glimpse of some dead and forgotten world, so different is it from the aspect of any other spot on earth.

"As I stood thus meditating, I turned my gaze from the landscape to the heavens where the myriad stars formed a gorgeous and fitting canopy for the wonders of the earthly scene. My attention was quickly riveted by a large red star close to the distant horizon. As I gazed upon it I felt a spell of overpowering fascination—it was Mars. . . ."

These words, written in 1911, might almost have been those of Percival Lowell. Instead they were those of a hitherto unknown writer who had once served in an undistinguished capacity with the U.S. Army in southern Arizona—hence the eyewitness feel of his prose. They were written at the very time Lowell was observing Mars with his telescope at Flagstaff. He was a man with an imagination quite as powerful as Lowell's, but unlike Lowell, he could ill afford a telescope. Instead of attempting to make his claims on science and reason, he made his appeal directly to the human emotions.

His name was Edgar Rice Burroughs. As Lowell's canals were on the verge of being banished from respectable science by men like Antoniadi, Burroughs secured a safe haven for them in the immortal realms of the imagination. There is no doubt where Burroughs received his primary inspiration; not from British science fiction pioneer H. G. Wells, as some would later allege, but from Lowell. In Burroughs's first science fiction novel, *A Princess of Mars*, he grandly and unmistakably called forth a Lowellian Mars of dead sea-bottoms, dry-dust deserts, canals, and hurtling moons. "Theirs is a hard and pitiless struggle for existence upon a dying planet," Burroughs wrote of his Martians. "The people had found it necessary to follow the receding waters until necessity had forced upon them their ultimate salvation, the so-called Martian canals. . . ."

Edgar Rice Burroughs was born in 1875 to middle-class prosperity in Chicago's West Side. The youngest of four boys, Burroughs was a sensitive child with a quick wit and a propensity for humor. A literary flare also appeared at an early age; he wrote rhymes at the age of five, was a prolific letter writer by the age of six, and had immersed himself in Greek mythology in high school, though he failed to recognize this literary passion until much later in life, when all his hopes and dreams had seemingly vanished from sight. But young Burroughs was not a scholar, and he made a much better storyteller than a student. Irwin Porges, Burroughs's biographer, says the covers and margins of his school textbooks are marred with drawings and scribbles, suggesting that here sat a bored, young dreamer, a man with limited attention for matters not of his liking, and that included his studies. What Burroughs wanted most at that point in his life was a little adventure and excitement, which he was soon to get. Fear of an epidemic of la grippe in 1891, forced George Tyler Burroughs, Edgar's father, to remove his son from school. And, much to young Burroughs's delight, he was sent to Cassia County, Idaho, to join his older brothers George and Harry on their cattle ranch.

Cassia County of the 1890s was everything Chicago was not. Part of America's raw frontier, Idaho's dusty wilderness spawned a litany of ruffians and storybook characters—men who roped wild horses, spurred opponents in the back during barroom brawls, and got shot while evading arrest. Although these colorful stories fueled young Burroughs's imagination and sharpened his powers of observation, the fledgling cowboy did not participate in any of these antics himself. He was but a ranch hand performing random tasks, like grubbing sage brush and driving a team of broncos to a "sulky plow." The hard work and long hours toughened him, but Burroughs admits he "had proven more or less of a flop as a chore boy," and he returned to school in Chicago. But the brief Idaho experience had made its mark. Burroughs had sampled a carefree adventurous life, and the gritty taste of the West would not soon leave him.

In 1891 Burroughs attended Phillips Academy in Andover, Massachusetts, where he indulged in natural science, history, and literature. But his innate disinterest in scholastic matters led him to be dismissed within a year. That same year his father decided to enroll him in the Michigan Military Academy, which had a "sub rosa reputation as a polite reform school." Despite the academy's hard, rough-and-tumble life, Burroughs still found himself in trouble, and, "as usual," he was under arrest for "various diverse infractions of discipline." He was by this time an ornery urban cowboy with an uncontrollable desire for independence.

But something clicked inside Burroughs when Captain Charles King became the academy's commandant in 1892. Not only was King a firm leader with high morals and a heart for justice, but he had established himself as a writer, having authored several novels about army life in the West. Burroughs's adoration for this stately soldier who had helped tame the West was close to worship. Toward the end of 1894 (the same year that Lowell first promulgated his Martian canal theory), and six months before his graduation from the academy, Burroughs decided on his future—he would try to become a commissioned officer in the army.

His enlistment occurred on May 13, 1896, and the eager tenderfoot was assigned to the Seventh Calvary at Fort Grant, Arizona Territory. Located at the foot of Mount Graham, Fort Grant was a living hell, a fort with a crude and unhealthy reputation. Its timber and adobe buildings did not keep out the rain and were in constant need of fixing. A decade before Burroughs arrived, a shortage of water led to the construction of an artificial cement-lined lake ("Lake Constance") with a water and sewage system in the middle of the fort's parade ground. There, amid the scorching sun-baked lands of the Arizona desert, in the presence of an artificial lake with waterways, Burroughs was subjected to a prisonlike form of hard labor that consisted of road work, ditch digging, and "boulevard building." The coincidence that Burroughs was slaving in a desert near an artificial lake, digging ditches during the very height of Lowell's Martian canal fervor, is hard to overlook. Certainly his days in the desert, working in the very state whose northern mountains supported Lowell's famous observatory, must have colored his Martian fantasies.

Further evidence can be found in one of his harrowing journeys into the Arizona wilderness. In 1896 the Federal government had confined the Apaches to a nearby post, and everybody expected their tethered rage to snap imminently. "We were always expecting boots and saddles and praying for it," a hopeful Burroughs wrote, "for war would have better than camp life." That opportunity came none too soon for Burroughs. A man and his daughter had been murdered on the Solomonsville Trail and their wagon burned. The notorious Apache Kid, a dangerous outlaw, and his band of cutthroats were suspected, and Burroughs's B Troop was called into action.

Despite the exhilaration Burroughs must have felt about finally having an adventure, the young soldier must have also been quite apprehensive about the nightmarish three-day journey across the Arizona mountains. The bloody savagery of an Apache rampage was not a campfire story to frighten youngsters but a harsh reality. Corporal Josh, Burroughs's only Indian friend and a former Apache renegade, had shared the following story with Burroughs; it tells how Josh made amends to the U.S. Calvary by answering to a reward for the Apache Kid. Although Josh did not capture the Kid, Burroughs writes that

> he did the next best thing and killed one of the kid's relatives, cut off his victim's head, put it in a gunny sack, tied it to the horn of saddle and rode up from the Sierra Madres in Mexico to Fort Grant, where he dumped the head onto the floor of the headquarters and asked for forgiveness and probably a reward.

Few people at the time, it seemed, felt the horror and injustice of such a barbaric act by our military. Although Burroughs's search for the Apache Kid ended in failure, the adventure found its way into *A Princess of Mars,* which begins with John Carter and a friend prospecting in Arizona Territory:

> Since we had entered the territory we had not seen a hostile Indian, and we had, therefore, become careless in the extreme, and were wont to ridicule the stories we had heard of the great numbers of these vicious marauders that were supposed to haunt the trails, taking their toll in lives and torture of every white party which fell into their merciless clutches. . . . I was positive now that the trailers were Apaches and that they wished to capture Powell alive for the fiendish pleasure of the torture, so I urged my horse onward at a most dangerous pace, hoping against hope that I would catch up with the red rascals before they attacked him.

Aside from the daily tension of possible attacks by the neighboring Apaches, the overall humdrum of enlisted life failed to capture Burroughs's adventurous spirit. The romance and excitement of his army training was largely an illusion, and the burgeoning soldier returned disappointed to Chicago. Now at a prime age of twenty-two, Burroughs had "no goals or directions, and no understanding of himself or his nature."

Then, on February 15, 1898, the U.S.S. *Maine* mysteriously exploded under a moonlit sky in Havana Harbor, Cuba. Of the 266 men who lost their lives, nearly all were enlisted men—men like Burroughs, who had dreamed of moving up in the world by serving their country. The incident that sparked the Spanish-American War also rekindled a flame in Burroughs's heart for military action. When Colonel Theodore Roosevelt called to assemble his Rough Riders (a volunteer cavalry that would become famous for making a victorious charge at the Battle of San Juan Hill in Cuba) Burroughs requested action. Alas, Roosevelt wrote that he could not see bringing in a "man from such a distance." All further attempts Burroughs made to enter the war ended in frustration. The young man's dream of becoming a commissioned officer had finally come to a sad end.

Sometime in June 1898 Burroughs opened a stationery store in Pocatello, Idaho; it didn't survive the year. "God never intended me for a retail merchant," the frustrated Burroughs penned. So, as was customary, Burroughs once again joined his brothers on their cattle ranch. "It was during this Idaho experience," Burroughs's biographer Irwin Porges reveals, that "Ed suffered an odd and distressing experience that he never forgot." It happened in a saloon when a quarrel erupted:

> In 1899 I received a heavy blow on the head which, while it opened up the scalp, did not fracture the skull, nor did it render me unconscious, but for six weeks or two months thereafter I was the victim of hallucinations, always after I had retired I would see figures standing beside my bed, usually shrouded. I invariably sat up and reached for them, but my hands went through them. I knew they were hallucinations caused by my injury and did not connect them in any way with the supernatural, in which I do not believe.

"Being a creator of fantasies of other worlds filled with unrealistic incidents that might be considered wilder than any hallucinations was one thing," Porges shares. "But as a man of science on a real world, he firmly rejected the improbable or unprovable." And it was this understanding of reality versus fantasy that would ultimately help catapult him to fame.

A survey of all the later happenings in his life from 1894 on made it plain that Burroughs did not take a serious view of life. Indeed, until Burroughs had picked up the pen in 1911, he was the very antithesis of Lowell. Burroughs had failed miserably as an entrepreneur. His long desire to become a commissioned officer in the military, to engage in battle and taste the blood of his enemy, also never materialized. Even his inexhaustible lust for adventure was continually compromised by the lack of some inner stimulus, excitement, or confrontation.

By 1911 Burroughs would sum up his life at that point simply as " a flop." Ironically, what saved Burroughs was not so much the pen, but the very trait that had led to Lowell's demise—*imagination.* Although Lowell himself believed that imagination was genius, he perceived that his colleagues looked upon it in a different light:

> This word to the routine rabble of science is a red rag to a bull; partly because it is beyond their conception, partly because they do not comprehend how it is used. To their thinking to call a man imaginative is to damn him; when, did they but know it, it is admitting the very genius they would fain deny. For all great work imagination is vital; just as necessary in science and business as it is in novels and art.

And so it was to be for Burroughs. A man who firmly rejected the improbable or unprovable, Burroughs used his imagination not to prove the existence of Martians with science (as Lowell tried to do) but to make them believable in his fiction. And so it was in that year of conquest and challenge, when territorial ambition and social revolution stalked the world in 1911, that Lowell's mysterious red planet became the perfect stage for Burroughs's fictitious hero, Captain John Carter of Virginia, who would go forth on a series of heroic odysseys on Mars, encountering the very beings Lowell had already primed a curious public about.

Unlike the peaceful Martians Lowell envisioned, Burroughs's Martians possessed the greed and desires of mortal men. On Barsoom (as Burroughs called his fictitious Mars), as on Earth, there were warring factions, religious beliefs based on superstition, beings of different color, and tiers of social classes. Burroughs created a credible fantasy based on human reality. While Lowell tried to convince the world that his dying Martians accepted their plight in peace and harmony, Burroughs's pages burned with Martian Darwinism, allowing only the fittest to survive. Burroughs made his Mars and its inhabitants recognizable, understandable, perhaps even sensible. In *A Princess of Mars* Burroughs did not completely ignore Lowell's imaginings, for he incorporated the Bostonian's superior beings into his plot:

> The story is supposedly from the manuscript of a Virginian soldier of fortune, who spends ten years on Mars, among the ferocious green men of that planet as well as with the highly developed and scientific race of

> dominant Martians, who closely resemble the inhabitants of earth, except as to color. It is a member of this latter race which gives the story its name and at the same time infuses the element of love into the narrative.

That Virginian soldier, John Carter, who could will himself to Barsoom (Mars), would roam the dead sea bottoms and subterranean chambers of that dying planet, facing death time and time again. At each turn of the page, readers would find Carter immersed in any number of exciting adventures or battles, performing heroic feats and chivalrous actions, or romancing Dejah Thoris, the only woman he had room in his heart for.

Clearly, if Burroughs could not spill the blood of his enemy on the battlefield in real life, he could do it on paper. And if he could not achieve his dreams on Earth, he could excel in his fantasies on Mars. And so, during fitless nights of sleep, Burroughs would lay awake fabricating exotic creatures and fantastic plots. "As he wrote," Porges explains, "the real world of the commonplace became the unreal one; it vanished, and in its place he conjured up a strange fierce civilization set in the midst of a dying planet. The new world closed around him, all sounds of the old were gone, and he was a man lost in a perilous land where science battled against savagery, beauty against ugliness."

With his imagination unleashed, Burroughs played out his life as a fictitious superhero who would live between the covers of his books. "That was the key," Porges reveals, "the prayer of the escapists—*not to be like other men.*" And John Carter was not like other men. He was, as Burroughs writes,

> a splendid specimen of manhood, standing a good two inches over six feet, broad of shoulder and narrow of hip, with the carriage of the trained fighting man. His features were regular and clear cut, his hair black and closely cropped, while his eyes were of a steel gray, reflecting a strong and loyal character, filled with fire and initiative. His manners were perfect, and his courtliness was that of a typical southern gentleman of the highest type.

That Captain John Carter was a superhuman version of Burroughs is undeniable; one could also argue that Captain John Carter has more than a touch of Captain Charles King in his character, for King represented everything young Burroughs had hoped to achieve in the military but failed to do. As noted earlier, after Burroughs wrote *A Princess of Mars*, some critics supposed that he had borrowed the ideas from H. G. Wells's *The War of the Worlds*.

But Burroughs claimed he had never read any fiction before he started writing *A Princess of Mars,* and he said so in a letter dated May 31, 1918, which he sent to Joseph Bray, an editor at A. C. McClurg & Company:

> Will you tell me, please, when H. G. Wells wrote his Martian stuff or rather when it appeared? One critic calls attention to the fact that this story of Wells' and another story which I never heard of, suggested my Princess of Mars. As a matter of fact, I never read Wells' story and mine was written in 1911, it is possible that it anticipated Wells. Just for curiosity I should like to know.

Porges also argues against such an absurd innuendo:

> Any theory that *The War of the Worlds* even "suggested" the *Princess of Mars* is without logical evidence. Wells' novel, written in his coldly precise style in an attempt to create scientific realism, bears no resemblance to Ed's freely imaginative work with its fantastic characters and setting. In Wells' plot, centered about an invasion of our planet from Mars, the Martians become grotesque monsters; he makes no effort to develop them as individuals or to characterize them. Ed creates a bizarre civilization on Mars; in doing so, he was concerned with neither reality nor with scientific plausibility, although he did supply sufficient and ingenious details to give some semblance of reality. Students of Burroughs attribute much of his success as a storyteller to his knack of making the impossible seem as if it could really happen. . . . Ed's concept of a story, in contrast to Wells', was exaggeratedly romantic; he utilized all the popular ingredients—a beautiful lady, a dashing hero, a warped, sadistic villain, and of course, a love that surmounted all Obstacles.

As was discussed earlier, some of the scenes and plots in *A Princess of Mars* were drawn from Burroughs's experiences in the Martian-like desert at Fort Grant in the Arizona Territory. One could also argue that the princess herself appears to be fashioned after an Apache woman. Of the Apache women Burroughs saw during his stay at Fort Grant, Burroughs wrote:

> We saw little or nothing of their women, though several that I did see among the younger ones were really beautiful. Their figures and carriages were magnificent and the utter contempt in which they held the white soldier was illuminating to say the least.

This impression is reflected in Burroughs's portrait of Dejah Thoris, his fictitious Princess of Mars, when John Carter first sees her:

> She was standing with her guards before the entrance to the audience chamber, and as I approached she gave me one haughty glance and turned her back full upon me. The act was so womanly, so earthly womanly, that though it stung my pride it also warmed my heart with a feeling of companionship. . . . Had a green Martian woman desired to show dislike or contempt she would, in all likelihood, have done it with a sword thrust or a movement of her trigger finger; but as their sentiments are mostly atrophied it would have required a serious injury to have aroused such passions in them.

Even Burroughs's description of a sunrise over the Arizona desert,

> It was now morning, and, with the customary lack of dawn which is a startling characteristic of Arizona, it had become daylight almost without warning,

bears a striking resemblance to his description of a fictitious sunset on Mars:

> There is no twilight on Mars. When the great orb of day disappears beneath the horizon the effect is precisely as that of extinguishing of a simple lamp within a chamber. From brilliant light you are plunged without warning into utter darkness.

If there is any similarity between *The War of the Worlds* and *A Princess of Mars*, it is that both works are vehicles for expressing their author's views of society. Indeed, both works were written during times of intense hardships for their authors. When Wells wrote *The War of the Worlds* in 1897, he had fallen ill with consumption and was supporting two households; his life was cramped and painful and looked likely to be brutally brief. Before Burroughs started writing *A Princess of Mars*, he was poor and destitute, about to give up: "I had to pawn Mrs. Burroughs' jewelry and my watch to buy food," he wrote.

Both men viewed society with a hardened heart, and both men escaped their harsh environments by creating worlds of fantasy. "There's a quality in the worst of my so-called 'pseudo-scientific' (imbecile adjective) stuff," Wells wrote, "which differentiates it from Jules Verne, e.g. just as Swift is differentiated from fantasia—isn't there? There is something other than either story-writing or artistic merit which has emerged through a series of my books. Something one might regard as a new system of ideas—'thought.' "

This "thought" was social criticism, and it is is not as unique as Wells had claimed it to be, for it has been the stuff of writing since words were first formed on paper. And in the realm of science fiction, disguising social commentary as works of fantasy was to became the very framework of the most popular books and movies—from Burroughs's *Tarzan of the Apes* to Bradbury's *Martian Chronicles*.

Burroughs wrote *A Princess of Mars* two years after the height of the Mars furor, when the scientific community was pitted against Lowell and his Martian canal theories, and when Lowell "frequently fulminated against science, and in fact all mankind, for failing to recognize and acknowledge the cosmic importance of his Mars work." Is it surprising, then, that Burroughs opens his second tale, *The Gods of Mars* (1913) with Captain John Carter in an Arizona tomb rising from the dead to speak to his nephew about his beloved Mars: His words are distinctly Lowellian:

> I know that the average human mind will not believe what it cannot grasp, and so I do not purpose being pilloried by the public, the pulpit, and the press, and held up as a colossal liar when I am but telling the simple truths which some day science will substantiate. Possibly the suggestions which I gained upon Mars, and the knowledge which I can set down in this chronicle, will aid in an earlier understanding of the mysteries of our sister planet; mysteries to you, but no longer mysteries to me.

To understand the stuff of this hero, the fantastic descriptions of planet Barsoom on which he adventured, and the intense social commentaries peppered throughout Burroughs's works, we need to look no further than into his past. For it was through Burroughs's life experiences that the world received a new perspective on Mars, one of lingering romance, endless desires, and social justice. And it was partly through Burroughs's prolific writing—he wrote eleven novels about John Carter's adventures—that the Martians were alive in the human psyche long after Lowell passed away in 1916.

12

War of the Worlds

As children tremble and fear everything in the blind darkness, so we in the light sometimes fear what is no more to be feared than the things children in the dark hold in terror. . . .

—Lucretius, *On the Nature of Things* (c. 60 B.C.E.)

Less than three years after Lowell's death Martians began to haunt the Earth. In the spring of 1919 the world's first amateur radio operator, Guglielmo Marconi of Italy, announced that several of his radio stations were picking up very strong signals "seeming to come from beyond the Earth." How fantastic, and perhaps hopeful, this discovery must have seemed, especially to the people of Europe. After celebrating an end to World War I in 1918, they watched the eastern and central parts of their worlds fall into chaos and revolution; during the spring of 1919 the Foundation of the Third Communist International was created to propagate communism and world revolution, Benito Mussolini founded the Italian fascist movement, and Romanian troops invaded Hungry. Could a signal from outer space mean that someone "out there" was watching us, maybe warning us about our destructive ways? The signal was not something that could easily be brushed aside with a guffaw, for Marconi was not a controversial figure like Lowell; he was an accepted genius with impeccable scientific credentials.

Born in Bologna on April 25, 1874, Guglielmo Marconi was the second son of a runaway marriage between Giuseppe Marconi, the son of a wealthy land owner, and Annie Jameson, daughter of Andrew Jameson of the Irish Whiskey Company. On July 20, 1897, Marconi established the world's first wireless telegraph company, and his research earned him the Nobel Prize in Physics in 1909. Thanks to Marconi's wireless invention, a message from the *S.S. Montrose* to New Scotland Yard led to the arrest of the infamous murderer Dr. Crippen and his mistress who were fleeing London for the Americas; also wireless distress calls from the *S.S. Titanic* in 1912 had saved 705 lives. Two years later Marconi was appointed a senator in Rome (a position that Schiaparelli had once held), and King George V of England awarded him the honorary title of Knight Grand Cross of the Victorian Order. Marconi was not, then, one to initiate a foolish prank. The mysterious signals that reached his radio stations had to have been real, but how to explain them?

Enter Nikola Tesla, a controversial and often mythologized electrical magician. Called the "forgotten father of technology" by some, a "madman" by others, Tesla harnessed the electrical current we use in our homes today; *he* invented the radio, fluorescent lighting, and the bladeless turbine. But in his spare moments, the electrical magician was also a basement Dr. Frankenstein. Fond of creating neighborhood-threatening electrical storms in his apartment laboratory, he once nearly knocked down a tall building by attaching a mysterious "black box" to its side. His fevered intellect was an arsenal of rabid ideas that bordered on black magic and science fantasy. Tesla talked of death rays that could destroy 10,000 airplanes at a distance of 675 kilometers (250 miles) and claimed to be able split the Earth in two.

Free electricity, time travel, ozone generators, thought machines, and anti-gravity airships were all part of Nikola Tesla's dark and mysterious world.

The son of a Serbian Orthodox priest, Tesla was born in present-day Croatia, then part of the Austro-Hungarian Empire, on July 9, 1856, just before the American Civil War. Tesla moved to the United States in 1884, where he worked for Thomas Edison—who quickly became a rival. A self-educated man, Edison disliked Tesla for being an "egghead." Tesla's taste for Edison was equally sour: "If Edison had a needle to find in a haystack, he would proceed at once with the diligence of a bee to examine straw after straw until he found the object of his search. I was a sorry witness of such doings, knowing that a little theory, a little calculation would have saved him ninety percent of his labor."

What destiny had brought together, arrogance would soon push apart. After a dispute with Edison over compensation—Edison had promised Tesla the magnificent sum of $50,000 if he could solve a host of problems with Edison's patented direct-current generators; when Tesla successfully completed this assignment and asked Edison for his money, Edison replied, "You obviously don't understand American humor"—Tesla donned up his bowler hat and stormed out. "A man always has two reasons for the things he does," Tesla once said, "a good one and a real one."

At the time of Tesla's departure, the nation was immersed in industrial progress, and inventions were materializing as fast as new computers are today. By 1898 Edison and Tesla were racing to see "who could boggle the minds of lesser mortals with the more outrageous claims," writes Margaret Cheney in her biography *Tesla: Man Out of Time*. Working in his basement, Tesla built equipment that exceeded anything ever designed before, equipment such as magnifying transmitters, which, he believed, had no limits—a message could be sent to Mars almost as easily as to Chicago, Tesla said, and Martians, he believed, were a "statistical certainty"; communication could be achieved by transmitting wireless messages by using the Earth or the upper atmosphere as a conductor. A year later he had built a gigantic "Tesla coil" (a device that produces extremely high voltage; its descendants are still used today in every television set), which he connected to a tall antenna in a laboratory in Colorado Springs. A year later in 1899 he asserted that this powerful invention had received signals from Mars.

It happened one night when the inventor heard strange rhythmic sounds emanating from his powerful and sensitive radio receiver. The only explanation for such a regular signal, he believed, was that beings on another planet (Mars being the most likely source) were establishing contact. Tesla let the world know of his discovery, which unleashed a thunderous critical response from E. S. Holden of Lick Observatory in California:

> [The signals come] probably from Mars, he guesses. It is sound philosophizing to examine all probable causes for an unexplained phenomenon before invoking improbable ones. Every experimenter will say that it is almost certain that Mr. Tesla has made an error, and the disturbances in question come from currents in our air or in the earth. . . . Why fasten the disturbances of Mr. Tesla's instrument on Mars? Are there no comets that will serve the purpose? . . . Until Mr. Tesla has shown his apparatus to other experimenters and convinced them as well as himself, it may safely be taken for granted that his signals do not come from Mars.

Holden's words were ineffectual. Certainly one thing an ingenious inventor like Tesla was not prepared to do was to disclose his creation to scientists with arid imaginations. To hell with his critics. Tesla was too thrilled and awe struck over the signals to waste time in pointless debate. He instead became obsessed with the idea of returning a signal to Mars.

That Tesla's "discovery" and ensuing ambition to contact the Martians came at the turn of the century was not overlooked by the press. To a scientist, the turn of century equals nothing more than one plus ninety-nine revolutions of the Earth about the Sun. But to the curious public, the dawning of a new century brings with it mystical overtones of impending promise or possible change. And who better was there to peer into the crystal ball of science than that almost supernaturally gifted "hurler of lightning," Nikola Tesla? Writing for *Century* magazine, Tesla discussed the energy sources and technologies of the future. The article was full of photographs and resounded with Tesla's predictions, including his intent to contact Mars, all of which thrust him further into the center of controversy.

The idea might have seemed crazy until Lowell's assistant Douglass noticed a prominent "projection" on the telescopic disk of Mars in December 1900.[2] Although it was nothing more than a cloud catching the last warming rays of sunlight on that distant planet, newspapers across the nation exclaimed that on the evening of December 7 Mars had been signaling Earth. Lights, it was reported, had suddenly shone out from upon the surface of the planet, lasted for some time, and then vanished.

In response to the brief but intense exposure of this event, Lowell announced that the "signaling part of it was a tale added by journalistic ingenuity." Garrett P. Serviss, science columnist for the Hearst newspapers, concurred:

> This will probably lead to a renewal of the suggestions made during the last preceding oppositions of Mars, that the inhabitants of that planet are signaling the Earth. . . . How deeply this idea has sunk in the popular imagination is indicated by a proposal . . . that special researches be undertaken for the purpose of solving the problem of interplanetary communication.

Tesla returned to the limelight. The press cheered on the electronic wizard in an article in the February 23, 1901, Pittsburgh *Dispatch.*

> The press at large has of late been having a good deal of fun with Nikola Tesla and his predictions. . . . Some of his sanguine conceptions, including the transmission of signals to Mars have evoked the opinion that it would be better for Mr. Tesla to predict less and do more in the line of performance.

Tesla did indeed return fire, but the volley did not come from his own vessel. No, his critics suddenly received an unexpected broadside from the east, when England's famous Lord Kelvin, a respected and learned mathematician and physicist, paid Tesla a visit. After a banquet in Kelvin's honor at Delmonico's restaurant in New York City, Kelvin shocked the scientific community by openly supporting Tesla and his beliefs about the Martians. New York, Lord Kelvin announced, was the "most marvelously lighted city in the world," and the only spot on Earth visible to Martians. Inspired by conversation, and perhaps inspired by some fine wine, Kelvin further declared that "Mars is signaling . . . to New York."

Those words screamed in the headlines of all the dailies. Kelvin's sentiments left Tesla's incredulous colleagues speechless. Not even Holden dared refute Lord Kelvin. Furthering Tesla's advantage, one Julian Hawthorne took Kelvin's claims a step further, writing that Martians have long been visiting the Earth and watching over humanity, only to return to Mars with the sad news that "they're not ready for us yet." But the birth of Nikola Tesla, he said, had changed their opinion. "Possibly," Hawthorne wrote, "they (the starry men) guide his development; who can tell?"

Thus, when Marconi picked up his extraterrestrial signal in 1919, Tesla could draw only one natural conclusion—that his rival had finally succeeded in achieving what he had been doing on a regular basis himself for the last two decades.

The impact of radio on society was swiftly coming. In but a few years the medium moved out of the shops of the privileged few and into the homes of the many. In 1922 Marconi and five other companies formed the British Broadcasting Company in London. Two years later, Columbia University in the United States began using radio for educational broadcasts. That year Mars sailed close to Earth, and radio listeners across the United States began detecting strange, unidentified signals from the red planet. News of the detections swept across the globe like a brushfire in a severe drought. And when Mars swung ever closer to the Earth in 1924, the Great Mars Experiment was conducted, and radio stations around the world were urged to simultaneously cease transmissions at specified intervals, so as not to interfere with any attempts by Mars to radio the earth. Amherst College astronomer David Peck Todd (a long-time advocate of Lowell's network of artificial canals) issued sensational reports that he had detected signals at wavelengths ranging from 5,000 to 30,000 meters (16,400 to 98,400 feet). Ironically, this is the portion of the radio spectrum that is least likely to penetrate Earth's ionosphere, either outward bound to Mars or inward bound to terrestrial listeners.

Throughout history each step forward in technology has spawned great leaps of human imagination. The "what if's" championed by Wells in his *The War of the Worlds,* the raw Martian imagery of Burroughs's Barsoom, now the Mars radio magic of Tesla and Marconi mushroomed in the fertile minds of the public. If Lowell's Martians cannot be seen, they can certainly be heard. And, so it was, that just as Mars was reaching yet another favorable opposition in October 1926, newspapers exploded with the headlines "Mars Message Waited [*sic*]." A report from London stated that "thousands of British radio enthusiasts will listen in tomorrow night for possible messages from Mars, which will be in a more favorable position for radio reception than it has been for 100 years."

The year 1926 was not a good one for Burroughs. He felt he was "through writing Martian and Tarzan yarns." But, excitement over the possibility of radio signals coming from Mars led the *London Daily Express* to ask Burroughs his opinion on what might be revealed when Earth and Mars neared:

> Winds, snows and marshes that astronomers have discovered on Mars indicate an atmosphere. Vast reclamation projects following the lines of interminable aqueducts presuppose rational inhabitants highly developed in engineering and agriculture, naturally suggesting other culture.

The voice of Lowell was speaking from beyond the grave. Tesla sprinkled more plausible Lowellian ideas into his own fantasies, which enriched the imagination of an open-minded public: "Aerial machines will be propelled around the Earth without a stop and the Sun's energy controlled to create lakes and rivers for motive purposes and transformation of arid deserts into fertile land." Spaceships, radio signals from Mars, mysterious flashes, scientific and literary corroboration. The stage had been fastidiously set for the most terrifying drama in radio history.

On Halloween evening, 1938, the Martians landed in the minds of millions of panic-stricken Americans. The "invasion" began promptly at 8:00 P.M. Eastern Standard Time, when Orson Welles and the cast of the Mercury Theatre on the Air took their places before a microphone at a New York studio of the Columbia Broadcasting System and began broadcasting Howard Koch's freely adapted version of H. G. Wells's *The War of the Worlds:*

> ANNOUNCER: The Columbia Broadcasting System and its affiliated stations present Orson Welles and the Mercury Theatre on the Air in *War of the Worlds* by H. G. Wells.
>
> THEME

> ANNOUNCER: Ladies and gentlemen: the director of the Mercury Theatre and star of these broadcasts, Orson Welles. . . .
>
> ORSON WELLES: We know now that in the early years of the twentieth century this world was being watched closely by intelligences greater than man's and yet as mortal as his own. We know now that as human beings busied themselves about their concerns they were scrutinized and studied, perhaps almost as narrowly as a man with a microscope might scrutinize the transient creatures that swarm and multiply in a drop of water. With infinite complacence people went to and fro over the Earth about their little affairs, serene in the assurance of their dominion over this small spinning fragment of solar driftwood which by chance or design man has inherited out of the dark mystery of Time and Space. Yet across an immense ethereal gulf, minds that are to our minds as ours are to the beasts in the jungle, intellects vast and cool and unsympathetic regarded this earth with envious eyes and slowly and surely drew their plans against us. In the thirty-ninth year of the twentieth century came the great disillusionment.

It was near the end of October. Business was better. The war scare was over. More men were back at work. Sales were picking up. On this particular evening, October 30, the Crossley service estimated that thirty-two million people were listening in on radios. . . .

The million listeners who missed Welles's introduction and the preceding announcement turned on their radios and began a frightful journey into a night of terror. Some tuned in just in time to hear the music of Ramon Raquello and his orchestra interrupted by this special news bulletin:

> Ladies and gentlemen, we interrupt our program of dance music to bring you a special bulletin from the Intercontinental Radio News. At twenty minutes before eight, central time, Professor Farrell of the Mount Jennings Observatory, Chicago, Illinois, reports observing several explosions of incandescent gas, occurring at regular intervals on the planet Mars.
>
> The spectroscope indicates the gas to be hydrogen and moving toward Earth with enormous velocity. Professor Pierson of the observatory at Princeton confirms Farrell's observation, and describes the phenomenon as (QUOTE) like a jet of blue flame shot from a gun. (UNQUOTE.) We now return you to the music of Ramon Raquello, playing for you in the Meridian Room of the Park Plaza Hotel, situated in downtown New York.

Little did the actors know their Halloween entertainment would be believed by so many people across the country. As the incredible one-hour drama unfolded, American citizens from Maine to California learned that Martians had landed at the Wilmarth farm in Grover's Mill, New Jersey; that the Martians were hideous beings, having appendages like grey snakes and V-shaped mouths with saliva dripping from their rimless and quivering lips; that they had emerged from their cylinders armed with heat rays; that all armed resistance sent against them met with horrifying death; that Martian cylinders were "falling like flies" all over the country; that the world was near an end.

Newspapers the following morning spoke of the "tidal wave of terror" that swept the nation. Long before the broadcast had ended, documents Hadley Cantril, in *The Invasion from Mars: A Study in the Psychology of Panic,* people all over the United States were praying, crying, fleeing frantically to escape death from the Martians. Some ran to rescue loved ones. Others telephoned farewells or warnings, hurried to inform neighbors, sought information from newspapers or radio stations, summoned ambulances and police cars.

"That Halloowe'en Boo sure had our family on its knees before the program was half over," Joseph Hendley from the Midwest told Cantril. "God knows but we prayed to Him last Sunday. . . . Lily got sick to her stomach. . . . Just as soon as we were convinced that this thing was real, how pretty all things on Earth seemed; how soon we put our trust in God." And in a New York suburb, Mrs. Delany hugged her radio, held a crucifix, and prayed while looking out an open window for falling meteors. "I also wanted to get a faint whiff of the gas," she said, "so that I would know when to close my window and hermetically seal my room with waterproof cement. . . . When the monsters were wading across the Hudson River and coming into New York, I wanted to run up on my roof and see what they looked like, but I could not leave my radio while it was telling me of their whereabouts."

Of the 1,700,000 residents who heard the broadcast, 28 percent believed it was a news bulletin. Seventy percent of those listeners were frightened or disturbed by it; about 1,200,000 people across the nation in all were affected.

Cantril argues that the unusual realism of the performance may be attributed to the fact that the early parts of the broadcast fell within the existing standards of judgment of the listeners. If a stimulus (in this case the performance) does not contradict what seems plausible, it is likely to be believed. Indeed, by the late 1930s radio was the most widely accepted vehicle for important announcements, and millions of Americans were intently listening to their radios for any late-breaking news on the impending war in Europe. "I was looking forward with some pleasure to the destruction of the entire human race and the end of the world, " said one of the people Cantril studied. "If we have Fascist domination of the world, there is no purpose in living anyway."

The Mercury Theatre's selection and portrayal of the strange events on Mars was very convincing. That a Professor Farrell of the Mount Jennings Observatory reported seeing several explosions of incandescent gas on Mars would be interesting but not surprising to the listening audience; top scientists had been seeing mysterious flashes on Mars for decades. That the spectroscope would indicate the gas to be hydrogen would also seem reasonable. Since the latter part of the nineteenth century scientists had been turning their spectroscopes to Mars to determine its atmospheric chemistry without success; their attempts to detect oxygen on the red planet in 1930 had also failed. Since hydrogen is the most abundant gas in the universe, why not hydrogen on Mars? (Of course, we now know that carbon dioxide is the principal gas of the Martian atmosphere.) Subliminally, the audience was at a disadvantage as well. For nearly three decades the public's imagination had been steeped in the Martian adventures created by Edgar Rice Burroughs. And popular radio plays and comic strips, such as "Flash Gordon" and "Buck Rogers," kept Americans strapped into their rocket ships for endless adventures to Mars and other planets. Armed with Teslaesque disintegrator guns, Americans continually waged imaginary war on extraterrestrial dictators. Indeed, transport cylinders, heat rays, and mad Martians were tightly woven into the fabric of the human psyche when the Welles broadcast hit the air.

And so, in the public's sinewy perception of an inhabited, warlike Mars, expectation triumphed by creating illusion. Panic ensued, spawned by a perceived "direct threat to life, to other lives, that one loved, as well as to all other cherished values," Cantril writes. "The Martians were destroying practically everything. . . . One was faced with the alternative of resigning oneself and all of one's values to complete annihilation or of making a desperate effort to escape from the field of danger, or of appealing to some higher power or stronger person whom one vaguely thought could destroy the oncoming enemy."

The following morning, H. G. Wells was not amused: "The dramatisation was made with a liberty that amounts to a complete rewriting and made the novel an entirely different story," he said. "It's a total unwarranted liberty." But the ruffled Wells soon had a change of heart when he learned that the radio broadcast helped boost the sales of what had been, until that time, one of his more obscure novels, and Wells allowed himself to be interviewed by Welles.

Welles's innocent (though many would argue contrived) radio drama had also made an indelible mark on history. That millions of Americans could be duped by a radio broadcast had far-reaching effects, prompting decades of research into mass hysteria. Clearly the European war of the late summer and early fall of 1938, when Nazi Germany then Soviet Russia invaded Poland, helped confuse the issue of the fictitious "war" with Mars that Halloween eve. Take for instance, Sylvia Holmes, a housewife in Newark, who panicked when she heard the radio announcer say, "Get the gas masks!" She thought she was going crazy: "It's a wonder my heart didn't fail me." Wanting to be with her husband and nephew (so they could all die together) Holmes ran outside and tried to hail a bus. People saw how excited she was; her reply to their questions was the same: "Don't you know New Jersey is destroyed by the Germans—it's on the radio."

Writing in the November 2, 1938, *New York World-Telegram,* columnist Heywood Broun stated the obvious: "The course of world history has affected national psychology. Jitters have come to roost. We have just gone through a laboratory demonstration of the fact that the peace of Munich hangs heavy on our heads, like a thundercloud."

Equally poignant was Dorothy Thompson's revelation in the *New York Tribune:* "All unwittingly, Mr. Orson Welles and the Mercury Theatre of the Air have made one of the most fascinating and important demonstrations of all time. They have proved that a few effective voices, accompanied by sound effects, can convince masses of people of a totally unreasonable, completely fantastic proposition as to create a nation-wide panic. . . . They have demonstrated more potently than any argument, demonstrated beyond a question of a doubt, the appalling dangers and enormous effectiveness of popular and theatrical demagoguery. . . . Hitler managed to scare all of Europe to its knees a month ago, but he at least had an army and an air force to back up his shrieking words. . . . But Mr. Welles scared thousands into demoralization with nothing at all."

The forties dawned blood red with the incursion of World War II and the development (and later the use) of the first atomic bombs. The threat of global nuclear war spawned a new genre of science fiction novels and radio dramas with themes of nuclear Armageddon. Arch Oboler, whose *Lights Out* radio dramas from the mid-1930s to the mid-1940s offered listeners the most chilling and gruesome sound effects on radio (including the sounds of stabbings, dentist drills, and people being turned inside out), entertained listeners with several such science fiction plays—"Rocket from Manhattan," for instance, as well as "Terror from Outer Space" (which aired as an episode on *Murder At Midnight*) preserved Oboler's passion for horror while instilling an air of Armageddon; "Immortal Gentleman" even introduced Einstein's relativistic concepts of space and time. But the most powerful voice to emerge from the shadows of that dark time came from a blossoming American novelist who first drafted his short stories on paper that butchers used to wrap their bloody meat.

Born in Waukegan, Illinois, on August 22, 1920, Ray Bradbury lived on a strict diet of science-fiction adventure novels by Edgar Rice Burroughs. By the age of ten, he would, to the consternation of family and friends, all but become the indomitable John Carter or would behave like a Martian thoat, "which, everyone knows, has eight legs," Bradbury divulges. Here was a child in love, in love with the fantastic worlds that enriched his imagination and made him feel alive. And his imagination knew no bounds: "I woke, called for my head, which crawled on spider legs from a pillow nearby, to sit itself back on my neck and name itself *Chessman* of Mars."

The impact of Burroughs on generations of youngsters cannot be denied. While other fantasy authors, like Jules Verne and Rudyard Kipling, were better writers than Burroughs, they were not better romantics. "Burroughs stands above all these by reason of his unreason," Bradbury explains, "because of the sheer romantic impossibility of Burroughs' Mars and its fairy tale people with green skin and the absolutely unscientific way John Crater traveled there. Being utterly impossible he was the perfect fast-moving chum for any ten-year-old boy."

Bradbury began writing short stories in 1931. For a salary, he sold newspapers on Los Angeles street corners from 1938 to 1942, during which time he sold his first short story and published his own magazine—for which he did most of the writing. He began writing full-time the following year, contributing numerous short stories to periodicals. In 1945 his short story "The Big Black and White Game" was selected for Best American Short Stories. But it was not until 1950 that he received his reputation as a leading writer of science fiction with the publication of *The Martian Chronicles.*

The Martian Chronicles is a collection of twenty-seven short stories following man's conquest of Mars (Bradbury wryly twists the plot of Wells's *The War of the Worlds,* making humans the invaders). The work has the flavor of an Edgar Rice Burroughs Martian adventure novel, sans superhero and chivalry, placing us in crystalline Martian homes, by meandering azure canals, or in ancient bone-chess cities near fossil seas. Bradbury raised the ante of realism by following the rules of science (not willing oneself to Mars like John Carter), though he did not dismiss the possibility of going beyond the traditional bounds of science, as long as it seemed reasonable; thus Bradbury's Martians can communicate with telepathy. "Science-fiction is the law-abiding citizen of imaginative literature," he notes, "obeying the rules, be they physical, social, or psychological, keeping regular hours, eating punctual meals; predictable, certain, sure."

But Bradbury also portrayed Mars like no one else had before. He looked at the red planet through the tinted eyes of Lowell. He wrote with the compassionate heart of Burroughs. His words flourished with the sensitivity of Robert Frost. And on his shoulders lay the futuristic concerns of the world.

> [The Martians] knew how to live with nature and get along with nature. They didn't try too hard to be all men and no animal. That's the mistake we made when Darwin showed up. We embraced him and Huxley, and Freud, all smiles. And then we discovered that Darwin and our religions didn't mix. Or at least we didn't think they did. We were fools. We tried

> to budge Darwin and Huxley and Freud. They wouldn't move very well. So, like idiots, we tried knocking down religion.
>
> We succeeded pretty well. We lost our faith and went around wondering what life was for. If art was not more than a frustrated outflinging of desire, if religion was no more than self-delusion, what good was life? Faith had always given us answers to all things. But it all went down the drain with Freud and Darwin. We were and still are a lost people.
>
> . . . [The Martians] knew how to combine science and religion so the two worked side by side, neither denying the other, each encircling the other.

Bradbury's portrayal of male Martians often mirrored the cold chauvinistic tendencies of Earthmen:

> "Keep your silly, feminine dreams to yourself! . . . Ridiculous, is it!" he almost screamed [at his wife]. "You should have heard yourself, fawning on him, talking to him, singing with him, oh gods, all night; you should have *heard* yourself!"

His depictions of Martian women usually reflected wanton sensuality:

> The young woman sat at the tiller bench quietly. Her wrists were as thin as icicles, her eyes as clear as the moons and as large, steady and white. The wind blew at her and, like an image on cold water, she rippled, silk standing out from her frail body in tatters of blue rain.

And when the Earthling Sam Parkhill ("First man on Mars with a hot-dog stand") shoots this frail and innocent Martian woman in cold blood, the illusion locked in our fuzzy minds that man is good suddenly vanishes in a wisp of diaphanous vapors:

> In the sunlight, snow melts, crystals evaporate into a steam, into nothing. In the firelight, vapors dance and vanish. In the core of a volcano, fragile things burst and disappear. The girl, in the gunfire, in the heat, in the concussion, folded like a soft scarf, melted like a crystal figurine. What was left of her, ice, snowflake, smoke, blew away in the wind. The tiller seat was empty.

In the end, global nuclear warfare flares up on Earth. The human settlers of Mars step onto the porches of their 1950-style Midwest, suburban homes and watch the "green star of Earth" erupt in flames:

> They stood on the porches and tried to believe in the existence of Earth, much as they had once tried to believe in the existence of Mars; it was a problem reversed. To all intents and purposes, Earth now was dead; they had been away from it for three or four years. Space was an anesthetic; seventy million miles of space numbed you, put memory to sleep, depopulated Earth, erased the past. . . . But now, tonight, the dead were risen, Earth was reinhabited, memory awoke, a million names were spoken: What was so-and-so doing tonight on Earth? What about this one and that one? The people on the porches glanced sidewise at each other's faces.

As the Cold War escalated in the 1950s, aliens invaded American households through the magic of television. Like Bradbury, movie producers were keenly aware of how to use Mars as a Trojan Horse, as a vehicle disguised to drive home statements about the overwhelming apprehension of America during the height of the anti-Communist furor. A new paradoxical image of Mars was emerging: Mars was "War," and its invaders could alter minds of innocent humans; Mars was "Hope," whose visitors were concerned with peace and the plight of the Earth. Two classic movies best illustrate this dichotomy of thought.

In *The Day the Earth Stood Still* (1951), a flying saucer landing near the White House, throws the nation's Capitol into a panic. A handsome extraterrestrial, Klaatu, steps out of the craft with a huge robot, Gort, who can shoot death rays at Klaatu's discretion. Although Klaatu came in peace, he is shot by a nervous soldier and is taken to a hospital; Klaatu tries to arrange a meeting with the leaders of the world, but they cannot agree on a meeting place. "I'm impatient with stupidity." Klaatu stresses, "My people have learned to live without it." After escaping from the hospital and making a futile attempt to contact the Earth's leading scientists (even they act stupid), Klaatu shuts down Earth's power for half an hour. He is hunted down by the military and is killed. But Gort miraculously revives Klaatu, and the handsome extraterrestrial introduces the world to the phrase, "Gort, Klaatu barada nikto," which essentially means, "Gort, don't wipe out these stupid humans." Instead, Klaatu leaves the Earth with a grave message—

that unless the people of Earth stop their nuclear arms race, which endangers the rest of the universe, Gort and the rest of Klaatu's robots will reduce the world "to a burnt-out cinder." "The choice," Klaatu declares "is yours."

The Invasion from Mars (1953) typifies American paranoia during the 1950s Communist-spy phobias. In it, a young boy awakens from a sound sleep to see a flying saucer land behind a hill near his house. Soon he realizes that Martians have burrowed underground and are stealing and altering the minds of the townspeople—a powerful metaphor for the pervasive presence of the unseen enemy. At first, no one listens to the boy—another strong metaphor for the alienating feeling a child must have when he becomes aware of something terribly wrong with the world but is powerless to do anything about it. Fearing the Martians have an unstoppable infrared weapon, the army moves in and the aliens are ultimately defeated. In the end, the boy awakens and discovers it was all a dream . . . until he sees a flying saucer land behind a hill near his house.

Note that the object that triggered the hysteria in both movies was a single event—a flying saucer landing. This is no coincidence. On July 24, 1948, the crew of an Eastern Air Lines DC-3, flying near Montgomery, Alabama, made headlines when they became the second group in the United States to report an Unidentified Flying Object (UFO). The *Atlanta Constitution*, a credible newspaper, carried a front-page headline that read: "Atlanta Pilots Report Wingless Monster." Thirteen months before their sighting, private flyer Kenneth Arnold saw a mysterious disk-shaped object flying near Mount Rainer in Washington State. "Barely a year before the Arnold incident," reveals renowned UFO investigator Philip Klass, "A U.S. Army Air Forces-sponsored study at the RAND Corporation 'Think Tank' had concluded that enlarged versions of the V-2 ballistic missiles developed by Germany during World War II could soon make it possible to orbit unmanned spacecraft around the Earth. The next step could be space travel to the moon and planets like Venus and Mars, where scientists as well as science-fiction writers had long speculated there might be intelligent life."[4]

Then in July 1947, a flying saucer allegedly crashed in the desert near Roswell, New Mexico. The *Times* (London), July 8, 1947, headlines screamed: "U.S. Army to Examine a Flying Disk." Closer to home, the *Roswell Daily Record* for the same day had headlined: "RAAF Captures Flying Saucer on Ranch in Roswell Region":

> The intelligence office of the 509th Bombardment group at Roswell Army Field announced at noon today, that the field has come into possession of a flying saucer. . . . Mr. and Mrs. Dan Wilmot apparently were the only persons in Roswell to have seen what they thought was a flying disk. . . . In appearance it looked oval in shape like two inverted saucers, faced mouth to mouth, or like two old type washbowls placed, together in the same fashion. The entire body glowed as though light were glowing through from inside, though not like it would inside, though not like it would be if a light were merely underneath.

When the military arrived they took the craft to the infamous Area 51 for study. A rash of UFO sightings across the nation followed. By the close of 1947 the Army Air Forces (Now the U.S. Air Force) was ordered to create a special office to investigate flying saucer mysteries. Although natural explanations for many of these incidents were forthcoming, the nation grew to believe that strange alien crafts were hiding in our skies and that their performance and design were alien to the technology of this Earth. Bookstores became littered with titles revealing the science fiction had become reality—that Earth was finally being invaded by mysterious creatures from distant planets.

By the spring of 1950 the Roswell incident was making new headlines. On March 8, 1950, a millionaire oil baron named Silas Newton, addressed a science class at the University of Denver in Colorado and spread tales of flying saucers and little green men. He also said that a certain friend who went by the pseudonym "Doctor Gee" had been working for the U.S. government when he was called out to Roswell, New Mexico, to investigate a UFO crash. "Gee" claimed a total of thirty-six bodies were removed from the craft and that the government was covering up an incredible incident. However, later official announcements would claim the UFO was a military balloon. Mumbles about a government cover-up grew louder across the nation (they persist to this day). Newton convinced another friend to publish a book in 1950 titled *Behind Flying Saucers*, which promulgated even more fantastic claims about spaceships and little green men.[5]

How incredible all this must have seemed to the aged Edgar Rice Burroughs as he finished his breakfast on Sunday morning March 19, 1950. His dreams seemed to have come full circle. Science fiction was becoming reality—the men were even green, like some of his his beings on Barsoom.

But Burroughs would not live to learn the truth. He died quietly that morning after sitting in bed and reading the comic pages. Newton, it turns out, was not an oil millionaire, but he was trying to sell a worthless device for finding oil. So Newton and a man named GeBauer were arrested. Not surprisingly, GeBauer turned out to the mysterious "Dr. Gee." GeBauer was not a scientist, and his stories about UFOs and little green men were fabrications.

Burroughs passed away at the age of seventy-four. He left behind a long trail of paper containing some of the most fantastic characters ever to reach the hands of young readers. "His greatest journey," Porges writes, "forever to be appreciated by his host of readers, began in his imagination. It . . . allowed him to soar through space and arrive, unconcerned with all boundaries and limitations, at his own teeming worlds. At first *his* worlds, they quickly became the pleasure and dream worlds of others—the eternal legacy of Edgar Rice Burroughs."

Reflecting on the impact of Burroughs on his own life, Ray Bradbury wrote, "His greatest gift was teaching me to look at Mars and ask to be taken home. . . . We have commuted because of Mr. Burroughs. Because of him we have printed the Moon. Because of him and men like him, one day in the next five centuries, we will commute forever, we will go away. . . . And never come back. And so live forever."

Part IV
Marsfall

13
Water, Water—Anywhere?

A dry and thirsty land, where no water is.
— Psalm 63

Mars, the fantastic canaled planet, born from Lowell's beliefs and glorified in Burroughs's writings, entered our lives at a time when astronomy was largely dominated by scientific uncertainty. At the turn of the century astronomers did not have the tools necessary to restrain the imagination, though many believed (or hoped) that photography and spectroscopy—whose astronomical applications were still in their infancy—would do so. At Lowell Observatory, however, the search was on to capture incontroversial photographic images of canals on Mars or to detect spectroscopic evidence for water on the planet; either discovery, they realized, would be a crowning achievement for technology and a vindication of their founder.

Photography of the planet began with Earl C. Slipher's 1905 efforts at the Lowell Observatory—eventually he amassed more than 100,000 images covering twenty-seven oppositions. Most of these images were obtained from Flagstaff, though Slipher went to Chile for the 1907 opposition of Mars and to South Africa for the 1954 opposition. He drew up a map in the late 1950s that was adopted by the U.S. Air Force, though in many ways it represented a decisive step backward from Antoniadi's 1930 map; it still showed a network of canals. Photographic studies were limited by the fact that even state-of-the-art emulsions required exposures of several seconds, long enough to blur the finer details. Thus the impressions of visual observers remained supreme.

In addition to visual and photographic studies, important work was done by observers using other kinds of instruments than the eyeball and camera—for instance, thermocouples were first used in the 1920s; these instruments electronically measured the small amounts of infrared radiation emanating from Mars, allowing the first direct determinations of the temperature in different parts of its surface. Most important, there were spectroscopic studies of the planet. Along with the telescope itself, the spectroscope has always been far and away the most useful of astronomical instruments.

The science of spectroscopy is based on a simple principle, first demonstrated by the nineteenth-century German chemists Robert Bunsen and Gustav Kirchoff: light from the Sun, Moon, planets or a star is passed through a slit; then, by means of a prism (or diffraction grating, a piece of glass on which closely spaced lines are etched), it is dispersed into a spectrum. Bunsen and Kirchoff demonstrated in 1859—the year of Darwin's *Origin of Species*—that a globe of heated gas under pressure, like the Sun, produces a continuous spectrum (rainbow of colors). When light from the Sun passes through a gas, such as that contained in the Sun's atmosphere, the chemical elements in the gas absorb light preferentially in certain specific positions in the spectrum to produce a series of superimposed dark lines (or, in some cases, bands), known in general as absorption lines or bands (or, in the case of the Sun, Fraunhofer lines, after their discoverer, the Bavarian optician Joseph Fraunhofer). The pattern of lines is characteristic for each element and effectively provides a signature of the chemical composition of the gas somewhat akin to the uniquely identifying pattern furnished to criminologists by a set of fingerprints.

Spectroscopic observers of Mars were always most interested in finding lines or bands in its spectrum indicative of the presence of water—for obvious reasons, since the whole question of possible life has always turned on the question of its water supply.

The water that fills the Earth's oceans—and any that may once have filled oceans on Mars—is believed ultimately to have come from the ices delivered by planetesimals from the outer solar system. Swept up by the planet's gravitational field, they added their mass to that of the accreting planet. Most of the Earth's supply probably arrived in this way within the first 100 million years of its formation. In addition to water, many of the components of the primitive atmosphere of the Earth, and even some organic compounds, probably had extraterrestrial origins.

The oceans formed early on from gases belched forth in volcanoes and fumaroles from the Earth's interior, and already, some four billion years ago, must have covered the entire planet. The Earth at that time was a seething and tempestuous place. Volcanoes may have surged upward in many places in the oceans; the crust was still thin and fragile. There were still monster impacts, some energetic enough to vaporize the oceans.

On the early Earth there was an abundance of thermal energy. Conditions on the planet may well have been similar to those that are now encountered only in the neighborhood of volcanic vents, featuring scalding temperatures. There was heat enough for many chemical reactions to occur rapidly that would not occur spontaneously at room temperatures at all. Extreme pressures near the ocean floor also would have served to force molecules together that otherwise would have preferred to remain unaffiliated.

In the neighborhood of deep-sea vents, water allowed the chemical reactions that would ultimately lead on to the evolution of primitive metabolism. Ever since the beginning, water has always been the essential solvent, "the stage and setting of life."[1] Even in sophisticated lifeforms such as ourselves, nutrients are transferred to cells in aqueous solution, and wastes are removed by the elimination of water. There is no other readily available solvent that would so neatly have served the purpose. This is true not only on Earth but presumably wherever else in the universe life has appeared. Thus, if life ever arose on Mars, it must have been in the presence of liquid water. It can even be said that life itself is a consequence of the unique properties of water, that wherever water cannot persist, life—the molecules of life—cannot function.

Living organisms are largely composed of water—usually between 50 and 90 percent of live weight (in humans, the figure is 75 percent). The very blood in our veins contains a solute whose composition is almost identical to that of sea water. It is no surprise that, despite the stark beauty and mystical allure of the desert, we are always and irresistibly drawn to water. Even on the desert, it is the oasis that most attracts us. Hermann Melville wrote in *Moby Dick*:

> Why is almost every robust boy with a robust healthy soul in him, at some time or other crazy to go to sea? Why upon your first voyage as a passenger, did you feel yourself such a mystical vibration, when first told that you and your ship were now out of sight of land? Why did the old Persians hold the sea holy? Why did the Greeks give it a separate deity, and own brother of Jove? Surely all this is not without meaning. And still deeper the meaning of that story of Narcissus, who because he could not grasp the tormenting, mild image he saw in the fountain, plunged into it and was drowned. But that same image, we ourselves see in all rivers and oceans. It is the image of the ungraspable phantom of life; and this is the key to it all.[2]

Water is life. The seas teem, as they always have, with the most abundant life. As the Earth's internal fires began to cool, life's niche in the neighborhood of hydrothermal vents became narrower and more specialized (though even today, there are still thermophilic bacteria that thrive in such places). As life advanced to land, it still required water—sometimes precious little, but the more precious that little. There are microorganisms able to live on the water adsorbed onto a single crystal of salt, there is a plant of the Namib Desert of Africa (*Welwitschia mirabilis*) that—by means of a single vertical root whose growth outraces the sinking of the rare rainfall into the soil—ekes out its existence on only a trace of annual rain water. Thus sustained, it is able to live for a thousand years.

Given water's fundamental importance to the development and sustenance of life on Earth, the existence of liquid water on the Martian surface has always been regarded as the sine qua non in the quest for life on Mars. The most recent theme of Martian exploration announced by NASA—"to follow the water"—has antecedents in the first investigations of Mars in the nineteenth century.

Sojourner, deployed by *Pathfinder* on the surface of Mars and able to capture the imagination of the public in a way that many more pretentious missions failed to do, bore the name of Sojourner Truth, the nineteenth-century black evangelist and reformer who advocated abolition and women's rights. Someday another space vehicle ought to be named for another prominent nineteenth-century suffragist, Carrie Nation, the temperance advocate famous (or notorious) for her demolition of barrooms with a hatchet. She believed, firmly and uncompromisingly, with the Greek poet Pindar: "Water is best."

For nineteenth-century astronomers such as Secchi and Schiaparelli, the quest for Martian water seemed eminently straightforward; water seemed to be literally present right before their eyes, since both took for granted that the dark areas of the planet were bodies of liquid water. Thus, in his *First Memoir*, summarizing his results at the 1877 opposition, Schiaparelli wrote:

> Based on the data of experience, we can readily accept the supposition that the bright areas on Mars are its continents, and the dark parts its seas. This probability is further enhanced from the appearance on our chart, where all appears to be disposed in a manner suggestive of the expansion of a liquid mass above an uneven surface. Thus all those streaks, which form furrows between the so-called seas and whose ample mouths are trumpet-like in shape, appear just as expected if the large dark regions are indeed seas, and the streaks the channels of communication between them.
>
> . . . [Moreover,] could we imagine vapors, clouds, and polar ices existing upon a wholly dry planet? The alternating waxing and waning of the two masses of the polar ices presupposes the transport of a vast quantity of substance from one hemisphere to the other. Transport on such a vast scale must take place partly through the movement of vapor, but also partly through liquid currents, as on Earth.[3]

In general, astronomers of the day were satisfied to follow William Herschel's suggestion that the polar caps consisted of frozen water, though there was at least one lonely dissenter. The Irish astronomer G. Johnstone

Stoney, using the recently formulated theory of gases of James Clerk Maxwell to calculate that Mars might not be massive enough to have hung onto much of its original water-supply, argued that the polar caps must consist of frozen deposits of the heavier gas carbon dioxide (dry ice). Resurrected again after the *Mariner 6* and *7* spacecraft flybys in 1969, Stoney's theory is now known to be true, in the qualified sense that the polar caps do indeed contain quantities of frozen carbon dioxide (though in the case of the north cap, overlying a more permanent cap made up of ordinary water-ice). However, it was largely disregarded by nineteenth-century astronomers, simply because it seemed that Martian water vapor had already been detected by pioneer spectroscopists.

In the case of the Moon or Mars, which shine by reflected sunlight, the spectrum will, in the first instance, be merely the solar spectrum, including the characteristic Fraunhofer lines. However, whereas the Moon has long been known to be, to all intents and purposes, airless, on Mars the sunlight will—before arriving at the spectroscope of an astronomer on Earth—have passed twice, once coming and once going, through its atmosphere. Thus, a comparison of the spectrum of the Moon with that of Mars should reveal slight intensifications of the lines corresponding to chemical elements present in the Martian atmosphere, including—if present—water vapor.

To detect water vapor in the atmosphere of Mars would, then, seem to be straightforward enough, involving nothing more than a side by side comparison of the spectra of the airless Moon with that of Mars. Preferably this would be carried out at a time when both are present in the same part of the sky (to insure that the light-path through the Earth's atmosphere is nearly the same). The experiment was duly attempted by the early workers in spectroscopy. The first was William Huggins, an English amateur astronomer who, after amassing a sizeable fortune in his family's silk shop in London, sold the business in his early thirties, moved with his elderly parents into a comfortable large house at Tulse Hill in south London, and henceforth devoted all of his time to astronomical research with a 20-centimeter (8-inch) Clark refractor he acquired from the well-known observer William Rutter Dawes. According to his own autobiographical notes, Huggins became dissatisfied with the "routine character of ordinary astronomical work," but was rescued by Bunsen and Kirchoff's 1859 papers on spectroscopy and their exciting spectroscopic demonstration, two years later, of the chemical composition of the Sun. These results Huggins experienced as "like the coming upon a spring of water in a dry and thirsty land."[4] He was also a "lateral thinker insofar as he possessed the ability to see around scientific corners."[5] By 1862, Huggins began systematically analyzing light—not from the Sun, but from the distant stars—by means of a spectroscope attached to his telescope. That year he also confirmed that the spectrum of Mars—then at a favorable opposition—exhibited the principal lines of the solar spectrum, which was to be expected, since Mars shines by reflected sunlight. In 1867, he went further and announced that he had found a series of bands in the spectrum of Mars not in the solar spectrum. These he identified as due to water vapor, since they were the same as bands seen when sunlight passes through the lower layers of the Earth's atmosphere (the so-called telluric bands).

As Huggins well knew, the presence of water vapor in the Earth's atmosphere—in massive quantities—was sure to confuse experiments aimed at the detection of water vapor on Mars, since bands produced by terrestrial water vapor were bound to be superimposed on the Martian spectrum. But Huggins found the Martian bands were somewhat strengthened relative to those in the Moon's spectrum, even when the latter was observed at a lower altitude in the sky (so that its light had to traverse a longer path through the Earth's atmosphere). Thus, he felt justified in concluding that the bands he observed in the spectrum of Mars had been produced at least in part by water vapor in the atmosphere of that planet.

Subsequently, Huggins's result was confirmed by other astronomers, who followed his method and used the spectroscope, in effect, as a divining rod for finding water on Mars. These astronomers included Angelo Secchi in Italy, Herman Vogel in Germany, and most notably Pierre Jules Janssen in France. Janssen had a particularly colorful career. He had started out as a bank teller and teacher, but turned to science in his early thirties—his first scientific work was a magnetic survey of Peru. He quickly gravitated to the exciting possibilities of spectroscopy in astronomical research, and in the 1860s made a careful study—from high in the Alps—of the absorption of the solar spectrum by the Earth's atmosphere. He concluded that most of the telluric lines superimposed on the solar spectrum were produced by water vapor. It is these lines on which he concentrated his attention in a May 1867 study of the spectrum of Mars, carried out from the

William Huggins (1824–1910). (Mary Lea Shane archives of the Lick Observatory)

summit of the 3,280-meter (10,741-foot) still-sulking volcano Etna in Sicily. The location was most appropriate. Here, according to ancient lore, is the pillar of the sky spewing out the waters that the sea pours into the whirlpool of the monster Charybdis. Here, the Greek philosopher Empedocles (c. 490-420 B.C.E.), allegedly hoping to demonstrate to his followers that he was a god, tossed himself into the crater, while a much later philosopher, Giordano Bruno (who was burned at the stake, in part, for his belief in the Copernican system) concluded from his studies that the volcano's activity resulted from the interaction of fire and water.

Janssen did not go to Mt. Etna specifically to observe the spectrum of Mars; the planet was far from the Earth, and its disk was small, but in spite of the difficulties Janssen—who had previously made himself thoroughly familiar with the absorption features of water vapor by passing a beam of light through a long tube filled with water in his laboratory at Meudon—confirmed the results of Huggins at sea-level. Because of the great altitude of Etna and the bitter cold near the summit, there was very little water above his station, and yet he weakly saw the water bands in the spectrum of Mars, though none in that of the Moon, which was then at lower altitude. In his discussion of these results he added a revealing comment:

> To the close analogies which already unite the planets of our system, a new and important character has now been added. All the planets form, accordingly, but one family; they revolve about the same central body giving them heat and light. They have each a year, seasons, an atmosphere. . . . Finally, water, which plays so important a part in all organized beings, is also an element common to the planets. These are powerful reasons to think that life is no exclusive privilege of our little Earth.[6]

Despite his brief campaign on Mars, Janssen was always most interested in the solar spectrum, and before the total eclipse of 1870—during the Prussian siege of Paris—he escaped from the city *en ballon*, and successfully landed within the path of totality in Algeria, only to be clouded out. He became the first director of the Meudon Observatory in 1875, and in 1890, when he was in his sixties, still pursuing his perennial quest for high-altitude observations, established an observatory on Mont Blanc, Europe's highest peak; he had to be carried by porters, sedan style, to the summit.

By then, the belief in actual seas on Mars was coming under attack from

Jules Janssen. (Mary Lea Shane archives of the Lick Observatory)

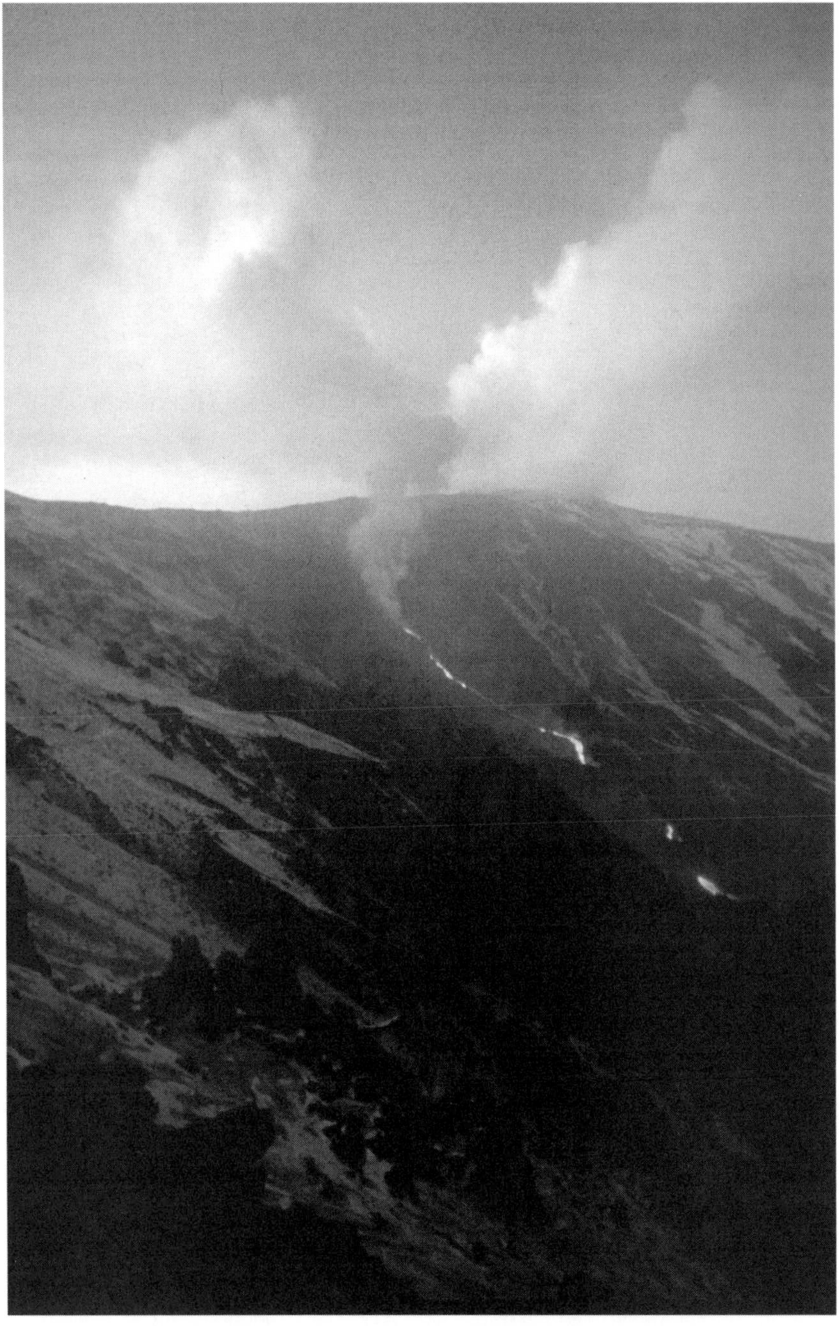

Mount Etna in eruption in 1991. ©Stephen and Donna O'Meara / Volcano Watch Intl.

Janssen borne by sedan chair to the summit of Mt. Blanc. (Courtesy Leo Aerts)

several quarters. The first dramatic reduction in the amount of water claimed for the planet was made during the observing campaign of 1894, when Pickering and Lowell established that the dark areas, despite their blue or green hues, could not be seas as had been assumed so long but were more likely vegetation. But they still believed that there were standing bodies of water in parts of the planet, notably around the polar caps. A dark blue collar, later known as the Lowell band, formed each Martian year around each melting cap, and was identified as consisting of a temporary sea of meltwater. This furnished, it seemed, direct evidence against the solid carbon dioxide theory of Johnstone Stoney, since under ordinary conditions carbon dioxide sublimes—passes directly from solid to vapor—and does not pass through the liquid phase at all. Moreover, there were, of course, abundant (if indirect) signs of the effect of water in what appeared to be the blooming of desert vegetation in the dark areas and along the canals.

In that same year 1894, W. W. Campbell, a young astronomer at the Lick Observatory, made a renewed attack with the spectroscope on the Martian water vapor question. He attached to the world's largest telescope at the time, the 91-centimeter (36-inch) refractor of the Lick Observatory, a much more powerful visual spectroscope than Huggins, Janssen, and their contemporaries had been able to use, which gave him a wider spectrum and thus allowed the detection of fainter lines or bands. Observing, moreover, in the late-summer and early-autumn dry season at Mt. Hamilton, where there was much less water than in England or France or any of the other European sites, Campbell set out to do what he at first thought would be "simple and easy." He assumed that if Huggins, Janssen, and the rest had been able to detect the bands of water vapor on Mars even under the extremely unfavorable conditions in which they had been forced to observe, with equipment that was primitive by his standard, the same result ought to have been glaringly obvious to him with his greatly superior means. What he actually found came as a great surprise. During ten nights that summer in which he attempted to compare the spectrum of Mars with that of the Moon, Campbell failed to detect any strengthening of the water vapor bands whatever. This did not, of course, prove that there was no water vapor on Mars, only—according to his calculations—that the amount present must be no more than one-fourth that above Mt. Hamilton on a dry summer night.[7]

Campbell's results were at once disputed by Huggins and Janssen, who repeated their earlier experiments and arrived at their same results. Janssen, in particular, made a great deal of the superior elevation of Mt. Etna compared with Mt. Hamilton.[8] The matter obviously was of the greatest importance to the whole question of possible life on Mars.

After V. M. Slipher joined the Lowell Observatory, Lowell assigned him the task of mastering spectroscopy, so that he could contend in this important arena. In this respect, Slipher was—in Campbell's opinion—"Lowell's man Friday." In the winter of 1908, when the air over Flagstaff was unusually dry, Slipher obtained spectrograms—photographs of the spectrum of Mars—supporting Huggins's and Janssen's earlier results. He believed they showed one of the more prominent bands due to water vapor, called the *a* band, strengthened in the Martian spectrum compared with that of the Moon. When Slipher described the results to Lowell, the latter had, characteristically, announced to the world that Slipher had succeeded in obtaining spectrographic evidence of water vapor on Mars, thereby confirming an important point in his theory. He later sent prints of Slipher's spectrograms for inclusion in the new edition of the *Encyclopaedia Britannica* where, Lowell wrote to Slipher, "they are sure to go 'thundering down the ages.' "[9]

W. W. Campbell with the spectroscope attached to the Lick Observatory refractor, used to search for Martian water vapor in 1894. (Mary Lea Shane archives of the Lick Observatory)

For good measure, Slipher also sent the spectrograms to Campbell, who—in noting that the *a* band was in the faint, almost invisible red end of the spectrum—was unimpressed. Campbell found that though in one of Slipher's spectrograms the band appeared to be intensified compared to the Moon's spectrum, it was not in another. He also noted that Mars had not been very near the Moon in the sky at the time the spectrograms were obtained. To George Ellery Hale of the Mt. Wilson Observatory, he confided his doubts:

> From the first, I have had no confidence in their reported evidence of water vapor, and these spectrograms do not change my opinion. The critical band lies just in the beginning of the region where Slipher's plates fall off exceedingly rapidly in sensitiveness, and we all know very well that in such regions the apparent contrasts may vary widely from the truth, both on the original negatives and the photographic copies. With the data now at hand, I believe this is the explanation of the apparent effect.[10]

As with such disputed features as the canals of Mars, it was obvious that the interpretation of the bands of the spectrum of Mars also depended very much on the viewpoint of the observer.

The following year, during August and September 1909—at almost the very moment when Antoniadi was beginning his epoch-making study of the planet with the great Meudon refractor—Campbell carried his quest for Martian water literally to new heights. As long ago as 1895, in response to Janssen's criticisms, he had resolved to take his spectroscopic equipment to a much greater elevation than Mt. Hamilton. He had his eye on Mt. Whitney, California's highest peak, from which he knew that most of the water vapor of the atmosphere of the Earth would be below him; conditions there would be highly sensitive for detecting water vapor on Mars, and Campbell resolved to make the summit—at 4,418 meters (14,495 feet,) an even greater elevation than Mt. Etna—his observing station.

For his telescope, Campbell used an 46-centimeter (18-inch) flat mirror—the size determined on the basis of the heaviest load a mule could transport up Mt. Whitney—which was turned by means of a clock drive so that it would feed the light into a fixed reflecting parabolic mirror 41-centimeter (16 inches) in diameter. The parabolic mirror in turn was tilted slightly so that it could reflect the light past the flat mirror into the slit of the spectroscope. A shelter was established on the summit, all the equipment was sent up in

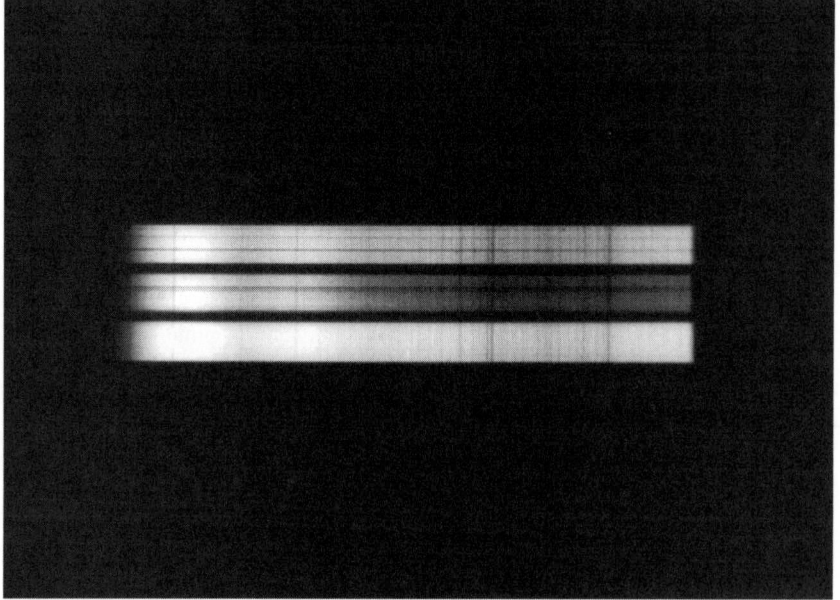

Spectrogram of Mars (center) and the Moon (top and bottom) taken by W. W. Campbell and his assistant Sebastian Albrecht from the summit of Mt. Whitney, in 1909. The water vapor bands in the visual region lie on either side of the strong sodium line about a third of the way from the right of the spectrum. Since they are essentially invisible on all these spectra, because of the dryness of the atmosphere over Mt. Whitney, Campbell concluded that there was very little water vapor on Mars. Note the red color of Mars shown by the weakness of its spectrum at the left (blue) end of the spectrum. (Courtesy Donald E. Osterbrock and Joseph Miller of the Lick Observatory)

advance, and Campbell and several assistants arrived on the summit on August 27 just as a thunder storm was in progress. Fortunately, the weather cleared on the night of September 1, and that night and the next Campbell obtained a series of exposures on the spectra Mars and the Moon. The spectrograms were developed on the summit and revealed that the notorious *a* band was weak on all of them; it was definitely no stronger in the spectrum of Mars than in that of the Moon. In 1894, this did not prove that there was no water vapor on Mars, only that the quantity present must be very slight—"much less . . . than was contained in the rarified and remarkably dry air . . . above Mount Whitney," he noted. And he added, "These observations do not prove that life does not or can not exist on Mars. The question of life under these conditions is the biologist's problem rather than the astronomer's."

Campbell went on to a great career as director of the Lick Observatory, and for many years was one of the ruling powers of American astronomy; finally—grown ill and depressed—he died at his own hand in 1938. His careful negative result would stand until 1963, when the detection of water vapor on Mars was made by Audouin Dollfus of France and independently by H. Spinrad, L. D. Kaplan, and G. Münch at Mt. Wilson Observatory in California using an extremely sensitive instrument that allowed them to look much farther into the infrared part of the spectrum (a region essentially invisible to the early pioneers of spectroscopy and to the relatively insensitive photographic plates used by Slipher and Campbell).

Dollfus was a daring French planetary astronomer who had been in pursuit of Martian water vapor for years. In May 1954 he ascended in a balloon to make observations of the Martian spectrum from a height of 7,000 meters (22,945 feet), more than twice the height of Mt. Etna. The balloon was launched at night from the terrace of the Meudon Observatory, close to the dome from which Antoniadi made his great observations and not far from the place where a statue of Janssen stands. He failed to detect an unambiguous signal of water in the Martian atmosphere. In April 1959 he tried again—this time stringing together a series of weather balloons and rising to a height of 14,000 meters (46,000 feet) in quest of this elusive result. Again his measurements were inconclusive, but in January 1963 he at last succeeded in detecting a trace of water vapor on Mars by means of a special telescope set up on the Jungfraujoch, a mountain pass high in the Swiss Alps.

The amount of water vapor was shockingly small. The Mt. Wilson group estimated that the equivalent thickness of liquid water, if all the atmospheric water were condensed onto the surface, would be only about 14 microns (thousandths of a meter), thus making Mars a far more arid desert than even the most arid deserts of Earth where the amount of precipitable water is at least on the order of 1,000 microns. The amount of water vapor on Mars fluctuates with the seasons, since much of it is released from the alternately melting polar caps, but on average it accounts for only about 0.04 percent of the pressure of the thin Martian atmosphere.

In total, the whole Martian atmosphere contains the equivalent of only about 4.8 cubic kilometers (1 cubic mile) of liquid water. Imagine three cubic miles of water dispersed over a planet with a surface area equal to that of all the continents of Earth. This will give some idea of the terrible reality of the Martian deserts.

In the motion picture *The Treasure of the Sierra Madre*, the salty old

Audouin Dollfus's April 1959 balloon ascension in quest of the elusive water vapor bands in the spectrum of Mars. Dollfus is standing in the gondola within the skeleton tube of the special telescope used on this flight. He was unable to detect water vapor on Mars on this occasion but succeeded in January 1963 with the same instrument mounted at a high-altitude station at Jungfraujoch in the Swiss Alps. (Courtesy of Audouin Dollfus)

miner played by Walter Huston quips that there are times when water is far more precious than gold. This would be emphatically true on Mars.

Schiaparelli christened one of the vast Saharan tracts of Mars Chryse—the Land of Gold. A century afterward it would serve as the landing site of *Viking 1*. Gold conjures up dreams of riches. But on Mars, there are no riches as great as those found in the smallest trickle of water in the deserts of Earth—much less the boundless treasures of our lakes and oceans. Mars is a desert more parched by far than the Atacama of South America where there are spots that have not tasted rain in a century, where a single summer shower brings riches far more precious than all the massed treasures of Croesus.

On Mars, it would be water—not gold—that would stir the fondest dreams.

14 Woodstock Mars

Men willingly believe what they wish.
—Julius Caesar,
De Bello Gallico III

The grandest and most tragic social experiment of a strange century—Soviet-style communism—contributed to a surrealistic midcentury world in which two superpowers created giant rockets aimed at each other. The spiritual ancestors of these rockets were starry-eyed dreamers such as Lucian of Somosata, who in 160 C.E. wrote of a voyage to the Moon, and the nineteenth-century French science fiction writer Jules Verne, who wrote of a cannon powerful enough to fire a projectile from the Earth to the Moon. Then there were the thinkers: Konstantin Tsiolkovsky, a nearly deaf teacher who developed the theory of rocket propulsion a year before the Wright brothers flew at Kitty Hawk and later wrote of rocket-powered interplanetary vehicles; Robert Hutchins Goddard, who was scorned as an eccentric by his contemporaries for building experimental rockets and firing them in the United States (in an editorial in the *New York Times*, he was accused of being ignorant of the most elementary principles of physics in imagining that a rocket could work in a vacuum!); and Hermann Oberth, a theorist from Austria-Hungary (now Romania) who, even though his doctoral dissertation on rocket design was rejected for being too improbable, sparked the rise of modern rockets in Europe through the German *Verein für Raumschiffahrt* (Society for Space Travel).

The immediate fathers of these rockets were a pragmatic group of German engineer-visionaries, like Wernher von Braun, who, after meeting Oberth in the mid-1920s, became enamored with the idea of interplanetary flight. Von Braun later made a pact with the devil of Nazism to acquire the funds for building rockets big enough to cross a continent. He was placed in charge of the German army's rocket station at Peenemünde, on the Baltic, where the sinister V-2 buzz-bombs were developed. They were, essentially, weapons of terror, and in the final desperate stages of the war were rained down on London and the Home Counties with much destruction and loss of life. (A biography of von Braun was called *I Aim at the Stars*, but an irreverent comic from the 1960s noted that the real title ought to have been *I Aim at the Stars but Sometimes Hit London*.)

Shortly before World War II ended, von Braun surrendered to the U.S. Army, bringing with him 120 of his engineers; other engineers surrendered to Russia, setting the stage for a rocket race to the heavens. At the time both the United States and Russia were more than a decade behind the Germans in rocket technology. In the euphoria of the postwar years, von Braun and his colleagues, plus magazine writers and a generation of starstruck youngsters, some of whom would later become NASA Mars scientists, believed that interplanetary flight was just around the corner. Around 1950, von Braun and his colleagues wrote a series of articles, beautifully illustrated by the pioneering space artist Chesley Bonestell, for the magazine *Colliers*. These articles—published in the days when most popular magazines still had content—showed the feasibility of multi-stage spacefaring rockets, instrumented satellites, space stations in orbits, landings on the Moon, and epic expeditions to Mars.

In a 1952 speech von Braun urged that the United States build a "manned satellite to curb Russia's military ambitions." A year later—as the United States was attempting to extricate itself from a military quagmire in Korea—he pointed out in his book *The Mars Project* that "the logistic requirements for a large elaborate expedition to Mars are no greater than those for a minor military operation extending over a limited theater of war."[1] His words fell on deaf ears. But by 1957, both Soviet Russia and the United States were planning to demonstrate their technological prowess by launching artificial satellites into Earth orbit as part of the 1957-58 International Geophysical Year. On October 4, 1957, the Russians—led by von Braun's equally brilliant counterpart, Sergei P. Korolev—astonished the world by launching the first artificial satellite, *Sputnik 1*, and ushering in the Space Age.

Claiming the lead in space technology, Soviet Russia now postured menacingly at the United States, which viewed the situation as a threat to national security. Having survived the Third Reich, von Braun became an American hero when he shot back America's reply four months later: using one of his rockets, America launched its first artificial satellite—the bullet-shaped *Explorer 1*. The man who once sent weapons of terror across the continents had now thrust humanity a step closer to achieving the centuries-old dream of interplanetary travel; indeed, von Braun would live to see men walk on the Moon.

Within months of the *Sputnik* and *Explorer* launches, a vigorous planetary scientific community began to organize in universities from Los Angeles to Moscow, promoting the idea of using the large existing intercontinental ballistic missile technology to expand humanity's horizons and to explore the planets.

In retrospect, it is apparent that Sputnik, more than any other development, shocked the West into recognizing that the socialist system had beaten it at its own game. Russian leaders saw space exploration as a way of establishing the credibility of their system while at the same time developing weapons of mass destruction (powered by rockets, of course), which they could use, if necessary, against the perceived threat of imperialistic capitalism. In 1961, recently elected president John F. Kennedy saw space exploration as the most likely means of galvanizing the country out of its Eisenhower-era complacency by pushing the nation's engineers to better efforts (and of curing his own political doldrums following the Cuban Bay of Pigs debacle). Scientists saw a chance to hitch their instruments to rockets bound for other worlds, where they could finally learn whether generations of thinkers about the cosmos and man's place in it had been right in supposing there might be other Earth-like worlds in the universe. The public saw a high-stakes adventure.

The most likely places where answers to these perennial questions might be found were Venus and Mars. At the time, Venus was a cloud-shrouded enigma; it might be covered with oceans, dense jungles, or deserts—no one knew. Even the period of its rotation was unknown. The Russians launched the first of many probes to Venus in February 1961, but lost contact with it long before it reached the planet. The Americans had the first success with *Mariner 2*, which swept by Venus in December 1962 showing that the planet was more like the Medieval notion of hell than it was like another Earth; conditions on the surface were extreme, owing to runaway greenhouse warming produced by the massive carbon-dioxide atmosphere, with the temperature reaching 477° C (890° F), well above the melting point of lead. Clearly there was no possible role for life there. That left Mars.

The Russians were again the pioneers; they launched several unsuccessful missions in the early days of spacefaring. One vehicle, *Mars 1*, set out in the fall of 1962 and reached a distance of over 100 million kilometers (62 million miles) from the Earth before its radio transmitter went dead. No useful information was obtained from it when it sailed silently and uselessly by the planet in June 1963. The first American spacecraft to Mars, *Mariners 3* and *4*, were launched in November 1964. *Mariner 3* failed ignominiously soon after launch when a fiberglass shroud on the front end of the rocket failed to separate; *Mariner 4*—launched on November 28, the three hundred and fifth anniversary of Christiaan Huygens's rough sketch showing the Syrtis Major region in unmistakable form—went off well; the shroud was ejected and the solar panels deployed, which would power the spacecraft on its seven and a half month journey to the red planet.

Although crude by today's standards, and resembling a Volkswagen-sized lampshade connected to a ceiling fan of solar panels, *Mariner 4* represented the cutting edge of technology at the time. It embodied NASA's

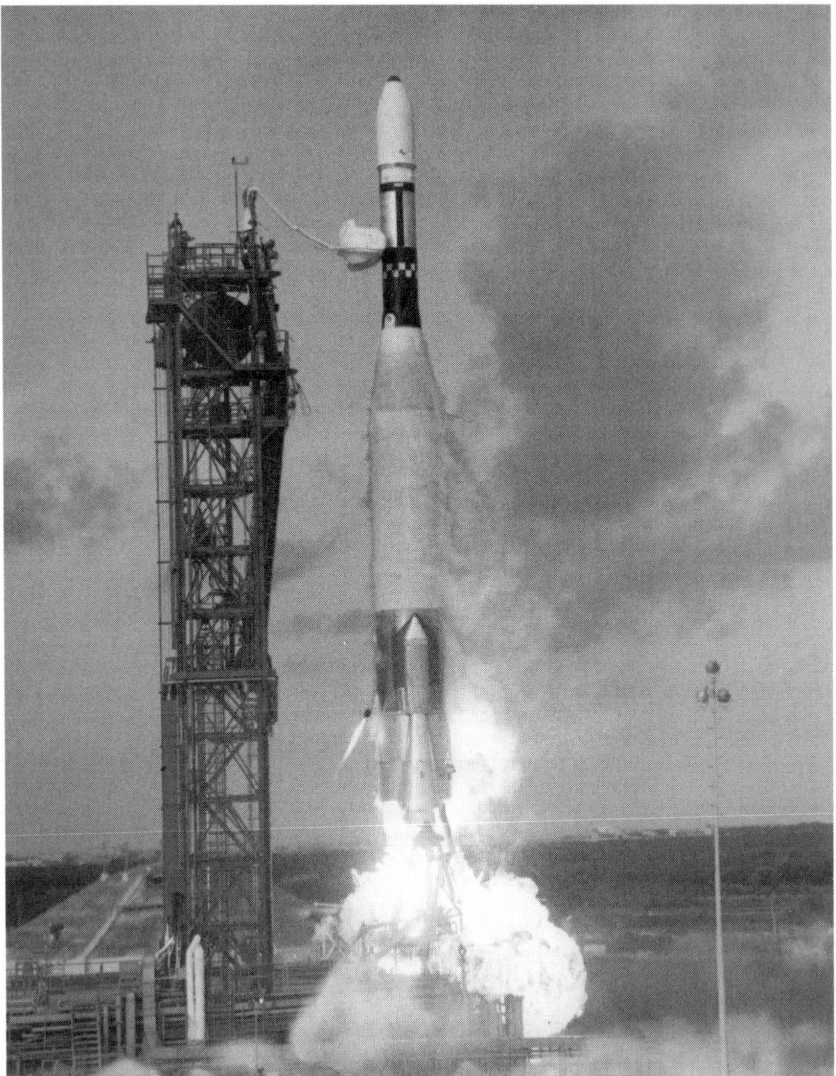

Launch of *Mariner 4*, November 28, 1964—305 years to the day after Huygens's sketch of the Syrtis Major region. (NASA)

original philosophy: spaceflight would be the testbed for the latest technical advances in electronics, miniaturization, computers, and innovative design. In those days, each new spacecraft was meant to be bigger and grander than the last. These bold leaps drove American technology forward. The philosophy lasted until the 1990s, when it was replaced by the "smaller, cheaper, faster" approach, designed to get more small probes off the ground but encouraging reliance on off-the-shelf modules instead of innovation.

Mariner 4 carried a number of sensitive instruments to measure the magnetic fields, dust particles, and interplanetary gas encountered on the way to Mars as well as sample their presence in the Martian environment. The radio transmitter would be used not only to transmit data but to make a crucial scientific measurement—one that had long eluded Earthbound observers. When the spacecraft passed behind Mars (in terms of its line-of-sight direction from the Earth) its radio signals would pass through the Martian atmosphere. Measurement of the resulting distortion of the radio signal would allow measures of the pressure, temperature, and density of the atmosphere. Measures of the magnetic field of Mars were also important in characterizing the planet, because a strong dipole field—that is, one with a north and south magnetic pole, like the Earth's—is thought to be generated by currents in a liquid iron core. A strong field of this type would suggest a sizable active core, still molten; a weak or patchy field would suggest a frozen, "dead" interior.

The most important instrumentation on board *Mariner 4* was the camera system. The camera could not be targeted on specific surface features, such as canals; instead, as *Mariner 4* flew past, the camera would simply snap a series of pictures covering a strip across the disk of Mars. Scientists would have to settle for what they could get.

On July 15, 1965 (Greenwich Mean Time), *Mariner 4* sailed 9,800 kilometers (6,120 miles) above the surface of Mars—about three planetary radii from the center. This large-miss trajectory was selected to avoid any chance of a crash on the surface; no one wanted to take the chance of contaminating the Martian soil with terrestrial microbes or organic molecules before it could be tested for native lifeforms.

The camera worked well enough, sending back a string of twenty-two "postage stamp" pictures of small regions on the disk. The first was a view of the limb, showing a section of the Amazonis desert. The rest of the series covered a discontinuous swath extending south and then eastward from Amazonis across Zephyria, Atlantis (the bright strip between the dark areas Cimmerium and Sirenum), Phaetontis, Memnonia. It took almost a week to transmit the data to Earth. The images with their coarse TV scanning lines were not great even by 1965 standards; a single photo with a good 35mm camera contained about twenty-five times the number of information bits of the entire *Mariner 4* photo set. Furthermore, the images had surprisingly low contrast; they appeared murky and hazy. (Designers had not counted on the dust, haze and mists that often veil Mars. Such may account for the poor quality of the images, but it's also possible the problem was more mundane, originating in a light-leak in the camera system.) Nonetheless—poor as they were—the *Mariner 4* images gave the first view of real topographic and geologic features on Mars instead of the broad shadings and shifting clouds that had been the domain of generations of telescopic observers. The features included impact craters, something like three hundred in all, in all sizes, including one in Mare Sirenum measuring 120 kilometers (75 miles) across. It was as if *Mariner 4* had simply photographed a strip of the Moon's surface.

Today, craters do not seem surprising on an alien world, but in 1965 they caused a shocked reappraisal of Mars. It is important to remember that in the early 1960s impact craters were only beginning to be recognized as an important phenomenon shaping planetary surfaces. Arizona's "Meteor Crater" (a misnamed feature that should really be known as "meteorite crater" since "meteor" refers to a bolide burning up in the atmosphere and "meteorite" to one reaching the ground) had been recognized for more than a century; it is located not far from Lowell's observatory at Flagstaff. But it was thought to be a freakish feature of no real consequence. Thousands of craters had been mapped on the surface of the Moon, but in the early 1960s they were still widely believed to be volcanic. Eugene Shoemaker, a geologist at the U.S. Geological Survey station in Flagstaff who would later go on to become the century's foremost asteroid scientist and codiscoverer of the famous Shoemaker-Levy 9 comet that impacted into Jupiter in 1994, had just completed his youthful research on the Arizona crater and was rapidly convincing his colleagues that the lunar craters were features of the same type. This would imply that both the Earth and Moon had been shelled, early in their history as worlds, by swarming shards of interplanetary debris.

Meanwhile, Canadian geologists were beginning to recognize numerous ancient, glacier-eroded impact craters in Canada, usually visible on aerial photos as precisely circular lakes. Canada proved to be an ideal hunting ground for ancient impact scars, because it is the several billion-year-old core (craton) of the North American continent—a stable region that has been relatively spared disruption by mountain building, volcanism, or plate tectonic forces.

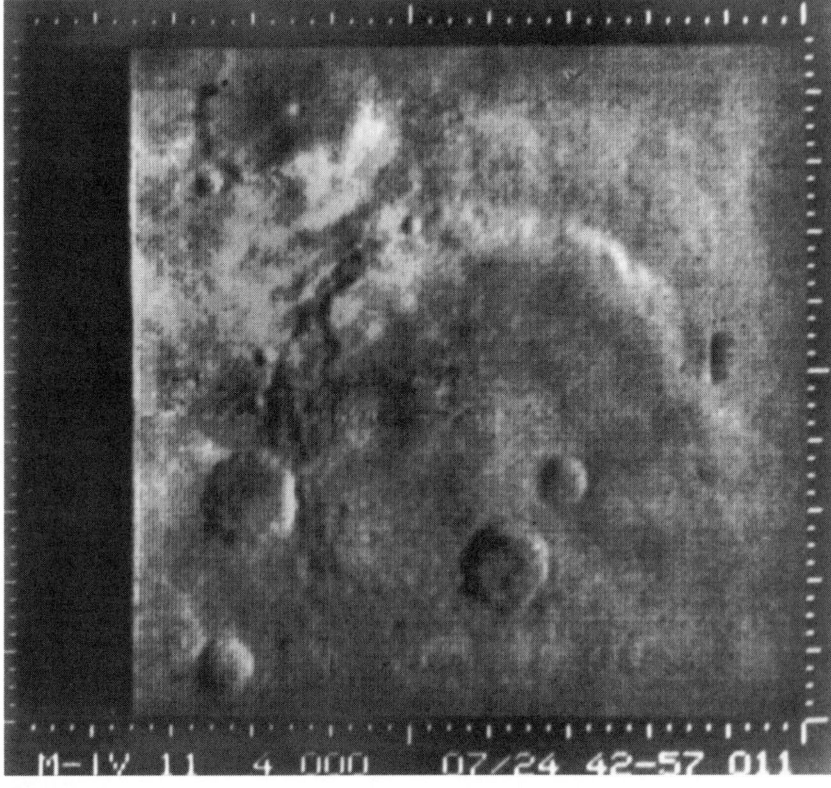

Large crater in Mare Sirenum—*Mariner 4* image. This crater was later named "Mariner." (NASA)

The upshot of all this work in the early 1960s was the recognition that ancient planetary surfaces in the solar system have accumulated many asteroid and meteorite hits. To put it the other way around, a very young surface, such as a lakebed deposit or a lava flow that is, say, only 100 million years old, is unlikely to have accumulated many hits. But if the surface is one to three billion years old like the Canadian shield, it will have many scattered craters, exactly like the dark lunar lava plains that make up the features of the "Man in the Moon." And if it is about four billion years, it will show the scars of the heaviest era of bombardment that accompanied planet formation—it will be virtually saturated with craters, shoulder to shoulder, cheek by jowl.

In 1965, the significance of all this research had not yet been felt, and *Mariner 4* scientists emerged from their first views of the image set somewhat shell-shocked. A few scientists—notably, Clyde Tombaugh, the discoverer of Pluto in 1930 and a keen-eyed student of the planets at the Lowell Observatory and later at New Mexico State University, and the Estonian-born Ernst J. Öpik—had suggested as long ago as the 1950s that the surface of Mars might well prove to be cratered, owing to the planet's proximity to the asteroid belt. Tombaugh even proposed that the "oases" of Lowell and Pickering might actually be craters. But they had had virtually no impact. In a 1976 book released to coincide with the forthcoming *Viking* lander missions, well-known Mars scientists Tim Mutch, Ray Arvidson, Jim Head, Kenneth Jones, and Steve Saunders reviewed the *Mariner 4* era. Recalling the remark by the *Mariner 4* team—that the craters were "not expected by most scientists"—they added with a touch of sarcasm that "in retrospect, it is difficult to imagine what they were expecting." But really it is not so difficult to imagine. They were men and women of their time, expecting answers to the mystery of the canals (despite passing over several of those mapped by classical observers, *Mariner 4* showed no sign of them). They were wondering if they would see evidence of Earth-like mountain ranges, canyons, even erupting volcanoes to explain the "flashes" and transient bright spots reported by observers ever since the late nineteenth century. The implicit paradigm was that only dead moons had craters; planets—at least the inner or so-called *terrestrial* planets—should have Earth-like features.

Taken at face value, the *Mariner 4* images seemed to reveal a world that was, in a word, Moon-like—its surface apparently old, battered, dead. This somber impression was reinforced by the failure of the spacecraft's instruments to detect a magnetic field and especially by the results of the radio-occultation experiment. Two hours after making its closest approach to the surface of Mars, *Mariner 4* passed behind the planet. Its radio signal was distorted by passage through the thin Martian atmosphere, and this was repeated when it emerged again from the night side. By analyzing the shape of the distortion it was possible to calculate the surface pressure at the two occultation points. The result was distressingly low—only 4.0 to 6.1 millibars (thousandths of a bar, where 1 bar is roughly equal to the surface pressure of the atmosphere of the Earth).

Only a few years earlier, in the early 1950s, the French astronomer Gerard de Vaucouleurs had carefully weighed all the evidence and suggested that a value around 85 millibars was probably about right; not far from the value of 87 millibars that Percival Lowell had adopted. The only pre-*Mariner* estimate even close to that of *Mariner 4* was the 1963 measure from Mt. Wilson Observatory, a byproduct of the search for water vapor in the atmosphere of Mars. The Mt. Wilson team had estimated the partial pressure of carbon dioxide on Mars as 4.2 millibars, putting the total atmospheric surface pressure at not more than 25 millibars—though even this drastic downward revision was not draconian enough, as it turned out, since they grossly underestimated the percent composition of carbon dioxide in the Martian atmosphere. As we now know, the Martian atmosphere is almost entirely—95 percent—carbon dioxide.

In view of these findings, it seemed only too likely that G. Johnstone Stoney's nineteenth-century theory that the polar caps were comprised of carbon-dioxide ice—Dry Ice—was in fact correct. At such low atmospheric pressures, liquid water—even in the relatively warmer equatorial regions of the planet—would be unstable on the surface. In their official summary of the *Mariner 4* results, Robert B. Leighton and the other members of the television team announced that "the heavily cratered surface of Mars must be very ancient—perhaps 2 to 5 billion years old . . . [and] it is difficult to believe that free water in quantities sufficient to form streams or fill oceans could have existed on Mars since that time."[2]

In the midst of this drastic downsizing of Martian expectations, Ernst Öpik counted up the impact craters in the *Mariner 4* pictures and compared them with size distributions of craters on the Moon. He found that in relative terms, Mars had fewer small craters than the Moon. Furthermore, many of the large old craters on Mars had shallower, flatter floors than the small young craters. Öpik surmised that some process on Mars, either present or past, was moving dust and sediments to fill in the craters. And William K. Hartmann, a scientist at G. P. Kuiper's Lunar and Planetary Laboratory in Tucson, who would later propose the currently accepted theory of the formation of the Moon from a large impact involving the primordial Earth and another planet, applied a similar analysis to terrestrial impact craters that had been identified up to that time. He found that the terrestrial features were even more depleted in small craters than those on Mars, a result of the obvious rapid destruction or infill by processes such as water transport and deposition of sediments, glaciation, plate tectonic activity, and the like. Thus, Mars was not so Moon-like after all, but intermediate between the Moon and Earth in terms of surface youthfulness and geologic activity. Maybe Mars wasn't so uninteresting after all.

At this point, NASA announced another pair of probes would be readied to take advantage of the launch window around the 1969 close approach of Mars. *Mariners 6* and *7* set out in February and March of 1969, respectively. After a few heart-stopping mishaps, such as *Mariner 7*'s temporary loss of stabilization and signal just before reaching Mars, the two probes arrived within a few days of each other around August 1 (just after the Apollo 11 lunar landing). Like *Mariner 4*, they were flyby missions, but this time the cameras included both wide-angle and telephoto lenses. During the long swing out to the planet, images of Mars were obtained for comparison with Earth-based images, while wide-angle views obtained during the closest approach provided far better coverage than the "postage stamp" images of *Mariner 4*.

Mariner 4 had provided coverage of only 1 percent of the planet's surface. The two probes of 1969 increased the coverage to 10 percent. Moreover, because the dark areas had always been the features which had most strongly seized the attention of Earth-based observers, they were given the highest priority. The flyby *Mariners* were directed selectively to the dark areas, mostly in the southern hemisphere.

The desolate impressions of a Moon-like Mars were very much in evidence; the by-now familiar craters were fairly ubiquitous, and included a number of frost-fringed features along the edge of the south polar cap—whether coated with water-ice or frozen carbon dioxide it was impossible to say. However, in addition to the lunar-like landscapes, there were some surprises as well. The large bright circular area of Hellas—classically regarded as an elevation, since it was a site where whitish clouds were frequently formed—proved to be a low-lying basin. Its interior was virtually featureless. This seemed to imply massive transport and deposition of dust sediments, certainly a nonlunar process. There was also an irregularly shaped lowland area, christened "chaotic terrain," centered on about 40°W, 15°S; it consisted of hillocks jumbled in higgledy-piggledy fashion, which looked as if formed by withdrawal of subsurface material, such as the local melting of permafrost or ice triggering collapse from below. This implied that frozen Mars had once experienced flowing water. (However, this possibility raised further questions: If ice had melted in restricted areas, what

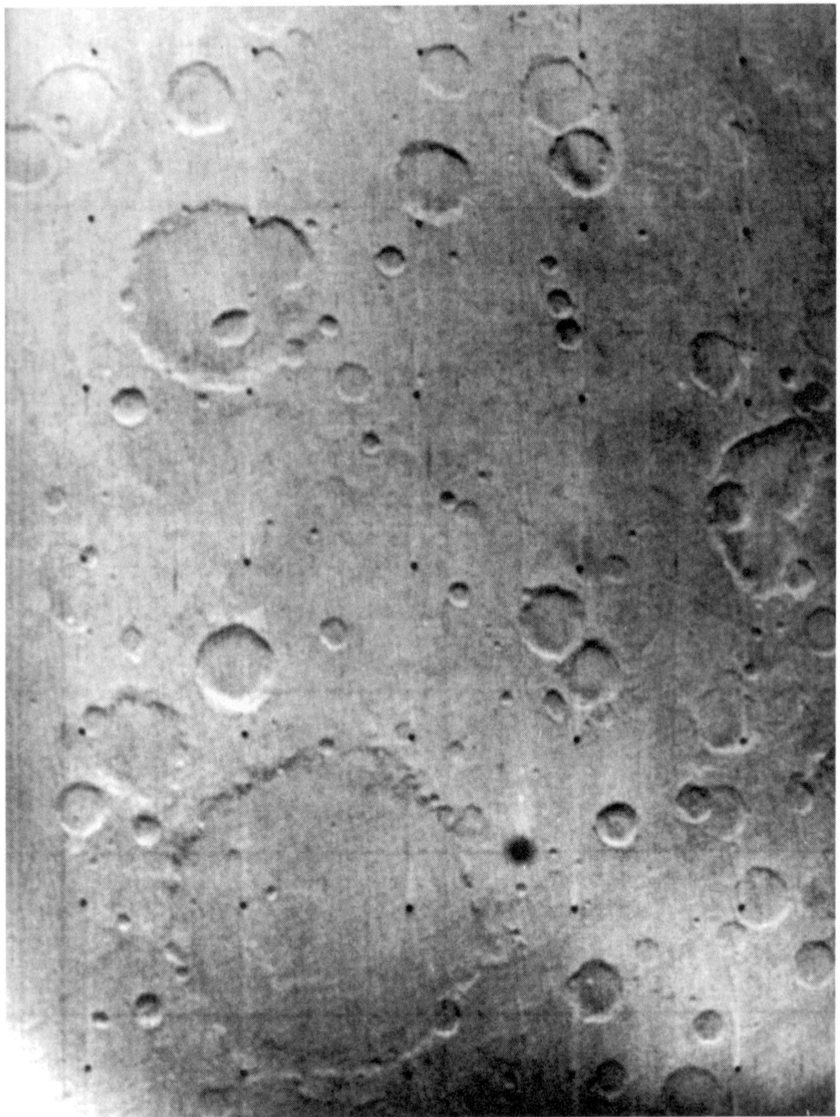

Mariner 6 "near-encounter" image of Mars showing lunar-like surface. (NASA)

was the localized source of heat? Did Mars have local geothermal or volcanic activity? Moreover, if liquid water had been involved in shaping the Martian surface in the past, where was the real evidence? Three separate space probes and hundreds of photos had turned up no real evidence of river channels, lakebed deposits, or shorelines.

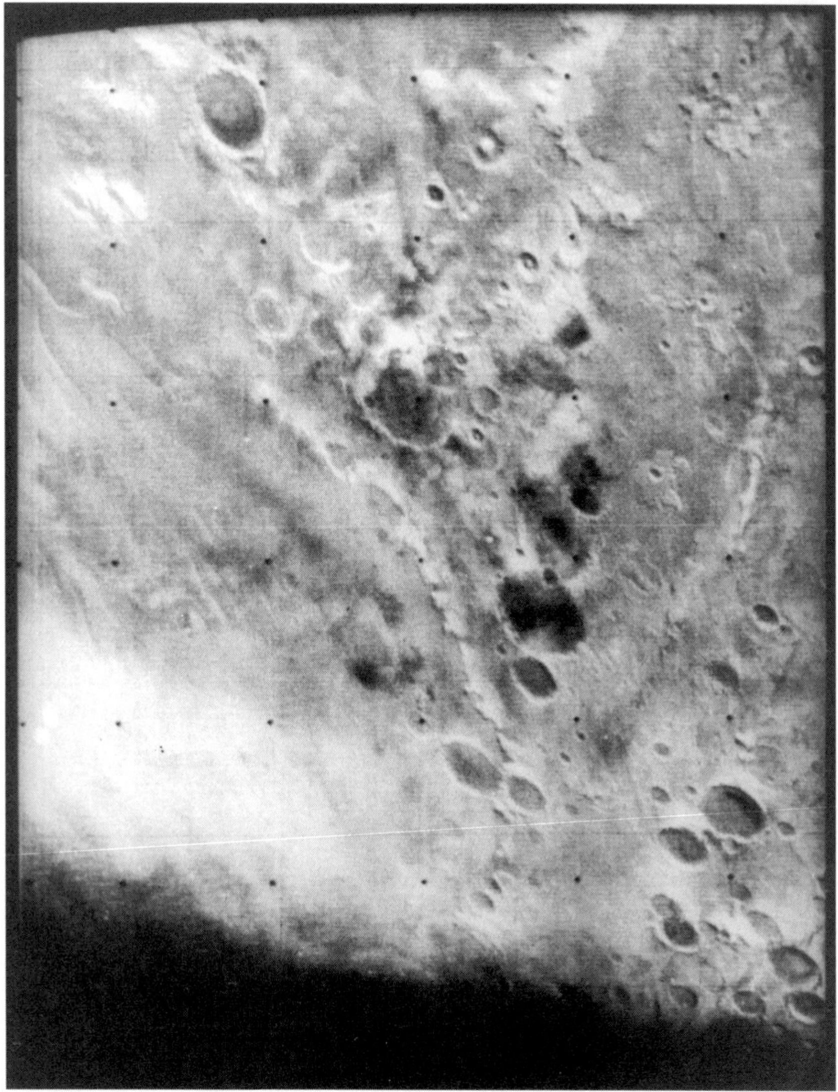

Mariner 7 view of carbon-dioxide frost-rimmed craters in south polar region of Mars. (NASA)

Apart from the imaging results, the rest of the findings from the two spacecraft added confirmation to what was already known. Instruments on board the two spacecraft registered the same low atmospheric pressures found by *Mariner 4*—thus *Mariner 6* found a pressure of 6.5 millibars in the Sinus Meridiani region, while *Mariner 7* found only 3.5 millibars over a region, Hellespontica Depressio, which had long been regarded from Earthbased observations as a depression (hence the name) but instead proved to be elevated. The temperature at the south polar cap was measured at –123° C (–190° F), almost exactly as expected if it were composed entirely of frozen carbon dioxide.

The politically and socially turbulent era of the 1960s ended with the drab and moonlike Mars of *Mariner 4* still fairly ensconced—though *Mariners 6* and *7* had added just enough qualifications to pique further interest. The Lowellian world of dry sea-bottoms, canals, and dying civilizations had faded like a dream and what Norman Horowitz has called the "delowellization of Mars" was complete. But it was also true that Mars was no Moon; the post-*Mariner 4* reaction had gone too far.

Had Mars ever been remotely Earth-like? This was the real question. But the only way to find out was to go back to Mars and do a complete mapping of all its features rather than attempt to extrapolate from a small subset of them.

15
The Brave New World of *Mariner 9*

Worlds on worlds are rolling ever
From creation to decay,
Like the bubbles on a river
Sparkling, bursting, borne away.

—Percy Bysshe Shelley, "Hellas"

There have been epic journeys in the history of human exploration of the solar system, journeys that rival the Earthbound adventures of Columbus or Magellan. There was Galileo's exploration of the mountains and craters of the Moon from his balcony in Padua; the systematic series of explorations by that Henry the Navigator of Mars, Schiaparelli, from the Palazzo of Brera in Milan; Percival Lowell's twenty-two-year odyssey at the telescope in Flagstaff; Antoniadi's September night of superlative vision at Meudon.

There have been farflung expeditions to the Moon and planets by spacecraft, such as the Russian Veneras' brave descents through the choking atmosphere of Venus to the hellish red surface of that sinister planet, the landings of astronauts and Lunokhods on the Moon, the *Voyagers*' grand and glorious voyages to the outer planets—Jupiter, Saturn, Uranus, Neptune.

But of all the planetary missions of this golden era of discovery, arguably the most significant in the sheer sweep and implication of its findings was *Mariner 9*. Before *Mariner 9*, our view of Mars—for at least a century the most compelling world beyond the Earth—was largely a matter of distant surmise based on fragmentary visions eked out by informed hunches and speculations. Now for the first time we began to see by the full light of Martian reality.

After the flyby *Mariners*, Mars seemed a place dead and uninviting; a world perhaps hardly more worth becoming intimately acquainted with than the Moon, though the latter at least offered the advantage of lying cosmically in our own backyard. In early spring 1971, no less than five spacecraft—three of them Russian and two American—were prepared for launch. The American plan, at least, was well publicized in advance, and called for two spacecraft being placed in closed orbits around Mars; the first, *Mariner 8*, would enter a highly inclined orbit allowing scrutiny of the polar areas, the other, *Mariner 9*, would be placed in a more nearly equatorial orbit. The Russians planned one orbiter-only mission; the other two missions were more ambitious and consisted—like the *Viking* probes later launched by the United States—of both lander and orbiter components. After entering Martian orbit, the landers were supposed to separate from the orbiters and, braking their descent through the Martian atmosphere partly by rocket thrusters and partly by parachutes, were to touch down gently on the surface.

Mariner 8 ended up in the Atlantic Ocean when the second stage of its launch vehicle failed to ignite, forcing mission planners to revise their plans for *Mariner 9*, which now called for its being placed in a compromise orbit allowing some coverage of both the polar areas and the rest of the planet's surface. The first Russian spacecraft ended in failure; it was unable to escape from Earth orbit owing to a miscue radioed to the on-board computer. However, *Mariner 9* and the two remaining Russian spacecraft, *Mars 2* and *Mars 3*, got away cleanly at the end of May 1971.

Mariner 9 was scheduled to reach Mars at the time of the most rapid shrinkage of the south polar cap, just as the markings in the southern hemisphere were undergoing their expected wave of darkening. However, in the meantime there were some dramatic developments on Mars.

During the summer of 1971 while *Mariner 9* and the two Russian spacecraft were heading to Mars, the planet was kept under close scrutiny from the Earth. It was approaching its first perihelic opposition of the spacecraft era and had not veered within 56 million kilometers (35 million miles) of the Earth since 1956. In July, a yellow dust cloud suddenly appeared over the great basin of Hellas; it soon subsided, but a haze of dust lingered over the region for two months. Then, on September 22—four months into the *Mariner 9* flight trajectory and still two months before its expected arrival at Mars—an intensely brilliant streak suddenly appeared over the desert region called Noachis. It was photographed by observers in South Africa, then tracked by observers at Lowell Observatory and New Mexico State University as it began to spread; for two days the core elongated only slowly, then the dust cloud began to expand rapidly to the west. By the end of September the whole region from Hellas to Noachis was obscured, while markings all the way around the planet were starting to fade. The main cloud continued to expand westward along the bright corridor of Hesperia (between Mare Cimmerium and Mare Tyrrhenum), and during most of October Mars looked for a while most un-Martian, becoming quite as bland and featureless as perennially cloud-decked Venus. (One of us [SJO] observed the swelling storm with Dennis Milon, who independently discovered the event with the 23-centimeter (9-inch) refractor of Harvard College Observatory. Through that same telescope O'Meara watched the planet's darkest features succumb to the onslaught of dust, which shimmered with a lemony glaze, until only fragments of the classical surface features remained—and these markings could only be identified by comparing the visual image with photographs taken by Milon over the course of the storm. Seeing dust obliterate entire "continents" on Mars made him feel a somber, yet beautiful, gloom.)

Thus began the Great Dust Storm of 1971. It was not the first time Mars

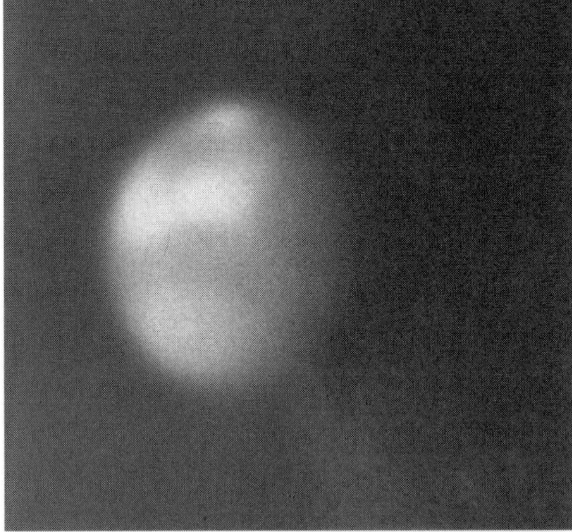

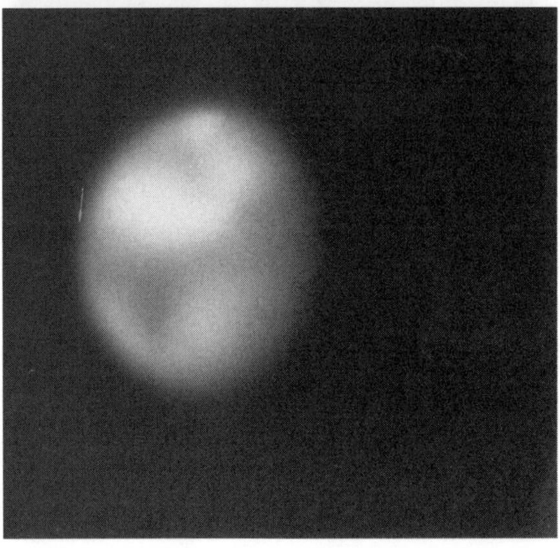

The 1971 dust cloud in Hellas appears as a bright haze near the center of the Martian disk. Photo by Dennis Milon with the 23-centimeter (9-inch) refractor at Harvard College Observatory. (Stephen O'Meara collection).

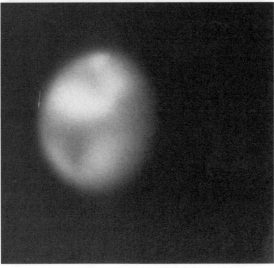

had been obscured by dust—Antoniadi had watched a large though not globe-encircling storm in August 1909. Again, in August 1924, the same observer noted that the entire planet was almost completely covered for a period "and presented a cream color similar to that of Jupiter." In one of his drawings, made on December 24, he showed only a single vague dusky patch on an otherwise featureless disk.

There had been other major dust storms in 1941 and 1956; the latter was particularly well observed, and like the 1971 event began with an intensely brilliant cloud elongating slowly at first before undergoing a rapid phase of expansion. However, the 1971 storm was the greatest so far on

Charles (Chick) F. Capen at the business end of the Lowell 61-centimeter (24-inch) refractor. (*Sky & Telescope* photograph)

record. Oddly enough, the possibility of a major storm had been predicted even before *Mariner 9* set out for Mars by a leading expert on Martian meteorology, Charles ("Chick") Capen of the Lowell Observatory, who noted—as indeed had Antoniadi as long ago as 1909—that though dust clouds were not particularly infrequent at other times, gigantic planet-encircling or planetwide storms seemed to occur just when Mars was near perihelion, when it receives forty percent more solar radiation than it does at aphelion. At these times the surface and lower atmosphere become warmer than normal. Atmospheric instabilities arise similar to those that produce swirling dust devils in arid regions on Earth. On Mars, certain regions are particularly susceptible, such as slopes or the boundaries of polar caps where there are sharp differences in temperature that enhance near-surface winds (thus Mars's dust clouds tend to arise preferentially in the same areas). Once aloft, the suspended dust itself becomes a major absorber of solar radiation and of heat being reradiated from the surface; this in turn produces further atmospheric temperature instabilities, more wind and more dust.

Apparently there are a number of factors that serve to amplify an initial disturbance, but the interplay of these factors is unpredictable—an example of a so-called chaotic phenomenon—so that though large-scale storms occur with increased probability at certain times, they are not an inevitable result. Capen was unusually well-informed in the historical record of Martian observation; but he was also lucky to some extent in his prediction of the Great Dust Storm of 1971.

The implications of the dust storm for mission planners were obvious, since it was apparent that by the time *Mariner 9* reached Mars, the atmosphere would not have had time to clear. The planet, indeed, was still hopelessly covered on November 10 when the spacecraft switched on its cameras some 800,000 kilometers (480,000 miles) out from Mars. Fortunately, the mission plan had been kept flexible; after *Mariner 9* was successfully inserted into orbit around Mars on November 14, it shut off its television cameras in order to conserve energy. The images it had so far obtained were singularly uninformative; the Martian disk was entirely lacking in detail except for four dusky spots, whose significance was unclear, though one of them was found to coincide in position with Schiaparelli's bright patch Nix Olympica (the Snows of Olympus).

By contrast, *Mars 2* and *3* were entirely preprogrammed. On November 27, *Mars 2* released its descent module as planned; it crashed. On December 2, *Mars 3* attempted the same maneuver; this time the descent module reached the surface safely and remained intact just long enough to plant a pennant containing the hammer-and-sickle insignia of the former Soviet Union and to switch on its television camera before contact was lost—possibly the spacecraft was blown over by the gale-force winds.

The two Russian orbiters fared little better; since they had been preprogrammed before launch, they could only carry out their imaging sequences automatically, obtaining an unrewarding series of views of an essentially blank disk. (Admittedly, other instruments on board the spacecraft sent back more useful information, including a series of measures of temperatures at various points around the planet; but all in all, the Russian Mars missions of 1971 had to be regarded as a sharp disappointment.)

All the hopes thus centered on the American *Mariner 9*, with its more flexible mission program that allowed it to patiently wait out the storm. By the end of November, the winds began to drop and the dust cleared suffi-

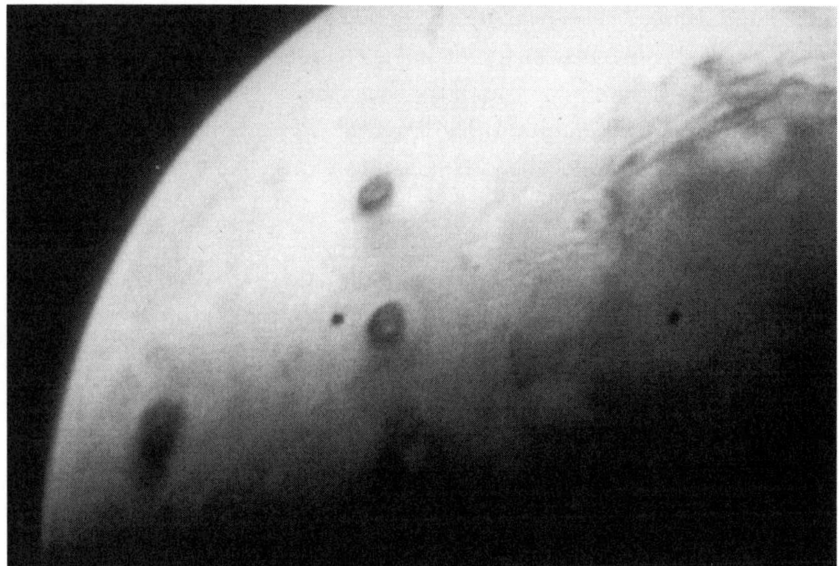

When *Mariner 9* first imaged Mars in 1971, the Martian disk was entirely blank except for four dusky spots—one of which was found to coincide in position with Schiaparelli's bright patch Nix Olympica (the Snows of Olympus). By the end of November, however, the the dust had cleared sufficiently for the dusky spots to show their true nature: their tops, rising above the dust, proved to be calderas atop the cones of enormous shield volcanoes. (NASA)

ciently for the dusky spots to show their true nature: their tops, rising above the dust, proved to be calderas atop enormous shield volcanoes. The grandest of all—the one in the position of Schiaparelli's Nix Olympica—was christened Olympus Mons, and measures 800 kilometers (480 miles) at its base and rises some 25 kilometers (15 miles) above the surrounding plains into the thin Martian air. The other great volcanoes in this part of Mars, called Tharsis on Schiaparelli's 1878 map, are Ascraeus Mons, Pavonis Mons, and Arsia Mons. They are spaced some 700 kilometers (420 miles) apart and aligned southwest-northeast along the crest of a great rise known as the Tharsis Bulge. All of these volcanoes are much larger than the most spectacular feature of the kind on Earth, the Hawaiian shield volcano Mauna Loa; by comparison the latter measures only 120 kilometers (70 miles) at its base and rises only 9 kilometers (5 miles) above the ocean floor.

The volcanoes of Hawaii were formed above a deep-seated mantle "plume"—a source of hot material upwelling from the zone of the Earth lying intermediate between the overlying rocky crust and the deeper molten core. In fact, Hawaii is near the end of a chain of volcanic islands whose age increases as one follows toward the northwest; among the others are Maui, Molokai, Oahu and Kaui. These islands formed in succession as the Pacific plate has ridden above the mantle plume, being carried by the movements of plate tectonics. But each of the Hawaiian volcanoes is relatively shortlived, remaining active for only a few million years. Chains of new volcanoes are then produced as the old ones are rafted away on the thin, mobile crust of the Earth. On Mars, plate tectonic processes never occurred. Thus, a volcano forming over a mantle plume remains active in the same location indefinitely and over hundreds of millions of years can build itself up to staggering proportions.

As the dust over Mars continued to subside, more and more landmarks began to emerge: by the first week in December the south polar cap was distinctly visible, while a view toward the Martian horizon taken on December 17 provided a first dramatic glimpse of the enormous canyon of Valles Marineris. It extends along the equator for 4,000 kilometers (2,400 miles), a full quarter of the way around the planet's circumference, and is believed to have been formed from a series of deep troughs that opened up as the crust in this part of the planet was buckled by the neighboring Tharsis rise.

Mariner 9 continued to send images—7,239 in all—until it exhausted its fuel on October 27, 1972. It had taken humans centuries to explore the confines of their own planet; centuries of bold emprise on the part of explorers like Hanno the Carthaginian, Vasco da Gama, Columbus, Magellan, Cook, Peary, Amundsen. In just under a year, *Mariner 9* opened up to the mind of man the entire surface of the red planet, from pole to pole, and in exquisite detail. The cratered terrrains of the flyby *Mariners* were there, but so was a hitherto hardly suspected brave new world of mountains, canyons, and—most remarkable of all—great channels and dry riverbeds attesting eloquently and unmistakably to a much more Earth-like Mars in the past. Whereas the flyby *Mariners* had emphasized Mars's moonlike face, at least some of the features revealed by *Mariner 9* showed clear analogies to features of the Earth. Thus, the great shield volcanoes of Tharsis resembled—apart from their much more massive scale—nothing so much as the great shield volcanoes of Hawaii; the volcanic plains of Syrtis Planitia appeared similar to the Deccan lava fields of India or the Columbia River Basalt Basin of the northwestern United States, and so on.

It did not take *Mariner 9* long to show that the albedo features—the classical dark and light markings so long and lovingly studied by observers from Earth—were not, in general, topographically significant. Thus, the prominent dark area Syrtis Major, once regarded as the basin of a long dried-up sea, proved to be an elevated plateau. Mare Acidalium, on the other hand, one of the largest dark areas in the northern hemisphere, is a relatively flat plain. Some of the bright areas—Hellas, Argyre—prove to be gigantic impact basins and mark low-lying spots on the planet; other bright areas, including the Tharsis rise and Elysium (which contains a number of shield volcanoes) are the most elevated.

The most important generalization about the Martian surface is the marked difference between the northern and southern halves of the planet—the Great Crustal Dichotomy. South of a circle inclined roughly 35° to the equator, the surface consists mostly of ancient, heavily cratered terrain; north of this circle lie younger, relatively smooth plains and volcanic features. The albedo markings are spread rather heedlessly over these more significant units of structure. In fact, the difference between light and dark areas reflects nothing more fundamental than the difference in dust-grain sizes; the dark areas contain a wider range of particles, the light areas are covered only with finer grains ("fines"). Because the flyby *Mariners* had been directed mainly over the southern hemisphere, where most of the prominent dark patches are located, they completely missed some of Mars's most intriguing features.

Despite the apparent blues and ochers reported by visual observers, the actual color of the planet appeared to be uniformly rust-red, owing to the ubiquitous presence (north and south) of oxidized dust produced by weathering of basaltic rocks on the planet; the so-called desert areas simply consist of finer, brighter, and more heavily oxidized, thus more intensely rust-red, particles (presumably, the greater degree of oxidation is due to the smaller size of the dust grains, since smaller grains will have a higher surface-to-volume ratio). The presence of dust is attested to not only by the shades but also by the shapes of the dark markings—for instance, Sinus Meridiani and Margaritifier Sinus end in forks. This gives them a highly windblown look, and windblown they are. In general, these features point along the direction dust is swept by prevailing Martian winds. The classical markings on Mars prove to be, then, mainly related to windblown dust.

Indeed, unlike the airless and moistureless Moon, Mars is a windy place. There are gentle breezes and gusts powerful enough to stir up dust in sufficient quantities to obscure the entire planet. *Mariner 9* revealed a plethora of windblown splotchy and streaky features, which make many parts of the planet look distinctly Antoniadiesque. The most striking of all are the comet-like tails that emerge from craters filled with dark material. They are encountered in great concentrations in Syrtis Major, where they appear as "shredded streaks," and are especially multitudinous on the inward-facing slopes of the enormous eroded basin of Isidis, located just east of the great Syrtis plateau. Long ago Antoniadi noted changes in the outlines of Syrtis Major, which he naturally tried to account for in terms of the vegetation theory then current. The shape of its hourglass changed, he found, with the seasons, becoming streaked and narrow in the spring, then widening in the autumn. Presumably the east-west shift he observed was produced by changing winds alternately blowing material up and down the slopes. If so, however, then the Martian circulation patterns cannot remain constant over time, since the change in width of the eastern side of Syrtis Major has not been observed now for several decades.

In addition to the streaky or "tailed" craters, there are also wind-eroded hills known as yardangs. Above all—and as well befits a desert planet—there are dunes. Most notably, there are vast fields of transverse dunes attesting to sand accumulation in the region between latitudes 75 and 85° N. Here they form the dusky collar long known as the "Lowell band," which surrounds the north polar cap. Often the dunes completely fill the floors of craters. In other parts of the planet, where sand is presumably more scarce, the characteristic form is the crescent-shaped dune known as a barchan.

The great dust storms, like the one that obscured the planet for several months in 1971, testify to the vast power of the Martian winds to transport volumes of dust. The winds are especially potent in moving fine materials. When Mars is closest to the Sun, wind speeds pick up because of the increased heating, moving sand by saltation, a process that causes large particles to bound and jump across the surface, stirring up finer particles that become windborne in the atmosphere. Thus particles of different sizes become separated. Temporary changes in the intensity of albedo features are produced in the wake of localized dust or planet-girdling dust storms as a fine dusty veneer is blown over wide areas of the planet. But this begs the

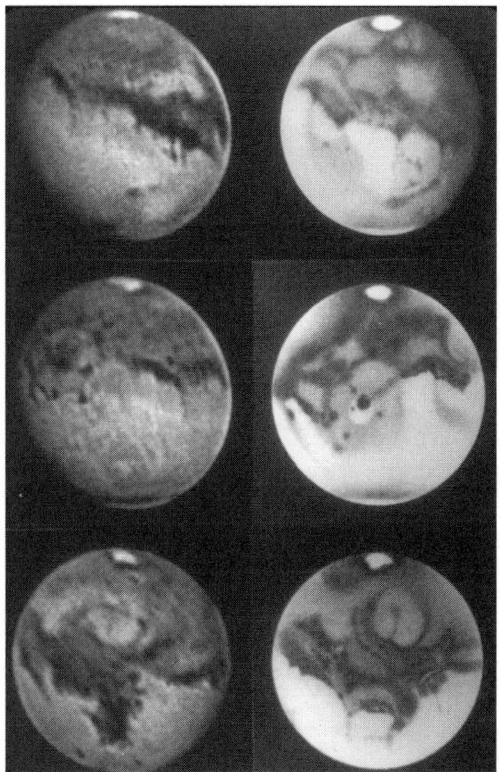

During the favorable 1988 apparition of Mars, Stephen Larson of the Lunar and Planetary Lab created these high-resolution images of Mars (left) with the 155-centimeter (61-inch) Catalina reflector atop Mount Lemmon in Arizona. At the urging of Carl Sagan, he compared the modern images with drawings made by Antoniadi in 1909 (right) and found that the large-scale surface features have not changed dramatically over the years. Dust can alter the appearance of affect small details. (Courtesy Steve Larson)

question why the whole planet has not, over the ages, been turned to a uniform brightness all over. The answer is that wind-erosion produces debris mainly in certain areas of Mars, such as Syrtis Planitia, where there are rocky outcrops of basalt; as the particles thus produced separate out and the fine materials are blown around the planet, they accumulate selectively in other areas, such as Tharsis, Arabia, and Elsyium. These areas contain only fine dust particles (fines). Since there are no larger particles in them to trigger the saltation process, once dust settles in them it cannot be removed. Instead it remains permanently in place. These areas of Mars are referred to as dust-sinks.

The overall yearly pattern is for material to be scoured off from regions like Syrtis Planitia and deposited in dust-sinks like Elysium. Immediately after a dust storm, the dark areas appear light because they are then wearing a veneer of lighter dust; thus the Syrtis Major always looks faint after a major storm. However, scouring action by the wind soon removes this veneer to re-expose the underlying basaltic bedrock, producing a revival in the darkness of these features. But the red basis of the famed wave of darkening is the increase in contrast between the dark areas and surrounding ocher areas that proceeds apace towards the equator every spring and reverses in the autumn, the pageant in which Lowell and other early observers of the planet saw evidence of the growth and decline of vegetation. So the wave of darkening is really a wave of brightening, as discovered by Charles F. Caper Jr. in the early 1970s.

Apart from its many observations of Mars, *Mariner 9* also obtained the first close-up images of the Martian moonlets, Phobos and Deimos, which had been discovered by Asaph Hall in 1877. It proved once and for all that they were not, as proposed by a Russian astronomer around 1960, hollow space stations launched by the Martians! Instead both appeared to be battered fragments of worlds, similar, no doubt, to the thousands of asteroids which flock in the zone between Mars and Jupiter. Indeed, gravitationally captured asteroids they undoubtedly are. *Mariner 9* imaged Phobos in considerable detail, showing it to be lopsided (27 × 19 kilometers or 16 × 14 miles) and pockmarked. In fact it looked, in the memorable words of one investigator, "just like a diseased potato."

Though *Mariner 9* turned some of our cherished dreams of Mars to dust, it revivified others. For one thing, it provided a detailed analysis of the composition of the polar caps. Earthbased observers had long followed the waxing and waning of the caps each Martian year, and tied the different behavior of the two caps to the idiosyncrasies of the seasons. Because of Mars's highly elliptical orbit, the southern hemisphere—which is tilted toward Earth when it is nearest the sun and away from Mars when it is farthest away—has long cold winters and short hot summers. Thus, the south polar cap grows to cover a vast area at its maximum extent in midwinter—it reaches as far south as 60° around its circumference, in places, such as the Argyre Basin, as far as 50° S latitude. However, despite its enormous surface area, the south polar cap is evidently of soufflé-like thinness, and must consist of little more than a thin garment of ice-coated dust-particles. Originally blown from equatorial latitudes during dust storms, the particles, on ascending into colder, higher latitudes, gather jackets of frozen carbon dioxide around them. At last, ballasted with this increased weight, they are no longer able to remain airborne, and settle out in a thin "snowfall" on the ground. During the summer, the insubstantial cap undergoes a torrid retreat to become no more than a small patch hardly visible from Earth. The northern hemisphere of Mars has less extreme seasons; its cap neither grows to the same vast extent, nor does it dwindle so completely.

In the wake of the flyby *Mariners*, most astronomers believed that the polar caps might consist entirely of frozen carbon dioxide. *Mariner 9* showed that this is the case only for the south polar cap. At its greatest extent, the south polar cap consists largely of a brilliant white expanse of frozen carbon dioxide, which quickly gasses away (or sublimes) with the arrival of spring and summer. Enough carbon dioxide is released in this way to cause a very perceptible increase in the atmospheric pressure at the surface (thus, the *Viking 1* lander of 1976–77 would record, on the ground on Mars, a pressure increase from 6.7 millibars in the southern hemisphere winter to 8.8 millibars in summer). Though the retreat of the south polar cap is dramatic, most summers, at least, it does not progress all the way, but a residual (permanent) cap of frozen carbon dioxide remains, with a characteristic swirl pattern produced by uneven removal of frost by wind from valleys; because of local topography, its center is offset by about 6° from the pole—a peculiarity which even Maraldi noted long ago. The frozen carbon dioxide buffers the temperature to the frost point of carbon dioxide (–125° C or –193° F at a surface pressure of 6.1 millibars).

The behavior of the north polar cap is quite different. When it emerges from a hood of cloud in the early northern hemisphere spring, it extends to as far as 65° N. At this stage it also consists of a seasonal cap made up mainly of frozen carbon dioxide; but—since the frost is laid down during the dust storm season—it is darker in hue than its southern counterpart, absorbs the solar heat more efficiently, and sublimates completely by the time of the northern hemisphere summer solstice. The removal of carbon dioxide ice exposes an underlying residual cap of water-ice. (Though not confirmed until the later *Viking* missions, the fact that this cap consisted of water-ice was already strongly indicated by the measurements obtained by *Mariner 9*.)

The north polar cap is a significant source of water vapor in the Martian atmosphere. The entire cap seems to contain, according to the most reasonable estimates, only about 1,200,000 cubic kilometers of water-ice; less than half the volume of Greenland's ice sheet. Not much for a whole planet with a surface area equal to the entire land area of the Earth. Of course this water exists permanently in the solid state. The rest of Mars's presently discernible allotment of water exists as delicate cirrus clouds.

What became of the rest of it?

Obviously water is scarce on Mars to an extent far beyond the dreams of Percival Lowell. Liquid water on the surface is nonexistent at the present time; at the low temperatures and meager atmospheric pressures on Mars, any that appeared would freeze or evaporate into the dry Martian air. But we're talking of Mars at the present time. What of the past?

We come at last to the most surprising discovery of *Mariner 9*, a discovery that completely revolutionized our ideas about Mars forever. Cold and frozen desert though it is now, a landscape littered with craters and dunes and lonely and forlorn beyond our ability to imagine, Mars may not have always been so—it was possibly a much more Earth-like world, perhaps even another Earth.

Mariner 9 showed that, in contrast with the Moon, the older craters on Mars are considerably weathered; erosion has taken place there. The younger features are surrounded with ejecta blankets that resemble mudflows and furnish evidence of subsurface permafrost or ice melting, produced as a slush of liquid water released by the energy of the impact mixed with dust and flowed across the surface. The mudflows appear only around craters above a certain size limit. Moreover, since near-equatorial features are generally crisp and well defined while craters of the same size appear sloshy in higher latitudes, it is evident that the subsurface ice must lie hidden at greater depths near the warmer equator and be exposed nearer to the surface in the colder polar latitudes.

Here was one indication of the presence of significant amounts of underground ice and water below the Martian surface. However, there were findings even more startling. *Mariner 9* imaged numerous sinuous valleys, typically a kilometer or two wide but some—Ma'adim Vallis, Al Quahira, and Nirgal Vallis—hundreds of kilometers long. The valleys form large branching networks. They are far from rare; indeed, they are widespread in the ancient, heavily cratered southern highlands. Though on the face of them they give every indication of having been cut by erosion of rock by slowly moving water like terrestrial river valleys, the fact that "individual trunk channels do not extend themselves, capture streams from adjacent basins, and control drainage over large areas" suggests, according to Michael Carr of the United

States Geological Survey, that "fluvial action on Mars was either short-lived, very intermittent, or not truly analogous to what occurs here."[1]

However that may be, since the small rivers that cut them would freeze rapidly under present Martian conditions, the conclusion seemed inescapable—Mars must have had a thicker atmosphere and been warmer at the time they formed. Some of the investigators who first examined the *Mariner 9* images even thought the valley networks furnished evidence that precipitation—rain, in other words—had formerly occurred on Mars; perhaps, they hoped, it had done so even in the relatively recent past when, owing to oscillations of Mars's axial tilt, large amounts of carbon dioxide could have been released from the polar caps to produce greenhouse warming and more moderate periods in the planet's climate.[2] However, the *Viking* orbiters of 1976 showed that there is now, and has been since the very early era of Mars's career as a world—the first billion years or so after its formation—far too little carbon dioxide in the polar caps, even if all were released at once, to drive temperatures above the melting point of water. Instead, if the channels were formed by water, it must have been through groundwater sapping, a process in which water released during melting of near-surface permafrost undermines the ground from below.

The valley networks appear in the ancient terrains on Mars that harken back to the first billion years or so of the planet's development, after the smaller-than-Earth Martian globe had formed through accretion of numerous smaller asteroidal bodies in the violent opening chapter of the solar system's history. At this time Mars was still undergoing massive bombardment from asteroidal debris and was more active volcanically than at any other time in its history. This period has been referred to as the Noachian period, because the prototypical region is Noachis Terra, Schiaparelli's "Land of Noah"; it spans the era from the time Mars first formed 4.5 billion years ago to about 3.8 billion years ago. According to what has been the standard view of the planet, if, as the valley networks seem to indicate, liquid water was able to exist on the surface of Mars at the time, the planet must have possessed a substantially thicker atmosphere, consisting of carbon dioxide and other greenhouse gases produced by degassing in volcanoes. It would also have been much warmer than now. According to estimates by Carr and others, there may once have been enough water to cover the entire surface uniformly to a depth of 500 meters (1,650 feet). By comparison, the water on Earth, if spread in a uniform layer, would make a layer 3 kilometers (1.8 miles) deep. Much of this water may have collected in a Noachian ocean, located in the smooth northern plains, where "ponded sediments, shoreline indicators, infilled craters and basins, spillover channels, pitted basin floors, whorled patterns of multiple ridges, and other evidence indicate the past existence of extensive lakes or temporary regional flooding."[3]

Alas, the period in which Mars experienced these primitive Eden-like conditions—if it ever existed—was brief. Most of the atmosphere and water was lost before the end of the heavy bombardment stage. Valley development on a planetary scale seems to have ceased. The vast northern ocean, if it existed, disappeared, and the planet settled into its severe post-Noachian climate of bitter cold and desert-like aridity.

It is clear that Mars lost at least 70 to 90 percent of its available water. Where did it go? Some of it would have been split apart into its constituent hydrogen and oxygen atoms by ultraviolet radiation from the Sun, a process that would have continued throughout the four billion years or so since the river networks were formed; the hydrogen would have escaped into space, the oxygen would have combined with ferrous Martian surface materials to turn the planet rust-red. Some of it—though only a little—remains trapped in the north polar cap. But most of it must still lie dormant near the surface as buried ice or, perhaps at greater depths, as liquid water. (A prime location to search for it is the large southern plateau—target of the failed Mars Polar Lander mission of 1999—which extends nearly 100 kilometers [60 miles] beyond the south polar cap's edge. It has been proposed that this vast plateau in the Martian antarctic might well consist mostly of buried ice, in which case it may prove to be one of the richest repositories of water on Mars.)

The evolution of Mars did not end 3.8 billion years ago. The planet has continued to be volcanically active, and intermittently some of its subsurface water seems to have been released onto the surface on a much larger scale than occurred during the Noachian period, which saw the heyday of the valley networks. This brings us to another of the Martian features first recorded by *Mariner 9*, the so-called outflow channels. Compared to the relatively tiny valley networks, these features are on a truly grand scale, typically measuring hundreds of kilometers long and tens of kilometers wide. They emerge fully formed in chaotic terrain, areas that have undergone widespread collapse and consist of jostled blocks slumped below the surrounding landscape and enclosed by inward facing cliffs and canyons. Several of the most remarkable outflow channels—the Ares, Tiu, and Simud Valles—originate in the chaotic terrain in Aurorae Sinus at the eastern end of the great Valles Marineris canyon complex; they flow northward and converge on the floor of Chryse Planitia, on the eastern edge of the Tharsis bulge with its massive shield volcanoes, where they merge with the low-lying plains of the high northern latitudes. A number of other outflow channels are found in Elysium Planitia, northwest of another volcanic province.

On Earth there is a landscape—exactly one—which resembles these remarkable landscapes on Mars.

In eastern Washington in the northwestern United States, a broad swath of the basaltic Columbia Plateau looks bizarre enough to be extraterrestrial. It consists of what from ground-level appears to be "elongated tracts of bare, or nearly bare, black rock carved into mazes of buttes and canyons," but from the air is found to make up an enormous plexus of stream channels, cataracts, island-like hills, and immense gravel bars. The region was first given its name of "Channeled Scabland" by J Harlen Bretz (J, without a period, which was actually his first name), a University of Chicago geologist who made the first careful study of the region in the 1920s. In his first paper on the subject, Bretz noted that the unique combination of topographic features found in the Channeled Scabland could have only one interpretation; it must be "the erosive record of large, high-gradient, glacier-born streams."[4] In other words, the Channeled Scabland had originated in a catastrophic flood (at the time the source of the flood was still unknown). His suggestion was immediately and almost universally denounced as outrageous—not to say heretical—by other geologists.[5] The reason for this hostile reaction was, simply, that when geology first emerged as a science in the nineteenth century it did so only by distancing itself from biblical notions of catastrophic floods and putting forward the notion that geological formations resulted from more gradual and uniform processes still in evidence today. By proposing that the only possible explanation for the Channeled Scabland was flooding on a catastrophic scale, Bretz seemed to be "flaunting catastrophe too vividly in the face of the uniformity that had lent scientific dignity to the interpretation of the history of the earth." However, Bretz persisted, and eventually was vindicated. It is now established that thirteen thousand years ago, during the last ice age, a glacial lake (Lake Missoula) that formed behind a dam of ice along the Montana border suddenly gave way, releasing several thousand square kilometers of water, a hundred meters high, across the Idaho panhandle; the torrent then rushed into eastern Washington and continued to push its way to the Pacific. The quantity of water involved, at its peak, was equal to 100 times the maximum flow of the Mississippi River. As Bretz described the stupendous scene:

> The volume of the invading water much exceeds the capacity of the existing streamways. The valleys entered become river channels, they brim over into neighboring ones, and minor divides within the system are crossed in hundreds of places. . . . All told, 2,800 square miles [7,200 square kilometers] of the region of are scoured clean onto the basalt bed rock, and 900 square miles [2,300 square kilometers] are buried in the debris deposited by these great rivers. The topographic features produced during this episode are wholly compounded of river-bottom modifications of the invaded and overswept drainage network of hills and valleys. Hundreds of cataract ledges, of isolated buttes of the bed rock, of gravel bars piled high above valley floors, and of island hills of the weaker overlying formations are left at the cessation of this episode. . . . The physiographic expression of the region is without parallel; it is unique, this channeled scabland of the Columbia Plateau.[6]

Unique it is—on Earth. But Mars, with its vast tracts of outflow channels, apparently presents even grander examples of channeled scablands. The discharge of water flowing across the Martian surface must have been vastly greater than that which formed the Channeled Scabland of eastern Washington; indeed, the floods that formed the outflow channels must have contained a quantity of water which achieved 1,000 to 10,000 times the maximum flow of the Mississippi. Where did all this water come from? The standard interpretation holds that on Mars, subsurface water was present in the form of confined aquifers, trapped under high pressure beneath a thick layer of permafrost. Some of these aquifers would have to have been of vast extent. The water would have been released explosively by faulting, impact, or any other process capable of breaching the overlying cap of permafrost—an event comparable to the failure of the ice dam that kept in check the ice age Lake Missoula, and leading to sudden catastrophic collapse of the overlying terrain to produce the jumbled blocks of chaos and the massive outflow channels.

Significantly, many of the outflow channels are found around Chryse

Basin, one of the lowest-lying regions on the planet; its margins might provide an ideal location for the generation of high artesian pressure. However released, water flowing across the surface would have rushed so violently that freezing would have been negligible, even under the current deep-freeze conditions that prevail on Mars. It is important to emphasize, then, that in contrast to the valley networks, their presence does not imply a more substantial atmosphere or a warmer climate at the time they formed. Moreover, these flooding events have evidently occurred intermittently over the history of the planet. From cratering count estimates, it seems that Ares, Kasei, Maja, and Vedra Valles formed between 2 and 3 billion years ago; but Mangala Vallis, in the upland region of Memnonia on the border of Amazonis Planitia, may be probably only about a billion years old, and Upper Tiu Vallis may have formed within the last half billion years.

Admittedly, the idea of vast volumes of water crashing across the Martian surface does seem almost far-fetched, given the planet's present state of extreme desiccation. We will say more about the whole question of Mars's water supply later, a subject that continues to be hotly debated. But for now we recall once more Percival Lowell's vision of the planet.

In his meditations on the evolution of worlds, Lowell suggested that Mars—with its smaller size and more rapid rate of cooling—was destined to race ahead of the Earth in what he regarded as an inevitable process of desertification. The dwindling of the planet's water supply precipitated the crisis that led, in his version of the planet, to the desperate feats of the canal-builders. At least he got some of the picture right. It's obvious that Mars lost any oceans it might once have had, and became—apart perhaps from the occasional short-lived torrents released from beneath the frozen rind of the planet in episodes of catastrophic flooding—a frigid, dry-as-a-bone desert. What of the Earth? Will it eventually follow suit, as Lowell envisaged? In his first book about the red planet, *Mars*, he wrote:

> A planet may in a very real sense be said to have life of its own, of which what we call life may or may not be a subsequent detail. It is born, has its fiery youth, sobers into middle age, and just before this happens brings forth, if it be going to do so at all, the creatures on its surface which are, in a sense, its offspring. The speed with which it runs through its gamut of change prior to production depends upon its size; for the smaller the body the quicker it cools. . . . Now, in the special case of Mars, we have

> before us the spectacle of a world relatively well on in years, a world much older than the Earth. To so much about his age Mars bears evidence on his face. He shows unmistakable signs of being old. Advancing planetary years have left their mark legible there. His continents are all smoothed down; his oceans have all dried up.[7]

If early Mars may have been in some respects Earth-like (just how much continues to be debated), recent research by Shigenori Murayama of the Tokyo Institute of Technology indicates that the Earth may go the way of Mars, at least in regards to its water supply. Since about 750 million years ago, seawater has been returning to mantle rock beneath the crust. Seven hundred fifty million years ago, at about the time of the Permian Ice Age (when the Earth was in the throes of the longest period of deep-freeze it has ever known), this loss of seawater caused the ocean levels to begin to drop, perhaps producing the first emergence of continents above water. At the present time, about 1.12 billion metric tons of ocean water are being lost every year. Murayama has estimated that it will take only another billion years for the Earth to be bereft of the rest of it.

Then the deep-blue Earth may turn into a dusty windblown rusted desert like Mars—or like Venus. At present, most of the Earth's carbon dioxide is locked up in its calcium carbonate rocks—some 300,000 times more carbon dioxide exists in this form than is circulating in the atmosphere. What keeps things in balance and maintains global temperatures at close to their present levels is the so-called carbonate-silicate cycle, which ultimately determines how much carbon dioxide is released into the atmosphere. Without going into all the details, the important point is that the carbonate-silicate cycle depends critically on the presence of the oceans. Without oceans, the Earth's massive allotment of carbon dioxide would be released into the atmosphere, producing a runaway greenhouse effect as on Venus—a planet that lost its oceans early in its history as a world and is now a stifling inferno where ground temperatures are sufficient to melt lead. The day is still remote, but come it will—a billion years hence, assuming the calculations do not need to be revised (at least there will be plenty of time to rework them!). Here is the sobering tale of planetary evolution.

Part V
The Abode
of Life?

16

Paradise Lost?

We also know how cruel the truth is, and we wonder whether delusion is not more consoling.

—Henri Poincare (1854–1912)

The longest journey in the history of mankind has been the search for our place in the cosmos. It has been an inner journey as much as an outer one. "Who are we? What are we? Where did we come from?" We see these "questions of all questions" symbolized in Stone Age artwork, vocalized in ancient creation chants, and molded into our classical myths and religious beliefs—whose strength of conviction has led men into conflict on the battlefield and in the halls of science. But the mystery of life is not confined to that on the Earth; it has long been a puzzle of cosmic proportions. From the sky people of Aboriginal Dreamtime to Lowell's dying Martians, the idea of extraterrestrial life has been stitched into the fabric of human imagination since the evolution of thought. But only in the past few decades has the human species begun to look seriously and systematically for evidence of life elsewhere. Only in the past few decades have humans been able to cross the gulf of space to gain a better understanding our planetary neighbors like Mars. (If the 4.6 billion years of Earth history were compressed into a single year, space exploration would have begun less than a tenth of a second ago.) And only in the past few decades has our race been capable of comprehending the true and profound vastness of space. (If we could shrink the Milky Way to the size of the North American continent, we would need an electron microscope to see our planet, which would be a speck one-millionth of an inch in diameter; of course, man would be infinitely smaller still.)

From a totally cosmic perspective, our host galaxy, the Milky Way, is not special; it is one of countless trillions of galaxies. Our Sun is not special; it is an average star among 200 billion others circling the Milky Way (every galaxy has billions of suns, many like our own). And, as we now know, our Sun is not the only star to have planets. "We find that we inhabit an insignificant planet of a hum-drum star," exobiologist Carl Sagan said, "lost in a galaxy tucked away in some forgotten corner of a universe in which there are far more galaxies than people. We make our world significant by the courage of our questions, and by the depth of our answers."[1]

One question Sagan sought to answer until his untimely death in 1996 is, "Are we alone?" He died not knowing the answer, nor do we still know the answer. Yet, if we follow our train of thought laid out in the preceding paragraph, we would conclude that life is not special to the Earth—a concept that has been, and still is, an unsettling prospect for many people. That's because we have been, and still are, "bedeviled by a natural and persisting sense of anthropomorphism," as the late Harvard astronomer Harlow Shapley espoused. "Correctives for our vanities are provided by modern science, but we still suffer relapses and return to believing that we are somehow important and supremely powerful and understanding. Of course we are not."[2]

From the cosmic perspective, it is hard to believe that Earth's thin blue

Carl Sagan. ©J. Kelly Beatty.

line could embrace the only biota in the universe. Sagan came to believe this early in his life. Born in Depression-era Brooklyn in 1934, Sagan was an avid reader who became fascinated with the stars before the age of eight—when he believed, as most children do, in life on other worlds. "It seemed absolutely certain to me that if the stars were like the Sun," he recalled, "there must be planets around them. And they must have life on them."[3] He also devoured Edgar Rice Burroughs's classic novels about Mars (his fictional "Barsoom"), which inspired him; Sagan particularly liked the phrase, "the hurtling moons of Barsoom." By high school the young voyager had graduated to the works of Arthur C. Clarke (who was also inspired by Burroughs). And it was one of Clarke's books, *Interplanetary Flight*, that would change, no, steer, the direction of his life:

> The challenge of the great spaces between the worlds is a stupendous one; but if we fail to meet it, the story of our race will be drawing to its close. Humanity will have turned its back upon the still-untrodden heights and will be descending again the long slope that stretches, across a thousand million years of time, down to the shores of the primeval sea.

That book also conveyed Clarke's own conviction that life exists on Mars:

> It is debatable whether Mars or Venus will be the first of the planets to be reached. . . . It is to Mars, however, that all thoughts will turn . . . for on

> Mars alone have we been able to detect what is almost certainly the existence of life. . . . It is believed that the "deserts" really are deserts, but the seas, like those of the Moon, are not water-covered. They are much more interesting, for they show seasonal changes which most astronomers now believe are due to the existence of vegetation.[4]

Sagan began transporting in his mind the experiences of humanity to other worlds: in an essay contest sponsored by the Roman Catholic Knights of Columbus, the young Jewish highbrow asked whether human contact with technologically advanced extraterrestrials would be as disastrous as contact with Europeans had been for Native Americans. This boldness of thought cost Carl his chance at becoming valedictorian of his class, for it convinced some people at Rahway High School that he was "*too* full of crazy ideas."

A major turning point in Sagan's life occurred in 1952 at the University of Chicago, where he was an undergraduate. That fall Sagan met Nobel Prize chemist Harold Clayton Urey, who introduced Sagan to his graduate student Stanley Miller. Miller was immersed in a extraordinary and important experiment that piqued Sagan's curiosity. Using a system of glass flasks, Miller was attempting to show that the precursors for life, amino acids, can be produced as a product of lightning acting on a primordial soup. Miller passed an electrical spark (symbolic of lightning) through a mixture of boiling water, ammonia, methane, and hydrogen—the gases then believed to constitute Earth's early atmosphere. Any molecules made by the reaction would fall into a trap at the bottom of the apparatus. This trap prevented the newly formed chemicals from being destroyed by the next spark. Eventually, Miller was able to produce a mixture containing very simple amino acids, the building blocks of proteins in all living things.

Sagan also attended Miller's colloquium on the experiment, and he left enraptured. It seemed that the natural emergence of living organisms from a primordial soup was not only possible but unavoidable—no miracles or supernatural agencies were needed. What's more, nothing in Miller's experiment was unique to Earth. If life could evolve under the harsh and primitive conditions of early Earth, so, too, could it on primitive Mars and other worlds. The results of this experiment led Sagan to blaze his own trail through life. He took one of Urey's undergraduate courses and wrote an honor's essay on the origin of life. "It was very naive," Sagan later admitted,

"I had the idea that in one fell swoop I could understand the origins of life, though I had not had much [training in] chemistry or biology." Indeed, the paper was riddled with misconceptions, and Urey didn't hesitate to castigate the budding biologist. Sagan did not cower at Urey's criticism but instead learned from it; he dusted himself off and marched forward to pioneer the new field of exobiology (the study of possible alien biochemistry and life forms).

In the mid-1950s to the early 1960s the chance of finding life on Mars looked pretty promising, as most popular books of the time suggested. "The fact that large, distinctly marked dark areas exist on Mars indicates that these surfaces cannot be dead," decreed Robert S. Richardson in his 1954 book *Exploring Mars*, "for no surface without the power to regenerate itself could withstand the continual inpouring of dust for ages. Hence the only reasonable explanation of the dark areas would seem to be that they consist of some living substance which stubbornly refuses to be obliterated by defying the sand drifts and feeding upon the dust itself."[5] In their 1962 encyclopedia of astronomy, Lucien Rudaux and Gerard de Vaucouleurs note that the "Martian vegetation, if it is such, sometimes behaves like terrestrial vegetation [in] our swamplands on Earth. . . . They give [us] what is the first recognisable evidence for the existence of life on another world."[6] Even the canals had not entirely disappeared from the 1960s literature, though theories of their creation went from the artificial to the natural: "The canals are very probably some sort of special surface feature resulting from the action of tectonic forces causing an alignment of a number of depressions, which, because they collected moisture, became relatively well adapted to support life."[7]

To some researchers, these beliefs still seemed fanciful and were driven by a desire to want to see life. Stephen Larson, who worked under Gerard P. Kuiper at the newly established Lunar and Planetary Laboratory in Tucson, said that serious Mars research in the 1960s was mainly comprised of creating maps of albedo features and monitoring dust-storm activity. "We never considered seriously the albedo features to be correlated with vegetation." Kuiper did investigate that possibility while he was at McDonald Observatory in Texas in the 1940s, taking infrared spectra with the powerful 2.1-meter (82-inch) reflector. But he concluded that contrast effects between gray albedo features and the surrounding salmon colored deserts caused the eye to *perceive* greenish tints in the greyish regions, and it was this perception that contributed in large part to the theories of vegetation (see Appendix B, "The Colors of Mars"). "We never really talked too much about life on Mars," Larson said. "We were just interested in Mars for the usual things: comparative planetology, geologic processes, and things like that. We were talking about wind blown sand on lava flows not about moss and forests. As for me, I didn't doubt that there were once conditions on Mars capable of supporting life. But were such conditions there long enough to allow life to form and evolve to a point where it could then adjust to the conditions that are there now?"[8]

Norman Horowitz, a colleague of Sagan, eventually answered that question in a most enlightening way. "If we admit the possibility that Mars once had a more favorable climate which was gradually transformed to the severe one . . . [of] today, and if we accept the possibility that life arose on the planet during this earlier epoch, then we cannot exclude the possibility that Martian life succeeded in adapting to the changing conditions and remains there still."[9]

In a 1961 article published by the National Academy of Science and the National Research Council, under a section titled "The Question of Life on Mars," Sagan concluded:

> The evidence taken as a whole is suggestive of life on Mars. In particular, the response to the availability of water vapor is just what is expected on a planet which is now relatively arid, but which once probably had much more surface water. The limited evidence we have is directly relevant only to the presence of microorganisms; there are no valid data for or against the existence of larger organisms and motile animals. . . . The ancient and exciting question of the possible existence of life on Mars will probably be answered in the next decade.

And he was partly right. As we have seen, on July 15, 1965, *Mariner 4* transmitted to Earth the first spacecraft images of the surface of Mars. And,

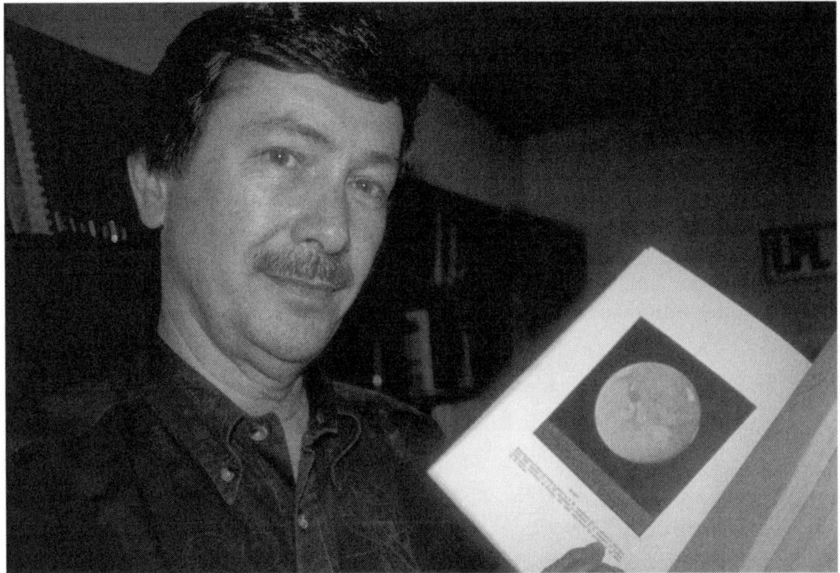

Stephen Larson worked under Gerard Kuiper at the Lunar and Planetary Laboratory, creating maps of Martian albedo features and monitoring duststorm activity. Here Larson displays a reproduction of a 1909 drawing by Antoniadi. © Stephen James O'Meara.

as we have seen, these images delivered a paralyzing punch to many scientific hopes and dreams by apparently turning Lowell's living planet into a floating corpse. By the end of 1965, the *New York Times* eulogized the Red Planet, calling it the Dead Planet. In a speech presented at a meeting of the Arizona Academy of Science Meeting of April 29, 1967, Kuiper announced that "*Mariner 4* seems to have done what these careful observers of the past half century were unable to do, namely, to destroy in the public mind the myth of the canals of Mars and all that it implied. This indicates, if such were necessary, that even reports by scientists may at times be found to be premature or foolish and that no subject is so well established that continued and more careful scientific investigation is superfluous."[10] To demonstrate just how ridiculous astronomers had been, he told the audience that Lowell's one-time associate, Harvard astronomer William H. Pickering, once speculated that "the Martian canals were hedges designed to prevent dust and vegetation from blowing from one area to another." President Lyndon B. Johnson was also comforted by the *Mariner* results. "As a member of a generation that Orson Welles scared out of its wits," he told a NASA group, "I must confess that I'm a little bit relieved that your photographs didn't show more signs of life out there."

Sagan, however, turned a deaf ear to such blatant rhetoric, and in a December 1967 *National Geographic* article, persuasively found a way to keep the canal controversy alive: "And the canals that cross the dusty seas, and at least some of the finer lines found by *Mariner 4*—as we interpret the evidence—turn out to be ridges comparable to the oceanic ridges and sea mounts that lace ocean bottoms on earth." *Mariner 6* and *7*, however, provided even more anticlimactic views of a lunar-like Mars, leading one team member to say, "We've got superb pictures . . . but what do they show? A dull landscape, as dead as a dodo."[11] But Sagan had the tenacity of a bacterium. To him, Mars was far from "dead," for the *Mariner* results were tentative at best. "Intelligent life on the Earth," he pronounced "would be entirely undetectable by photography in reflected sunlight unless about 100-meter (330-foot) resolution was achieved, at which point the urban and agricultural geometry of our technological civilization would become strikingly evident."[12] *Mariner 9* did have that resolution, and when it arrived at Mars in 1971—and became the first spacecraft to orbit that planet—its images revealed no signs of civilized life, not that Sagan believed it would; he was simply making a point about the limited resolution of the previous spacecraft. *Mariner 9* did, however, show volcanic formations and evidence for water—dry river beds and gullies carved by flash floods, as Sagan and others interpreted them.

But not all mission scientists were convinced that these features were carved by water. Hal Masursky, head of the *Mariner 9* imaging team, argued that the features could just as easily have been carved by lava flows. Either way, Mars, the former Dead Planet, had at least a new geologic face and a possible faint pulse. As *Mariner 9* proceeded to resolve details to within one-tenth of a kilometer, a renewed fervor ensued over Mars. "Our image of a cratered, static Mars," Masursky said, "was replaced by one of a dynamic and fascinatingly complex world that called out for further exploration."[13] The possibility of life had returned to the red planet. Sagan was euphoric.

Over the years Sagan had become as quixotic about the possibility of life on Mars as Lowell had been about his civilized race of dying Martians. And, like Lowell, Sagan could woo the public, communicating his views about the possibilities of life on Mars—no matter how complex or controversial—with eloquence and ease. Sagan quickly became an international celebrity who shared his musings about life through books, television and radio; one writer for *Time* dubbed him "exobiology's most energetic and articulate spokesman."[14]

But the Sagan the public enjoyed on the screen was not the Sagan his colleagues encountered in the halls of academia. "He wore his Optimist hat in public, when he talked blithely about the possibility (however remote) of 'advanced life forms' on Mars," biographer Keay Davidson explains, "but in his conversations with colleagues, he often donned his Skeptic hat." But at times Sagan was a master at wearing both hats simultaneously. "Look," he'd argue, "here is a niche in which you can imagine life. And don't you have to know more about that niche, or look directly for life, before you exclude it?"

In 1975, one year before two *Viking* landers would set down on the red planet's surface, Sagan was back in the public eye declaring, "We are only now beginning an adequate reconnaissance of our neighboring world. There is no question that astonishments and delights await us."[15]

July 20, 1976. A day of infamy. At 4:13 P.M. local Mars time, the Viking *1* Lander—NASA's first emissary to the red planet whose primary mission was to search for life—parachuted onto the surface of Chryse Planitia, a plain in the north temperate hemisphere of Mars. Sagan watched the historical event unfold from the Jet Propulsion Laboratory's Theodore von Karman Auditorium in Pasadena. Based on *Viking Orbiter* images, which showed the region as being relatively smooth and featureless, Sagan couldn't help but imagine that the lander had safely touched down on soft desert sands, like a toy truck dropped into a sandbox. (In 1975, a JPL artist showed such a "sandbox" with patches of moss in an illustration of the landing site based loosely on Saganesque visions.) But as *Viking* turned on its electronic eye and began transmitting the first panorama of that romantic red desert—first named by Schiaparelli, furrowed by Lowell, and transformed by Burroughs into a land of "soft and soundless moss"—it became clear that, at least in a macrobiotic sense, Mars was dead.

Viking orbiter image showing three of the great Tharsis volcanoes at left, the Grand Canyon of Mars—Valles Marineris—extending across the upper half of the globe, and regions of chaotic terrain and outflow channels reaching northwards from the Valles Marineris in the middle and right parts of the image to the plains in the far north which may once have harbored a primordial sea (Oceanus Borealis). (USGS—Flagstaff, Arizona)

Viking 1 had landed near the mouth of an ancient outflow channel—among a shoal of boulders that stretched 3 kilometers (2 miles) into the distance all around the craft. The lander narrowly escaped impacting one boulder large enough to smash or destroy it. Had the scientists not known better, they would have guessed that the craft had taken a wrong turn at Mars, returned to Earth, and perhaps landed in the rubble-strewn caldera of Maui's Haleakala volcano.

When *Viking 1* landed on Mars in July 1976, the view was disappointing—especially to those hoping to see signs of life. The craft landed near the mouth of an ancient outflow channel, among a shoal of boulders that stretched two miles into the distance all around the craft. This picture of Mars was taken on July 21—the day following the craft's successful landing. The local time on Mars is approximately noon. The view is southeast from the *Viking*. (NASA)

Sagan looked upon the image with despair: "There was not a hint of life—no bushes, no trees, no cactus, no giraffes, antelopes, or rabbits." Sagan had long believed, and popularized in his book *Other Worlds*, if there was going to be life in a macrobiotic sense, it would be "polar bears"— not real polar bears but large lifeforms whose size would protect against the cold, dry, and perhaps ultraviolet of the Martian environment as well. Even in the late 1960s some researchers were looking at the kangaroo rat as a terrestrial analog for macrobiotic life on Mars—this animal can survive for long periods without liquid water, for it obtains all the moisture it needs by the oxidation of the carbohydrates in its food.[16] The disappointing *Viking* images turned hallucinatory when, looking at the panorama, *Viking* scientists began, in a mirthful way, seeing in the play of light and shadows, an oasis with mangrove-like trees near a shimmering lake, "chicken tracks" in the soil (actually the tracks of wind-blown pebbles), and rocks of curious symmetrical shapes (like a muffler or a clog); one rock even appeared to have the letter "B" scribbled on it (caused by shadowing of surface grains on the rock or by a dark stain produced by weathering)—a "B," Sagan thought, for Burroughs's "Barsoom." The "B" was a "delightful interruption during the mission's difficult schedule," said Gerald Soffen, project scientist during the *Viking* mission, "but no scientist seriously considered it anything more than an odd coincidence of geometric form and lighting."[17]

Eleven days after *Viking* touched down, Sagan found himself confronted by a press thirsty for information about whether life existed on Mars. Sagan, who had given himself the task of scrutinizing the first incoming images for signs of movement on the Martian surface, could only reply, "So far, no rock has obviously got up and moved away."[18]

When a second *Viking Lander* touched down on a vast northern plain called Utopia on September 3, 1976, it offered no further hope of large lifeforms. The panoramic view of the site was no less a forest of rocks than the *Viking 1* site had been. There were differences, of course, the most striking being that the rocks had extensive pitting—the kind of vesicular holes one would find in volcanic rocks on Earth. Although the sites were geological wonderlands, they were biological bombs.

Inevitably, one segment of the public was not so convinced that NASA failed to find life on Mars and sensed a "cover up." Shortly after *Viking 1* had landed, NASA released a *Viking Orbiter* image showing a great stone "face" 1.5 kilometers (.9 miles) across staring up from a place called Cydonia in the Elysium region of Mars; the interplay of light and shadow on this natural mesa-like rock formation caused some Earthlings to share in the Martian hallucinatory effects. A myth soon emerged that the "Face" was engineered by Martians—the survivors of an interplanetary war that left the surface of Mars pockmarked and ravaged.[19] Of course there is no more a Face of Mars than there is a Man in the Moon, but a tabloid-fueled public soon spawned new theories of a dying race on our neighbor world; Lowell would have been amused in a sardonic sense. Meanwhile, the scientific battle over Martian life had not ended just yet. Although it was clear that macrobiotic life did not exist, the surface could contain evidence of microbiotic life—an idea Sagan championed. And the two *Viking* landers were designed specifically to explore that possibility.

The question of how to detect organisms on Mars, should they exist, had been carefully considered by the biologists. Rather than just asking,

Viking 2 touched down on terrain similar to that of *Viking 1*. The shiny muffler-like object at the bottom of the frame is not of Martian origin. It is an aluminum instrument cover that was ejected on September 5, 1976, two days after *Viking 2* landed. It struck the porous rock at the bottom of the picture, bounced about 20 inches, hit the surface again and bounced another 20 inches. The scar left by the second bounce is faintly visible halfway between the shroud and the rock it struck. (NASA)

"Is there life on Mars?" they also wondered, "If there is life on Mars, is it of different origin than terrestrial life?" (Life could be carbon based, as it is on Earth, but some scientists had also speculated that extraterrestrial life could be silicon based.) Of course, before the *Viking* designers built their experiments to detect life, they had to *define* "life." In the grandest sense, life has countless definitions, ranging from the religious view (a miracle) to the more scientific view (a self-reproducing "machine"). Sagan, who was by far the most imaginative and optimistic of the *Viking* scientists, did not like the traditional scientific definition of life: something that consumes energy, moves, and reproduces. "My automobile eats and breathes and metabolizes and moves," he said. "Crystals grow and even reproduce."[20] For him the key was genetics. Automobiles might mimic some properties of life, Sagan said, but they did not carry a genetic code or evolve; they rust. Unfortunately, no *Viking* experiment would be able to look for the genetic attributes of any Martian life, nor would the experiments last long enough to see if that life would evolve. (There was, incidentally, abundant evidence of *rust* on Mars!)

Norman Horowitz, one of the biological experiment designers, concluded that any life on Mars must be made up of organic molecules that contained carbon atoms. What makes carbon the most likely component of life, Horowitz said, is its ability to combine in myriad ways with other elements allowing "strange and wonderful creatures to develop." In the end, the *Viking* designers equipped each lander with a 3-meter- (10-foot-) long sampling arm and a $55 million ($165 million today) biology lab capable of detecting a wide spectrum of microscopic life within about 12 square meters of the lander. The biologists designed three experiments:

1. Pyrolytic release experiment. The sampling arm scoops up a tiny sample (0.1 gram) of Martian soil and places it inside the test chamber of the biology lab. Carbon dioxide and carbon monoxide labeled with the radioactive isotope carbon-14 are then admitted, the mixture is incubated under a sunlamp for several days, and everything is heated to break down (pyrolyze) any organic compounds present. Finally, hydrogen gas is admitted into the chamber to sweep the pyrolysis products into a gas chromatograph and mass spectrograph capable of detecting carbon-14. Since any organisms present should carry out metabolic processes during which they will assimilate carbon-14 from the gas in the chamber, detection of carbon-14 would be considered a positive result. However, this in and of itself would not be entirely conclusive, since a first peak of radioactivity might conceivably be due to chemical processes not involving living organisms. In order to rule out this latter possibility, other samples (serving as controls) are sterilized by heating before the carbon source is admitted.

2. Labeled release experiment. Again, a sample of Martian material is placed into the chamber, and a moist nutrient material containing carbon-14 is added. Any Martian organisms present will metabolize the nutrient material and release carbon-14-labeled gas, which is then registered by the detector.

3. Gas exchange experiment (popularly known as the "chicken soup" experiment). At the beginning of the experiment, the atmosphere within the chamber consists of carbon dioxide and the inert gases helium and krypton; a nutrient material and water vapor are added to the soil sample. On sud-

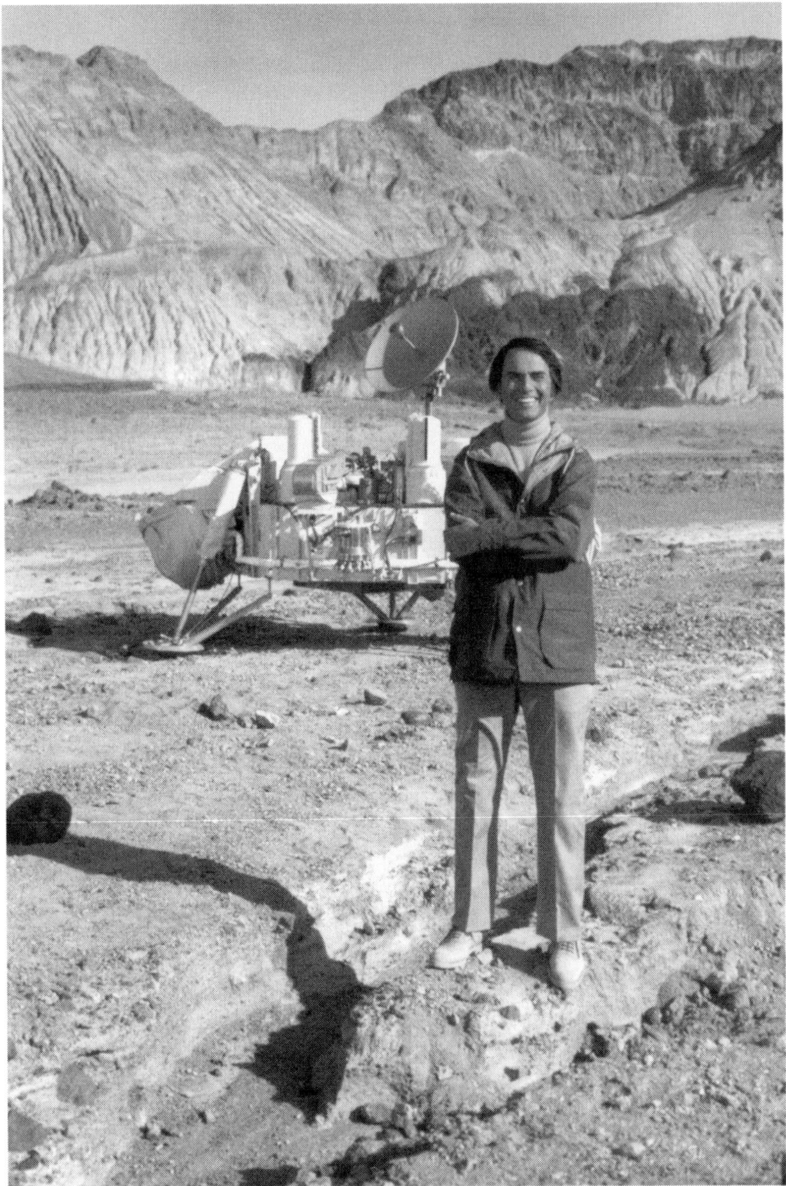

Carl Sagan on a mock Mars with a *Viking* Lander in the background. Sagan hoped the craft would have detected life. But he did not like the traditional scientific definition of life: something that consumes energy, moves, and reproduces. "My automobile eats and breathes and metabolizes and moves." he said. Instead he leaned toward genetics. Unfortunately, no *Viking* experiment would be able to look for genetic attributes of any Martian life, nor would the experiments last long enough to see if that life would evolve. (*Sky & Telescope* archives)

denly finding themselves in a water- and nutrient-rich environment, the Martian organisms are expected to respond with a vigorous spurt of metabolism, resulting in the sudden buildup of gases in the chamber.

Apart from these three experiments, a mass spectrograph was designed to make sensitive measurements in a direct attempt to detect organic materials on Mars.

How likely was it, the researchers wondered, that *Viking* would find life on Mars? The bets ran the gamut. Bruce Murray, "an honest-to-God, card-carrying geologist," said the chances were zilch. Horowitz, who designed the pyrolytic-release experiment, put the odds at "not quite zero." Harold Klein, head of *Viking*'s biology team, gave it a 1 in 50 chance. Sagan took the agnostic approach: There was either life or no life, so he guessed 50 percent. Team member Clark Chapman believed the odds were much less.

The results did not settle any bets. The pyrolytic release experiment showed two peaks, and at first was felt to be weakly positive; however, later attempts to duplicate the effect were unsuccessful. The labeled release experiment showed an immediate—and startling—rise in the level of carbon-14 radioactivity immediately after the nutrient was introduced into the chamber. This data strip seemed to attest to a positive reaction, so much so that the experiment team immediately rushed out and ordered a bottle of champagne. The "chicken soup" experiment also produced dramatic and unexpected results; when the samples were humidified, there was a sudden burst of oxygen—something that had never occurred in earlier tests with terrestrial samples. However, there was a very weak response when the nutrient material was added.

On the whole, the consensus was that, instead of being produced by organisms of some kind, the chemical reactions observed were entirely due to a highly oxidizing substance in the rust red Martian soil, perhaps iron peroxide or superoxide. Somehow, intense ultraviolet radiation from the Sun passing through the thin Martian atmosphere had turned the soil viciously corrosive, making it full of chemicals that would burn your flesh if you dared to step in it. Before these results, Horowitz said he'd gladly eat a spoonful of Martian soil on a salad, though he now retracted that offer.[21] Some of the organic compounds in the nutrient would have been sensitive to oxidizing materials. The same exotic chemistry can explain the evolution of the large amounts of oxygen when water vapor was added to the gas-exchange experiment. The fact that the mass spectrograph failed to identify any organic compounds (except for some known contaminants such as methylchloride and freon-E) appeared to argue strongly against biological explanations for the results. On the other hand, the data from the labeled release experiment remained in dispute, and a small minority of scientists still maintain, even today, that the *Viking* results provided positive evidence for the existence of microorganisms on Mars.

Overall, though, the feeling was one of dismay. For Sagan, the results were depressing. A few scoops of Martian soil, and *poof!* Mars was once again declared biologically dead. It was chilling to hear the results. Until the advent of the Space Age (in fact, just up until the *Viking* Mission), the universe had been a playground for all manner of imagined life. Lowell had his intelligent race of civilized Martians, while Flammarion believed that even Venus and the other planets had inhabitants. In the 1700s William Herschel believed that extraterrestrials might live inside the cool core of the Sun, looking out at the universe through sunspots.[22] Of course, the further back we travel in time the more supernatural the heavens had seemed, the more they were regarded as realms occupied by deities and overlords; indeed, as we have discussed earlier, the stars and planets themselves were living entities to aboriginal peoples. Ironically, as technology brought us ever closer to achieving the summit of our "mountain Mars," our visions of life on the planet diminished proportionally. It was as if we were looking for life through the wrong end of the telescope. As Mars's surface loomed closer in our view, life went from being an intelligent race of people, to tracts of forests, to patches of moss. Finally to a cold and rocky wasteland devoid of life. From a biological viewpoint, the long and arduous journey to the surface of Mars paralleled that of the enigmatic loner and Norwegian explorer Carl Lumholtz (one of the last great Victorian pioneers) who rode into the remote canyons of Mexico on "a fool's errand"—to try to pry secrets from the ancient cliff-dwelling Anasazi, a culture that had faded away six centuries earlier. Although Lumholtz never found his lost people, in the end the experience taught him a "new philosophy of life," and made him uncertain of his place in the universe.[23]

At one point during the *Viking* biology experiments, Sagan became concerned about the (relatively) high temperatures under which all the experiments had been conducted. "It's as if the Martians sent equipment to Earth that detected life only at 200° Fahrenheit," he said. Ironically, Sagan and his team members had no idea just how tenacious life could be. The double irony is that a momentous new discovery about microscopic life on Earth had made that knowledge available three weeks after *Viking 2* touched down on Mars—but the news was ignored by the press and by NASA; why get people excited about microscopic life on Earth when *Viking* had them mesmerized over the possibility of microscopic life on Mars? Unfortunately, the news would have told the *Viking* scientists that they were looking for life in the wrong place. If microscopic life existed on Mars, it would be hidden *inside* rocks, not in the soil.

The story of life in rocks actually dates to 1961, when Hungarian born microbiologist Imre Friedmann received a piece of limestone from Israel's scorching Negev Desert. Inside the rock was a curious green, copperlike layer. Tests showed it to be a living membrane of blue-green algae; Friedmann dubbed the organisms "cryptoendoliths," meaning "things that hide inside rock." The algae survived the blistering heat at the surface by living off small pockets of water just a few millimeters inside the porous rock. "How innocent, how happy, indeed how comfortable life might be," Pliny the Elder once said, "if it coveted nothing from anywhere other than the surface of the Earth."[24]

If life could survive in harsh desert environments, Friedmann postulated, might it not also survive in the opposite extreme? To secure evidence, Friedmann proposed searching for life in the rocks of Antarctica's Dry Valleys. But his idea was met with "stone cold" resistance. In the 1960s NASA tested prototypes of *Viking*'s biology experiments in the Dry Valleys and found the soil sterile, so why would anyone embrace some newcomer waving around a crazy theory about life in rocks?[25] Friedmann's luck changed in 1973 when he met Wolf Vishniac, a biologist with the *Viking* mission. Vishniac's biology experiment (the only one that required Martian microbes to be able to grow in a liquid water medium) had just ended up on the cutting room floor—a cost-saving measure by NASA that destroyed a decade of Vishniac's lifework. Like Friedmann, Vishniac did not believe that the Antarctic soil was sterile. Determined to prove that the NASA experiments missed the microbes, he went to Antarctica himself; he promised Friedmann he'd return him a rock from the South Pole. But this act was "almost foolhardy bravado," William Poundstone explains in his biography of Carl Sagan. Having failed a physical required of those going to Antarctica (childhood polio had stunted his right arm), "he got a senator to pull some strings for him," Poundstone reveals. "He also had himself excused from taking the navy survival course, normally demanded of scientists doing Antarctic fieldwork."

Vishniac and a colleague, Zeddie Bowen, arrived at McMurdo Station on the Ross Ice Shelf in November 1973. Together they would journey to a dry valley near Mount Baldr, to set up a series of nutrient-glazed glass slides on which Vishniac intended to capture soil cultures. One month later, on December 10, Vishniac embarked alone on a twelve-hour hike to retrieve the slides. Bowen remained at a campsite to await a supply plane. "We went off alone on several occasions," Bowen explained, "always in good weather and with an expected route and timetable. The route was not dangerous."[26] But when Vishniac did not return on time, Bowen went looking for him expecting, at worst, he had broken an ankle. Bowen found Vishniac, but his body had fallen off a 150-meter (500-foot) cliff and tumbled several times on a sheer slope beneath an ice field between two mountains. Vishniac had followed a different route to the Valley; he slipped and fell to his death. At the suggestion of Sagan, a crater was named in Vishniac's honor for his pioneering efforts in the search for life on Mars; the crater lies at the same southern latitude where Vishniac had perished following his curiosity.

The news devastated Friedmann. Not only had he lost a comrade but his dreams of learning the secrets of life in Antarctic rocks perished with his friend . . . until he received a letter in March 1974 from Vishniac's wife, Helen, who had just received a box from Antarctica with her husband's belongings; among the items she found were some rocks with Friedmann's name on them. The rocks were a godsend, for within a few millimeters of the crust Friedmann found a perfect specimen of blue-green algae, which meant that life could survive in an environment where the temperature rises above freezing no more than one or two days each year. Vishniac's rocks proved that life had extreme moxie.

So life exists in Antarctic rocks. So what? Steven Dutch of the University of Wisconsin at Green Bay says that before Antarctica drifted away from Pangaea, life there enjoyed a temperate climate. "There is a vast difference between survival of a few lifeforms in a slowly worsening environment," he cautions, "as opposed to evolution in an equally harsh environment." Enclaves, he says, are a common theme in science fiction—like Lowell's civilization holding on to small spots on an otherwise lifeless world. Change is the one constant in nature. On Earth, if a cataclysm destroys life in one spot, migrants from elsewhere rapidly recolonize it. But on a truly hostile world, Dutch says, such recolonization may be impossible. The environment in between may be too harsh, or there may be no air or water to transport organisms. "When one enclave dies," Dutch proclaims, "it is not recolonized, and if a new favorable spot appears, nothing may be able to get to it. When the last enclave dies, that's it."

But if life on Earth could survive the slow migration from a temperate environment to an antarctic environment, might not life have survived on Mars—if Mars was once temperate? In other words, is it possible that Mars could have been at some remote time in the past more Earth-like?

Less than a billion years after its creation, the infant planet Mars, a world one-fourth the size of our Earth, was in many ways already extraordinary. When the primordial bombardment ended 3.8 billion years ago, and Mars's seething molten surface began to cool, water vapor—and several tens to hundreds of times as much carbon dioxide and other greenhouse gases—would have been freed from the cooling rock. The volume of gas would have been dense enough to trigger the onset of global warming. Thus, although Mars lies in a frigid realm of space one-third farther away from the Sun than the Earth, its climate would have been temperate enough to support liquid water on its surface.

Although the amount of water and how long it lasted is still unknown, it now seems quite certain that liquid water once lapped in waves upon the shores of Mars, perhaps in an ocean so vast that it would have covered one-third of the planet's surface to a depth of up to 1.5 kilometers (1 mile). Impacts from rogue, water-bearing comets could have added to the wetness of early Mars. The oceans would have covered the depressed northern plains of the planet; water percolating through the porous rock would have gravitated to that low-lying region. In the north, active volcanoes would have erupted with spectacular force, flooding the surface with syrupy lava and scattering fertile ash upon the land. Beneath the roiling waves it would not be difficult to imagine thermal vents along the planet's volcanic ridges releasing sulfur-rich nutrients into a darkened ocean world.

At the time of the *Viking* landings, no one imagined that life could have secured a foothold in such a deep, dark, and volcanically active environment. It would have been absurd even to postulate such a claim. But an astounding discovery in 1977 once again turned the world of science on its head.

One year after *Viking* landed on Mars, a team of geophysicists and oceanographers took *Alvin*—the world's first deep-sea diving submarine—to a mid-ocean ridge near the Galapagos Islands off Ecuador. At a depth of 2.5 kilometers (1.5 miles), the researchers found an abundance of fresh lava, the first warm-water springs ever discovered in the abyss, and a rich and lush concentration of life in the most bizarre forms—the strangest of which were snakelike "things" in ten-foot-long tubes with no mouths, guts, or anuses—they live in symbiosis with bacteria that pack their bodies; as the worms absorb oxygen through extended plumelike structures, the bacteria use it to break down hydrogen sulfide, which becomes food for their hosts. These giant tubeworms form part of a complex deep-sea food chain in an ecosystem powered by volcanic minerals and heat—not sunlight. Black, turbulent clouds rising through mineralized chimneys (called "black smokers") spout metal-sulfide minerals from the seafloor, which feed and nurture the bizarre life forms. Even more astounding was the discovery of chemosynthetic bacteria swarming inside the hot vents. The microbes can withstand heat (up to 350° C or 660° F) that would kill all other forms of life. Volcanoes, largely noted for destroying life, were suddenly found to support it at active thermal areas along submarine rifts.

Conventional wisdom says when you get beyond the boiling point of water you can't have life. But if conventional wisdom ruled science we'd still believe that the Sun orbits the Earth and that rats arise spontaneously from bran and old rags (as the seventeenth-century Flemish physician and psychologist Jan Baptista van Helmont proposed).[27] "The foibles of our anthropocentric focus are driven home by the whole history of deep exploration," Pulitzer Prize winning author William Broad shares in his book *The Universe Below: Discovering the Secrets of the Deep Sea*. "At almost every juncture, our imaginations and intuitions failed us. Generations of scientists dismissed the abyss (a dismissive word in some respects) as inert and irrelevant, as geologically dead and having only a thin population of bizarre fish . . . they were wrong, impressively so."[28]

It took years for the scientists to fully understand the significance of their discoveries, but they knew instinctively that the ecosystem they had discovered was unlike anything people had seen before. "We all started jumping up and down," researcher John Edmond recalled. "We were dancing off the walls. It was chaos. It was so completely new and unexpected that everyone was fighting to dive. There was so much to learn. It was a discovery cruise. It was like Columbus."[29]

Later expeditions to other hydrothermal vents discovered even more surprises. Among the the vent microbes were archaebacteria, the most ancient life form, present three to four billion years ago when life first appeared on Earth. And based on experiments with bacteria collected from the first hot vents in the Galapagos, it was discovered that vent bacteria can reproduce at the outrageous temperature of 250° C (482° F).

Microbiologist John Baross and geologists Jack Corliss and Sarah Hoffman, both formerly of Oregon State University, took the discoveries to the next level. In a controversial paper, the researchers proposed that billions of years ago, the chemical precursors of life had been present deep in the interiors of the hot vents, and that these substances had been heated and transformed, little by little, into complex, self-replicating molecules. The vents, they said, were "ideal reactors."[30] Life, they suggested, might not have begun in a primordial soup but at the bottom of the ocean at hydrothermal vents. Life, they argued, evolved in step with the formation of the seas.

The unorthodox idea was immediately shunned or given little thought. Corliss reacted by saying,"It's amazing how resistant science can be to an idea." Over the years new evidence mounted in their favor. Today the theory that life originated at active hydrothermal vents forms the very foundation of a new belief that life thrives along hydrothermal vents in an ocean below the ice-covered surface of Europa, one of Jupiter's four Galilean moons. (The idea is so compelling that NASA has made the exploration of Europa one of its top priorities. "If we could go tomorrow, we would," said one mission planner.)[31]

When molecular biologists traced back the ancestry of all living species using a form of RNA as a guide, the roots led them to microbiota living at extremely and inhospitably hot environments—not only in the smoking chimneys beneath the sea but in the throats of geysers, bubbling hot springs, and steaming pools found in Earth's natural geothermal areas like Yellowstone in the United States and Rotorua in New Zealand;

microbes have also been discovered in volcanic basalt two miles below the Earth's surface (these deep-rock creatures have a very low metabolic rate, reproduce perhaps once a century, and get their energy from water and basalt, which produces a little bit of hydrogen). Today, conventional wisdom says it is not surprising that the *Viking* landers did not find life in the soil of Mars, for conventional wisdom now says that if life did exist on Mars, it would have survived not on, but below, the surface. Friedmann and Vishniac, those rogue warriors of unconventional thinking, had the key to unlocking the greatest secrets of Mars all along.

Could water, the incubator of life on Earth, have also been the incubator of life on Mars? Its presence on Mars certainly would argue strongly in favor of life. But if Mars had water, it did not last. As the interior of the red planet cooled, volcanic activity with its release of carbon dioxide into the atmosphere waned, triggering a climatic reversal and the onset of global cooling. The once hospitable temperatures plummeted well below freezing. Life, if it existed, could still have survived in water beneath its surface (as scientists now believe it may on Europa). But two billion years ago, the Martian oceans froze entirely; if a great sea ever existed on Mars, it would have then become a mammoth glacier covering some thirty million square kilometers. Sagan and David Wallace of Cornell postulated that the only likely source for a body of water on Mars at this point in its history would be geothermal or impact melting of the ice. Occasionally a series of catastrophic floods would burst out of the ground at canyon walls and heads. Rushing downslope in a torrent of water, mud, boulders, and sand, huge blocks of rock would have been displaced up to ten kilometers on a side. Sagan and Wallace computed that these ice rivers would carve channels hundreds of kilometers long—then freeze-dry over tens of millennia, leaving the dry channels we see in the *Viking* and other spacecraft imagery.

Sagan, who suffered from *myelodysplasia* (a disease of the bone marrow), did not live long enough to see the striking *Mars Global Surveyor* images showing clear signs that liquid water may have seeped onto the surface from underground reservoirs in the relatively recent geologic past. The relative freshness of these features indicate that liquid water might have flowed on Mars as recently as a million years ago, maybe yesterday. That liquid water might still exist in some areas at depths of less than 500 meters (1,640 feet) beneath the surface of Mars intrigues biologists, because any Mars microbes could conceivably still live there. "If an alien civilization contacted me," quipped NASA exobiologist Chris McKay, "and asked what kind of life we have on Earth, I'd say 'water-based.' Water is essential for all life we know of, and wherever we find water, we find life."[32]

Sagan did live to see the greatest irony in the search for Martian life. In May 1996, seven months before his death, NASA announced that a team of nine researchers revealed startling new evidence that primitive life might have existed on Mars. What's more, the evidence was not a product of man's ingenuity, or of his billion-dollar efforts to land spacecraft on Mars to test the soil; the evidence literally fell from the sky in the most primitive fashion.

Sixteen million years ago an asteroid impact on Mars blasted rocks off the surface and jettisoned them into space. One orphaned stone wandered through the solar system until thirteen thousand years ago, it fell rather uneventfully onto the Allan Hills ice field in Antarctica. About two kilograms (four pounds) of this "lamp of earthly flame," to quote Shelly's "Epipsychidion," survived the blazing journey through our atmosphere. The burned stone sat in frigid isolation until an American search team chanced upon the interplanetary survivor on December 27, 1984—it stood out from the snow like a plump chocolate chip in a scoop of vanilla ice cream. Since it was the first meteorite discovered in 1984 from the Allan Hills area, it was designated ALH84001. Roberta Score, one of the searchers, recalls that it was one of the greenest meteorites she'd ever seen among the hundreds of Antarctic finds. "I've always thought that rock was weird," she said.[33]

And weird it was. The rock, initially misidentified as a chip off an old asteroid called Vesta, was found in 1996 to hail from Mars. Unlike the other twelve Martian meteorites known at the time (which are no older than 1.3 billion years), ALH840001 dated to 4.5 billion years; this rock thus experienced virtually the whole of Martian history and may be part of the planet's initial crust.

Sagan had just returned home after a bone-marrow operation when he learned of rumors leaking from NASA that fossils had been found in the meteorite. Sagan must have smiled a weak smile, as he recalled what he prophetically said two years earlier about Martian meteorites—that there had been no reports of microbes in them . . . "so far." The news was officially announced in the August 16, 1996, issue of *Science*. Although Sagan had reviewed and approved that article, he didn't forget his mantra that "extraordinary claims require extraordinary evidence."

The problem with finding extraordinary evidence to confirm the existence of primitive life on Mars is that no one knows anything about past life (never mind present life) on Mars. Lacking a clear picture of what kind of life might have existed on the red planet, we can only acknowledge our ignorance and evaluate the evidence based on what we know of ancient fossil life on Earth. It's a starting point at least.

No one questions that ALH84001 came from Mars. That much is clear. Its chemical composition is consistent with data collected from the *Viking* landers. And everyone seems to agree that the rock must have crystallized slowly from magma before it was shocked by a nearby impact 3.8 to 4.0 billion years ago—eons before being blasted toward Earth in another impact. ALH84001 then spent some time under water that was abundantly charged with carbon dioxide. Perhaps it did so more than once; the cracks and pores in the rock could even have been created by carbon dioxide percolating through the rocks.[34]

What scientists do question is the claim that primitive bacteria once lived in the cracks and pores of the rock. Officially, managers at NASA have adopted an attitude of "skeptical fascination" with the results. The controversy began when Christopher Romanek, then working with a NASA-Standard University team, first noticed that the rock contains some strange-looking carbonate globules no more than 250 microns (0.25 millimeter) across. The pancakelike blobs display orange-brown centers surrounded by alternating dark and bright rims, which have been likened to Oreo cookies; such globules have not been found in any of the other Martian meteorites. The layers appear to be mineral deposits laid down in a warm, hospitable, and fluid (possibly water) environment. If the globules are of Martian origin, they imply that Mars had a temperate climate in the remote past. The cracks and pores in the rocks then could have served as safe havens for water-born microbial cells and colonies to anchor in—as they do on Earth.

The team also found structures in the rims of the carbonate globules

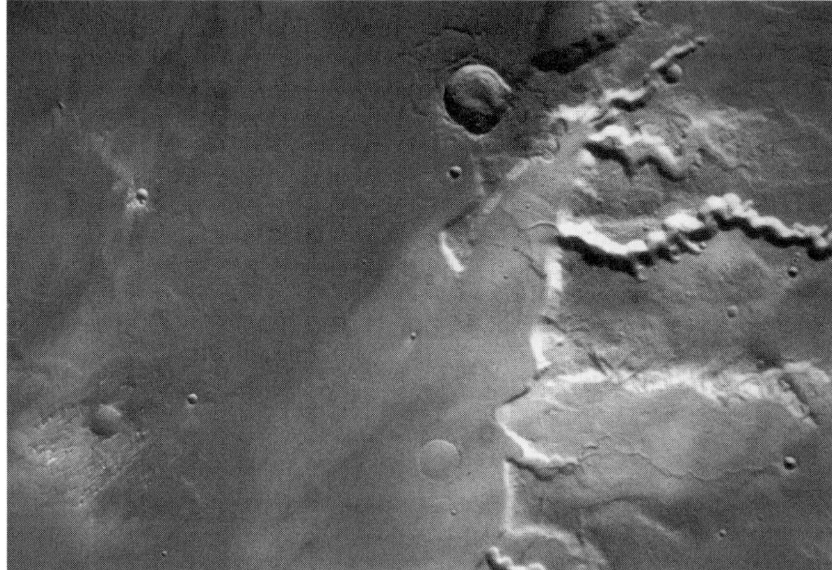

In the past a denser Martian atmosphere may have allowed water to flow on Mars. As this *Viking* orbiter image shows, many features resemble shorelines, gorges, riverbeds and islands suggest that great rivers and oceans once marked the planet. Thee lumpy regions surrounding the impact craters suggests permafrost may be present in the Martian soil. (NASA)

similar in size and shape to the fossilized remains of modern terrestrial bacteria. While these structures are very small, they are within the size limit of known nanobacteria (50-200 nanometers). However, firm evidence that these bacteria-like structures are truly the fossilized remains of Martian bacteria has not been forthcoming. Some of the features have been interpreted as the remains of biofilms and their associated microbial communities. Biofilms are produced by *terrestrial* bacteria as a protective device against times of environmental stress. When found in the fossil record on Earth, biofilms are considered strong evidence of bacterial colonies in ancient rocks. It is possible that some of the clusters of microfossil-like features in ALH84001 might be colonies, although that interpretation depends on whether the individual features truly are fossilized microbes.

Within the carbonates, the NASA-Stanford team also found minerals that could be associated with life. They found iron oxides and sulfides—which can be produced by anaerobic (oxygen-hating) bacteria and other microbes. They also found magnetite, a form of iron whose size, structure, and purity are identical to those produced by some terrestrial bacteria, but they match no known nonbiologic form of magnetite; on Earth, magnetite particles in some species of bacteria provide them with the ability to sense magnetic fields. The structures, by the way, are remarkably small; you can fit about a billion of these on the head of a pin.

ALH84001. (NASA)

The most compelling evidence is that the meteorite's globules are infused with organic molecules known as polycyclic aromatic hydrocarbons (PAHs). Some of these PAHs may be a unique product of bacterial decay that flowed in when the carbonates were deposited. Recent data show that the PAHs most likely came from Mars. Ordinarily their presence would not indicate biologic activity—PAHs are also found in other meteorites and in star-forming clouds of gas in interstellar space—but the PAHs in ALH84001 are much simpler. They're what you'd expect to to find when simple organic matter decays.

But we are still "bedeviled by a natural and persisting sense of anthropomorphism." Opponents have claimed the fossil nanobacteria are natural bumps in the rock or artifacts created when the samples were being prepared for electron microscopy. Some adversaries have found evidence that the carbonate and magnetic crystals formed at temperatures too high to support life. Still others have voiced concerns that, because the rock sat on Earth for thirteen thousand years, the structures we see are all terrestrial. The carbonate globules do appear to be from Mars, but they, too, could be contaminated with earthly microbes.

The researchers who introduced the fossil evidence have admitted that some of the features in ALH84001 (originally identified as being suggestive of fossil organisms) may have actually been caused by the process of preparing a sample or by the result of weathering. But other structures, they claim, are definitely not the result of human or geological intervention and cannot be ignored. So the jury is still out.[35] In one of his last essays, Sagan cautioned that "the evidence for life on Mars is not yet extraordinary enough," but added that the discovery opens up the entire field of Martian exobiology. "Science is far from a perfect instrument of knowledge," Sagan admits in his *The Demon Haunted World*. "It's just the best we have."

As Sagan's colleagues continued to battle over the possibility of life in this little rock—and it continues today, with the weight of opinion gradually tilting in favor of the skeptics—Sagan watched quietly from the sidelines; he was struggling with his own battle—the possibility that his own life was really over. By December 1996 his illness had progressed to a critical stage. And as the sparkle receded from his eyes, his wife Annie Druyan stood by him, gripping his hand. "What a wonderfully lived life," she said to him, then repeated over and over again. "With pride and joy in our love, I let you go. Without fear. June 1. June 1. For keeps."[36] On December 20, Carl Sagan "lost the one thing he spent his life searching for but never found."

If we learn beyond a shadow of a doubt that ALH84001 contains fossilized microbes from Mars, we may have reached the threshold of understanding the origins of life on Earth. "We are strangers and sojourners, soft dots on the rock," Annie Dillard mused while in the Galapagos. And it is, to use another Annie Dillard phrase, "the imaginary, and impossible, extreme" that concerns us now in matters concerning ALH84001.[37] And it is the imaginary, and impossible, extreme that concerns us now in matters concerning ALH84001—for the very presence of that stone on Earth shows us that life can, in principle, be transported between worlds. The question is, "Did life begin on Earth and travel to Mars, or did life originate on Mars then travel to Earth?"

In his book, *The Fifth Miracle*, physicist Paul Davies concludes, "It is . . . inevitable that life from Earth has reached Mars . . . that is why I am certain that there was life on Mars in the past, and may well be life there today." The problem with this argument is that, once again, we find life on

Earth somehow "central" or important (though Davies, of course, does offer the obvious alternative, as well). "But who shall dwell in these worlds if they be inhabited," Kepler wondered. "Are we or they Lords of the World? . . . And how are all things made for man?"[38] The fact is, since Mars is smaller than the Earth, it would have cooled faster shortly after its formation. Conditions suitable for life, therefore, would have also evolved faster. And since Mars has one-tenth the mass of the Earth, its gravitational field is weaker, making it easier for rocks to flee from the surface into space after an impact; likewise, Earth's stronger gravity is more efficient at sweeping up wandering stones in space. Statistically it is much more favorable for life to be transported from Mars to Earth. Of all the rocks blasted from the surface of Mars into orbit around the Sun, about 1 in 15 will eventually collide with the Earth. In fact, about half a ton of fragments blasted off Mars millions of years ago arrives on Earth every year—though we have in our possession only thirteen Martian meteorites so far; meteorites, which look like many other stones on Earth, are tremendously difficult to discover—unless they happen to be exposed on ice—and a large percentage of them are, of course, likely to be sitting at the bottom of Earth's oceans.

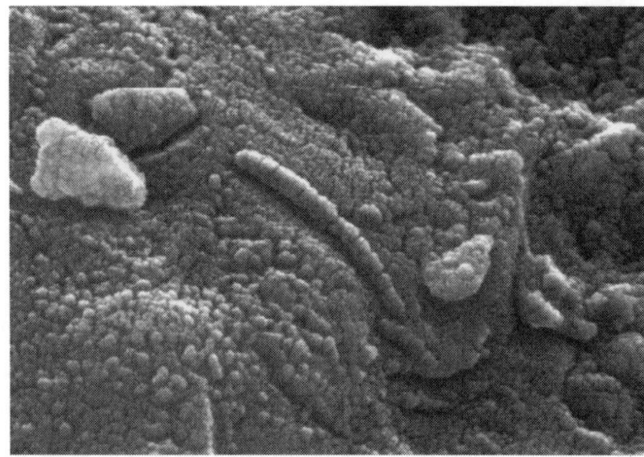

Electron microscope image of unusual worm-like structural form—a possible microfossil—that is less than 1.100th the width of a human hair. (NASA)

To survive the trip to Earth—which could take thousands or millions of years—the lifeforms would have to endure freezing temperatures, deadly cosmic rays, and ultraviolet radiation. The freezing temperatures, it turns out, might actually help the organisms survive cryogenically (in deep freeze), while the stone around it provides shelter from radiation and cosmic rays.

Isn't it ironic that in his conclusion of *The War of the Worlds,* H. G. Wells has his tentacled, large-brained octopus-like Martians—who arrived in ships that blazed through the night like shooting stars before impacting the Earth and flinging sand and gravel "violently in every direction over the heath"—succumbing to terrestrial bacteria?

At any rate, in all the bodies of the Martians that were examined after the war, no bacteria except those already known as terrestrial species were found.

The real irony is that if microbiotic life evolved first on Mars (before it did on Earth), and if a Martian rock teeming with microbes found its way to our sterile world, and those microbes survived, our search for Martian life is over—it is here on Earth. If true, Lowell was closer to his beloved Martians than he could ever have dreamed. He was, and we are, them.

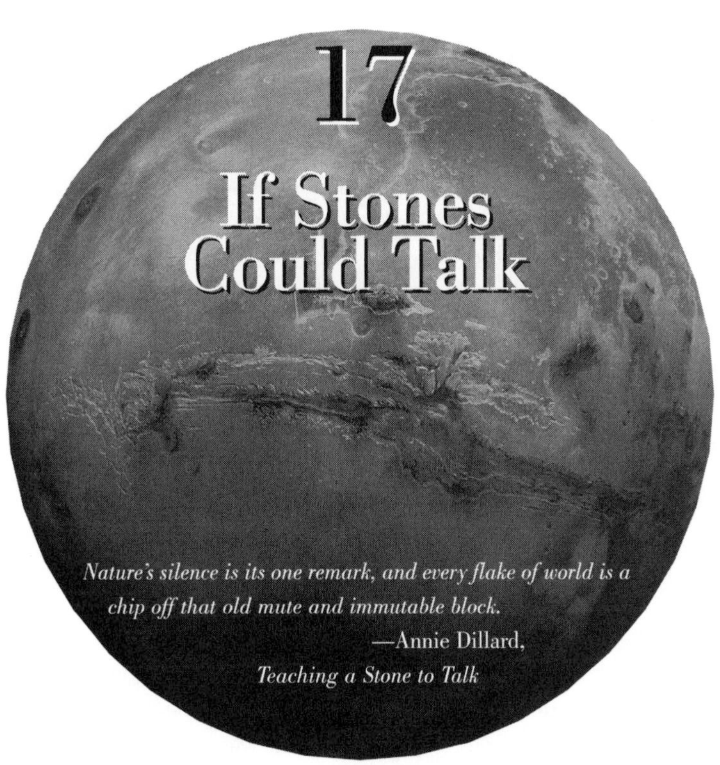

17
If Stones Could Talk

Nature's silence is its one remark, and every flake of world is a chip off that old mute and immutable block.

—Annie Dillard, *Teaching a Stone to Talk*

At 8:43 in the morning on January 18, 2000, a space rock the size of a cabin cruiser—but one weighing 60 times as much (200 metric tons)—ripped into Earth's atmosphere over western Canada at 10 kilometers/second (6 miles/second). The air around the meteor ignited, transforming the solid mass into a multicolored fireball that outshone the Sun in brightness. Surprised residents in a

remote area between Atlin, British Columbia, and Carcross, Yukon Territory, saw the fireball streak across the morning sky and light up the surrounding landscape. Some reported sizzling sounds and peculiar smells. Minutes later the fireball exploded with an energy equal to one-third the power of the atomic bomb dropped over Hiroshima. When the shockwaves generated by the blast reached the Earth, houses shook, and the ground trembled enough to affect regional seismographs. The explosion was also detected from orbit by two U.S. Department of Defense satellites. Some residents feared for their children. Others rushed outside to photograph or videotape the smoke trail left behind by the vaporized rock.

Though unusually dramatic, the event itself was not uncommon. Every day the Earth is bombarded by 80 to 100 metric tons of space debris. But most of this debris is microscopic. We see this burning dust every time we spot a shooting star. What's rare, however, is for a large chunk of space rock to survive its journey through our atmosphere and to wallop the Earth's surface near a populated region. And what's most extremely rare is for the surviving fragments to be picked up soon after the fall.

But on January 25, a week after the Yukon fireball exploded, outdoorsman and fishing-camp operator Jim Brook found several chunks of it while driving his pickup truck across the ice-covered Taku Arm of Tagish Lake. Fortunately, Peter Brown, a meteor scientist at the University of Western Ontario (who was investigating the blast) had been in contact with Brook shortly after the explosion. Brown had explained to Brook what meteorite fragments would look like, and he showed him how to collect them if he ever encountered any. On the day of his discovery Brook says he was keeping his eyes peeled for meteorites; he had been fooled several times already by wolf droppings. But the black objects he saw on the ice on January 25 clearly were not skat. "You don't find rocks a half mile out from shore on a lake," he explained.[1] He said he could also see the melted outer crust.

Following Brown's instructions, Brook carefully collected the rocks, covering his fingers with clean plastic and placing the meteorites in clean plastic bags. After only ninety minutes of total search on January 25 and 26, Brook had sealed up several dozen fragments whose total weight was almost one kilogram. He then kept the samples in a freezer—to minimize the potential loss of organic materials and other volatile compounds that might exist in the fragments.

Michael Zolensky, a meteoriticist at NASA's Johnson Space Center in Houston, analyzed the samples and found the meteorites to be a type of carbonaceous chondrite—a rare, organically rich, charcoal-like class of meteorites that probably hail from the asteroid belt between Mars and Jupiter; it's possible the samples predate the solar system. Brook's find is all the more important given that it was collected only a week after the object entered the Earth's atmosphere, so it had little time to be contaminated—it was never touched by human hands. In contrast, chondrites discovered on the Antarctic icesheets have been exposed, in some cases, ten thousand years or more. The Yukon meteorite is the first meteorite to fall in a cold arctic area, to be quickly recovered, and then to be transferred to a laboratory for inspection without thawing.[2]

Brown and a team of scientists returned to Tagish Lake in April 2000. They harvested a new crop of fragments, the largest of which was a piece weighing 250 grams. To date, 500 fragments have been recovered over an area measuring 10 kilometers (6 miles) by 2 kilometers (1.2 miles).[3]

The Yukon meteorite—now officially designated the Tagish Lake Meteorite—holds many distinctions: it is the first carbonaceous chondrite found just after landfall since the Murchison (Australia) meteorite of 1969, the first to be studied using modern techniques, the largest meteorite find in Canadian history, and the largest ever recorded over land by an orbiting satellite. "Of all the times I dreamed of finding meteorites, I never thought of finding them like this," says Alan Hildebrand, planetary scientist in the Department of Geology and Geophysics at the University of Calgary and an investigation coleader. "One day while I was picking pieces of meteorite out of porous ice I thought that the experience must be a bit like sampling on the surface of a comet. We believe these to be the most fragile meteorites ever recovered."[4]

The excitement this find has generated in the scientific community cannot be understated. Carbonaceous chondrites contain significant amounts of carbon, primarily in the form of organic compounds similar to those found in living organisms on Earth. Amino acids, for example, have been identified in other carbonaceous chondrites, including a large number of amino acids that do *not* occur naturally on Earth. The Tagish Lake samples, then, are of extreme importance; since they have remained frozen after their fall, the rocks should still contain the primordial signatures of ancient water (the essential substance for life) and amino acids—the basic building blocks of life. If the Tagish Lake Meteorite fragments do contain these "seeds of life," then it would be hard not to imagine the possibility that life on Earth could have had an extraterrestrial origin—a theory (Panspermia) first advanced by Swedish chemist Svante Arrhenius in the nineteenth century. The Tagish Lake Meteorite could then hold the key to unlocking the secrets of the origins of life. "There's nothing like this [meteorite] on Earth," Zolensky said. "You're looking back at your ancestors here in a bucket of ice."[5]

There is an unspoken message here as well. In the 1960s, scientists argued that carbonaceous chondrites contain microfossils. Yet no one believed the data because of the contamination issue. If the Tagish Lake Meteorite also contains microfossils, we will have no choice but to rethink our origins. So the excitement is clear. Given the recent news that the Martian meteorite ALH 84001 might also contain microfossils, and that other space rocks may contain the building blocks of life, we may be on the verge of the greatest revelation in the history of humankind.

Ever since the dawn of humanity, when man first looked to the stars with a sense of understanding and place, we have been humbled by a succession of revelations—discoveries that have affected our lives and thoughts. Each revelation has shown us that the Earth does not possess a commanding place in this universe. "If there is some grandeur in our position in space and time," the late Harvard astronomer Harlow Shapley once said, "I fail to find it."[6] Yet many still cling to the tiresome creed that we are somehow special, very special—that humans are more important than any other living creature on Earth, that we are outside our environment (not a part of it), both on Earth and in space.

We do not learn our lessons well.

Four Great Revelations

The first revelation was Copernicus's doctrine that removed the Earth from the center of the universe, ending 1,000 years of egocentrism; but the acceptance cost some believers their lives or their credibility. In 1600 Giordano Bruno was burned at the stake as a heretic for promoting the Copernican view (and for believing in the plurality of worlds). Galileo Galilei was also tried as a heretic for promoting his views that telescopic observations lent credence to the heliocentric theory. But the church's stance on the Copernican doctrine was simple: it was "foolish and philosophically absurd and formally heretical."[7] Galileo called anyone who did not believe that the Earth moves "imbeciles," "mental pygmies," "dumb idols," and "hardly deserving to be called human beings."[8] Summoned before the Inquisition, Galileo was ordered to abjure the Copernican system. He complied—thus, escaping the fate of Giordano Bruno and depriving the Roman public of "the spectacle of another heretic dragged to Campo di Fiori with his tongue pierced by one iron spike and another driven into his palate to prevent the utterance of blasphemies, then stripped of his clothes and immolated on the stake."[9] With time, the silence was broken, and the Copernican theory was accepted—even by the church.

The second revelation removed the Sun (and our solar system) from the center of the universe—this time without any violence from the church. In the eighteenth century, human understanding of "the universe" was limited to the Milky Way, which William Herschel modeled after making extensive star counts through his telescope. His observations revealed (falsely) that the Sun was situated at the center of the universe, which he portrayed as a wafer-like metropolis of stars surrounded by an elliptical disk of suburban suns. And there we remained, at the center of it all, until the beginning of the twentieth century—when Harlow Shapley in 1920 announced that his research on the distances and placements of globular star clusters around the hub of our galaxy revealed that our Sun (and therefore the Earth) does not hold a central position in the Milky Way. It is off to one side in a region tens of thousands of light years from the true galactic center. "Man, the so-called crowning glory of Creation," Shapley said, "is revealed to be peripheral, off-center."[10]

The third revelation occurred only four years later, when Edwin

Hubble used the clockwork regularity of pulsating stars in the Great Andromeda Nebula to discover that this nebula, and certain other hazy patches in the sky (which were long believed to be part of the Milky Way) were not nebulae or clouds at all, but themselves resplendent accumulations of suns—island universes floating in space beyond the gravitational grasp of our own galaxy. What was once accepted as "ours" suddenly belonged to no one. At about the same time, Einstein added that we are no more at the center of the universe than anyone else. Interestingly, Giordano Bruno had believed this before he was burned at the stake, and William Herschel had also hinted at it in his own belief in a plurality of worlds. The fuzzy nebulae Herschel saw through his magnificent telescope, he said, "are probably much larger than our own system; and, being also extended, the inhabitants of the planets that attend the stars which compose them must likewise perceive the same phaenomena. For which reason they may also be called milky ways."[11]

The fourth, and certainly not the final, revelation is that our solar system is not unique among the stars. We have held on to that belief as long as possible. Prior to 1995, many people, including scientists, believed that our solar system was unique.[12] But advances in telescope technology have now allowed us to discover other extrasolar planetary systems. So the time has come for us to accept the fact that our Sun and its family of planets hold no preeminent position among the stars. We are but one of countless planetary systems that must populate the Milky Way. To date we know of fifty new worlds with at least a half dozen others suspected, and that number will only increase as telescope technology evolves. Extrasolar planet hunter Geoffry Marcy (University of California) reports that we are now seeing for the first time numerous hints of full families of planets.[13] There are undoubtedly innumerable other planetary systems surrounding the billions of stars populating each of the uncounted billions of galaxies in the universe.

So what remains of man's importance in the universe? The answer is life. And, as we have said, we may be standing now on the threshold of understanding that mystery of all mysteries. And the key to understanding life may be in our own "backyards," in the pieces of stone that fell from the sky—some from Mars, some from the Asteroid Belt, some perhaps from comets.

A Meteor streaks across the northern skies over Hawaii. ©Donna and Stephen O'Meara / Volcano Watch International.

What will it take for humanity to accept the ultimate possibility that life may be an inevitable consequence of the laws of physics and chemistry working in concert under the right conditions—not only the conditions we enjoy here on Earth but also on Mars, Europa, and elsewhere in the universe? Paul Davies, Professor of Natural History at the University of Adelaide, South Australia, strongly believes in this contention for, he says, it is based on the adoption of three philosophical principles: (1) *the Principle of Uniformity of Nature*, which states that the laws of nature are the same throughout the universe, so the physical processes responsible for life on Earth can also produce life elsewhere; (2) *the Principle of Plenitude*, which states that that which is possible in nature tends to be realized; and (3) *the Cooperation Principle*, which mirror's Shapley's argument that the Earth does not occupy a special position or status in the universe.[14]

We can apply the same principles to inanimate objects as well, such as oceans on Mars. Certainly the physical processes responsible for creating oceans on Earth would also apply to Mars, given the right conditions. We have already seen that it is deemed quite probable that oceans existed (albeit geologically briefly) in the planet's early history. If an ocean once existed on Mars, the second philosophical principle says we are destined to find evidence of it. Indeed, while researchers were investigating the Tagish Lake Meteorite for clues to the origins of life, news suddenly broke in June 2000 that researchers from Arizona State University had extracted salt from the interior of a 1.2 billion-year-old Martian meteorite that landed in Nakhla, Egypt, after a 1911 meteor shower. The salt, says Carleton Moore (Arizona State University), was originally present in Martian water. Apparently, salt water leaked into the rock and evaporated, depositing sodium, chlorine, and other ions within it.

The news of Martian salt came only one day after images from the *Mars Global Surveyor* spacecraft revealed titillating evidence that water might have flowed on the Martian surface in the recent past. The only significant difference between the salty elements found in the Martian meteorite and those present in ocean water on Earth was the amount of calcium, which was much higher in the Mars rock. Moore believes that the lower calcium concentration in Earth's seawater may be due to the mineral being removed biologically by plants, corals, and shellfish. When the Nakhla meteorite left Mars 1.2 billion years ago, life on Earth had not yet evolved to these higher forms (shells only appear in the fossil record about 600 million years ago).

As if to prove Davies' third philosophical principle, Moore concludes, "There was apparently a uniformity between the planets. The inference that the early Martian ocean was very similar to our current ocean also implies that the early Earth's ocean may have been very similar to what it is today."[15]

The Earth and Mars both formed out of the swirling solar nebula 4.5 billion years ago. They shared a common birth. At first, apart from their different masses—Mars contained only a tenth of the matter of the Earth—they seemed twins tied to a common destiny. Both sustained the violence of the early epoch of the solar system, when left-over debris from the formation of the planets rained down torrentially on those still-embryonic worlds, battering their surfaces, leaving them stark landscapes full of impact craters. The Earth was smitten by nothing less than a planet-sized interloper, perhaps even larger than Mars itself; fragments of the colossal wreck gathered together to form the Moon.

Although the early Sun burned with only some 30 percent of its present heat, there was an abundance of energy within the still seething and youthful planets Mars and Earth. Planets release pent-up energy by tectonic and volcanic forces. Volcanoes are notorious producers of carbon dioxide and other greenhouse gases, which might have set the stage for global warming on Mars. Despite the weaker Sun, temperatures on the surface of Mars might have been warm enough, for what was geologically speaking one brief shining moment, to sustain liquid water and salty seas. At hydrothermal vents beneath the waves, life could have been taking hold. Recent calculations have shown that the temperature of magma in a primordial planet like Mars would have been about 200° C (392° F) hotter than it would be in an old planet that has largely let its internal heat escape by radiation into space. This finding is important because higher initial temperatures of spewing volcanic gases are more favorable for organic synthesis; thus, they might have contributed to the production of the organic compounds required for the emergence of life on an ocean floor.

But the water on Mars did not last. As the interior of the red planet cooled, volcanic activity and its incessant release of carbon dioxide waned. The climate changed. Temperatures dipped well below freezing and the water—perhaps gradually, perhaps quite abruptly—turned to ice. Life, if it ever existed, could only survive at mineral-rich geysers or hot springs below the surface, beneath the deadpan outer covering of wind-blown sand, volcanic ash, and ice. Two billion years ago, maybe more, thick ice would have capped the north and south poles of Mars. The oceans, too, would have all but frozen solid. Occasionally, still-liquid groundwater beneath the ice would have burst through, unleashing fantastic floods that rushed down slopes in a torrent of water, mud, boulders, and sand. The floods would have carved the distinctive broad-based channels we see in images today. After the water froze, it was covered by the planet's wind-blown sand and volcanic ash.

And though Mars may look dead in still photographs, there may still be life in that old world yet. Much of the ice sheet may still be present in the northern plains of Mars, buried under a veneer of dust and volcanic ejecta. Liquid water might yet flow several miles underground, a possibility which intrigues biologists, because any tenacious Martian microbes could conceivably thrive in the subterranean rock. Just follow the water, and it may

Earth's and Mars's primordial seas probably dashed against burning volcanic coastlines, as depicted in this photo taken on the southeast coast of Hawaii. © Donna and Stephen O'Meara / Volcano Watch International.

lead to life. And while no Krakatau-like volcanic plumes have been seen on Mars, recent studies of volcanic landforms have shown that Mars may not be geologically dead; lava may have erupted on the surface within the last ten million years (young geologically). James W. Head III (Brown University) says that recent volcanism could have heated the planet's icy subsurface and liberated water in the upper Martian crust. William K. Hartmann (Planetary Science Institute) adds that the recent discovery of water flows in the high latitudes of Mars are easily explained by the new discoveries of youthful lava flows.[16]

While life was perhaps struggling to survive on Mars, life on primitive Earth probably had its own problems getting started. The surface of primordial Earth was a violent world—hot, seething, and bombarded by deadly solar radiation. As on Mars, life probably had its start deep beneath its newly formed oceans, near deep-sea volcanic vents, with the complex shuffling of organic chemicals that still takes place in the vicinity of the mid-ocean ridges.

Only some 3.8 billion years ago did the Earth become stable enough—and steady-going enough—to build up a stable crust; only then did it begin to form the first protocontinents (at first submerged beneath the planet-covering ocean). We know the date approximately because this is when the heavy bombardment of the Moon also started to die down. Not coincidentally, this seems to be the age of the oldest sedimentary rocks on Earth—grizzled veterans that escaped chance destruction by impact or by the inexorable grind of plate tectonics; they are found in a only few places, such as Minnesota and western Greenland. (One of us [W.S.] has on the bookshelf an unimposing piece of grey-banded pinkish rock, gneiss, which he found at an outcrop at Morton, Minnesota, not 80 kilometers (50 miles) from where he has his home. It is staggering to think that by chance it has survived for over three billion years, and was formed at about the time lava flows began filling the ancient basins of the Moon; [S.J.O.] owns a piece of the Issua series from western Greenland.)

Once conditions became suitable, life seems to have formed very quickly and evolved rapidly on Earth. There is indirect evidence—from studies of carbon isotopes found in the 3.8-billion-year-old gneisses of the Issua series—that living organisms may have existed on the Earth already by then. Various lines of evidence suggest that the first lifeforms were hyperthermophilic bacteria, which thrived near volcanic vents at the bottom of the sea. Fossils of ancient threadlike organisms that flourished in the volcano-heated ocean have recently been found at the Sulfur Springs deposit, in the Pilbara region of Australia, a timeless region that is now a dry rocky desert but was once an ancient seabed. They have been dated to 3.2 billion years ago. These bacteria were sulfur-feeding, able to exploit what is now an unconventional source of energy but one that was readily available in the hot, sulfurous primordial world. They are able to metabolize sulfur compounds in order to gain the energy they need for life. Instead of originating in a quiet warm surfical pond, as Charles Darwin once famously suggested, the true birthplace of life on Earth seems to have been an environment more closely resembling Medieval notions of hell.

For the next almost three billion years life on Earth consisted exclusively of microscopic, single-celled organisms. Only in the Cambrian "explosion," which occurred some 500 million years ago at the end of an era of great ice ages, just after the solar system completed its passage through the Norma arm of the Milky Way spiral and the cores of the early continents gathered into a giant supercontinent, did the first multicellular life forms

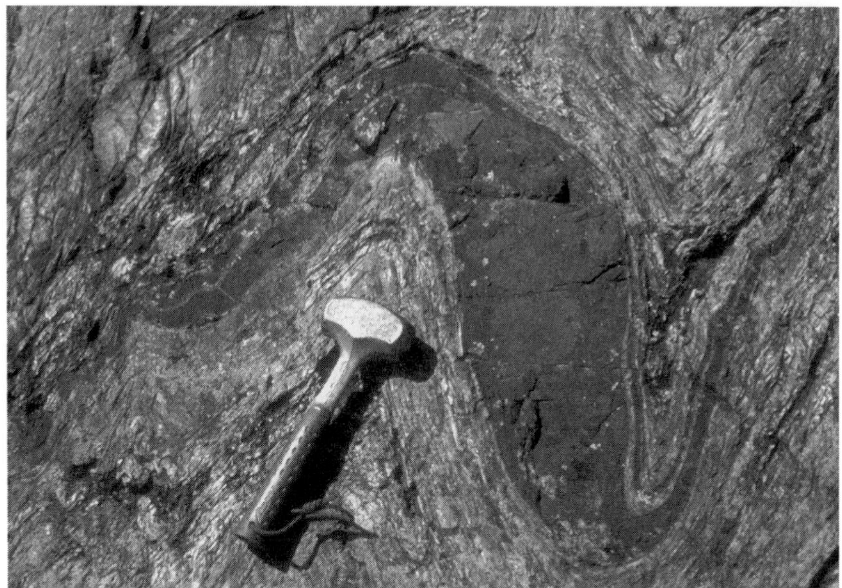

Exposed at the edge of a glacier (*facing page*) is an outcropping of 3.8-billion-year-old gneisses (*above*) of the Issua series, from western Greenland. (O'Meara collection)

arise. One of the assumptions of early planetary evolutionists such as Percival Lowell was that life, once formed, must develop into higher—that is, more complex—forms, including, eventually, intelligent life. "Nor is this outcome in any sense a circumstance accidental to the earth," Lowell wrote; "it is an inevitable phase in the evolution of organisms."

But the conclusion does not follow from the premise. In fact, as Harvard paleontologist Stephen Jay Gould has pointed out, it may well be that simple, unicellular life "arises as a predictable result of organic chemistry and the physics of self-organizing systems wherever planets exist with the right constituents and conditions—undoubtedly a common occurrence in our vast universe." But this hardly means that predictions can be made about the direction taken by life from these basic beginnings. Instead of following an inevitable course as Lowell envisaged, "the pathway to consciousness . . . ," Gould argues, "must be viewed as a tortuous track rutted with uncountable obstacles and festooned with innumerable alternative branches. Any repetition of our earthly route on another planet therefore becomes wildly improbable."[17]

In our own solar system, we know of at least two planets where the right constituents and conditions seem to have existed for life—microbial life—to have formed: Earth and Mars. Early Mars—at least if we accept the standard warm, wet interpretation of its features—seems to have had oceans and volcanic vents no less than the primordial Earth. Were evidence of microbial life on Mars—unequivocal evidence, as unequivocal as the fossilized microbes found in the rocks of the Pilbara—ever produced, it would be an event of profound importance; it would lead to the conclusion that such life must be exceedingly prevalent in the wider universe. There must be billions of planets even in our own galaxy where these preconditions exist.

But such a discovery, profound as it would be, would still not tell us how prevalent intelligent life itself may be in the universe. For even if life is rampantly abundant—a "cosmic imperative" in the phrase of Nobel Prize-winning biologist Christian De Duve—the chances of intelligent life occurring may still be infinitesimal. After all, of the billions of species that have appeared on Earth since life first formed sometime between four and three and a half billion years ago, only one—*Homo sapiens*—has emerged that is able to ponder the question: are we alone? Even on the scale of the galaxy, we may be unique—a flickering light in the cosmic wind, perhaps too unstable and impractical to last for long, a freakish aberration, not an inevitability.

The Great Attempt—a piloted mission to Mars—still lies ahead, and we cannot yet predict its outcome, but hopefully we have said enough to show that Mars is a place like no other. It is a place with all the allure of a New World, which unfolds before us with the sweep and grandeur of the American West. It is a frontier that pulls us with magnetic intensity. It is not only a planet with thin blue clouds, lilac sunrises and sunsets, and orange-brown noon-day skies—strange and riveting as all of those no doubt are; it is not only a geologist's paradise of dry river-beds and volcanoes towering higher than the Hawaiian shield volcanoes of the Earth, or a planet of abortive plate tectonics whose huge canyons stretch a sixth of the way around its circumference.

Compelling as all of these may be, in the final analysis none is the real reason we want to explore the planet. We want to explore it because it is Mars. It is the Mars of romance, a fire-opal shimmering in the telescope. It is Percival Lowell's Mars, Edgar Rice Burroughs's Barsoom. If we explore Mars, it will be in large part because it is not only a world in space but a place in the human imagination. To reach Mars will not only be an adventure but also a vast entertainment for our inquisitive and novelty-seeking species: it is the Everest that looms before us, the shadow of a magnitude that draws us on and has the potential to become the defining theme of the twenty-first century, a century that may well be remembered as the Martian Century. We will reach for it simply because it is the grandest thing we can imagine, because it provides us with a goal and a sense of purpose. It projects us forward from our often blood-stained and tarnished past into a future bright with promise for our still youthful species. It is our Pyramids, our Parthenon, our Cathedrals. Perhaps one day we will even build cathedrals on the plains of Chryse or in the old flood basin of Ares Vallis: thin tapering spires and dream-arches suspended like spider's webs, delicately wrought gossamer structures of crystal glass and thin clear Martian air. The Cathedrals of Mars.

For our hearts desire we have chosen—Mars.

> What shall I do to be forever known
> And make the age to come my own?
> (Abrahan Cowley, "The Motto")

Other generations will have to find other goals, other pinnacles for the human spirit to reach at. Journeying to Mars is what we, of our generation, must do to be forever known and make the age to come our own.

Mars is tied up with the whole story of the human spirit—and more than human spirit, since we are merely the dandelion-seed at the tip-top of the whole living structure of life, the lightest and most readily airborne—or spaceborne—of all the species that inhabit and have inhabited this jewel of the planets. We represent in some part the whole struggle of life out of the seas and onto the dry lands—the first mountings of living things, now halting and skittish, now assured and masterful, into the round ocean of air.

Man has touched the Moon. It's possible he will touch Mars. If he does, it will be in large part because Mars is not only a world in space but a place in the human imagination. (NASA)

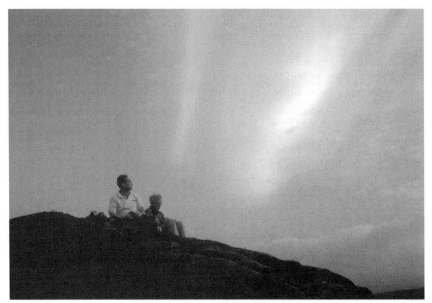

Author Sheehan and planetary astronomer William K. Hartmann contemplate the sky from the lonely lava fields of Hawaii. © Stephen James O'Meara.

Now life in the shape of forked creatures—erect-standing, agile-fingered, large-brained—reaches for something more precarious even than craggy rock-face jutting from sea-surge, as inviting as the blue, bountiful, long-unconquered ocean of air. Life reaches for a fin-hold in the cosmic ocean, an aerie among the shining realms of stars.

As we ponder Mars one last time as it moves across the curtain of the night, wandering among the multitude of background stars, we return to the primitive feeling with which we began our adventure—the primitive awe and terror that must have gripped our earliest ancestors whenever they first saw feelingly the star-filled night. It is the feeling Pascal captured when he wrote, "The eternal silence of these infinite spaces terrifies me." What is this strange world into which we have been flung? Is the cosmos a home, or are we outcasts in a vast and inhospitable void of stars that will remain forever strange and alien to us?

We have especially felt an unsettling sense of planetary loneliness in the out-of-the-way places on Earth—hiking in the rugged deserts of the Australian outback, or puttering in a small dingy at night in the sea near Stewart Island, south of New Zealand, with the electric pulsations of aurora australis playing over the chill Antarctic seas and the Moon setting in splendor in a bank of clouds—a haunting and evocative rounded fragment of a planetary collision that took place at the beginning of time, when life was at most a twinkle in the planetary eye. We have felt the unsettling loneliness standing among the scorching stones of Hawaii, where primitive forces still erupt in waves of molten madness, spreading new land into the sea and creating blank spaces of delightful mystery.

What if the Earth itself is a kind of lonely Stewart or Hawaiian Island in the vast cosmic ocean? Do we inhabit our planet, or are we marooned upon it?

We question the night sky for the answers to these perennial questions. Mars has been the most communicative of all the bodies to which we have posed them. Still, even its answers thus far have only been in riddles, and the night sky remains an eternal silence.

Epilogue
The Mars of Global Surveyor

By the year 2000, we had managed to conjure up a quite delicious Mars for ourselves—again. Though the present-day Mars is inhospitably cold and dry, there seemed to be compelling evidence that things had once been otherwise. Early Mars, at least, was warm and wet—there had been shallow seas, whose outlines we still seemed to discern in the northern plains. There were volcanoes. Put those together and one seems to have the ingredients for the precursors of biomolecules—of metabolism and life itself.

But was it all an illusion once again? There was no question that vast quantities of water had once flowed on Mars. The question was from what cause—and for how long. Local sources of heat—impacts or volcanic eruptions—might cause sudden, short-lived episodes of water-flow across the surface that were unsustained. In order for life to have gained a foothold, it couldn't have disappeared right away—it would have had to remain on the surface for an extended period of time. Increasingly, that proposition has come to seem unlikely.

In the *Mars Global Surveyor* images, some features that first looked as if they had been produced by running water—notably sinuous channels forming from young gullies on crater-rims and tumbling into fan-shaped debris on the crater floors—seem not to have been formed by mudflows after all but by underground streams harbored beneath retreating glaciers. They look strikingly similar to features formed in this way found by NASA/Ames researcher Pascal Lee in an impact crater at Devon Island, in northern Canada. Thus, they fail to provide the evidence at first hoped for that liquid flowed recently on the Martian surface, in geological terms (as we've seen, water is highly unstable on the surface at the present time because of Mars's extremely cold and wispy-thin atmosphere).

Even the shorelines of ancient seas are no longer so clearcut. Perhaps Mars never had oceans but only smaller bodies of water-like lakes. The idea that the huge outflow channels were formed by processes analogous to those that created the Channeled Scabland of eastern Washington, involving the release of massive quantities of water on the surface, also proves to be, as it were, less than water-tight. Nick Hoffman of La Trobe University, Australia, has emphasized the difficulty in this model of recharging the aquifer—the underground reservoir-source of water—on a planet without rainfall. Moreover, he calculates that at least ten times as much water would have been needed to produce rapid flows—as opposed to sluggish and sticky mud creep, which wouldn't have produced the observed features—than the volume of the chaotic collapse zones where the floods supposedly originated. As so often happens in the history of past studies of Mars, it seems likely that we have been misled by false terrestrial analogies. Hoffman suggests that many of the flow features on Mars were actually formed by processes involving the other volatile on Mars—carbon dioxide. He suggests that although carbon dioxide would not be stable on Mars's surface, at a depth of several hundred meters it might form liquid streams, which would remain intact under a seal of water-ice permafrost able to keep it from percolating up through cracks in the Martian soil. When disturbed—say by a volcanic eruption or a meteorite strike—the carbon dioxide would vaporize in explosive fashion, creating a fluidized flow of dust and rock fragments. In Hoffman's view, it was this process—not water flowing on the surface—that produced the chaotic terrains and outflow channels of Mars.

Hoffman adds that the young Sun—which would only have been 85 percent as warming as now during the period when the outflow channels formed—was insufficient to overcome Mars's greater distance from the Sun, and never succeeded in sustaining a dense, warm atmosphere on the planet, even with the huge amounts of carbon dioxide and other greenhouse gases that would have been belched out by its volcanoes. Being smaller than the Earth, its interior heat also would have leaked out more quickly. Thus, during its evolution as a world, Mars might have quickly settled into its present cold dry and dusty climate regime. Hoffman calls this the "White Mars" interpretation, and in his published version suggests that liquid water might not have been present on the Martian surface for most of the last four billion years or so since the heavy-meteoritic bombardment of the planets began to wind down.[1] For the record, he suggests that between about 3.9 and 3.7 billion years ago—which is the period during which life seems to have originated on Earth—there may have been "a more complex transition period. Major bombardment still occurred, ranging from basin-forming impacts to craters of Chicxulub proportions [the impact that spelled the doom of the dinosaurs on Earth]. As a result, intervals of peace and quiet with near-present conditions were probably interspersed by energetic episodes in the wake of each major impact, or cluster of minor ones." During this complex transitional period Mars *might* have become warm enough for the polar caps to release all their carbon dioxide into the atmosphere, warm enough at the equator for liquid water to have formed.[2] But again it wouldn't have lasted, and without planetary oceans, there would have been no safe haven from the rampaging impacts such as those enjoyed by living organisms in the vicinity of the deep-ocean vents on Earth during the same period.

Regardless of whether water once flowed on Mars, the fact that it hasn't done so for aeons is demonstrated by what are undoubtedly some of the most important recent observations ever to have been made of the red planet. Geological maps of Mars created using data from the Thermal Emission Spectrometer aboard *Mars Global Surveyor* revealed large areas of the planet rich in the greenish iron-magnesium silicate mineral olivine. Abundant olivine is found scattered across the dark-basaltic volcanic areas on Mars—there is a particularly rich outcrop on the small plateau at Nili Fossae, in northern Syrtis Major; other exposures include olivine-rimmed craters. In all, olivine is spread over an expanse of a million square miles of the Martian surface. (The Thermal Emission Spectrometer also found large exposures of rock containing coarse-grained hematite, the iron-rich mineral which had long been believed to account for the ruddiness of the parts of the planet.)

On the Earth, olivine is thought to be the primary component of the mantle, and is a constituent of olivine-rich, mantle-derived basalts; but apart from a few unusual places, such as the "green beaches" of Hawaii, where the tiny grains of olivine giving them their color are renewed by fresh material from eroding volcanic rock faces, it is seldom a significant component of surface sediments. The reason is that olivine rapidly erodes in a wet atmosphere. The presence of so much olivine on Mars shows that very little weathering has occurred on the surface of the planet for billions of years. During all that time, Mars has been bitingly cold and monotonously dry; its water supply has remained trapped in the frozen state below the surface, and has rarely—if ever—existed in liquid form above ground.

In the history of the telescopic exploration of Mars, observers were long held spellbound by the blues and greens that they saw in the dark areas of the planet. These colors suggested, by obvious terrestrial analogy, either the expanses of great seas or of large tracts of vegetation. It was later shown that the tantalizing colors seen by the old observers were illusory—all in the eye of those who beheld them (see Appendix B: "The Colors of Mars"). The blues and green are formed by simultaneous contrast—the tendency of the eye to bleed blue- or green-tinges into neutral- or even warm-colored dark areas surrounded by ocher or ruddy deserts. Swamped by such illusory colors, the true greens of Mars's olivine outcrops would presumably remain forever beyond reach of the telescopic eye.

Who would have guessed that when eventually real greens were found on Mars, they should have such different implications, and instead of demonstrating the existence of seas or of lush burgeoning tracts of vegetation, the real Martian greens should prove to be the pale sickly cast of a changeless and unfeeling mineral-world—the gray-greens of a landscape of stark rocky outcrops that has preserved itself, as if hermetically sealed, from every condition prerequisite for life.

For now, Mars—the master illusionist—has once again transformed itself. Gone is the world of our hopes, with its warm, wet, and hospitable climate (even if that existed only briefly and billions of years ago). Mars has become "itself, itself alone." Whereas yesterday—in our dreams—it was a world balmy with oceans and pleasant summers, today we are wide-awake, and it has become once more a place cold, bleak, unearthly.

At the moment, we seem almost to have returned back to where we started before the *Mariner 9* mission quickened new life from the ashes of our fading romance with the red planet; we are almost back in the grim gray days of the flyby *Mariners*. We seem to be stricken once more with a bad case of cosmic loneliness.

But then that has always been the way with Mars. Given the past changes in our Martian fortunes, who is to say that the planet is not once more masquerading? Who is to say that it will not—like a hardy seed lying dormant beneath the snow of a long winter—come once more to life, and in so doing once more quicken our fondest hopes of life beyond Earth?

Appendix A

A Square Old Yellow Book of Mars

Excerpts from the correspondence of Giovanni Virginio Schiaparelli (translated from the French and Italian by William Sheehan)

Giovanni Schiaparelli's *Memoria Prima*, which appeared in 1878, included the first map of the planet on which the positions were determined by micrometric measures. The same work introduced the nomenclature that serves as the basis of that still in use today, and, of course, the notorious Martian canal network.

Schiaparelli followed this important publication with a series of memoirs on later oppositions (through 1890). However, in addition to these published works, Schiaparelli carried on a fascinating—and in some ways more candid—commentary about the planet with his colleagues, Otto Struve and François Terby.

This correspondence has never been published in English. In reading it in the original languages, I felt rather like the nineteenth-century English poet Robert Browning, who discovered a parchment-covered book in one of the book stalls in the Piazza San Lorenzo in Florence. The book, Browning found, was the complete history of a Roman murder case, "the pleadings and counter-pleadings, the depositions of defendants and witnesses," and served as the basis of Browning's poetic masterpiece, "The Ring and the Book":

> Do you see this square old yellow Book, I toss
> I' the air, and catch again, and twirl about
> By crumpled vellum covers,—pure crude fact
> Secreted from man's life when hearts beat hard,
> And brains, high-blooded, ticked two centuries since?

Would that some Browning would take up the notebooks and letters of Schiaparelli for similar poetic treatment. In the meantime, I present here some excerpts from the "square old yellow Book of Mars"—written when the "heart beat hard and the brain, high-blooded, ticked"—of the Master Martian of his age.

To François Terby, Nov. 20, 1877

An areographer completely unknown seeks your permission to present a small essay on the planet of your predilection. Having devoted myself to the task during the months of September and October 1877. . . . I was able to establish on the planet a network of sixty-two points, and envelop it, as it were, in a canvas, on which I placed the lesser details with the aid of twenty-five complete drawings and a large number of partial sketches. The enclosed map is the modest result of this little survey. To a certain extent, I have tried to render the relative intensities of the hues in the spaces called seas; on the continental spaces, the gradations are so delicate I have had to leave them blank. But I have indicated the gradations of tone in those doubtful spaces which probably represent submerged regions of varying depth.

To Otto von Struve, Nov. 23, 1877

On November 4, I concluded my observations of the topography of Mars. I have now carried out the necessary calculations to produce a topographic map of the southern hemisphere of the planet. . . . This work proves the excellent definition of our lens, surpassing all I had dared hope for this class of objects.

What I find most remarkable is the complicated system of dark lines (or *canali*), which run into the seas enveloping the whole planet. There is a great deal of uncertainty about the measures of these features; but I can't believe they would be seen so distinctly if they were less than 50 or 60 kilometers wide. Often they become nebulous or indeterminate: thus one can assume that they must divide into several branches, each branch too narrow to be made out distinctly. As for the other features, it is clear from our map that they strongly resemble the map of the Earth, with continents and oceans. And yet one cannot speak properly of continents, since all of them there are broken up into numerous islands. It could be the limits of the lands and seas are not very definite on Mars, as is said to have been the case on Earth during the Carboniferous era.

The fecundity of the details, to which many more will probably be added by better observers equipped with larger lenses, has impressed me with the need to find a system of names. . . . This is a question which ought probably to be addressed by our Astronomical Society, in order to prevent the perquisites of Mars from falling to such mean ambitions as those of MM. Proctor and Flammarion.

To Struve, Jan. 4, 1878

To return to the denomination of the markings of the planet, I send you another copy of my map, with the names I have given to the objects I have recorded in the order in which I have given them. At first, I counted on using the names of Proctor; but his map (and also, to a lesser extent, Flammarion's) is so poor that I wasted a great deal of time trying to orient myself to it. Finally, as I found it necessary to record my observations quickly, and as it was necessary to avoid all chance of ambiguity, I began to populate the drawings with names from the *Odyssey*; then I began adding others from the Argonauts, and so produced a melange of mythical and poetic geographies: this explains the curious mixture and disorder which you will find there. If I send you the names, it is only to show that I have more or less accepted your idea of using [for the *canali*] the names of the rivers in the *Iliad*. But meanwhile I await the nomenclature that will be approved by the Astronomical Society. It would be well if some scholar, with poetic sensibilities, were charged with arranging everything in an appropriate manner.

. . . In October [1877] the atmosphere of the planet was admirably clear, and I was able to make out the dark markings all the way to the pole; the two large islands of Thyle I and II stood out clearly, and if other lands existed in those latitudes they, too, would have been seen.

In the southern hemisphere, the clouds of Mars disappeared almost completely by the beginning of September, though I could not quite rule out the persistence of a mist covering the shallow seas of Mare Erythraeum. Over the marsh-land that I call Noachis these mists hung stubbornly to the place as late as December. I was for a long time unsure of my ability to make anything out at all in this variable whitish mass, but in the end I seem to have succeeded: from what I can tell, it appears to be a low-land. Unfortunately, the planet is now so far away, I am unable to say more.

To Struve, July 6, 1878

The two chambers [the Chamber of Deptuties and the Senate of the Kingdom of Italy] have yet to approve the expenditure of 250 thousand francs in order to build a refractor of 18 inches for the Brera Observatory. But I am now hopeful that it is to be done. At the end of April, having finished my memoir on Mars (of which the first copies were distributed the day before yesterday . . .), I made an excursion to Rome to present it to the [Society of the] Lynxes. The President of the Ministers and the Minister of Public Instruction attended the meeting, and I made a popular exhibition of my work, and in explaining my map took note of the fact that it had been made with only a small lens. I then alluded to the much greater telescopes of Washington and Gateshead with which it would be possible to do so much more, etc. I dared express the wish that Italy might one day have a similar lens. This declaration pleased many; it was roundly applauded, and discussed around the city, with the result that two or three days later I was summoned to present my work at the Quirinal [palace], in order to explain to Their Majesties [King Humberto and Queen Margherita] that Mars seems to be a world but little different from our own. Using a little of the Flammarionesque style, I pulled the affair off well enough. The queen was quite shocked at the distortions of latitude in the Mercator projection, and found the stereographic projections showed [Mars] much more naturally. This famous lady is a person of amazing affability. . . . They were, in the end, so completely enchanted that, in referring to the advantage of larger glasses, I resolved to tempt them with the project of a large glass of our own. *Aut nunc, aut nunquam*! I remembered our old octagon room, eleven meters in diameter, constructed by [Ruggiero] Boscovich, and I proposed converting it into a rotating cupola; I also imagined putting, on the large pillar of masonry at the center of the room, an equatorial of 18–20 inches. The Academy of the Lynxes, to which I had recommended the project, placed it in the hands of the President and the Minister; and it was duly approved by the Chamber of Deputies and the Senate.

[Referring to the studies of Nathaniel Green at Madeira:] The most curious part of this whole affair [of the *canali*] is that some of the objects of which Mr. Green entirely denies the existence have been seen splendidly, and with low powers, without going to Madeira. . . . I think that in the present case, before he speaks of *illusions*, he ought to wait and study my results, which I have promised to send him in due course. For me the conclusion of this curious discussion . . . is that in England there are some strongly exaggerated ideas about the power of reflectors which will not hold up to scrutiny.

To Struve, Feb. 19, 1879

I see that in America and in England my work is not as much approved as I might wish. They have a right not to accept a result of which there is no greater guarantee than the testimony of a single observer. But I am prepared to await calmly and confidently the corroborations of other observers, who given the progress in optics and the art of observing will not, I hope, be too far in the future. Beyond that, I have heard of nothing except for the singular discussion held during the meeting of the Royal Astronomical Society on April 12, 1878. Referring to [one of my drawings], which I had sent Mr. Green, there were some comments neither serious nor worthy of such an august body, nor of science itself. Sir George Biddell Airy was right to break off their chatter by saying: "I fear we are trifling with the time of the Society." I believe that those who have condemned me will change their minds if only they have read my memoir, which at the time had not yet been published. I don't understand why Mr. Green should worry so much. His drawings made at Madeira are excellent, and accord with mine as far as one could expect of a reflector, in which the definition is bound to be considerably less than in the refractor of Milan. All that he saw, I saw also: he should be pleased, as I am, with the wonderful agreement, instead of talking about optical illusions! I await with impatience the drawings made by M. [Etienne] Trouvelot with the 26-inch refractor of Washington. I had hoped that these drawings would serve to corroborate my observations, but according to M. [F. A. T.] Winnecke's letter, they cannot see in America so much as I can here in a humble 8-inch. To tell the truth, this 8-inch is very well achromatized for the less refrangible part of the spectrum [red light], and this could well be a reason for the whole mystery. If Mars were bluish or purplish, things might well be otherwise. In any case, I propose to attend to these remarks in an honest and unbiased fashion; my work is far from perfect, and I will be only too happy to learn of any shortcomings so I may correct them.

From Charles Burton, Dec. 8, 1879

I fancy from a comparison of my sketches with your beautiful map [and] drawings that I have dimly seen forms analogous to if not identical with the canals which you have there shown.

To Terby, Dec. 11, 1879

Regarding clouds, I don't know what to say. This year I don't find any! In 1877 it is possible that clouds occupied part of Ausonia and all of Hellas, also Noachis and probably a great part of the continents north of the Great Diaphragm. But in 1879 these continents show all their details unmistakably, except for the part between the river of the Laestrygonians and the Ocean below Tharsis. South of the Great Diaphragm, there is no trace of clouds. Mare Erythraeum has always been completely clear.

To Struve, Jan. 6, 1880

The current opposition of Mars is almost at an end, and the observations I am pursuing again involve its meteorology and topography. If I was happy in 1877, I have been even more so in 1879. In the space of three months I was able to make useful observations on sixty nights, and ten or twelve of these were nothing less than superb: the image appeared in the field of the instrument like a painting, absolutely motionless, of indescribable beauty. All the formations of my map [of 1877] have been seen again, with the sole exception of Juventae Fons: it is true however that the region in which it lies could not be examined well until December, when the diameter of the planet was reduced to 13". I was also able to study a considerable portion of the northern hemisphere, of which the map this time will reach as far as 60 degrees. The most interesting result is that the dark stripes or channels are persistent features, though the width and visibility of some of them are subject to periodic and very considerable variations. These variations could not be the result of clouds. Instead, the most natural explanation for them is that they are due to extensive flooding.

To Terby, May 3, 1880

I would regret becoming the innocent cause of the division of areographers into opposing camps. Mr. Green has every right not to accept as definitive some details which he could not make out with an instrument which was certainly very good. But rather than oppose himself to me, he would have done better to suspend his judgment.

I would further regret your adherence and faith in my observations becoming an obstacle in your dealings with other areographers. I hope that this is not so! and that an attitude of partisanship will not enter into these discussions, which will never advance by the mere statement of opinions but only by the diligent seeking-out of the facts. Happily, it is not possible that the lens of Milan is the only one in the world capable of showing so many of these details. . . .

Argyre has been the very last thing visible during the opposition of 1879–80. It was so white that it looked almost like one of the polar spots.

From Green, June 3, 1881

Many thanks for the little map of Mars. I am delighted with it and consider it the most like the planet I have seen of yours. All the great points I can recognize. Tho' I cannot follow you in the sharp lines *of the canals. In several of the places where you draw a sharp line I have seen a softened tone of gentle shading and I cannot but think that some of the difference between our views is due, to the different way in which we draw (or try to express) what we have seen.*

To Rev. T. W. Webb, April 1882

What can the double lines signify? It is an embarrassing question, and we cannot hope for a good answer until they have been well studied through a certain number of oppositions. I will affirm this much to you: they are rectilinear, or nearly rectilinear, and their aspect, without bends or irregularities, has not been exaggerated in my drawings. My earlier maps do show a certain tendency to represent these lines under an irregular aspect, a tendency produced by the idea of having, before my eye, forms analogous to those of the Earth. But in truth these bands are so uniform in tint and in width, that any irregularities, if they exist, are too small to be seen with my instrument.

To Terby, May 14, 1882

[Referring to an article Terby had published on the geminations in the journal *Mondes*:]

I find your confidence in me touching, for it has required considerable courage and faith in order to announce, on the affirmation of a single observer, some facts so extraordinary that their very appearance must engender suspicion. I am especially appreciative, given that my reports have been generally received with such coolness and incredulity. Not that I wish to complain: these scientific questions cannot be resolved on the basis of anyone's word.

It appears that in England they look at my efforts with amusement; this from a people known for their gravity. Nevertheless, I hope they will consider their instruments and not judge them exclusively by aperture or size, but only compare them to the definition and power for these researches of our instruments here, and so, with open minds, set out to verify these aspects of Mars in 1884. I hope I deserve so much; for it is really a great misfortune to have all to oneself the ability to see so many beautiful things.

To Terby, Nov. 6, 1883

Newton says somewhere in the *Principia* that whenever one is searching for the explanation of some phenomenon in nature, it is better to resort first to the reason which provides the simplest and most natural explanation. I ask you to apply this rule to my long silence, which has been owing to the unhappy combination of heavy work with a decrease of health and vigor, obliging me to lay aside my correspondence as well as several other works to which I attach interest. Must I confess to you that for several months I have done little more with Mercury [Schiaparelli had begun a close study of that planet in 1881–82]? And that the extremely important observations of Mars made at the opposition of 1881–82, which I had hoped to publish, remain buried for the most part in my notebooks? . . .

As for Mars, I do not intend to abandon it, and will sacrifice to him all other opportunities, if necessary. Unfortunately, at present conditions are not very favorable here. We have unusually cold weather which means a nearly continuous agitation of the atmosphere. When I have attempted to observe here, the agitation has been so great that I have been unable to survey the configurations of the surface. All I could see is that the north polar cap is again very large, and bounded by some darkish spaces.

To Landerer, April 1885

[Responding to a suggestion that the geminations might be produced by eye-fatigue:]

I have repeated the experiments you suggested, and this is what I find. I watch the target with varying degrees of attentiveness, and it is always the same. If I watch it with close attention, and endeavor to fix the eye on it continuously, in order to see the smallest details on its circumference, I can do so for only some fifteen or twenty seconds at a time; after that the eye gets tired, and as I continue to watch the view becomes more and more blurry and more and more confused. It is then necessary for me to rest for a few moments: after which, recovered from my fatigue, I see the simple and very definite target again as at the beginning. But I must say it is impossible for me to produce a doubling by eye-fatigue. . . .

With respect to the canals of Mars, I was able to separate some of the most evident of them at the last opposition. Despite the extremely unfavorable conditions, I need hardly say that the contours of the continent and of the disk of the planet both appeared to me perfectly simple; and I made several measures around the axis of the lens with my eye, and also tried different oculars around this axis. But since the wires of the micrometer always appeared perfectly simple, the explanation [of the geminations] can hardly be a question of monocular diplopia.

To Terby, May 11, 1886

I have plunged once again into areography, and always find something in my observations that had escaped me. It is a New World, this world of Mars, believe me, and it will be necessary for us to conquer it little by little as a prize. It will be a less difficult and less bloody conquest than the exploits of Cortes and Pizarro. There are, however, but ten observers occupied with it even during the favorable periods of the oppositions. But how many important things must escape us simply due to bad timing, especially because of the interval of 30 days and more which must pass before we can again study a given region of the planet. So it becomes absolutely necessary for several observers, scattered through different terrestrial longitudes, to chronicle the numerous and gigantic events occurring there, and with remarkable rapidity given the greatness of the spaces they cover.

To Henri Perrotin (telegram), March 29, 1886

Pray look at Mars great double line observed here March 27 and 28 across Chryse and Tharsis length sixty degrees width ten degrees separation very easy.

From Perrotin, May 16, 1886

Our observations have been made with the 14-inch lens at Nice on 15, 23, 24, and 25 April and lastly 11 May. On 11, M. Trépied, doctor of the Algiers observatory, and M. Thollon and I could vouch for the accuracy of your drawing: we easily saw the double line crossing Chryse, to which you had called our attention recently. . . .

To Perrotin, May 1886

By your observations at Nice it is to be hoped that the single and double lines of Mars will enter the lists of incontestable facts.

To Terby, May 28, 1888

I am writing a few lines to alert you (if it is even necessary) that we have a gemination so beautiful that I believe you will finally see it without difficulty. The long track of the Euphrates is presented exactly as it is shown here. . . .

From Terby, June 3, 1888

I must thank you for your letter of May 28 alerting me to the gemination of the Euphrates. . . . As you requested, I made every effort to succeed in this observation: yesterday, June 2, I had some particularly favorable conditions—favorable enough to allow, I should think, some decisive finding. . . . But I didn't see the Euphrates, despite the most sustained attention.

To Terby, June 7, 1888

I urge you not to become discouraged. . . . It may be that the inability to make out such details has been owing to the state of your atmosphere; it may be you will be more successful tomorrow or the next day. It sometimes happens that the images here appear perfectly steady, and yet one still sees very little: a kind of veil seems to be thrown over the disk, for no apparent reason. Some experiments I have made here lead me to believe that at such times atmospheric tremors are present, but their amplitude is so small that the eye is unable to notice them except for their general effects mentioned above. I will give you a striking example: I believed I saw the planet well enough on May 9, 25, and 27, and began to be almost satisfied to have noticed three or four geminations. But I was unprepared for the happiness I experienced on June 2 and 4, and then only did I begin to understand the true power of a 19-inch aperture on Mars. Then the memorable nights of 1879–80 and also of 1882 returned for the first time, and I had some again those wonderful images as exquisite as a steel engraving, and reveled in the magic of the details. A magnifying power of 650x was no longer sufficient to show everything that was visible; and my only regret was that the disk was reduced to only 12" in diameter. Not only was I able to confirm the gemination of the Nepenthes (*quantum mutatus ab illo!*) and the reappearance of the Lacus Triton of 1877, but I saw the Lacus Moeris, imaged as a tiny point but perfectly visible and plainly separated from the Syrtis Major.

The Euphrates is again entirely double; but this is less apparent than on May 27 and 30. However, yesterday it appeared so once again, though the two tracks were slightly blurred and the part below Lacus Ismenius came out better than the part above it. [The two *canali*] Callirrhoe and Protonilus are two very narrow geminations, but perfectly geometrical and very dark, Callirhoe especially.

The Oxus was greatly faded, and lately I have not seen it, while on the other hand the Indus has reappeared. The Hiddekel is nearly invisible; the Gehon a little darker; it goes off toward a small lake, and leaves it as two lines on the right toward the Lacus Niliacus. But what is more extraordinary and unexpected are the changes that have occurred in the last month in the Boreosyrtis and the surrounding regions. The sketch that I give of it is not definitive, for there are some small details which I will need to reexamine; however, of the geminations and their disposition I have no doubt, and they are strangely entangled. What could all this mean? Evidently the planet has some fixed geographical features resembling those of the Earth, with gulfs, channels, etc., irregularly laid out. Comes a certain moment, they all depart in order to make room for these ridiculous polygonations and geminations, which evidently represent the previous state approximately, but it is a gross mask, and I say almost ridiculous.

Appendix B
The Colors of Mars

It is ironic that in the study of Mars, the two figures who had the greatest influence should have presented such remarkable contrasts. The first, Giovanni Schiaparelli, was colorblind, yet his eye was remarkably sensitive to slight nuances in the shadings on the Martian disk, that allowed him to make out the delicate markings which he represented schematically as the amazing network of *canali* on the planet. His descriptions of the planet, too, are clinical and colorless. He was almost Olympian in his cautious reserve and persistently refused to speculate on the ultimate meaning of his observations.

The other most-important figure in the history of Martian observation, Percival Lowell, evoked the subtle colors of the planet in colorful prose. He was a romantic, eking out, from meager suggestions on the Martian disk—a few linear markings here, a few washes of color there—a highly detailed picture of Martian conditions and of Martian life. Though the illusory nature of the canals is now well-known, the world that Lowell conjured up with his imagination, which proved to be far more powerful than his telescope, depended as much on changes in color as on his tessellated maps of the planet. But though the canals have been widely discussed, the colors of Mars have received less notice by historians and interpreters of the lore of the planet.

Lowell's observing notebooks are full of references to the subtle colors of the disk. The following, for instance, are from 1894 :

> June 2. None of the dark parts really darker than a gray.
>
> Hellas and southern Ausonia one continuous rosy-orange band, distinct but fainter than equatorial continent. The rosy-orange tint of the land much more striking than the green-gray of the shaded parts.
>
> June 7. Nothing visible except pale-green tint of seas and orange of lands.
>
> June 9. Colors superb: brilliant rose-orange and livid bluish-green.
>
> June 15. Color of seas changed from green to blue with the dawn. Have previously noticed the change of color of the continental areas from rosy-orange to rosy-red on similar occasions of the turning of night into day. Our daylight, therefore, adds blue light.
>
> June 20. It is worth noting again how faintly differentiated are the dark markings from the light all over the planet.
>
> {Lowell absent in Boston all of July–late August}
>
> August 20. Colors beautiful: continent and island S[outh] rose-orange, seas blue.
>
> Cimmerium Sea greenish blue all over.
>
> August 22. Colors of the planet those of a fire-opal.
>
> August 24. N[orth] region intense green.
>
> {Lowell absent in Boston September}
>
> October 27. Hesperia and all other markings much fainter than at August presentation.
>
> October 31. Dark areas pale blue, usual sky-color.

Summing up, Lowell claimed that in June, the high southern latitude containing the two Thyles and Argyre II on the map were blue-green; by October, he found the same region was chiefly yellowish. There were also changes in many of the smaller details. What they added up to, he alleged, was "a whole-sale transformation of the blue-green regions into orange-ocher ones . . . in progress upon that other world." In fact such sweeping changes are not exactly borne out by his observing notebooks; in October the dark areas were more or less as they had been in June—"pale blue, the usual sky-color."

The changes were, in fact, less of tint than of tone. As Lowell admitted in his later opus, *Mars and Its Canals*: "Usually the change of hue seems essentially one of tone; the blue-green fades out, getting less and less pronounced, until in extreme cases only ocher is left behind. It acts as if the darker color were superimposed upon the lighter and could be to a greater or less extent removed. This is . . . what was seen in 1894 at Flagstaff."

Of course Lowell was only too eager to demonstrate that the dark areas consisted of vast tracts of vegetation on the planet, showing seasonal changes of tint from spring verdure to autumn sere, though in passing it should be noted that even the Lowellian deduction of vegetation from the blue-green tint of these areas was hazardous, at best, being based on unjustified extrapolation from the colors familiar from terrestrial plant-life. Recall that on Earth photosynthesis is carried out by green plants, which contain the green pigment chlorophyll. The structure of the chlorophyll molecule includes a porphyrin ring similar to that in hemoglobin but surrounding an atom of magnesium instead of iron. The main forms of chlorophyll, chlorophylls a and b, have very strong absorption bands in the violet and red parts of the spectrum, but absorb very little in the yellow and green, which explains why plants look yellow-green; a chlorophyll molecule with a different profile of absorption might equally well have been seized on by natural selection, in which case we might now have red meadows, brown glades, and purple fields. Though Lowell often stressed that on Mars "no creatures resembling us" would be found, he seems to have tacitly assumed a resemblance between Martian and terrestrial plant-life.

But he was not alone. So did E. M. Antoniadi, who not only confirmed but embellished Lowell's palette of colors. Writing in 1924, Antoniadi claimed that "not only the green areas but also the grayish or blue surfaces turned under my eyes to brown, lilac-brown, or even carmine. . . . It was almost exactly the color of leaves which fall seasonally from trees in summer and autumn in our latitudes." Though he vehemently disputed Lowell's theories about the canals, Antoniadi never doubted that Mars was the abode of abundant vegetative life.

Indeed, though it was widely agreed after Antoniadi's great campaign at the 1909 opposition that the linelike markings on Mars were illusory—products of the eye's unfailing tendency to link together various irregular details at the threshold of vision—the possibility that the Martian colors might partake of similarly significant subjective contributions apparently went ungrasped. The theory of color-perception abounds in its own perplexities, as had been recognized by the French dye specialist M. E. Chevreul in the first half of the nineteenth century. As Director of Dyeing at the Manufactures Royal de Gobelins, the national tapestry workshop, he was called in to investigate chronic complaints of the fading of blues and violets in tapestries. To his surprise, he found that the colors in the tapestries were as bright and unfaded as intended; the real problem was that the apparent intensity of a color depends to a significant extent on the hue and brightness of its surroundings, an effect which Chevrel described as simultaneous contrast. Simultaneous contrast causes colored highlights to impart their complementary hue to adjacent low-luminosity or neutral features.

Viewed against a bright ocher background, a dark neutral marking will—because of simultaneous contrast—take on an illusory bluish-green cast. Regarded from this perspective, Percival Lowell's careful observations of the colors of Mars prove to have been nothing more than compulsive records of this physiological effect, an effect having nothing to do with Martian reality at all.

Here it is of interest to recall some results obtained by William K. Hartmann, an astronomer-artist who observed Mars in 1988 with the 61 cm (24-inch) Cassegrain reflector at the summit of the 4,200 meter (13,800 foot) shield volcano Mauna Kea, in Hawaii. Hartmann found the bright deserts "pale orange like what you might find at the junction of orange sherbet and vanilla ice cream." The dark markings looked bluish-gray at the eyepiece, but he later found they could be realistically depicted in an acrylic painting using only pigments on the warm (reddish-brown) side of neutral—a textbook display of simultaneous contrast. Note: "There are," according to

Andrew T. Young of San Diego State University, "other effects involved in addition to simultaneous contrast: unless one uses a reflector and an eyepiece with good color correction and a small secondary spectrum, even a little spillover of short-wavelength light from the bright areas into the nearby dark features will color them bluish or greenish. Observations with refractors are obviously seriously suspect. Another problem is that the visual system tends to accept the brightest parts of the scene as 'white.' On Mars, that's usually a polar cap. But the caps are actually somewhat yellow from dust in and above their surface; so again this shifts all perceived colors to the blue."

During the favorably close approach of Mars in the summer of 1988, one of us (O'Meara) used the 1.52-meter (60-inch) reflector atop Mt. Wilson to study the red planet. He was immediately impressed not so much with the amount of detail visible on the planet's surface, but with the purity of the colors that washed over it in layers of pastel pigments. Vast white polar hazes covered the high northern latitudes, while, further south the clouds thinned into a mesh of glacial blue cirrus; their thin and wispy nature mimicked the horse's tails seen on cool crisp winter mornings on Earth. They formed a skrim over the blackened mass of Olympus Mons where a thick white orographic cloud buttressed its windward slope. Continuing north, the faint scattering of blue light faded into the cream-colored sands covering the vast Oceanus and Amazonis deserts. If any red was seen, it was only during moments of imagining that the desert sands glinted with spectral radiance on a microscopic scale—flashes of red and green light entered his eye like beads of fractured sunlight scintillating in a dew drop. Opposing these colors to the south was a vast sea of what seemed undeniably spring green bordering the desert regions north of the south polar cap. And yet other dark features—Solis Lacus, Mare Sirenum, Mare Cimmerium—showed no hint of blue or green anywhere, instead appearing a characteristic chocolate lavender, the same color O'Meara saw in the mesas and hills in the deserts of southern California from an altitude of 6,000 meters (20,000 feet).

O'Meara also experimented with stopping down the telescope's aperture, to as small as 61-centimeter (24 inches), the same as Lowell's telescope. To his surprise, he discovered the image immediately lost any semblance of its "true" color. The planet was transformed into an ocher or smoggy-yellow blob with only hints of greenish or bluish tints seeming to fringe the borders of the darkest (now drab gray-brown) regions, while the cream-colored sands had been replaced by expanses of ocher. Under these conditions Mars reverted to the classical world of optical illusions.

Almost end of story. But at least one region—the Syrtis Major—does sometimes exhibit genuine bluish tints—true blues, not merely the illusory hints caused by simultaneous contrast with the surrounding deserts. Every Martian year around the time of the Summer Solstice in the Northern Hemisphere, a localized (i.e., topographic) cloud forms over Syrtis Major and portions of the adjoining Libya Basin, and usually persists through early summer. Named by the late Lowell Observatory astronomer Charles F. Capen the "Syrtis Blue Cloud," the blue color is formed by scattering of light by the cloud's aerosols and ice crystals. (Of course, here too there is an illusion at work: it is the blue cloud that makes Syrtis Major appear to change color; there is no change in Syrtis Major itself.)

The Martian tourist to the vast volcanic landscape now known as Syrtis Planitia would find a plateau reaching as far as the eye could see, strewn with dark basaltic rocks, sheets of windblown dust, and dunes; a magnificent desolation, a region wild beyond all imagining. But if the tourist arrived during the early Northern Hemisphere summer—at the time the region was covered by the Syrtis Blue Cloud—he or she might be presented with a beguilingly Earth-like sky. Unusual on Mars, it would almost repay the journey to this forlorn region of the planet. It would serve as a reminder of the long deceptive and mirage-like image of Mars as the likeness of Earth, in which Syrtis Major—now sea, now tract of Martian vegetation, and finally broken and rugged plateau—long played a particularly convincing role. Now see it for what it is—no sea with Martian sailing vessels here; no vegetation-covered sea-bottom of Barsoom. Instead the Syrtis is a desert plateau as vast as the Deccan Plateau of India, or the Parana basin of South America—a region of ferocious gusts, bitter cold thin air, unconquerable loneliness, and, once each Martian year, Earth-like skies of cornflower blue.

Appendix C
Exploring Mars with Your Telescope

What goes on upon all those distant globes? Are they worlds, or are they mere masses of matter? Are physical forces alone at work there, or has evolution begotten something more complex, something not unakin to what we know on Earth as life?

—Percival Lowell,
Mars, 1895

Given the influence Mars has had on humanity throughout time, one could easily imagine that the planet has loomed forever large in the night sky, that it is our constant companion—there to see whenever we feel the urge to contemplate its nature. But Mars is a fickle friend. It flares to prominence only once every other year and only for a few short weeks. Although the planet can be seen in the sky for several months at a time, it is not always conspicuous; the planet waxes and wanes in brightness depending on its distance from Earth. Most of the time Mars is far away, so it appears only modestly bright to the naked eye, rivaling a star, say, in the Big Dipper. But when closest, it can outshine all other celestial bodies except for the Sun, Moon, and Venus.

An apparition of Mars (meaning the several-month stretch when the planet is visible) begins in the east, in the early morning sky shortly before sunrise; it ends when the planet slips into the evening twilight and sets shortly after the Sun. At these extremes, the planet is rather dim and virtually unrecognizable but for its color. It is when Mars rises in the east as the Sun sets in the west (the *opposition* point) that the planet burns brightly enough to pull at our heart strings. That's when scores of amateur astronomers turn their telescopes to that fiery beacon and try to glimpse details on the planet's surface.

Not all oppositions of Mars are equal, thanks to a quirk in the planet's orbit. Although both Earth and Mars have elliptical orbits, Earth's is nearly circular while that of Mars is highly eccentric (greatly out of round). So the distance between Earth and Mars changes with each successive opposition. When Mars is closest to the Sun in its orbit, it is at *perihelion;* when farthest away, it is at *aphelion.* Clearly then, perihelic oppositions are the most favorable to observe, because that is when Mars is nearest to the Sun and the Earth at the same time.

The very best perihelic oppositions occur about every 15 or 17 years; that's when Mars sails within 56 million kilometers (35 million miles) of Earth. During the worst *aphelic* oppositions, the red planet comes no closer than about 102 million kilometers (62 million miles).

Favorable oppositions of Mars always occur during late summer or early fall, as seen from the Northern Hemisphere; unfavorable oppositions always occur during the cold and harsh winter months. As we write this chapter, astronomers around the world are gearing up for the extremely favorable opposition of August 2003, when the red planet will sweep within 56 million kilometers (35 million miles) of the Earth and be slightly closer than at any time in recorded history—in other words, closer than at any time since the Pyramids were built, Troy's towers burned, and Rome rose and fell (see appendix F).

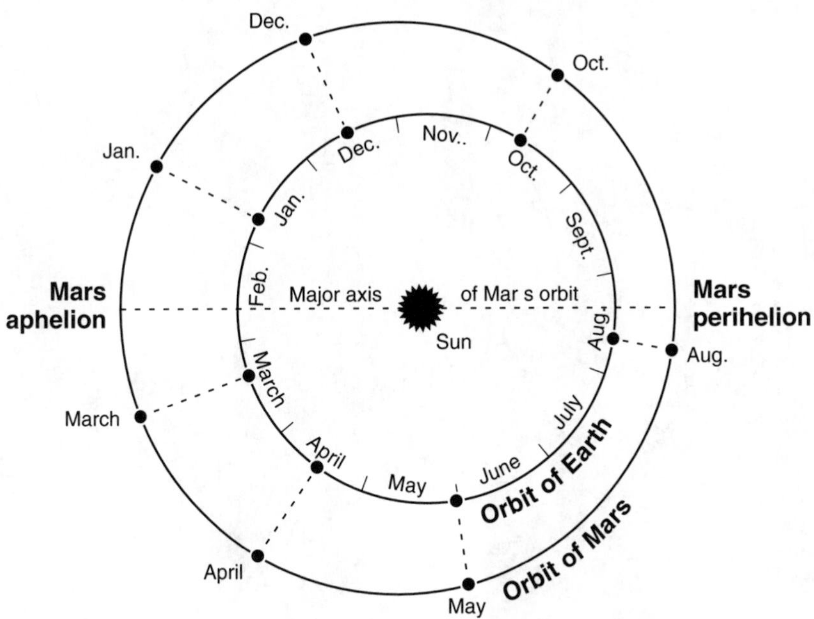

THROUGH THE TELESCOPE

Mars is a small world measuring a mere 6,780 kilometers (4,200 miles) in diameter; its size is intermediate between the Earth and the Moon. Thus, even when Mars is closest to Earth (which is 140 times the distance of the Moon from the Earth), its disk appears impressively small through a telescope. During favorable oppositions, Mars appears more than 70 times smaller than does the Moon. During unfavorable oppositions, the disk of Mars shrinks to nearly half that size. When smallest—before and after opposition—the planet diminishes to a minuscule dot 300 times smaller than the apparent diameter of the Moon; so if the Moon were the size of a baseball, Mars would then appear to be the size of a pea.

Careful observers should be able to detect small changes in the planet's phase. The disk of Mars is full at opposition. Before and after opposition the disk of Mars displays a slight phase proof that Mars shines by the reflected light of our Sun. At greatest phase, Mars is 89 percent illuminated and

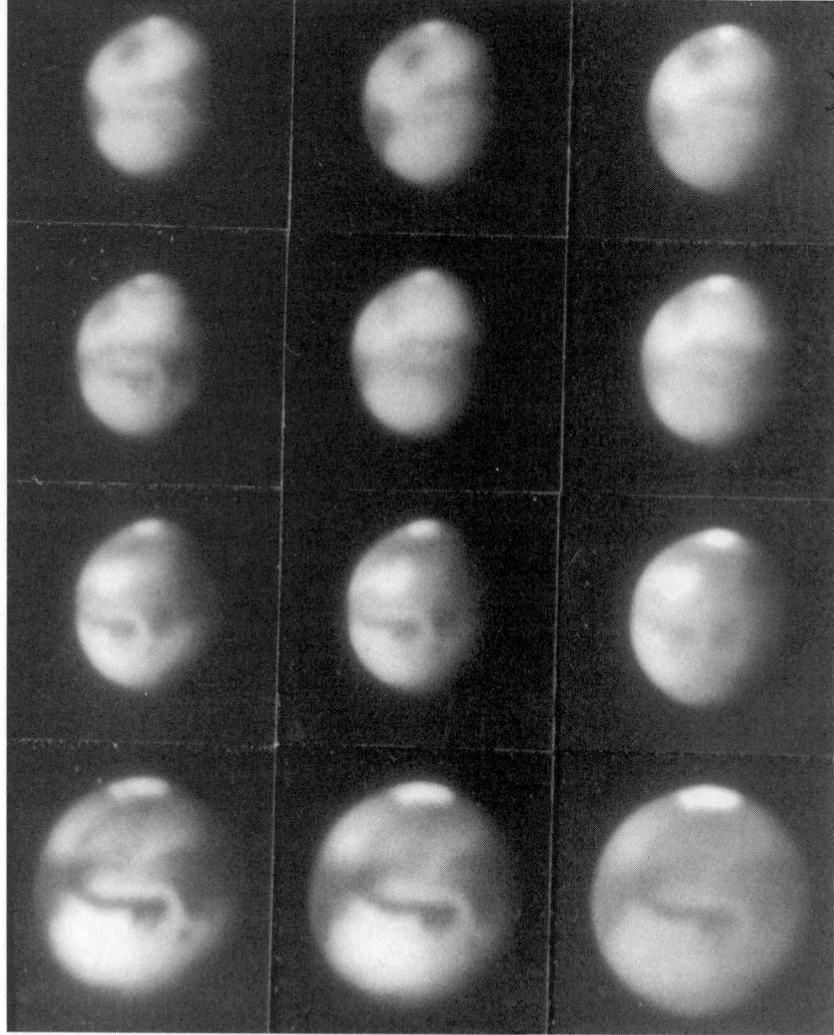

As Mars approaches opposition, its disk grows. Series taken in 1971 by Dennis Milon with the 23-centimeter (9-inch) refractor at Harvard College Observatory. Note the dust storm near the center of the disk and how it changes shape over time. Note also the small change in phase of the planet and the growing south polar cap. (O'Meara Collection)

looks like the Moon seen three days from full. (Mars can never be seen in a crescent, new, or quarter phase, because its orbit lies outside the Earth's.) Even Galileo thought he could make it out: "If I mistake not, I think I already perceive that he is not perfectly round."[1] (Perhaps he was only guilty of wishful thinking.)

No matter what the size or phase of Mars, details (such as the planet's polar caps, dark surface markings, and clouds) can be seen whenever the Earth's atmosphere is calm and steady. During the best oppositions, from the Northern Hemisphere Mars is always low in the sky, so atmospheric turbulence may cause Mars to shimmer, boil, or blur. Although the disk of Mars is smaller during aphelic oppositions, Mars is higher in the sky, which is a distinct advantage, since it can be observed through less of the Earth's atmosphere. That is why most skilled planetary observers are patient observers. They usually study the planet for an hour or more, waiting for rare moments when the atmosphere is steady and subtle details flush into view.

What details you see depends on which "face" of Mars is present when you look. If you scan the map below, you will notice that about two-thirds of the planet is covered by light areas—the famous deserts of Mars; if the greatest desert regions are facing Earth, few dark markings will be present when you look. The dark regions, on the other hand, have remained largely unchanged since they were first drawn in the 1600s, and are a most intriguing sight.

The Dutch astronomer Christiaan Huygens was the first to spy a dark feature (a V-shaped marking) on November 28, 1659. By watching that marking rotate, Huygens was able to detect a slight shift in its position during the time he kept it under observation; when he turned his telescope toward the planet again, on December 1, he found that it had returned to very nearly the same place on the disk. Thus, he noted in his journal, "The rotation of Mars, like that of the Earth, seems to have a period of 24 hours."[2] Today we know the planet spins on its axis in 24 hours, 37 minutes, and 23 seconds, slightly longer than our own day. If we were to observe Mars at the same time night after night, we would see its surface features appear to "back up" by about 9° each night, causing an illusory retrograde rotation in about 36 days.[3]

Color

First-time observers might be surprised that the color of Mars through a telescope does not appear blood red. "Seen through a telescope, Mars is not so red as it appears to the naked eye," writes Martha Evans Martins in her

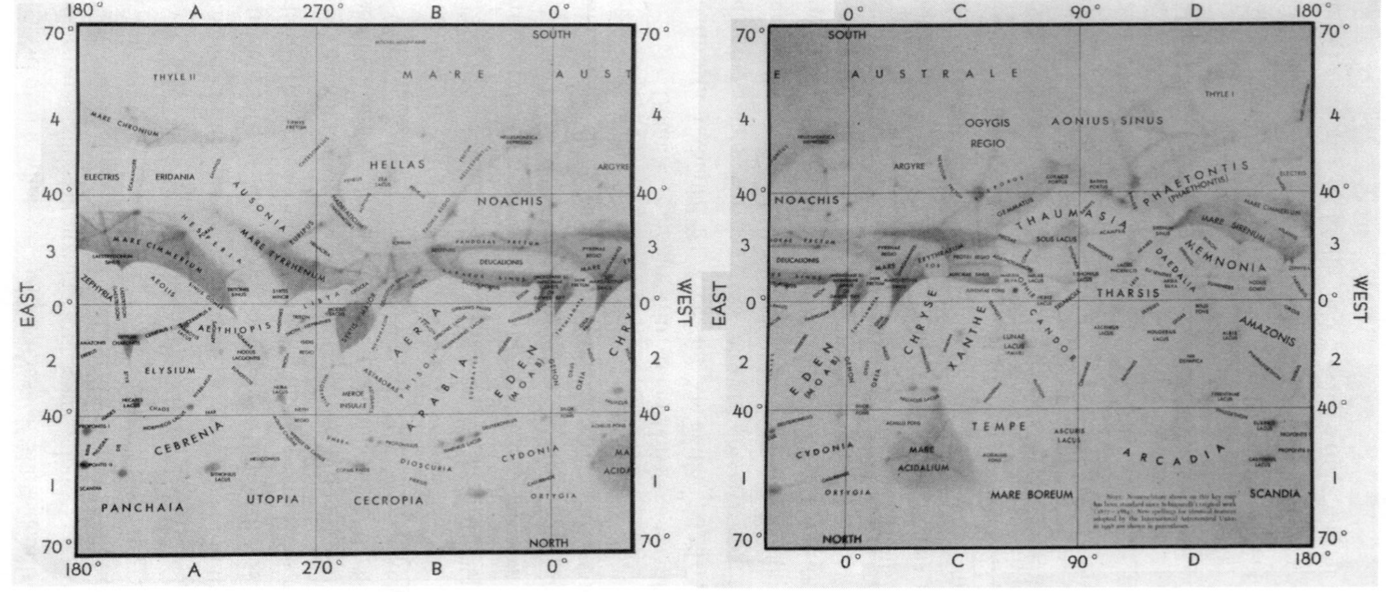

These Mars maps, based on observations made by Earl C. Slipher and Percival Lowell, show the principal surface features, including the illusory canals. The nomenclature is based primarily on Schiaparelli's. (O'Meara Collection)

1912 work *The Way of the Planets*. "One of the best observers of it has compared it to an opal, and it surely has some of the qualities of an opal in the diversity of aspect that it shows to different observers from different points of view."[4]

Indeed, romantic expressions of the planet's color abound. At the turn of the century Camille Flammarion described the colors of Mars as follows:

> It has been agreed to term *sea* the parts that are lightly tinged with green, and to give the name of *continent* to the spots coloured yellow. That is the hue of the Martian soil itself, which would resemble that of the Sahara, or, to take a less arid region, that seen on the line between Marseilles and Nice, in the vicinity of Esterel; or perhaps to some peculiar vegetation. During ascents in a balloon, I have often remarked that the hue of ripe corn, with the sun shining on it, is precisely that presented to us by the continents of Mars in the best hours of observation.[5]

Others have seen the sands of Mars as coral, salmon, orange-pink, reddish-yellow, red sandstone, and so on. The color effects are sensitive to seeing conditions, the telescope's aperture size, the disk size, and Martian seasonal effects. During the southern hemisphere summer, when there is often a great deal of dust in the atmosphere, the contrast of the markings is more subdued; the desert areas are then apt to appear more yellowish or even lemon, while the dark areas appear neutral gray or brownish. At the aphelic oppositions, when dust is generally absent, the apparent bluish tints can be rather striking. Various subjective effects also play a role in what one sees, including differences in the response curves of pigment-sensing proteins, or visual pigments, from one individual to the next; the extreme case is complete insensitivity of one or more pigments, also known as color blindness.

Recent studies of Mars made during the *Mars Pathfinder* Mission show that, up close, the red planet is surprisingly "un-red." Matthew Golombek, the project scientist on the *Mars Pathfinder* mission, says the surface "actually shows up as butterscotch or butternut. In every case where there was careful work done, from *Viking* to *Global Surveyor* to *Pathfinder* to the Hubble Space Telescope, it's actually brownish yellow."[6] The color of Mars is a direct reflection of the amounts of hematic dust, an iron-rich material that forms as a product of weathering and coats the planet like a mantle of rust.

Ice Caps

The most obvious features on Mars (especially through small telescopes) are its brilliant, snow-white polar caps. As on Earth, the ice caps of Mars display seasonal changes. But the changes on Mars are more dramatic. For example, if you were to watch the south polar cap for an entire Martian year, starting with the spring thaw, you would see the great ice sheet (which can extend half way to the planet's equator) start to fracture and shrink until, by the end of Martian summer, nothing remains of it but a tiny island of ice near the south pole; this carbon dioxide frost cap generally fails to disappear completely, though it may be invisible to small-telescope users at this time. As autumn on Mars approaches, the cap then starts to swell, reaching its maximum extent once again in the dead of Martian winter.

The solid north polar cap behaves slightly differently. During much of the Martian autumn and winter, the cap lays hidden beneath a cloudy polar hood. The cap emerges from this hood at the start of spring. In general, the retreat of the north cap is quite symmetrical. In late spring, the cap becomes fissured, then a bright mass, known as Olympia, breaks off. In most years the seasonal carbon dioxide frost cap evaporates off completely, leaving a residual water ice remnant. As it retreats, the north polar cap appears to be surrounded with a dark collar, sometimes known as the Lowell band, which was once regarded as a shallow sea but coincides in position with a wide swath of sand dunes.

Mars has seasons because, like the Earth, its axis is tilted. The axial tilt of Mars is 25.2° compared to Earth's 23.5°. Therefore, we can see either the north cap or the south cap but not usually both at the same time. Which cap we see when we look through our telescopes depends, once again, on the type of opposition—perihelic or aphelic. The south polar cap is tilted toward the Earth at perihelic oppositions, while the north polar cap is tilted toward us at aphelic oppositions. While the length of seasons on Earth are generally almost equal (because our orbit is nearly circular), the length of a Martian season can vary by as much as fifty-two days (again, because the orbit of Mars is greatly eccentric). Seasons on Earth are also not in synch with those on Mars; the axis of Mars does not point to Polaris (our North Star) but toward the star Deneb in Cygnus the Swan. If we observe Mars in the summer, the corresponding season on Mars will be autumn. Finally,

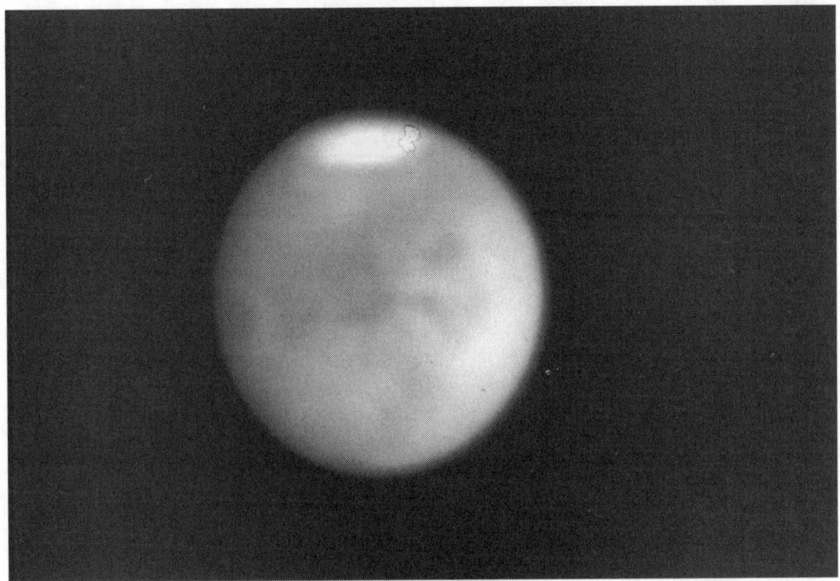

During Martian spring, the south polar cap is quite extensive (top), but by the end of summer, nothing remains of it but a tiny island of ice near the south pole (bottom). South is up. (Courtesy Stephen Larson.)

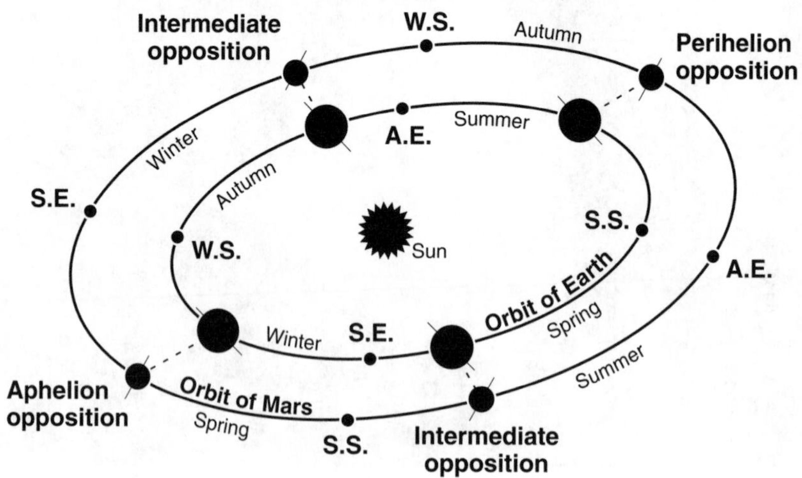

since a year on Mars is almost twice as long as a year on Earth, seasons on Mars last correspondingly twice as long.

Wave of Darkening

The dark features of Mars (which we discuss in more detail below) also display "seasonal" changes that seem to occur in concert with the shrinking polar caps—namely, as the cap shrinks, a "wave of darkening" sweeps from the pole toward the equator, traveling at a rate of 30 kilometers (19 miles) per day.[7] At it does so, dark features appear to become more robust, they spread out into the deserts and seem to take on a greenish tinge. As autumn approaches the green is replaced with a more "muddy brown" coloration. Had an observer on another planet seen such changes on Earth, he or she might conclude that the "wave of darkening" was related to vegetation and how it reacts to our planet's changing seasons. It would be reasonable to think, then, that as the polar ices on Mars melt, water flows into areas of vegetation and helps them to green, until cooler weather returned and the vegetation fades and browns. Indeed, the skilled astronomer-artist Etienne

L. Trouvelot promoted this theory as early as 1884: "One could believe . . . these changing grayish areas are due to Martian vegetation undergoing seasonal changes."[8]

Of course, this cannot be the case, for we now know that Mars has no vegetation. So what causes the well-documented darkening? The late great Mars observer Charles Capen solved the problem by showing that the "wave of darkening" is actually a "wave of brightening." The features only appear to darken because the adjacent deserts have brightened during early spring. Confirmation of this process comes from *Viking* lander photographs, which show fresh dust deposits covered by winter frosts being uncovered during Martian spring when the frost sublimes away.[9]

Clouds

Although the Martian atmosphere is thin and generally clear, clouds, much like those on Earth, do appear occasionally and are bright enough to be seen in small telescopes. Most often clouds, hazes, and frosts can be seen on the planet's limbs. Morning clouds never rotate far onto the disk; these clouds form during the cool Martian night but quickly disperse in the warmth of morning. Tiny patches of surface frost can persist for much of the Martian day, but larger telescopes are generally needed to see them. The most impressive and brightest clouds generally appear on the evening limb and can rival the polar caps in brilliance; this can be a source of confusion for beginning Mars observers who are trying to orient themselves to the planet because Mars will appear to have two polar caps but at right angles.

In 1907 E. C. Slipher of Lowell of Observatory spied a most remarkable cloud spectacle. That year he noticed a curious W-shaped formation of bright white clouds in the planet's Tharsis region. But an intense study of the peculiar grouping was not undertaken until 1954, when they were seen to form almost every afternoon for a period of more than three weeks. The clouds were intermittently seen in successive years, and they remained a mystery until 1971 when the *Mariner* 9 spacecraft revealed that the W clouds formed as winds passed over the towering volcanoes of Mars in the Tharsis region. They are especially prevalent during Martian spring and summer. These orographic clouds (composed of water vapor) begin forming on the upper slopes of the volcanoes around local noon. Telescopically, though, they are best seen in the late afternoon (Mars time), about two hours before they reach the planet's evening limb and rotate out of view.

Occasionally, faint, wispy bands of clouds can be seen crossing the planet's equator. These high clouds, akin to our cirrus (indeed they are sometimes referred to as "Martian cirrus"), are composed of carbon dioxide ice crystals; they appear to be related to the thawing of the Martian polar caps for they appear twice each Martian year—once after the south polar cap sublimates and once after the north polar cap sublimates.

The most famous of all the Martian clouds are the dust events due to intense wind storms. Small dust clouds kicked up by the Martian winds travel at average speeds of about 15 to 50 km/hr (10 to 30 mi/hr) and may persist for a few days before they dissipate. These minor atmospheric disturbances tend to hug the desert borders of the dark areas, and though they can travel "inland" they hardly ever make great progress. More remarkable are the global storms. Though rare, they can blot out large areas for many days or weeks or even months. As we have seen, the fantastic dust storm of 1971 obscured all dark surface features except for the highest volcanic peaks. In 1909 Antoniadi noted that though minor dust activity can occur at any time, the most intense storms occur during the perihelic oppositions. At that time Mars is closest to the Sun and there is maximum heating at the surface. The driving force of the dust appears to be strong convection currents and turbulence in the atmosphere. During the great dust storms, initial wind speeds can peak at 100 km/hr (60 mi/hr) before they diminish to 60 km/hr (37 mi/hr) after the first day.

Seasoned Mars observers use colored filters to help them differentiate the different clouds. Undoubtedly there is no other planet for which their use is more indispensable, and the serious Martian observer simply cannot afford to do without them. A yellow filter (Wratten 12 or 15) increases the contrast of the dark areas with the background—this is what Schiaparelli used, and it always brought the markings out "like spots of India ink." Orange (W21 and W23A) and red (W25) also will increase the contrast of surface details and assist in the identification of dust clouds. Green (W58), blue (W44A), and blue-violet (W47) filters help observers to differentiate the elevation of different frosts and clouds. If a cloud appears brighter in blue light than it does in green or orange light, it is an atmospheric cloud.

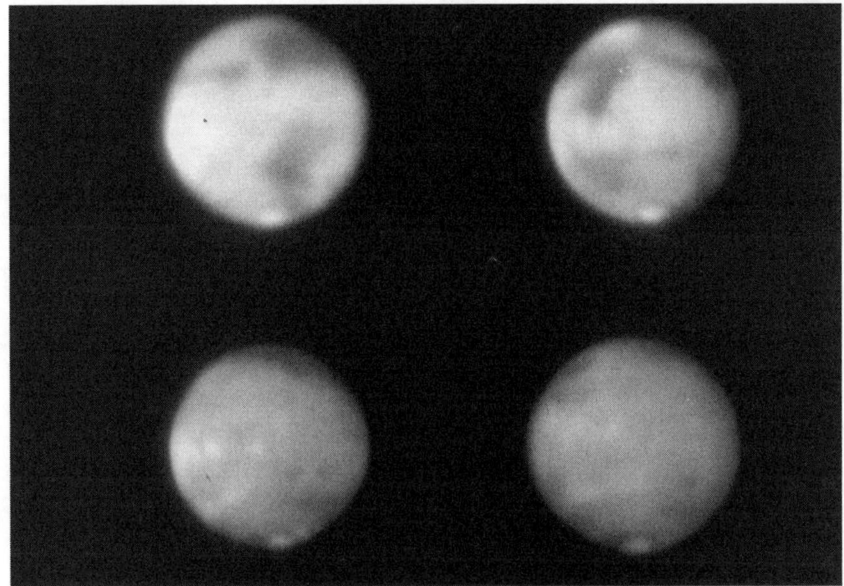

Clouds on Mars. The image at upper left shows a very cloudy morning limb (at right) and a small white north polar cap. The image at upper right reveals a bright cloud covering the great Hellas Basin (at top); note that this cloud is not the south solar cap, for the north polar cap is clearly in view (at bottom). The image at bottom left shows the famous "W" cloud, which appears as a series of white dots at the center and left side of the planet. And the photo at bottom right shows bright evening clouds (at left), a haze over Hellas (at top) and faint traces of equatorial banding. (Courtesy Stephen Larson).

If the bright feature is most pronounced in a green filter, but dim in blue and blue-violet light, it is undoubtedly a lower-level fog. Bright spots with sharp boundaries that show up best in green and yellow light but dim in blue light is most likely surface frosts. Fogs usually form in valleys and basins while frosts appear in cool, light albedo features, such as the floors of large craters. Since some of these filters are quite dense, they require telescopes with fairly large light grasp—the blue-violet filter (W47) needs at least 22.5 centimeters (9 inches). Generally speaking, surface details are invisible in the blue and blue-violet filters, but one should be on the lookout for the so-called blue clearings. (Once the subject of much speculation, they have now been explained rather mundanely as the result of phase-angle effects of light-scattering by airborne dust; this causes occasional enhancement of low-contrast differences between the light and dark areas in blue light, especially for a few days around the time of opposition.)

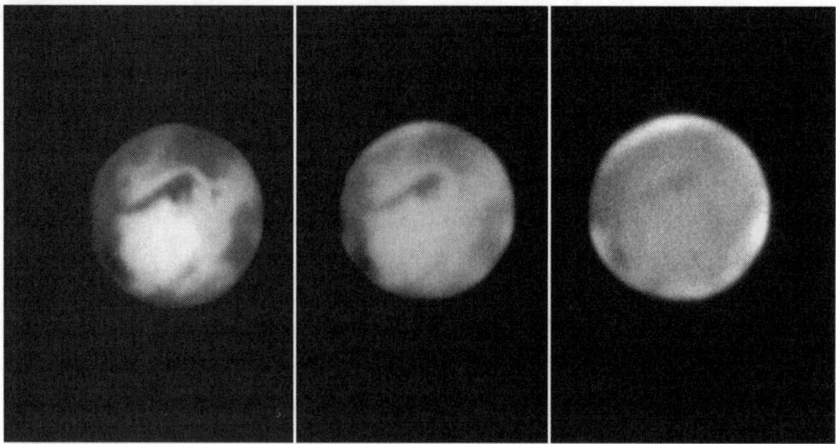

Observers use colored filters to emphasize various features on Mars. Here is Mars in red light (left), green light (middle), and blue light (right). Red light enhances surface detail, while blue light brings out atmospheric phenomena. Green is good for detecting frosts. (Courtesy Stephen Larson)

A Global Tour of the Principal Features of Mars

The observer who wishes to become familiar with the main aspects of the planet as seen in a modest telescope may find the following guide of some use (to follow along, please refer to the the maps in this appendix on page 350). In addition to the main telescopic markings (albedo features), we highlight aspects of the topography of each Martian region, which, though not directly visible, are convenient to keep in mind when orienting oneself to the disk. We include four Hubble Space Telescope Images to further enhance the experience.

We begin our tour with the Sinus Sabaeus (Terra Sabaea), since this is the region through which the 0° meridian passes. The serpentine ribbon of Sinus Sabaeus runs just south of the equator and terminates in the Sinus Meridiani (Terra Meridiani), whose two northward-pointing forks are still sometimes referred to as Dawes's forked bay. The point between the forks, christened Fastigium Aryn by Schiaparelli, is the zero of Martian longitudes—or, more precisely, the small crater in this position known as Airy is. The forked appearance is not always apparent, but at times it can be distinct in only a 15-centimeter (6-inch) telescope.

South of Sinus Sabaeus are the moderately bright regions of Deucalion and Noachis. Their ancient and heavily cratered terrain dates back to the middle Noachian period of heavy bombardment, four billion years ago. The brighter equatorial continent to the north is also heavily cratered and is known as Arabia; among its leading craters are Schiaparelli, which lies just on the border between Sinus Sabaeus and Arabia—it was often seen as a circular brightish patch by E. M. Antoniadi. Again, though, none of these features can be seen with modest telescopes.

A view of Mars showing Meridiani Terra (old names Meridiani Sinus or Dawes's forked bay) on upper left, followed onto the disk by Margaritifer Terra (Margaritifer Sinus), with its beak-like extension, and the great canyon system of Valles Marineris. The large smooth dark area toward the bottom (north) of the figure is Acidalia Planitia (Mare Acidalium). Note the swirling cloud just above and to the right of the south polar cap. (Hubble Space Telescope photograph, NASA)

To the west of Sinus Sabaeus lies Margaritifer Sinus (Margaritifer Terra), whose beaklike extension sometimes appears broken off at the end. The Ares Valles, one of the largest Martian outflow channels, courses through the region on its way to Xanthe Terra to the northwest; Xanthe Terra is also the site of the great Tiu, Simud, and Shalbatana channels, in which spacecraft photographs have shown lemniscate islands and alluvial plains suggestive of massive flooding. These features originate in western Margaritifer Sinus in the rough-and-tumble region known as "chaotic terrain." The flooding that took place here was on a catastrophic scale—much greater than anything ever seen on Earth. With good seeing, one can see even in modest telescopes that this is a region of complex formation.

The dusky region south of Margaritifer Sinus is occupied by Mare Erythraeum, whose boundary is rather ill-defined; however, there is one notable feature: the large circular formation of Argyre, which lies at about latitude 50° S. It is a splendid feature, 1,500 kilometers (900 miles) across, and was formed by a huge impact late in the era of heavy bombardment. The impact was so violent that the debris fell in several concentric rings; the innermost ring is very rugged and forms the basin's rim, of which the northern part is known as the Nereidum Montes; the southern is known as the Charitum Montes. The basin's floor tends to be covered with frost in the southern hemisphere winter, which causes it to appear brilliant at times.

North of Xanthe Terra is the plain of Chryse Terra, in the middle of which lies the *Viking 1* landing site; still farther north is Mare Acidalium (Acidalia Planitia), one of the vast northern plains. Mare Acidalium is among the most prominent features during the aphelic oppositions, when the northern hemisphere is tilted toward the Earth. One sometimes forgets the scale of what is being unfolded in the telescope; Mars is a small world, but since it has no oceans, its land area is equal to that of the Earth, and Mare Acidalium covers an area equal to about a quarter of the continental United States. In recent years, the extension of Mare Acidalium, Nilokeras, has been prominent enough to be made out easily in small telescopes.

As Mars rotates, Sinus Meridiani passes off the disk and the Solis Lacus region comes into view. Solis Lacus is a variable albedo feature centered within the bright circular region that Schiaparelli called Thaumasia Felix—the Land of Wonders. It was clearly visible in the 1830s, when Beer and Mädler drew it as small and round; by the 1860s it had become noticeably elongated in an east-west direction. In 1877, Schiaparelli and Trouvelot found it nearly round but slightly elongated north and south. Its east-west elongation was again evident in 1879, and this was the way it generally was figured (though with minor changes) until 1926, when it underwent a radical transformation. In that year Antoniadi found that it curved toward the northwest, at a right angle to its usual direction. In 1939 it was found to be made up of a number of small spots, and its form remained large and complex through the 1970s. In the 1990s, however, it has become smaller and rounder again. Obviously Solis Lacus is one of the most variable regions on the planet, which is hardly surprising given that the plain

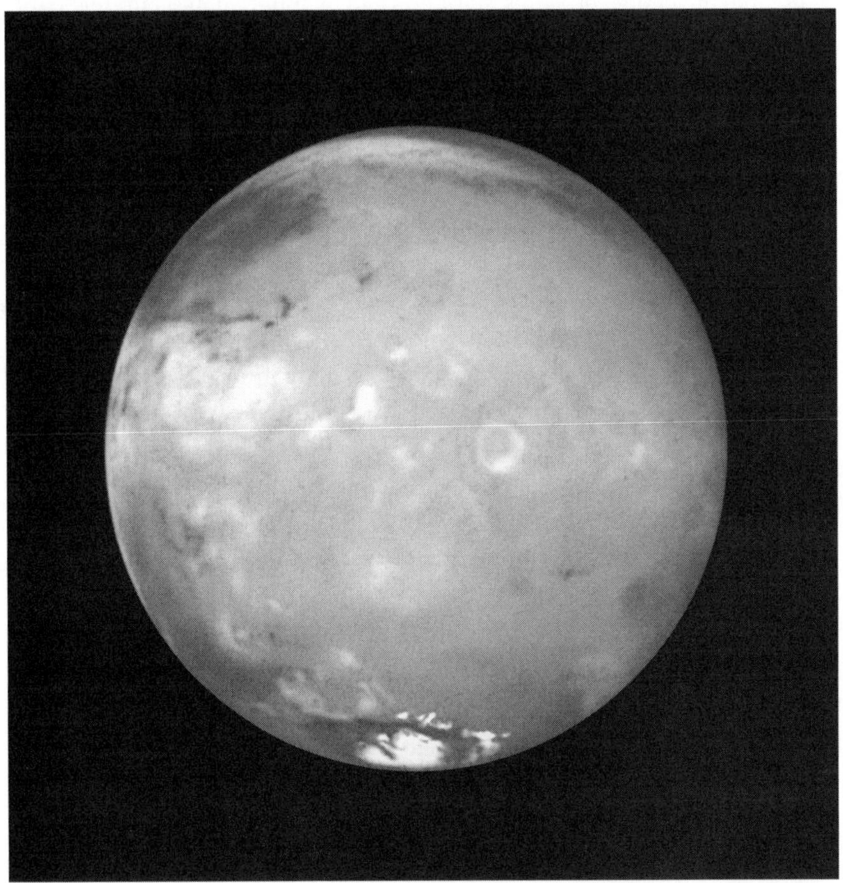

The image shows Mare Acidalium (bottom of image) and Valles Marineris passing out of view. The great volcanic region of Tharsis is in the middle of the disk—note the bright ring of the shield volcano Olympus Mons. (Hubble Space Telescope photograph, NASA)

located here, Solis Planum, is one of the areas long associated with the initiation of duststorm activity.

The great Valles Marineris canyon system runs through the region just south of the equator, its system of interconnected canyons running east and west from Margaritifer Chaos to the complex Noctis Labyrinthus. The Martian canyons are on a stupendous scale compared with the Grand Canyon of the Colorado River; at their widest point, in Melas canyon, the span reaches a width of 200 kilometers (120 miles). Thus, because of the curvature of the planet, if one stood on the north rim of the canyon, the walls of the south canyon would be completely below the horizon! Even in a small telescope, the course of Valles Marineris can be followed as a curving, dark, threadlike line; this feature was known as Agathadaemon on the canal-filled maps of the classical era.

South and west of the Valles Marineris complex are the great volcanic plains associated with the huge Tharsis bulge. In a small telescope, this enormous region extending from the edge of Mare Sirenum to the north pole appears bland and featureless, but since the spacecraft explorations it has become one of the most famous regions on Mars, for here lie the great shield volcanoes. Arsia Mons, Pavonis Mons, and Ascraeus Mons run along a southwest-to-northeast line, and Olympus Mons, the tallest mountain in the solar system, is located at longitude 130° W and latitude 20° N. In modest telescopes, one can sometimes make out faint dusky patches in these locations, or, more commonly, whitish patches—the latter, of course, was the form in which Schiaparelli saw one of them when he discovered Olympus Mons long ago and christened it Nix Olympica (Snows of Olympus). The volcanoes are often overhung by clouds—use a blue filter; the shield of Olympus Mons, though it rises some 25 kilometers (16 miles) above the surrounding plains, is 800 kilometers (500 miles) across at the base, so that the slope is not very steep—only about 6°. Thus, immense as Olympus is, its shadow even at the terminator (the dividing line between day and night on Mars) is not within the reach of Earth-based observers.

We continue to follow the features that come into view as Mars rotates. What Schiaparelli called the "Great Diaphragm" of the southern hemisphere begins with the strip of Mare Sirenum, which projects eastward toward Solis Lacus; this swath of darkness broadens as it continues on through Mare Tyrrhenum and breaks into a complex of smaller patches—-

A bright cloud hangs over Olympus Mons at the left limb of the planet. The desert regions of Amazonis Planitia (center) and Elysium Planitia (right) are well presented, and the straggling dark areas of Terra Sirenum and Terra Cimmerium, which overlie an ancient cratered terrain (Hubble Space Telescope photograph, NASA)

Antoniadi's "leopard skin." The broken or mottled appearance is partly controlled by the underlying relief and indicates the action of the wind depositing and sweeping away materials of different colors. The landforms consist of the rough, cratered terrain that occupies so much of the southern hemisphere of Mars; but these topographical features can only be inferred by the telescopic observer—they are nowhere directly observable. Between Mare Sirenum and Mare Tyrrhenum is a lighter-albedo band, Hesperia Planum, which precedes the large, roughly rectangular darkish patch of Mare Tyrrhenum onto the disk. The latter ends in the northward-pointing wedge of Syrtis Minor. Schiaparelli, inspired by his maritime view of Mars, thought that Hesperia was a floodplain or marsh lying between the two adjacent seas, a reasonable supposition at the time; but the spacecraft photographs have shown that it is a geologically distinct unit, the Hesperian system, which consists of ridged plains overlying the older cratered terrain of Noachian age.

The northern hemisphere in this part of the planet is dominated by the bright plains of Amazonis Planitia and Elysium Planitia, over which bright clouds are often seen. The latter is the site of the great Elysium volcanoes—Albor Tholus, Elysium Mons, and Hecates Tholus, of which nothing, of course, can be made out in modest telescopes. Nevertheless, it is always worth looking with the "mind's eye" and recalling that the volcanoes here are inferior only to those of Tharsis itself! One can make out a dark patch, Trivium Charontis-Cerberus, which has been rather faint in recent years. The Elysium basin often appears as a brightish patch and is sometimes cloud covered. Though the region has been largely inundated by volcanoes, part of the basin's rim still stands above the volcanic plains and forms a mountain range, the Phlegra Montes, which was identified in the spacecraft photographs.

At aphelic oppositions one can make out Utopia Planitia—landing site of the *Viking 2* spacecraft—in the extreme north, and the dark plains of Vastitas Borealis. The region between 75° and 85° S is peppered with sand dunes.

We come finally to the most celebrated area of Mars: Syrtis Major (Syrtis Major Planitia). The prominent, dark Syrtis Major is clearly shown in a 1659 drawing by Christiaan Huygens. A low-relief shield volcano has now been identified within Syrtis Major whose eruptions were the source of the dark materials covering the region; indeed, the whole region is an elevated volcanic plateau. The southern part of Syrtis Major is streaked and mottled, owing to wind action, and there are large dune fields within its great expanse. In the southwest, close to where the Sinus Sabaeus branches off, lies the great crater Huygens—it is partly filled by dark material and can sometimes be glimpsed from Earth. The peculiar Deltoton Sinus consists of three arcuate, semicircular "bays," or so Antoniadi described them when he first saw them with the great Meudon refractor in 1909.

There are two huge basins in the Syrtis Major region of the planet: Isidis Planitia, which encroaches on Syrtis Major from the northeast, and Hellas, which lies directly to the south and is by far the most prominent

The most recognizable face of Mars. Syrtis Major Planitia (Syrtis Major) lies at the center of the disk; once thought to be a dried-up Martian seabed, it is actually a windswept plateau, centered on a low-relief shield volcano (the source of the scattered dark materials that cover this part of the surface). The bright area near the top of the photograph (far south) is not a polar cap but the cloud-covered Hellas basin, the largest impact-basin on the planet. The north polar cap is at the bottom of the image while on the left-hand limb is a cloud feature over the elevated volcanic region of Elysium Planitia. (Hubble Space Telescope photograph, NASA)

basin on Mars. Hellas is 2,100 kilometers (1,300 miles) across and is enclosed on the east by the darkish strip of Mare Hadriaticum (Hadriaca Patera), and on the west by that of Hellespontus. In winter the Hellas basin is often partly or wholly filled with clouds. There are some elusive and evidently variable albedo markings; Schiaparelli sketched crisscrossing canals there, the Peneus and Alpheus; and in 1892, J. M. Schaeberle of Lick Observatory and Stanley Williams, a British amateur, figured a prominent dark patch near the basin's center, which Antoniadi later named Zea Lacus. This has returned to prominence in recent years—it was very marked at the 1988 opposition.

We have now followed Mars through a complete rotation, and we return once more to our starting point, Sinus Sabaeus. The Martian features have been described in the order in which they appear in the true rotation of the planet. In fact, however, since it is not possible to follow Mars through a complete rotation in a single night, and since the early evening hours are often the most convenient for viewing, in practical terms the observer tends to pursue the slow apparent drift of the markings in backward order from night to night—thus the Sinus Sabaeus gives way to Syrtis Major, followed successively by Mare Tyrrhenum, Mare Sirenum, Solis Lacus, and Margaritifer Sinus.

The details we have described here are, in a sense, superficial. What one actually sees will depend on a variety of factors: the stability of Earth's atmosphere, the size of the telescope, the size of Mars, which face of Mars is presented toward Earth, the season on Mars, dust activity, and the skill of the observer. Mars is a subtle world, one full of both intricate and imagined details. History has shown that the planet has revealed itself only to those who care. We do not expect first-time observers to come away from the eyepiece with a complete understanding of what he or she has seen. Nor do we expect novice observers to see much. As Shakespeare writes, "Oft expectation fails, and most oft / there / Where most it promises."[10] Mars is a difficult object to observe, but there is none more rewarding; the observer's interest is always piqued by the ever-changing panorama of polar caps, dark markings, and clouds and dust storms. If there is an ultimate reward from observing the red planet, it is knowing that we are continuing an age-old tradition—one that began long ago in some aboriginal dreamtime, one that enamored the greatest astronomical observers and science fiction writers of our times, and one that promises to continue to lure in new "Martians," even to the utmost age of human wonder and imagination.

Appendix D
Table of Data for the Planet Mars

Table of Data for the Planet Mars

Orbital Data

Semimajor axis	227,940,000 km (1.52366 a.u.)
Eccentricity	0.0934
Inclination	1.8504°
Longitude of ascending node	49.59°
Longitude of perihelion	335.94°
Mean orbital velocity	24.13 km/sec
Mean synodic period	779.94 days
Mean sidereal motion	0.5204°/day

PHYSICAL ELEMENTS

Axial inclination	25.19°
Length of sidereal day	24 hr, 37 min, 22.66 sec
Mean orbital period	686.98 Earth days
	669.60 Martian solar days
Diameter	6,779.84 kilometers
Polar compression	0.006
Surface area (Earth = 1)	0.2825
Volume (Earth = 1)	0.1504
Mass (Earth = 1)	0.1074
Density (water = 1)	3.93
Mean escape velocity	5.027 km/sec

Sources: H. H. Kieffer, B. M. Jakosky, C. W. Snyder, and M. S. Matthews, eds., *Mars* (Tucson: University of Arizona Press, 1993).

Appendix E
The Satellites of Mars

	Phobos	Deimos
Mean distance from Mars	9,378 km	23,459 km
Sidereal period	7 hr, 39 min, 13.84 sec	30 hr, 17 min, 54.87 sec
Eccentricity	0.0152	0.0002
Inclination	1.03°	1.83°
Diameter	26.6 × 22.2 × 18.6 km	15.2 × 12.42 × 10.8 km

Source: H. H. Kieffer, B. M. Jakosky, C. W. Snyder, and M. S. Matthews, eds., *Mars* (Tucson: University of Arizona Press, 1993).

Appendix F

Oppositions of Mars, 2001–2035

The table below gives the opposition date, the planet's position in the sky in terms of its right ascension (RA; the planet's celestial longitude, from 9 to 24 hours, with the hour lines increasing toward celestial east) and its declination north or south of the celestial equator (the latter is particularly important because, for northern observers, a far southerly declination infers that the planet must be viewed through a longer path of the Earth's atmosphere, which diminishes the view); the apparent size of the disk in seconds of arc; and the distance of the planet in *millions* of kilometers and *millions* of miles. Owing to the slight inclination of Mars's orbit to that of the Earth, the minimum separation between the two bodies can actually occur in few days before or after the opposition date.

Opposition Date	**RA**	**Declination**	**Disk (seconds of arc)**	**Distance (in millions) (km)**	**(miles)**
2001 Jun 13	17h 28 m	–26° 30'	20.5"	68.2	42.4
2003 Aug 28	22h 38m	–15° 48'	25.1"	55.8	34.7
2005 Nov 7	02h 51m	+15° 53'	19.8"	70.3	43.7
2007 Dec 28	06h 12m	+26° 46'	15.5"	89.7	55.8
2010 Jan 29	08h 54m	+22° 09'	14.0"	99.3	61.7
2012 Mar 3	11h 52m	+10° 17'	14.0"	100.8	62.6
2014 Apr 8	13h 14m	–05° 08'	15.1"	92.9	57.7
2016 May 22	15h 58m	–21° 39'	18.4"	76.1	47.3
2018 Jul 27	20h 33m	–25° 30'	24.1"	57.7	35.9
2020 Oct 13	01h 22m	+05° 26'	22.3"	62.7	38.9
2022 Dec 8	04h 59m	+25° 00'	16.9"	82.3	51.1
2025 Jan 16	07h 56m	+25° 07'	14.4"	96.2	59.8
2027 Feb 19	10h 18m	+15° 23'	13.8"	101.4	63.0
2029 Mar 25	12h 23m	+01° 04'	14.4"	97.1	60.3
2031 May 4	14h 46 m	–15° 29'	16.9"	83.6	52.0
2033 Jun 27	18h 30m	–27° 50'	22.0"	63.9	39.7
2035 Sept 15	23h 43m	–08° 01'	24.5"	57.1	35.5

Source: William Sheehan, *The Planet Mars* (Tucson: University of Arizona Press, 1996).

Appendix G

Table of the Most Favorable Oppositions, 3000 B.C.E. to 3000 C.E.

COMPUTED BY E. MYLES STANDISH, JET PROPULSION LABORATORY

Dr. Standish's note: "The Earth-Mars distance is a rather complicated function of the mutual inclination between the two orbits, the relative location of Earth's aphelion and mars's perihelion from teh mutual line of the nodes, and the actual positions of Earth and Mars is their orbits. It seems that the Earth's aphelion and Mars's aphelion have been drifting toward the line of nodes over the past several thousands of years, so that the mutual approaches have been generally decreasing.

"The table gives the closest approaches of Earth to Mars between the years 3000 B.C.E. and 3000 C.E. The upcoming opposition of 2003 is the eighth closest during that whole period, and the closest at any time since 3000 B.C.E.

date	**distance a.u.**	**miles**	**kilometers**
2729 Sep 08	.37200418	34 579 948	55 651 033
2650 Sep 03	.37200785	34 580 289	55 651 582
2934 Sep 05	.37217270	34 595 613	55 676 243
2287 Aug 28	.37225400	34 603 170	55 688 405
2808 Sep 11	.37230224	34 607 655	55 695 623
2571 Aug 30	.37238224	34 615 091	55 707 590
2366 Sep 02	.37238878	34 615 699	55 708 568
2003 Aug 27	.37271825	34 646 418	55 758 006
2208 Aug 24	.37278352	34 653 322	55 769 117
1924 Aug 22	.37284581	34 658 183	55 776 939

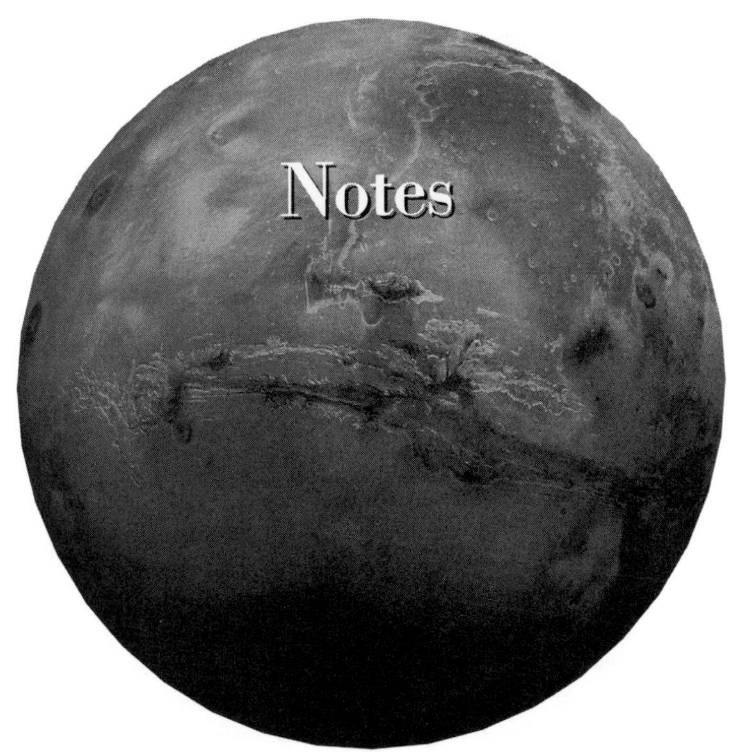

Notes

Preface

1. Daniel J. Boorstin, *The Discoverers: A History of Man's Search to Know His World and Himself* (New York: Random House, 1983), pp. 82–83.

2. Quoted in Daniel J. Boorstin, *The Creators: A History of Heroes of the Imagination* (New York: Random House, 1992), p. 345.

1. Lilac Dawn

General references: Paul Raeburn and Matt Golembek, *Mars: Uncovering the Secrets of the Red Planet* (Washington, D.C.: The National Geographic Society, 1998); Donna Shirley with Danelle Morton, *Managing Martians* (New York: Broadway Books, 1998); Carolyn Collins Petersen, "Welcome to Mars," *Sky & Tele-*

scope 94, no. 4 (1997): 34; William R. Newcott, "Return to Mars," *National Geographic* (August 1998): 6.

2. Mars in the Solar System

General references: J. Kelly Beatty, Carolyn Collins Petersen, and Andrew Chaikin, eds., *The New Solar System* (Cambridge, Mass.: Sky Publishing Corporation and Cambridge, England: Cambridge University Press, 4th edition, 1999); William Sheehan, *Worlds in the Sky: A History of Planetary Discovery from Earliest Times to Viking and Magellan* (Tucson: University of Arizona Press, 1992).

3. Wanderers and Wonderers

General references: John Allman, *Evolving Brains* (New York: Scientific American Library, 1999); Barry Cunliffs, ed., *The Oxford Illustrated Prehistory of Europe* (Oxford and New York: Oxford University Press, 1997); Christian de Duve, *Vital Dust: Life as a Cosmic Imperative* (New York: Basic Books, 1995); *Larousse Encyclopaedia of Mythology* (Prometheus Press, 1959); A. Pannekoek, *A History of Astronomy* (1961; reprint, New York: Dover Publications, 1989).

1. "Witness to the Creation: Mary Leakey, 1913–1996," *Newsweek*, 23 December 1996, p. 74.

2. Allman, *Evolving Brains*, p. 128.

3. Douglas C. Wallace, "What Mitochondrial DNA Says about Human Migrations," *Scientific American* 277, no. 2 (1997): 46–47.

4. Paul G. Bahn and Jean Vertut, *Journey through the Ice Age* (London: Weidenfeld and Nicholson, 1997).

5. Ian Tattersall, *Becoming Human: Evolution and Human Uniqueness* (San Diego: Harcourt, Brace, & Co. 1999).

6. R. L. Gregory, *Eye and Brain: The Psychology of Seeing*, 3d. ed. (New York and Toronto: McGraw-Hill, World University Library, 1977), p. 219.

7. Owen Gingerich, "The Origin of the Zodiac," *Sky & Telescope* 67, no. 3 (1984): 218–20.

8. Stephen J. O'Meara, "Tales from the Pacific," *Sky & Telescope* 72, no. 1 (1986): 73–75.

9. Roslynn Haynes, Raymond Haynes, David Malin, and Richard McGee, *Explorers of the Southern Sky: A History of Australian Astronomy* (Cambridge: Cambridge University Press, 1996).

10. Alex A. Gurshtein, "Prehistory of Zodiac Dating: three strata of Upper Paleolithic Constellations," *Vistas in Astronomy* 39 (1995): 347–62.

11. Pannekoek, *History of Astronomy*, p. 41.

12. Ibid., p. 38.

13. Camille Flammarion, *Astronomy for the Amateur* [originally titled *Astronomy for Women*], trans. Frances A. Welby (London: Thomas Nelson and Sons, 1904), p. 137.

14. For more details, see John D. Barrow, "Study in Scarlet: The Sources of Colour Vision," in *The Artful Universe* (Oxford: Clarendon Press, 1995), pp. 174–85.

15. Johannes Kepler, *New Astronomy*, trans. William H. Donahue (Cambridge: Cambridge University Press, 1992), p. 118.

16. Pannekoek, *History of Astronomy*, pp. 39–40.

4. The Untrackable Star

General references: J. L. E. Dreyer, *A History of Astronomy from Thales to Kepler* (1906; reprint, New York: Dover, 1953); Owen Gingerich, *The Eye of Heaven: Ptolemy, Copernicus, Kepler* (New York: American Institute of Physics, 1993); T. Heath, *Aristarchus of Samos: The Ancient Copernicus* (1930; reprint, New York: Dover, 1981); James S. Romm, *The Edges of the Earth in Ancient Thought: Geography, Exploration, and Fiction* (Princeton: Princeton University Press, 1992); W. H. Stahl, "Aristarchus of Samos," and G. J. Toomer, "Ptolemy," in *Dictionary of Scientific Biography*, ed. C. C. Gillispie (New York: Scribner, 1970).

1. Bruno Snell, *The Discovery of the Mind in Greek Philosophy and Literature*, translated by T. G. Rosenmeyer (1953; reprint, New York: Dover, 1982), p. v.

2. The Greeks were not the only seafarers. In the fifth century B.C.E., Phoenicians under Hanno the Carthaginian pushed far beyond the Pillars of Hercules into the "outer sea" (the Atlantic), and followed the African coast at least as far as the modern-day Sierra Leone before the increasing terror of his crew compelled him to turn back.

3. Aristotle, *Metaphysics*, I.5; 985 b 23–986 b 8.

4. *Doxographists*, Act.ii.30; 361.

5. William R. Ivins Jr., *Art and Geometry: A Study in Space Intuitions* (1946; reprint, New York: Dover, 1964), pp. 16–17.

6. Boorstin, *The Discoverers*, p. 151.

7. Ibid., p. 99.

8. Owen Gingerich, *The Eye of Heaven*, p. 8.

9. S. Angus, *The Mystery-Religions: A Study in the Religious Background of Early Christianity* (1928; reprint, New York: Dover, 1975), p. 169.

10. Bertrand Russell, *History of Western Philosophy and Its Connection with Political and Social Circumstances from Earliest Times to the Present Day*, 2d ed. (London: George Allen & Unwin Ltd., 1961), p. 269.

11. Walter Prescott Webb, *The Great Frontier* (Austin: University of Texas Press, 1964), p. 2.

5. The War with Mars

General references: Max Caspar, *Kepler*, trans. C. Doris Hellman (New York: Dover, 1993); Michael J. Crowe, *Theories of the World from Antiquity to the Copernican Revolution* (New York: Dover, 1990); Johannes Kepler, *New Astronomy*, trans. William H. Donahue (Cambridge: Cambridge University Press, 1992); Arthur Koestler, *The Sleepwalkers* (New York: Grosset & Dunlap, 1959); Victor E. Thoren, *The Lord of Uraniborg: A Biography of Tycho Brahe* (Cambridge: Cambridge University Press, 1990).

1. Boorstin, *The Discoverers*, p. 162.

2. Noel M. Swerdlow, "The Derivation and First Draft of Copernicus's Planetary Theory," *Proceedings of the American Philosophical Society* 117 (1973): 423–512.

3. Quoted in Crowe, *Theories of the World*, p. 133.

4. Quoted in J. L. E. Dreyer, *Tycho Brahe: A Picture of Scientific Life and Work in the Sixteenth Century* (Edinburgh: Adam & Charles Black, 1890), p. 14.

5. Ibid., p. 27.

6. Caspar, *Kepler*, p. 34.

7. Ibid., p. 102.

8. Ibid., p. 123.

9. Kepler, *New Astronomy*, p. 185.

10. Caspar, *Kepler*, p. 201.

11. Ibid., p. 195.

Chapter 6. The Sails of Imagination

General references: Steven J. Dick, *Plurality of Worlds: The Origins of the Extraterrestrial Life Debate from Democritus to Kant* (Cambridge: Cambridge University Press, 1982); Bernard le Bovier de Fontenelle, *Conversations on the Plurality of*

Worlds, trans. H. A. Hargreaves (Berkeley: University of California Press, 1990); Camille Flammarion, *La Planète Mars, et ses conditions habitabilité* (Paris: Gauthier-Villars et Fils, 1892); Galileo Galilei, *Sidereus Nuncius or the Sidereal Messenger*, trans. Albert Van Helden (Chicago and London: University of Chicago Press, 1989); Samuel Eliot Morison, *The European Discovery of America: The Southern Voyages, A.D. 1492–1616* (New York and Oxford: Oxford University Press, 1974); William Sheehan, *The Planet Mars: A History of Observation and Discovery* (Tucson: University of Arizona Press, 1996); William Sheehan and Thomas A. Dobbins, *Epic Moon: A History of Lunar Exploration in the Age of the Telescope* (Richmond, Va.: Willmann-Bell, 2001).

1. Webb, *The Great Frontier*, p. 9.

2. Review of Germán Arciniegas, *Caribbean: Sea of the New World*, *New York Times*, 11 August 1946.

3. Webb, *The Great Frontier*, p. 13.

4. John Maynard Keynes, *A Treatise on Money* (New York: Harcourt, Brace & Co., 1930), vol. 2, p. 154, n. 3.

5. Quoted in E. A. Whitaker, "Selenography in the Seventeenth Century," in *Planetary Astronomy from the Renaissance to the Rise of Astrophysics*, vol. 2, part A, *of The General History of Astronomy*, ed. R. Taton and C. Wilson (Cambridge: Cambridge University Press, 1989), pp. 120–21.

6. Quoted in Koestler, *The Sleepwalkers*, pp. 372–73.

7. Galileo Galilei, *Le Opere di Galileo Galilei*, Edizione Nationale, 20 vols., ed. Antonio Favaro (Florence: G. Barbera, 1890–1909), vol. 10, p. 503.

8. Fontenelle, *Conversations*, p. 52.

9. Christiaan Huygens, *The Celestial Worlds Discover'd: Or, Conjectures Concerning the Inhabitants, Plants and Productions of the Worlds in the Planets* (London, 1698), p. 21; quoted in Dick, *The Plurality of Worlds*, p. 130.

7. Mappers of Strange Seas

1. Richard J. McKim, "Telescopic Martian Dust Storms: A Narrative and Catalogue," in *Memoirs of the British Astronomical Association* 44 (June 1999): 14–15.

2. W. Herschel, "On the remarkable appearances at the polar regions of the planet Mars, the inclination of its axis, the position of its poles, and its spheroidal figure; with a few hints relating to its real diameter and atmosphere" (1784), in *The Scientific Papers of Sir William Herschel* (London, 1912), vol. 1, p. 156.

3. A. Secchi, "Osservazioni di Marte, fatte durante l'opposizione del 1858," in *Memorie dell'Osservatorio del Collegio Romano* (Rome, 1859).

4. W. R. Dawes, "On the Planet Mars," *Monthly Notices of the Royal Astronomical Society* 25 (1865): 225–68.

8. "A Less Difficult and Bloody Conquest"

General references: Jürgen Blunck, *Mars and its Satellites: a detailed commentary on the nomenclature* (Hicksville, N.Y.: Exposition Press, 1977); Michael J. Crowe, *The Extraterrestrial Life Debate 1750–1910: The Idea of a Plurality of Worlds from Kant to Lowell* (Cambridge: Cambridge University Press, 1986); Giovanni Virginio Schiaparelli, *Corrispondenza su Marte*, vol. 1 (1877–1889) (Pisa: Domus Galilaeana, 1963); Schiaparelli, "Osservazioni astronomiche e fisiche sulll asse di rotazione e sulla topografia del pianeta Marte," *Memoria* 1 (1877–1878), in *Le Opere di G. V. Schiaparelli*, vol. 1 (Milan, 1930); also the English translation thereof: *Astronomical and Physical Observations of the Axis of Rotation and the Topography of the Planet Mars: First Memoir, 1877–1878*, translated by William Sheehan (San Francisco: Association of Lunar and Planetary Observers, 1996); Denis Mack Smith, *Italy and its Monarchy* (New Haven and London: Yale University Press, 1989).

Passages from the correspondence of Giovanni Schiaparelli were translated from the Italian or French by William Sheehan.

1. Percival Lowell, *Mars and its Canals* (New York: Macmillan, 1906), p. 11.

2. N. E. Green, "Observations of Mars, at Madeira in Aug. and Sept., 1877," *Memoirs of the Royal Astronomical Society* 40 (1878): 123–40.

3. Schiaparelli, *Corrispondenza*, vol. 1, p. xx.

4. Schiaparelli, "Osservazioni," in *Le Opera*, vol. 1, pp. 11–12.

5. Boorstin, *The Discoverers*, p. 152.

6. Schiaparelli to Terby, 20 November 1877; in *Corrispondenza*, vol. 1, p. 5.

7. Schiaparelli, "Osservazioni," in *Opera*, vol. 1, p. 61.

8. Schiaparelli to Struve, 4 January 1878; in *Corrispondenza*, vol. 1, pp. 10–11.

9. Schiaparelli, "Osservazioni," in *Opera*, vol. 1, p. 61.

10. Schiaparelli, "Il Pianeta Marte" (1893), trans. William H. Pickering as "The Planet Mars," *Astronomy and Astro-Physics* 13 (1894): 635–40, 714–23: 638–39.

11. Quoted in William J. Walter, *The Space Age* (New York: Random House, 1992), p. 114.

12. Schiaparelli, "Il pianeta Marte ed I moderni telescopi" (1878), in *Opere*, vol. 1, p. 188.

13. Schiaparelli, *Corrispondenza*, vol. 1, p. 7.

14. Schiaparelli to Struve, 6 January 1880; in *Corrispondenza*, vol. 1, p. 41.

15. Schiaparelli to Struve, 6 July 1878; in *Corrispondenza*, vol. 1, p. 16.

16. Schiaparelli to Terby, 11 May 1886; in *Corrispondenza*, vol. 1, p. 150.

17. Schiaparelli to Terby, 28 May 1888; in *Corrispondenza*, vol. 1, p. 199. Terby to Schiaparelli, 3 June 1888; in Corrispondenza, vol. 1, p. 201.

18. Schiaparelli to Terby, 7 June 1888; in Corrispondenza, vol. 1, p. 203.

19. W. H. Pickering, "Mars," in *Astronomy and Astro-Physics* 11 (1892): 668–72.

20. Schiaparelli, "The Planet Mars," p. 719.

Sidebar: A Color-Blind Astronomer

The principal sources referred to are: Joseph Ashbrook, "Father Hell's Reputation," in *The Astronomical Scrapbook* (Cambridge, Mass.: Sky Publishing, 1984), pp. 218–21; William Sheehan, "Giovanni Schiaparelli and Mars: The Views of a Colorblind Astronomer," *Journal of the British Astronomical Association* 107, no. 1 (1997): 11–15; Andrew Young and Andrew Chaikin, "What Color Is the Solar System?" *Sky & Telescope* 69 (1985): 399–403.

9. Lowellian Mars

1. Hoyt, *Lowell and Mars*, p. 12.

2. Willy Ley, *Watchers of the Skies* (New York: Viking, 1966), p. 300.

3. Barrett Wendell to Robert White-Thompson, 23 June 1900, in M. A. DeWolfe Howe, *Barrett Wendell and his Letters* (Boston, 1924), p. 137. This passage was called to our attention by David Strauss.

4. Katharine Bigelow Lawrence Lowell to Percival Lowell, undated letters, Lowell Observatory archives.

5. Amy Lowell, "Sevenels, Brookline, Mass.," *Touchstone* 7 (1920): 210–18.

6. Quoted in Hoyt, *Lowell and Mars*, p. 15.

7. Quoted in ibid., p. 16.

8. Percival Lowell to Barrett Wendell, April 24, 1877; Wendell papers, Houghton Library, Harvard University. Called to our attention by David Strauss.

9. Lears, *No Place of Grace*, p. 229. Before going to Japan, said a friend, Bigelow had known "more about the mountains of the moon than he knew about his own soul."

10. David Strauss, "The 'Far East' in the American Mind, 1883–1894: Percival Lowell's Decisive Impact," *Journal of American-East Asian Relations* 2 (1993): 217–41.

11. For that matter, genes for mood disorders seem to have run true in the family quite as much as those for literary and mathematical abilities. See A. Myerson and R. D. Boyle, "The incidence of manic-depressive psychosis in certain socially important families: preliminary report," *American Journal of Psychiatry* 98 (1941): 11–21. Several of the Lowells, including Percival, seem to have experienced marked hypomanic states along with depressions, and Robert Lowell, poet of a later generation, was clearly manic-depressive and suffered frequent hospitalizations for manic psychosis.

12. Camille Flammarion, *La Planete Mars*, vol. 1, p. 591.

13. Quoted in ibid., p. 510.

14. Percival Lowell, "The Lowell Observatory and Its Work," text of address given to the Boston Scientific Society, 22 May 1894; *Boston Commonwealth*, 26 May 1894.

15. David Strauss, "Percival Lowell, W. H. Pickering, and the Founding of the Lowell Observatory," *Annals of Science* 51 (1994): 37–58.

16. Seth C. Chandler Jr. to E. S. Holden, 4 September 1895; Mary Lea Shane archives of the Lick Observatory.

17. Anthony Storr, *Churchill's Black Dog, Kafka's Mice and Other Phenomena of the Human Mind* (New York: Grove Press, 1988), pp. 4–5.

18. Webb, *The Great Frontier*, p. 6.

19. Frederick Jackson Turner, *The Frontier in American History* (1953; reprint, New York: Dover, 1996), p. 1.

20. Observing log book, Lowell Observatory archives.

21. Percival Lowell, "Mars: Spring Phenomena," *Popular Astronomy* 2 (1894): 99.

22. Percival Lowell, "Seasonal Changes in the Surface of the Planet," *Annals of the Lowell Observatory* (1898), vol. 1, p. 83.

23. Lowell, "Mars: Spring Phenomena," p. 99.

24. Lowell, "Seasonal Changes," p. 83.

25. Perhaps concentrating on small planetary images in the solitude of a lonely observatory is a hitherto unappreciated method for inducing hypnosis. It is not unlike concentrating on entoptic phenomena—luminous internally produced moving shapes familiar to sufferers from migraines, including geometric forms such as grids, zigzags, dots, and spirals, which appear when subjects close their eyes and concentrate on what they see. This is said to provide "an easily achieved, agreeable, and captivating inner visual experience . . . when the subject becomes absorbed in this inner focusing of attention, typical signs of a trance state (immo-

bility, slow regular breathing, etc.) become evident." See John F. Hunchak, "Hypnotic Induction by Entoptic Phenomena," *The American Journal of Clinical Hypnosis* 22, no. 4 (1983): 223–24. It has been suggested that entoptic phenomena may account for the puzzling abstract figures that grace Upper Paleolithic cave art. The Paleolithic artists too worked—as astronomers do—in dark, lonely places. See J. D. Lewis-Williams and T. A. Dowson, "The Signs of All Times: entoptic phenomena in Upper Paleolithic art," *Current Anthropology* 29, no. 2 (1988): 201–45.

26. Percival Lowell, "Mars: Oases," *Popular Astronomy* 2 (1895): 261.

27. Ferris Greenslet, *The Lowells and their Seven Worlds*, p. 366.

28. Flammarion, *La Planète Mars*, vol. 1, p. 515.

29. Schiaparelli to Terby, 30 November 1896; in *Corrispondenza su Marte*, vol. II (1890–1900) (Pisa: Domus Galileana, 1976), p. 219.

30. Percival Lowell, *Mars*, pp. 208–209.

31. T. J. Jackson Lears, *No Place of Grace*, p. 236.

32. Percival Lowell, *Mars and Its Canals*, p. 376.

33. Percival Lowell, private diary from 1904; communicated by David Strauss

34. Percival Lowell, *Mars as the Abode of Life*, p. 134.

35. Ibid., p. 142.

36. Ibid., p. 143.

37. Ibid., pp. 215–16.

38. Schiaparelli to Lowell, 2 September 1909; Lowell Observatory archives. Schiaparelli died on July 4, 1910.

39. Frederic J. Stimson to Barrett Wendell, 1 January 1917; Wendell papers, Houghton Library, Harvard University.

40. William E. Leuchtenburg, *In the Shadow of FDR* (Ithaca, N.Y.: Cornell University Press, 1983), pp. viii–ix, quoting a speech by Adolph Berle given shortly after President Franklin D. Roosevelt's death.

The excerpt from Percival Lowell's poem, "Mars," is from an unpublished manuscript in the Lowell Observatory archives.

General references: Ferris Greenslet, *The Lowells and their Seven Worlds* (Boston: Houghton, Mifflin & Co., 1946); William Graves Hoyt, *Lowell and Mars* (Tucson: University of Arizona Press, 1976) and *Planets X and Pluto* (Tucson: University of Arizona Press, 1980); T. J. Jackson Lears, *No Place of Grace: Antimodernism and the Transformation of American Culture, 1880–1920* (Chicago: University of Chicago Press); A. L. Lowell, *Biography of Percival Lowell* (Boston: Houghton, Mifflin & Co., 1935); William Lowell Putnam, *The Explorers of Mars Hill: A Centennial History of Lowell Observatory* (West Kennebunk, Maine: Phoenix, 1994); David Strauss, *Percival Lowell: The Culture and Science of a Boston Brahmin* (Cambridge, Mass.: Harvard University Press, 2001).

In addition, Lowell's own books still make fascinating reading, especially: *Mars* (Boston: Houghton, Mifflin & Co., 1895), *Mars and Its Canals* (New York: Macmillan, 1906), and *Mars as the Abode of Life* (New York: MacMillan, 1908).

10. La Grande Lunette

1. Clarence E. Dutton, *The Physical Geology of the Grand Cañon District*, in *United States Geological Survey, 2nd Annual Report, 1880–1881* (Washington, D.C.: U.S. Government Printing Office, 1882) pp. 86–87.

2. Ibid., p. 87.

3. E. W. Maunder, *Journal of the Transactions of the Victoria Institute* 44 (1912): 85, quoted in Richard McKim, "The Life and Times of E. M. Antoniadi, 1870–1944, Part I: An Astronomer in the Making," *Journal of the British Astronomical Association* 103, no. 4 (1993): 164.

4. Noel Barber, *Lords of the Golden Horn* (London: Macmillan, 1973).

5. P. M. Ryves, *Journal of the British Astronomical Association* 55 (1945): 163, quoted in McKim, "The Life and Times of E. M. Antoniadi," p. 164.

6. Gary W. Kronk, *Comets: A Descriptive Catalog* (Hillside, N.J.: Enslow Publishers, Inc., 1984).

7. William Graves Hoyt, *Lowell and Mars*, p. 15.

8. William Sheehan, *The Immortal Fire Within: The Life and Work of Edward Emerson Barnard* (Cambridge, England: Cambridge University Press, 1995), p. 4.

9. Percival Lowell, *Mars*, p. 209.

10. Noel Barber, *Lords of the Golden Horn*, p. 176.

11. Richard McKim, "The Life and Times of E. M. Antoniadi," p. 164.

12. Hoyt, *Lowell and Mars*, p. 71.

13. Jürgen Blunk, *Mars and Its Satellites* (New York: Exposition Press, 1982), p. 42.

14. Camille Flammarion, *Dreams of an Astronomer* (Boston: D. Appelton and Company, 1923), p. 114.

15. John Ruskin, *The Elements of Drawing* (1904; reprint, New York: Dover Publications, 1971), p. 120.

16. Richard McKim, *Journal of the British Astronomical Association* 103, no. 4 (1993): 168.

17. Ibid., p. 169.

18. Richard J. McKim, "Telescopic Martian Dust Storms: A Narrative and Catalogue," *Memoirs of the British Astronomical Association* 44 (June 1999): 37.

19. Robert Frost, "Time Out," *The Poetry of Robert Frost* (New York: Henry

Holt and Company, 1979), p. 355.

20. E. M. Antoniadi, *The Planet Mars,* trans. Patrick Moore (Devon, England: Keith Reid Ltd., 1975).

21. R. J. Trumpler, "Visual and Photographic Observations of Mars," *Publications of the Astronomical Society of the Pacific* 36 (1924): 263.

22. Hoyt, *Lowell and Mars*, p. 171.

23. E. M. Antoniadi to P. Lowell, 15 November 1909, Lowell Observatory Archives.

24. Antoniadi, *The Planet Mars*, pp. 225–26.

25. Ibid, p. 67.

26. Richard McKim, "The Life and Times of E. M. Antoniadi, 1874–1944, Part II: The Meudan Years," *Journal of the British Astronomical Association* 103, no. 5 (1993): 225.

11. Invaders from Mars

General references: William Sheehan, *Planets and Perception* (Tucson: University of Arizona Press, 1988); Irwin Porges, *Edgar Rice Burroughs: The Man Who Created Tarzan* (Provo: Brigham Young University Press, 1975); Lovat Dickson, *H. G. Wells: His Turbulent Life and Times* (New York: Athenaeum, 1969); Herbert George Wells, *Experiment in Autobiography* (New York: The Macmillan Co., 1934); Edgar Rice Burroughs, *A Princess of Mars* (1912; reprint, New York: Ballantine Books, 1963).

12. War of the Worlds

General references: Ray Bradbury, *The Martian Chronicles* (New York: Bantam Books, 1979); General Electric, "300 Years of History—Marconi Centenary 1897–1997"; Marc J. Seifer, *Wizard: The Life and Times of Nikola Tesla, Biography of a Genius* (Secaucus: Birch Lane Press, Carol Publishing Group, 1996); Margaret, Cheney, *Tesla: Man Out of Time* (New York: Dell Publishing, 1981); Nikola Tesla, *On My Inventions: The Autobiography of Nikola Tesla*, ed. Ben Johnston (New York: Hart Brothers, 1982); Irwin Porges, *Edgar Rice Burroughs: The Man Who Created Tarzan* (Provo: Brigham Young University Press, 1975); Lovat Dickson, *H. G. Wells: His Turbulent Life and Times* (New York: Athenaeum, 1969); Herbert George Wells, *Experiment in Autobiography* (New York: The Macmillan Co., 1934); Hadley Cantril, *The Invasion from Mars* (Princeton: Princeton University Press, 1940).

1. Lowell, *Mars*, pp. 202, 208.

2. Ibid., p. 76.

3. William R. Corliss, *Mysterious Universe* (Glen Arm, Md.: Sourcebook, 1979).

4. Philip J. Klass, *UFOs Explained* (New York: Vintage Books, Random House, 1974).

5. Donald Cohen, *Creatures from UFOs* (New York: Simon and Schuster, 1978).

13. Water, water—anywhere?

General references: Bruce Jakosky, *The Search for Life on Other Planets* (Cambridge: Cambridge University Press, 1998); Donald E. Osterbrock, John R. Gustafson, and W. J. Shiloh Unruh, *Eye on the Sky: Lick Observatory's First Century* (Berkeley: University of California Press, 1988); Earl C. Slipher, *Mars: The Photographic Story* (Flagstaff, Ariz.: Northland Press, 1962); Malcolm Walter, *The Search for Life on Mars* (Cambridge, Mass.: Perseus, 1999).

1. Philip Morrison, "HOH and Life Elsewhere," *Scientific American* (May 1997): 117.

2. Herman Melville, *Moby Dick*, Great Books of the Western World (Chicago: Encyclopaedia Britannica, 1952), pp. 2–3.

3. Schiaparelli, *Astronomical and Physical Observations*, pp. 48–49.

4. William Huggins, "The New Astronomy: A Personal Retrospect," *Nineteenth Century* 41 (1897): 907–29.

5. Allan Chapman, *The Victorian Amateur Astronomer: Independent Astronomical Research in Britain, 1820–1920* (Chichester: Praxis, 1998), p. 115.

6. Quoted in Crowe, *The Extraterrestrial Life Debate*, p. 363.

7. W. W. Campbell, "The Spectrum of Mars," *Publications of the Astronomical Society of the Pacific* 6 (1894): 228–36. For an account of Campbell's spectroscopic studies of Mars in 1894 and his 1909 expedition to the summit of Mt. Whitney, see Donald E. Osterbrock, "To Climb the Highest Mountain: W. W. Campbell's 1909 Mars expedition to Mount Whitney," *Journal for the History of Astronomy* 20 (1989): 77–97.

8. J. Janssen, "Sur la presencé de la vapeur d'eau dans l'atmosphére de la planète Mars," *Comptes Rendus des Séances de l'Académie des Sciences* 121, 233–37.

9. Percival Lowell to V. M. Slipher, 16 March 1908; Lowell Observatory archives.

10. W. W. Campbell to G. E. Hale, 11 May 1908; Mary Lea Shane archives of the Lick Observatory.

14. Woodstock Mars

General references: Samuel Glasstone, *The Book of Mars* (Washington, D.C.: National Aeronautics and Space Administration SP-179, 1968) and Thomas A. Mutch, Raymond E. Arvidson, James W. Head III, Kenneth L. Jones, and R. Stephen Saunders, *The Geology of Mars* (Princeton, N.J.: Princeton University Press, 1976).

1. Wernher von Braun, *The Mars Project* (1991; reprint, Urbana: University of Illinois Press, 1953), p. xv.

2. R. B. Leighton et. al., *Mariner Mars 1964 Project Report: Television Experiment*, Part I: Investigators' Report (Pasadena: Calif.: Jet Propulsion Laboratory Technical Report 32-884, part 1, 1967).

15. The Brave New World of *Mariner 9*

General references: Victor R. Baker, *The Channels of Mars* (Austin: The University of Texas Press, 1982); Michael H. Carr, *The Surface of Mars* (New Haven: Yale University Press, 1981); William K. Hartmann and Odell Raper, *The New Mars: The Discoveries of Mariner 9* (Washington, D.C.: National Aeronautics and Space Administration, 1974).

1. Carr, "Mars," in *The New Solar System*, 4th rev. ed., p. 153.

2. C. Sagan, O. B. Toon, and P. J. Gierasch, "Climatic Change on Mars," *Science* 181 (1973): 1045–49.

3. V. R. Baker, R. G. Strom, V. C. Gulick, J. S. Kargel, G. Komatsu, and V. S. Kale, "Ancient Oceans, Ice Sheets, and the Hydrological Cycle on Mars," *Nature* 352 (1991): 589–94.

4. J. Harlen Bretz, "The Channeled Scablands of the Columbia Plateau," *Journal of Geology* 31, no. 8 (1923): 617–49.

5. Victor R. Baker, "The Spokane Flood Controversy and the Martian Outflow Channels," *Science* 202 (1978): 1249–56.

6. J Harlan Bretz, "The Channeled Scabland of Eastern Washington," *Geographical Review* 18 (1928): 446–77.

7. N. Hoffman, "White Mars: A New Model for Mars's Surface and Atmosphere Based on CO_2," *Icarus* 146 (2000): 326–42.

16. Paradise Lost?

General references: William Poundstone, *Carl Sagan: A Life in the Cosmos* (Henry Holt and Company, 1999); Keay Davidson, *Carl Sagan: A Life* (John Wiley and Sons, 1999).

1. Carl Sagan, "The Solar System," *Scientific American* (January 1975).
2. Harlow Shapley, *The View from a Distant Star: Man's Future in the Universe* (New York: Basic Books, 1963), p. 33.
3. Raeburn and Golembete, *Mars*, p. 76.
4. Arthur C. Clarke, *Interplanetary Flight: An Introduction to Astronautics* (New York: Harper, 1951), p. 135.
5. Robert S. Richardson, *Exploring Mars* (New York: McGraw-Hill Book Company, 1954), p. 127.
6. Lucien Rudaux and G. de Vaucouleurs, *Larousse Encyclopedia of Astronomy* (New York: Prometheus Press, 1962), p. 199.
7. Ibid, p. 200.
8. Private communication.
9. Glasstone, *The Book of Mars*, p. 217.
10. Gerard Kuiper, "Condon Report," Appendix C, p. 1312 (1967).
11. David McNab and James Younger, *The Planets* (New Haven: Yale University Press, 1999), p. 91.
12. Carl Sagan, "The Solar System," in *The Solar System* (San Francisco: W. H. Freeman, 1975), p. 7.
13. Harold Masursky, in *The New Solar System*, 1st ed. (Cambridge, England: Cambridge University Press, and Cambridge, Mass.: Sky Publishing Corporation, 1981), p. 83.
14. *Time* (December 13, 1971), pp. 50–52.
15. Carl Sagan, "The Solar System," p. 7.
16. Glasstone, *The Book of Mars*, p. 217.
17. Gerald Soffen, "Life on Mars?" in *The New Solar System*, 1st ed., p. 94.
18. McNab and Younger, *The Planets*, p. 193.
19. Carl Sagan, *The Demon-Haunted World* (New York: Ballantine Books, 1996), p. 53.
20. Paul Raeburn and Golembelc, *Mars*, p. 86.
21. McNab and Younger, *The Planets*, p. 195.
22. Frank White, *The SETI Factor* (New York: Walker and Company, 1990), p. 71.
23. Paul Salopek, "Pilgrimage Through the Sierra Madre," *National Geographic* (June 2000): 56.

24. Pliny the Elder, *Natural History* (New York: Penguin Books, 1991), p. 286.

25. McNab and Younger, *The Planets*, p. 203.

26. Ricki Lewis, "Researchers' Deaths Inspire Actions To Improve Safety," *The Scientist* 11, no. 21 (October 27, 1997): 1.

27. William Broad, *The Universe Below: Discovering the Secrets of the Deep Sea* (New York: Touchstone Books, 1997), p. 331.

28. Victoria A. Kaharl, *Water Baby: The Story of* Alvin (Oxford: Oxford University Press, 1990), p. 175.

29. Broad, *The Universe Below*, p. 112.

30. McNab James Younger, *The Planets*, p. 212.

31. Ibid., page 204.

32. J. Kelly Beatty, "Life from Ancient Mars?" *Sky & Telescope* 92, no. 4 (1996): 18.

33. Everett K. Gibson Jr., David S. McKay, Kathie Thomas-Keprta, Frances Westall, and Christopher A. Romanek, "The ALH84001 announcement at T+2 Years: How Well Does This Piece of Mars Meet Accepted Criteria for Evidence of Ancient Life?"

34. Poundstone, *Carl Sagan*, p. 379.

35. Annie Dillard, *Teaching a Stone to Talk: Expeditions and Encounters* (New York: Harper Perennial, 1992).

36. Kepler, quoted in Burton, *The Anatomy of Melancholy*, epigram in H. G. Wells, *The War of the Worlds*.

17. If Stones Could Talk

1. Robin Summerfield, "Meteorite Debris May Unlock Secrets," *Calgary Herald* (June 1, 2000).

2. "Largest Meteorite Find in Canadian History," University of Calgary press release (May 31, 2000).

3. "More Pieces of Rare Meteorite Recovered," *Sky & Telescope* 100. no. 3 (2000): 18.

4. "Largest Meteorite Find in Canadian History," University of Calgary press release (May 31, 2000).

5. Summerfield, "Meteorite Debris May Unlock Secrets."

6. Harlow Shapley, *Of Stars and Men: Human Response to an Expanding Universe* (New York: Beacon Press, 1958), p. 9.

7. A. Pannekoek, *A History of Astronomy* (New York: Dover Publications, 1961), p. 233.

8. Rocky Kolb, *Blind Watchers of the Sky* (Oxford, England: Helix Books, 1996), p. 107.

9. Ibid., p. 108.

10. Harlow Shapley, *Beyond the Observatory* (New York: Charles Scribner's Sons, 1967), p. 18.

11. Richard Berendzen, Richard Hart, and Daniel Seely, *Man Discovers the Galaxies* (New York: Columbia University Press, 1984), p. 12.

12. Dennis L. Mammana and Donald W. McCarthy Jr., *Other Suns. Other Worlds?* (New York: St. Martin's Press, 1995), p. 214.

13. "Extrasolar Planets Aplenty," *Sky & Telescope* 100, no. 5 (2000): 24.

14. Paul Davies, *Are We Alone?* (New York: Basic Books, 1995), p. 22.

15. "Meteorite Research Indicates Mars Had Earth-like Oceans," University of Arizona Press Release (June 23, 2000).

16. "Recent Volcanism on Mars," *Sky & Telescope* 100, no. 4 (2000): 34.

17. Stephen Jay Gould, "War of the Worldviews," in *Natural History*, (December 1996–January 1997), pp. 22–33.

Epilogue. The Mars of Global Surveyor

1. Nick Hoffman, "White Mars: A New Model for Mars's Surface and Atmosphere based on CO2," *Icarus* 146 (2000): 326–42.

2. Personal communication to William Sheehan, 10 December 2000.

Appendix B. The Colors of Mars

The principal sources referred to are: William K. Hartmann, "Mars from Mauna Kea," *Sky & Telescope* 77, no. 5 (1989): 4; and William Sheehan and Thomas A. Dobbins, "The Colors of Mars: Reality and Illusion," *Sky & Telescope* 97, no. 4 (1999): 116–20.

Appendix C. Exploring Mars with Your Telescope

General reference: William Sheehan, *The Planet Mars* (Tucson: University of Arizona Press, 1996).

1. George F. Chambers, *The Story of the Solar System* (New York: D. Appleton and Company, 1904), p. 101.

2. Camille Flammarion, *La planète Mars et ses conditions d'habitabilité*, vol. 1 (Paris: Gauthier-Villars, 1892), p. 16.

3. Jeffrey D. Beish and Charles F. Capen, *Mars Observer's Handbook* (Pasadena, Calif.: The Planetary Society, 1986), p. 3.

4. Martha Evans Martins, *The Way of the Planets* (New York: Harper & Brothers, 1912), p. 172.

5. Camille Flammarion, *Astronomy for the Amateur*, p. 143.

6. Andrew Bridges, Chief Pasadena Correspondent, Space.com, posted: 12:44 P.M. ET 29 (November 1999).

7. Glasstone, *The Book of Mars*, p. 115.

8. Ibid., p. 117.

9. Beish and Capen, *Mars Observer's Handbook*, p. 20.

10. William Shakespeare, *All's Well That Ends Well*, 2.1.145.

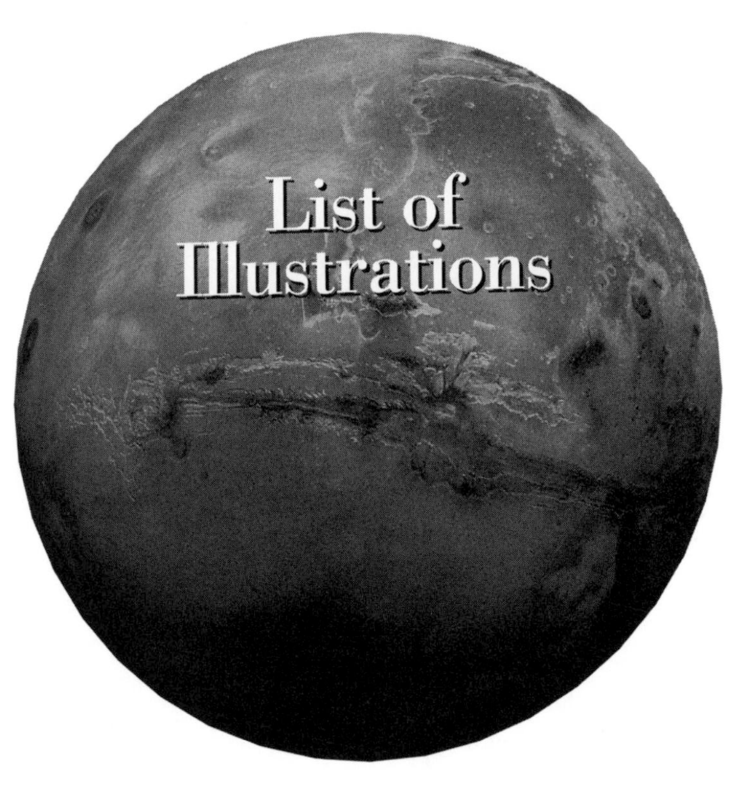
List of
Illustrations

Index